From the Beloved Author of
A Many-Splendored Thing
Comes an Epic Affair of the Heart . . .

.. *Till Morning Comes* ..

HAN SUYIN "has hit a double jackpot with her latest novel. Han is a perceptive, sensitive and eloquent . . . observer and interpreter of the chaotic times and vast complexities of her homeland. . . . The Chinese characters, from the upper middle-class Jens of Shanghai, to the peasants, soldiers and villains are memorably etched. Stephanie is presented vividly . . . Jen Yong is a marvel. . . . The second part of the jackpot is the love story."
—*Chicago Sun-Times*

"HAN SUYIN'S *Till Morning Comes* spans the whole sweep of the past fifty years of China's turbulence and the roller-coaster of Chinese-American relations in a dramatic love story of an American woman and a Chinese man. Everything is there—Chiang Kaishek, Mao Tsetung, Chou Enlai, Richard Nixon, McCarthy, the FBI, The Cultural Revolution—but at the heart it is a love story of two fine people, a man and a woman, caught up in a whirlwind."
—Harrison Salisbury

"Readers who love love should read this special story of romantic love, love of heritage, country, and love of life."
—*Houston Chronicle*

"Engaging and convincing . . . An empathic view of an often bewildering period and society—and a fascinating counterweight to the more elitist *Spring Moon*."
—*Kirkus Reviews*

"A fascinating novel . . . on how it is to live while heaven and earth change place—again and again . . . Han Suyin's gift is for sketching deftly and sparely a city, a season, a dialect."

—*The Washington Post*

"An eloquent and highly moving love story . . . Only Han Suyin could have written so beautifully detailed a book about China's upheavals."

—*Los Angeles Herald-Examiner*

"When Han Suyin was able to return to China . . . she said she would write a truly great love story. This is it. The novel is beautifully done. It can be read as a story on many levels, but on each it is engrossing and enthralling."

—*The Indianapolis News*

"A sweeping story of passion . . . A portrait of life under Mao as well as a stunning saga of the power of enduring love."

—*The Chattanooga Times*

till morning comes

han suyin

BANTAM BOOKS
TORONTO · NEW YORK · LONDON · SYDNEY

TILL MORNING COMES
Bantam Hardcover edition / July 1982
Bantam rack-size edition / June 1983

All rights reserved.
Copyright © 1982 by Han Suyin.
Cover art copyright © 1983 by Max Ginsburg.
Frontispiece adapted from Edgar Snow's China,
Copyright © 1980 by Lois Wheeler Snow.
Reprinted by permission of Random House, Inc.

This book may not be reproduced in whole or in part, by
mimeograph or any other means, without permission.
For information address: Bantam Books, Inc.

Library of Congress Cataloging in Publication Data
Han, Suyin.
Till morning comes.
I. Title.
PR6015.A4674T5   823'.912   81-19150
ISBN 0-553-23270-3   AACR2

Published simultaneously in the United States and Canada

Bantam Books are published by Bantam Books, Inc. Its trademark, consisting of the words "Bantam Books" and the por-
trayal of a rooster, is Registered in U.S. Patent and Trademark
Office and in other countries. Marca Registrada. Bantam
Books, Inc., 666 Fifth Avenue, New York, New York 10103.

PRINTED IN THE UNITED STATES OF AMERICA

H   0 9 8 7 6 5 4 3 2 1

To Cathy, Therese and Theodora
who have helped me so much

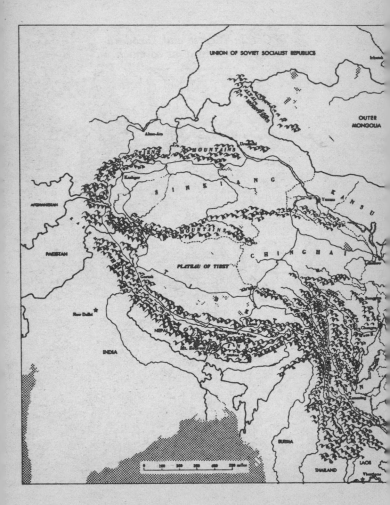

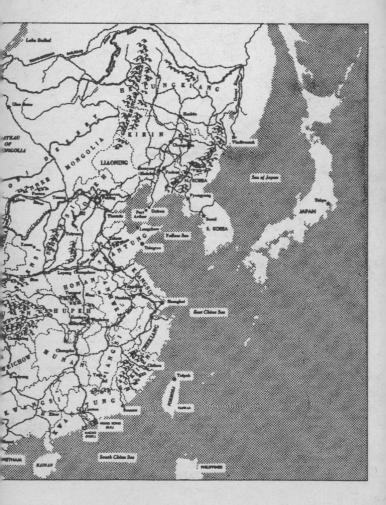

till
morning
comes

one

THE city woke, wrenching John Moore out of the sweaty torpor which was sleep in Chungking's sweltering summer. He had hated this dawn cacophony when he had first come to the beleaguered city in 1939. Hated its sprawl of blistered habitations, the stridency and the smell, the crowds, the crowds, human blight disfiguring the crested, rocky peninsula lapped by its two rivers, the mighty Yangtze and the beautiful Chialing.

But this was summer 1944, five years later. John Moore now loved this war-scarred city precisely because it was a perpetual assault upon his senses, a perpetual reminder of heroism and its betrayal. The squalor and the noise, the discomfort of Chungking's furnace summers and fog-smothered winters, were challenges which he missed when he was away on leave, as if part of him was rooted in this treeless rock.

Five years ago, when he was thirty, and imbued with great certainties about good and evil, he had come to China as a fledgling reporter. It was a journey to a great war pitting the embattled Chinese people against the Japanese invaders.

City after city, province after province had fallen, but still the stubborn people did not give up. Still they would not surrender.

Nanking, Shanghai, Wuhan, all had fallen. The government of Chiang Kaishek had retreated to Chungking, in faraway Szechuan province.

And then the Japanese had bombed the overcrowded city, and burnt it down, in May 1939.

But the people's spirit was unbroken. They patched up, and among the cinders and ash they lived, and laughed, and worked. How they worked! The city had been rebuilt, and bombed again. And again . . . John Moore had shared in this renewal, this tenacity. He had then understood why Americans in China fell in love. With China. With its people.

His articles on the war had won him renown. He had, through them, acquired a solid craftsmanship and a reputation for integrity in reporting.

But now things were going awry. Heroism was present still, but so was disillusion, bitterness. The rhetoric of resistance rang hollow, almost derisive.

For the Chiang Kaishek government, popular in 1938, 1939, was now hated. Corruption, despotism had destroyed its image.

And John Moore woke up each day in Chungking wondering how he would be able to inform his American readers about the government of Chiang Kaishek, the Kuomintang, yet at the same time not disillusion them to the extent of thinking the Chinese people were no longer worth helping.

For a little over two years these bone-eroding doubts had inhabited his spirit and were reflected in cautiously balanced think-pieces, which his editors queried. They, like the American public, had been immersed for years in an image of China—which he too had contrived to project—as a radiant epic of courage. And now the note of doubt he introduced was disconcerting. Especially to Lance Clark, the owner of the prestigious newspaper he worked for, who would never admit any disenchantment, any flaw with Chiang Kaishek.

John felt comforted by the cheerful bawling of the waking streets, while the sun sprang out of the Great River and immediately another sweltering day began. He discerned in this uncouth and perpetual cacophony that foolish energy which makes mankind keep on its appointed journey through life, laughing and loving and rejoicing as if manipulating eternity rather than hastening towards that ultimate engulfing shadow where all noise and agitation cease.

Things fell into perspective; the hubbub lessened his anxiety, diminished the worry of having to tell his fellow Americans that there might be a grave political crisis in China and that this crisis would inevitably involve America.

He lay back under the mosquito net, and his ears picked

out the neigh of the water carriers, swinging their wooden pails full of gold-brown water, coming up from the river, eight hundred feet below and almost a mile and a half away. They climbed, with staccato heaves and grunts, the steep cobbles of the staircase track up the cliff, and their cries of "beware" mixed with the jocular shouts of "lend a light" from the descending file of excrement bearers. Upon the backs of the latter, wood barrels leaked a pungent slime, treasure for the rice fields which nourished the over-crowded city. Water carriers and dung collectors spattering liquid of almost the same color on the cobbles of the climbing streets.

He raised the net, placed his feet upon the wooden floor already warm with seeping heat, and heard the bugles of reveille from the nearby soldiers' camp. Kuomintang soldiers' camps all over Chungking; machine guns fixed on concrete blocks at crossroads. Not against the Japanese, but because of restlessness among their own people.

A few hundred young voices now launched into the Nationalist anthem. John walked to the ceramic jar in the corner and sluiced himself with the half gourd provided; the water flowed onto his skin, cooling him for a short while. He listened to the song. At one time it had brought tears to his eyes, stirred his guts. It had meant valiance, conjured up visions of nobility, of defiance against frightful odds. But now the chant reminded him of the recruiting camp he had visited. The recruiting camps of the Kuomintang were not open to inspection, but John Moore had insisted. Because he had seen, on the roads out of the city and among the fields, soldiers—or rather ambling skeletons in uniform—dragging themselves, followed by officers beating them with sticks.

Inadvertently, due to an error in date made by the Information Ministry, he had arrived at the camp a week earlier than he had been expected. . . . And the horror of it remained with him.

He had seen the peasants tied together so they would not run away, pressganged off the fields, small, wizened, some emaciated, waiting to be untied, sitting in their own filth. In their huddle they even carried a corpse, for one of them had died on the way and no one had noticed. How long had they waited and not been fed? "More soldiers die in the recruiting camps because they are not given any food, than

3

on any hypothetical battlefield," John Moore wrote, and provoked a furor. But the phantom battalions of the dead went on drawing pay and the pay seeped into the pockets of the officers. And nothing was changed.

The water trickled off him into the tin tub in which he stood. He dried himself, applied talcum to his heat rash, the neck, the scrotum, under the armpits. Not yet six in the morning and already the sun was a white blindness in a sky opaque with heat. No respite from the heat. All day the sun baked the rock and the houses; at night the rock and the houses oozed back the heat like treacle into the air.

John pulled on a shirt and noted the sudden bark and roar of the common toilet down the corridor. Terry Longworth. The man's bowels were still a mess. Everyone in Chungking suffered from bouts of diarrhea, and dysentery and cholera were never unlikely. Terry had nearly died of some complicated infection while in North Burma that May, slogging along with General Joseph W. Stilwell, known as Vinegar Joe, the American commander who was attempting to reconquer the Burma Road for China. Who was trying to retrain the armies of Chiang Kaishek. Who was furiously denouncing Chiang Kaishek.

Terry had written magnificent pieces about Stilwell, about the Chinese battalions Stilwell was training; John Moore hoped that Terry would get a Pulitzer for his work. He deserved it. And it would help, in Terry's situation.

He heard Stephanie Ryder laugh. It sounded as Stephanie looked, cool, joyous, and he felt a winged desire which hurried him out of his room and down the stairs.

Stephanie, undimmed by heat, or by any sorrow. Although Alan Kersh had died less than three months ago, Stephanie was vibrant with youth and the savor of youth.

She was framed by the gate to the courtyard of the Press Hostel, where the foreign newsmen lived. She wore light sandals and a pale dress; her arms were raised, pinning up her brown hair with its flecks of bronze, using a tortoise shell pin to leave the nape of her neck free. She smiled at him, saying "Hello John," and then answered Alistair Choate who teetered near her. "But of course I know how to get there, Alistair. I went there yesterday, but I didn't have my camera with me. I want to take some snapshots of the people."

"You should have someone with you, Stephanie. These

4

people are not altogether trustworthy. They're a pretty desperate lot, they'll try to get money out of you."

John felt the skin of his face tighten, as it always did when Alistair expressed his scorn of the poor, the beggars. It was that streak of idealism in him, incurable. God knows, the people here suffered enough, poor bastards, without having someone well-fed and secure like Alistair showering his contempt upon their misery.

There was also the unspoken rivalry over Stephanie. For the foreign correspondents the scarcity of women was one of Chungking's ordeals—and Stephanie, who had landed the previous week, caused shock waves of lust. Except for Terry Longworth, who had Rosamond and wanted to marry her, the men hung about Stephanie, eager, somewhat expectant. But her eyes swept them all with a friendliness almost insulting in its innocence. John had realized that her smile, the toss of her head was not an invitation, but a natural joyousness, a happy puppy frame of mind which had nothing to do with sexual innuendo. She's innocent as a cloud, John thought. He wanted to protect her, protect that candor of hers. Yet Alan Kersh had written to John, his best friend: "You'll see my new girl . . . Stephanie's delightful. . . . She's got brains, ambition . . . and is she good in bed. . . ."

And now remembering Alan's vulgar reference to Stephanie made John angry—if one could be angry with a dead man. A failing Don Juan. He had screwed the letter up, thrown it in his wastepaper basket.

Stephanie was beautiful. She had eyes even darker than her hair, with the same bronze flecks. Her face held a luminous quality, an inner glow which was the juice and sap of almost shocking youth. She seemed within an hour to be many women at once: accessible, yet distant, warm and outgoing, yet given to sudden farawayness. She looked small and fragile, but was compactly slim. She was both docile and combative. She was just twenty-one. And her soft, frank gaze had made John Moore feel weak, shaken with desire and love.

"It's going to be *very* hot," said Alistair, pleading. "And the beggars will be buzzing round you like flies."

"I think Stephanie can take care of herself," said John.

"There's a press conference at ten," said Alistair.

"I'll be back by then," said Stephanie. "Chungking is no hotter than Dallas, Alistair. You should've been in Dallas in

5

the heat wave, last year. . . ." And waving a cheerful hand, she walked away, her smile and her wide-eyed child look effacing petulance.

The two men watched her go, stepping lightly in the alley between the banana trees and the oleander, passing the gate with its two armed soldiers on guard, and into the track which sloped to the crowded main road.

They turned to each other, aware of the seething resentment and frustration induced by Stephanie's presence.

"I hear Clarence Gauss is leaving. Too bad. I enjoyed those poetry sessions of his," drawled Alistair.

"He knows the country well," replied John.

"We all suffer from that illusion after a while. We think we know China because we've stayed here. We never shall know the Chinese; they neither think nor react as we do. They are a maverick among nations and always will be. It's bad for an ambassador like Gauss—or even mere newsmen like us—to become *too* emotionally involved with China."

The waspish innuendo stung John, who walked away from him into the dining room. He tore off a page from the calendar stuck on the wall, as he did every day. The calendar had on each page the photograph of a Chinese girl, hair permanent waved, smiling. It was an advertisement for the high-class brothel up the road. The cook and waiters of the Press Hostel had probably been promised a cut if they could bring real American dollars to the brothel.

It was August 25, 1944. The radio spluttered, roared, a voice spoke of the liberation of Paris the previous day. The head waiter Old Sung—whom everyone called Boy although he was white-haired and who served forty years at the Cathay Hotel in Shanghai before walking to Chungking, because he would not serve the Japanese conquerors—set a plate of ham and eggs along with butter and toast in front of John. The butter began to melt in its dish. John felt the sweat dribble down his neck, down his rib cage. Strange that for a short while, looking at Stephanie, he had totally forgotten the heat.

The track led Stephanie to the circular main road, where the crowds of morning jostled, men and women in worn clothes, with heat-blenched faces, pressing without hurry

6

to their work, waving fans in their hands. Carriers in verminous rags swung the bamboo chairs, called *huakan*, in which men and women reclined, carried to their destination. This was the only mode of conveyance in the rock city with its climbing streets, apart from occasional overcrowded buses along the main roads, and the sleek limousines of the mighty, the officials, the wealthy.

Stephanie crossed the main road as it elbowed round a small hillock covered with derelict bone-bleached houses, went down a reeking lane, fetid with urine, where a lopsided balcony offered flamboyant dahlias. Filth oozed out of every open doorway, and in the darkness were eyes, eyes that watched her passing.

Always people, people . . . a press and an urgency of people. Nowhere was one ever alone. Always faces and eyes and voices. Never a corner without its human being. The city was an immense untidy anthill, and all its inhabitants ants, crawling upon each other. . . . Magnificence and squalor. Delicacy and brutality. Beauty and vicious ugliness. Cheek by jowl. Always together. *I never thought it could be like this.*

Within a week of her arrival Stephanie had discovered how far from reality were the illusions which still prevailed in America about the Nationalist government sited in Chungking. Revolted by what she saw after her first walk in the streets she had gone to John Moore. "I'm stunned, I'm shocked, it's unbelievable."

John Moore had calmed her. Had spoken of the courage, the steadfastness of the people. "Do not judge too quickly. There are also admirable things. University students and professors from all over China, refusing to stay in areas conquered by the Japanese, have trekked, walked inland with all their staff and their students. Old men and young, young women and old ones have given up everything to serve their country. Old Sung, our waiter, abandoned his home to walk three thousand miles to come here. Remember, it's the people who matter . . . as for the government . . ." He shrugged. "It's a long tale and a sad one."

The endless human labor. The endless *degradation* of labor. This was what appalled Stephanie. Here labor was not ennobling toil, giving man his raison d'être. Here work made ugly not only the bodies but also the spirits of men and women and children. They had deformed rib cages,

7

calluses like cushions on their shoulders and their backs, suppurating wounds and ulcers between their legs and on their faces. The children had the look of old midgets with bellies swollen with hunger and worms. The women were ravaged with childbearing; their wombs dropped between their thighs before they were thirty years old. And this hideousness also bred a savagery in the strife for survival. They hit and were hit and there was no pity at all for the weak—and the babies died like flies, or were thrown into the cesspits.

Stephanie set her teeth, fought the nausea that rose, rose and made her mouth bitter. *Now that I'm here, I'm going to see it through*. She would record the besmirched vision, for along with horror and disgust another feeling grew in her: a strange feeling of involvement, a gathering and fusion within herself which was rage, indignation that human beings should have to endure such an existence. And a desire to do something about it. Indifference was the unpardonable crime. Stephanie could not remain indifferent. . . .

On the road a young boy was dragging himself backwards on his buttocks, his legs trailing behind him at an impossible angle, useless. Perhaps it was polio, perhaps a car accident. No one looked, no one helped as the boy painfully reached a stoop by the road, and then gave Stephanie a radiant smile. Stephanie groped for money to give, and after giving felt ashamed.

Stephanie had been twenty and in her last year at Radcliffe, majoring in Asian history, when Alan Kersh had come to lecture on the Sino-Japanese war. She had attended the lecture and afterwards asked questions. He had answered, his eyes raking her over, and asked her out to dinner. Stephanie thought that he was fascinating, was flustered at his attentions. And he persisted. After a while she thought that perhaps she was a little in love with him.

Alan Kersh was good-looking, debonair, and had a reputation as greatly successful with women. But he was forty-one and married, and she had steadfastly refused to sleep with him. At first.

She had standards inculcated into her by her upbringing. One did *not* sleep around. One did not sleep with married men. Besides, she was not altogether certain that she loved him. He excited her, fascinated her, but . . .

"Don't go the whole way until you're sure," Helen Wilkes, her best friend and a year older, had advised. And how could she be sure?

Alan then told her that he would divorce his wife and marry her. He also asked her to come with him to China; they could be together. And he pulled strings to get her a job as cub reporter for HERE, a magazine becoming rapidly successful. He did not tell Stephanie that his own wife, Sybil, was on the staff of HERE. HERE offered to send her to China to do some exclusive reporting on women at war. Stephanie accepted a year's contract. A year . . . *then I'll know what I really want to do*.

And then it had happened.

Not in a hotel, nor in Alan's flat, but on the settee of the living room in her parents' home in Dallas. Alan, who still had a month of his four months of home vacation, came down to Dallas. He called; they would go to a movie. It was raining. Her parents and Jimmy, her brother, were not at home that afternoon. He had begun to kiss her tenderly, then savagely. The rain was like curtains enfolding them, its lullaby was insidious, erotic. She gave, he took, and she had been possessed.

It had been neither painful nor pleasurable, merely something accomplished, a curiosity satisfied. She wondered, afterwards, that she had felt no transporting joy, none of the ecstasy promised. She had noticed a slight patch of baldness beginning in the center of Alan's thick hair when, afterwards, his head rested upon her breast.

"We'll be together in China," Alan told her, crushing her to him. "Stephanie, it will be . . . heaven. I love you so."

Five days later, Alan's car collided with another car in a rainstorm, and he was dead. Stephanie wept. Rather copiously. Preserved Alan's photographs, his three letters. And within a month her assignment for China had materialized; and she left, flying across the Atlantic to Lisbon, and by day hops on American planes to Chungking.

"I'll sure be able to see history in the making there," she said to her father.

"Just you take care of yourself and use your head, baby," Heston Ryder had replied.

Dad was great. He had not objected to her going off to China. He believed in audacity, adventure. Even for a girl. Above all, he loved her greatly, for she shared with him a certain fearlessness, a disregard of physical discomfort, a vigor of spirit and body, and that beauty which comes with it. On their holidays he had taken her and Jimmy, five years younger than she, trekking in the woods, camping sometimes for days on end. "A woman's got to know how to cope," he said. And this tradition of hardship as a thing to be coped with, a pioneer kind of challenge, was a solid bond between them.

As for her mother, Isabelle de Gersant, French aristocrat, wilting and pale in the too vital air of Texas, she had stared at her daughter and kissed her goodbye with cool and perfect manners, the usual bland look that raised between them an impalpable fence, a boundary across which they maintained with each other a scrupulous politeness. Mother enjoined her to be careful, always to drink boiled water, and said she would not forget to pray that all would be well. "My uncle had a servant from Shanghai," she recalled. "I believe his name was Wang. I wonder if by any chance you might meet some of his relatives."

Stephanie arrived in Chungking. Alan's memory did not prove a source of prolonged grief. The days contained longer and longer periods in which he was totally absent from her thoughts. He was absent from her dreams, and her waking hours were so full of indignation, disgust, and a growing empathy for the people who endured so much, that no time was left for him. Alan began to seem like an unfocused snapshot, a printed shadow, and no stab of memory or sudden tightening of the heart came to her on mention of his name.

Stephanie reached the cliff edge, where the city wall crumbled into a morass of stone and rubble. Five hundred feet below the spoon-shaped peninsula on which the city was built, the Yangtze River furled and unfurled its ochre waters like golden brocade. The stream was swollen with the melted mass of its Himalayan snows and had risen nearly a hundred feet that summer, wiping away some thousands of the derelict hovels sprouting too near its edge. The bat-sailed junks afloat seemed helpless as insects skimming the pellicle of a precipitous summer cascade, and the boatmen steered desperately while they chanted incantations of lament and defiance to the Great River.

Down a goat track in front of Stephanie was a fungoid growth of shacks; the effluvia of sweat, urine, and excreta, distinct, all-pervasive, enveloped her. One quarter of Chungking's two million people dwelt in these clusters which grew from the offal of the city, upon the garbage dumps, or whatever was rejected, thrown away, unwanted. The slum-dwellers lived off the city's putrescence and mushroomed mightily from its ordure. What did they do for food, for water? How did the children survive? Here was a story and Stephanie wanted to write it. She clutched her camera, her sandaled feet slipping on the crumbling rock and debris—and heard the screaming. She was now level with the first huddle of shacks.

They were pushing the men and the women out of their hovels, hitting them with rifle butts, knocking the flimsy bamboo props which supported roofs of cardboard, tarpaulin, rotten planks held in place by a piece of string, so that they fell in clouds of dirt and ash. Soldiers. Unkempt, dirty, and vicious. The kind that were beaten by their officers, and in turn beat the helpless people. They smashed earthenware jars; water spilt into the dust.

The women were screaming. A rhythmic wail, almost as if they sang. Agile and fleet children ran between the uniformed men, avoiding swinging rifle butts, picking up here a glass bottle, there a broken pan or some rags. They hugged these rescued treasures to their thin bodies and raced away towards the river, rolling down the slopes almost to the water's edge.

Why, why? Stephanie's mind raced back to the newsmen's talk. "Clearing the slums—they knock down those poor squatters' hovels, drag the men away to those death camps called recruiting camps—it's called keeping the city clean. . . ."

She raised her camera, pressed the button. Once, twice, three times. The soldiers had not yet seen her. They were now rifle-whipping the men, collecting them into a group, tying them with rope to each other. The women now threw themselves at the soldiers, screaming, suddenly ferocious, protecting their men, their men who were being taken away like cattle. Some thrust their own bodies under the soldiers' rifles.

The young woman, large-bellied and heaving painfully, came out of the last hut, leaning on a boy. Her breath was a harsh whisper, her face and hair wet with the sweat of labor. She walked up to the officer in charge. He was handsome, young, immaculate. He stood a little away, attended by two soldiers with fixed bayonets, watching the scene. He held a handkerchief covering his nose and mouth. The woman knelt in front of him, pointing to her belly, bowing to the ground then raising her face to him and again pointing to her belly. And her son also knelt, knocked his forehead on the ground, lifted his head, and again sank his face to the dust.

The officer looked down at them. He put his handkerchief in his pocket, took a step backwards, raised his leather-shod foot, and kicked the young woman in the belly.

And then Stephanie was upon him, pushing him so that he staggered, pushing him and shouting: "Oh you bastard, you dirty bastard, how can you, how can you . . ."

His two guards sprang at her, twisting her arms behind her back, and the officer was shouting and slapping her, swinging his fist and punching her face. A bright red spurt of blood gushed from her nose, fell on her dress. "Aiyah," shouted the soldiers, frightened, and let go of her. Blood. Spilling blood always caused panic, fear . . . blood, a live thing which called to Heaven for vengeance. Blood for blood.

The officer stopped, gasped, his face livid with rage and now with fear. This was a foreigner, a foreign woman, almost certainly an American. . . . Stephanie wiped her streaming nose with the back of her hand, still shouting: "You hit her, you kicked her . . . you monster . . ." She saw his hatred, also his fear. He turned, barked an order. The soldiers came running, they formed into ranks. And suddenly all of them were marching away, marching off behind the officer, who never looked back.

"God," said Stephanie. "Oh my God." She was shaking, trembling with anger. She put her head back, trying to staunch her nosebleed. Her dress stuck to her with sweat. She didn't have a handkerchief. *I mustn't faint or be sick.* She breathed hard, squeezed her arms tight against her chest, trying to control her shaking.

The woman lay where she had fallen, her face like gray

putty, her lips blue. The little boy crouched by her side, grasping her hand, moaning softly, "Ma, Ma." The bulging belly had a life of its own, and it stirred, moved. This galvanized Stephanie. *Must get her to a hospital. . . .*

"Doctor!" she shouted, using the loud voice of those who speak to the deaf, looking at the massed slum people who stood in glazed silence in a circle round her, their eyes upon her. "Doctor," she repeated. "Doctor!" she said again helplessly. *Oh Lord, what's the Chinese for doctor?*

The little boy seemed to guess. He spoke to the others in a high piping voice, and suddenly they were pressing forward; women coming to lift the prone body, men bringing a broken bamboo chair held together with thongs of split bamboo. Hands lifted the woman into it. Voices were raised, expostulating, explaining. The men placed the chair poles on their shoulders, shoulders grooved by long years of carrying such poles, and they all looked at Stephanie expectantly. She began walking in front of them, walking, as she wiped her face, wiped her nose, which had not stopped bleeding, with her hand.

Jen Yong slipped his hand under the child's head and raised it off the bed. The neck did not bend; rigid as a board, the body came off the mattress. Tuberculous meningitis. The child would die. There was no cure. He washed his hands at the enamel basin filled with pink disinfectant water.

He was tired. He had been up eighteen hours, and this was the third tuberculous meningitis of the night. But summer in Chungking was a harvest of death. Death went on the rampage among the suffocating streets and alleys; ravaged the overcrowded shacks and tenements. Dehydrated babies with dysentery, gangrene, three women comatose with malaria . . . a man vomiting blood, a ruptured appendix, a miner with a broken back . . . a case of tetanus, several beriberi cases . . . that had been his night in the emergency ward.

"We must send the child home," said Jen Yong wearily to Nurse Sha. He knew that family. Another child had been brought in the same condition the previous year. The father had large cavities in both lungs and smoked opium. He infected his children, his wife, his colleagues in the crowded bank where he was a clerk.

Tuberculosis was so common, so prevalent in the teeming city. And not only among the poor. It had now increased alarmingly among undernourished school teachers, university professors, students. With the uncontrolled inflation most of them could no longer buy enough to eat.

"Tell the father, Nurse Sha." Nurse Sha, solid as a concrete block, talked to the child's father. He ignored her and spat, hawking up a gluey mess upon the floor. She pointed to the spittoon. He ground his spittle into the floor with his heel. His young wife squatted on her haunches by him, nursing the new baby. She had the large brilliant eyes and beautiful skin of a Szechuan girl. Regularly he bartered her body to other men for money to buy opium.

"You must take the child home. There is nothing we can do, we have no bed," said Nurse Sha in her peremptory, unanswerable manner. The wife smiled brilliantly and looked up at her husband. He spat again, pretended he did not understand.

Stolid, squat-bodied Nurse Sha had walked from Shantung province, in North China. With two hundred of her schoolmates she had left Tsinan when the Japanese took the city in 1938. In Chungking she had studied nursing, and she was now in charge of several wards. She was devoted, tireless, bouncing back from the stream of daily tragedies with such brisk cheerfulness, such total absence of any emotion that at times Jen Yong felt gooseflesh creep over him. She was utterly unimaginative, and she was extremely competent. She had become almost indispensable to him, for Jen Yong was thin-skinned, could never refuse a patient without feeling remorseful; and when he had to harden his heart and send someone away to die in unrelieved agony he was anguished for a good while. He had become dependent on Nurse Sha for her efficient brutal unfeelingness, which spared him much fretting and worry. She never felt guilty about refusing to admit someone. . . .

"We cannot spare a bed," Jen Yong said.

Nurse Sha firmly placed the child in his father's arms. He immediately shifted the body upon his wife's shoulders, and she began to strap her dying son upon her back, because she would have to carry the new baby in her arms. Jen Yong escaped. He walked to the doctors' common room, removed his white coat, and sighing with tiredness poured himself a cup of hot water from the thermos flask on the table. Tea leaves were now too costly even for the doctors. He sipped, then stretched and yawned. He would go back to the dormitory and sleep, sleep.

Through the open door he saw Old Wang shambling in the corridor, holding a freshly washed spittoon in either hand. Old Wang bowed and murmured "Doctor" and Jen Yong merely nodded. He must not be seen talking to Old Wang.

Old Wang and he met almost once a week, at night, but this was part of Jen Yong's other life.

Another life. Another China. One which held out hope, promise for its people. It had all begun way back in 1935. The Japanese had already taken Manchuria, were steadily invading North China. And in all China's universities and high schools, young students angrily demanded resistance to Japan, paraded in the streets, held demonstrations.

And were hosed down, shot down, jailed by Chiang Kaishek, who did not want to fight the Japanese invaders; who went on making ruinous military expeditions in war against the Chinese Communists. . . .

And then, in 1936, Chiang Kaishek had been captured by the Communists. The whole world thought he would be killed. But instead he emerged from captivity to announce that the Communists and he had come to a united front alliance—against Japan!

Never had Chiang been so popular. And Jen Yong, and so many like him, had been carried by a great wave of patriotism into believing Chiang Kaishek would keep his promise. From 1938 to 1941, Jen Yong had believed and hoped.

But by 1941, when Chiang quietly ordered his armies to stop fighting Japan, to let the Communists bear the brunt of the fighting—while he again begun attacking his allies, the Communists—Jen Yong had changed. . . .

Not only he, but hundreds, thousands of the non-Communist intelligentsia now watched with growing despair the disintegration by corruption of the Kuomintang; its tyranny, the overwhelming power of the secret police.

Hundreds of young people—high school and university graduates, writers, teachers—began to slip away from Chungking to Yenan, the major stronghold of the Communist guerillas. Because nothing mattered but this fierce love for China, for China—and the red guerillas were patriotic. Even among those who, like Yong, rejected Communist dogma, the Communist Party had gained great prestige since 1937. And now, all over China, behind Japanese lines, in conquered territory, and even in Chungking, heart and center of Chiang Kaishek's power, clandestine Communist organizations were mushrooming.

Old Wang, he of the apathetic silly face, who only said "aye, aye, coming" when anyone called him, was the head of the branch organization within the hospital.

By day he cleaned spittoons and bedpans, shuffling into the wards to collect the filthy receptacles. He hauled two buckets of muddy river water and stood them next to the public latrines in the hospital grounds. There he worked, cleaning the utensils, emptying the water into the latrines. It was rumored that he sold the latrine produce, precious manure, to the night soil bearers for the fields round the city.

The basement where he slept housed discarded and broken equipment: bits of rubber tubing, disused enamel basins, shreds of lint, wads of unusable cotton wool. Pink-bellied rats squeaked and scampered there, and it was said that Old Wang caught them and flayed them and sold their skins.

Old Wang gave directives to Jen Yong. When Jen Yong had requested permission to leave Chungking, to serve on the guerilla battlefields, Old Wang had consulted the leadership and replied: "No, not for the time being. You are more useful in Chungking. You train people, collect medicines for us . . . you must stay."

Jen Yong had stayed. His latest batch of trainees would now leave for Yenan.

"It will be Sunday," Old Wang had said to Jen Yong.

Sunday was the hospital's annual picnic day. There would be about two to three hundred people, students and nurses, doctors and their families, at the Hot Springs Park. But there would be five people less when they returned to the city. Five people who would be smuggled out of Chungking that day, who would, in various disguises and with faked permits, travel to Yenan. Five, trained by Dr. Jen Yong.

Jen Yong walked to the hospital side exit. From it a track

16

crept up a hillock. Upon it stood several buildings of gray brick. One of them was the dormitory for the hospital doctors.

"Dr. Jen, Dr. Jen." Nurse Li of the emergency ward, a fine sweat of distress upon her face, was behind him. "We've got a serious case and Dr. Liu is busy with a hemorrhage. . . . Could you please . . ."

Jen's first reaction was weary anger. I've been up all night, he thought sullenly, but already his feet were following hers, retracing their steps, entering the emergency ward.

He shoved through the crowded room; the smell gripped his throat and he wondered how delicate Nurse Li could endure the stench, eight hours every day. Lying on a stretcher was a woman with a large belly; her face gray putty, her breathing imperceptible. By the stretcher stood a young foreign woman, with blood on her dress and a red welt across her face.

"This American woman brought the patient," said Nurse Li in Chinese as she wound the blood pressure apparatus round the patient's arm. "Only 50/80, Doctor, I can't feel her pulse."

Jen Yong's hands moved on the belly, his stethoscope picked up the baby's heartbeat. Fast and amazingly clear. "What happened?" he asked in English, turning to Stephanie.

"She was kicked in the belly by an officer . . . I was there," said Stephanie.

He saw, herded in a corner, the three *huakan* bearers, the little boy. They secreted that particular foul odor of the utterly poor.

"It's bad, isn't it?" said Stephanie.

"Ruptured uterus, I think," said Jen Yong. "Set up a drip, Nurse Li."

"She's still alive?" queried Stephanie.

"Yes . . ." He looked at Stephanie's dress and then at her face. His head was spinning with tiredness. Through a blur he saw that she was pretty, and he smiled. "Are you a missionary, madam?"

"No, I'm a newspaperwoman," said Stephanie.

The ward helpers began to wheel the stretcher away. Jen Yong said: "Thank you for bringing the patient, madam."

"Miss. Ryder. Stephanie Ryder."

"My name is Jen Yong. Perhaps you'd like to telephone later. Find out the patient's condition."

"Yes, I'll do that," said Stephanie. He was thin and tired, very tired. She liked his hands. They had been so deft and gentle upon the woman.

He straightened, willing his tiredness away, and walked out of the room.

"Let me give you a hot towel to wipe your face," said Nurse Li to Stephanie. "And oh, your dress . . ."

"Don't worry," said Stephanie. "Cold water will take the stains out."

Nurse Li's face lit up. She thought: What a nice foreigner . . . so simple. She gave Stephanie an ointment. "Apply twice a day to your face. And please call the hospital about nine o'clock tonight. Dr. Jen does ward rounds at that time."

"I'll do that, and thanks, Nurse," said Stephanie.

Nurse Li smiled at her. "*We* thank you . . . for caring," she replied.

Stephanie walked out, followed by eyes, the inescapable eyes of the teeming crowd, watching the foreign woman who had brought a Chinese slum-dweller to the hospital. It parted in front of her like smooth water. But she was not aware of the reverence, only that the sun was harsh and that her face was sore. And that she looked a mess. And her camera was gone. What had she done with it? Where had she left it?

Oh cripes, that would have been some picture. She walked back along the main road. No one seemed to notice the blood on her dress.

Jen Yong. An easy name to remember. He would have been good-looking anywhere. Not brawny, only slightly taller than herself, not at all the rugged he-man type. But a man. So sure of himself. Moving so neatly. And that mop of blue-black hair, those eyes with the flying eyebrows. A slim nose. He was built like a precision instrument, or like one of those polished jade statues. His skin.

"Nice," she said aloud.

She came in view of the yellow brick wall surrounding the Press Hostel. Two two-storied buildings, brick below, wattle and plaster above, with green shutters. In front ran a verandah, where the newsmen sat at night, slapping at mosquitoes and drinking the strong local liquor, *maotai*. At the

18

gate the sentinels stood, rifles with fixed bayonets on their shoulders. They were supposed to protect the foreigners from robbers and "bad elements," or so the newsmen were told. "What nonsense. It's to keep the people from coming to talk to us," John Moore had told Stephanie. The Kuomintang government did not want unmonitored contact between foreigners and the Chinese people. . . .

No one was in the hall; her colleagues must be at the press conference in the Ministry of Information building on the hillock opposite the hostel. She went up the stairs to her room, washed, and changed her dress.

Secretary Hung opened the door, clicked his heels, and shouted: "Your Excellency, the foreign newsmen have assembled."

Henry Wong, Chief Information Officer, External Affairs Department, pushed his armchair back with dignified weariness. He resented Secretary Hung's "alert and active" manner. But a new directive from Number One Big Wind (a current nickname for Chiang Kaishek; the other nickname, taken up with relish by Stilwell, was Old Peanut, because Chiang was bald) had enforced upon government officials a demeanor copied from the German Nazis, and threatened that anyone who "threw away the face of the country by slouching or waddling" would be shot.

Henry Wong had had a bad night. Meena had massaged his neck muscles, but that had not dispelled the headache. He slumped back in his chair, trying to compose his spirit before confronting the newsmen.

Every time he had a press conference ahead of him, the headache arrived first.

Before the Sino-Japanese war, being Chinese was not something to crow about. For decades, for almost a century, China had been bullied, invaded, colonized, despised, humiliated. The Sick Man of Asia. Henry remembered the sign at the entrance to the park in his native Shanghai: "No dogs or Chinamen admitted." Western scholars admired China's ancient civilization but remained totally callous about China's present misery.

Then suddenly, because of the war, China was no longer servile, passive, despicable, cowardly. The Chinese were fighting back. There was no longer any gap between intellectuals such as Henry Wong, an American-educated official in the Chiang Kaishek government, and his own people. Until then, Henry had felt cut off, ashamed of the poverty of China, secretly ashamed of being Chinese. But the war had made Chinese poverty heroic, glorious. Rags became mantles full of stars. To endure and to suffer under Japanese bombings became the Odyssey. All over the world foreign newsmen wrote glowingly of China, of her people's indomitable courage. Never mind that they were poor. They were brave . . . they fought for Freedom!

The foreign newsmen in China had reveled in being able to live in, to share, the primitive conditions. They were awed by the people's valor and wrote articles praising the war effort of the Kuomintang.

As Chief Information Officer, Henry had made good friends of the foreign newsmen. He had been congratulated by his superiors on his handling of information. And if some of the human interest stories enshrined in many a book in America had been more than embellished, nevertheless it was true that the morale of the people had been high, their heroism believable.

And then in 1941 Chiang Kaishek's mania had started again: charging "lack of discipline," he ordered the massacre of several units of the Communist New Fourth Army. Unfortunately, the people killed had been doctors, nurses, and their patients—thousands of them.

The foreign newsmen had reacted badly. Diplomats warned that a renewal of civil war in China would be disastrous for the allied cause, because now China's war had become part of the Second World War. That astute and clever Communist, Chou Enlai, had been in Chungking at the time. Although hemmed in by Chiang's Secret Police, he had talked to foreign newsmen, had made an excellent impression on them. And the whole population of the city had gathered to listen to Chou Enlai saying that, despite the attacks, the Communists would fulfill their duty as patriots and continue to fight Japan.

Henry Wong's headaches began when he realized that Old Peanut loved his power above all reason, above all common sense.

The foreign newsmen had finally learned that only the Communist armies had been fighting Japan in the last five years.

Chiang Kaishek had held Henry Wong responsible. Summoned him for a dressing down. Henry's heart still faltered when he thought of Chiang's cold fury. A few people never returned from such an encounter. They were shot. (Madame Chiang, American educated, had saved Henry, pointing out to her husband that Americans would be very upset should a Harvard man be shot out of hand.)

Henry had created special teams in his department; called them the Verification Bureau. Their job was to think up stories for the newsmen.

He arranged impromptu visits to recruiting camps. One of these visits had gone very wrong: the clerk in charge (who later had been shot), being a Szechuanese, had mistaken the word *four* for *ten*—pronounced almost alike. As a result, John Moore had arrived at the camp on the fourth of April instead of the tenth.

Other visits had been more successful. Visiting editors and VIPs loved to visit military camps, to come in physical contact with genuine Chinese soldiers. They could not know that handpicked members of the Kuomintang youth league, chosen for their sturdiness, were made available for the occasion, as were cooks from the Secret Police who produced meals the real soldiers had never dreamed of.

The weekly press conference was now an ordeal. Confronted with an array of maps to indicate mythical campaigns against Japanese divisions (how the Verification Bureau sweated to produce these maps!), Terry Longworth (filing five hundred words a day) had pointed out that the enemy's "defeats and withdrawals" had resulted in a further five hundred-mile Japanese advance. Reuters' quiet little man (two thousand words a day), adding up the Japanese proclaimed killed in the last six months, had come up with a total which was more than all the existing Japanese divisions in China.

Henry smiled at the newsmen. His smile pleaded: You know, and I know, that I'm lying. But I've got to live.

As if the British and the Americans didn't lie, thought Henry resentfully. Look at Winston Churchill, closing the

Burma Road to China right in the middle of 1942, saying it was "necessary," because he wanted America to concentrate her war effort on Europe . . . because he didn't want America meddling in Britain's Asian colonies, in India. . . .

The Americans hoped to keep Chiang Kaishek fighting. Roosevelt both cajoled and threatened Chiang, wrote him angry letters, sent Vice President Wallace, sent Stilwell. . . . They did not understand Chiang. And Chiang only understood POWER. The real issue was power. Nothing else mattered to him. Nothing else mattered to the Communists either.

But now there was Yenan. Where the Communists had landed after the Long March. And in Yenan a man had emerged, Mao Tsetung. Seconded by that extraordinarily able scholar and revolutionary, Chou Enlai.

In Yenan, against all odds, the Communists had thrived, expanded, and Roosevelt wanted to know more about them.

Chiang Kaishek had had to agree to an American military observer mission to Yenan.

The mission had arrived there on July 22 and was sending reports, favorable reports, directly to Washington, bypassing Chungking's censors.

To make matters worse, in May of 1944, the Japanese had begun a major offensive to wipe out the dozens of American air bases set up within the last three years in unconquered Chinese territory.

And Chiang Kaishek had ordered his armies *not* to fight the Japanese. *Not* to protect the American air bases.

To the great fury of the Americans, some air bases had been overrun by the Japanese. But the Communists had cleverly mobilized the village people, the peasantry in their areas, to rescue American airmen. About a hundred pilots, mechanics, and other personnel had been saved. Everyone knew it.

And everyone wondered how Henry Wong would explain Chiang's strange aversion to fight Japan?

The three censors were waiting for Henry Wong at the door of the press room. Within it, the correspondents could be heard talking among themselves; two electric fans whirred noisily above their heads.

And here was John Moore, rising to greet him. "Good to see you," said John Moore, shaking his hand. John knew that Henry Wong would be subject to a barrage of unpleasant questions. It was almost like a bull fight, with Henry the gentle bull trying to look as if he enjoyed being gored.

Henry smiled bleakly at John Moore, said, "My dear John, I'm glad to see you," and bracing his shoulders, entered the room and began to lie.

two

THE operating theater reeked of blood. Jellied clots were squished on the tiled floor under the cotton boots of the doctors and the nurses.

The woman's uterus had ruptured. She was alive, but the baby had died.

David Eanes worked carefully and quickly, mumbling of post-operative shock.

"What have we given her, Claudia?" Head Nurse Claudia Preaux, the statuesque French-Canadian in charge of the blood bank, stood in a corner.

"Three. We don't have another bottle, Dr. Eanes."

"Oh well," said Eanes, "she'll have to make do, won't she?" He regularly gave blood, as did Jen Yong. But now, due to the soaring prices of food, the doctors were as undernourished as the populace and donations were dropping off.

Among the people there were very few volunteers; the Chinese feared bloodletting. Nurse Preaux (who herself gave as much as she could) kept combing the diplomatic corps, the missionaries, the foreign newsmen, and the American military personnel. Among the Chinese officials, the mayor and Henry Wong and his wife, Meena, were also donors, which was remarkable. Not one of the well-fed military commanders would give.

The operation was almost over. Both surgeons were exhausted, dripping sweat, their clothes clinging to their backs, buttocks, and thighs.

"David, you go, your patients are waiting, I'll close her up," said Jen Yong.

"But you've been up all afternoon yesterday and all night, Yong," David protested.

24

"A few minutes more won't hurt," said Yong, smiling behind his mask. He was too exhausted to feel tired. David Eanes had done the main job, Jen Yong only trusting himself to assist.

Eanes ripped off his rubber gloves and started stripping on his way to the shower. Yong finished the last suture, swabbed mercurochrome, attended to the bandaging, checked the blood pressure. He felt unsteady with oversweating. He would drink some water, take a spoonful of salt. He checked once again, then went off to the shower. Exhaustion had now induced in him a tranced state. He could no longer feel anything, except a vague soreness coursing up and down his body. His head seemed to float unconnected with the rest of him. His legs wavered, the floor came up to meet his feet.

"Dr. Jen Yong?"

Outside the doctors' common room stood a man, lean and youngish, not in uniform but with a vague air of wearing one.

"I am Dr. Jen."

The man bowed, he had excellent manners. "My lowly name is Tsing, of the Second Bureau." He took out a card, presented it with both hands to Jen Yong. "If I may solicit a few moments of your valuable time . . ."

Jen felt a pinch in his throat, a constriction of the chest. A slight tremor shook his hand as he took the visiting card. Second Bureau. That meant the Secret Police. Political. Had someone talked too much? Would he have time to warn Old Wang?

"Certainly, Colonel Tsing."

Jen went to the capped thermos flask, poured out two cups of hot water, indicated to Tsing the settee, place of honor. "Please." All this formality while he tried to steady himself.

Tsing received the cup in both hands. "Your inferior brother is too honored," he said using the classically courteous phrase. His eyes gleamed as he sat upon a chair, sipped with just the right amount of relish, put the cup down, and cleared his throat. "Dr. Jen, your great reputation has reached all ears. We know we can rely on you."

"You evaluate me too highly, Colonel Tsing."

"My superiors hold you in great esteem. Very great. Hence I have been sent . . . it concerns a ridiculously small affair . . . the patient brought in this morning by a foreign woman."

Jen relaxed. Tsing noted the relief, as he had noted the tremor of Jen's fingers holding his visiting card. He sucked his teeth respectfully.

"The foreign woman interfered when a unit of our army was obtaining recruits. She assaulted the officer-in-charge, Major Hsu. He is now in a hospital, suffering from an internal chest wound."

"Wounded?" said Jen, vast incredulity in his polite voice. "I find it hard to believe that a woman, even foreign, could wound an officer of our valorous army."

Tsing's ears noted the sarcasm, his eyes bored into Jen Yong. "Our doctors have examined Major Hsu and reported on his condition. . . ."

"The patient brought in appears to have been grievously hurt," said Jen Yong. "We had to operate urgently. . . ."

Tsing again sucked his teeth. "According to many witnesses, the woman fell down and hurt herself. . . ."

So that was to be the story.

"Major Hsu is well-connected, although employed in a somewhat lowly post at the moment," Tsing continued. "He is young, but has promise. He is . . . trusted."

This meant that Hsu was a protégé of someone high up in the Secret Police and that he would soon begin to climb its echelons.

Tsing continued: "Miss Ryder—that is the name of the American—has committed a serious offense, interfering needlessly with slum clearance. We do not wish any unpleasantness to occur; we hope the case can be settled without . . . trouble."

Jen Yong put his cup down. "As a medical person with no influence, I can only state that the patient's condition was extremely serious."

"No one actually saw her being struck," replied Tsing blandly.

Jen Yong noted the blandness, swollen with menace. And suddenly he saw Stephanie's face, the welt across it, the blood on her dress. He remembered her smile. That smile, so unconscious of danger! So open! Suddenly she was in front of him, and he was staring at her eyes with their golden pinpoints, like stars in a velvet night, like . . .

He shook himself, rubbed his tired face. Stephanie's image lingered with him.

"I shall certainly note what you have told me, Colonel Tsing."

Tsing rose, murmuring apologies, suave and mannerly, master of the situation. He bowed several times to Jen Yong, but there was a little mockery in his exaggerated politeness.

Jen Yong walked through the emergency ward. He had to reassure Nurse Li. Undoubtedly Tsing had been to emergency while he was operating and questioned the staff.

Nurse Li was filling a syringe, and by the way she looked at him he knew that she was worried. He stood near her and said in a low voice: "It was about the patient brought in this morning. Nothing else." She nodded. There was no need to alert the Organization.

He walked out into the sun, squinting at the glare as he climbed the pathway to the doctors' dormitory. His eyes were sore and he kept them half shut and Stephanie was there, dancing beneath the lids. And he heard her voice. I'm hallucinating, he thought. Ryder. Stephanie Ryder. She was beautiful. He did not notice the little boy squatting by the pathway, who now rose and followed him.

Stephanie had let down the bamboo screen in front of her window and lay on her bed in the semi-darkness under the whirring electric fan. She was trying to digest the episode. To put it in words. In a little while she would hurl herself at her portable typewriter and write it all down. Write down the indignation which burnt in her.

The newsmen had returned from the press conference. Alistair Choate stood outside her door. He knocked.

"Stephanie, are you there? Are you all right?"

"Yes, Alistair, but I'm lying down. I've got a bit of a headache."

"I warned you about the heat. . . . Would you like me to bring you anything?"

"Thanks, but I'll be up in a moment."

"See you at lunch," said Alistair.

She heard his feet depart, the creak of the badly jointed wood floor.

Then John Moore was knocking at her door and Stephanie opened to him. She felt safe with John.

"I thought you'd be at the press conference. . . . Good God, Stephanie, what's happened to your face?"

Stephanie chuckled, a forlorn and defiant sob. "I got into some trouble, John." She told him the story. "I'm going to write it up—it was awful. . . ."

John listened, impassive. Then he sat on her chair, crossed his legs.

"Stephanie, listen. Your story would never pass the censors. And if it *did* get by, I doubt whether your readers would believe it. It's too . . . melodramatic. They're not ready for that kind of stuff. Not yet, anyway."

Stephanie threw up her head in the coltish way she had and said angrily: "I've *got* to do something about this. I can't just forget it."

"Stephanie, please, if you want to write the story do so by all means, write it out of you. But don't send it yet. Remember, it's not just that one man hitting a poor pregnant woman. It's the system which breeds that kind of brutality. And that system is very very old, a couple of thousand years old, or more. . . ."

"But it's monstrous," replied Stephanie angrily. "Surely you don't expect me to condone this kind of thing."

"Let me tell you a story," said John. "I've got a friend— let's call him Peter, an Englishman. He's teaching English at the university here. He's a bit of a poet too. He used to like walking in the hills. But one morning he met two soldiers carrying something in a basket slung on a pole between them. It was a man, another soldier, moaning a bit. Just moaning. Peter stopped to watch. The two soldiers got to a bit of soft ground and put down the big basket. They also had two spades slung on the pole, and they began to dig. They dug a hole, and the soldier in the basket kept moaning, a very monotonous sound, Peter said. And when the hole had been dug, the two soldiers took the basket and tipped it and the man fell into the hole. Then they covered it with earth and stamped it down and went away. And Peter just stood there. He didn't move."

Stephanie covered her face. "Oh God," she whispered, "oh God in Heaven."

"Peter is still around," said John Moore. "He still gets a bit wild-eyed when he remembers. . . ."

"I would have dug up the man," said Stephanie. "Even with my bare hands . . . dug him up . . ."

"*You* would, Stephanie. But Peter didn't. Because he couldn't, he was paralyzed . . . paralyzed by something in the air, something that got hold of him. . . . So many of us, even the best, have felt it . . . this shocking inertia . . . because there's just too much cruelty, too much. Daily, hourly, every second of the day. . . . And anyway, the story would be censored out, both here and at home. . . . Remember, in times of war, certain things cannot be said, if it's damaging to ourselves or to our allies. Wars are won by myths that foster confidence, sacrifice. People back home still cling to the myth of Chiang Kaishek. Even Teddy White, when he wrote what he saw, had some of his dispatches edited out of recognition."

"No wonder people are going over to Yenan," said Stephanie. "I couldn't understand why communism should attract them. But after today I'm beginning to understand. . . ."

"We've got a mission there now to find out what they're really like," said John. "I don't like communism either, but there have been a lot of good reports about Yenan—from every American and Englishman who went there. Besides, I hear they're not all dyed-in-the-wool Communists, mostly just very patriotic Chinese."

He told her about his own bone-eroding doubts, the problem of writing about China in a fair and balanced way. They had tormented him for over two years. "We've got to keep balanced, Stephanie, not let one incident affect us too much."

"But what's happened today is just damn hard for me to take, John. I don't know how I can write anything fit to print after this. . . ."

Henry Wong entered his bedroom for the usual after lunch siesta, a habit which seven years in America had not changed. He heaved his body onto the Beautyrest mattress. Meena's second cousin, assistant director of the Transport Bureau, had brought it by truck over the Burma Road in early 1942. He patted the pillows, closed his eyes. The telephone rang.

"Oh blast it," said Henry. *"Wei,"* he shouted into the mouthpiece. Secretary Hung, stammering with fright, told him that General Yee wanted to see him. Immediately.

General Yee. The Defense Ministry. This might mean Number One Big Wind; and as he thought once again of appearing before Chiang Kaishek, Henry felt his lower limbs grow flaccid.

As he dressed, Henry's mind raced over the morning press conference. Had he been wrongly reported? Would he be shot? Old Peanut had shot seventeen young commanders suspected of a plot against him earlier that year. . . .

What have I done wrong?

When Terry Longworth had quoted General Stilwell (whom Terry idolized) as to the obstacles encountered "not from the Japanese enemy, but from Chungking," Henry Wong had replied that General Stilwell's zeal and competence were well-known, but he must remember the immense difficulties China labored under. When Dangforth of AP had asked how much of the one hundred million dollars recently given to China by Roosevelt had simply disappeared into the pockets of Chiang's commanders, Henry had said that in all countries inventories and budgets were not always accessible to ordinary scrutiny, especially in time of war. John Moore, whom Henry considered a good friend, had also been acerbic. But Henry would always forgive John, knowing John would not betray him. For one night, when his tongue had loosened, he had told John of his cousin, in Yenan with the Communists. "All of us have family on both sides," he had said, thinking of Madame Chiang, whose beautiful sister, Madame Sun Yatsen, also sided with the reds. And confided that, at times, he himself was tempted to swap horses. . . .

General Yee's residence overlooked the beautiful Chialing River; summer silt did not invade its waters, it glowed with opal tinges between pale gray cliffs surmounted by clumps of camphor and Chinese oak and pine. Yee awaited Henry in the living room, with its carved furniture inlaid with Tali marble, each piece a surrealist landscape. He was a short man, agile of mind, "round within and round without," able to see every facet of a question, able to adapt his mind to any situation. His nickname was Winner Takes All, for he also had phenomenal luck at the game of mahjong.

He shadowboxed every morning for an hour and for another hour practiced calligraphy. "Be at ease, Henry. Take off your jacket. In this heat it is only possible to think clearly in loose apparel."

Yee poured Dragon Well tea, brought all the way from far Hangchow. War or no war, he kept up his collection of precious teas. He also continued to admire Japan. He had, the previous year, while on an inspection tour of the apocryphal "frontline," called upon the Japanese commander in charge. The Western press had been puzzled and even indignant about this act of courtesy between gentlemen of the same profession. But killing and getting killed was a matter for the lowborn, those who were expendable, whose lives or deaths did not matter in the least to the planet or to the history of Man. Generals did not kill each other. They sat, drank tea together, exchanged poems, and planned the games of a war in which other men died.

Yee came to the point. "A disagreeable incident, Henry. A foreign newspaperwoman tried to hinder the clearing of a slum by a squad of soldiers. She struck the young major in charge, in front of his men. He lost face, of course. Now it happens that his father and General Tai Lee's father were sworn brothers. . . ."

General Tai Lee. The Scorpion, the *éminence grise*, head of the Secret Police. To be feared even more than Chiang Kaishek.

Henry said: "I shall enquire." But Yee waved this away.

"Publicity would be inopportune. Curbing irresponsible reporting is your job. I do not think the matter is of any importance, except that the young woman may write it up. You must persuade her not to do so."

"I am most incompetent," began Henry. The self-deprecatory stance was ritual good manners.

Yee again waved this away. "Americans are somewhat naïve. We must be patient, educate them in—ah—wisdom. I do not wish the Secret Police to go overboard in this matter. They sometimes . . . ah, lack judgment. I hear they are circulating a document enjoining much harsher treatment of our left-leaning intellectuals. This is *not* good. Intellectuals are important, they must not be ill-treated. It is unwise." Yee fanned himself, and in the silence only the roar and swell of the noon cicadas accompanied the soft

31

strokes of his fan. "The press is powerful in America . . . we must be careful to—ah—avoid undue publicity."

"I understand, General," said Henry.

Henry left, far happier than he had been on arrival. The Secret Police was always ready to start a witch hunt. He would invite the young woman to his house. Stephanie Ryder. Texas. Radcliffe. He had signed her accreditation card. He would turn Meena on to her. Schools, orphanages, refugee camps, even a guerilla heroine or two. . . . She would get stories to write about; enough to dispel the unpleasant impression, to show that it was an isolated event. . . .

And, reasoned Henry, the head of the Secret Police, Tai Lee, must also be worried. Because if Chiang heard of the incident, he might—he just might—bark out: "Shoot Major Hsu." If he was in one of his disciplinary moods. And to prove himself democratic.

The matter must be handled carefully. The censors must be alerted, a watch set on Stephanie's letters. Henry Wong sighed. No afternoon nap today.

Jen Yong awoke. Immediately Stephanie's voice, her face, were there with him. He looked at his watch. It was seven at night. He had missed the evening meal, which was at six, but the cook had kept some food for him.

Jen Yong shared a small brick bungalow with nine other doctors. Four of them, including Yong, were bachelors and lived together in one room. The other five had wives and children, and each family occupied one room. They shared a cook, a cleaner, and a washerwoman. Because inflation was uncontrollable, half the monthly wage of the doctors was paid in rice, and the price of rice per picul of weight became the basic accounting unit. There was no family allowance, and families with numerous children frequently went hungry. Meat was eaten once a week, sometimes only once a month. The unmarried were slightly luckier, except that three of the bachelor doctors supported relatives on their meager stipend. Two of them, engaged for the last four years, could not afford to marry. In their spare time, they tried to do private practice or coach students to supplement their income.

Jen Yong was deemed lucky. He did not have to send money to relatives, for his family in Japanese-occupied Shanghai was wealthy. He shared his rice with those who had not enough, and also bought extras such as peanuts or sugar for the children.

Jen Yong sluiced himself clean in the common washroom, then ate his evening meal. He could hear his neighbor, Dr. Liu, teaching his two children, and upstairs Mrs. Wan speaking with her husband. The walls were so thin that every noise came through them easily. The Wans had three children and a fourth was coming. Jen Yong had offered to share his tiny space with the eldest Wan boy. The boy had moved in with him, and the room now held five bodies.

Dusk had fallen and the heat poured out of every stone as he walked back to the hospital for the evening ward rounds. How silly he had been, not to tell her when to telephone. And perhaps she would not telephone. Perhaps . . . How could he find her again? A newspaperwoman, she had said . . . Stephanie Ryder . . . The syllables filled his mouth with coolness, with delight.

A small boy stood in the heat-dense shadows as Jen Yong reached the end of the pathway. A beggar. His hand went to his pocket, but the boy bowed and said *"Taifu,"* calling him by his title of doctor, and then stood humbly, looking down at the ground, ready to kneel, to knock his head on the ground in supplication. The boy was a typical Szechuanese: stunted, his bones bent by too much hard work too early, deprived in every limb. But his eyes were large and bright, and he had high cheekbones; and he carried himself with that competent small swagger which was typical of the people of his province. They always bounced back after every blow, every calamity. . . . This boy knew pain and suffering, but he also had the wry humor of his kind, and in his humility there was dignity.

Jen Yong, coming from the big coastal city of Shanghai had fallen in love with the tough fierce people of Szechuan. He loved their brash and singing chatter. And how they talked! Great tales, long as unending dragons in battle array! He had often sat on the low stone wall bordering the winding road past the hospital, listening to them—for in this part of China even the beggars made poetry. And he, the man from Shanghai, sophisticated and affluent, felt the throb and pulse of his country here, in the devastated and noisome city. And it was the drums of hope he heard, beating steadily, beating the song of the future.

"What do you want, little devil?"

A term of endearment. Everyone used it. The Communist underground was especially good at recruiting such boys. During the Long March hundreds of them had followed the red armies. They had learnt to read, to write, to fight; some of them now commanded guerilla battalions. Oh, thought Jen Yong, how much talent in my people, so many of these beggars are potential doctors and scientists. . . . Oh, who will begin to give them their birthright if people like myself do not try?

"My mother was brought to doctor this morning by the foreign lady. I have not dared disturb the doctor . . . may I ask how my mother is?"

Of course, there had been a boy, holding the patient's hand. Her son.

"I am just going to see your mother. Come with me." He put out a hand, meaning to place it on the boy's shoulder, but the boy raised an arm, shielding his face, shrinking as if he might be hit. Then he stopped himself midway, flashing his teeth, grinning sheepishly. Jen's hand rested lightly on the ragged shirt. It was stiff with dirt. "What is your name? How old are you this year?"

"My family name is Liang; my small name is Little Pond. I am fifteen years old."

He looks twelve, thought Jen Yong. The Szechuanese always added a year to their age, sometimes two. He was probably fourteen. Many like him were being taken into the recruiting camps; taken off the fields where they worked, planting or harvesting rice. They carried guns too tall for them. They starved and died quickly.

Little Pond limped.

"Your leg is bad?" asked Yong.

"I was helping my Pa to pull a cart with a load of great stones. I was pushing behind the cart. The stones were for our landlord who wanted a fine tomb." His father had stumbled, the cart had backed, his leg was caught under the wheel. "But I became well again, *Taifu*. This spring my Pa was taken by the army from our landlord's fields. The landlord threw us out, Ma and I, because we could not till the land. . . . I tried hard, but I could not work as father did. And so we came to the city."

34

Jen Yong said: "This is great bitterness for you, so young."

Little Pond replied, imitating the adults he had heard, "Before the down-river people came here, we were poor. But we owned two things: our spit and our shit. Now even this is taken from us."

Jen Yong said: "It is not our fault, we came here because we were driven away by the Japanese."

"Is that true?" said Little Pond. And then: "I spoke a great wrong, for you come from down-the-river, and you do good to our people."

They had reached the hospital and Jen Yong was apprehensive. "Little Pond, your mother was very ill. We tried our best to save her life."

"I know," said Little Pond. His voice was colorless in the sultry dark heat which clogged all gestures and feelings. "*Taifu* has given blood for my Ma."

"Who told you that?"

"I heard it."

The people's grapevine; whispers among the long files of water carriers and dung carriers and chair carriers and all the other bearers of loads, bearing the load of war and tyranny. They generated a careful small breeze of words which went through walls and fortresses and prisons and nourished the city's mind.

"I did not give blood to your mother. This blood was given by many people, Chinese and foreign. . . . All blood is the same, all over the world . . . did you know that?"

"I did not know," said Little Pond.

They went up to the ward. Liang Ma was alive. Her face was still waxen, her nostrils pinched, her breath almost imperceptible. But she was alive. Jen Yong checked the bottle of glucose saline dripping into her arm. He checked the urine catheter. He wrote on the file, ordering an injection of vitamin B.

"The baby did not live, Little Pond."

"Was it a man child or a girl slave?" asked Little Pond in his neutral voice.

"A man child."

"This blood debt is written in my heart, *Taifu*," said Little Pond.

Jen Yong said, "Have you eaten?" and again put his hand to his pocket.

Little Pond shook his head. "I have eaten, *Taifu*," he lied.

35

He knew the question was a dismissal. Had he not come into the hospital with a doctor, he would have been thrown out. Because he was so dirty, because he smelt so bad. Ma lay there, in a clean bed, along with twenty or more other women, in a big room. Everything was so clean, Little Pond felt he dirtied the place with his presence. "I am going now, *Taifu*."

"Come again tomorrow night to see your mother," said Jen Yong. He would tell Nurse Sha and the other nurses to let the boy in. The hospital rules were strict. It was impossible to allow visits, except in first class. The common wards would overflow with people, bringing their lice and their squalor. But Jen Yong wrote a special note for Nurse Sha and Nurse Li to allow Little Pond to see his mother for a few minutes at night, and gave the note to the boy.

Old Wang sat with Prosperity Tang in the basement. Tang was burly and looked like a well-to-do shopkeeper. He wore a long robe of Neichiang linen and cool handwoven slippers. His hands were very clean and he laughed fatly, as becomes a man who earns good money. Actually, Prosperity Tang was the Party secretary in charge of the district underground. But no one knew it. He had played the role of a small trader, solely occupied with making money, for sixteen years.

Prosperity Tang came to the hospital to buy discards and rejects: old broken boxes of cardboard and plywood; unusable cotton bandages, so dirty they could no longer be rewashed and sterilized, but useful for patching winter clothes. Scraps of paper. Bottles with broken tops. Worn rubber tubing . . . all of it valuable, precious even. To stuff a pallet, patch a garment, mend a jacket, block a hole in a roof or wall. Half the population of Chungking bought litter and turned it to use. A single rusty nail, a spool of thread, a battered spoon . . . all could be used.

Prosperity Tang had a contract with the hospital accountant for buying the hospital garbage. He used his visits to converse with Old Wang, who lived amid the offal in the basement. Wang reported to Tang on the progress of the Party's infiltration among the staff and students of the teaching hospital. Now he gave Tang the news about Tsing of the

Secret Police coming to see Jen Yong. "It was because of this woman brought to the hospital by an American. It is a pity that attention was drawn upon Dr. Jen."

Tang nodded. Both men knew the danger of being noticed, even casually. Invisibility was the perfect protection, and Jen Yong had been unknown to the Secret Police. Never had he been mixed up with any meeting, demonstration, or group deemed suspect. Old Wang had impressed upon him how much he must avoid being noticed, and Jen Yong had stuck to surgery. He had even been derided by some progressive students for his lack of concern with "the nation's problems." He had shown discipline and discretion. Much depended on how Jen Yong had reacted to Tsing and whether the latter would pursue the matter or not. It was to be hoped that Jen Yong had not betrayed himself by a show of nerves; had not indicated anything but compliance, even servility. . . .

"Be careful and yet more careful on Sunday," Tang advised. This was a wonderful opportunity: a bus available, one fully protected because a certain warlord's underlings were traveling in it . . . too good a chance to miss smuggling five valuable medical personnel to Yenan.

Then the two men talked of Stephanie. "It was a good thing she did," insisted Tang. "She seems a woman of courage. I shall report the incident to the upper level." Tang tried to convey to Wang the new thinking about Americans among the leaders of the Communist Party. Americans, said Tang, were not all imperialists. American newsmen were being useful, reporting favorably on the victories of the Communist Eighth Route Army, on Yenan, on the benevolent policies of the Party towards the peasantry. "There are many good Americans and they can be a great help to us," said Prosperity Tang. "Comrade Chu Deh, our commander in chief, has told the Americans that we have twenty divisions ready to fight Japan. If only the Americans give us the needed weapons, we can hasten victory and thus spare the lives of American soldiers. This American woman has done a good deed. We must try to interest her in our work. Tell this to Dr. Jen Yong." He wagged his head. "Ha, to see her strike that muddled turtle egg . . . how happy it would have made me to watch it!"

Jen Yong had gone through the surgery wards checking every patient. Nurse Sha was not on duty that evening and Nurse Tsai, pale and slim, the skin of her face so fine that it always looked powdered, went the rounds with him. She did not bustle and exclaim as did Nurse Sha, who was occasionally overpowering in her zeal. Nurse Tsai was very quiet, and he found her presence restful. He often wondered whether Nurse Tsai belonged to the Organization. There was that feeling about her, that quiet absorption, but also a certain watchfulness. The underground taught its members reticence, self-control. Each person connected with it only knew two others, no more. A precaution in case of betrayal. Jen Yong knew Old Wang and Nurse Li. Nurse Tsai's soft cotton slippers made no noise upon the cement floor. She did everything delicately and with great concentration. She had some faint streaks of white in her hair.

Yong finished the round and dawdled. He read again Liang Ma's file. The name of the foreign woman was there. Nurse Li had noted it down . . . Stephanie Ryder. She had said she would telephone.

This urge to hear her voice.

It grew upon him. Hear her voice. Her voice.

He sat, looking at the files but not really seeing them. He saw, instead, her face. Her eyes. The flecks of light in the deep, velvet brown of the irises. Oh she is beautiful, beautiful, his heart cried. And she is brave. Imagine her rushing at the bully, hitting him and being hit! He saw her dress, and the grace of her, uncaring of her appearance, the blood upon her dress. And she had brought Liang Ma to him. The slum people had followed her. They had followed a foreigner. . . . Never had anything like this happened before. In so many cases the victim was left to die; no one dared to intervene or help in any way, but this time it had not been so.

The telephone hanging on the wall began its shrill intermittence. Nurse Tsai went to it, unhooked the speaking tube, listened, then turned: "Dr. Jen, someone is calling for you."

But Jen Yong was already by her side, hand outstretched. He noted the surprise on Tsai's face at his unseemly haste.

"Wei, wei," he said in the telephone and then, fearful that she might misunderstand and hang up on him, he said: "This is Jen Yong speaking."

Her voice with that lilt of gladness, like the toss of a child's head: "Stephanie Ryder, Dr. Jen. How is our patient?"

Our. Jen Yong almost staggered under the bliss of that word. "She is alive, Miss Ryder. We could not save the baby. But the mother is doing well."

"I'm glad." She paused. "Is there anything else I can do? Would she need anything?"

"I don't think so . . ." And then there was nothing else to say. Jen Yong groped, frantic, for a sentence, a few words, but his mind refused to function. Yet he must keep her on the telephone. He must hear her voice, he must . . . "Thank you for remembering, remembering to ring up . . . ."

"But of course . . . I was concerned." A laugh. Oh that laugh. It filled him. All his life he had waited for the marvel of that laugh. "As you may know, Dr. Jen, I'm a reporter, I've been in China only a week." She too was extending herself, prolonging the conversation, giving him clues about herself, which he could pursue.

"You are a very brave woman, Miss Ryder. Very few people would have done what you did."

"I'm just impulsive, Dr. Jen." Again that smile in her voice. Again the dead end of words.

Jen felt his heart stammer. He breathed hard. He wanted to say "Please don't hang up . . . I want to go on talking to you," but he said instead: "Our people will be grateful to you. Always."

After a pause, Stephanie replied politely, "I'm sorry if I'm detaining you. You must be very busy."

"Oh no. I'm not busy. Have you . . . have you eaten?" (Of course she must have eaten. How imbecilic of him to ask.)

And Stephanie chuckled, a very small clear chuckle. And he was imploring her silently . . . *Please, oh please, let me hear you laugh, see you smile.*

"No, I have not had dinner yet. And you?"

"No . . ." he lied frantically. And wildly unbelieving of his own outrageous daring, he added: "Perhaps, if you are not too tired, would you like to come out . . . to eat something. . . ." And then he thought, in a panic, how much

39

will this cost? I must go back and get my money . . . I must borrow some money. I may not have enough . . . good restaurants are expensive.

"Yes," said Stephanie, "I'd like that. I'd like to eat at the street stalls. I've often gone by them, but there's been no one to take me."

"They're not good enough," said Jen Yong, panicky again. "The food is too spicy . . . and not clean. You are not used to it. We must go to a restaurant."

"But I've wanted to eat at the street stalls ever since I came to Chungking, Dr. Jen. Will you take me? Please?"

Stephanie was waiting on the track outside the sentinel box and saw Jen Yong walk up the path. She walked down to meet him. She was totally unselfconscious in doing so. Today's encounter seemed to her a good opportunity to make a friend on her own. A Chinese friend. Chosen by herself. She knew he would not be allowed into the Press Hostel by the soldiers on guard at the gate, and to spare him the humiliation—inflicted upon him by his own countrymen—she had waited outside. Now she smiled, and took a few steps towards him.

She did not know that Jen Yong had never in his life been out alone with a woman; that he had never had a love affair. Which was not strange in his country, in his society.

She thought: he looks awfully nice. I want to talk with him. And Jen Yong approached, his heart beating, and thought that she was the most wonderful being on earth, and knew that he loved her.

"Good evening," she said brightly, extending her hand to shake; and he did not answer because he was looking at her, and so he smiled, shook her hand, and they walked side by side to the road. In the nights of Chungking the rats came out of the sewers, out of the open ditches, bold masters of the city, to gaze at the people. Stephanie stared, fascinated, at a family of rats gamboling by the large open sewer which ran next to the path to the hostel. Baby rats played, squeaking around their fat and somnolent mother. "Do they come out every night?"

"Yes . . . in the summer. But in the larger streets we shall not see so many of them," said Jen Yong.

Earthenware lamps, their wicks dipped in oil, glimmered in clusters all along the streets, puncturing the darkness, adding a starlight luminosity to its haze. The shops remained open almost till dawn, since in Chungking's summer, people could not sleep. They strolled in the night until exhaustion pushed them into stupor—a stupor abridged by the ferocious return of the despotic sun at dawn, exploding out of the river and laying its slaughtering rays upon all.

Silence fell upon Stephanie and Yong, silence tentative, filled with grace, with intimation of trust. Stephanie broke it. "I've only been here a week, Dr. Jen, and everyone tells me that Szechuan food is the most deliciously spicy in China." And somehow she too found small, easy things to say as they walked under a night sky powdered with stardust. He looked at the sky, and then at Stephanie's face. Oh let me remember forever this moment of pure happiness, he prayed. Her face was lovely and he could smell her body. He loved her smell. It stirred him and poetry lines floated up to him:

> I smelt the odor of her clothes
> And she became once more present to me
> And I wept

He shivered, and knew then how much he would suffer, loving her. The trap of love had closed upon him, and he could not, would not, escape. . . .

Stephanie was saying, "Have you ever been to the States?"

And he was replying, "Never . . . but I hope to do so one day. Perhaps when the war is over. America has great knowledge. . . . We need the knowledge, we are so backward." And then he talked of surgery, of operations. "We lack a great many things we need, but after the war . . ."

Oh, he thought, why do I say such heavy, pompous things? I do not know how to speak to her. "Forgive me, I do not know how to talk to a woman. You see, I have never been out with a woman alone. Always there has been someone—a, a . . ."

"Chaperone," said Stephanie, and turned to him with gentle warmth. "I've only been a week in Chungking. No, ten days today. I've noticed that very few of us have Chinese friends. Except among the officials, of course. I'm glad I could

41

meet with you, you can tell me so much about this country. You see, as a newspaperwoman, I want to pick your brains."

Jen Yong said, a little solemnly: "I would so much like to be your friend. Always."

She then spoke about Texas. "Where I come from it's so different. Few people, lots and lots of space, you can ride a horse for half a day and not meet anyone . . . but I'm glad I came, even though everything's strange. . . ." When she talked she did not look right or left, or heed her own words. He guided her gently, not touching her; he wanted so much to touch her, and listen and remember every word.

They had now reached the streets where food stalls on both sides set out their trestle tables and their long benches. Here there were hurricane lamps hanging from poles; noise and shouting and a great commotion of people. Jen Yong said: "If you do not like it, please say so. We can then go to a restaurant." He carried a large amount of money with him. A thick bundle of paper money filled his jacket pocket. He had borrowed, borrowed, sold his rice rations for a month.

She smiled. "This is fine. I love eating in the open."

They sat at a stall, and Stephanie saw without surprise that she was the only foreigner there. Politely the stallkeeper laid out a special bench and table for them. The flavor of the *maotoudze*, that mixture of tripe, kidney, liver, brain of ox, and pig simmered in spice, seized the air, filled the street with pungency. Jen ordered and paid the bill immediately, fearful that prices might rise while they ate. For this was inflation; every evening prices were higher than in the morning.

Most of the money on him came from Dr. Liu, his best friend. Liu had grinned understandingly and given him all that he had. Liu had been married for fourteen years. It had been a child-marriage. He had not seen his wife for the past six years, for she had remained in Japanese-occupied territory to look after his old parents. And now that they were separated, Liu had fallen in love with the small child-wife whom he had taken, one dark night, but never known, even when she had borne him two sons. "When the war is over and I go back," he said, "I shall tell my wife that I love her. I have never said the word *love* to her." His wife had become a reason for living and enduring, and dreaming.

"Enjoy yourself, old Jen," Liu said.

Jen Yong blushed: "It is not . . ." he began, then turned crimson; Liu laughed, then sang a snatch from a love song as Jen went out.

Now here was the face of love, of all delight, in the flicker of the brownish stall lights, and Jen Yong looked at Stephanie, and she caught him staring and touched her cheek.

"Does it show?"

"What?"

"The mark . . . you know." She had thought he looked at her welt.

Jen said with an effort: "I want to kill the man who hit you. . . ."

"But I hit him first," said Stephanie. "I pushed him hard. And I'm only sorry that I seem to have lost my camera in the process." She told him about the snapshots she had taken.

Jen Yong said: "You are . . . very brave."

"I was very angry. . . . Tell me, how can the people put up with this kind of brutality?"

"It will not be forever," he said quietly.

The *maotoudze* came and Stephanie tackled it. She choked, and the tears came to her eyes, but she swallowed, in between mouthfuls opening her mouth wide and exhaling. "My, it *is* spicy."

Jen Yong ordered tea. "On no account drink cold water when you eat Szechuan spicy food, Miss Ryder." There he was, being prim again.

She gulped, tears standing in her eyes. "In Texas we have a hotpot soup, very spicy, lots of red peppers. . . . It's a Mexican recipe, and it's great for a hangover."

"What is hangover?"

She explained, and then he became extravagant and ordered a bottle of maotai wine, and his tongue was unloosened. He spoke about his work, about Chungking, about his coming from graduation in Shanghai to Szechuan, six years ago. Walking away from Japanese occupation—walking with his fellow students and his professors, though sometimes they were lucky and caught buses. They crossed rivers on barges, but mostly they walked. It took four months. "So we came and set up a medical school in Chungking, and I've been working at the hospital. It was founded by American medical missionaries. We'll go home when the war is won."

Between them gleamed the steaming copper dish; the

43

owner bustled about them, pressing more meat and vegetables upon them.

Stephanie talked about her father, Heston Ryder, and about her mother, who was part French, part Hungarian, and an aristocrat. "Her family was quite straight-laced, I guess, but she fell in love with Dad. And left Europe and came to America with him. Dad's great. He's a hundred percent Texan and he thinks that's better than royalty. He builds airplanes—he designed an engine. And," she added softly, with love, "he's let me come here by myself because he thinks women should be independent."

"Perhaps not all women," smiled Jen Yong. "Perhaps only his daughter, because you are like him."

She flushed. "How perceptive you are. It's true that my mother is different. She's . . . more remote. It's her upbringing. But I guess she was plucky in her own way. If she could leave her family and background, and all for love, why shouldn't I come to China for . . ." she stopped, "for adventure," she ended, her face a little clouded, as Alan Kersh came up in her mind, and she brushed the memory away.

Jen Yong would remember this pause, the shadow which crossed her face and then left it. Later this memory would torment him. He would never be able to rid himself entirely of it. But he said as she paused, "I too liked adventure when I was younger, and one day, with two companions, I set off to wander like the heroes of our legends, roaming our own country to learn its vastness. And we walked through seven provinces."

It had lasted over five months; he had been nineteen, and it was then he had been horrified by the discovery of his people's savage misery.

"Before that walk, I'd never left Shanghai. I never knew how unhappy my country was. I saw at times the streets with beggars, women and men sitting and selling their children, putting a twig of hawthorn in the hair of the little girls for sale . . . but somehow I did not think further. And then after my walk I began to read, to enquire, and I knew that being a doctor was not enough. . . . I had to think of national salvation for my people."

He saw Stephanie's puzzled look at the words: national salvation. "All my generation have thought of saving the country, it's bone deep with us. It's due to history, to decades of shame and humiliation. In schools and universi-

44

ties since the 1930s we've marched and held demonstrations. Against outside invasion, against the colonial powers, against exploitation. For national salvation. I cannot remember *not* being involved, but it became absolute certainty with me after I had walked through my country. Then I knew I had to give myself . . . to my country."

He went on speaking of the years since he was born—wars and their ravages, a rosary of woe. "And now it continues. Look at what happened yesterday. What you saw was an example . . . but the Chinese people won't let this horror go on forever!"

Stephanie heard the fervor, the resolution. This explained the trek of so many youths away from Chungking. To Yenan. They believed the Communists would save China, put things right. . . . But was that true? Was Yong a Communist? She must ask him . . . but perhaps he would be upset.

"We don't like communism in America," she said tentatively, "the authoritarianism, the lack of freedom . . ."

He smiled, polite, noncommittal. He did not explain or defend.

They rose and walked away. On all the streets were would-be sleepers; people had pulled their narrow pallets out on the sidewalks; unhooked doors from their frames and lay upon them, fanning themselves, trying to coax sleep, some moaning aloud with the torment of heat. "Chungking is the only city I know where it is hotter at night than in the day," said Jen Yong.

They walked to the Watching Heaven Gate, where steps of stone went down, down to the muscled and vital Yangtze, to the docks and the ferry. One could feel the river, even in the darkness one felt its waters moving, a press of water fretting away the rock. And on the narrow shore were people, fanning and squatting; and the night lengthened in front of them, the houses dwindled as they—young man and woman—loitered, silent now in a companionable silence.

The city ended in a mixture of rice fields and groves of bamboo and thatched huts, and farther on lay the pale semicircular tombs of a cemetery. Obviously a wealthy man's private cemetery; the poor could not afford monuments and inscriptions to commemorate them.

Yong said: "I know a poem, I think it was written by someone who, like us, stood one night outside a city.

> *Ancient tombs lie thicker than the grass*
> *And new graves now infringe on trodden roads.*
> *Beyond the city wall no empty ground remains,*
> *Inside the city people soon grow old. . . .*

"It's as true today as it was a thousand years ago. Our living land is a land of cemeteries; you'll see them everywhere among the fields. All over the north. Round earthen mounds. In the south, people put the bones of the dead in earthenware jars. . . . There should be less dying and more living, I think."

Stephanie said: "Your generation will change all this. . . . The way you talk about national salvation, the way you feel . . ."

"Only if we bestir ourselves mightily."

How formal and how charming, thought Stephanie. He spoke such clipped precise English. He did not know the current American idioms. He must have learnt the language mainly by reading.

"You're teaching me a good deal. I feel less of a stranger now."

Jen Yong said: "We cannot change China without help. We need America. Only America can help us to help ourselves. But America must understand us, Miss Ryder."

"Please don't call me Miss Ryder. Stephanie is my name. We're kind of informal in my country."

"Stephanie." He savored it. "It is beautiful as you are beautiful, within my mouth and beautiful to my ears." He said it gravely, an acknowledgment of her gift. For it was a giving. She had given her name into his keeping. "And my name is Yong."

"Yong," she said. "Easy to remember."

He never wanted to leave her side, he wanted to go on forever walking with her, but the cherished one must be protected, cared for. And it was getting late, so he took her back, walking slowly, fearing that she might become tired, fearing to strain the moment's felicity, fearing to bore her. And Stephanie, a little mortified, thought: Have I done something to displease him? Why does he want to leave me? But perhaps here it's the man who says it's time to go home. And when they reached the hostel gate, they shook hands formally and Stephanie said: "I've enjoyed myself very much. I hope you will call me again, Yong."

"Yes," said Jen Yong, "yes," and then with an effort, "I will be waiting. . . ."

"Fine," she said, not quite understanding what he meant and a little surprised by his choice of the word *waiting*. "Goodnight, Yong."

"Goodnight . . . Stephanie."

He stood, staring at the hostel wall. The soldiers sat in the sentinel box. He could not enter. He stayed at the gate, trying to peer at the building, but the soldiers wordlessly waved him away. And he was ravaged by love, swept by such a turmoil of passion that he could only walk, walk, walk the night away, until the sudden dawn drove him back to work.

After the last clearance raid, the slum-dwellers moved a mile and a quarter farther down the loop of the river and perched timid new shanties on another slope. This one was a garbage site, nauseating with excreta and mangy dogs nosing the filth-strewn ground. The children were sent to scavenge throughout the city to bring back whatever could be used. Little Pond's neighbor, Uncle Yu the One-eyed, who had helped them before, helped him again to put together a bamboo pole, topped by some frayed tarpaulin, to contrive a lean-to.

"When Big Sister Liang returns from the hospital she will have protection against the rain," said One-eyed Yu.

"Thank you, Uncle Yu," said Little Pond politely. He would also repay this debt of kindness. Uncle Yu was a professional beggar. He queued, with other beggars, at the back doors of restaurants. When the slops were thrown out, Uncle Yu fought for them; he usually managed to eat some mouthfuls before moving on to another restaurant.

One-eyed Yu was one of the three men who had borne the bamboo chair in which Mother Liang had been taken to the hospital. And he was worried, because he had the foreign woman's camera. She had put it down, unheeding, when she had rushed forward . . . and oh, how they remembered her onslaught! Within a day they had found for her a name, tenderly culled from their trove of legends. Yi Niang, the Valorous Maiden, the bold spirit who fought and conquered demons and ghosts. No matter that she had assumed the guise of a foreigner. All things were possible to spirits, said One-eyed Yu.

But the black taking-likeness box. How could it be restored to her? No one dared to carry it to her, for if the police saw a poor man with the foreign taking-likeness machine he would immediately accuse the carrier of theft and beat him insensible, and Valorous Maiden would not recover it.

"I will speak of this with Jen *Taifu*," said Little Pond importantly, "he will find a way."

Little Pond had acquired big face now. He told everyone about his mother lying in a clean, clean bed, without a hole anywhere, a blanket over her. He told of bottles, and healthy blood going into her body. Blood which saved life. Even foreigners gave blood, he said.

"Aiyah, a foreigner's blood . . . that will turn Sister Liang into a foreign devil. . . . How can she ever be one of us again?" wailed Old Grandmother Wu, who nursed a gangrenous foot which stank abominably. Her words carried weight, even though she had no coffin to her name and sent her grandchildren begging for money to buy her one. She had saved a clean jacket for her funeral and she would be buried in it. She had asked her son to dig the grave deep, so that no one would disinter her body to get at the jacket.

Little Pond said: "Old Grandmother, Jen *Taifu* says that all blood is the same, everywhere . . . foreign or Chinese. . . . Dr. Jen also has given blood."

"How can down-the-river people's blood be the same as our blood?" asked Grandmother Wu. And around her the women nodded, a little frightened that Sister Liang should have foreign blood poured into her body. Little Pond felt that perhaps, perhaps his mother would be changed; but he shut his eyes and clung fervently to Dr. Jen's voice, to his words. Ma would still be Ma.

As dawn came with its small coolness which lasted no longer than a few breaths, before the sun scowled once again upon the earth, Little Pond decided that he would go to the hospital and wait for the doctor and tell him about the camera. But first he must scavenge, or steal, or beg . . . for he had to eat. One day, he would grow up and be a man, like his father. He would avenge his mother and his unborn brother. He slept, cradled by his hatred and his love, and both greatly comforted him.

Colonel Tsing of the Secret Police was told about Jen Yong and Stephanie eating together at the stalls and afterwards walking about together. The report made no mention of immoral contact.

Tsing became increasingly curious about Jen Yong. He could not forget that slight tremor of his hands, the sudden twitch of an eyelid. . . . There is a devil somewhere, he thought. Jen Yong came from a wealthy Shanghai family. The family had remained in Shanghai, but Jen's father did not collaborate with the Japanese, Jen Yong himself had no known radical leanings. But he had walked and eaten with the foreign woman, the very one who had struck Major Hsu, and that very night they had talked animatedly. Was the foreign woman eager to taste Chinese manhood? Dr. Jen was indeed very handsome. Even so, it was extremely uncommon for a foreign woman to go out with a Chinese. . . . *There is a devil at the heart of this*.

Colonel Tsing was a clever man, a man who smelt the air, whose perceptions were like an insect's antennae. He judged people by their aura, by the smell of fear, the sourness of anger, their body emanations. He had a talent for discovering crypto-Communists, because he knew a great deal about their manifold covers, their patience, their infiltration of every service, every government department. Anyone too honest, too virtuous, or anyone in the least way remarkable *could* be a red. All antennae out, like a reconnoitering insect, he had walked the hospital corridors, had noticed Nurse Li's sharp, clever face. But this was a hospital with American Red Cross connections. Some of the doctors were foreigners. This is a place the reds might choose, he thought. To conceal their people. But he would have to proceed with great care.

In a room of the clinic reserved for Secret Police personnel and their families, Major Hsu, whose personal name was Towering Cloud, sat in his underpants with a bandage on his chest, eating watermelon and spitting the seeds over the verandah balustrade. The woman with him was short, with frizzy hair and big buttocks. She was pleasant and fanned him untiringly. The bandage was evidence that he had sustained "severe blows."

Hsu Towering Cloud was the son by affection of the top man in the Secret Police, General Tai Lee. Although he had been performing a lowly job (slum clearance), he knew that as soon as a satisfactory opening could be created he would move up. And what had happened to him had been a stroke of luck.

A foreigner, a mad woman, had rushed upon him and struck him. The foreigner being American, the incident had to be handled very carefully. Towering Cloud would be compensated for loss of face in front of his soldiers. But he must not say a word. Otherwise—if the American made a fuss—Toppled Cloud would become his nickname. . . .

The singsong girl started humming noisily. "Go and prepare a bath for me," Hsu ordered. She rose obediently, waddling to the bathroom. He heard the faucets creak, the rush of water.

The girl came back, a towel on her arm, a smile upon her face. "Let me massage you," she said, "Big Brother . . ."

He was pleased. In a better job, he would be able to afford many women, submissive, large of buttock, small of foot. He plunged into the bath and dreamt of carving the American woman's face, slowly, with a small knife.

Henry and Meena Wong threw a cocktail party at their home. With that artless informality only achieved through rigorous planning, Meena circulated among her guests, her accent flawless Wellesley. She was petite, well-rounded, and well-liked. She never said anything malicious about anyone. "I think it is marvelous the way you put up with our Chungking weather," she told Stephanie. "Look at you—fresh as a rose." Shrewdly, she had gauged the girl. Intelligent, but without any guile, "Heaven honest." She piloted Stephanie towards Henry, chatting of their nostalgia for the States. "We both spent some years there, he at Harvard, and myself at Wellesley." Of her two sons, at Yale and Princeton, of possible mutual friends, mentioning professors, editors . . . "Alan Kersh was *such* a friend of ours," she said. And waited to see Stephanie wince. But Stephanie looked at Meena with tranquil brown eyes.

"Alan got me my job here," she replied.

Oh dear, thought Meena. Alan brought out almost a girl a year, though he stuck to his wife Sybil no matter how many girls, nor how beautiful. Sybil had been Meena's classmate at Wellesley.

"Henry," she called, "here's Stephanie Ryder. You've been dying to talk to her."

"Welcome, welcome to our Sino-American family," boomed Henry. "Would you like a brandy ginger ale? Good brandy is hard to come by . . . but we laid in a small supply, which thank God was not bombed, before the Burma Road was closed in 1942." He was agreeable but not unctuous. Was there anything particular Stephanie would like to investigate? Then without waiting for an answer he launched into a program for her. Orphanages and schools, clinics, meeting women who had fought the Japanese, and of course perhaps an interview with Madame Chiang Kaishek. "We'll do all we can, just let us know what you need for the magazine. . . ."

Stephanie shifted her weight from one foot to the other. She was touched by the kindness, the obvious well-meaning of Henry Wong. He was a nice man. Not his fault if the system was rotten. She looked at him with that steady naked gaze which some men found unnerving. "I'm not happy about some of the things I've seen," she began.

Henry sighed. "Oh, my dear, do you think I am? We've got twenty-five million refugees. . . . It was Teddy White, incidentally, who found out the number for us . . . those who walked away from the Japanese to come here. We have enormous problems . . . we're trying to stamp out corruption . . . if you see anything you don't like, *please* come and tell me, or tell Meena. So that something can be done to wipe out that kind of evil." Henry Wong energetically swiped at the air. Stephanie took a sip of her drink, and Henry went on. "Of course, one's first impulse is to rush off a denunciation. I am all for exposing everything . . . but there must be balance . . . objectivity . . . we're fighting a big war. We're under great strain. And . . ." here he wagged a solemn finger, "it's not only the external threat of Japan.

There's a great danger at our very heart. Communism. The reds are everywhere, infiltrating, spreading unrest. Their propaganda is very effective. Even some of your colleagues, Miss Ryder, are being taken in."

Stephanie said: "Perhaps we should be given an opportunity to judge for ourselves."

"And so you shall," Henry Wong replied. "But at the moment, with the Japanese trying a last desperate thrust at us—which we are dealing with adequately, although we are so handicapped by lack of equipment—we've got to be more than careful." Again he held up a solemn finger. "And we must always ask ourselves: Will this or that piece of writing discourage the war effort? Weaken the resolve to win the war? I constantly have to face this problem," said Henry gravely.

Stephanie smiled. "I get the point."

"Good." Henry beamed. "You're young, my dear, give yourself time."

"I'd also want to go to Yenan," interrupted Stephanie. "I feel I ought to. To get balance, objectivity."

Henry had expected this. Urbanely, he parried: "Why not? A lot of Americans are there already. They're taken round, only shown what the reds want them to write about . . . but . . ." he shrugged, "time will tell."

Meena gravitated to Terry Longworth and Alistair Choate. With them was Rosamond Chen, the woman Terry loved and wanted to marry. Rosamond was exquisitely pretty, very well educated, and divorced. She was fifteen years older than Terry but she looked a girlish eighteen, with flawless ivory face and lacquer black hair. Terry wanted to divorce his American wife, Blanche, to marry Rosamond. Everyone knew it.

Rosamond was exceptionally outspoken for a Chinese girl, almost trenchant in her remarks, which was a major disadvantage in Chungking. She worked as liaison officer in a ministry, and a campaign had been led against her by the wife of a certain government official. She had been accused of being the mistress of the minister. It had been a vicious campaign, with every high official's wife suddenly becoming a monument of virtuous indignation. For a while, all

Chungking talked of nothing else, and Madame Chiang had pointedly omitted Rosamond from her monthly tea and cake party for the Women's Association for War Relief. Only Meena continued to invite her, but of course never at parties with Chinese officials and their wives. Only with Westerners.

Rosamond was eager to marry Terry and leave Chungking. "Here I've got a scarlet letter printed on my forehead," she said. "The most dreadful things are going on, but the officials behave as if all China's miseries were due to *my* so-called immorality." She tried to pretend she did not care, but it hurt her badly.

"I think Stephanie's utterly charming," said Meena. "Don't you think so, Rosamond?"

"Terry finds her a little overwhelming. He says she's too wholesome," replied Rosamond, "but I think she's great . . . defending the slum people, hitting that man who kicked a pregnant woman, going out to dinner with a Chinese doctor. She's making the whole place sit up and take notice."

"Where did you hear all this?" asked Alistair.

"Why, the whole city knows it," said Rosamond, "or am I talking too much? . . ."

Alistair looked at Stephanie across the room. She looked so beautiful, as if buoyed by emanations from an unknown planet. All this since her slum tour three days ago . . . She had refused to go out to dinner with him, saying she was busy. Alistair had suspected John Moore. What a bitch, he thought, his neck tight with rage. Stephanie—and a Chink. Bitch, bitch . . .

three

SUNDAY was suffocating. Tigerish heat clamped upon the city. The bleached sky needled one's eyes, and everyone hoped for rain.

The hospital's once-a-year outing was proceeding. Around a hundred men, women, children, babies and toddlers, families of the staff, had come in three shaky motor buses which hiccupped up the slopes, and slid down them with unsure brakes. Once inside the Hot Springs Gardens, they spread among the lotus ponds, bamboo groves, artificial hillocks with their hexagonal pavilions. The adults fanned and ate chunks of red watermelon, carefully preserving the seeds to take home; the children, heat drowsy, drooped, played a little around the waterfall, dipping their hands and feet in the ponds. Women sat in small groups, many with babies in their laps, and others with their own large bellies. They fanned and talked and sighed because of the heat, and mopped their faces.

Three male nurses and two doctors, one of them a woman, would leave the park, unperceived, and from there proceed to Sian, and on to the Communist base in Yenan in the north. They would run the blockade of Secret Police and road patrols all the way.

Usually the Organization only filtered one or two people at a time—five was a large number. But police surveillance of the goldfish trail had slackened. The inflation also helped. Bribery was a legitimate way of surviving, and the Organization used it copiously.

Yet unexpectedly, today a large number of plainclothes Secret Police stalked about the park. Their walk betrayed them. Also the fact that they kept their jackets on, to conceal the pistols in their belts.

It had been arranged that the five would saunter casually to the toilets, one by one. And from the toilets a door, apparently locked, but to which the key had been obtained, led to the kitchen of the park restaurant. And from the kitchen (the cook was a Party member), they would be picked up to start their journey.

But the paved alley to the toilets was now blocked by three plainclothes men and there were two more in the restaurant. Fortunately, they had not thought of the kitchen.

Jen Yong looked for Nurse Li. She was with a group of women. He noticed the tiny line between her brows. "Follow the plan," he said, passing her, scarcely moving his lips.

Nurse Li strolled to a family group of three adults and seven children, and started chatting with them. And someone from that group detached himself and went to look at the lotus pond, and spoke to someone else. And so the network was mobilized. For the emergency plan. In case of a hitch.

"Excuse me Dr. Jen," said a voice behind Jen Yong. It was Nurse Sha, beaming, her hands raised, offering him a bunch of grapes. "I bought them from the Shapingpa store, Dr. Jen, won't you have some?"

Watching the maneuver, Yong smiled absently, picked at a grape. "Thank you, Nurse Sha." And walked away, leaving Nurse Sha holding the grapes, holding her offer of love.

A small crowd of boisterous and whooping children was now assembled as in a game, jostling, shouting, and pushing their way down the steps to the latrines, surrounding the three plainclothes men standing on the path. Behind them came a bustle of parents, as if suddenly a frenzy for the relieving of bladders and bowels had seized them all. The latrines and the restaurant nearby were thus cut off from the main alley of the garden. Yet another group of men pushed to the restaurant, loudly ordering meals. They blocked the kitchen.

Suddenly, from the artificial rockery rose a clamor, loud angry exclamations.

People turned to each other.

"What's happened?"

"Has there been an accident?"

Then—"Get the police, get the police!"

The plainclothes men in the park rushed towards the rockery, abandoning the kitchen and the latrines.

In the rockery was a group of nurses holding pamphlets printed on rough paper, of the kind regularly plastered on the walls of Chungking, and as regularly torn down by the police. A plainclothes man reached for them, but Nurse Tsai (for it was she who had been selected by the Organization for this task) held them back.

"No, I am taking them to the Public Security Bureau."

"Big sister," said the policeman politely, "*we* are the Public Security Bureau."

"How can I believe you?" said Nurse Tsai. "Perhaps you planted this red-bandit propaganda here, and now you wish to remove it."

The policeman extracted his card from his pocket. Nurse Tsai peered at it. "Policeman Wu Hsingfa," she read aloud.

"My friends here are also of the police," said Wu. The plainclothes men had now gathered in a threatening group, their revolvers jutting visibly from their waistbands. Nurse Tsai gave Wu the two pamphlets in her hand.

"You had better search the whole park, Police Officer Wu, there may be more of these things about."

Wu glanced at the pamphlets he held in his hand. They were the usual caricatures of fat officials guzzling food or drinking wine, while below them skeletons piled up in a small mountain of skulls and bones.

Peace was restored. And the five had made their getaway. The picnic outing proceeded. Jen Yong left early and took a *huakan* chair part of the way back to the hospital.

Nurse Sha saw him leave; she still had the basket of grapes in her hand. She had been bold, overbold, offering them to him in public. Now she rushed to offer the grapes to others. "Nurse Li, Nurse Tsai, please have some grapes, it will cool you after the excitement." Both nurses ate some grapes and told Nurse Sha how good they were. But Nurse Sha had seen Jen Yong leave, leave the picnic, and now the day for her was but a parched extent of hours to wait, until the next ward round, when she would be with him again.

Later in the afternoon the families strolled back to the buses. Nurse Sha noticed an absence.

"Dr. Liu, Dr. Liu . . . I don't see Dr. Lao anywhere. . . . She sat next to me when we came."

"She is probably in one of the other buses," said Dr. Liu.

Nurse Sha frowned. She had a feeling that she had missed something.

"Have you seen Dr. Lao?" asked Nurse Sha of Nurse Tsai.

"Dr. Lao . . . didn't she leave early?" said Nurse Tsai. "I thought I saw her leave . . ."

The buses started. Nurse Sha climbed into hers.

The young public security man, Quo, stood by the gate and watched the buses heave off. He had heard Nurse Sha's question about Dr. Lao. He paid attention only because her accent was the same as his: Shantung province. Shantung people were not many in Chungking.

Jen Yong spent the rest of the day working. He was compiling a book, translating into Chinese the gist of the surgery articles he collected from Western medical magazines. The magazines were five, six years old, for nothing new had come in since 1939. With the war, surgery was advancing enormously in America, in Europe. New drugs were being discovered. Antibiotics. Painstakingly, he searched for the new knowledge and translated it.

In the evening, after his usual cold water sluicing and spare meal, he walked to the hospital. Nurse Sha was there. It was her turn for night duty. He did the ward rounds with her; she trailed behind him, arms clutching ward files, her flat loud voice reporting on every patient. Mother Liang was much better. She could sit up and smile. Hemoglobin was sixty-five now.

"Has her son come to see her?"

"Only once, Dr. Jen." Nurse Sha paused. The round was over. "Dr. Jen, those grapes. I've brought some more which I kept at home. Won't you please take some? They are good for digestion, especially in hot weather. . . . Doctors who work as hard as you do should look after their health."

Jen felt slightly annoyed. How persistent she was. Grapes. Grapes. The luscious globular fruit. Yet he did not like them particularly. He did not see the yearning in Nurse Sha's eyes. He said: "I'll take a few."

Happily, Nurse Sha went to her ward table in the corridor. On it stood a small basket with a bunch of translucent green grapes, the cow udder variety, the best, expensive.

"Here, take them, Dr. Jen, take them." She pressed the basket into his hands. He tried to push it back but she laughed stridently, "No, no, no, you must take them . . . I bought them for you. . . ."

"Thank you, you are too kind, Nurse Sha." He was afraid of hurting her feelings. He was embarrassed. Holding the basket awkwardly, he went out of the ward down the corridor to the doctors' room. And then down the back staircase to the basement. On a Sunday night very few people were about and perhaps he could see Old Wang.

Old Wang was eating his bowl of semi-husked rice and some pickles. That was his meal. Jen Yong placed the basket of grapes in front of him. "Someone gave them to me, please have some." He went on: "The five have gone. But there were many special police in the garden. . . . I wonder why they suspected us."

Old Wang said: "A directive was issued only two days ago by the Scorpion, Tai Lee. Any gathering of intellectuals is now subject to reinforced vigilance, searches. There will soon be raids in the universities." After a pause, he went on: "About this American newspaperwoman. We have reported the matter to the leadership. The leadership thinks she may be very useful. We must cultivate such people. It will be part of your duty to see that she helps. . . ."

Jen Yong felt anger mounting, accumulating in him. He said, his voice hardening: "This is a personal matter, I do not wish her to be unknowingly involved in the work we are doing. She is . . . a person I admire and respect."

Old Wang's body seemed to shrink upon itself. He scooped up the rest of the rice in his bowl, swallowed it slowly, giving himself time. He burped. He put the bowl down and let silence come, silence like a wall, walling off Jen Yong.

In the long, heavy silence, Jen Yong said, not aware that he spoke aloud: "I will not take advantage of her. I care for her. I love her." And Old Wang sitting walled by his own silence found the words scandalous, shocking.

Love. Repugnant word. Word which could not be used publicly in China. This was immorality, lust, uxoriousness. In China's villages, no one ever spoke of love. No one uttered the word. And here was Jen Yong, saying aloud: I care, I love. He had no sense of shame, no sense of propriety. Of course, he was, after all, the offspring of a capitalist. Jen's ancestors were exploiters, evil people who had many women, who raped village girls. They had crushed people such as Old Wang, generation after generation. Wang thought: Your class and my class . . . we are enemies . . . we shall always be enemies . . . we do not stand under the same Heaven together. Even though Jen was now rendering service to the Organization, he remained a vacillating intellectual, untrustworthy, needing constant surveillance, guidance . . . he might even become a danger to the Organization.

The deed done in the darkness of the night. That is what Jen Yong was talking about, openly, openly. . . . The deed of man and woman—shame!

In Old Wang's village, a new bride had to be beaten on her wedding night. It was the custom.

When Old Wang was twelve, he had seen a sight: a woman of the village who had committed adultery. She had been tied on a horse, naked, a big wooden stake driven between her legs, and paraded round the village. He remembered the red blood flowing down the flanks of the horse . . . the long unwound black hair of the woman, streaming down the horse, like her blood.

Old Wang himself had never been able to afford a wife. His sexual life, at forty, consisted only of fierce dreams in which the woman on the white horse came back, and he saw her mouth open, he heard again the jeers, the laughter. It made him wet his pallet.

Wang had become a Party member. The Party had given him worth, dignity. Had taught him to read and to write, to plan and to scheme. And to obey. Then it had given him authority. He developed astuteness, patience, silence, tenacity. He also discovered love. A fierce love for the Party. He would die for the Party. Cheerfully. Nothing else really mattered. No woman would ever take the place of the Party. . . .

Now he cleared his throat, veiled his eyes with placidity, looked at Jen Yong. But Jen Yong had forgotten him. He was dreaming, dreaming of that woman, upon his face his yearning all too plain.

I love her . . . I love her. She means more to me than almost anything else on earth, thought Jen Yong. He was now launched into a discovery of himself. He was helpless, as the boatmen on the Great River are helpless in the flood.

And on what rocks, what whirlpools in the narrow gorges of passion would he be broken? *My whole life is changed. I only think of seeing her again. I must be allowed to love. . . .*

Old Wang coughed and Jen Yong said, "Old Wang, please understand me. It is the first time . . . that I . . . feel this way."

Old Wang nodded. "I am only a poor peasant, uneducated. Many things escape me. I am not an intellectual. But the Party protects intellectuals. We must understand. I shall report to the upper level." He thought: To me you are no longer reliable. A cold fury possessed him now. He hated Jen Yong. Hated the nakedness of the man's desire. But he merely rose to wash his rice bowl and chopsticks, and set them back on the small shelf above his pallet. Placid. Almost stupid in his movements.

"I shall not fail the Organization," said Jen Yong, "but she . . . she cannot be used in any way."

Old Wang nodded. "I shall transmit your point of view to the upper level. The Organization will certainly listen to your ideas."

Jen Yong rose. He said: "I'm going now," and left. And he left the basket of grapes behind.

Old Wang went outside to walk some paces around the hospital courtyard. He carried in his hand the basket of grapes, picking at them slowly. If anyone asked him, he would say: "A rich man forgot them in the hospital." He ate and ate. Not that he liked grapes. But they were luxury, costly beyond dreams. As he ate he thought of Dr. Jen Yong, able to afford such food. . . .

Nurse Sha, on her way back to the nurses' quarters, saw Old Wang standing by the hospital gate, her small basket of grapes in his hand, eating the fruit, spitting the seeds onto the sidewalk. Cow udder grapes. Hers.

Little Pond came very late on Monday night to see his mother. He sidled into the emergency ward where everyone now knew him. The nurses on duty often pressed upon him something to eat; he always said politely: "I have eaten to my full." They gave him a dumpling saved from their noon meal, a piece of beancurd, some cooked rice. Little

Pond bowed low; always refused the gifts three times before accepting, although hunger twisted his belly. He thought the nurses were fairies, they smelt so clean, they looked so beautiful, and oh those white, white gowns they wore! He knew that he stank. His trousers held together by string, almost exposed his buttocks. But the nurses did not throw him out. Except Nurse Sha who grumbled: "Don't bring your lice into my wards."

In the hospital he grew taller in his own mind; the kindness he met made him feel he did not limp.

He walked towards the ward and saw a foreigner coming towards him, frighteningly tall, with glasses and a huge nose. How ugly he was! But he had a doctor's white dress, and Little Pond bowed. And the foreigner said to him in excellent Chinese: "Ah you want to see your mother. She's much better. Come with me."

The big foreigner retraced his steps. He was taking Little Pond to his mother. Walking with Little Pond, not at all angry with him for being poor and for stinking.

A foreign woman was standing by his mother's bed. Oh marvel, lifting his heart to exultation, it was the Valorous Maiden! She turned her head and saw him, and saw the foreign doctor. She smiled at him, said, "You've come," in Chinese; and the two foreigners talked in their language, shook hands, and the tall ugly man gave Little Pond a tap on the shoulder and said: "All goes well. Your mother will be out of the hospital in two or three weeks."

Little Pond said to Valorous Maiden in Chinese: "I thank you . . . I wish to lay down my life for you. Heaven may disintegrate and earth fall to shards, but my heart shall not change."

And Stephanie Ryder did not understand all the words but guessed gratitude, and patted Little Pond's shoulder, and said in Chinese and then in English: "Your mama. Good. Very good. *Hao.*"

"Good, *Hao,*" repeated Little Pond, beaming.

Little Pond thus learned two English words that night. "Mama good," he said.

Stephanie clapped her hands and said, "Yes."

That was Little Pond's third English word: "Yes."

Liang Ma was propped up on a clean pillow, and it made Little Pond's skin itch to look at all that cleanliness. Her eyes were open, she smiled and said: "Son, oh son . . . "

And because he now replaced his father, and was the male of the family, he said in a voice he tried to make gruff:

"Ma, I have brought you some oranges. Here. Eat them."

Gruff. One spoke gruffly, to hide one's love.

Two small oranges. He had carried twenty baskets of Neichiang oranges up the steps from the river boats to the fruit stalls, all day. Sixty-four steps on the stairs every time. At the end he had received half a bowl of rice, an old pair of straw sandals, and two oranges. He put the oranges in Ma's hand, which lay on the sheet. She smiled as she fingered their slippery skin. Her smile was all the sweetness of living to him.

Valorous Maiden continued to say words which sounded pleasant to the ear; Ma smiled at her, as if she understood. Little Pond stood ravished, grinning at both, saying, "Yes, yes."

And then Nurse Sha came in. She was a taut tight body in a white gown; an inner fury made her bones brittle, so that Little Pond knew she creaked as she moved. "I must wash the ill person, it is time to go," she said. Peremptory. He bowed. He always bowed when he encountered a brutal gesture or an insulting manner. It deflected calamity. Until the day he would stand straight, tall in mind, tall in body, he would bow, to placate all the furies.

The foreign woman said in English something which sounded like a question. It had the name Dr. Jen among the words. And Nurse Sha replied, wagging her head. The foreign woman then smiled at his mother and walked away, and he followed her out of the hospital, but from a distance. He did not dare to walk *with* her.

He wanted to tell her: I have your take-likeness box. I keep it safe at night, and Uncle One-eyed Yu keeps it by day. But we cannot bring it to you. I must ask Dr. Jen to come where we live and bring it to you. But he could not say all this to her. He would have to see Jen *Taifu*, talk to him.

Once outside the hospital, Valorous Maiden looked hesitant, as if she did not quite know what she would do next. Then she turned to him, smiled, took his hand and put money in it. He shook his head.

"No, no."

But she said, "Yes, please," only he did not understand "please."

Then she walked away, down the road, with that walk of hers which fascinated him. It was so certain, as if the earth were safe, as if there were no dangers and no disasters and adversities, no demons and bullying landlords every time one took a step.

He squatted in his usual place by the roadside to wait for Jen Yong. He closed his eyes and thought of his mother and also of Nurse Sha. And he wondered why Nurse Sha disliked Valorous Maiden so much, why Nurse Sha, who had enough to eat, was angry all the time.

Stephanie was kept busy. Meena Wong took her to see orphanages. The orphans were beribboned, well-dressed children, bursting with health. She visited model refugee camps. The refugee grandmothers knitted sweaters for the soldiers. They were so well dressed that, compared to the city denizens, they looked affluent. With a twinge of sadness Stephanie noted the artificiality of the arranged shows. But John Moore had advised her to be mutely observant. "Everything important is said by silence," he had told her. "They know, as you know, that this is all baloney, but what d'you want them to do? Henry's got to take you to these places. Don't give him trouble, will you? He's a good guy."

Stephanie wrote a long article, contrasting with mild innuendo the almost paradisaical conditions in these centers run by the Kuomintang government for a few, a very few of the human wreckage of war, and the ordinary life of the citizenry in Chungking. She also mentioned the slum clearance, its cruelty and uselessness. "The slum-dwellers just pick up whatever has been scattered by the wanton brutality of the soldiers, and once again they rebuild their hovels somewhere else." She did not mention her own grueling experience. That could wait. . . .

The article passed. No one from censorship asked her to alter it.

She read dispatches, ate with her colleagues, drank with them, and on the verandah in the evening spent long hours arguing, talking about China. For that was really the only topic; everything else in the world receded a little, and China was the center of their preoccupations.

"Whether we like it or not, China and what's going to happen to her will count a great deal in the future," said John Moore.

But Alistair Choate would disagree. "There's a kind of catching disease about, the 'love China, love the Chinese' malady," he said, not looking at Stephanie. "It's a fascination with the dinosaur. China's still prehistoric, a before-the-flood phenomenon, always reacting in ways we can't grasp. The Chinese are the most racist people in the world. Nothing exists for them but China and they'll use anything and anyone to make China powerful once again."

Stephanie became acquainted with the liquor brewed from orange peel and sugar which Teddy White, whom everyone spoke of with reverence, had invented. She acquired a taste for *maotai*, the fiery liquor of Szechuan. And there was no sign from Jen Yong. Mortified by his silence, she felt like telephoning again, then refrained. He had said he would wait. . . . Wait for what? He was a surgeon, busy.

She wrote letters to Dad and to Isabelle. She concentrated on reassuring Dad. "The heat doesn't bother me, it's like Dallas." She went into lavish descriptions of the magnificent scenery and the hideous living conditions. "But we are privileged . . . we get all the food we want, because we pay in American dollars. We're very well looked after."

She was thinking of writing a book. On Chinese women and their contribution to the war. HERE wanted some human interest stories, warm and touching. She studied the reports from the American military mission in Yenan. The mission, sent by request of President Roosevelt, was nicknamed the "Dixie" Mission. "Because they're in rebel territory," John Moore explained to Stephanie. "The Communist bases in North China are all outside the jurisdiction of the Kuomintang government."

The reports were unanimously favorable. The Americans seemed impressed with the honesty, the social justice, the people's obvious enthusiasm, the excellent condition of the Eighth Route Army soldiers. All this came out of the dispatches, and in Stephanie the urge grew to see for herself, to understand the promise held out for the Chinese people. Perhaps Yong was right when he said that everything would have to change. She wanted to see him, to talk to him. . . .

HERE sent her a cable praising her first two articles on Chungking and urging her to visit "guerilla areas." A major report had come out in America on the guerillas. Were there guerilla women? She cabled back, saying that she would try to find out.

Meanwhile, the Japanese offensive grew calamitously. A thrust of thirty divisions threatened the rice bowl province of Hunan. Should Hunan be occupied, the food situation in Chungking would become extremely precarious. Chiang Kaishek shot a few rice hoarders to show he was doing something about it.

"But he's ordering his military commanders *not* to fight the Japanese," John told her. "Retreat, retreat. They're letting the Japanese overrun every camp, every military position."

"But why, why?" asked Stephanie.

"Why?" John shook his head. "Peanut's tortuous brain. Let America fight Japan, deal with Japan . . . all *he* wants to fight is Yenan . . . so he's storing up money and guns, and keeping his best divisions off the battlefields. . . ."

Roosevelt's messages to Chiang became increasingly irritable, and Joseph Stilwell was saying openly that Old Peanut should retire. "So long as he's in command there'll be just one unholy mess," said Vinegar Joe to everyone he met.

The days went by. Three, four, five.

Stephanie acquired a Chinese teacher with whom she would study the language two hours a night three times a week: prim, bespectacled Miss Soo, sexless as a worker bee, a schoolmarm who coached in her spare time to keep from starving on her meager salary.

Five days. Yong had said he would telephone, and Stephanie felt restless. Increasingly, she thought of him. She did not know that Yong had no money left and was in debt to his friends. That pride forbade him to take her out before he could repay the money he owed.

She had been to the hospital to see Liang Ma. And met her little son. He smelt bad, but what a wonderful face he had, large eyes and high wide cheekbones, and such a smile! And then a nurse had come in and Stephanie had

asked whether Dr. Jen would be coming. "Dr. Jen has
finished his rounds, he has gone home," the nurse had
replied. She had left the hospital, wandered a little, as if
. . . . as if she might meet him. And then, angry with herself,
had gone home.

Now in the darkness she lay under the wheeling fan. She
felt fragmented, unable to collect herself. As if her self was
made up of several pieces that could not come together.

It's the heat.

Pull yourself together, Stephanie. Think of your work.
Your next article is due. . . .

She remembered the well-groomed women Meena had
introduced her to: the Committee for Refugee Relief. Delightful champagne conversation, satin smooth flattery laced
with silken innuendo. Tea and cakes. And then mahjong.
Benevolent, charitable ladies doing their bit for the war.
Stephanie did not play mahjong.

Yong. Yong was really concerned. Really working. He
said things in such a surprising way. The words he used
were like . . . like flower petals, neat, prim. They had a
newness to them. And he was unconscious of his handsome-
ness. His hands. His face. The slim taut body so easy in its
clothes. She felt different, so very good with him.

Why did he not telephone?

She went to her window and peered into the moving
darkness of the street. Pale flitting shadows, people walking
in clusters, dappling the night with movement and the hum
of their voices. She decided to go for a walk. To join the
crowd drifting in the streets, searching for slumber. She
should have asked Little Pond where he lived now. Stephanie had returned to the slum area but it had become an
abandoned litter of ash and dirt. Where had the people
gone?

She *would* go for a walk.

She reached the road, stepping lightly. There was a small
peal of thunder, and a sudden wind gust throwing up limp
volleys of dust. The rain, long awaited, now arrived hesitantly, shedding tepid and scattered drops, then an encouraging spatter. And suddenly it began to rain, really rain.
And all over Chungking city came the many-voiced "aaah"

66

of relief, and eager faces were raised towards Heaven, dispensing coolness, at last.

She walked in the steady drizzle, a word unknown to her until, four days ago, a Reuters correspondent had used it. "Watch for the first autumn drizzle," he had said. Alan Kersh had hated water from the sky, while she loved walking into it, feeling it upon her face and arms, feeling blessed. . . . Alan had always carried a large umbrella with him, and she had laughed. "I catch cold easily," he had said, a little crossly.

Yong. She would ask him: "Do you like walking in the rain?"

Rain. More earnest now, steadying its beat, pouring with willingness; and gaiety returning, the listless heat-shriveled people yelling in mock fright and true pleasure, pretending to run for cover, exhilarated by the benison of water, and running back into it to feel it on their faces, their arms. She reached the bend of the road where scattered oil lamps spread like yellow stars among the shops on either side. And she saw him, walking towards her, walking in the rain, no umbrella, coming to her, holding a parcel covered in yellow oilcloth in his hand. He had a loose shirt on, faded and worn from frequent washing. He wore sandals. No one stood between them in the populous street. For them, everyone else had vanished in a cloud of unknowing.

"I was just going for a walk, and here you are, Yong."

"I was coming to you." He held the parcel out to her. "Your camera. The slum people return it to you."

"Oh great! My pictures! I thought I'd lost them! How did you get it?"

He told her. Little Pond had reached him, waited for him, taken him to the new slums. . . .

"They kept it for you. They took turns watching it until I could come and collect it."

They stood smiling at each other. And Stephanie felt stirred. Felt the juices of her body moving softly, softly, and no longer heard or saw the street, the rain.

Only Yong.

"Let us walk," said Yong.

Three days after his first meeting with Stephanie, Jen Yong had gone to the Eanes's. The turmoil in him had not abated. He felt compassless, disoriented. He needed advice, a voice that he could trust. Not his friend Liu, who smiled knowingly and sang a love poem, "Ah, the jade pallor of her face!" when he saw Yong. Yong needed a foreigner, but one who was also a little Chinese.

David Eanes and his wife, Jessica, were medical missionaries. They too had come to believe in that other China beyond the mountains, whose beacon name was Yenan. And what propelled them towards Yenan was Christianity.

David was "third generation"—son and grandson of missionaries. All his life, from childhood onwards, he had listened to memories of China. Praying and teaching and working in China. He really knew no other land, not even his own Canada, as well as China. It was in David's house that Jen Yong coached medical students. This coaching was known as "Bible discussion afternoon." Yet the Eaneses knew well that it was actually Yenan-oriented discussion of events.

Under the Chiang government any comment on "social affairs" was illegal, but a foreign missionary's house was safe, and the foreign missionaries had books by such people as Jack Belden, Edgar Snow, Harrison Forman. They had newspapers from abroad, which *did* comment on the true state of things in China.

It was to David that Yong, with many innuendoes, conveyed the distraught landscape of his mind. "I have met a young lady of high moral character and courage," he began. And went on, round and round, quoting from the classics, to attenuate the impact of what he wanted to say. And David, knowing the primness of the Chinese language, its concealment of passion under phrases of depreciation and minimization, understood immediately that Jen Yong was in love for the first time in his life, and probably for the last time in his life.

"I hope to become the sincere friend of Miss Ryder," said Jen Yong. Which meant that he wanted to cherish her forever, that he loved her passionately, and wanted to marry her.

Jessica said, "I am happy for you, Yong. Please bring her here, whenever you wish."

Jen Yong said, "I do not wish to compromise her. My work . . ."

They understood.

"Perhaps she too, as a news reporter, wants to see something more of China than Chungking," said David Eanes. "Perhaps she wants to discuss things with you."

"You've got to trust yourself," said Jessica.

When Yong rose to leave, after having borrowed five American dollars (and with five American dollars Yong became a rich man) Jessica said: "Yong, we Westerners are clumsy in speech. We often cannot understand feelings unless they are spelt out in simple words, in a way which sounds indelicate and brutal to you Chinese. Remember, she is American. She'll expect *you* to tell her what you think, what you feel. Frankly."

Jen Yong nodded. "Thank you, Jessica, for telling me. I will remember . . . " And then he thought this would be the greatest ordeal of all. How did one tell a foreign woman that one was hopelessly in love with her? And how did one do it frankly?

The rain had cooled the night, and the air about them was clear and delightful. They walked, untired, untiring. Stephanie would remember this as a walk into the time of her own being. Always, later, those hours of walking in Chungking came back, when she and Yong were carried, sustained, almost floating above the dank and dreary streets.

They reached the orange groves of the reserved park, a little above the city. Soldiers were at the iron gates, but Stephanie was a foreigner and so they went through unhindered.

And Yong talked.

"I am doing work which the government does not approve of," said Jen Yong. "It is good work, but it could become dangerous."

"You mean . . . you're working for the reds?"

"I train medical staff for the guerillas who are fighting Japan," he replied. "I do not believe in communism, but I believe in patriotism. And the Communists are patriots. My generation is so desperate that it will believe in the devil if the devil will do good for China. . . ."

"What I've seen here has made me understand the attraction of Yenan," said Stephanie. "A lot of my colleagues, hardheaded newsmen, are also impressed. But communism is such a fanatic faith. . . . I feel I should go there to see for myself." She looked at him full in the face. "Why don't you go? Why d'you stay here?"

And because he could not tell her what role he played here, he replied, "Perhaps it's my destiny. I stayed here and now we have met."

"You're being evasive," she said.

"I'm a patriot," repeated Yong obstinately. "If you go to Yenan I shall be happy; you will go as an observer. You will not be . . . involved. And I do not want to influence you in any way."

"You're not influencing me. You're helping me to see clearly. That's all."

He turned to her then; her face was luminous in the darkness. Her perfume came to his nostrils, and he wanted to put his arms around her. He wanted . . . the effort to control himself kept him immobile as a drop of water withdrawn in its round concentration upon itself. "I have no words for my feelings. Because they are too new, too new for me," he said.

The way he said simple things . . .

"Then," she said, "let us just walk. Words aren't always needed, are they?"

Their shoulders touched, inadvertently. And he felt the shock, electric, a clear blaze through him.

They were now back in front of the Press Hostel. He handed her the camera and extracted from his pocket a slim book of poems. "It's a very old book, Stephanie. Perhaps you will read it one day."

"I'm learning Chinese," said Stephanie. "Three times a week."

They stood, and longing overwhelmed him. He wanted to put his arms around her, but said unsteadily: "It's very late. . . ."

She said: "Goodnight, Yong. Don't wait too long before calling me up."

"Stephanie," he said.

"Yes?" She paused, looking at him with a smile which waited. . . .

But he could no longer follow Jessica's advice. He could

not say "I love you." Not yet. He said "Goodnight" in a choked voice, and stood, holding himself in.

She turned then, walked past the guards into the hostel. He watched the darkness empty of her. Watched a very long time.

Stephanie's teacher Miss Soo made her a proposal the following week. Would Stephanie like to visit the school where she taught?

"I'd love to see your school," said Stephanie.

"But we must take a conveyance, it is too far," said Miss Soo. Stephanie knew that Miss Soo could not afford a bamboo chair, a *huakan*, but would probably insist on paying. She must find a way around the teacher's pride.

Stephanie lay uncomfortably in the *huakan*—she always found the half-horizontal reclining awkward. It was impossible to raise one's head without unbalancing the carriers, without inflicting pain on their shoulders. And going uphill, one's feet were above one's head, which induced a feeling of helplessness. She journeyed with Miss Soo out of the city and through the fields of rice and rape seed to a small fuzzy hill dotted with huts. These were the actual school buildings, of wattle daubed with plaster, crooked roofs, tiles merely laid on, so that during the bombings they flew off the roof frame and could be picked up and relaid. Among the flimsy buildings was an incongruous old temple of wood and stone with brick floors, functioning as the main classroom. Here four hundred girls, with pigtails or with bobbed hair, chanted their lessons. There was a basketball court and a volleyball court, and the rooms of the dormitory, with their three-tiered planks for beds, were very clean. She shook hands with a dozen teachers, all sober looking women with the same conventual, ascetic air about them as Miss Soo. And then Miss Soo took her to her own room, a cell with three narrow camp beds, a shelf of books, and the usual enamel basins on their wooden stands. She shared the cell with two other teachers, but at the moment, save for herself and Stephanie, it was empty.

Miss Soo poured the ritual cup of boiling water and then said: "I have brought you here to talk to you, Miss Ryder." Suddenly she had changed, was precise and resolute and

71

ardent. "We know that you are interested in writing about the true conditions in China. We decided to trust you. Would you like to visit some villages where you can really see the people liberated from exploitation?"

Stephanie was surprised and yet not surprised. Nothing was surprising in this surprising country; people all had multiple lives. All of them, like the spirits in fairy tales, were and were not what they seemed. They shifted from one personality to another. Because life required a multiplicity of being. There was Yong, helping the Yenan reds and yet not a real Communist. . . . Miss Soo, highly recommended by a Kuomintang official, was also probably a Communist sympathizer. She looked a prim celibate. Perhaps she had a torrid, passionate love life?

"How can this be managed?" asked Stephanie, circumspect, learning to fashion her talk the Chinese way, which is always to leave an element of doubt, query, enquiry for further parley. For it blocks conversation to monopolize all its issues with arrogant certainty.

"You would not be gone very long, say a month at the most," said Miss Soo, who had the irritating Chinese habit of pursuing her own train of thought before answering a question. "We welcome friends. We want them to know the truth. We show them the true state of affairs. Not little show pieces, like the Chungking authorities."

"I understand there must be government permission," Stephanie probed.

Teacher Soo said: "Of course, to visit Yenan there must be government permission. As a correspondent, you could visit Yenan now that many Americans are there. But our proposal is different. It is an area where no foreigners have been. We think you could write truthfully about it."

We.

Who was *we*? Stephanie knew she must not ask. This was too good an opportunity to miss. A real, not arranged trip. And then later she could go to Yenan.

"I'll have to think it over," she said. "But of course I'd be very happy to see some places besides Chungking. But why bring me here to tell me? Couldn't you speak at the hostel?"

"There are unfriendly eyes and ears in your hostel. There are none in my room," said Teacher Soo. She grinned and looked elfin-charming. "We like you," she said.

"Perhaps for the time being we should cut off all contact with Dr. Jen," said Old Wang to Prosperity Tang, giving him a full account of Jen Yong's scandalous conduct.

Prosperity Tang shook his head. "Comrade Wang, we must understand these intellectuals. The policy of the Party is to make friends with them now; later on we shall remould their thinking. Jen Yong has the defects of his class, but he is most useful. Most. It is good that there should be a bond between him and the American woman. They can be much more useful if they are linked by personal feelings."

However, it would require tact, good handling. Old Wang could not handle it, that was obvious. Tang would refer to upper level. Old Wang had his limitations. He was thorough, reliable, but a peasant. He did not understand that a true Communist must know how to work with all kinds of people, even with reactionaries.

And perhaps it was time that Jen Yong should leave Chungking for Yenan. He could teach there, organize medical units. Things were changing very fast. The upper level had called for expansion of work. . . . As for the American woman, a trusty female comrade was in touch with her. All the American newsmen wanted to make contact, to get to Yenan, to write reports on Yenan. But because Stephanie wrote for a magazine with mass appeal, the upper level had resolved to give her something special.

Prosperity Tang, who had taken a great liking to Stephanie though he had not seen her in the flesh, decided to speed up the matter.

"I seem to have acquired new eyes, Dad," wrote Stephanie to her father, "or rather a greater feeling of outrage at the human condition which I encounter here. There are countless episodes that somehow compel one not to be merely a witness, but to actively take part. Many of us feel the same way. I don't know whether it is because we are Americans and our puritan conscience propels us in the direction of trying to better the world—whether we understand what we're trying to do or not. But something MUST

73

be done for the Chinese people. The Kuomintang is unbelievably corrupt, and one hears of peasant uprisings and forced grain levies all the time.

"How all this can be changed I don't know—but it must," she concluded. She thought of Jen Yong, who was involved in the change, but did not mention him in her letter.

Yong. He would not leave her body or her mind in peace.

It had happened, when their shoulders had touched.

She had felt it then. Running through her. Desire.

She had wanted him then. Suddenly knowing what it meant, to *want* a man.

She was unsteady walking back to the hostel, and he had tried to tell her something. Something about himself. And her.

"Stephanie," he'd said. And she'd waited. But it would not come. And so she had turned, walked away.

There was the book of poetry he had given her. She had begun reading one poem with Miss Soo.

> *The gourd has still its bitter leaves*
> *And deep the crossing at the ford.*
> *I wait my lord.*

" 'I wait my lord.' It's beautiful," said Stephanie.

"It is very feudal," said Miss Soo primly.

Lying under the fan, in the darkness, she wanted the telephone to ring. Yong.

four

COLONEL Tsing of the Second Bureau was happy.

Three weeks had elapsed since his first encounter with Dr. Jen. And now something had occurred which made it possible for him not only to arrest the young surgeon but, more to the point, to destroy a branch of the Communist underground.

Had Tsing not circulated among his subordinates a crisp alert to collect every piece of information, rumor, or gossip about Jen Yong, a valuable item might not have reached him. It would have been buried among thousands of unchecked details in the files.

Eight months ago, three medical graduates had left Chungking for Yenan. One of them, a woman, was caught in the Kuomintang blockade maintained to prevent the seepage of the intelligentsia to Yenan. Reeducation internment camps housed those who were caught. After some weeks of rigorous questioning, a few beatings, having hot peppers put in her anus and vagina and toothpicks introduced under her fingernails, the woman had broken down. She had mentioned Jen Yong as the doctor who had trained her. She had also given the names of the two other trainees, both of them tutored by Dr. Jen.

Lieutenant Colonel Hsu sat on a chair next to Tsing's, behind the massive desk. He too was happy.

There is no pleasure more delightful in its extent, depravity, and savor than revenge. And now revenge was on its way.

Sipping chrysanthemum tea, Tsing proceeded with the plans. In front of him stood the detectives who had been watching the hospital picnic in the park on that Sunday.

"Why did the nurses make such an uproar about the

pamphlets?" mused Tsing. "It is not in the nature of a woman to do so. Women always pretend they have not *seen* unpleasant things. Did you ask yourself this question, Officer Wu?"

Officer Wu had not asked himself this question. "May I report to Colonel: The nurses created a commotion. We had to respond."

"And so all of you gathered together and went on a search for more of these silly handbills." Tsing was bland, and his blandness was fearsome. He consulted the reports in front of him. "Anything else strange about this party? You had your men at the park entrance gate. Did they see anything?"

He noted a small movement from a young detective standing in the second row. "Yes . . . Inspector Quo."

"Report to Colonel: I do not know if what I say is useful. . . . Colonel, please extend leniency to me." Quo had a terrible northern accent. Tsing thought northerners slow and dull: they only knew how to obey and to die.

"Speak," he said, already uninterested.

"I was standing by the motor buses when the hospital party left, and I heard one nurse say: 'Where is Dr. Lao?' Then someone replied, 'I think Dr. Lao left early,' but the first woman appeared puzzled. The nurse who asked came from my province of Shantung, and it drew my attention," added Quo. He blushed. Perhaps he had said too much. "I could not ascertain whether Dr. Lao was man or woman."

Tsing closed his eyes. He said: "Find this Dr. Lao and bring him or her to me."

Nurse Sha thumped briskly down the lane from the nurses' dormitory to the hospital. It was early morning, but she prided herself on turning up in the wards ten minutes earlier than anyone else. She owned a watch, an object she cared for, because its steady ticking made her less lonely.

Nurse Sha was feeling unwell. Her mind kept on circling around the incident. Kept on, like a persistent fly.

She had followed Jen Yong out of the hospital the day after discovering Old Wang eating *her* grapes.

She had seen Jen Yong walk towards his dormitory, Little

Pond come to him, and then both had walked away together. She had followed.

And Jen Yong had gone to the slum and emerged, carrying a parcel wrapped in a piece of oilcloth. It was raining, but he did not seem to care. She followed, wiping the raindrops from her face.

And on the curving road there she was—the foreign woman in her pale dress and bare arms and that casque of bronze hair—coming down the street, a street suddenly different because of her.

Nurse Sha could not see Yong's face, only his back and the back of his head. But that was all she saw in the wards, following him. His back, straight, slim-loined. And the way his hair grew. So cleanly. And the neat ears. It made her limp. It made her feel like screaming. She became wet between her legs, following him, following him around the ward, saying yes, Doctor, yes, and taking notes . . . and looking, looking at him, hoping he would turn his head, smile at her.

That night, she had heard Stephanie's voice. Under her feet a rat whooshed past. She had turned into a dark lane, enough . . . enough. The foreign woman. A fox. A painted devil. And Dr. Jen going with her—oh how could he, how could he be so foolish, so blind? She would only bring harm to him. . . .

"Big Sister Sha."

Her face swiveled on its short neck, unsmiling, hostile. In the morning light, a young man, neatly dressed, stood by the wall which circled the hospital compound.

"Who are you?"

"Big Sister Sha, I would request a favor from you. . . ."

"If you want anything, go to emergency," barked Nurse Sha brusquely. "I have no time . . ."

"It concerns Dr. Jen Yong," the young man said.

Nurse Sha stopped.

"What about Dr. Jen?"

"I am a friend of his. He is in danger. Friends of Dr. Jen should try to help him."

Nurse Sha's nostrils flared. Her face became brick red. She said, "Hng," and shoved forwards.

"Truly, I am a friend. Dr. Jen saved my brother's life. . . .

77

But if you have no time now, perhaps we can talk later in the day."

"Speak what you want to say, but quickly." She raised her arm, looked at her watch.

"My name is Quo," said the man, "and I am from public security." He added, "You and I are from the same village, Big Sister Sha."

True. His accents were the accents of her home.

Nurse Sha thought of the long days on the road, walking to Chungking, walking away from war and disaster, away from her family. She thought of Jen Yong, and her grapes, and the hateful foreign woman. She looked at Quo. He seemed respectful, averting his eyes. And he talked as she talked. "Speak then," said Nurse Sha.

Stephanie felt the sweat trickle down the back of her knees as she walked the narrow lanes. A funeral went by her, a hasty affair. A rough-hewn wooden coffin, planks disjointed, scarcely covered over with a rented cloth, its bearers bickering angrily, the widow and her son clad in white homespun, fanning themselves and forgetting to lament loudly the departed.

Rosamond Chen had asked Stephanie to lunch. The address was in the Chang Family Garden, which was not a garden but a staircase street running steeply down to the river. A house of brick nestled here, in the shade of a stunted tree.

Rosamond had stood watching at the upper floor window for Stephanie. "So glad you could come," she said, opening the door. They crossed the shop on the lower floor—it was a pharmacy—and went up the wooden stairs together.

Rosamond's living room was soberly pleasant. A few well-preserved furniture pieces—a jute carpet, crimson, a large window, an electric fan. In one armchair sat a slim girl dressed in a faded blue student gown, wearing white socks and black cloth shoes. On her lap was a bag with a red cross upon it. "My friend, Yee Meiling," said Rosamond. "She is a distant relative of mine. But then all of us Chinese seem related to each other; we keep our family lineage records from generation to generation, and we have at least sixteen grades of cousinship in our extended family system."

She and Meiling laughed, putting Stephanie at ease. Yee Meiling had a nice smile, her two front teeth bent slightly towards each other. She had studied ballet in England after finishing university, but when the Sino-Japanese war began she had given up ballet, returned from England, and was now an administrator in the Chinese Red Cross. She had a mouth too wide for the average Chinese girl, but she was small-boned and charming, and Stephanie found her easy to talk to.

They spoke as women who feel at ease with each other, in small sentences, with bursts of description and explanation; and Stephanie found Meiling listening attentively, asking her questions. Dallas. Radcliffe. Why had she come to China? Meiling said carelessly: "I see your magazine. I thought you'd written quite a lovely article about the orphanages. . . ." She laughed merrily, easing her Red Cross bag off her lap.

Rosamond had a good cook, a gaunt woman who had bought a little Szechuan girl and was training her. "I've also been teaching her to cook Western food," said Rosamond.

They sat at the table, served by the little girl. She had a round face and beautiful eyes, and her name was Pomegranate.

Stephanie handled chopsticks expertly. She enjoyed the food. "You learn very fast," said Rosamond. "Perhaps because you have no prejudices. It's difficult not to be prejudiced."

"Let me walk you home," said Meiling when Stephanie rose to go. And when they were walking up the staircase street, she said casually, "Have you thought about Teacher Soo's suggestion? We really would like you to visit our liberated villages, to see for yourself the real China—the one we're trying to build."

Stephanie halted. Teacher Soo, Yee Meiling of the Red Cross, Rosamond perhaps, and Yong . . . all of them. Involved in this below-the-surface *other* China.

"Why, yes," she said. "I'd like to write a piece about guerilla women. And of course I want to go to Yenan."

"Everyone is going to Yenan, to spend a few days, write an article," said Meiling. "There's a weekly plane now that the American Dixie Mission is there. But *we* thought you'd like something special for your magazine."

We.

The telephone in Jen Yong's dormitory hung on the wall of the passageway. The static was abominable, and Jen Yong had to shout: "Miss Ryder, the American lady journalist."

"Miss Lighter," said the grainy voice of the reception manager. "And who are you?" Jen Yong told him, had to repeat his name three times. Mrs. Wan from upstairs came out of her room, hovered over the stairwell, listening. She liked to air her belly, magnificently round with the life growing in it.

It took a great deal of time for the voice at the Press Hostel to return. "She is not here."

"May I trouble you to tell her . . ."

But the man had hung up. Jen Yong cursed, "Son of a turtle." Had it been a foreigner calling, the voice at the other end would have been courteous, even servile.

He wanted to see her. Talk with her. He had to tell her. That he loved her, loved her, and of course wanted to marry her. But would she be able to live in China? Was he not insane, was he not forcing himself upon her? *I'm crazy, she'll never want this kind of life, never. . . .* He thought of all the difficulties, like the treacherous rocks of the Yangtze which suddenly struck at the frail junks and broke them.

Yet there were such couples. In Shanghai, in Peking. He had seen them. One of his professors had married a foreigner. Stephanie was gifted with a rapture for living which also promised a disregard of difficulties. She was too fearless to plan for contingencies. She neither calculated nor schemed. She thought it was sufficient to fashion a life for herself by wanting and going for what she wanted. Was it right to take advantage of it?

What could his love bring her but a hemming in, a cage for the eagle, and the eagle would die or become a common crow. *What have I got to offer her?* A hard life, a bitter one. He loved her, he was lost in that great whirl of wings which was love, but what would it do to Stephanie?

And did Stephanie care for him? Or was it just curiosity? He would die if she laughed at him.

Passionately he reasoned, and dispassionate wisdom told him that it was madness.

At seven the next morning he began once again his battle

with the manager of the Press Hostel at the other end of the telephone. And finally, after twenty minutes, he got Stephanie.

"Stephanie Ryder here," she said crisply.

"Good morning, Stephanie . . . this is Yong," he said.

"Oh," she said with a note of pleasure, and then, because of his formality, also formal: "Good morning, Yong."

Oh are we going to start all over again, all over again having no words, no words to say what we really feel . . . ?

"I want so much to see you, Stephanie."

"Do you?" she said. And suddenly, through the silence, an awareness of his hurt, his pain came to her. "I'm being silly. . . . I want to see you too. Very much."

"I always say the wrong thing, Stephanie. Bear with me."

She chuckled. "Wait till I start speaking Chinese," she said.

Oh that voice, that laughter. He would never listen enough to the music of her voice. And he began to laugh and relief flooded over them and he whispered to her in Chinese: "Oh I am yours, and this contents me, full pleased with my pain."

And she asked, "What did you say?"

He replied, "I've told you something in my language which I cannot say in yours, Stephanie."

Stephanie said, "Is it in the book of poems you gave me?" She would never tell him that she had asked prim Teacher Soo: "What is the Chinese word for love?" And Teacher Soo, scarlet-faced, had told her there were many words, depending on whether one addressed children, parents, or . . . or . . .

"Lover," Stephanie had said bluntly.

"A gentleman one is married to," Miss Soo had corrected.

"Stephanie, I'm so afraid to cause you . . . difficulties."

"I hadn't thought of it that way, Yong. I can't really believe that doing what is right can hurt anyone."

Mrs. Wan was now coming down the stairs with the children; she smiled at Jen Yong with a great deal of understanding and started humming . . . as Liu had done . . .

Jen Yong was furious.

"Stephanie, could we meet this afternoon?" He told her that David Eanes and Jessica had invited both of them to tea. "Can you come? And after tea we'll go across the river, in the ferry, and, and . . ."

"And we'll talk," said Stephanie. "Yes of course, I'll come."

She would tell him that she was going on a tour of some liberated villages. He would be happy then. *You see, Yong, I am involved in caring*. There is only one deadly sin, the sin of not caring. This would show him that she was not afraid. That the work he was doing could only be right if it was good for the people. *I'm against communism, Yong, but I'll keep an open mind till I see what they're really like*.

She went to get her letters at the reception desk, and there was the note from Jessica Eanes asking her to tea that afternoon.

The Secret Police swooped down on the doctors' dormitory right after the noon meal.

The plainclothes men walked in, asking the doctors' help in clearing certain matters. The telephone was disconnected. Dr. Jen, Dr. Liu, Dr. Fan, Dr. Wan were all taken away in a police van.

The raid extended to the nurses' dormitory. Nurse Li was arrested as she slept. She had been on night duty. Nurse Tsai, however, was forgotten. Colonel Tsing himself walked into the hospital to arrest Old Wang—but Old Wang was not to be found. And though the plainclothes men ransacked the cellar, they found not a scrap of paper, nothing. Only some very old patched clothes, three spittoons, and a bedpan Old Wang had not had time to clean.

David and Jessica Eanes looked forward to having Jen Yong and Stephanie to tea. David had invited other friends. Since his bungalow was a good half mile away from the hospital, he did not know of the raid. No one had dared—or been able—to telephone to him.

At four o'clock Stephanie walked to the Eanes's bungalow, situated on a small promontory clad in camphor and oleander. She had passed the hospital gate and noted that it looked surprisingly deserted. Usually a great many patients and their relatives hung around. She decided to visit Little

Pond's mother, Liang Ma, right after tea. Her heart was light, and she stepped lightly. She would be seeing Yong.

The gray brick bungalow was of the usual missionary type—functional, slightly shabby, but comfortably furnished. David Eanes came to the door. "So glad you could come." He pumped her hand vigorously. "Jessica, here's our guest."

Jessica, tall, pale, with fair hair and washed-out blue eyes, smiled at Stephanie with a rush of affection. Like David, she was China missionary offspring and spoke Chinese fluently. She had known Pearl Sydenstricker before she became famous as Pearl Buck. "We've heard so much about you from our friend Jen Yong," she said, "and the whole city knows how you saved that woman. Now I'd like you to meet Professor and Mrs. Chang Shou, and Hsiao Lu, the poet. He writes both in English *and* in Chinese, and he's translating *Macbeth*."

Hsiao Lu had a broad humorous face. He laughed a great deal and told acerbic stories. When the Japanese came into Peking, he said, he had tried to flee but went in the wrong direction and walked into a whole battalion of them, complete with tanks. "They thought anyone stupid enough to walk *towards* them could not be an intellectual, so they did not shoot me. I told them I was a silk merchant. They slapped my face, and I bowed to thank them, and they were happy and let me go."

Hsiao Lu could not make a living merely writing poetry, books did not sell, so he did translation work for the Ministry of Culture, as well as teaching at the university. "I missed going as an interpreter with your Dixie Mission to Yenan," he said. "The ministry thought a poet would not be politically reliable . . . although my father is a big shot—a warlord, no less. I am ashamed of him, and he is ashamed of me. So we can meet without friction, knowing exactly how we feel about each other."

A thin, fairly tall man with a pointed face and owlish spectacles, in a threadbare robe so worn it seemed to hang together only by its patches, said in a beautiful musical voice: "I've heard a great deal about you from my friends David and Jessica." It was Professor Chang. Diminutive Mrs. Chang simply shook hands. "My wife does not speak English," said Professor Chang, "but she loves parties." Professor Chang Shou was a sociologist and historian of some eminence. He said to Stephanie: "You must be disturbed at what you see of China now. But change is coming, Miss Ryder. Oh yes. It is bound to come. All of us are working for a democratic China."

"I'm glad to hear you say so, Professor," she replied politely.

The telephone rang and David went to it. He was away for quite a while. Jessica was passing the plates of cake and the teacups when he returned, perceptibly grim.

"I'm sorry, Jen Yong won't be able to come . . . he's been delayed," he said to Stephanie, and caught Jessica's eye.

Professor Chang looked up quickly and rose, smoothing his frayed robe. "I'm afraid we've overstayed. My wife and I *must* be getting back. We only dropped in for a moment to meet you, Miss Ryder. It's been a great honor. Come, Hsiao Lu, you must go with us. . . ."

Hsiao Lu looked at Chang's face and rose obediently. He did a small Chinese obeisance to Jessica, putting his hands together, fingers tucked in, and wagging them up and down three times. "Lovely lady, I shall come back next week to bore you with my latest poem," he said brightly. And to Stephanie: "Miss Ryder, I am composing a poem about you."

Stephanie also rose to go. She felt exhausted, drained. Jen Yong was not coming, not coming. Jessica smiled at her, but there was something tired about the corners of her mouth. "My dear, we've been so *happy* to see you; sorry Yong was delayed . . ."

"Let me walk you back to the Press Hostel," said David.

"Oh please don't bother." Stephanie tried to look cheerful. "I was going to drop by the hospital, to see Liang Ma."

"Put it off until tomorrow or the next day," Eanes replied.

"Why? Isn't she well?"

"She's fine, but the hospital is extremely busy today; we're rearranging the wards. . . ."

"Is that why there were so few patients around the main gates?" asked Stephanie.

"Exactly," said Eanes. "Exactly." He walked her firmly up the road, away from the hospital. "Let me show you a picturesque corner of the city. I used to come here as a child, to look at the two rivers meeting, the blue of the Chialing merging with the yellow waters of the Yangtze. . . ." All the way to the Press Hostel, Eanes stuck to her, babbling of his youth in China. And when he left her, he wrung her hand. "Stephanie, I'll be calling you, very soon."

Feeling uneasy, Stephanie went to her room, washed, thought of telephoning, and finally, at a loss, went down to the lounge. Alistair was there.

"Stephanie, no doubt you've heard—there's been a police raid at the hospital and also at the university—a number of Communist suspects have been detained."

Stephanie became pale. Even her lips were bloodless. Yong. That's why he had not come. "Are you sure, Alistair?"

"Positive, m'dear. The crackdown had to come. Now I wonder . . ."

But Stephanie was no longer listening. She had walked out, out, down the path, down the road, to the hospital. She walked quickly, unaware of the people turning to look at her. The gates were not closed, but even the emergency room was empty of patients. There was a nurse, pale, tired, sitting at the desk.

Stephanie walked into the surgical ward. In Liang Ma's bed was another patient. The occupants of the other beds did not look at her.

"Liang Ma, where is Liang Ma?"

No one answered her. Stonily, they were all looking away. Or they kept their eyes closed.

She heard the grinding noise of wheels in the corridor. A young nurse was pushing a trolley with surgical dressings towards the ward. Stephanie walked up to her. The nurse looked up, shrank back as if in fear.

Stephanie said haltingly: "Dr. Jen Yong."

"No, don't know," said the nurse. Then in Chinese she repeated: "I do not know." And pushed her trolley to the far end of the ward.

Stephanie went back to emergency. There the pale tired nurse was bandaging the hand of a whimpering child. Stephanie waited until she had finished and then said, "Dr. Jen Yong . . . where can I find him?" Nurse Tsai (for it was she) looked at Stephanie. A long, long look, then she shook her head.

"I don't understand English," she said in Chinese.

Stephanie felt a wave of hot anger rise in her. God in Heaven, all these people so scared. She clenched her hands. "Jen *Taifu*, where is he?" she said slowly in Chinese. "I want Jen *Taifu*."

Nurse Tsai did not answer, went on with her work, as if Stephanie did not exist.

Stephanie walked out. Stood looking up and down the road. Yong. Yong. Maybe he would suddenly be there. She saw someone in the dusk, looking like Yong. She hurried behind him; yes, it might be . . . but it was not.

She was back in the Press Hostel. Looked for a message. No message. She knocked on John Moore's door.

"Come in," shouted John.

"Stephanie!" John Moore was surprised. He was at his typewriter, the fan was on, loud and whirring. He got up. "Stephanie, what a nice surprise."

"John, I think my friend, the Chinese surgeon I told you about, Dr. Jen, I think he may have been arrested."

John Moore went to the cupboard and took out a bottle of brandy and two glasses. "Let's have a pick-me-up first," he said. Stephanie shook her head, but he handed her the glass. "You'll find that in our profession, Stephanie, it's sometimes the only way to stand up to the flak. There's been a directive concerning Communist activities in Chungking. Tai Lee, the head of the Secret Police, has decided to make a big show. Your friend may indeed be in trouble."

"But John, it's so absurd. You told me yourself there's supposed to be a united front. And there are Americans staying with the Communists in Yenan."

John looked at her. He wanted to say: Stephanie . . . you're crazy. Why'd you have to fall for a Chinese? The whole city knew that Stephanie Ryder had picked a Chinese doctor. Had gone out twice with him. Which just wasn't done. Western women did *not* go out with Chinese men. Yet even as he thought this, he *knew:* Stephanie was not like other women. She had . . . something so natural about her. She was so straight-arrow.

For a wild moment he was glad that Jen Yong had been arrested, but then he saw Stephanie's face, the pupils widened with fear for Jen Yong. What a cad I am, he thought. He put his arm around her. "Stephanie, don't take it too hard. The hospital board will protest, and the Chiang government can't afford to really harm an intellectual . . . there'd be too much of an uproar."

"Poets and writers and students have been shot," said Stephanie. "You told me yourself about their pouring red pepper down the nostrils of a young girl at the university, and, and . . ."

John looked away. "I'll call Henry Wong tomorrow. He might be able to help. . . ."

"Henry! He'll be no help! What about us? Can't we do something?" She fought rising hysteria.

"Stephanie," said John quietly, "hold it, hold it."

Stephanie buried her face in her hands. "I'm sorry, John . . . I . . ."

"I promise you I'll do all I can . . . but technically, the doctors are *not* arrested . . . merely held for questioning."

Stephanie rose, tried a small, shaky smile. "I'm grateful, John. I'm sorry I got . . . upset. I'll go now. And thanks."

"Stephanie, I understand." He hesitated. "I've never met your friend. . . . I guess he was . . . involved; so many of them are."

But Stephanie only nodded, then smiled, and was gone, leaving that small desperate child's smile with him.

For several days Liang Ma had been well enough to move about, even if slowly. Her abdomen was still stiffly bandaged because the incision refused to heal. The stitches had been taken off and then the wound had burst open. A young doctor had stitched her up again, and now she shuffled about, eager to serve; she helped the other patients, fed them, washed their faces and hands. She would also help with the bedpans.

Go she must, one day. But she hoped, by making herself useful, that someone among the doctors and the nurses would say: Let Liang Ma stay and work here. She had watched the cleaning women scrubbing the floors, had watched Old Wang cleaning the spittoons, the bedpans. She never failed to call him Wang Ta Yeh—Grandfather Wang. To work in this hospital—ah, that would be to ascend to the highest paradise of delight. And she was a quick, hard-working woman, not slothful. . . .

But the hard-eyed, fox-faced men had come, and the terror they spread had reached into her brain, and she remembered the soldiers, and something gave way in her.

They called the nurses out, pushed the patients out of bed, searching everywhere. They had pistols, not rifles. But they were rough.

And Liang Ma knew that it was all her fault. It was her fate, a bitter fate pursuing her throughout this life, pursuing those who helped her. The monster had followed her, right into the hospital.

"A thin destiny, a child bringing misfortune." So the astrologer had said when she had been born. Her mother had sold her at a bargain, as a child bride, when she was seven and able to work. The groom-to-be was five years younger than she. She had carried him on her back for a few months, a drudge to the family who bought her, and, when he died of scarlet fever, of course it had been her fault. Wearing coarse white, she had wailed at his funeral, and on the return from the grave her hand had been taken by a strange woman. She had been sold before she could reenter the house and wreak more misfortune upon the family.

She had worked and been beaten and at seventeen she had been sold again, to a poor peasant. He did not beat her unduly, though she did not conceive for many years. And then happiness had come. Little Pond had been born. She felt her ill luck had turned. The astrologer, casting his horoscope, said the man child had a strong destiny. He would become . . . a lord of battles, a prestigious commander. And for some years it was truly as if the demon of mischance had forgotten her.

Little Pond was thirteen when she conceived again. That spring her man had been taken away by the soldiers, and she and Little Pond had become vagrants and gone to the city to beg.

Now they had come back, the terrible men who beat and kicked as they pleased. And they had taken Jen *Taifu* away. It was her fault. Her sins were heavy as Mount Tai, and how could she expiate?

"Liang Ma."

She raised her head from the corner where she huddled, fearing to infect more people with her bad luck. Nurse Sha stood above her, her brows met above her nose, her face was dark with hatred. "You have brought ill luck with you, Liang Ma. You are an evil woman."

Liang Ma bowed her head. It was true, she had brought dreadfulness to Jen *Taifu*, to the hospital. Nurse Sha walked off, thumping her feet as usual, and Liang Ma rose and went to the latrines. She found in her hand the belt of a hospital robe. The robe belonged to another patient, who was afraid of catching cold even in tiger weather, and wore it on top of her hospital jacket and trousers. The belt had found its way into Liang Ma's hand.

The toilet was a squatting one, a flush toilet; an arm projected with a chain at its end. Liang Ma had been taught by the nurses to pull the chain; water flushed through to clean the toilet, a thoroughly extravagant way of disposing of so much good manure that could have been used on the fields. But now this arm had another use. She threw the belt over it, after making a loop for her neck. She stood on a bamboo stool, which older patients used to steady themselves while defecating. She sighed, thinking of Little Pond. "Son," she said. "Son." Little Pond had a strong and good destiny. She must not harm it. She slid off into emptiness.

Nurse Sha turned her body on her summer sleeping mat. She stared at the ceiling and an evil face leered at her from the darkness. She was damp with sweat.

"Ill luck . . . she brought us all ill luck," she muttered.

What had she said? Nothing, really nothing at all. Detective Quo, who came from her province, had asked her a few questions.

She had told Quo how wonderful Dr. Jen was. He coached students in his spare time; he had given half his bed space to the son of another doctor.

"He is attractive to foreign women," Quo had needled her. Strange that Dr. Jen was still unmarried. He needed a helpmate, a steady, chaste woman. Foreign women were lustful and dissolute. Chinese women were virtuous and did not seek to pluck flower-pleasure beyond the wall.

That was true, Nurse Sha had said. And almost cried aloud, seeing Stephanie's face, Jen Yong walking towards her.

Quo's manner to Nurse Sha was full of respect and admiration. Then they had talked of Dr. Lao's absence after the picnic in the park. Nurse Sha said that Dr. Lao had left to visit her parents. "That is what is said in the hospital." Yes, Dr. Lao was a woman.

Quo had left, thanking her. "This will help Dr. Jen," he said.

Nurse Sha groaned. Not she. She had not hurt Jen Yong. It was the American fox-woman, with her face, her hair.

Teacher Soo always looked the same, as if she was put away on a tidy shelf between the lessons she gave to Stephanie. A neat toy which never needed dusting or washing, for she did not appear to sweat. Her faded face was always clean, as was her blue dress; her hair never grew longer or was cut shorter. She was ageless, odorless, deathless.

"Miss Ryder, today is our lesson six. Writing and receiving letters, telegrams, etc., will be the subject of our lesson. Please repeat after me: 'Dear friend Postman, is there a letter for me?'"

Stephanie repeated, Soo gently correcting her tones.

"Yes, there is a letter for you." And Stephanie repeated the phrase.

"Ah, I see it is from my friend. I have been waiting for it."

"I have been waiting for it. . . ." Stephanie repeated.

"Friend Postman enquires: 'What does your friend write?'" And Stephanie repeated it.

"He writes that I must not worry. I must do my work. I must trust that all will be well."

Stephanie stared. "Teacher, I . . ."

Teacher Soo put a finger to her lips.

"Now we write," said Teacher Soo.

She wrote: "Everything is arranged for you to travel to the villages. It is best that you should leave Chungking at the moment. It will be easier for your friend if you are in safety with us."

"Please copy these characters," said Teacher Soo.

Stephanie read. She looked up. Teacher Soo was watching her. Teacher Soo put out a small dry hand and clutched Stephanie's hand.

And Stephanie understood. This was a message from Yong.

Rosamond appeared the next day and took Stephanie for a stroll.

"You should go, Stephanie. Staying in Chungking may *harm* him. They may try to use you to bully Jen Yong . . . make him admit certain things."

"But will he be told?"

Rosamond laughed. "I'm not . . . one of them. I've only been asked to help in this case because I come and go easily among foreigners. You understand?"

Stephanie packed a bag; she would be gone perhaps two weeks, perhaps three, Meiling had said. Meiling would come to fetch her.

That evening she wrote to her parents, telling them she would be away for a fortnight or three weeks. ". . . not to worry . . . I've got a marvelous opportunity to see something of the real China . . . and all on my own."

She left a message for John Moore, who was away.

"Dear John,

"This is just to you. I'm going to some villages. I've had a message from Yong. Somehow I trust what I've been told."

She had given John her roll of film, the one she had taken in the slums. "Better have it developed at home," John had said. "I've got a friend at the embassy, we'll have it back within a month."

The room boy knocked at her door and handed her some letters. The post had come.

There was a letter from her father.

"I've been reading the newspapers and the Japs seem to be getting on. Hope they won't reach Chungking. I've got Chungking down on the map—all these Chinese names are difficult for us. . . . I've also bought a book, all about the Yangtze gorges . . . now a river like that, it's quite a problem. But if the silt is controlled, it could be a great source of electric power. . . ."

Some lines from her mother in her neat handwriting, unlike the scrawl of her father's hand. "We have read your fascinating letters with much interest. Asiatics are used to poverty, I'm sure they can be happy with much less than what we would require."

And from Jimmy, a scrawl so much like his father's. "Sis,

don't forget to bring yourself home in one piece. And I'd like some of those Chinese stamps. . . ."

A wave of homesickness came over her. Oh, what was she doing here? In this monstrous bog of a land which was sucking her into its belly?

She saw the cool quad of Radcliffe, the soft-eyed balm of the green lawns and clean cobbled streets of Cambridge. She saw the wide-rolling plains of Texas, the grandeur of its limitless horizons. . . . And now she had launched herself into this steamy, compelling quagmire of people, people . . . and she was worried about a Chinese who was in jail, a Chinese young man called Yong. And she'd only been out twice with him. But merely thinking about him made her tingle, made her damp. *I am falling in love. . . .*

There was a knock on her door. It was Meiling.

Stephanie slung her camera across her shoulder. Meiling carried her Red Cross bag like a badge. It showed what she was, and the guards at the gate saluted her. They had let *her* through. General Yee's daughter.

"You must be a big shot," said Stephanie.

"Not me," said Meiling. "My father is. And he doesn't like the Secret Police."

She saw Stephanie's strained face. Hesitant. Unusual slowness in picking up her packed bag.

"What is it?" asked Meiling.

"It's . . . look, I'm leaving Chungking, like running away, and Yong's in jail. I . . ."

"Stephanie." Meiling put a hand on her shoulder, a gesture of trust. "Please believe that we care for him. It is for the best that he should not worry about you while he's in jail. . . ."

"How will he know?"

"We have our methods."

Again that *we*. All pervasive, all encompassing.

Stephanie picked up her bag and followed Meiling. She told the hostel reception manager she would be away for a week, perhaps ten days.

92

five

THE *huakan* swayed up the narrow stone track of the cliff to the Buddhist temple. Around the temple were groves of oak and camphor and gingko trees, with small earth god shrines at their foot. The view of the river gorges blurred by mist, of the valleys with their alternating wooded ridges and fields and sparkling rivulets, was enchanting.

"This is called Halfway to Heaven Peak," said Meiling. "We rest here tonight. My father often comes here to meditate."

Meiling stepped into the smooth, pale gray temple courtyard. An acolyte in a black robe was waiting and led them to the spacious room they would occupy. "Buddhist temples always have rooms for weary travelers," said Meiling. Here was cleanliness and silence underscored by the evening melody of a single oriole, and also coolness, far above the sultry teeming city.

Night fell abruptly. In the light of the small clay lamps disposed on the table, Stephanie and Meiling ate a vegetarian meal; so clever was the cook that the beancurd was made up to look like meat and chicken, and tasted as such. And there was the clean room with two beds. After washing themselves, they lay down in the darkness. The night carried the first hint of autumn. There was a faint smell of incense and the distant sound of chanting. "The monks are at their prayers," said Meiling. The monks avoided their presence because they were women. Only the acolyte with shaven head, who was chosen to serve them, would approach them. But he kept his eyes on the ground, not looking at them.

Meiling and Stephanie lay relaxed in the darkness, talking. "I've often wanted to stay here, just forget everything

and stay," said Meiling. "Unfortunately, it's not possible."
She sighed softly and abruptly fell asleep. And Stephanie
also felt blessed languor, her limbs at ease. Her mind
soothed. Yong was in jail. But here, in this Buddhist temple, living took on immortal texture. And even jail seemed
clad with the garment of the Blessed One, for whom all
suffering is but the way to bliss.

The sun rose with great splendor and there was breakfast,
a meal of rice gruel, hot stuffed buns, and tea. Stephanie
realized she would greatly miss coffee on this trip of hers.
She'd forgotten to take a tin of coffee powder, available in
Chungking for the foreigners.

"Meiling, you haven't told me very much. Where am I
going exactly?"

"To a liberated district," said Meiling. "Villages which are
on the borderline between Yenan and Chungking."

"Sounds quite fascinating," said Stephanie. "We always
think in terms of absolutes, but here you live cheek by jowl
with your enemy. . . ."

"More than cheek by jowl. We are intimate enemies. No
enemy is absolute, Stephanie. Today's friend may be tomorrow's foe. . . ."

"Meiling, I've been thinking. Could I send a message,
just a few words, to Yong?"

Meiling frowned slightly. "Written messages are always
dangerous; we do everything by word of mouth."

"Why?"

"Stephanie, the Kuomintang is not stupid. . . . They
look in wastepaper baskets, they steam open all the
mail. . . . We shall certainly pass a spoken message, it's just
as good."

Stephanie had begun to learn a wisdom beyond the
conventional gestures of rationality of her own country.

Meiling had said to her the night before: "You are vulnerable in Chungking. Yong will be worried about you.
Remember, it all began with your hitting a Secret Police
man. They might try to revenge themselves. He cares for
you. . . ."

Now Meiling became brisk, matter-of-fact.

"I wish I could go the whole way with you, Stephanie,
but I cannot. Reliable people will look after you. You'll be
safe, and it'll be an experience you'll never forget. Write
about it."

They trod the stone path, lighthearted in the morning light, until they came to a road where a small group of people stood waiting with their luggage. There were men and women but no young children, which was already odd.

"My father has stamped all the twenty-seven permits you need," Meiling had said. "You don't know my father. Chiang hates him but can't do anything to him. Father knows how to take care of himself."

After a few minutes of waiting, a bus came up the road, a lopsided shambling wreck; half of its springs were gone, it sagged on the right side. But it was able to stagger on, and did.

From inside the bus came a short girl who shook Meiling's hand. "Stephanie, this is Yuyu, she will care for you all the way." Yuyu had another woman to help her, Panpan, who seized Stephanie's bag and stowed it at the back of the bus. Stephanie climbed in and waved goodbye to Meiling.

The bus trip lasted ten days and not four, as Meiling had asserted. Stephanie now wore Chinese trousers and top, both of blue cotton. They had been given to her by Yuyu when the bus stopped for the night. "You wear," said Yuyu, who was laconic in the extreme, for she translated directly from Chinese, which has no tenses, no gender, no singular or plural.

Stephanie learnt what it was to travel as a Chinese in China.

The roads were havoc, potholes and dust, none of them paved. There were frequent stops to let the bus motor cool. That very afternoon a leak developed, and the bus stalled. Everyone waited. Evening came with a great splash of pink and gold, isolating the bus and its passengers, while the driver and his two helpers alternately hit the motor with spanners or went with a tin can to a nearby brook for water.

The efforts to repair the motor having failed, everyone prepared to spend the night sitting up in the stalled machine.

Stephanie wanted to ask "What's happening?" but forbore. She remembered in time that Yuyu, who sat impassively, like a small Buddha, not looking at the driver and his helpers, was in charge of her. Asking would imply an unquiet mind, a querulous lack of trust, discourtesy.

Deep night fell with a violet sweetness. And then came peasants with lanterns, and the passengers walked to a village. Somehow villagers had been recruited, parleys accomplished, shelter sought and found.

Stephanie, Yuyu, and Panpan shared a room which was simply a roof and three wattle and mud walls and a cot. Stephanie was given the cot and Yuyu and Panpan squeezed together on a mat on the floor. The cot was a plank on four legs, and within ten minutes the bedbugs had come out from the wood and were feasting on her.

Bite, bite. She felt the burning pain, and slapped again and again. Another and another. "Yuyu," she said, "I'm being bitten." Yuyu rose, lighted the wick in the earthenware cup with a sulfur match. The smell of the match was strong in the air. She came to Stephanie's bed. Stephanie saw the weals on her own arms and legs.

"My God," she said.

"Bedbugs," said Yuyu matter-of-factly.

"I know they're bedbugs. Well for heaven's sake, let's get rid of them."

"Everywhere bedbugs," said Yuyu, as if objection to bedbugs could not be entertained.

"I can't sleep with those damn things crawling all over me," said Stephanie. "Can't you do something?"

Yuyu and Panpan looked at each other, looked at the cot. A battalion of bedbugs was now marching openly across it towards Stephanie. Panpan said something and went out. She returned with a tin.

"DDT," said Yuyu. They sprayed Stephanie's cot. Surrounded by DDT, she fell into slumber. The next morning, she noticed Panpan stowing the DDT can in her bedroll.

And so it was to be, everywhere. Stopping at squalid inns, Yuyu and Panpan would douse Stephanie's bedframe with boiling water, spray the mats with DDT. "Now perhaps sleep," said Yuyu, resigned to someone who attracts bedbugs as lightning rods do lightning.

Besides the bedbug-infested nights, there was the ever-repeated ordeal of the latrines. Never, thought Stephanie, have I ever thought so much, so continuously, been so obsessed by my own excretory body functions. Never had these been performed in such abominable surroundings.

Latrines were a hole or a row of holes set between stones slippery with urine and over which one squatted without anything to hang onto. Below the hole was the common sewer, and Stephanie stared, with fascinated horror, at the gold and silver moving mass of maggots. Constipation was the result. Stephanie sat for hours with heaving insides in a bus which shook and rumbled. Then spurts of diarrhea took the place of constipation and she endured further shame—that of having to ask that the bus stop by the roadside so she could relieve herself in the fields, with Yuyu and Panpan trying to shield her from the view of anyone peering to see if it was true that foreign women had foxtails hanging between their legs.

And thus centered upon the primitive functions of her body, upon sleeping, eating, excreting, she spent long spans of daytime sunk in semi-stupor, time lost forever, because her brain shut off. It had to shut off to endure discomfort—save for rare and lovely moments when the horizon began to bleed a sunset, or when the pre-dawn grayness yielded to a great rush of light, washing the world with the freshness of resumed life after that similitude of death which is sleep.

There were police barricades. Almost every day, sometimes twice or three times a day, the bus would cross checkpoints. An officer in uniform, accompanied by two or three soldiers with rifles at the ready, would enter the bus. Yuyu and Panpan carried with them letters, documents with imposing red stamps. The officer would stare at Stephanie, argue, look at her passport. Yuyu would hand him a letter which carried three very large red stamps. Then the officer would go away to consult someone while the whole bus waited. None of the other passengers spoke to her, but on the third day a woman who had bought some small apples at a stall pressed two into her hand, smiling.

"Eat, eat, good to eat," she said to Stephanie.

The passengers changed; almost every day some got out, others came in. They occasionally spoke to each other, a few words. But mostly they seemed entirely unaware of the others.

Each person carried an enamel basin to wash in. Yuyu strove to supply enough warm water for Stephanie, who seemed to need much washing every day. "I give you bath when we get there," said Yuyu.

"But we've been five days on the way, Yuyu. *When* do we get there?"

"Maybe tomorrow," said Yuyu.

"But I was told three, four days at the most."

"Tomorrow," repeated peremptory Yuyu.

There were fewer bedbugs now and Yuyu noted this.

"Foreign blood different taste, but now you eat Chinese food, your smell change," she said.

"They don't bite us," said Panpan.

And indeed their skin was flawless.

Panpan carried the bags, ran errands, brought Stephanie food and water, and spoke Chinese with her. "You learn quickly." And when Yuyu was trying to get the best room at the inn for Stephanie, or was composing a menu for Stephanie's sensitive bowels, she would talk. "We like you," she said one day, squeezing Stephanie's hand. "Me, your little sister, learn many things from you. You have big gallbladder." Which meant courage, the gallbladder being its seat. Stephanie was pleased at the compliment.

Everywhere, all the time, people. Never, never free from eyes, faces, bodies, shuffling, noise, smells. People staring, crowding, pressing, shoving. And the smell of excreta, all the time, permeating everything. And so many, so many big-bellied pregnant women, everywhere!

On the sixth day everything went wrong; the bus had broken down, fortunately not too far from a small town. The inn was the foulest yet, the privy a quagmire with rooting black pigs, and Stephanie's stomach had heaved, she had retched and thrown up. Yuyu, impassive, watched and said: "You wait." And pretty soon a hag-like creature carrying a large jar came into the room. She was almost totally bald save for a small artificial bun tied at the back of her head by a few remaining strands of her own hair. She set the jar down in the middle of the room and motioned to Stephanie to take off her trousers. Stephanie used the jar, which was empty and had been cleaned, though odor clung to it. Suddenly looking up, she found the paper window of her room punctured with a score of holes, each hole inhabited by an eye. This was too much; she started shouting:

"Goddam sons of bitches, bastards," she screamed, hastily pulling up her trousers.

Yuyu returned and asked, "What you say?"

Angry tears streamed down Stephanie's cheeks as she

pointed to the window. "Those bastards, goddammit, I want to wring their goddam necks."

"You tired, better rest," said Yuyu. The word *rest* was Yuyu's fallback for every situation. "We rest," she would say when the bus broke down.

"Sorry, Yuyu, I lost my temper. You care for me and look after me. I'm sorry to lose my temper."

"You bad temper," said Yuyu. "All foreigners big angry. Always angry. No use. You lose bad temper is good." And Stephanie knew the word lose was not understood by Yuyu.

Anger. The *ch'i* or essence, breath of one's skin, was the name of anger in Chinese. Stephanie lay down and suddenly the whole episode became farcical, hilarious. She began to laugh, laugh with herself. *Oh Yong, Yong, I wish you were here with me. . . . Always patient. Unruffled.*

She missed him now. Missed him. *Yong, now I am beginning to know your country. I'm beginning to understand how much there is to change. I know better how you feel. I know I love. . . .*

Her heart tightened. He was in jail. . . . Would he be out by the time she was back? Meiling seemed to think so.

On the eighth day they stayed at yet another small town, and it had rained, a sudden downpour. The unpaved dirt street was a meander of mud in which the bus slithered to a stop in front of the inn. The room was cleaner than usual, and the beds astonishingly clean. The room was on a top floor, and there would be no prying eyes. Panpan and Yuyu established themselves in a corner on one bed, Stephanie in the other. "We sleep well tonight," said Panpan.

The moaning began. It came from the next room, the partition merely a thickness of plaster. The moans alternated with little screams. Somewhere else a game of mahjong was proceeding; a clatter of tiles slapped on the table, and shouts of triumph or desolation. After about half an hour Stephanie said quietly:

"Yuyu."

"Yes," said Yuyu. She awoke immediately when someone called her name.

"There's someone in pain next door."

"We don't know this person, you rest," said Yuyu, not moving.

"But it worries me."

Panpan rose and went into the next room. There were

whispers. Stephanie could hear voices expostulating. After a few minutes Panpan returned.

"Woman having baby. You rest."

The moans were now stifled; they sounded as if they were coming through a thick towel. And Stephanie then realized that Panpan must have told the woman that there was a foreigner next door who was inconvenienced by her moans. Meanwhile the mahjong game rose to a crescendo; a furious argument began and was suddenly extinguished, and someone began to sing, piercingly, Chinese opera.

Then there were muffled sounds again, and smothered screaming, and voices, and then sobbing. Stephanie fell asleep and dreamt of her mother. Her mother was holding the mouth of a very large black bag open and saying: "You must get into this bag, Stephanie." And inside the bag, smiling at her, waiting for her, was Little Pond's mother with a towel wound around her head.

"Now we go." Yuyu was shaking her by the shoulder. Stephanie had fallen asleep at last.

"Did the woman have her baby?" asked Stephanie.

"Don't know," said Yuyu.

Panpan, devoted to Stephanie's foreign whims, one of which was pointless curiosity, went away and returned. "Baby dead."

Dawn still wrapped the small town in fine blue mist and made all things a little distant. The bus took off, and now they were climbing, twisting on a mountain road across a huddle of low, time-worn hills, with here and there a small pagoda, like a lookout tower, and the thatched roofs of villages spreading in the valleys. They too had changed; their walls were now of ochre-colored clay. The land was no longer so green and bamboo clumps were scarce. There were ridges of mottled limestone streaking the flanks of the humped promontories herding the valleys in which the bus now coursed. The road had suddenly improved.

And the next day they crossed the weathered ridges into an endless plain—a haze of pale ochre, dry and almost treeless. Fields of tall rye stood clumped around the scattered villages whose yellow clay houses and roofs of thatch crouched indistinguishable from the sallow-faced earth they sprang from. The air was dry, the sky blue and very high, whiskered with wispy cloud. It was the north in the effulgence of its one good season, autumn. Autumn swung across the land, stirring odors of pale smoke and the first golden leaves atop the scarce trees.

Stephanie's bus companions now unwound. Two middle-aged women who had sat next to her without a word for the last three days now spoke to her in English. Both of them resembled Teacher Soo in their self-contained quietness, their neat features and hair, smooth faces, every physical trait wrought with the utmost economy.

"We are nearing our destination; there is democracy and friendship here," said one of them in very formal but flawless English.

"It has been a pleasure to have you as our travel companion, Miss Ryder," said the other. "We all know America is a truly democratic country."

"It is a memory we shall treasure all our lives," they chorused.

And Stephanie, in a daze of tiredness, of stunned exhaustion, smiled tremulously and said, "Thank you." They did not tell her their names and left the bus shortly afterwards. It would be many years before Stephanie saw them again.

In the pale amethyst glow of an evening reluctant to end, the bus halted and Yuyu said, "We have arrived." They came down, and waiting for them was a boy, perhaps thirteen or fourteen, dressed in a short black tunic and trousers. He wore a pair of hand-stitched cloth shoes with very white sole edges, which showed they were new. As the bus lurched away, Stephanie waved at the other passengers and they waved back.

In Indian file, following the boy, the three women walked the skin-colored path between the tall spears of rye in the increasing darkness. In less than half an hour they had reached a village. No lights showed. No sound save their feet bruising dry stalks on the ground.

The boy knocked softly and spoke at the wooden door of one house. It opened. When they had entered, the door was shut and Stephanie heard the furry snap of a match. A woman in soldier's gray uniform, with a cap on her head, leggings, and straw sandals, held the match to a small lamp. The room was neat, with a table and four chairs along the wall. The floor was of tamped brick. Along another wall was a long and narrow table and upon it a glass case containing a row of wooden tablets. The family altar, the soul-tablets of ancestors. Beyond loomed another room, curtained off by a blue cloth hanging. The soldier-woman motioned Stephanie to enter it. Panpan followed with the lamp and Stephanie's bag. The room was half-filled with a platform of clay and brick—the *kang*, or stove-bed of North China. Its hollow inside harbored an oven space. In the fierce winter a small fire was lit to heat it.

"This room for you," said Yuyu. "Was landlord's house, landlord run away. Would you like bath?"

"A bath! That would be wonderful, Yuyu."

Everything was clean, clean. The quilt on the *kang* was spotless.

"Yuyu, I don't hear dogs barking in this village."

At every halt on the road there had been dogs, fearsome mongrels, mangy, skeletal, howling at visitors, howling at night.

"We kill all dogs," said Yuyu.

"Why?"

"Dogs bad. Make noise when fighters come. We kill all dogs. Landlord dogs, running dogs, Japanese dogs . . ." Yuyu suddenly burst into hearty, fruity laughter; her stolid face looked happy as she went on. "Kill dogs, bedbugs, traitors, Japanese."

The soldier-woman unfolded the quilt, plumping it with both hands. "This is Comrade Heng. She kill Japanese devils very good," said Yuyu, her head nodding towards the soldier-woman. "She good fighter. She look after you like sister."

Stephanie awoke. Oh marvel, rapture. She was clean, clean! Cleanliness was extraordinary, outrageous well-being, sensual fulfillment!! For the first time in nine days, the food last night had been served on a clean table. There were no flies. There had been a coarse bread with a nutty flavor, two boiled eggs, and some cabbage. It had all tasted good, so good. Comrade Heng had served her. She was deft and tranquil, despite the long pistol with a wooden handle slung into her belt. She smiled when Stephanie said:

"The food is wonderful. Thank you, Comrade Heng."

"We are all sisters," she replied. She had a low, contralto voice.

And when Stephanie had eaten, Heng, Yuyu, and Pan-pan had carried in a large wooden tub and then, in relays, brought kettles of boiling water to fill it. And Stephanie had had her first bath in nine days and reveled in it, discovering the ecstasy of feeling her own body, her own flesh and bones beneath the silk of skin. She had washed her hair and Heng stood by her, untiringly pouring more water, and then began to knead her neck muscles, knead her spine between the shoulder blades. And Stephanie abandoned herself to Sister Heng's strong gentle hands. Massage. It was Heaven. . . .

The sun streamed through the papered window above the *kang*. Cocooned in the quilt, she had slept, plunged into exquisite sleep, deep and dreamless. She rose and found a new cloth quilted jacket and blue trousers laid out for her, all with the exemplary stiffness of new cotton. And cloth shoes with very white soles. Such care and thought, and so much *expense*, in a land where clean water was so rare, where a new jacket was talked about for at least a year . . .

She walked out of the house looking for the latrine, and in the sunfilled street was Sister Heng, waiting for her. Sister Heng grinned, showing splendid even teeth, and indicated the thatched outhouse. The hole had been freshly dug: two bricks, dry and clean, for her feet on either side—no one had used it. Privacy. Sister Heng extracted the usual yellow toilet paper from her jacket pocket. (The coarse yellow paper was ubiquitous. Boiled from straw and pounded and rolled into sheets, it was dried by sticking on house walls.) She handed some sheets to Stephanie. Stephanie felt the world was a friendly place as she accepted the gift.

The world *was* friendly. This was a different China. A clean village. No peering. There were women in blue, young boys and girls coming and going. Sweeping. Carrying rice and cabbage in baskets slung on poles. They walked briskly. They did not stare at Stephanie.

This is a liberated village. Meiling told me. Not under Kuomintang rule. Under the rule of Yenan. Yong, this is what you've been working for. . . . And she felt bruised by his not being here to share her joy of discovery.

She returned to the house and found the basin full of

warm water for her to wash her hands and face. On the table in the main room was a large bowl of hot millet gruel, some steamed white buns, and a plate of pickled cabbage. Yuyu then appeared, bristling with new energy.

"Please eat breakfast, people wait for you," she said.

"Why are they waiting for me?" asked Stephanie, her mouth full of hot gruel.

"Welcome meeting," explained Yuyu tersely and sat on the bench to watch Stephanie eat. She had changed into a gray soldier's jacket and trousers and wore straw sandals like Sister Heng.

They walked down the village street together and no one was about, except the abundant sun spilling its benison upon the crouched houses and the purple battalions of rye. They came to the village threshing floor of beaten earth, hard as stone with generations of stamping, crossed a small humped stone bridge over a parched brook bed, walked to a clump of old trees, under which nestled the curved roof of a small brick temple.

"Village temple, now school," said Yuyu.

"What is the name of the village, Yuyu?"

"River Fork," replied Yuyu. "There was big river here, now dry."

"But there is water?"

"Yes," said Yuyu, "water in well."

In front of the small temple, grouped like the ancestors' tablets in a hierarchy of age, was the village population: in front about twenty children, from five-year-olds to fourteen-year-olds; behind them about thirty women, some in soldier's garb like Sister Heng, others in blue faded jackets and trousers; and behind them a few old men, white towel cloths on their heads like bandanas. Two of them had thin white beards. They held small paper flags, red, white, and blue, and waved them at her, shouting in unison: "Welcome, welcome, American friend."

And behind the marshaled village, lolling against the black pillars of the temple's stone platform, were two men in green battle fatigues. Americans. "No," said Stephanie, incredulous, "oh, no."

"Oh, yes," said one of them as they came towards her, one tall and one short, both of them grinning. "Hi there, welcome to River Fork village." They hugged her and Stephanie hugged them back.

"What a welcome, what a lovely, lovely welcome," she said.

"We were told you'd come late last night. But the people wanted to make a real good show, a welcome party, so we had to wait until this morning when you woke up. I'm Bill Haynes and this is Dick Steiner."

"I'm Stephanie Ryder," said Stephanie.

"Attention please," called Yuyu, clapping her hands to interrupt. Obediently, the Americans stood while the children intoned discordantly, "For he's a jolly good fellow . . ."

"I taught them that. I've been teaching the kids a lot of stuff since we got here three weeks ago," said Bill Haynes proudly.

Now Sister Heng strode up smartly and made a speech in Chinese, and everyone clapped again.

The children now dispersed with high sweet yells; the women walked purposefully back to their houses, leaving only the old men, who sat on two stone benches in front of the temple or stood in the sun, puffing on short straight pipes with soapstone mouthpieces, and watching the three Americans.

Bill Haynes was tall with blue eyes in a face all chin and Adam's apple. He jingled coins in his pocket, his feet beat a measure, he hummed and he grinned and moved all the time, teetering or pulling at his cap. Dick Steiner was Jewish, swarthy, voluble. Both were airmen who had been stationed in one of the American bases in east China.

"We knew the Japanese were moving in on us," Bill Haynes told her. "Our radio kept on about Japanese columns advancing. But the Kuomintang commander told us we were safe. He was a fat, happy guy, and we believed him. Then one day he got his men together and marched off. 'We have orders to attack the enemy,' he said. 'You are safe. Tomorrow some more of our troops come to look after you.' He shook hands with us. We were about forty Americans in the base, and that night the Jap planes attacked, strafing us, machine-gunning, shooting up the gasoline tanks—it was just like a small Pearl Harbor."

"Bill and I were lucky," said Dick Steiner. "We ran out, right to the edge of the field, and made it to a plane that had fuel. Don't ask me how we did it, but we took off. Our radio was all static, we couldn't get anything, we hoped other planes got away. We just headed straight out, and they didn't come after us . . . maybe too busy pounding the planes on the field. What a mess."

Then they had run out of fuel.

"We parachuted out and just hid in the fields all day. We didn't know where the hell we were. But out here the villages are close, there isn't much waste land and no cover. And the villagers were looking for us, combing the fields, calling and waving their lanterns. At first we thought they might be pro-Jap, but they shouted: '*Meikuo pongyou, meikuo pongyou,*' American friend, American friend, so we decided to trust them. Anyway, we couldn't hide forever, we'd had nothing to eat or drink for a couple of days, so Bill shouted back at them: 'Come and get us.'"

"They were great," Bill took over, "they fed us and hid us in the day, when there were Kuomintang patrols. At night they moved us from village to village. They even carried our uniforms for us. We're wearing them today in your honor. I think they want to send us on to Yenan. They say there are a lot of saved American airmen there. And then last night the girl who speaks English told us that an American newspaperwoman was coming. God were we happy."

"I guess they want you to write us up," said Dick Steiner with a grin. "Maybe that's why they brought you here . . ."

"Maybe," said Stephanie. Of course. That must have been the plan of the mysterious *We*.

"It's a great story, and of course I'll write it up," she said.

The three sat in the balmy sun, and no one bothered them. Even the old men had gone, except one who occasionally shuffled a few steps nearer and then withdrew to his original stoop, like a cautiously prying sparrow.

Bill Haynes was full of discovery of the liberated village. "There's no meat here, nothing on the hoof, just hens for eggs." There was no tea, no coffee, no sugar.

Bill's so American desire to improve matters had blazed. "They could increase their crops, plant corn." He was a farm boy, his father owned two thousand acres at home. "They're damn good farmers, they just need better seed, some machinery. But God, their fields are so small here."

He had gone to the fields and scooped earth up in his

hand and felt it, and thought of ways of improving the soil. He had walked to the small river a little over half a mile away, and by gesturing started the idea of digging a canal to bring the water to River Fork, which no longer had a river, only the dry, stone-ridden bed of a vanished brook.

"What bugs me," said Dick, "is there are no men here." No men below fifty or above fifteen. Only the few old men who sunned themselves and did no work except mind the children. "And the youngest kid is four years old. And there's only one pregnant woman in the bunch."

"I think this is a guerilla village," Bill said. "The women do everything—plant and reap; they also drill, they're the militia. I guess their men are guerillas fighting the Japs. . . ."

Stephanie felt happy. She had been right to trust. Trust Meiling. Trust Yong.

Yong. These villagers are Yong's people. These are men and women proud of themselves, redeemed. *Oh Yong, now I understand your passion. You want to make a better world for your people. And here, maybe, I'm seeing its beginning. . . .*

The women militia of River Fork did their morning exercise on the threshing ground to the strident sound of a whistle. They bent and stretched, swung their arms. They stamped, they ran, shouting: one, two, three, four. They swung their rifles into their hands and back onto their shoulders.

When the drill ended, Sister Heng made a speech, consulting a slip of paper. Then the militia women sang the "Internationale," removing the caps from their short-cropped hair. A little later they sat at school desks in the main hall of the temple, each woman with a pencil and a small notebook. Others went on sentinel duty around the village.

Dudu, the only pregnant woman of the village, did not do the drill. She sat at a school desk, her belly protruding from her soldier's jacket; the gap revealed her stomach, clothed in a white cotton camisole. When class was over she did not join the others but walked up to Bill who strolled with Stephanie, enjoying the sun. Her round face shone, her cheeks were apple red, and a grin stretched her wide mouth. Bill put his arm around her.

"Stephanie, meet my special friend, Dudu."

"Welcome," said Dudu.

"I taught her that," said Bill. Bill walked a few steps with Dudu, he speaking English and she Chinese, neither understanding the other, but stopping occasionally to laugh together. And Dudu laughed because she was the proud carrier of another life, so hallowed that she could put her hand on the shoulder of a man, even a foreigner like Bill, and no one would think ill of it.

"We were in pretty poor shape when we arrived. . . . We had the usual dysentery and we were both verminous," said Bill, "and it's Dudu who cared for us. She shaved our heads and beards, she washed our clothes. . . . She's got a mean hand with a razor." Showing concern, he pointed to Dudu's belly.

"Everything okay?" he asked.

And Dudu raised her thumb in the universal gesture.

"Okay," she said.

"I taught her that too," said Bill.

Dudu went away, waddling a little.

"She'll have the baby any day now."

After the usual noon rest—all village China sleeps after the noon meal—Bill took Stephanie to the village grinding stone—two round stones atop each other, fitted with an arm and a harness for a mule. But there was no mule, and Bill had volunteered to grind, pushing the grindstone, while Sister Heng and pregnant Dudu fed in the grain.

On their doorsteps sat women, stitching cloth shoes. Their long thick needles went in and out of the many layers of white cotton that made the soles. A thousand stitches to every sole. "Those shoes are for the guerillas," said Dick Steiner. "In every village we went through, women were making shoes."

And then the bags of grain were empty. Bill Haynes took off his harness and was again a gangling shy American from Iowa. "I enjoyed that," he said. They strolled back through the village. On the doorsteps youngsters were sharpening scythes with long wood handles.

"Tomorrow we harvest," said Bill. He squinted towards the fields. "Guess we'll all be busy getting it in before the cold starts."

When it was night, although they were sleepy, they still didn't want to part. They talked of home, and they talked of River Fork village.

"Do you know *when* they intend to send you on to Yenan?" asked Stephanie.

"They don't tell us anything," said Dick, "not until they've fixed everything the way they want."

"That's just what I don't like. I don't like being manipulated and not told," Bill growled.

That's my impression too at times—of being somehow manipulated, thought Stephanie. But they *must* plan for us, they're responsible for us. She lay down, rolled in her quilt. It was blissful just to lie there. And to think of Yong. Yong. Was he still in jail? I want to see him, I'm hungry for him. Now that I am beginning to know his world . . . his China.

Tomorrow she'd tell Yuyu firmly: Now I want to go back to Chungking—it's been a wonderful trip and a unique one—I've enough material for at least six major articles, but I want to get back. And then her whole body felt the yearning. She wanted him, yes, she did . . . she wanted Yong to make love to her.

The next morning harvesting began. Sister Heng blew small blasts on the whistle which hung on her belt. The militia women stood as on parade. One at the head of each furrow, scythe in hand. Sister Heng again blew on her whistle and they began cutting the stalks, swinging in perfect time.

An old man with so many wrinkles on his face that he looked like an extravagant doodle came up with hand sickles and gave one each to Bill and Dick.

And Bill became another man, heir to five thousand years of farming. Spare of gesture, he cut neat and straight, laying the sheaves to his left, swinging the blade with clean strokes. With him an unheard rhythm began pulsing through the field, homage to the sun's bounty, to life and the growing of the grain.

Dick came to Stephanie. He was giving up, seeing his efforts futile next to Bill's.

"Have you thought what a great story this is—Bill going through the rye in a Chinese village?"

Stephanie said, "I'll take a photograph," and ran back to the village to get her camera. She pointed it at the field, and suddenly all the women were running away with sharp cries of distress, covering their faces. And Sister Heng came up to Stephanie, waving her hands violently in front of her face.

"They don't want their photographs taken," said Dick.

Throughout the trip Yuyu had not allowed Stephanie to use her camera. "People here no good," she had said. But Stephanie now guessed that superstition was at the root— just as the "plain people" of Pennsylvania disliked having their portraits captured on film. So she took a snap of Bill and Dick standing in the rye, and they clowned a bit, making faces to relieve the unease and the fear the camera had aroused among the women. Dick decorated himself with cut stalks like an American Indian feather headdress. They photographed Stephanie holding a sickle. The women stood on the field's far edge, watching them.

Soon Yuyu came marching up, righteous as a school-mistress. "Time your food," she said briskly.

"Already? It's not even ten," said Stephanie, consulting her watch.

"Time eat," repeated Yuyu. It was an order.

"I haven't seen Dudu this morning," said Bill to bridge the awkwardness.

"Having baby," said Yuyu.

"It's her first baby . . . is a doctor looking after her?" asked Bill.

Yuyu turned on him. "Why you ask?" she said.

"Because I'm concerned, that's why. I happen to like Dudu, and I hope there's a doctor, in case . . ." said Bill.

"Comrade Dudu good comrade, strong," Yuyu interrupted. And then severely, to Stephanie: "Must not take photographs of people. I give you second warning."

"Oh nuts," said Stephanie wearily. "What's wrong with taking a photograph of people harvesting?"

Yuyu did not reply; she now wore her usual look of righteous patience as she marched the three to their house where the bowls and chopsticks had been laid. Eggs, cabbage, and millet. Stephanie was angry. *Yuyu must stop ordering me about.*

Bill was dimmed, like a snuffed candle. One big hand lay between his knees, and he jiggled coins in his pocket

(American dimes, for God's sake, Dick said) with the other. Bill was happy with the things of earth, his spirit as joyful when he trod the fields of China as it was when he worked the earth in his native Iowa.

"I'd really like to come back here and work with these people when this crummy war is over," he would say. Now he slouched or paced restlessly, because Dudu was having a baby.

"Cut it out, Bill, you're not the father," said Dick.

"That Yuyu, she'd make one hell of a warden at Sing Sing," said Bill.

"She means well, but her English is pretty limited," Dick explained.

Sleep in the afternoon. And Yong. The sun began to melt into the saffron and purple of the sky, and Stephanie melted, dreamed of Yong—those oh-so-gentle hands caressing her, that slender, taut body possessing her, as his spirit already possessed her.

The cold came suddenly upon the iridescent plain. Stephanie put on the fur-lined jacket she had brought with her. Bill and Dick returned, walking back from the fields. Bill had again inquired about Dudu from Sister Heng and been told "Baby coming." They sat, waiting for the evening meal, and there was a burst of firecrackers and Stephanie said: "Not another celebration . . ."

But Dick had jumped up: "Machine guns." The relentless chatter like a ticker tape machine and a faint clamor like the distant rumor of the sea. "We're being attacked. . . ."

They rushed out of the house and there was Yuyu running towards them in the village street.

"Come." She grasped Stephanie's hand strongly. "Enemy. Quick."

"Wait a bit, what about Dudu?" said Bill, running behind her.

Yuyu pulled Stephanie on. "Must save you." Dick and Bill ran with her, and now there were precipitate rifle shots and a vague screaming. Yuyu and Stephanie reached the village well—with its windlass, rope, and pail—round-rimmed upon its stone platform. The water level was ten feet down. "Go in," said Yuyu and jumped into the well, splashing, looking up with water to her waist. "Jump," she said again.

Stephanie turned and saw that only Dick stood with her by the rim. "Where's Bill?"

"You'd better jump, Stephanie," said Dick.

Stephanie jumped, and hit the water, and staggered up as the water splashed around her. Dick stared down at her, waved his hand, and was gone.

"Dick, Dick," cried Stephanie, and found Yuyu's hand clamped upon her mouth.

"Follow me." Yuyu crouched under the water level, disappeared beneath it, not letting go of Stephanie's hand. And Stephanie perforce went under the water with her, closing nostrils and mouth. Her head scraped the margin of the well's inner wall, and then she emerged into a pocket of darkness and air.

Yuyu hoisted herself up on a shelf of banked earth and stone, where she groped for and found a flashlight. "Here," she said, shining the light so that Stephanie could see how to clamber onto the shelf. In front of them opened the black gullet of a narrow tunnel. Yuyu went into it, squeezing herself on all fours, and Stephanie followed her. After what was probably only half an hour but seemed much longer, Stephanie felt fresh air upon her face; the earth was drier under her hands, some sand and gravel even flaked off as they emerged into a scooped-out cave, obviously man-made—for as Yuyu flashed her light briefly, a pickaxe gleamed, still stuck in the ground.

The cave was round-walled and small, but at its outer end was an opening giving into the night, barred by a tangle of brush. Yuyu went to it, parting the boughs, and looked out. "Village burning," she said.

In the distance was the redness of a fire licking the rim of darkness, and Stephanie thought of the harvested sheaves upon the threshing ground. Cinders now. She was wet, mud had caked on her hands and trousers. She shivered, took off her jacket, wrung the water out, put it on again. The cave was still warm with the contained heat of the day, but it was getting colder.

Darkness and time stretched upon them, and in their wet clothes they sat and dozed and woke. During those hours Yuyu talked, still in those short peremptory sentences of hers. Told her own story.

"My family live in red base. One of the first ones. All of the people want revolution. Then the Kuomintang armies

112

come. Papa, they hack him to death . . . could not even tell his face. Mama, all the soldiers upon her, and then they stab with bayonets between her legs." Yuyu herself had been overlooked, concealed in a hole dug in the floor by her father. Even then peasants in North China scooped tunnels and holes in the loose yellow earth to escape the soldiery, as they did later to escape the Japanese. When the soldiers had left she had been rescued by people from another village, who had run away in time. "Then I join Party when I am nineteen. I do what Party says, because Party is great, glorious, and correct. The Party train me. I learn culture. If no Party, I am dead, or a beggar."

Stephanie shivered.

"How come the Japanese got here, Yuyu? If the Party was so well organized, your people should have had warning."

Yuyu's lips were drawn; she hissed, "Not Japanese. Kuomintang troops attack us. Kuomintang help Japanese kill us. Traitors. Running dogs, running dogs . . ."

Towards mid-morning, as Stephanie drowsed, her body began to react strangely. She felt wretchedly hot, then cold, and her brain conjured vivid fantasies. Her hands felt clammy, her forehead very hot. Her throat was sore. She slumbered fitfully, dreamed Jen Yong was with her, but the dream kept fragmenting, she could not put it together. And now she ached in every bone; pain, radiating through her body, almost splitting her skull. Outside, someone was calling softly. Yuyu went to the opening and peered out. A voice. A hand parting the branches. She came back to Stephanie. "We return now," she said. Staggering, clenching her teeth against the ague which shook her, Stephanie followed Yuyu back the way they had come.

Cinders flew lazily in a small breeze come from nowhere. The whole village smelt of the burning. On the village street, in uncomfortable sprawls, lay a body or two in the khaki uniform of the Japanese "puppet troops"—Chinese in the employ of Japan.

Sister Heng and other women were carrying stretchers piled with bodies. The bodies of dead villagers. They walked towards the fields with them. Dick Steiner came out

113

of a house whose door swung brokenly. His arms were bare, and his face gray with ash and weariness.

"Stephanie," he said. "You're okay? Thank God."

"Dick. Dick, where's Bill?"

"Later," said Dick and walked swiftly after the stretchers.

Yuyu led Stephanie back to her room. The soul-tablets of the ancestors strewed the ground. Stephanie's bag and camera had gone and so had the quilt. Stephanie lay on the *kang*. Her teeth chattered. Excruciating pain in her jaws, in her head.

"I think I'm not well," she said to Yuyu.

Yuyu put a hand on her forehead. "Fever," she said, and went out, and came back with a dirty, ragged quilt. She began to undress Stephanie, rolled her in the quilt. Later, Sister Heng came and with sturdy deft hands rubbed and pummeled Stephanie and then gave her a hot drink which was strong and thick and had an acrid taste and smell, as of cinnamon and cloves. And Stephanie lapsed into a sleep which was no sleep but a voyage through strange fantastic scenery, full of anguish and silent screaming.

Night came but the village did not sleep. People worked, and there were moans from some of the houses. Stephanie staggered up, put on her clothes. They had dried, stretched on a line above a small stove. She went out and there were guerilla women, carrying things, going here or there, purposeful. When they saw her they shook their heads and gently pushed her back. "Water. Drink," croaked Stephanie. Tremors shook her from head to foot. She rolled back into her quilt, felt icy cold, got up, and vomited, a painful process since she had not eaten for twenty hours. "My head, my head." It ached so that she could not bear it.

And then it was light and she was a little better, and Dick Steiner was by the *kang's* side.

"You're like a furnace, Stephanie. Fever."

"What's happened to Bill, Dick? You've got to tell me."

Dick sat on the *kang's* edge. "I'll tell you. We were attacked by around fifty soldiers. Not Japs. Chinese. They went into each house, shooting and killing, and the girls tried to put up a fight—they sniped and ran, and Bill and I, we picked up a couple of rifles and we too started sniping.

"Bill got to Dudu all right. She was in a room, she'd just had the baby, it was still tied to her, but there were four of them there stabbing Dudu and the baby with their bay-

114

onets—and Bill went right into them—threw himself
straight at them. . . . I was just behind him and I couldn't
fire, but I hit one man. Then one of them flashed a light on
him and shouted 'American' and that seemed to scare them
all and they rushed out. . . . But they'd stabbed Bill, Stephanie, he'd thrown himself over Dudu and the baby . . . it
was still tied to its mother. . . ."

Nightmare took over, a monstrous, luminous rainbow of
terror. She was screaming and sweating, and Sister Heng
came in, and rubbed her, and pinched her neck and shoulders, and they again gave her that thick cinnamon brew,
thick as mud, to take the fever away.

The next morning the fever had dropped. Yuyu came in
with hot gruel and hot water to wash Stephanie. Stephanie
staggered up and began to dress. Her throat was sore, and
she could swallow only a few mouthfuls of the hot gruel.

"You better," stated Yuyu.

"Yes," said Stephanie.

"Now we have meeting, at temple," continued Yuyu.
"For American hero, Bill Haynes. Our Party hear about
attack. Send brother soldiers to us."

They watched the guerillas arrive. Men in rumpled gray,
moving easily, not in time, walking into the village single
file, with their guns across their backs. Around twenty of
them. Where had they come from? How had they been
alerted? Yuyu came to Dick and to Stephanie with the man
who appeared to be the leader. A young man with a round,
unlined face. Dick and he shook hands. And then he shook
hands with Stephanie.

Bill Haynes lay in state in the inner room of the temple;
above him the statue of the Buddha Kuanyin, the Compas-
sionate One, stared down. And now the guerillas lined up
and came one by one over the threshold, filing in solemnly
and saluting Bill. Dick and Stephanie filed in too, and the
wounded—who had been moved to makeshift beds in the
classroom—looked across the courtyard, sharing in the ceremony. They would dig a grave that day—a deep one, for
Bill who had so loved the earth, who had longed to make it
fruitful. He would rest in this village forever.

Yuyu said: "Comrades now making coffin for brave American."

"Where is Panpan?" asked Stephanie, her voice hoarse.

Yuyu said: "Panpan is sacrifice," which meant that she had been killed.

Four guerillas now lifted the door upon which Bill lay. The women had washed him clean, and he wore his khaki jacket but Chinese trousers and cloth shoes—new, the white soles had never trod the ground.

A pit had been dug beyond the clump of trees which shaded the temple. Out of the doors which had not burnt, a coffin had been fashioned, tied together with hemp cord made of twisted stalks of rye. The leader then stood by the coffin and started a speech. Yuyu translated: "The comrade fighter, he says Bill Haynes true friend of Chinese people . . . Haynes give life in service of people against imperialism. He sacrifice for revolution. Chinese people never forget. . . ." Solemnly, the guerilla leader advanced with both hands outstretched, again shook Dick's hands, shook Stephanie's hands. "Comrade say, famous American lady journalist must write truth, how Kuomintang break word, attack people. But final victory is the people."

And now there was an expectant pause. Everyone waited for Dick, for Stephanie. Stephanie could hardly whisper now, her throat was so sore, and that terrible, blistering headache had begun again. Dick cleared his throat, frantically groped for words—what could he say? What came up from him was the Jewish Kaddish for the dead; would it be appropriate for Christian Bill Haynes?

Yit-ga-dal ve-yit-ka-dash she-mei ra-ba be-al-ma di-ve-ra chi-re-u-tei, ve-yam-lich mal-chu-tei be-cha-yei-chun u-ve-yo-mei-chon u-ve-cha-yei de-chul beit Yis-ra-eil, ba-a-ga-la u-vi-ze-man ka-riv, ve-i-me-ru a-mein.

Glorified and sanctified be God's great name throughout the world which He has created according to His will. May His kingdom soon prevail, in our own day, our own lives, and the life of all Israel, and let us say: Amen.

Yuyu said: "I don't understand what you speak. What is it?"

"It means not be afraid of death," said Dick, falling into Yuyu's English.

"Bill, goodbye, Bill," said Stephanie and made the sign of the cross.

Four guerillas slid the coffin into the pit.

They assembled again, but now on the threshing floor. Seven of the women militia dragged another woman not in uniform, hands bound behind her, one whose face was streaked with tears and dust. "Traitor," said Yuyu to Dick and Stephanie. "She brings the bandits here." They pushed the woman to her knees. She knelt. A board on which was written "Traitor, Running Dog, Spy" was hung about her neck. The old men and the children began to shout, the men guerillas stood in a circle, while their chief, like a judge, listened to the women who one by one stepped out, fingers pointing furiously, voices shrieking at the kneeling woman.

"Accusation meeting," said Yuyu. And now in unison, the women were shouting slogans, heaping imprecations upon the woman: "Death to the traitor . . . death . . . kill the running dog!" and the small crowd was getting more and more excited.

"Six children, five woman comrades, all dead," said Yuyu, "also American friend," and she too began to shout "Kill, kill."

"What's the evidence?" said Dick to Yuyu. Dick was now supporting Stephanie who was unable to stand.

Yuyu glared at him. "What you mean? Evidence? We know," she said. And to Stephanie: "You have fever again?"

And now, swiftly, everyone moved. The guerilla women came forward and started to beat the kneeling figure with their rifle butts, swinging them up and bringing them down upon her. The other village women came; some had sticks, others had hoes, all of them clustered about the kneeling figure, beating her. Yuyu shouted, her eyes shone, she was excited. "Beat, beat, beat the running dog to death," she shouted. She turned happily to Stephanie, yelling "I beat," and ran forward, holding a flashlight aloft, and pushed to the center of the group, and brought the flashlight down, again and again.

"It's for Panpan. She used to wear a flashlight," thought Stephanie blearily.

Nothing could be seen of the woman now, only the bent backs, the heads. Nothing but a moan, gagged, covered by the furious shrieks, the dull sound of blows. "Let's go," said Dick, grimly. And they turned back, and Dick lay Stephanie on the *kang*, and covered her with a quilt, and sat on the edge, his arms about the quilt, and began to weep.

Yuyu came back and saw them.

"You not watch," she said reproachfully to Dick.

"She is very sick," Dick replied.

Yuyu touched Stephanie's forehead. It was burning with fever. For the first time Yuyu looked uneasy.

The same door which had served as stretcher to carry Bill Haynes to the temple would carry Stephanie, wrapped in a quilt, away from River Fork village.

The guerillas relayed themselves. They ran, light and fleet, and Yuyu ran by the stretcher and so did Dick. Stephanie was raging with fever and delirious. Yuyu fed her water, sponged her face. Cleaned her. They rested at intervals. Not a word. They saved their strength for this running. They never stopped; and they also carried Dick when he collapsed with exhaustion the next day. And thus within two days they covered the distance to the truck which had arrived from Yenan.

But Stephanie would not know this. She would never know of this race to reach the doctors in the truck; nor would she know that, because the Yenan base had only a single small truck, which also served as ambulance, she and Dick were carried in it, while the emergency medical personnel sent out to River Fork village would do forced marches on the way back. . . . .

One day she awoke clear-headed, although so weak that it was a major enterprise for her to lift her head, to look at the soft light which came through the window. A latticed window with a rounded top.

She was once again in a cave, in the womb of earth. But

the cave was warm, its walls were buttressed with brick and plastered white. The floor was smooth brick. Again she lay on a warm *kang*, but now on a mattress. There was a table, a chair, a metal stove with a pipe going through a neat hole. . . . Where was she? Above her head the ceiling arched, concave. She touched her face, relearning herself. She held up her hand. What an extraordinary thing was a hand! How marvelous were fingers! And now bending over her was Meiling, or perhaps it was not Meiling but someone very much like Meiling, who smiled at her.

"Meiling," said Stephanie. But the Meiling-like person shook her head and said in Chinese: "I am not Meiling, I am Loumei."

Then a swarthy, heavily built man came in who said in the best Southern drawl she'd ever heard: "Well, well, Stephanie Ryder, I reckon you've pulled through."

Stephanie closed her eyes. She must be home, despite the circular womb of earth round her, despite . . . "Yong," said Stephanie. Weight, savor, need in the word. "Yong."

"You'll be seeing Jen Yong soon, he's fine. Guess you'll be seein' a lot of old friends 'round here."

Stephanie kept her eyes shut, to hold on to that interlude of bliss. All disquiet melted away.

"Where am I?"

"You're in Yenan, sister. And I'm Lionel Shaggin. South Carolina, Spartanburg. You've been a very sick girl, Texas, but now you're doin' fine." She felt the cool, strong hand of the sun-bronzed man upon her cheek. "You sleep well now. Plenty of time to talk. Tomorrow." She felt the smile upon her new face. Her mind, her body were new. She was new born. In a new world. She slept.

119

SIX

THEY lay on the rotting planks to which shreds of matting adhered, gummed with the exudates of so many bodies before them. The prison was an abandoned air-raid shelter, deep-hewn in the cliffs of Chungking's South Bank, partitioned by concrete walls into six dungeons.

The autumn fog swirled like smoke into every hole and crevice. In the prison it was always damp; water tadpoled from each seam, the mud floor was alive with crawling things. Twice a day the prisoners were led out—in the morning to wash at one of the ten faucets lined along cement troughs; in the evening for an airing and a walk in the courtyard, a walk which lasted an hour, during which they were allowed to wander at will and even to talk to each other.

There were about two hundred of them in this jail, which was for political prisoners from all parts of Kuomintang China.

Jen Yong grew accustomed to the lice, the discomfort of sleeping wedged tight between other bodies, all in a row on a shelf. There were fifty-two people in his dungeon, No. 3, twenty-six to each side. All of the inmates were intellectuals—two poets, three journalists, several professors, many middle-school teachers. And a musician who had brought with him a small mouth harmonica and entertained the prisoners with a few airs every morning. On occasion he played the "Internationale."

The dungeon had its hierarchy. There was Professor Tseng, in jail already a year for spreading "an alien doctrine" among his students. He was dying of tuberculosis,

120

which had been diagnosed by X-ray two years previously. He tried to smother his coughing at night by stuffing rags into his mouth. The inmates had asked that he be transferred to a hospital. And one day all the prisoners in the four dungeons had gone on hunger strike for him. Professor Tseng had been taken to the hospital. But after a week he had been returned, with a bottle of brown cough mixture. He was said to have nothing wrong, nothing except "a slight weakness of the lungs."

The Organization was also present in the jail in the shape of its Party representative. But no one knew who the Party representative was, except the Party men. And no one knew who they were. The Party did not issue Party cards. It would have been a death sentence for the card-carrier. Everything was done by word of mouth. Party couriers did not carry documents. They stored everything in their heads.

In the jail there was the discipline, the prudence, even the sanctions imposed by the Party. This created solidarity, sustaining companionship, which endured even after release for many years.

This was the fraternity which Jen Yong found when he reached No. 3 dungeon. After a period during which he was checked, as each new arrival was checked, confirmation from the Organization about his reliability must have come in. Also the fact that he was not a Party member. It implied, therefore, that he could be trusted, but not with top-level decisions, not with ongoing policies.

Jen Yong's first interrogation occurred four weeks after his arrest. That afternoon a young student had been dragged in bleeding after a beating which had flayed his back. His dungeon mates placed him nearest to the heavy wooden door, the prized corner, the one with the most fresh air from the grilled aperture. Jen Yong examined him and thought he might have a broken rib. Perhaps two. There was nothing to put on his wounds. Soon the lice and bedbugs and other insects that plagued them were crawling towards the helpless, bruised body. The inmates relayed themselves to keep them off him. When the blood had dried they carefully put the student's jacket back on him. They fed him spoonfuls of rice and boiled water.

It was the courtly Colonel Tsing who received Jen Yong in an airy room, part of a building which topped the cliff above the jail. From its windows Jen could see the rock-city of Chungking pale and ghostly, color drained. The river was a marbled mass of water, half drowned in sky and the same no-color as the sky.

Tsing greeted Jen Yong with exquisite courtesy, apologized for the "unworthy accommodation" of the jail. He called "Serve tea," and a black-garbed subaltern placed in front of them a tea whose scent was a delight to inhale. Tsing spoke with gentle civility. "Dr. Jen, I have come here myself to spare you the trip through the city, an uncomfortable one, as it is the custom to chain heavily those we transport from one place to another. I am much grieved by the treatment you have received. . . . I will take it upon myself, because of our friendship, to offer you a warm bath. . . . Prepare a bath!" he shouted, and "Aye" was the response from an invisible servant and Jen Yong heard the faucets turned.

A bath . . . tea . . . surcease from itch, filth, the disgust of his own odors, offered to him so urbanely. "Colonel Tsing, I thank you . . ." and then he saw the smile widen slightly on Tsing's face, his patient, expectant air . . . and remembered the beaten student. He stiffened. He would have to go back to the dungeon, and the others, seeing him come back clean, what would they think? "I thank you . . . but I am not thirsty. Nor do I want a bath."

"Dr. Jen, it grieves me. . . . Perhaps I should make my heart clearer to you. We know that you are not a Party member; that you are an idealist. I would like to do something for you, for I admire your rectitude."

Jen Yong sat stolidly. The perfume of the tea invaded his nostrils, drove him almost mad with its reminder of past and delicate delights. Tea . . . his father and his grandfather had been tea connoisseurs. And he himself yearned for its fragrance, its conjuring of a world of art, beauty, gracefulness.

"There is a favor I would like to ask you, Colonel Tsing. Professor Tseng in our dungeon is dying of tuberculosis. He should be in a hospital. The germs are infecting other people. And there is also a young man badly beaten. I think he may have a broken rib. He too should be in the hospital. The dungeons are in abominable condition. They should be cleaned and fumigated."

"I shall attend to it immediately, Dr. Jen." Tsing jumped

up, theatrically started shouting orders. "Clean up the dungeons with disinfectant! Telephone to the hospital to send an ambulance . . . report to me here."

There were shouts of "Yes, yes, immediately," the sound of booted feet hurrying. Tsing, a Napoleon, came back to his desk, sighing, absentmindedly handing a cigarette to Jen.

Jen waved it away politely. "I do not smoke."

"I have to attend to everything," said Tsing, "everything. . . . The lower levels are rude, uncultivated people. Alas, it is a pity that the detention sector does not come under me. If it did, conditions would not be the same."

"If I may further impose, Colonel Tsing," said Jen Yong, "we also need vitamin B pills. We cannot survive merely on rice and a little cabbage. Some of my dungeon companions are getting swollen with beriberi. . . ."

Colonel Tsing nodded. "I shall see to it. Is there anything else you can tell me about the other prisoners? About their needs, their families? Do they receive news of their families? . . ."

"I know nothing of their families," said Jen Yong, avoiding the trap.

Courteously, Colonel Tsing bowed. "We must have another talk very soon, Dr. Jen. . . . Meanwhile, I shall see to it that your wishes are followed."

Jen Yong was returned to the dungeon. Incredibly, within an hour the vitamin B pills had arrived, and the young student was taken to the hospital. But he returned the next day, with a clean bandage around his chest; and three days later he was again taken out for interrogation, from which he did not return.

The next week an attempt at fumigation took place. The prisoners stood in the courtyard, while the dungeons were sprayed with DDT. "You certainly have an influential friend somewhere," smiled old Professor Tseng. Again he had been taken to the hospital after copiously coughing blood, and again was returned.

"They play with us as a cat plays with a mouse," said the musician, blowing on his harmonica. He was composing a prison anthem full of anger, defiance, sorrow, with catchy snatches of nostalgia. For nostalgia was a sustaining element in jail conversation.

During that week, however, the attitude of the inmates

towards Jen Yong changed. It began with the journalist and the poet who slept on either side of him and who now, without hurry, turned their backs to him when they lay down. Suddenly, no one addressed him directly, included him in their talk. They had cut him off. Ostracized him. The evening walk was the greatest ordeal of all. He walked alone, no one with him.

What had he done, or not done? This was agony, suffering worse than the lice, this shunning by kindred spirits, their suspicion. *I am not betraying them. Someone must be fabricating gossip. . . .*

It is hard to be utterly silent; to walk, to eat, to sleep with fifty-one other men without exchanging a word. Stephanie, her voice, her face sustained him. Stephanie . . . she must know by now he had been arrested. He was anguished for her. . . . Could they hurt her? She was vulnerable.

Again and again, as a man counting treasure, he saw her walking towards him in the rain, heard the gladness in her voice, and dreamt he was making love to her. His manhood spent itself, and he ground his teeth in silence. Oh, she was sea-treasure of torment and bliss, and his very cells were changed by knowledge of her existence.

The second time he was brought to Tsing was just before the evening meal. In Tsing's elegant room the table was set. A white tablecloth. Chopsticks and fine porcelain from China's greatest kiln. From the kitchen the smell of food wafted into the room. "My cook is one of the best available," said Tsing cheerfully. He suggested a duck and some mushrooms from Yunnan province, famous for its mushrooms.

Yong said, "I am not hungry . . ." He swallowed the saliva which filled his mouth.

Jen Yong returned hungry to the dungeon. He sat in silence on his bunk. No one spoke to him. He lay back and then Professor Tseng broke the silence. "Have you eaten, Old Jen," he enquired hoarsely. His larynx was now covered with ulcers.

"No," said Jen Yong. The dungeon absorbed his statement.

Two days later one of the journalists came to him in the courtyard. "Friend, your students have reached their destination. They send their regards. Your friend is also safe. Under good care."

And it was over; he was reintegrated. But what had been the cause for the sudden suspicion? He would never know, for this was the way it was—paranoiac suspicion could be generated by the smallest incident.

He now helped with the information channel. One of the guards, whose foul-mouthed oaths and insults to the prisoners were daily occurrences, was in fact a Party underground courier.

News came now. The Kuomintang had decided on a propaganda move. Release of some political prisoners to impress the Americans, for the press in America had been writing about atrocious conditions in jails and in the Kuomintang reeducation camps.

But action was not immediate and more days went by. Professor Tseng was now dying by the hour. He could no longer talk. His fellow prisoners took turns feeding him, cleaning him. The guards allowed them to bring water from the taps into the dungeon, so that they might wash him. On the third day Professor Tseng died. He hiccoughed for some hours, vomited, was incontinent, a gush of blood came from his mouth, and he was dead.

That evening the food given to the prisoners was better than it had been for a very long time. Instead of only rice with small bits of cabbage, which they received twice a day, three small squares of pork each, equivalent to a quarter ounce of meat, and a steamed bun were added. "It is Moon Festival night," explained the jailer. Moon Festival. In the Western calendar it was October 12. The inmates laughed. Fancy forgetting the Moon Festival! For with Tseng's death, they had forgotten.

That night something like gaiety pervaded the dungeon. The prisoners wanted to watch the moon, and the guards obligingly allowed them out in the courtyard for ten minutes. But a haze covered the sky, covered the moon's glow. Nevertheless, they recited poetry to her, playing the games of wit that scholars play, for a while forgetting their misery.

The detainees had unanimously voted to refuse a release unless all in the dungeons were released together, not just a selected few. "Chiang, that old turtle's egg wants to impress the Americans by letting only a few go, creating confusion . . ." This was the word that went around. They renewed their pledge that night. All, or no one, would accept freedom.

About an hour later Jen Yong was called. Another encounter with Tsing.

The moon through the open windows of Tsing's reception room was now high and full, wondrously round. Yong thought of Stephanie, and his heart smote him. The moon made him sentimental. He saw her face, her skin and eyes glowing in the opalescent light of the night sky. Emotion overwhelmed him so that he forgot to be careful, forgot Tsing's astute malice. Oh to be with Stephanie on a night like this!

"Ah, Dr. Jen, you contemplate the moon. . . . Tonight is when the fullness of the year's harvest fills our hearts with joy, and our souls turn to poetry, to love." There was wine, fragrant, and mooncakes, and from far down the road, the lovely murmur of people out to stroll in the moonlight. "Please, please have some wine," urged Tsing. "You will soon be released, Dr. Jen. The Communists already know it, and I am sure you know it too. We know they have a most efficient news system. Our magnanimous leader has decided on an amnesty for political prisoners. Hence, you may taste wine and eat a piece of mooncake without feeling that you betray your companions. I shall send wine and mooncakes to all of them, tonight."

Again he shouted in his theatrical way: "Let mooncakes and wine be brought to all our guests." And again there were the unseen voices, the precipitate feet doing his bidding. Jen Yong then accepted a small piece of mooncake and tried not to wolf it down. He sipped the wine, his palate rediscovering its pleasure. He had almost forgotten the savor of wine. Stephanie. He looked at the moon and finished his wine. His glass was immediately refilled.

"Elder Brother Jen, I see that your soul is that of a poet, your hands that of a healer of men. . . . Your heart understands the range of human feelings. Let us drink also to love, then talk of love. Love . . . We Chinese have a deep understanding of it. Not like Westerners, who mix it with vulgarity, with obscenity. They have no morals, their women are only too willingly seduced. . . ." He riffled negligently in a drawer of his desk, took out a letter in English, looked at it, smiling, then passed it to Jen Yong. "Elder Brother, you read their language . . . see what they write to each other. . . ."

And Jen Yong, because he was drunk and disarmed, read:

Dear John,

I've been wondering how long it would take you to come around to my view, but your last letter seems to indicate a change of heart. You'll be glad to hear that I'm on my way back, hopefully by June. And not alone. You'll see my new girl. Stephanie Ryder. Stephanie's delightful. She's got brains, ambition, but an even better body, and is she good in bed . . .

Jen Yong did not read further. He sat stunned, the blood withdrawing from his lips, his face, his limbs, beginning a frantic drumming and roaring in his ears. Tsing had turned his back on him, but was watching him in the long mirror he had placed for this purpose at the end of the room. Had he faced Yong, the latter might have struck him. "Ah," said Tsing, as if to himself, knowing Yong had stopped reading, watching his face and the hand which had replaced the paper on the table and remained, struck with palsy, in midair. "It concerns the person who brought us to know each other. That impetuous American girl. Elder Brother, I wish you happiness . . . but wild horses return to their wilderness. . . ."

Yong stood up. He would murder Tsing. He staggered forward, and then, shaking with the effort, controlled himself. "You vile thing," he said. "Pure gold goes through fire untouched. Let me never see you again. Earth has not space enough for both of us upon it."

He went back to the dungeon, lay down, and told his fellow prisoners that he had drunk some wine. "Perhaps I was wrong to do so."

"No," said the journalist. "We have also drunk wine, with our guards."

Stephanie . . . her smile, her walk, her hair . . . he remembered every little thing, every minute he had spent with her. The vibrations of her voice, eating the hot and spicy *maotoudze,* tears streaming down her cheeks and her saying "Oh, but in Dallas we *do* eat chili, chili pot, it's Mexican, it's supposed to cure a hangover."

Stephanie, oh Stephanie . . . "good in bed." Another man. Or was it other men? How many? The poet put a hand on his arm. "Friend, has something happened?"

"No. I drank wine. I . . . am not used to it." He had

wanted to take her in his arms, to crush her to him. He had not done so. Because he loved her too much, adored her. Every step she took, the way she turned her head. She was only twenty-one. His jaws were clenched so hard that they hurt. He must not weep, he must not cry out his fury, his anguish.

"Friend," said the poet, "whatever these devils say to hurt us, do not believe it. Have faith."

He clasped the hand on his arm. "It is nothing. It is nothing."

He lay all night long, unmoving, while the pain grew in him, gigantic. Now he understood what Jessica had meant. Why his last meeting with Stephanie seemed to have gone a little awry. She had expected more aggressiveness from him. He had thought her a virgin, to be treated with utter tenderness, with renouncing of his own desire. He ground his teeth, buried his head in the crook of his arm and drew up his legs and shrank upon himself, a fetus withered before birth.

The detainees were all released—although a few days later, some were to be rearrested.

Their hair was trimmed by the prison barber. Jen Yong thus returned to his dormitory looking as if he had just come back from work, or a walk, except that he was much thinner, a little unsteady on his legs. He went back to his room, past the sleepy gatekeeper, who saluted him as if he had never left. Dr. Liu, Dr. Fan rose from their beds and welcomed him with rapture, and the young boy who shared his space jumped up and said: "Uncle, you're back!" and ran to tell his parents. Dr. Liu went to telephone David Eanes, to tell him that Jen Yong was back. A little later David came striding from his bungalow and the news spread through the hospital. The cook grinned as he laid breakfast, and pressed Yong to eat. He had made special dumplings, having sent his wife to market to beg the butcher for meat.

Dr. Liu and Dr. Fan had only been held a few days, not in jail but in the police headquarters, along with Dr. Wan. And this, of course, was not surprising. Neither of them was involved with the Organization. As for Nurse Li, the wife of the police officer who had interrogated her was an old schoolmate of hers; they had let her go after a fortnight.

They were all sympathetic. They had all helped when they could. Not enough to get involved, just enough to get by, in case . . .

In case the Communists came to power.

Jen Yong understood this very well. There were the utterly dedicated believers, and around them, in ever widening circles, the semi-dedicated, the sympathizers, and then that vast mass (the outer circling of the whirlpool) of those who wanted to be always on the winning side, whatever happened. And this was only human, natural, to be expected.

Jen Yong tried to eat, said he was glad the hospital had not been unduly harmed. David Eanes said: "I've got news for you, Yong. The Chinese and American Red Cross have decided to send a joint medical team to Yenan for six months. It's one of the good things that's taking place now. We all agreed to put your name down to go. We thought that might get you out of jail sooner."

Everyone laughed at the irony of events. After years of blockade, and after Yong's arrest because he trained personnel for the northern front, here were the Americans organizing a convoy of medical equipment, drugs, and medical personnel to go to Yenan! A regular weekly plane now flew between Yenan and Chungking—a mere five-hour journey. And all because the American observer mission kept on sending good reports about Yenan to Washington. The American officers had visited the real fighting fronts. No spurious maps, no fake statistics. The Red Eighth Route Army was well trained, the soldiers well treated. There was a great sense of togetherness.

And foreign newsmen now frequently flew in and out. Almost to the man, their reports about the Communist base were favorable. Honesty, integrity, hard work, real concern for the people—and the support of the population.

"Good, very good," said Jen Yong, nodding his head at the news. But he was listless, and there was a morosity about him that surprised David.

Maybe he's exhausted, David thought. I hope he's not getting tuberculosis, he's so thin. "You're tired, Yong. You just rest for a few days, put on some weight. . . . The team won't leave for a couple of weeks, we're waiting for the

American expert who's to go with you." He wanted to talk to Yong about Stephanie, but there were too many people about, and David knew Yong's reticence. "I'll come to see you tomorrow," he said, rising to leave.

Jen Yong slept, rose to eat, to welcome visitors, students. At night, he left the room to walk, walk in the city. Pacing the winding streets. Standing to stare at the river swathed in mist. He was a ghost among the wraithlike people, for the fog took all color and substance away and even the noise was hushed. Only the long hoots of the ferries seemed to tear the fog's density. He saw a boy squatting in the white shadow of the track and thought it was Little Pond. "Little Pond," he said aloud and came near. But this was a beggar child with two white stones for eyes. He put some money into the outstretched hand.

And then, suddenly, normality was restored to him. Everything fell into place. What had happened to him? How could he, Jen Yong, sink into such a morass of self-pity? How could he be so odiously self-centered? Stephanie. If he loved her, how could he monopolize her *being*? A red haze came over him when he thought of her with another man, but he put this vision away and recalled her as she stood by the stretcher of Liang Ma, in emergency, with the angry welt across her face. The Valorous Maiden, intrepid beyond his imagining. Pure gold which fears not dross nor fire. And now he raged against himself. To fall into the trap laid out by Tsing, and all because of a letter, the moon, some verses, and a cup of wine! Who knew whether this letter was not a fake?

Stephanie. "Your friend is in good hands" had been the message relayed to him in prison. He had immediately assumed it was Stephanie. It meant she was being protected . . . but where was she? She had talked to him about going to Yenan, to see for herself. . . .

Telephoning the Press Hostel was hopeless. He would go and wait at the gate, just wait, wait for her—how often in his night walks he had circled, circled the wall around the hostel until dawn. . . . Or ask David and Jessica to telephone the hostel. They were foreigners and if they asked to speak to Stephanie on the telephone, even now in the small hours of the night, the hostel manager would not put them off.

And there was Old Wang. He had been so dulled, sunk

130

into his lethargy and pain that he had not even tried to see Old Wang. . . .

And Nurse Li. Tsing implied that she had talked, betrayed him . . . he did not believe it.

In a passion of guilt and remorse he now almost ran to the Eanes' house.

David and Jessica were surprised at Jen Yong's before breakfast visit. They plied him with biscuits and the remains of the chocolate cake which Jessica had baked for their wedding anniversary four days previously. For this she had used the very last bar of chocolate sent to her from home in 1942.

"Stephanie Ryder," said Jen Yong bluntly, "have you seen her?"

"She's in Yenan. I thought you knew, Yong."

And David told him of Stephanie leaving for a tour of some liberated villages. "We heard it from John Moore who got back the other day. She was in a liberated village on the edge of the no man's land between the Communist and the Kuomintang territories. She met two American airmen who had been saved by the peasants. Shortly after, the village was attacked by Kuomintang troops disguised as Jap puppets. One of the airmen was killed, but Stephanie was taken to Yenan. She was ill, Yong, but she's now recovered."

Jessica turned to David. "Why don't we try to reach John Moore, David. He could tell Yong all about it himself."

"Good idea," said David.

But Yong interrupted, "No, no, please don't bother. I must go now," and took abrupt leave.

Jessica noticed his face. It had changed at mention of John Moore. A wing of darkness had come upon it, replacing the joy which had suffused all of him when he listened to David's account of Stephanie in Yenan.

And Yong, rushing out, striving hard to fight his pain, his jealousy, walked, walked, stumbling into other bodies, not even aware till angry insults made him mumble "Excuse me . . ." John Moore. The man to whom the letter about Stephanie had been written. He had seen Stephanie, seen her in Yenan.

It took him an hour to calm himself down. And then he felt exhausted.

Whatever she does, I shall always love her. I must begin to learn how to love her. Oh, it was difficult and painful, but he would do it. *Even if I have to renew my very bones, I'll go on loving her.*

He would soon be going to Yenan. Then everything would be clear. In Yenan, away from pestiferous, squalid Chungking, everything would become clear again, clean again, clean as Stephanie was clean. . . .

In the surgical wards, Dr. Nee had taken Jen Yong's place. "I shall not be able to accomplish as much as you, Dr. Jen," said Nee cheerfully, and then plunged into discussion of operations under the stringent shortages which had become worse, not better, despite the reopened Burma Road. "And it's even worse in Yenan, where you're going. No rubber gloves, no catgut, no needles, no swabs, not even mercurochrome . . . I understand they're trying to make needles and syringes and they repair test tubes themselves."

Nurse Sha stood behind Dr. Nee, as she had stood behind Jen Yong.

"Nurse Sha, thank you for your great help to me all these years," said Jen Yong.

"Aiyah, Dr. Jen, don't go to Yenan; there is work enough here for two surgeons," said Nurse Sha. She looked haggard. Her face was creased and Jen Yong was shocked by the discord in her, which pulled awry the cords in her neck and made her voice shrill. As she spoke, he had the impression he was hearing crockery smashed.

Something was grievously wrong with Nurse Sha, and Jen Yong, with the new clarity which love and jail had given him, now knew that somehow he had wronged her. But how? Not wilfully. He had simply not seen her as another human being, as a woman. She had been a presence, eager, subservient, serving him, protecting him, and he had used her.

He said gently: "I hear Liang Ma took her own life. You looked after her well, Nurse Sha. I intend to search for Little Pond, her son, before I leave."

Nurse Sha said: "Liang Ma was a bitter life, a no-luck life. It was the will of Heaven, Doctor. You should not give yourself so much trouble. Her son came, and he was told his mother had died and to come with a coffin or take her away to bury her, but he never returned. Not a filial son."

Jen Yong wanted to say: But he is so poor. . . . However, this might hurt her. He shook hands with her. Her hand was small, plump, with a good moist skin. She should get married. . . . He went away and Nurse Sha looked at his back, looked at him until only the empty corridor remained in her eyes.

The slum was a black excrescence in the moonlight. This is where Little Pond had led him to retrieve Stephanie's camera.

Yong was sweating, although the night was clammy. The slum was a black beast watching him. He called: "*Wei*, Liang Little Pond, Little Pond." He walked the narrow lane between the smelly shacks. A man was suddenly there, in the fog.

"Who are you looking for?"

"Uncle, I am looking for a young boy, his family name is Liang, his own name Little Pond."

"There is no one of that name here," said the man. He was just a vague shape with no firm outline in the fog. He did not go away. Merely stood there. And then Jen Yong felt beings taking shape in the darkness, surrounding him. Thick specters, more and more of them, pressing in on him.

Perhaps they would kill him for his clothes, for the money he had . . . perhaps. But he must not show any fear. So he talked about Liang Ma, and how Liang Ma had killed herself because the police had come to the hospital and she was afraid, and now he was searching for her son Little Pond, and when he had finished the man spoke again. "He has gone away. We do not know where he is."

They did not trust him. They could not trust him. Liang Ma had died. He had not been able to protect her. Would his visit now do them harm? That was the way they reasoned. And now they murmured and pressed forward, ever nearer, forcing him slowly away from the lane entrance.

"Doctor, I have very bad eyes—can you give me some medicine?"

"Doctor, my son cannot move his legs. . . ."

"Doctor . . ."

They crowded him, suffocating him with their terrible smell, their scabs, the sheer weight of their suffering bodies, magnified by the fog, which seemed to enlarge their substance.

He had not been born in a slum. He came from the privileged class and he knew it and they knew it. Everything was different, his smell, his manner of talk, his bones . . . his entrails did not react the same way.

Words lied, brains lied. Only the body did not lie. And their bodies moved to his, knowing him alien, as cells move to devour a strange intruder. Soon they would stretch their hands, tear his clothes, tear him to pieces. . . .

The man who spoke first came to his rescue. "If Little Pond comes back, we shall let him know, *Taifu*." The others ceased to whine, and that tight, impenetrable wall of bodies, each head a battlement, gave way. They would let him go. He took all the money in his pocket. What was the use of money? A thick wad was scarcely enough to buy a cigarette.

"Uncle, please use this, it is all I have."

Tsui Sea Dragon had a wart on his chin from which a long hair grew downwards. His wife Chaste Wisdom had a cast in her left eye. The ugliness of the couple was reassuring. They both were Kuomintang moles, ensconced in the Communist underground.

Just as the Communists infiltrated the echelons of the Kuomintang establishment, so Chiang's Secret Police inserted their agents into the planetary outer rings which surrounded the Communist party.

It had been very difficult to do this while Chou Enlai had headed the Liaison Bureau between Communists and Kuomintang—a bureau set up in 1938 for the joint war effort against Japan. Chou Enlai was able, both audacious and prudent, his mind so subtle he would already have seen the reverse of every situation before the obverse had been talked into being. He had organized the Communist underground in the whole of southwest China. He held a tight discipline, and it was not easy to insert a needle, to get a drop of water into his setup. He also charmed all the foreigners, because he was aristocratic looking, cultured, irresistible.

The Tsai-Bo couple were excellent spies. They were both middle-school teachers—a good cover, for it was among middle-school teachers and students that Communist propaganda was most successful. They would now be going to Yenan. They would be isolated for months, for years, unable to tell who was with or against them save by body-talk—the way they would button a coat, pass a teacup, the way they would begin a conversation. . . .

Lieutenant Colonel Hsu Towering Cloud, now second in command to Colonel Tsing, sat across from them in the restaurant and entreated them to eat their fill. "Eat well, this is your last good meal, you will soon be eating only red-bandit boiled millet." They laughed. He continued: "There is an American journalist there, a woman. She is writing vicious articles against us in the press abroad." The Communists were treating Stephanie Ryder with special care, he said. They had smuggled her out of Chungking because they had great hopes of her being able to help them. They had also ordered a young doctor, Jen Yong, who was part of their network, to become her lover.

"You may be able to tell certain people about her dissolute life," suggested Hsu. "At the moment, the red bandits use everything, everyone. They even supply girls to the Americans in Yenan."

"We understand," chorused the couple. Morality. It was always possible to destroy someone by hints of sexual license—whether in Yenan or Chungking.

The three left the restaurant, burping with gastronomic appreciation. They walked through the fog-soft street. Chaste Wisdom stopped at a shop to buy some dried chili beef. "Only a little," warned her husband, "we must not look affluent."

A beggar boy saw them pass. He noted that they looked pleased, and one man had a wart on his chin. But the beggar boy squatting by the garbage mostly saw Hsu. He flattened himself into the fog, bending his body, scrabbling in the noisome heap. That was the man who had killed his mother. . . .

135

Little Pond had gone to see Ma on the night of the police raid. No crowd in the front courtyard. No noise, no screams. No one in emergency, save a young nurse who sat under the lamplight looking small and frightened. He bowed to her. She stared at him.

"Aunt, I come to see my mother."

The young nurse did not know anything. Little Pond explained, showed Yong's letter.

She said: "Visitors are not allowed."

"Dr. Jen said I could come at night," he implored.

The nurse was trying to look stiff, but she was all softness, her flesh was gentle, round, and white in her uniform. "Wait here," she said. She was gone a long time. And no one came. No one was about. The emergency dressers talked to each other in low voices in a corner. Is there no accident, no death, no sickness tonight? thought Little Pond.

The nurse came back, and with her was a new doctor, a corpulent man, who said, "Your mother . . . something happened to her. The police came to the hospital, and your mother she . . . she . . ."

"They took Ma away?"

"No . . . you better come with me."

Nurse Sha, stiff and tight, a mound of tight uneasy flesh, was there. "Nurse Sha," said the doctor, "this is the son of patient Liang Ma. Please do what's necessary." And the doctor walked quickly away. The ward was silent, no one moaned. In the beds the patients stared at Little Pond. In the bed where Ma had lain lay another woman.

Nurse Sha talked very loud, for all the ward to hear. "Aiyah, your mother had a bitter fate. It was her destiny. She hanged herself because she was afraid of the police. What was there to be afraid of? Nothing. No crime, no fear. But perhaps she had done wrong things and so she was afraid. . . ."

"Ma . . . Please to ask the *Taifu* . . . Dr. Jen . . . he will make Ma better. . . ."

"Ha! you and your Ma. It is because of you that the police came and took Dr. Jen away. Now come to see your Ma."

There was Ma, in a small room, on a bed of brick and cement. On her face was laid a piece of coarse straw paper. "Ma." He grasped her hand: it was cold, so cold.

"Don't look at her face, a devil is there," said Nurse Sha.

"You must buy a coffin and take her away, we cannot keep her."

Little Pond went back to the slum. He told Uncle Yu One-eyed that Ma was dead. The police had come to the hospital and taken away Jen *Taifu*. There was no coffin to bury Ma.

Uncle Yu said there was no way to buy a coffin. And so the soul of Ma would hang about and would return to search for Little Pond, because he had been unfilial, unable to bury his Ma decently, in a good coffin, to mourn her with paper money.

Uncle Yu did not speak for a long time while Little Pond cried silently, cried standing up, straight, like a man. Uncle Yu then shuffled away saying: "What can one do about fate? It was Sister Liang's bitter fate. . . ." And Little Pond knew that the people of the slum would not want him to stay. Liang Ma's ghost, unburied, would return to look for him. Would harass them.

He took his bundle of belongings: the torn jacket which had been Pa's, which Pa had had no time to put on when the soldiers took him away from the field; a tin spoon; a small used tin can; the pair of straw shoes he had earned by working, which he had kept for Ma; a felt cap which had belonged to Pa, which he used in winter. He walked out of the slum and no one asked him where he would go.

And now, almost two moons after Ma's death, he had seen the man who had kicked Ma, killed his brother in Ma's belly.

Now he followed, followed the man.

The river was November low; from it emerged the elongated island which served as Chungking's flying field in the winter, until the melting snows in May made the river rise and bury the island under water. From it the planes took off: for Kunming, the capital of Yunnan province, over the hump of the Himalayas at seventeen thousand feet to Mitkyna in North Burma, on to Calcutta, to Cairo, to Lisbon . . . across the Atlantic to America, via Tenerife in the Canaries . . . The island in the river was a link to the world.

Officials crowded the wooden building which served as a

waiting room. They were seeing off a famous American editor. He had had long interviews with Generalissimo Chiang Kaishek and Madame, and he was convinced that Chiang would fashion a democratic government after the war. "You're lucky to have such an enlightened head of state," he said to Henry Wong, and Henry beamed. The protocol officer, the assistant minister of foreign affairs, and the secretary of finance rearranged their respectful circle surrounding the Great Editor. He had been in Chungking all of four days.

Terry Longworth and Rosamond Chen huddled together, away from the official group. Terry was going home on temporary leave. He was still plagued with bouts of dysentery, which left him shaken and gaunt; and he was having trouble with his editor over the story on Joseph Stilwell, who had now been recalled.

Now it was Pat Hurley, Roosevelt's personal envoy, a man the Chinese called No. 2 Big Wind (among even less complimentary nicknames), who was influencing American policy. Hurley liked Chiang Kaishek. Hurley had gotten rid of Stilwell. . . .

Terry snorted as he heard the visiting fireman, as he called the Great Editor, proclaim that China was a great democracy. "Rosamond, the man's either an utter fool, or . . ."

"Hush dearest," said Rosamond, "hush." He subsided.

"I'll be back in February, Rosamond. . . . I'll get a divorce from Blanche. . . ."

Rosamond smiled faintly, said matter-of-factly, "You'll be spending Christmas with your children, Terry darling."

Terry protested, "Rosamond, *trust* me. I . . ."

"I do trust *you*," she said with an intonation which held so many nuances.

Towering Cloud Hsu was there. He loved airfields. Loved to watch the winged machines roar up into the sky. At airports one could also occasionally see foreign women.

He watched Rosamond and Terry with interest. But always, just behind his retina, was one face, one body. A face capped by bronze hair, a face he hated, wanted to ravage . . .

John Moore, face weathered by the Yenan wind, was also at the airport. He had returned from Yenan a few days previously, and had spent an hour the night before in long and furious argument with the Great Editor.

"Don't tell me what to think, I *know* what I've seen," the Editor had shouted.

Now he had come to see the man off. He watched the solid barrage of smooth, silken officials around the Editor, flattering him. The Chinese could charm the hind leg off a donkey, he thought. Their flattery was so subtle, so smooth, they seduced by food, and by smiles, and oh, how they could lie!

John had seen Stephanie in Yenan. He had been flown in with other newspapermen from Chungking, and he brought her a pile of mail, a toothbrush, soap, coffee, sugar. Stephanie, although still very weak and in bed when he had seen her, was well cared for. She sat up and smiled to greet him. "We've all missed you," he said, kissing her lightly, feeling his belly churn as longing rose in him. Oh, how he loved her, wanted her, and her beauty smote him, and her frailty. "Your story's hit the headlines, Stephanie—you should go home and tell America what it's like, they'll trust your words, you're a heroine."

"Not me," she said. "Bill Haynes and Dick Steiner. And the guerilla girls. I only got sick waiting in my wet clothes all night. I didn't even shoot one of those murderers, dammit!"

They had talked, and she had mentioned Jen Yong. "He's coming here," she had said, and her cheeks had glowed, and her eyes sparkled. Obviously she was in love, or thought she was, with the Chinese doctor.

Diffidently, he had attempted to reason with her. "I don't want to interfere, Stephanie, but it's not easy, you know, I mean . . ."

"You mean my being in love with a Chinese," she had replied, with that full child-glance of hers, and then she had smiled, tossed her head. "I'll take a chance."

It was obvious that she had made up her mind, ignoring the risks, the difficulties. . . . Her smile showed how unconscious she was of his own love for her. He was just a good friend, good old John. . . .

She had given him letters to take to Chungking, one for Jen Yong, one to the Eanes, and a long one to her parents.

Back in Chungking, he had dropped Stephanie's letter to Yong in the hostel post box, handed the Eanes her letter to them, and since he would soon be leaving for America, he would take Stephanie's letter to her parents with him.

The letter to Yong was removed from the post box and added to the Secret Police file on Dr. Jen Yong.

seven

you coming to the party, Texas?"

"Oh sure, you bet, Spartanburg."

Feeble humor, but nostalgia for America. Nostalgic as the name for the American military observer group in Yenan: the Dixie Mission.

Stephanie rose from the warm *kang*, put on her overcoat lined with goatskin and the fur cap hanging on the wall hook. She opened the wooden door of the cave and the icy wind threw a handful of frozen sand into her face.

"Ugh."

Lionel Shaggin and Loumei stood there, and Loumei took her arm, for Stephanie was still unsteady. "Sure you'll be all right?" asked Lionel.

"I'm fine," said Stephanie, wiping her face.

"D'you need more lanolin, Stephanie? I've got a tin. Genuine purified sheep fat. Best face cream in the world."

Stephanie thought how pained fastidious Isabelle would be to see her daughter go to a party in a bulky padded jacket and trousers of gray homespun, her face glistening with mutton fat.

The three walked slowly down the track which led from the caves to the valley bottom. There stood a building which served as main lecture hall, theater, and on Saturday nights as dance hall for the honored guests of Yenan.

These were mainly American: not only the observer mission, but transient journalists, and some permanent foreign residents. They rated top cave treatment, first class burrows, with neat plaster on the wall, brick floors, iron stoves for heating, a good wooden door, and a window with panes of glass instead of paper.

Shaggin lit the way with his flashlight. From all over the cliff side, firefly sparks punctured the night, people flash-lighting their way to the dance hall.

Yenan, Enduring Peace. A city four thousand years old that was almost erased by Japanese bombing in 1940. It now housed around forty thousand people in its burrows, dug out of the loess cliffs banking the Yen River.

Here had come the ragged remnants of the Communist armies after the Long March. They had scooped caves out of the cliffs, tiered one above the other, neat as the cells of a beehive. A style of dwelling sparing of building material, warm in winter, cool in summer.

"You've really made medical history," Shaggin had told Stephanie as soon as she could sit up. "Double pneumonia *and* malignant malaria, combined. Dr. Mehta diagnosed the malaria. He's from Bengal, so he knew. You got the last of our Atabrine injections, and you pulled through the pneumonia all by yourself." There were five Indian, one German, two Japanese, and a Russian doctor in Yenan.

But Stephanie still suffered from persistent anemia; she was also exhausted by very heavy and prolonged periods. And, as there was not enough cotton wool or cloth in Yenan to accommodate the women's normal monthly needs, the usual abrasive yellow straw paper had to be used.

Shaggin's Chinese wife Loumei, who had nursed Steph-anie to recovery, knew not a word of English. She was a gifted singer, from a conservative wealthy family. Like so many young people, she had run away to Yenan, to the revolution. There she had met and married Lionel Shaggin, one of that band of Westerners who fought fascism in the late 20s and the 30s, the Spanish War and China. The most famous of them all had been the Canadian Dr. Norman Bethune who had died operating on wounded guerillas.

In the long hours she lay slowly recovering, Stephanie talked to Loumei and to Lionel about Jen Yong. "We have a common bond, sister," Loumei had told her. "We have both crossed the frontiers which nations erect, to open wider the doors of understanding."

As soon as she could sit up on the warm *kang*, Stephanie had been provided with a small table straddled across her legs and had begun to write the story of her journey to

River Fork village, of her meeting with the two American airmen, and life at Yenan. She was glad to get back to work.

The party was being held by the Dixie Mission. In austere Yenan the Americans fell back on their tradition of creating their own entertainment.

Saturday night was dance night. It had now become a fixture. Decision of the top Party leaders. To accommodate the honored guests from America.

The latter, after a couple of months in Yenan, had courteously complained of lack of female company, of social intercourse.

A roster of reliable and attractive girls had been drawn up. Students from the Art Academy. There would, of course, be no sex. No sex at all. But the Americans would have female dancing partners, smiling and chattering, since that was what they wanted. All very proper.

Colonel David Barrett, the erudite, portly head of the military mission, was the heart and soul of the parties. His Chinese was both erudite and perfect. He even punned in Chinese, and this was not liked by the supercilious young Kuomintang colonel he had dealt with in Chungking, who had treated him as an inferior barbarian. "Colonel Tang used to give me the very smallest stool he could find for me to sit on, knowing I could only place half a cheek on it. Nothing is more unsettling to a man engaged in serious negotiations concerning guns and anti-aircraft than such fundamental instability."

Stephanie and the Shaggins walked down to the hall. Their breath smoked in the frozen air, and Stephanie was panting when they entered it. "How are you feeling, sister? Perhaps you shouldn't try to do so much." Shaggin was anxious. Stephanie was so pale and breathless.

"I'll just sit for a while." She headed for one of the stools lining the wall, and Loumei helped her take off her heavy coat and fur cap.

The hall was lit with kerosene lamps, shedding spotty illumination upon a five-man orchestra on a small platform. Two violins, a trombone, a drum, and an out-of-tune piano. About forty couples stomped energetically on the gray cement floor. Their padded garments made them look like portly teddy bears; even the closest hugging would only crush some inch of quilt without furthering proximity.

"Good evening, Miss Ryder. Miss Ryder—I say good evening." Exuberant, agile Dr. Mehta from Bengal shook Stephanie's hands, beamed upon her. His long-lashed eyes shone with the brilliance of ebony, his thin face worked all its muscles. Mehta had given blood to Stephanie when she had needed a transfusion. "I say . . . you look so beautiful. A little bit thin—" (he squeezed playfully the thick padding)—"but more beautiful than ever. . . ."

Mehta had been a revolutionary in India, and the British had put a price on his head for terrorism. He now swung Stephanie in a gentle foxtrot of his own invention, talking all the time. "Had an extraordinary two hours with the Chinese comrades. . . . Bless them, they're so earnest, you know, so sincere, but they've got such literal minds, you know, *literal*. I was joking, saying that after Indian independence we'd go on learning English, and that Nehru was an English aristocrat as well as a Kashmiri Brahmin. But they upbraided me, gently, of course, but oh, it took such a long time, they gave me a real lecture on the fact that I was not being serious-minded about politics. . . ."

The parties were occasion for much talk, stimulating, innovative, farsighted, looking deep into a future which seemed at the time fantastic. And the guests were impressive in their diversity.

Two State Department officials—tall and gangling John Service, fiery John Paton Davies—were there. Both of them offspring of American missionaries in China, of that generation which had produced John Hersey and Pearl Buck, and for whom China was another homeland, one which could not be separated, emotionally, from their own America.

Service and Davies had a conception of America's role in China which echoed the one Stephanie had heard from Jen Yong. In reports, they urged their government seriously to consider Yenan as an alternative to the rotting Chiang Kai-shek regime:

> The Communists . . . have the people of China with them. They operate an authority which we may dislike intensely because of its lack of freedom in the American sense; but certainly ninety percent of the

people in their areas have found social justice, equality, the beginning of some sort of a fair deal under their auspices. . . .

The Dixie Mission was worried about Pat Hurley, Roosevelt's personal representative. Hurley had made a lightning, unannounced visit to Yenan in October, and had gone away in triumph with a letter from Mao Tsetung to President Roosevelt.

"My dear President Roosevelt," wrote Mao. "I am greatly honored in receiving your personal representative General Patrick Hurley. . . . We have congenially discussed all the problems concerning the unity of all Chinese people and all the military forces for the defeat of Japan and reconstruction of China. For this I have offered an agreement. . . .

"The people of China and the people of the United States have a traditional and deep-rooted friendship. I hope . . . the two great nations will continue to march together for . . . the establishment of a lasting world peace, and the reconstruction of a democratic China."

The five-point agreement had been approved by Hurley. But back in Chungking, he had changed his mind. "Madame Chiang went to work on him, and he was like putty in her hands," said Service. Hurley had gone back on everything he had said in Yenan.

The American military observers had recommended to their government that America give the Communists twenty million dollars in weaponry to help them arm the twenty divisions they had to fight Japan.

"But Hurley thinks all ai ' should go to Chiang Kaishek alone. And in that case there's bound to be civil war," Service concluded now. And Davies, who was standing nearby, agreed.

"Mao and Chou and the other Chinese leaders are ready to fly to America at any time," said Davies. "They are NOT Communists in the Russian sense. They've proved it. Mao got the Chinese Party out of the Comintern way back in 1937, and Stalin's never forgiven him for this."

"The Chinese Communists are now so strong that they can look forward to the postwar control of at least North China," Davies added forcefully.

"D'you really believe that?" asked Stephanie. "D'you

think Chiang Kaishek has no chance at all?" She was thinking of a "balanced" article for HERE.

Service answered, "I think he has, if he throws out his Secret Police. If he promotes the liberals in his own government—and there are many of them—then he has got a chance."

Despite her physical weakness, Stephanie loved the parties. Relishing the talk, the American atmosphere, the feeling of being almost at home in Yenan. Never had she so well understood Yong's dedication as when she listened to her fellow Americans in Yenan.

And in her mind and body grew not only love, but regard. Admiration. She now yearned for Yong. He was coming, Lionel had said it. She would wait for him here. And tell him that she loved him and understood him, that she too was becoming involved.

Here, she felt, was a replica of early Christianity, frugal and sober, hard-working, undaunted, with a faith that could displace mountains. Above all, here was access and approach to the ordinary people of China.

Here she felt close to Yong. She now thought of him with enchantment. And love thus came to her, love not only a physical reality but also that most marvelous hold of all, a conjunction of minds. For love which feeds on love alone soon turns into nothingness. But now her love seemed soldered by a common cause, and one of utmost nobility— an alliance which would endure when passion grew cold, which would renew passion even when all else was spent.

Not the political, but the humanist aspect of Yenan had convinced her of this.

And the marriage of Loumei with Lionel Shaggin, and other interracial marriages, here seemed entirely normal. She waited for Yong. Never, it seemed to her, had she been so truly happy as during these days waiting for him to come. . . .

A drum boomed, reverberating in the confined hall, and the Japanese contingent marched in to much hand clapping. There were some sixty Japanese, some of them war prisoners who had now gone over to the Chinese Red Army. While no one else among the Allies could boast of having made Japanese converts, the Communists of Yenan had succeeded. Almost four hundred Japanese prisoners of war

146

now cooperated with the guerilla armies of Yenan on various fronts. They worked in radio broadcasting, propagandizing their own armies against the war. There were also two Japanese doctors.

The Japanese had dyed their rough homespun tunics in ochre and blue and tied red scarfs round their heads for the show. They wielded sticks with great abandon in mock fight, and uttered wild cries, leaping about in a ferocious manner and beating with great energy on two large drums of donkey hide. It was wonderful and wild, and everyone clapped and shouted "Encore."

Stephanie felt her shoulder grasped. "Enjoying yourself, Stephanie? That's right. That's good. The news is excellent, don't you think? We all rejoice. How about a little dance, eh? Warm us up." It was Herbert Luger, the head of the English language section of the radio.

Herbert Luger and his wife Alicia were American Communist Party members who had come to help the Chinese revolution. Ardent and righteous, his conversation a daisy chain of slogans, Herbert Luger had taken upon himself the task of educating Stephanie in politics. He did it with crusading enthusiasm, and reminded Stephanie of Somerset Maugham's missionary in *Rain:* tenacious, clinging, and inclined to much roaming over Stephanie's shoulders and waist.

"I'll sit a while, I'm tired," she smiled.

But Herb took Stephanie's smile as welcoming, and sat down beside her.

"Hear you're writing a series of articles on life in Yenan . . . that's good, that's excellent, Stephanie. We need to get the information across, keep up the good work. But I don't think you're giving the correct political view. How can you ever project these momentous historical events unless you have a correct political stance? Now the materialist viewpoint . . ."

"I judge for myself, Herb," Stephanie snapped.

But he wouldn't give up. "Stephanie, your mental resistance is natural; it's class struggle. Your class resists correct thinking because it wishes to go on crushing the proletariat. You don't *want* to remold your thinking to acquire the proper world concept. . . . Why, what's the matter?"

For Stephanie had stiffened. Abruptly. Suddenly she was running towards the entrance, with its heavy padded curtain in front of the doorway to keep out the cold. A man had just come in, who stamped his feet in their thin shoes, who wore a thin coat and a muffler and a cap, and whose eyes searched the hall. And she ran towards him, ran, calling his name, heedless of the surprised glances; the couples who swiveled heads at they danced.

Jen Yong saw her, and his mouth said Stephanie. He held out both arms to her, and she went into them and clasped him tight and his arms folded around her, tight and hard, and the padded jacket notwithstanding she felt her whole body melt and fuse with his. "Yong," she said. "Yong, I knew you would come."

"Stephanie, oh my dear love," he said, "my dear love."

"And I love you, Yong. I waited for you."

"Excuse me," a cool voice cut in. Close to Jen Yong, with proprietary closeness, stood a woman, oval-faced, staring at Stephanie with unconcealed spite. Jen Yong said, slightly slackening his tight embrace, "Stephanie, this is my Fourth Aunt Jen Ping."

And Jen Ping said: "Fancy both of us being here, and only meeting tonight through my nephew."

Then Shaggin was there, with Loumei, and Jen Ping took over the introductions. "Dr. Shaggin, this is Dr. Jen Yong, Red Cross team."

Shaggin shook hands. "So glad you've arrived, Dr. Jen. I've heard so much about your excellent work. . . . Where are the others of the team?"

"I came ahead," said Yong, "an army truck gave me a lift. The rest of the team will be here tomorrow."

It's for me, thought Stephanie, he came ahead of the team.

"My nephew hasn't changed his clothes or eaten a meal," said Jen Ping accusingly. "I think he needs to rest."

Jen Yong said, "I wanted to see Stephanie first."

Jen Ping glowered. "You'll catch pneumonia in these thin clothes."

Other people were now crowding around them, for any new arrival meant great excitement in Yenan. Herbert Luger shoved forwards. "How do, comrade. My name is Herb Luger, I work at the broadcasting station. I will announce your arrival if I can interview you. What's your name?" He put his arm around Stephanie. "Well now,

148

Stephanie, you wouldn't dance with me . . . but I guess it was for a good reason, yes, a good reason . . ."

Yong's face darkened, stiffened. He was suddenly angry, and he said: "Please take your arm off Miss Ryder." And Herbert Luger, startled, did so.

"Oh, I've been so longing to see you, Yong," said Stephanie.

Jen Ping again cut in: "I am the person responsible for lodging medical personnel. I'm afraid we have to go."

Shaggin said gravely, "Stephanie, I think it's time we all went home. She's been pretty sick," he told Yong, "malignant malaria and pneumonia, hemoglobin still only sixty-five percent. You all can talk tomorrow."

"I'll see you tomorrow then," said Stephanie to Yong. She felt on the verge of tears, both of happiness and dismay, for now there was a brooding, angry look in his eyes.

Yong nodded. "Goodnight, Stephanie," he said abruptly, and looked at her with longing and distress; and then he was gone into the icy night, with his Fourth Aunt Jen Ping following him.

Damn Herb Luger, thought Stephanie, lying on the *kang*. She was totally exhausted but she could not sleep. Yong, Yong was in Yenan. But he could not be with her. She longed for him. Longed to the point of fainting.

Herb Luger. Thickskinned, loudmouthed, and always touching, touching, this incurable mania for flesh contact. He would put his hand on someone's knee while he talked, and the unhappy captive would wriggle faintly while remaining subject to a fine spray of Herbert's saliva and to the unstoppable flow of his jargon. The Centipede. That was his Chinese nickname.

Surely, thought Stephanie, Yong can't have taken Herb Luger's gesture seriously. He's got too much sense . . . but that darkness on his face . . .

She rose in the colorless dawn, filled a large copper kettle with water from the brown ceramic jar which stood in a corner, and set it on the small stove which she had refilled with coal balls. When the water was hot, she poured it in her basin and washed herself, standing as near the stove as

149

possible. Then, already exhausted, she lay back on the bed, her head spinning.

Stephanie was favored in that she had a copper kettle and constant hot water because of the small iron stove, whose funnel went through the window. Even the leaders only had open braziers of charcoal, which gave off poisonous fumes and could not be kept on at night. And in many caves the only heat was that exhaled by its occupants. Every other day Wei Bamboo Shoot, the country girl who looked after her, carried two pails of water up from the river to fill Stephanie's ceramic jar. And because Stephanie was not strong enough to face the cold, outdoor latrine, Bamboo Shoot brought in and took out a blue ceramic pot, on which Stephanie sat and which was concealed in a corner by a folding screen of wood.

The latrines in use by all the cave dwellers were rows of holes, either dug in a wooden board or simply on bricks over a dry trench. They were semi-roofed against rain or snow, but otherwise wide open to the air, protected from view only by a low wall. In the winter, waste matter froze as soon as it fell, and a high glistening spike of it rose almost to the rear of the squatter. Each latrine therefore had an iron crowbar or pick standing by the wall, to smash the spike when it grew too high. In the spring, when the thaw came, the dry trench was emptied into compost heaps, to be used ultimately in the fields as fertilizer.

Having washed and combed her hair, Stephanie waited. For Yong. He will come after the early meal. After the noon meal. But the afternoon lengthened, night fell, and Yong did not come.

Perhaps he has been delayed; he must be at the hospital. She waited for Lionel Shaggin to return. He would bring news of Yong. But Shaggin merely said there was a meeting next day to welcome the Red Cross team, and that the Americans were invited, including of course Stephanie. "If you feel up to it." She was too proud to enquire about Yong. . . .

Night came and then morning. A desolation of freezing half-light which took an effort of spirit and body to surmount. Stephanie and Loumei walked down to the hall in the valley. It was the same hall used for the weekly dances. There the reception for the Red Cross team would take place.

The nurses of the hospital came, chirruping and laughing. They were mostly boys, carrying their small stools with them, sitting at the far end of the hall and lining the walls. But there were also a few girls and women. The doctors, recognized by the mufflers around their necks and their goatskin caps, came sedately in a group. Yong was with them, and also his Fourth Aunt, Comrade Jen Ping, standing next to him as if guarding him. Yong walked towards Stephanie. He was so pale, even his lips were pale. Stephanie felt again that formless bruise within her chest as he said her name "Stephanie" with such gravity. But she smiled at him, her eyes giving all of herself to him. "Stephanie, please wait a few days for me. I have . . . some matters to arrange. Please trust me."

"Of course, Yong, I'll wait. I love you."

"And I adore you," said Yong and turned away.

The Party secretary of the medical service, Comrade Pu, climbed on the platform and spoke at length. The burly American representative, Dr. Hagen, made a brief speech, and then everyone rose and Stephanie saw Party Secretary Pu look in her direction, look and find her, and then Jen Ping was talking to him and he was nodding, nodding. And Yong was surrounded by people, surrounded, besieged, a thick wall of people in quilted coats around him. And they frowned at her—no, she was hallucinating, it could not be—they were forming a wall to keep Yong from reaching her, because he was looking at her, he was trying to reach her but everyone was barring the way, talking to him, smiling at him, and Party Secretary Pu also, talking and standing so that Yong had to turn his back upon Stephanie.

And then Loumei was grabbing her arm and saying, "Let us go home Stephanie. You must rest."

And when she was outside the hall, Stephanie began to cry, very softly, wiping her eyes and feeling the tears sting her cheeks.

Back in her cave, Loumei helped Stephanie to lie on the *kang* and sat, holding her hand. "Dear sister, do not wound your heart. There are wicked people who delight in hurting such as you. But both of you are sincere and have no guile. And all will be well."

"But why, why, Loumei? What have we done that's so wrong? Why can't Yong come to see me? He loves me, and I love him."

151

"You are both young, beautiful. You, Stephanie, are impetuous, never concealing anything. All of us conceal . . . we have done it for centuries. Because some people just hate beautiful things. They want to cause suffering. It is the heritage of the past. The Chinese people are still very medieval, Stephanie, very puritan, especially in matters of sex.

"And now a cabal is starting. About Jen's morality. About you. Yong is fighting, for both of you. He does not want people to talk about you. He honors you too much and he wants others to honor you. . . . Do you understand?"

"No, I don't," said Stephanie, weak and angry. "It's our personal lives. No one has any right to interfere. . . ."

Loumei shook her head. "That is the American way. Personal privacy. Personal feelings. But here we are at war and in a war there must be collective discipline.

"Yong came specially to the dance hall to see you. He had no permission to attend the dance. He took a lift from a truck . . . all to come to see you. He broke discipline."

"And I balled up everything," said Stephanie. Vividly she saw it now: she had walked into Yong's arms in full view of everyone, and oh, the wonderful, wonderful feeling of his arms about her . . .

"Trust," said Loumei. "All will be well."

All Yenan was buzzing with the tale. Stephanie could almost feel the cave city vibrate with the tremor of scandal. So many mouths busy, so many ears eagerly receptive. From cave to cave. At night. Behind the impassive faces, the friendly smiles, that vein of eager malice. Talk. Yong. And she.

In the morning in front of her cave, there were people, staring. When she emerged to go to the Shaggins' cave, as she did every day, they walked away quietly, turning back their heads to look at her. This had never happened before.

Bamboo Shoot came as usual to fill the thermos flask and take out the toilet jar. Stephanie, looking at her round face, the cheeks apple red, skin roughened by the wind (no lanolin for her), wondered whether she too was talking about her. Her habits, her periods with their overflow of

152

blood, needing so much paper, so much coarse yellow paper to staunch it.

Women. Watching her.

"I feel flayed by their curiosity," wrote Stephanie in the diary she fitfully kept. "Curiosity which deems itself legitimate in this society where every person's business is everybody's business."

And now she found herself invaded by something like guilt. Her clean pride became almost furtive shame. "What was wrong with that hug?" she wrote. "It isn't even as if we'd kissed. . . . I know the Chinese abhor kissing in public. It's outrage to them. But we . . . we merely hugged." Then she was angry at herself for making excuses about that pure and joyful act, unsullied as lightning. She lay on the *kang*, weak-boned, feeling the lassitude of bitterness. She saw Yong as she had last seen him, surrounded by other men, protected and hemmed in by a thick uniform gray wall of men's backs and bulky coats. All alike, all talking to him, talking to him so that he could not reach her.

Another day edged slowly into its darkness. Dr. Mehta and Dr. Oburo, the Japanese doctor, came to the Shaggins' for dinner, and in honor of the guests there were small pieces of chicken, and from a store of honey, culled from the beehives of the previous summer, Loumei had made small round cakes with flour of maize and sesame seeds. There were also dry persimmon slices to chew. And of course stone bottles of the Yen valley liquor, heady and rough and strong. And the talk was of many things, how not to suffer from frostbite, and the number of new babies born, and the war, the war, and how the Kuomintang blockade, lifted for a while, was being clamped down again. And the small clusters of women gawking at her now seemed unimportant.

Be strong, my heart. And trust.

Lionel said as she left: "Don't worry, sister, everything's going to be fine."

Stephanie awoke and slept, washed, ate, walked a little and wrote. She wrote the articles she had promised to HERE. She organized her notes. She went to the cooperative store in the valley to buy the handmade writing paper available to those who had tickets (as she did)—everything was rationed. One could see the paper being made in the back of the store: the vats boiling, the paste being churned by men with tall wooden spoons, the paste coming out between two rollers, the workers who pedaled the machine to press it into sheets, in the drying room the round-cheeked girls who scissored it, or sat and stitched the leaves into copy books, pads, notebooks.

Finally on the fifth day, Party Secretary Pu, potbellied and jolly and a little asthmatic in the stabbing winter air, came to see her, accompanied by two younger men in gray with cloth caps. Pu told Stephanie that the articles she had published in America were "very correct" and "much appreciated." She would soon have an interview with some of the leaders, as she had requested. He begged her to be careful of her health, to let him know whether she was in need of anything, and then settled down to the heart of the matter. He began to ask her questions. About her family, and why she had come to China. The two young men took notes.

Stephanie replied. Her father had worked as a keeper of cows (she did not mention that he owned a ranch). Now he was building airplanes.

"Ah, an industrial worker," said Comrade Pu respectfully.

"No, well, he is an engineer, and he owns the plant," said Stephanie. Comrade Pu nodded. The two young men scribbled busily. She had a brother. No, they did not have many servants. . . .

"How many *mus* of land does your father own?"

"I don't think he is a landlord," she replied truthfully, and added, "but he owns an oil field." And since being a landlord-farmer was heinous, but no one owned an oil field in China, Comrade Pu did not know how to deal with this piece of information.

And because Stephanie realized this was part of the battle for respectability that Yong was waging, she was cautious. No, she herself owned no property. Yes, she had to work for a living. Yes, her father also worked for a living.

Secretary Pu withdrew, with more exhortation that she value her precious health and not go out too much. "It is very cold outside," he repeated.

The next day, unconventionally knocking at her door, came Sa Fei with her husband Liu Ming.

Sa Fei was a famous woman writer, brilliant and well-educated, who had been a militant Communist in Shanghai in the 1930s, proclaiming women's liberation and free love. Free union between the sexes had then been *the* revolutionary standard. Marriage was considered bourgeois.

But when the Communist Party core had left Shanghai and joined the rural bases organized by Mao Tsetung, they found peasant puritanism prevailed; here the manners and ideas of the big city appeared monstrously libertine. Sa Fei had had to stop talking of free love.

Liu Ming, Sa Fei's husband, was a small man, six years younger than his wife. He was of poor peasant stock, but he had begun to make poetry and recite his poems in his village before he could read or write. When he was nine, the village people had collected enough money to pay for a teacher for him. At nineteen he had begun to write, had written a saga of village life which, wonder of wonders, found its way to Shanghai and had been published.

At the time, the Party was looking for someone who could write about China's villages and revolution in the countryside. There was such *thickness* to the peasants' fury, to their despair, to their hopes . . . something city people could not put into words. None of the city born, city bred writers, could do it. Liu Ming's stories were something new, exciting, and revolutionary. It was also stunningly good writing. He became famous.

Sa Fei read his book while she was in jail. When she was released, she tracked him down to the tiny hamlet where he lived and wrote, and she broke all convention by saying to him, "I have come to stay with you. Will you have me?"

"Since then we have been together," Sa Fei told Stephanie. She clasped Stephanie's hand, her lively black eyes fixed upon her. "We have come to tell you not to be downcast; we sympathize with you. Many of us have had more or less similar experiences."

Stephanie felt lighter; she had felt so lonely, so cut off.

"It's good of you to come to tell me."

Sa Fei came again and again to see Stephanie. She talked at length of village life. "When you are better I'll take you to the villages around Yenan." Child marriage, selling of girls, prostitution were now prohibited in the territory, although the peasants still clung to some old customs. Sa Fei spoke bitterly about the fetish of virginity, still so strong. "Our Chinese men, even revolutionaries, still insist on virginity for their brides. There have been so many tragedies because that small spot of blood on the sheet was not present the day after. . . ." In the past, brides were beaten to death, or dismembered, or impaled on wooden poles for "unchastity."

One afternoon Sa Fei came riding a pony and leading one after her. The typical northern pony, scarcely larger than a donkey, with thick rough winter coat, a large head, and fat, funny legs. These ponies never cantered or galloped, they could only trot, trot briskly, and that is what they did untiringly. She and Stephanie trotted across the Yen River stone bridge to the Art Academy. It had been a Catholic church with a spire, very French provincial, built by the Lazarist Mission. The priests had gone many years previously. Now the Art Academy students, musicians and singers and actors, were quartered on the cliff, drilled with caves like Swiss cheese, flanking the old church. Eight hundred students lived on this slope, six to eight to a cave, for even cave homes were scarce.

"Even married couples do not always live together," Sa Fei told Stephanie. "Only the upper level leaders, army commanders, some very famous intellectuals, are allowed to share a cave with their wives." The young people who wanted to marry were told to wait, wait till the war was over.

There were guest caves for married couples. In turn, about once a month, couples were allowed to spend the night together in privacy. Thus Sa Fei and Liu Ming only cohabited once every four weeks. "In America too, many girls must be waiting, waiting for their loved ones, many wives waiting for their husbands," said eloquent Sa Fei, her eyes moist. "Stephanie, write to the American women, say that we want this war to finish so that their men can return home. . . ."

And after that Stephanie felt ashamed of her relative comfort. A cave to herself. Warm water for washing, a stove. And Yong. Yong, who loved her.

Herb Luger's wife, Alicia, in the condescending tone she adopted for people who were not "of the Party," said to

Stephanie: "The Chinese comrades have asked Herb and me about you."

"Why?" Stephanie tried not to sound too annoyed.

"They always ask our opinion about other foreigners. It shows the leadership's trust in us."

"How nice for you," said Stephanie. Now what *could* Alicia say about her?

The battle of silences and glances, of innuendoes and whispers, the battle in which Yong was engaged for her sake, how long would it last? When would Yong come to her? She became used to lying awake, wide-eyed, staring in the darkness, waiting for that first hint of grayness at the window which meant another morning. *I won't give in. I won't. Yong won't give in either.* Perhaps this testing was an initiation rite, tribal in a way, necessary too. To see if she and Yong were steadfast enough . . .

The comrade in charge of the registration office for marriages, Comrade Lo, was a jocund and portly woman who had had seven children, four of whom were still alive. Two were soldiers in the Eighth Route Army, the third and fourth were girls studying at the Yenan Art Academy.

Once a month, Comrade Lo slept with her army husband, Comrade Meng, who was posted twelve and a half miles away and only returned for this "family visit" every four weeks. Both accounted themselves fortunate, and the love between them was ample and contented.

Comrade Lo heard much talk about Stephanie, and about Dr. Jen Yong. She was to attend a spontaneous people's meeting at which "the case" would be discussed, a meeting inspired by Comrade Bo Chaste Wisdom, newly arrived from Chungking.

There was a great to-do about this American honored guest and Dr. Jen. No one knew how it had started, but Comrade Bo Chaste Wisdom was now talking. Talking about conduct which was a *danger* to socialist morality.

An American woman who did not belong to any progressive organization, who had come to Yenan, who had thrown herself into a public embrace with a Chinese doctor of the Red Cross team. They had hugged each other in public! Someone had even heard them say "I love you." In public!

This American woman was well known to have had several affairs in Chungking, said Chaste Wisdom. And there had also been episodes with Dr. Jen Yong.

How could one condone such license? Members of the Red Cross team who had come with Dr. Jen Yong reported his leaving the team and getting a lift on a truck to Yenan, and then rushing to the dance hall. "And they embraced there, in public," repeated Chaste Wisdom in shocked tones.

Comrade Lo, feeling great unease, had asked for further clarification. Dimly she wondered why they should have a meeting on the matter. Dr. Jen was not even a Party member. . . . If only her Old Partner, her husband, had been there! But he was not due for another week.

Comrade Yuyu was also at the meeting. She mentioned finding Dick Steiner on the same *kang* as Stephanie. "But she was very ill, and he was outside the quilt. There was no unseemly contact."

"Ah, but it *could* have happened, had not Comrade Yuyu intervened," interjected Chaste Wisdom.

Never, except in the case of Chairman Mao himself, when he had divorced his wife to marry a young actress from Shanghai, had there been so much excitement in Yenan.

Jen Yong and Stephanie's story now evoked dreams, dreams of bewitchment through beauty. Everyone knew how unsettling were love, beauty. It churned up the body cells, made the mouth water, it made both the young and old glaze-eyed—it was the high sky's lonely cloud, the music of wind in mountain pines. Beauty took one's mind away from revolutionary duty.

Excitement clamped the throats of the forty-odd women present, most of them primary school teachers or nurses. They queried every minute detail to prolong the delightful shocking moments. "Was the quilt thick or thin?" Yuyu was asked. "Was male-female contact possible, even with interposed quilt?"

After the meeting the women left. Nothing had been decided. But it had been a wonderfully gossipy meeting. Comrade Lo spoke about it to her husband, Meng, when he came on his monthly visit. Meng said, frowning: "But this meeting should not have been held. None of you had a right to criticize—it is not a political matter." And Comrade Lo felt very much abashed.

eight

"NEPHEW," Jen Ping said, "who is this American?"

"You have heard, Fourth Aunt. She is a newspaper-woman. Stephanie Ryder. I met her in Chungking. I want to marry her."

"Have you thought about your parents? About the Family? Do you plan to introduce barbarous foreign blood into it? She has made a spectacle of herself, flinging herself at you. And I have heard rumors. I hear she is not a virgin . . . has no restraint . . ."

Yong winced. He felt the blow as if he were hit, but answered equably, "She has the frankness of her people. I intend to marry her," he repeated. "Such prejudice, Fourth Aunt, is not . . . progressive."

Jen Ping laughed a little, to smooth the way for further unpleasantness. She said: "I am a Party member and I have no prejudice. But . . . we have a duty to the Family, to the generations before and after us. You are your father's only son. You must ponder this. You cannot bring spoilt goods into the Jen House."

"She is a person I honor and revere, and I will never marry anyone else, Fourth Aunt."

Jen Ping rose. "Nephew, how will you serve the revolution, serve your country, your people, with a foreign wife?"

He watched the darkness filling the arched cave, streaming down the scooped walls, deepening on the brick floor surrounding the *kang*. Jen Ping had given him her own cave, which she shared with four other women. All five of them had amiably moved themselves in among their friends on other *kangs*, in other caves.

Tomorrow he would resume the life of the dormitory, of the space shared, the odor, the noise, the presence of other bodies. Tonight the darkness was a cocoon of silk, great wings of silk which bore him back to his childhood. There was a slight odor of woman, which made him think of his mother. . . .

Oh, she had those moth eyebrows, was of that pallor which glowed with the palest rose. She was all beauty, his mother, all loveliness. He remembered the birdlike ring of her voice . . . and knew why Stephanie's voice had stirred him. The same melodic quality, the same vibrant echo.

Mother. Her amusement, her anger, her pride. There was a beautiful anger in Mother. But she did not own that rush of joy, spontaneous, irresistible, which was the splendor of Stephanie.

He was the only son. Mother's anger was never turned against him. It turned on others, on his sisters, on Father. When she was angry, the servants lost their alert gestures and lumbered; and Father would sit in his study and wield his brush, trying to write, and tear up what he wrote, for his fingers lost their poise. Yong would come to him, and Father would show him scrolls, discourse on painters, but his heart was not in it; his eyes roamed, he fueled the empty air with words, waiting for Mother to give him back his life. He was madly in love with his wife, and everyone knew it.

Mother. She cared for everyone in the Big Family; but she would turn and say to him: "But *you* are a man, my son," and so he would know her need to be protected, cared for. And so he assumed his boyhood and then his manhood easily, unafraid. He would never have to raise his voice. He learned to control himself as a man does. His family tradition taught behavior; his mother taught him honor.

Mother came from a lineage of scholars, among whom had been reformists—intellectuals bred in the old mandarin-ate who had broken their own tradition and had wanted to change China, to bring China into the modern age. And had been put to death for it. Her feet had not been bound, and she had studied in one of the first schools opened to girls in China. She read a great deal, all that was accessible to her. Reading seemed to feed that strange bright fury of hers, a rage for life, but well-controlled; for she had been married to Father (despite her family's reputation for modernism) at sixteen, when Father was nineteen—a family arrangement. And after that she had cared for the Family, extinguishing her own dreams for herself.

Surely she had wanted to do something else, to study, to carve her own destiny. Perhaps she had been headstrong, and so her family had bridled her with marriage. Perhaps.

Father had fallen in love with his wife and had never fallen out of that love. Forever he would say, before making a decision, "Let me think." And that meant he would discuss it with Mother. And one day he had said to his son: "She was my destiny. I want no other."

Yong remembered Father folding up his white silk sleeve over his blue gown, playing with her eyebrow pencils, the unguents upon her dressing table; in front of the triple oval mirror, Father watched Mother making up, his eyes adoring and helpless. "Here," he would say with a fake gruffness, handing her some cosmetic she was searching for and he had found. And then she would reward him with a smile and he would be happy, for she was not angry but had smiled at him.

Father had no anger about him. It had been gouged out of him by his own father, whose temper was notorious. Only kindness remained, a gentle absentmindedness, a dread of hurting people and all living things. He was, however, also a successful businessman.

Grandfather had governed the Family. Until Mother had come and had taken away power from Grandfather, reversing the patriarchal reign. She ruled in ways more subtle, and even more absolute. When Grandfather raged, broke porcelain, shouted, beat those around him, his two concubines were helpless. Mother would be summoned. Grave and attentive, respectful but not servile, she would smile, charm the old man into good humor, have the shards swept; the weepers were consoled, Grandfather's composure restored—in the Big Family all was again grace, harmony.

There were so many relatives coming and going in that large house. Father's brothers, sisters, cousins, their children. Bringing their lives and their woes, their whispers and their joy. To Mother.

Sixth Aunt, Jen Jen, Jen meaning patience, Father's

younger sister, was widowed even before her wedding, her fiancé having died. "She should marry again," said Mother. But Grandfather would not allow it. It was not virtuous for a widow to remarry. Now her nickname was Widow; she would forever remain Widow.

And Fourth Aunt, Jen Ping, was Father's older sister. She was a girl with fire and spirit, and she had run away from the Family. She had become a Communist, as many youths from wealthy families had done. The Family did not mention her name. Prudently. But she could always count on them, of course.

By 1940, every family in China of any worth or standing, had at least one member who was with the Communists, or at least a sympathizer.

Jen Ping had been shocked that Stephanie had walked into his arms.

Yet that had been the most wonderful moment of his life.

Stephanie. Coming to him through the throng of dancers, coming into his arms so simply, so utterly herself. He shivered with happiness, love, desire. He did not care that she might have slept with other men. He would be her husband and love her, love her with all of himself. And Mother would understand, would approve.

The members of the Red Cross team were assigned their living quarters in caves next to the hospital, which itself consisted of row upon row of interconnected caves, eight to ten patients to each cave.

Yong was assigned a teaching schedule in the afternoon, an operating schedule in the morning. "Surgeons are what we require most; none of us is really a surgeon," said Dr. Mehta with his usual frankness. "So you are going to be very busy, Dr. Jen."

Mehta had taken to Jen Yong right away, and applauded Stephanie's open gesture of love. As he put it to Shaggin: "Jolly good show, Lionel. A great romance, and they're a lovely couple."

"Some people had a somewhat different reaction," Shaggin said. He disliked the intense, though silent disapproval which Stephanie's gesture had caused. He was aware that a persistent and malicious campaign against Stephanie and Yong was going around.

"Nephew," said Jen Ping that evening, "the Party secretary would like to speak with you."

Secretary Pu's headquarters were in a house in the valley, near the old town wall—all that was left of the razed and burnt-out city of Yenan after the Japanese bombings of 1940.

After some polite preliminary enquiries about Yong's health and his lodgings, Comrade Pu cleared his throat and began. "Dr. Jen, there seems to have been an incident, which should be clarified."

Jen Yong said: "Party Secretary Pu, here are the circumstances." He related how he had met Stephanie in Chungking and what she had done for the slum people. He took his time, telling the tale meticulously, omitting nothing. Knowing that they would go again and again over the material, seeking flaws, contradictions.

Yong told reticently about his jail experience and being taunted by Colonel Tsing over Stephanie. "I consider this was deliberate Kuomintang propaganda to confuse me, to confuse our people, to make them suspect their friends.

"Ours is a correct relationship, Party Secretary Pu. I have not formed any previous attachment. Nor, so far as I know, has Miss Ryder. She is young, only twenty-one years old. She is impulsive and innocent, and she has the frank manners of her country. As you know, in America friends hug each other openly. She embraced me as a friend. She was happy to see me. Can this be accounted immorality?"

"This is complicated, very very complicated . . ." began Pu. "In fact, it is a situation full of contradictions." He moved some papers in front of him, moved and smoothed them. "As you know, we are at a great historical moment. Friendship and good relations with international friends are important; but our revolutionary work is also important. To be deviated by personal attachment from the important task which is yours—er, but of course," he added precipitately, "we can only *advise* you."

"I intend to ask Miss Ryder whether she will marry me,"

Yong replied. "I believe that we can work together, Party Secretary Pu, both contribute to efforts for a new China."

"We are not against international friendship—and Miss Ryder is an honored guest," said Pu. "Because of her serious illness we placed an entire cave at her disposal. But of course, you could not share it . . . the housing regulations . . ."

Yong understood that he would not be allowed to cohabit with Stephanie in that cave, since this might break the equalitarianism of the social order. Secretary Pu was seeking refuge in regulations. What counted was not love, but the rules concerning cave allotment.

"I have no intention to ask for privileges," said Yong. But he knew the problem would not end there.

He could not go to Stephanie. Must not be seen near her cave. Let him be seen but once talking with her, outside her door, and forever she would be labeled a lustful, uncontrolled woman. . . . But would Stephanie understand? Nothing in her culture would have prepared her for this strange and deliberate absence of presence. How could he tell her: I must prove that I love you by *not* coming to see you?

What Yong was to achieve was older than any party; it went back to all the traditions of romantic love, of yearning and dreams and self-control. He would slay the dragon of malice by his fortitude and emerge the victor, to claim her, the Flawless One of all men's dreams.

During the next three weeks, almost every other night after an exhausting day of operating and teaching, Jen Yong went to meetings. Groups organized themselves to talk with him, to "study the medical situation." Medical staff listened to him expounding surgical procedures. Never was there any reference to Stephanie. Yet all thoughts were coiled round her, her relationship to him.

Among his students, as he lectured, he could feel the stir of excitement, the curiosity. The sharp sting of a hundred curious, jeering eyes, probing, searching for a weakness in him.

And always there was Jen Ping. She would wait until he had finished an operation and was removing his sterile gown. She would then say earnestly, "Nephew . . . people are still talking, we must discuss what to do. . . ."

And Jen Yong would reply with a hint of contempt, "Fourth Aunt, do not worry. When the moon rises, the dogs bark."

Yong often began operating with the morning sun and ended when the sunlight failed. There was no electric light. He also did manual labor, as did the rest of the medical staff. He went down to the river to haul pails of water back for the hospital. With a pickaxe he broke the ice and shoved chunks of it into the pails. Heaving the pails on the pole across his shoulder, he would carry them back, step by step, climbing the cliff to the hospital. He would pour the ice blocks into the big tin cans set on top of long stoves, where they would melt. Hot water. Boiled water for the surgical instruments. There was kerosene which came by camelback from the inland northwest. Later, there would be a small generator— the generator used by the American Dixie Mission for their radio; after the mission's departure, it would be converted to produce electric light for the hospital. . . .

Yong slept with four other men in a cave. He had a bath once every ten days in the public bath house. He appeared serene. He had not an ounce of fat upon him, he was all smooth muscle, deceptively frail looking yet endowed with formidable endurance. He could always call upon himself for yet another ounce of doing, another hour of labor. And the one thing that sustained him was the knowledge that Stephanie had not gone away. She was here, she waited, and the tide was turning, would turn . . .

Many people were now in favor of Yong and Stephanie.

"He is a good doctor. . . ."

"Why should anyone try to find fault with him? He is twenty-eight, not married, they love each other. . . ."

"Whose business is it anyway? They are not Party members, Party discipline does not apply. . . ."

"She is a pretty foreigner, and very polite . . . they make a very beautiful pair. . . ."

All the world loves a couple in love: "Why all the fuss? The foreign woman has written well about us. . . ."

Public opinion was veering, approving of the romance, a mounting chorus of voices against the gossip.

Yong hungered for a glimpse of Stephanie, the shadow of her shadow. "Oh let me but see her walking in that confident joyous way of hers," he would pray to no god. He went about from one task to another, while within him roared a great fire of longing. He knew where she lived . . . next door to the Shaggins, only three rows of caves and one ridge away from him. *Not* to walk in that direction, *not* to attempt to see her. . . . His mouth dried and his throat was sore with the agony of it.

One evening Party Secretary Pu's aide came to him.

"Party Secretary Pu would like to have a talk with you." The aide smiled. "You have won," said the smile.

Yong had been assigned a small Mongolian pony because some of the places he had to visit in the course of his medical duties were three to four miles away, some over six miles away.

On his pony, Yong trotted down to the valley to Pu's office.

Pu tried to look cheerful. "Dr. Jen, your case was referred to the upper level. The leadership has agreed to your demand. Your proposed union with Miss Ryder appears to be founded on a spirit of genuine internationalism. You may now follow the proper procedure."

"I thank you for your efforts on my behalf, Party Secretary Pu," replied Yong.

"You have established a fairly good relationship with the masses," said Pu sourly. Which meant that Yong was popular.

Yong left. Pu watched him and sighed. Some people had all the luck.

Yong spurred his pony up the cliff, hurrying it savagely, dismounted and gave the reins to the stable boy and walked down the track, one ridge and three rows of caves down, on winged feet. As he had walked that summer night in the rain in Chungking, walked to meet his love, his love.

The frantic sand wind had folded itself away and stillness reigned in a night of many stars and no moon.

Too beautiful a night to sleep, thought Stephanie. She

had returned from dinner with the Shaggins; Lionel had harped on the fact that she had lost four more pounds. "Texas, what's the matter with you? You're not picking up."

"But I'm feeling fine, Lionel." She wasn't going to leave. She thought of those Victorian women, always going into a decline, and all for love. She wasn't going into a decline. She waited, knowing that Yong was fighting, fighting some battle she could only figure out imperfectly. Something hazy and illogical but which had to do with his own people.

A beautiful night, stars like forget-me-nots speckling the dark pool of space. She did not take a flashlight but walked out, feeling the ground with her feet in their warm felt boots. She felt at ease in the starlight, a swimmer comfortable with the sustaining sea.

The track went down to the valley, but it also wound up around the cliff curve, climbing to another row of caves. She chose the upper way, to test her strength.

Someone was walking down, walking down with quick sure steps. She knew the steps. Stood still, unbelieving, then believing and then seeing him. And she felt herself filling with gladness, with sheer joy, even before he had halted.

There he is.

They stood near to each other, almost afraid to touch, almost . . . as they had done when everything was simple and everything had begun. But the night sheathed them in starlight and so they came together, merging in each other's arms and without any words.

She released him and said: "Yong, you've won, haven't you?"

"*We* have won, Stephanie."

"You must tell me how it went. You must tell me why . . . but not now, not tonight."

"I will tell you one day, but not now. Now I have come to you, and I don't want to talk of anything else except . . . except that I love you."

They walked slowly back, holding each other, holding each other forever. They passed the cave where Shaggin and Loumei lived. Loumei had a baby coming; Stephanie had seen her stitching little baby shoes.

"Stephanie, you gave me the strength to fight . . . you walked across the dance hall, to me. So few women would have done that. No Chinese woman would have been so . . . courageous. I felt like an immortal then."

"I never thought for a moment it was going to cause such a fuss," said Stephanie.

He stopped, faced her. Strained, serious, with deep solemnity. "Stephanie, oh Stephanie, let us marry. I want to be with you in this life, and not only in this one, but life after life, if any other lives exist. . . . I shall never have enough of you, never enough . . ."

And Stephanie was moved by his intensity. *He really means it . . . he really means eternity.* It was a notion so romantic, so old-fashioned . . . but so right too. The immortality of love. "I don't know about other lives, Yong, but this life is good enough for me if I'm with you. Sure I want to marry you. I love you, all of you, even the parts that I don't always understand."

They had reached her cave, and he took the key from her hand and opened the door for her. The matchbox was on the table by the door, and she struck a match, lighting the kerosene lamp. The smell of sulfur came to her nostrils and she remembered Sister Heng, in River Fork village, lighting a lamp. River Fork had changed her, changed her life. She looked at Yong in the soft golden light. I, too, won't have enough of a lifetime to look at him, she thought.

And said: "Stay with me tonight, Yong."

Yong heard the early stir of the caves long before the window had lighted into faint grayness—the beat of feet, hastening to the dusty flat square where military drill was practiced; the voices, in unison, crying out: one, two, three, four. And then the guerilla marching song.

Then came the tinkle of bells on the pack trains of camels and donkeys carrying coal and cotton, kerosene and firewood, winding their processions into Yenan.

Stephanie lay in his arms, light and naked and pale; and he marveled at the miracle of her body, the dearness of her, the delight of her warmth, the silk of her skin. He knew then again that surge and ache coursing down his loins, swelling him against her back. But he would not wake her, for she slept deeply, drowned in sleep, like a child.

His body and Stephanie's had met in abandon, in total

inexperience. Gravely they had gone to bed with a sense of magic, of a rite God-given in its goodness. Love had given them art, and tenderness, and skill. Passion had not left them in doubt. They had not fumbled awkwardly. There had been no shame, only the adoration of a man who trusted his love, his fingers and eyes and mouth, a woman whose spirit soared, impetuous and unafraid. Stephanie had led him to her body so naturally, without hurry, and both had reached together the climax of their passion. And it had seemed only right, only what had to be, only what was normal, expected, a confirmation of their choosing each other. And then they had lain quietly, locked in each other's arms, and she had fallen asleep first.

He smiled, thinking of the wonder of their being together. She was his to care for, to cherish. And he would care . . . oh, how he did care! But he knew also that she was weak, that she bled too much, was pale with anemia. Lionel Shaggin had told him how he worried about her. She must leave Yenan because here she would not recover easily. Due to the Kuomintang blockade, the necessary drugs were simply not available.

"No," Stephanie had said, clinging to him. "No, Yong, give me another month. When spring comes I shall be better. I'm happy here with you—I'm writing a book." On a small borrowed typewriter, which belonged to a member of the Dixie Mission, she had set herself to writing about Yenan.

"Teach me your poems, Yong," she had said. Her Chinese was now fluent, and she was possessed by a great desire to perfect her mastery of the language. All the Americans she had met in Yenan spoke fluent Chinese.

"Teach me," she had said to Yong.

And he recited to her, from memory, the poems of love of the Book of Odes, and wrote them down for her. For the book, as well as her camera, her clothes, her notes, had all disappeared in the raid on River Fork village.

All perishable things became immortal only in love, only in love—and he was holding not only the body of a woman, but a small eternity of delight. "Ah, there will be no other Heaven for me, nowhere in this life, nor in any life to come, but you," he told the sleeping Stephanie.

Stephanie stirred a little, quivering in her sleep. He put his hand on her hair, gentle as if to quiet a child. She was so thin, he could see in her features the traces of her long illness, a slight waxiness where there had been a glow of health. He worried.

On the morning after their first night together, Yong applied for a registration of marriage.

The upper level approved. In fact, it was rumored that Chou Enlai had said: "What's wrong with marrying a foreigner?"

Comrade Lo was much relieved. She had become uneasy about the meeting regarding Jen Yong and Stephanie. Especially when her husband Meng had growled: "That has nothing to do with politics."

As the news spread throughout Yenan, Comrade Lo said to the women who dropped in: "I was *always* in favor of Dr. Jen and the American woman. They are such a handsome couple. Truly a pair of mandarin ducks." Mandarin ducks stay together until death, symbols of eternal love.

The cabal against Jen Yong and Stephanie, spun out of thin air, vanished as swiftly as the wind when it dies at dawn without a whisper.

And Comrade Lo beamed when Stephanie and Jen Yong came to register their intent to marry. She said: "This is true internationalism," and shook hands with both of them.

The marriage took place two days after Christmas. Lionel Shaggin and Loumei, Yuyu and Bamboo Shoot, Sa Fei and Liu Ming, the Red Cross team, the entire Dixie Mission, all came to the ceremony. Party Secretary Pu came, and his bound-foot wife. They clapped hands as Stephanie and Yong wrote their names down on the register and were issued marriage certificates with a big red stamp. Yong and Stephanie wore red flowers of satin ribbon pinned to their quilted jackets.

Afterwards there was a party in the Shaggins' cave. Pu shook hands with everyone and modestly hinted that it was all his doing.

"Mrs. Jen, your marriage is an act of faith in the future," said a high Chinese official, whose wife was Austrian. His presence lent official approval to the wedding.

Stephanie had told Yong straightaway about Alan Kersh. Unsparingly. He had listened, listened. Then he had asked: "Who is John Moore?"

She had said, her face lighting up with happiness, "Oh

John, he's such a good guy. A real good friend—he's the one who took out my letter to you, Yong. He was here for a week, came to see me."

"I never got the letter," said Yong. He was relieved. John Moore was not, had never been a lover. He would never tell Stephanie of Alan Kersh's letter to John Moore. "He knew Alan Kersh, yes?"

"Yes. Alan mentioned they were good friends."

Apart from a technical flaw, an "accident," he was the first man she had loved. And it pleased him. Yet he was angry with the dead man Alan for writing that letter, for being so careless of Stephanie's reputation. And John Moore, so stupid too, so careless, throwing the letter away, not destroying it. So that the Secret Police, hunting through the wastepaper baskets, could recover it. Stephanie must never know. "Mr. Kersh must have been an intelligent man," he said gravely, almost hypocritically to Stephanie, relapsing into stilted English. "Otherwise you would not have liked him."

And she did not catch the fury, the disgust, the contempt for Alan which he put in the word "intelligent."

"You really don't mind my not being a virgin, Yong? I was told Chinese men are very concerned about that. But then, so are a lot of Americans."

"You are a virgin to me, Stephanie. Even now you are a virgin. Your spirit is incapable of impurity. You can never do anything ugly or mean." She was pure gold, incorruptible. And to keep her so was what mattered to him. More than anything said about him and his male honor which demanded that his wife be "unspoilt goods." She would always be Stephanie. "I'll give you a Chinese name, dear wife," he said. "Your name will be Spring Snow." Because the snow in spring was sudden, and fell upon apple blossom, and did not destroy it.

There were two New Year's celebrations in Yenan: one was the solar calendar first of January, the second was the traditional moon calendar New Year, known as the Spring Festival, which took place several weeks later.

Peasant women then put red thread in the pigtails of their daughters. They cut out of red paper scenes of good luck and cheer, to paste on their window panes. The village scribe was kept busy writing scrolls of good luck verse, which were pasted to house doors.

The Art Academy students of Yenan practiced new plays, skits, and songs. From the villages around Yenan came the peasants, congregating in large tents of matting to watch the performances. All the shows had a political message, but it was great fun for the fun-starved peasantry. There was folk singing and dancing of the *yangko*, the dance associated with fertility and sowing time, which the Communists made their own.

And now the sun was bright, and Yenan sparkled. Soon it would be warmer, with only an occasional flurry of snow. The peasants dressed their children in bright clothes and sang the wild and beautiful songs of the deserts and of the plains.

On Sundays, Jen Yong had a free half-day. Then he and Stephanie went visiting or received friends in her cave. Jen Yong got on easily with the Americans. In no time at all, he was reciting Chinese poems to David Barrett, while the latter was translating limericks in Chinese.

They now had their own special friends. Sa Fei and her husband Liu Ming. Lionel Shaggin and Loumei. These formed the core of an enchanted circle in which they moved. And it seemed to Stephanie that all the world should be like this, a mixture of diverse races, each bringing its own wealth of knowledge and love to a common hearth.

At night, lying in Yong's arms, Stephanie would bask in happiness. How ridiculous they were, those who predicted disaster in a mixed marriage! On the contrary, it was added enrichment.

Jen Yong shouldered part of the work of Bamboo Shoot, carrying the water for Stephanie's bath up from the river. The pole left a dark bruise and the beginning of a callus on his shoulder. Stephanie objected and Jen Yong laughed.

"After a while, there will only be a callus, and I shall be able to carry twice as much."

But that he should willingly blemish—however slightly—his beautiful body hurt Stephanie. "You don't have to do this work, Yong."

"Why not, my beloved?" He took her hands in his, looking at her with so much adoration, so entirely given to her that sometimes it hurt her to feel the intensity of his love; he was without reserve; he was so vulnerable. "I love you. I want to serve you. You need care, you are still weak. And I want you to be accepted as my partner as well as my wife . . . do you understand?"

"I see, darling, but does that mean carrying water pails?"

"It means that and everything else. I want to show these people what it is to be in love. I am learning from Comrade Bamboo Shoot the craft of housework," said Jen Yong, stroking her hair. "I cannot get over your hair, the color. You carry the sun in your hair."

He would clean the cave on Sundays. Empty the stove of its ashes. Bring in the bullet-like black coal balls. He would even quietly get up early to empty Stephanie's toilet jar and clean it in the common latrine.

And one day he brought back two clucking hens. Bamboo Shoot and he scooped a small burrow for the hens out of the cliff face, just outside the cave, lined it with straw, and made an inner shelf. "This is how the peasants do it," he said. "Now you shall have your own eggs for breakfast."

In mid-February Shaggin took another blood test from Stephanie and became more worried than ever.

The hope of a relaxation of the blockade had not been fulfilled. In fact, the blockade had been tightened. As a result, the diet was poor, especially in winter. Millet, sweet potatoes baked in warm ashes, goat meat occasionally, very rarely pork, or eggs. Soon there would be no more medicines left. None were coming through. Herb Luger asked Stephanie to make an appeal on the English-language broadcast of Radio Yenan for medical supplies. She did so. "The small amount that came two months ago has been used, and well used. Not a pill, not a drop, has been squandered. There is need for more drugs, more sulfonamides, especially because pneumonia is so common among the babies." Stephanie did not know how feeble Radio Yenan was; it never would reach America. But it reached Chungking, and was duly monitored by the American Embassy there.

After examining Stephanie once again, Lionel Shaggin called a medical consultation with Mehta and Yong.

"I'm afraid Stephanie isn't going to get better if she stays here," he said gravely. "You know what that means, Yong."

Yong knew. He too had been worried. But he had fooled himself, thought that with love, with care . . . "She will have to go back to America," he said, looking at Lionel Shaggin and at Mehta. "I think that would be the best."

He came to her cave a little late that night. Stephanie was happy and excited, faint color in her cheeks, because she had just had a letter from Jimmy, to whom she'd written about marrying Yong. "Good for you, Sis, he sounds terrific," Jimmy had written back. Her parents had not yet replied.

"Stephanie, my dearest, why did you not tell me that you fainted when you were walking with Sa Fei the other day?"

"Yong, it was nothing, I was just tired and I blacked out."

"You get blackouts, you become breathless so easily, your blood count is too low." He was stern. "My darling, listen. I've talked with Shaggin and Mehta. As a doctor, not as your husband. I realize that I've been thoughtless and selfish. I should have insisted that you return home, to America, when you did not improve. . . ."

"Yong, I wouldn't have gone. Yong, I love you, I want to stay with you." She clung to him, so lovely, so frail too. She began to cry a little, half weakness, half love.

"I'm a selfish idiot," he raged. "I wanted you so much, I told myself you would get well . . . but now there's no other way."

"No, Yong, I don't want to go. Not yet. The war will be over soon; I'll rest a lot, and then we'll go to America, together. . . ."

She had been on iron pills for the past four months, and it had done no good, no good at all. Her body was not absorbing the iron. And now the hospital in Yenan had run out of iron pills.

"Stephanie, I'll soon have to leave for a tour of the field units. I'll be away for at least sixteen weeks. I have to go . . . and who will look after you then?" He did not say: "And if you become pregnant, in your condition." But he was thinking it, and she knew he was.

They lay in bed that night, near to each other, a strained nearness. And Stephanie cried a little; she was so tired, yes; and yes, at times she had wanted to go home. "But I love you so much, Yong. How can I leave you?"

174

"My darling, it's only for a short while. Two, three months . . ." Besides, had she not told him that her editor wanted her to return to discuss a book? She would get strong so quickly in America. "I have married a famous woman," he said gaily. "After the war you will be roaming the world, writing for important newspapers; your name will be everywhere, and I shall stay home and look after the children and wait for you and love you." And then Stephanie began to chuckle and whoop with laughter.

"I got so much better when you made love to me, my darling. . . . Please make love to me."

And he did, but holding himself, so as to pleasure her without tiring her. And all the subtleties of loving came to him, because he cared so much.

Everything was cleared very quickly. Too quickly, thought Stephanie, when confronted with imminent departure. So many friends came to see her, to wish her a good journey. Jen Ping also came, with unruffled brow, one afternoon. "I'm sorry that we have not seen much of each other," she said. "I come to wish you a safe journey to visit your parents." Jen Ping sat stiffly, sipping the cup of boiled water Stephanie gave her, nibbling a hard round cake Yong had baked.

Finally, one cold morning towards the end of February the airplane waited while the neutral sky spread bland light upon the pockmarked cliffs and the harsh landscape of yellow sand.

"You will come back, Stephanie," Yong murmured, "strong and well, and we shall be together, forever." And Stephanie brushed the tears from her eyes, and the door of the Dakota clanked into place.

The plane became a gray speck in the sky. Yong stared, eyes upward, would not let go of the sky with his eyes. Herb Luger put his arm around him, dragged him away, and started spraying him with saliva and slogans.

"Hope you told Stephanie to do some talks to the American masses. I've given her the names of a couple of my friends."

Yong nodded. Nodded, heard not a word.

nine

THEY stood side by side, their eyes upon the converted Liberator in its jungle paint, propellors whirling lazily to a stop as the machine halted upon the sun-drenched tarmac. "One of ours," said Heston Ryder. Transport and combat planes for the Pacific war were turned out by the hundreds every week, and Ryder Aircraft Corporation of Dallas was building engines for them.

As he stood waiting for his daughter to step out of the airplane, Heston thought of the splendid machines that would dominate the world. The war would be won by air power, no doubt about it. Air power was smashing the Nazis. It would finish off the Japs. It would make America the greatest power the world had ever seen.

He saw that Isabelle was in one of her faraway moods and anger flooded him. That ice queen look of hers, which he had once admired, now made him want to use filthy words. He had withdrawn from her, plunging into his man's world, a world of heady action, massive power, of technological magic, creating a metropolis of industry out of the once-sleepy town of Dallas, transforming the Lone Star State of Texas into the powerhouse of America.

"There she blows, Mom," said Jimmy, who was reading navy books. Jimmy was crazy about ships now. He was crazy about many things. He hovered forever among a haze of enthusiasms. He was sixteen years old.

The aircraft had disgorged its passengers and, indeed, there she was. Heston Ryder began to run. He ran across the landing field, ignoring the shouts of uniformed men, the brandishing of weaponry, knowing that no one would dare to arrest him for this breach of rules. "That's Heston Ryder . . ." He could hear them say it as he ran towards his daughter. And Stephanie, seeing her father, also began to run, body askew from the weight of her bag.

"Dad . . . oh, Dad . . ."

"Stephanie." He swept her into his arms with the same gesture as when she was seven and he swung her high in the air, while she chuckled with delight. "Oh baby . . . I've missed you . . . let's have a look at you . . . we'll have to fatten you up, Steph . . . my, what a time you've had. . . ."

"It wasn't bad, Dad . . . it was quite wonderful really." But already he had picked up her bag, had his arm around her, and was walking her towards Isabelle and Jimmy. Jimmy had wanted to run, but his mother put a restraining hand on his arm. Isabelle kissed her daughter and said, cool as always, "My very dear, it is marvelous to have you back." Then Jimmy was hugging her, taller than she was, his face still a little boy's face. "Hey, Sis . . . Gee whiz, my buddies all loved reading about you. . . . You're their favorite pinup. . . ."

And then friends, crowding around her. The Iveses and the Rayburns, the Stirlings and the Crockers. All shrieking their affection, gesturing, hugging, their faces working. Strange, thought Stephanie, responding with hugs, with delight, working her face in imitation. Strange to see faces showing their feelings so nakedly . . .

Press photographers, journalists jostled, shouting questions at her, but Heston Ryder was firm. "My daughter has returned from China for a medical checkup and a rest. She's had a pretty tough time. . . . You all've read about it in the papers. . . . No, no interviews . . . not at the moment . . . Soon as she's fit again . . ."

One woman piped up: "There's been a report that you married a Chinese doctor, Miss Ryder. . . ."

Heston: "Ma'am, have a heart, she's exhausted. We'll hold a special press conference for you ladies soon as she's rested up."

And smiling heartily, cheerfully. "The kid's worn out . . . coming all thataway . . ."

He propelled her towards the Lincoln, a gleaming obedient machine of power and grace. One of a good many such cars waiting, with their black uniformed chauffeurs standing by them.

"Horace, Miss Stephanie is back," said Heston Ryder.

Horace touched his cap and Stephanie shook his hand. "My, it's good to see you, Miss Stephanie. Lord knows we all've missed you."

And Stephanie, who now had the manners of Yenan, went on shaking his hand. "I'm very glad to see you, Horace, how've you been?" Forgetting he was a servant, a black, speaking to him without that slight crispness in the voice which forbids familiarity.

"Now mind you drive us home carefully, Horace," said her father, putting Horace back in his place. And to Stephanie, concerned: "How you feeling, honey? You look peaked. . . ."

"Twenty-six hours from Lisbon, Dad. Been on this trip about ten days in all."

And her mother said, "You'll be able to sleep, my dear. In your own room."

How clean, how large, how magnificent everything was! An amplitude of space, of air and sun; a limitless blue sky above the great wide earth. "We've found some more oil gushers, Steph," said her father. "Near Abilene. Look there . . ." He pointed to the horizon where concourses of cranes thrust skywards. The dim roar of bulldozers came to them through the open car windows. "This little state of ours is building every kind of gun and aircraft you can think of, baby."

Stephanie could not miss the new buildings of the growing city, growing powerful and beautiful. This was the heart of things, victory was fashioned here. "Yep, baby, we're winning the war right here," said Heston Ryder.

Dad and Texas. Drive, energy, power, a vitality so enormous it took on the whole world and changed it. And this was Stephanie's heritage—this drive to change things. It was the spirit that had led her to China, to the Yenan caves . . . and to Jen Yong. She smiled and her father, looking at her in the mirror, smiled back.

They were moving towards home. The quiet of green lawns, white buildings, magnolias radiant with blossom. "Still our old shack, Steph, but we're getting a new one. Wait till you see it. . . . It's quite something."

"It's got forty rooms, two swimming pools, sixty acres of garden and three patios," said Jimmy. Stephanie noticed his voice was breaking, he was on the edge of manhood. He

178

longed to tell Stephanie that he was taking flying lessons and that Dad had promised him his own small plane. He longed to tell Sis oh so many many things . . . that, for instance, he didn't really like war. . . .

There were three new servants, Carlotta, Lucy, and Adam, besides Horace and Abel, Minnie and Mignonette, standing to welcome Stephanie on the graceful stone porch.

Isabelle glided in her usual way across the living room, her walk perfection. French furniture, Isabelle's gift to the New World she had married, in the graceful room. Pale shades. Understated wealth. Stephanie glanced at the settee. Was it really the scene of that brief sprawl of bodies, hers and Alan's, an embrace which had determined her going to China? Now it was not even something to be ashamed of. Yong had made it totally neutral.

"Would you like to eat, Stephanie, are you hungry?" Isabelle, doing her housewife-mother act. Conveying through it her cool lassitude. Stephanie shook her head, and her mother took her upstairs to her own room. The shades were drawn, the bed inviting, with pale pink satin sheets. She sighed and kicked off her shoes, and found her mother staring at her. As she stared, off and on, throughout the car drive, a searching look, as if she were learning her daughter's face anew.

Stephanie smiled, the kind of smile she used to give to her mother to show that all was well, that she harbored no resentment, although the smile also emphasized the reticence always present, a wall of glass between them.

"I'm absolutely exhausted, Mom."

Isabelle nodded. "Just ring if you want anything, my dear. Lucy will look after you. I'll wait for you to wake up." She bent to touch Stephanie's cheek with her lips and was gone.

Stephanie slept on through the afternoon and the night, only waking drowsily to go to the bathroom, at first having forgotten where it was and having to grope for the light switch to find its door. At one point she was aware of hushed voices, of soft footfalls around her bed. She had always slept well, dropping into a deep, dreamless state, a child whose body rhythms work with fearless precision. And now she

179

woke with the same exact suddenness, very hungry. She had slept almost twenty hours.

She pressed the bell. Lucy appeared, magically brought orange juice and eggs and bacon and toast and coffee . . .

It was coffee she had missed most in China. Coffee. Now it tasted acrid, but it was like a drug—once started, one had to go on drinking it.

Lucy ran a bath, and Stephanie luxuriated in the warm scented water. She shampooed her hair, enjoying once again the pleasure of her body, knowledge of her body, sensuous touch and perception of a self all too soon dismayed by age. It was now a body too thin, too quickly tired. The bathroom scales showed that she was fifteen pounds under her normal weight. Her face did not show much alteration, but the bones of her hips protruded through her skin and her ribs showed starkly. And her short hair was badly cut and it had dulled. Yong said she had trapped the sun in her hair! Jen Yong . . . the syllables were like smooth pleasant pebbles in her mouth. She wanted his arms around her. . . .

Isabelle was waiting for her with Lucy, when she came out of the bath wrapped in a white terry cloth robe. The shades were up, the afternoon sun streamed in with bright joy, bringing the odor of mown grass and honeysuckle. Everything was fragrant, luxurious, and clean, and the three women were reflected in the tall mirrors, their gestures unhurried. Isabelle held out a dressing gown with lace at its cuffs and collar. All this here was commonplace, was taken for granted. As Lucy dried her hair, brushing and waving it, Stephanie remembered Bamboo Shoot bringing up the pails of water, tipping them into the brown ceramic jar which stood in a corner of the cave. . . . High-cheekboned Bamboo Shoot, who worked and worked, worked of her own free will, for she was not paid for her service to Stephanie. And Jen Yong, scooping out the stove, his surgeon's hands gray with ashes.

Isabelle said: "Thinking of China, Stephanie?"

"Yes, how did you guess? . . ."

"Perhaps because I have been thinking of France," she replied, and added cryptically, "Saviors always smash things, don't they? . . ." Then she changed, changing mood, subject, and her voice. "Your father has arranged for some doctors to see you. We are both worried about your health. We could telephone them, if you'd like to see them now . . . or tomorrow, as you wish."

Stephanie grinned. "I guessed Dad would have at least three specialists lined up waiting for me."

"Your father enjoys wielding his new power. . . ." said Isabelle in that neutral tone which gave no clue to her feelings. "The war has been good for him, for Texas. . . ."

Lucy was cleaning the bathroom. Stephanie heard the water gushing from the taps, whooshing down the drain. So much water. So much water. Stephanie saw Jen Yong lugging the pails of ice blocks on a bamboo pole, all the way from the river up the cliff, heaving them all the way. *I won't let this corrupt me . . . I won't.*

"I've often thought," said Isabelle, "they are very lucky in America, Stephanie. The war has made them prosperous." She said *they* with mordant detachment. She had no share in it.

Always there was this bitterness, Stephanie thought, this acidity welling up, and why was it so? A surfeit, overabundance of luxury had driven Isabelle away from her husband, her surroundings. She had no appetite for enjoyment, no hunger for success. To preserve herself she had walled herself away, even from Stephanie, who was too much like her father. But was wealth a crime? Was it wrong to own and handle power? Heston Ryder built aircraft. Was he evil to have become rich because he knew how to build good airplanes?

Stephanie brushed away these thoughts darting like minnows. She opened the cupboard to choose a dress. Her dresses, waiting for her—lovely smooth silks, and knits, and the colors . . .

"You are too thin," said her mother. "We shall have to get you some new clothes. You cannot wear these."

Stephanie turned to her, hoping to talk to her, hoping the barrier between them would come down. "I wouldn't know how to make up—I've almost forgotten," she said. "We used to rub lanolin on our faces in the winter. . . ." But Isabelle was no longer listening, she was back in her own world, self-possessed and estranged.

"If you are ready, it is best to telephone the doctors. They are waiting to see you."

Dr. Baxter, Dr. Daniels, and Dr. Rozinski were in charge of Stephanie's checkup. Heston Ryder had mustered the best. Baxter and Rozinski had flown in from New York. Two days were spent in checking, X-raying, blood testing Stephanie by the latest methods. She was pronounced healthy, save for a mild intestinal infection and a fairly serious anemia due to the destruction of so many blood cells during her bout of malaria. The problem was to build up her hemoglobin, replace the iron she lacked. She had not been able to absorb the iron in the pills given to her by mouth. The doctors suggested that the pills might have been inert, the iron already in a state which rendered it ineffective.

Heston listened to the medical reports, frowning. "Now we've got to fatten you up, Stephanie, build you up. You need a lot of good meat in you. Dammit, they can't have fed you well out there."

"But Dad, as I wrote to you, it was difficult to get any meat, I was given the very best there was. . . ."

"We'll go down to the ranch and you'll be fit in no time," Heston interrupted. "Thank God you came home," he added.

Stephanie found herself on a course of pills and injections, of sun and pure air at the ranch. The four-hundred-acre spread lay in rolling country; it took in half a small valley, shaded by live oak and pine. It was Heston Ryder's latest acquisition, and the ranch house was elegant white with portico and pillars. "It's all yours, Stephanie," he said, waving a hand over its expanse. "Guess you're the one that takes after me, baby. You sit a horse better than any other gal in the county." And there they were, the beautiful horses, five of them, guided by Mexican cowboys. "Our own boys have gone off to the war, Steph. I'm training these no-good Mexicans—lazy as mules—got to be on top of them all the time."

Sun, and the great noble wind of the plain, stirring the grass. And friends coming to the ranch to see her in a phalanx of beautiful cars. And nothing to do, for there were a dozen willing hands—black hands, brown hands—to turn on the bath, to wave her hair, to lay out her clothes. Two nurses on duty merely to see that she took her pills, re-

182

ceived her injections. She slept and woke and ate, and all the girls she'd grown up with came to visit her.

"Oh, darling, too too fabulous, I've read all about your adventures."

"You mean you really lived in a cave, a hole dug in a hillside?"

Yes, she would say with a wave of nostalgia for her cave, yes. And they would say: "How thrilling!"

"Stephanie, I'm so proud, so *overawed* to be with you!" That was elegant Christine Ponsonby, her best friend in Dallas. Christine had married at seventeen and already had two children. Her husband came with her. David Ponsonby was working on hush-hush new military projects. He wore a uniform.

Most of the young men, the beaus she had dated in high school, were at the war. Dallas newspapers were filled with their exploits. "Looks as if it's Texas that's winning the war almost single-handed," Stephanie commented after a few days of perusing the press.

"Well, baby, we've got more boys out there in the Pacific than damn-all the rest of America," said Heston. And he believed it.

Very swiftly Stephanie perceived that one subject could never be talked about with Dad. And that was Yong. Her husband.

Whenever someone would say "Well now you're back, thank goodness" and she would reply "But I intend to go back to China. You see I am . . ." her father would interrupt smoothly "Baby, you're not quite fit yet . . . have to build up your strength," and he would turn the conversation back to Texas—Texas agriculture, Texas steers, Texas oil—and the war.

"We're feeding the whole of Europe," said Heston. "And don't you all forget it." He would talk about breeding cattle for starving Europe and how the lend-lease ships came and went, ploughing the Atlantic, supplying Europe. He would talk of the generosity of America, deploying her wings of gold over the world. "God, but I'm proud of being American" he would say.

Whenever Stephanie would start to describe Yenan, the caves, China, her father would interrupt and turn to the growth of Dallas, the returning veterans. "We're mighty proud of our boys, Stephanie, mighty proud. We're going to find jobs for all of them when they come home. . . . We have the biggest veteran fund. We'll put all the guys through college . . . no boy from Texas is ever going to be forgotten."

It was like a small conspiracy circling about her, a nice conspiracy made up of smiles, affection, jokes, heartiness. Hearts of gold, lavishly dispensing gifts and goodies all over the world, shutting out China. Shutting out Jen Yong and all those like him, whose lives were meager and poor, but whose spirit was shining with hope.

And, basking in the languor of late March, the effulgent magnolia already leafing, its luminous petals strewn on the grass, Stephanie found herself shrinking at the thought of returning to discomfort—the outhouse latrines, the rasping straw paper, the lack of water . . . the lice . . .

But there was also a strange restlessness within her. In two weeks she had gained five pounds and her hemoglobin had increased. However, a new emptiness possessed her, so that she awoke, startled, at night, in the lovely wood-paneled bedroom, and felt as if she had lost a part of herself. Here, in total luxury, she walked about, rode a lovely mare called Tara, felt the wind through her hair like hands—and her heart cried out:

"Yong, Yong, I am losing myself . . . losing you."

Stephanie wrote to her publisher, Vance Marston of Marston House. He had cabled her as soon as the story of River Fork village had made headlines. He had sent her a contract for a book. Now that she was back in America, he telephoned, asking her to come to New York as soon as she was able. "We think it's great stuff, we'd like to publish it by the autumn," he said. And HERE magazine wanted to discuss a new contract with her. "You're one of our star reporters," they wrote.

Then came a letter from John Moore: "Stephanie, I'm in Washington for a couple of months. There's a lot I want to talk over with you, but Texas is a bit far for me."

The boondocks, thought Stephanie, resentful, suddenly all Texan. John thinks this is the backwoods. . . .

Radcliffe wanted her to lecture about her experiences in China. "We feel very proud of your achievements," wrote Professor Moslyn, head of the history department.

But Stephanie first had to talk to her father. She needed to talk about herself, about Jen Yong. Because Jen Yong had almost disappeared, and that frightened her. By refusing to listen, Dad was spiriting him out of existence.

"Stephanie," said Isabelle, "tell me about your husband." She said it in that weary, blanched voice of hers, as if she had been deprived of blood. Of the two of us, she sounds the more anemic, thought her daughter unkindly.

Isabelle's taste was faultless. She wore discreet muted colors, mauve and pale pink and an indefinite pearl gray; but this effacement suited her, and with her dark eyes and her white skin she looked like a Marie Laurencin.

For the more vivid Stephanie, Isabelle suggested eggshell white, shades of gold, or clear jade. Neiman-Marcus carried a new range of spring fashions and Stephanie bought three dresses and a suit of caramel color which set off her skin and her eyes; and then she wondered how she would ever wear these clothes in Yenan, or in Chungking.

Isabelle had resented Stephanie from the very day of her daughter's birth. It had been a long, painful, agonizing delivery; but Stephanie had come out of the exhausted Isabelle yelling, and Heston had fallen in love with this furious, screaming little bit of life. "She's full of guts," he had said, claiming her and scarcely looking at his wife, forgetting her pain in his delight with his daughter.

And now Stephanie was a woman, and a woman in love. Love had given her face, her body something which could not be described. A quality of beauty, unforgettable. But her father does not wish to see it . . . he is jealous, thought Isabelle, pleased.

Perhaps the time had come to make her daughter her friend. Even an ally, against Heston's killing vitality. Isabelle had loved Heston, but he had always overpowered her, overborne her. . . .

Isabelle de Quincy de Gersant came from a bone-tired, aristocratic family with excellent manners and an exquisite way of shrinking from the raw, energetic new world around them. Yet she had married that new world, not knowing that it would almost extinguish her.

Now she would reach out to Stephanie, talking as a woman talks to another woman.

"What is your husband like, Stephanie? Please tell me. I would like to know."

Stephanie's eyes rested upon her mother. She said, groping for words, "Yong . . . I cannot really describe him, Mom, because everything here is so different." At times Yong here became a fugitive black and white shade, as if even his existence were not altogether real.

"I think he's—he's remarkable . . . he's good, he's noble, he's patriotic . . . I can't explain." She thought, I love him, I love him. But talking about him makes him become someone I've read about, not a man I've known, made love with, whom I hunger for . . .

Isabelle nodded. "Love never can explain the loved one, my dear. It is the essence of wild unreason."

"When you married Dad, Mom, was it also something you couldn't help doing?"

Isabelle smiled faintly and, with platinum precision, ignored the question, making it sound impertinent, and said: "You must know that your father finds it difficult to accept your marriage. To a Chinese. He always finds it difficult to accept what he has not planned for those he loves. He cannot imagine that they should have desires separate from his own."

"If Dad met Yong, he would like him."

"Perhaps you've grown a little out of this world of ours. Your father is certain that your husband will not fit into his scheme of things, the one he is building. . . ."

"Dad's not used to the idea of me being married, period. He'll come around to it."

Isabelle changed the subject. "It won't be easy for you, living in China. Perhaps Yong will come to America, live here . . ."

"He won't. Live here forever, I mean. He loves his country, wants to help his own people." And now suddenly Yong was back with her, and she was sure, sure of him, of herself. "I too have changed. I know I won't be content until I share a little in this dream which moves Yong and others like him . . . to do something good for his world. . . ."

Isabelle looked at her daughter with delicate gravity. "Stephanie, you are in a state of grace at the moment, and long may you remain so. Because you have chosen something either infinitely worthwhile or which will destroy you. . . . But you have not chosen mediocrity and meanness. . . ."

And for the first time in their lives, there was understanding, even love between them, unimpeded.

Since January 1945, American armies had turned the tide of war everywhere, in Europe and in Asia.

In Europe victory was near. Air power was pulverizing the enemy's last cities and its industries. Hitler was in a bunker, awaiting his end. Night after night the bombers sallied forth, dropping a maelstrom of fire and death upon Germany.

In the Pacific, marines landed on every island, storming the beaches; it was a magnificent story, and the name of Douglas MacArthur was on all lips as the U.S. drove steadily towards Japan.

Air power had abolished the need for massive mobilization of infantry. Japan could be bombed from the Pacific Islands more efficiently than from air bases in China.

The need for Chinese armies was no longer pressing.

Roosevelt's preoccupation was no longer to keep China fighting but to come to terms with Russia in fashioning the postwar world. For it would be Russia that would be the great power-to-come, a challenger of the United States.

Generals with cascades of medals on their chests came down to Dallas. They met with Heston Ryder. Heston, wearing a checked shirt, handmade boots and a ten-gallon hat, took them down to the ranch. They ate steaks in the outdoor patio, while Mexican cowboys provided guitar music.

They talked business.

Europe needed rebuilding. Europe needed so much. Only America could help.

The generals were angry with Roosevelt because of Yalta—where he and Stalin, watched by Churchill, had divided the world. Very angry. They muttered that he'd given too much to Stalin, far too much. Stopped the Americans from advancing in Germany and given Poland to Russia . . . .

Some people, somewhere in Washington, were giving the President all the wrong advice.

Thus the rumor of a red-inspired conspiracy against America began. And in Texas a great many people would believe it.

Stephanie had been home almost a month. She had gained ten pounds. The new, stronger ferrous compound and the vitamin pills, plus another course of effective anti-malarial drugs to wipe out any possibility of recurrence, had worked wonders. American doctors, because of the many new diseases the GIs had brought back from the wide arena of war, had an armory of drugs, the best in the world.

She received a letter from Lionel Shaggin, enclosing one from Yong. "Our friends here are still doing their best to explain the Chinese situation to Washington," wrote Lionel. "Perhaps you will be able to put things in perspective—but it seems that some of the worst possible advice has prevailed."

Yong wrote:

Spring Snow,

Sudden and lovely as a storm of flower petals, time is a bird with the day-long voice that says your name. It is cold here but in the silence I hear your laughter and I am warm. I cannot tell you anything about where I am, nor what I do. The courier is waiting, he will not be back for six weeks. So I write to you and distance is abolished. My letter is a sea shell, to whisper the sea sound of your name: Stephanie. Spring Snow. Stephanie the singing tide.

All men must measure their living by something beyond themselves; some measure it with the years that pace by, as if they walked towards sighting distance of their own dissolving. Others erect landmarks, carving the deeds of other men and their own. But I measure my life by your presence, which absence does not take away. The knowledge of your being is a keeping grace, bright as the newest morning. And I am content forever.

And thus Yong was back, back with her, in a sweet season of assurance. Such strength, such unfolding of power beyond all the kingdoms of earth.

She would leave for New York. She could no longer stay home. Home was blessed and lovely, and she would want to return. But first she must leave. Because Dad would not acknowledge Yong.

"I'll *make* him do it."

That evening two businessmen came to dinner. They were in uniform: honorary U.S. Army colonels. This enabled them to hop onto the shuttle Dakota to and from Europe. Europe was a vast workyard, full of the ringing sound of future American factories. Europe would know a prodigious rebirth, thanks to American help. The Marshall Plan.

The honorary colonels scoured France and Italy for treasures, antiques and paintings. "This is the time, Heston. You ought to get yourself over there."

"Guess you're right," said Heston, not looking towards Isabelle, who sat at the head of the long table. "My wife and I plan to go over to Paris someday real soon."

"England's the place," said one of the men. "So many of those big families can't hold on to their stuff, it's all coming out of their castles. Taxes, you know. But you've got to know your way around. . . ."

Heston's architect for his new house was also at dinner. He had suggested importing some 17th-century woodwork from a certain manor in southern France for Heston's new house. "I've been dealing with them. It's a family that went over to Pétain . . . they're anxious now to get to Switzerland before de Gaulle shoots them."

Isabelle, impassive, sat like sculptured crystal. Her face only became a little more withdrawn as she raised her glass of water to her lips. She always, deliberately, drank water now that Heston served French wines (imported at fabulous cost).

Isabelle's whole family had sided with Pétain. Of course. So many of the French had done so, although they were now getting on the Resistance bandwagon. At least one of her aristocratic cousins had been caught and shot before he could escape to Spain.

"Stephanie, perhaps you'd like to go over to Europe with us, help us choose the stuff for the new house. . . ." said Heston to his daughter.

189

"Afraid I can't, Dad. I plan to go to New York real soon. And I guess the magazine will be sending me back to China," said Stephanie. She turned conversationally to the colonel next to her. "My husband is a Chinese surgeon. At the moment he's operating on one of the battle fronts, up in north China. . . ."

"A surgeon, eh? My, that's great, that's terrific," said the man heartily. He looked at Stephanie's bare hand.

"No wedding rings in a Chinese marriage," she said, flushing, feeling she had committed an indiscretion.

Skillfully, the colonel's wife turned to Heston. "Heston, did you read about the new hospital we're building downtown? There'll be a special wing for handicapped veterans. . . ."

No one referred again to China. But there was some talk of Roosevelt and his liberal friends, all of them "soft-headed about communism."

"I guess the ladies don't want to hear any more about Washington politics," said Heston, and Isabelle, contriving to look martyred, rose to take the women to the living room. Stephanie went with them. They talked brightly of parties to come, of Easter so soon, next week, of buying Easter gifts for the disabled GIs.

The guests said their goodbyes, Heston waving from the front door at their departing cars.

"Dad, I want to speak to you."

"Sure, Steph. Go ahead." Heston went to the bar, poured a brandy in a balloon glass, offered it to Isabelle, who refused it, and kept it for himself. "Want a brandy, Stephanie? Best Napoleon . . . Now what's on your mind?"

"I'm going back to China, Dad. I'm going back to my husband."

"Dr. Baxter thinks you'll need at least another three months."

"I'm taking *all* the pills, and I can see the doctors in New York. I don't want to hang around doing nothing, Dad."

"Doing nothing," said Heston. "By heck, there's so much to do here, baby. So much. Why, this is the very heart of it all, right here in Dallas . . ."

"Dad, Dallas is great and I love you all, but I'm married to a man in China. You don't seem to want to know it . . . and everybody seems to duck their heads when I want to talk about it. . . ."

"Honey," said Heston. "You *think* you've married some guy out there. A Chinese. Okay, okay. I've got nothing against anyone, maybe he's a fine guy, a very fine guy, but it's not really a marriage. You were in very poor shape, Steph, just out of coma, and maybe you were being influenced. Now you should give yourself a chance . . . get well again and think things over."

"Dad, there were around thirty Americans in Yenan, a whole military mission, State Department people, also American doctors. I was *not* being influenced. It was even difficult getting the marriage permit. I *wanted* to marry Yong. Because I love him."

"I'm not saying you don't, Steph." Heston was reasonable, entirely at ease. He swirled the brandy around in the balloon glass thoughtfully, the way Isabelle had taught him to do when they were both in Paris twenty-three years ago and she had been, for him, the key to the discovery of France's sophisticated marvels, of good taste and chic, of debonair civility.

How quickly he had learnt! Now he was using this acquired knowledge, civility, persuasiveness, on his daughter. Hell, she hadn't married just any Chinaman. He was sure of that. But it was still some kind of a fellow-traveler, a pinko, since he was working up there with the reds in Yenan . . . Oh, Steph, baby, my baby, he thought, I'd put the whole world at your feet, and you want to go to China!

"There's something in all this which *does* worry me, honey. I confess, I'm here in Dallas. It's still a smallish town and I'm just a plain, simple man. I guess Dallas isn't a big city like New York—not a metropolis—not yet, but I've got friends in Washington, good friends, and they keep pretty much in touch with things. And they've been talking to me. They've come down here to talk to me. In fact, I'm afraid that some of these guys you mention, these Americans out there in China, have pulled the wool over your eyes. . . . Not only yours. A lot of people have been taken in by them. People in the government, including that red-lover Roosevelt."

"What are you talking about, Dad? I don't understand."

"I'm talking about the red conspiracy, about world communism," said Heston. "That's what I'm talking about, Stephanie. Theodore White, and Gunther Stein, and Harrison Forman, and a lot of other fools, all of them writing books and articles praising the commies. And you-all over there were being sweet-talked into joining the conspiracy, honey. They use people, a lot of innocent people like you. Brainwash them. Why, they've even got some of our top scientists working for them. And I don't fancy my little girl being right in the middle of it, being used . . . These people are smart, *they* knew who you were."

"Dad, it isn't so, it isn't. You don't know them. If you'd been there, if you'd seen them, you'd be on their side too. Why, they're the only people who can pull China together . . . the only ones in China who've been fighting Japan. They're honest, Dad . . ."

"They're mighty clever, mighty clever," said Heston.

He finished his drink, put it down gently. Easy does it, he thought. Steph, oh my darling. Your daddy ain't about to give up looking after his little girl. "I'm not against your marrying anyone you really care for, baby. I'd even welcome this fella, if he's good to my daughter. . . . But he's got to prove to me he's not a Communist. I can't have my daughter being married to a red. . . ."

"Dad, listen. Yong is *not* a Communist. He loves his country. The Communist leaders in China want to be friends with America. They *need* America. Why, they said it to me, they said it to all of us. Their two top leaders offered to fly to Washington for talks with the President . . . I know it; they want and need us."

"And they wanted us to give them guns for their armies," said Heston sarcastically. "And then they'd have turned on us. I am telling you, now that we've beaten the Krauts, we're going to have to clean up a bigger sonuvabitch mess. The Russians, why, if it wasn't for us, Stalin would've been pushed right back into Siberia . . . and sometimes I think we should've let the Krauts push him."

Isabelle looked at her silk skirt and rearranged its pleats with satisfaction. "Heston," she said, "your daughter Stephanie is in love, and *married*." But neither Heston nor Stephanie appeared to pay attention to her definitive statement.

Stephanie rose. "I'm going to New York tomorrow, Dad," she said. "And I'm going to ask my magazine to send me back to China as soon as possible."

"Honey, you've got to do what you think is right," said Heston, reluctantly recognizing his own stubborn streak in her. "But my feeling is you're going to find out, the hard way." He put an arm around his daughter, easy and over-powering in his gentleness. "Remember, Steph, you're a Ryder. You come back, anytime you want, you hear?"

Heston lay awake in the wide bed next to Isabelle. He heard her light breath, knew her sleepless as he was, and was afraid to break the fragile but long-lasting truce between them. For on this complicity of silence his marriage rested.

Isabelle. 1921. Summer in Paris, with the rain making the gray roofs shine and lacquering the sidewalks. Scurrying girls, prettier than ever, peach faces under their flowery umbrellas. He was twenty-one years old and he strolled along the bookshops near the Luxembourg gardens, and there was Isabelle, carrying a voluminous bag, books in her arms, an umbrella, and her legs tangled in the leash of a small barking poodle which was trying to assault an elderly gentleman with a cane. He had disentangled her, they had walked together, the sun had come out and built rainbows in every puddle. He had fallen in love.

He had bought an atlas of America and showed her where Texas was, where Dallas was. He had told her—but with reticence, for he was already a man who did not bluster to get what he wanted, preferring to let others feel the palpable worth of him—that he had volunteered at not quite seventeen for the Lafayette Escadrille which had gone to France and to war. That First War to end all wars.

Isabelle had taken him to the house where she lived with her mother. In Rheims, in the shadow of the great cathedral. He then discovered France, the full extent and weight of her, her manners and mannerisms, her extraordinary radiance and her pettiness. Her love of liberty and her fundamental authoritarianism. French love for quarrel, fury, and argument, dedication to a logical arrangement of ideas, never mind if it was unhitched to reality. He had sharpened his wits against their supremely arrogant logic. He had visited quiet museums, theatres where poetry was spouted by the hour. But the greatest surprise of all was the day Isabelle came to him in deep black. Black hat, coat, dress, stockings, shoes, bag, white face covered with black

193

veil, almost no make-up. "Darling, what's happened?" A death in the family obviously, a major grief, the white face proclaimed.

And Isabelle had said: "It is the anniversary of the beheading of Her Majesty Queen Marie Antoinette."

Sonuvabitch, the death of a French queen in 1792—and this was 1921. . . .

Isabelle's mother, the Countess de Quincy de Gersant, questioned Heston a great deal when he asked to marry her daughter.

The result had been a polite refusal. He was not a Catholic, and it happened that one of Isabelle's uncles was a canon of the Church, that another one, the Duc de Quincy-Lombelle, owned a chateau and a very ancient name, and that none of them would agree to his marrying Isabelle. . . .

"I shall always love you," said Isabelle. But already on her lovely face he saw the resignation, that languor of too thin a blood, an end-of-family decline, a lassitude of the spirit. Resignation. She would always love him. But she would marry her Catholic cousin.

Heston had then kidnapped her. Literally. Had taken her away for a final walk to say goodbye decorously one afternoon, and she had never returned because he had the train tickets ready for Paris. When she had said, "But my clothes . . . my mother" (in that order), he had said, "I'll take care of it all." And kissed her and felt her fragile bones (how fine-boned and even-skinned she was. Not a hair on her legs or arms, skin like silk, thanks to a Hungarian ancestor) and made her sit in the train.

There had been the hotel. A room for her.

She had yielded. All the way, at last. And looked at him afterwards and said gravely: "I have committed a mortal sin for love."

He had married her. In Paris. Found a Baptist clergyman in Paris and gotten himself married. And she had said: "But it is heresy . . . my mother . . ."

He had taken her to America. And she seemed gay, happy. And Stephanie had been born.

Then he began to make money. He had bought land, ten thousand acres near Houston at a time when no one wanted land because it was the Depression. And it had turned out to be gusher land. Oil.

Isabelle still seemed contented, though at times unaccountably sad. And her way of responding to sex had changed. He put it down to her mother having died refusing to see her renegade daughter. Isabelle had inherited no money, only the furniture. He had it brought from France, shipped to Dallas, to make her feel less homesick.

Only in 1937, when Stephanie was fourteen years old, did Heston begin to perceive that things were very wrong. It had to do with Stephanie . . . it had nothing to do with Stephanie. Surely a mother loved her child? But Stephanie's vigor, her shining, seemed to deplete her mother. Watching her daughter, Isabelle grew older.

So it was to Stephanie that Heston returned in the ever-changing evening with its sudden twilight making all the colors of sky and earth more vivid. It was Stephanie who liked to trek with him, who went with him to the woods and the mountains, exploring the wondrous land of America. Isabelle never wanted to camp, to rough it. And she wilted, visibly, in spirit if not in the flesh, when they were all three together. She punished them with uninterest. An indifference which was worse than anything he had ever known.

She wasn't ill. She wasn't too thin. Just evanescent. He'd tried everything, given her everything, everything. He exhausted himself on her body, thinking she wanted more love-making. Anxiously peering at her face, afterwards. Her face. Resigned, well-bred sadness in her face. Remembering: "But this is a mortal sin . . ."

He'd really done everything he could. Put a lot of money in her name. Shares. Bought an apartment in New York, property in Houston for her. . . . She could shop like a princess without even enquiring about cost . . . but it all turned to cinders, everything went colorless when it reached her.

Then had come May 1940 and the debacle in France. And suddenly Isabelle had said that she must leave, go into the Free French forces in London . . . she must enroll . . .

Of course it was crazy. "Belle, you're helping to win the war here, darling. Being with me. We're going to build the planes that will knock off the Germans. Besides, what about Jimmy?" Jimmy was a wistful child, dreamy. He didn't like rodeos, horses, cockfights. He loved ships, however, and now Heston paid for flying lessons. . . . The boy might turn out all right, if his mother didn't fill him up with non-sense. . . .

Isabelle had become very pious. Going to church every day.

"I should think your kneecaps must've been worn out by now," he had teased her.

But she had looked at him gravely. "God is merciful to sinners who pray, *mon ami*."

Sinners. A dutiful wife, submitting. Sonuvabitch, it drove a man to drink, to the whores.

He could not help it if, at the dinners they gave, his friends would mention how the French had run away in May 1940 "and our boys went in and did the job for them."

Isabelle sat, outrageously superior, drinking water, saying in her exquisite courteous manner, which was worse than a razor blade across one's face, "The weather has turned quite windy, do you not think."

When Paris was liberated in August of 1944, he'd let Isabelle return, to find her family.

Within two months she was back. Palely she had said: "My two uncles, my cousin Paul," the guy she was supposed to marry, "were shot as collaborators with the Germans."

She lived and walked, a precise ghost.

In his house.

And now she was encouraging Stephanie in her madness. Encouraging the girl to go back to China. In order to bring him down.

But he wouldn't let her spoil Stephanie. He wouldn't. He flexed his fingers. Flexed and then unflexed them. He would fight for his baby. Steph, oh Steph my darling girl . . .

They sat in the roseate glow of the Algonquin's oak-paneled dining room, solaced by reminiscence, comic in retrospect, of Chungking's massive discomforts.

"Remember how we managed to wash in one small enameled basin?"

"Remember that gin Teddy White brewed out of orange peel and fermented cane sugar?"

John Moore had come up from Washington to meet

Stephanie in New York. And they talked, feeling the comfort of trust, of events shared. John was returning to Chungking very soon. "Hurley persists in saying that Chiang *is* the Nationalist government and we've got a commitment to him."

"It's because the Yenan leaders are Communists," said Stephanie. "In Dallas, the word makes people hysterical. They think we've all been brainwashed, that we've joined a Communist world conspiracy, if we say *anything* good about a red."

"Only people completely out of touch could think that," said John Moore.

"I wouldn't say my father is out of touch. . . ." said Stephanie, and they both laughed.

They sauntered down Forty-fourth Street onto Fifth Avenue, flowed with the Easter crowd, good-natured, unhurried. Spring in the air, and one could smell lilac. The department stores were bright with Easter gifts, the flower shops staked great sprays of forsythia right on the pavement. The sky vouchsafed that particular gleam of blue which is found only in New York. Cobalt light bounced off the spires and towers of Manhattan. The streets, canyons of the marching millions, became roads to delight as the spring afternoon lengthened, and everywhere women wore new, delightful hats, with veiling and sprigs of flowers.

And Stephanie thought John Moore the nicest companion she could have to saunter with in New York. Except for Yong.

For a moment Stephanie dreamed of Yong and her father meeting, not in Dallas, but here in New York. Dad was too strong in Dallas; the earth beneath his feet nourished him with gusty life. He would tower above Yong, and Yong would be outsubstanced. But in the bigness of New York, Yong would stand up well to Dad. And then Dad would like him, and not insist that he was a red.

New York was the focus for correspondents from all quarters of the world, more so even than Washington. They came to New York to meet, to talk, to argue, to renew the sap of life with each other's vitality, with scoops and facts and myths.

The "China hands" were even more prone than others to getting together, swapping stories, and slaking their nostalgia. They felt they had a war experience unmatched any-

197

where else. China had provided them with such a range of difficulties and challenges, had strained their bodies and their minds with so much anger and delight, bafflement and horror, had repelled them with monumental squalor, molded them with its smooth enchantment. Many would never recover from China. They would remain displaced persons, harboring vivid memories, a permanent fury of life, for many years.

Isabelle had insisted that Stephanie use her apartment on Sixty-eighth and Park Avenue, but it was at John Moore's apartment (eccentrically kept spotless by John's maiden aunt, who was totally deaf and always worried that Japanese submarines might enter New York harbor—for years she had kept watch, going every afternoon to the Hudson, scrutinizing the pewter water for periscopes) that the China hands assembled.

Terry Longworth, who was having difficulties both with his newspaper editor and with his wife Blanche, was vehement in argument, drowning his unhappiness in whiskey and words. When John Moore mentioned that Jack Service, the State Department representative of the Dixie Mission, had just arrived in Washington—he had had a last interview with Mao Tsetung on April 1—"April Fools' Day," Terry said bitterly. "Washington's already turned thumbs down on Yenan. . . ." He downed another bourbon. "D'you know what? I'm being reassigned. My boss says I'm too involved in the China scene . . . 'You're losing your objectivity,' he says. I'm reassigned to Dublin, Ireland. Ireland. For God's sake." This meant the end of his career, and he knew it. "And Blanche won't give me a divorce. Says I'm just going through a temporary infatuation."

"Terry, I'm so sorry . . ." Stephanie felt inadequate in the face of Terry's frustration.

Terry looked bleak. "I'm not good company tonight, Stephanie . . ." He was thinking of resigning, going free-lance, writing a book. "I've got a friend in Paris. Maybe I could get Rosamond to come to France."

"If I can do anything, Terry . . . I plan to get back to Chungking in July . . . I'll certainly see Rosamond."

Terry's eyes grew dim and faraway with a coat of tears. Angrily, harshly, he poured himself another drink. "I won't let Rosamond go by default, Stephanie, I won't."

"Terry," said Michael Anstruther, "you shouldn't expect *gratitude* from any bureaucracy."

Michael Anstruther represented a major English newspaper and was occasionally in New York, where he knew everyone. He had been in Singapore when Singapore had fallen to the Japanese, and had escaped almost by miracle. He looked deceptively slight, but his slenderness concealed great endurance. There were other things he concealed, for instance the fact that he was homosexual. But he bore himself with such dignity and was so discreet in his conduct that no one even mentioned it. He liked the company of beautiful girls, and dated some of the best-looking women in Washington. "Stephanie," he said now, "if I can do anything for you, let me know." He smiled at her, shy and deliberate, daring her to understand.

"Thanks, Michael, I will." Stephanie returned his smile.

Vance Marston, chief editor at Marston House, was jubilant over Stephanie's manuscript. He took her to dinner at the 21 Club and watched her with surprise. She was not the hard-boiled, sophisticated career woman he had expected, a breed he often took to dinner, deploying his sex appeal but careful never to go too far. She was a trustful, vulnerable girl, whose open delight in life stirred him. "An excellent thing in your manuscript is that it gives us a vivid picture of how people live, and especially how women in China manage," he said. She had conveyed the bleakness, the discomfort, the valiance, that daily small courage of women who get up at dawn to repeat unendingly the same labor—lighting fires, boiling water, tending babies, washing clothes, cooking . . . all things renewed and destroyed every twenty-four hours. The brassy call of trumpets in the morning rousing the sleepy girls from the *kangs,* getting them to stumble out, to line up for drill, shouldering too heavy rifles and practicing shooting, and yet remaining totally female. Nothing diminished the haunting obsession with daily chores, unalleviated by any mechanical device.

Stephanie had managed to portray this season of fortitude as a generator of strength.

"Stephanie, you can pick your own assignment," Halway Mandel, glossy-haired and suave, the shrewd and successful vice president of HERE magazine, greeted her effusively.

"China," she said. "I'm married in China, Hal, remember?"

Mandel rubbed his hands with open glee. "We expect a lot of pieces from you about what it's like to be the wife of a surgeon in China at war."

The women readership of HERE had responded well to Stephanie's articles, and Mandel was pleased with the offers from women's clubs and women's magazines for lectures and reprints. "It's the love interest," he told her. "A lovely woman, and you're in love. And in one of your articles, there's something about a Chinese woman writer and about married couples only being together on Saturday nights . . . but we'd like more, we'd like something to show that war *doesn't* make women masculine. That all they want is a normal, happy home life. Now that the war is almost over, we're launching articles to get women back to their real job, the home. The men will be returning from all over the world and we want them to feel that whatever's happened, the American girl has been waiting, waiting for marriage and children and . . ."

"Cooking, washing, and cleaning," suggested Stephanie absentmindedly, suddenly seeing Yong crouched over the stove, mixing millet and water to make dumplings for her. . . .

"Precisely," said Mandel, a little startled. How abrupt she was.

Stephanie went to Radcliffe to give the lecture she had promised. She was back among the graceful old buildings flanked by smooth lawns and meditative trees. Some of her classmates came to meet her, and a class reunion was held in her honor.

The story of River Fork village had become part of the curriculum in social sciences. And her marriage to a Chinese surgeon elicited admiration and even a little envy. "Just fancy, she had the guts to go ahead and do it," said her classmates. Gracefully they showered compliments upon her.

"Stephanie looks glorious, a bit like the Winged Victory but with her head on," said Camilla Waring, her best friend at Radcliffe, who was now championing schools for black children in Boston.

The news of Roosevelt's death, on April 12, sent Stephanie to the telephone to find John Moore. "It's the passing of an era," John said. "Roosevelt gave meaning, a vocation, greatness to our land."

Stephanie rang up her father. "It's quite a blow, Dad, he was a very great man."

"Well, now," said Heston, "I think he was getting pretty soft in the head, sweetheart."

He sounded, Stephanie thought, rather pleased. "Now don't overdo things, Steph. How much do you weigh now? Dr. Baxter says your hemoglobin is up to eighty-five percent. How about y'all coming down our way real soon?" He was attentive, affectionate, and they had nothing to say to each other. . . .

It was Victory in Europe Day, May in New York, Manhattan joyful under a dappled sky, throngs covering the asphalt streets, hugging and kissing. And girls in light sleeveless dresses were carrying roses, pinning them on the jackets of any man in uniform who happened by.

America had won the war. The movie houses showed European mobs welcoming the GIs, hugging them, kissing them, filling their tanks with flowers.

Isabelle came to New York, looking beautiful and blighted in a soft gray suit. Beauty can choose desolation as its dwelling place, and Isabelle had chosen.

"I am going to France, Stephanie. Your father wants to buy some antiques." The word in her mouth bristled of contempt. "It is always the craze, I think, for people who have no past to try to acquire the past of others."

Stephanie suppressed the sharp retort which came to her lips. It was unfair to Dad. Dad had an eye for beautiful things, and it was not only the past he loved. He also loved that new, exciting, beautiful future. Yes, it was true, he had a passion for acquiring beautiful things.

201

"Dad has got good taste," she replied, evenly.

Isabelle's mouth twisted faintly. "That is evident," she said.

Isabelle straightened her straight back. "I shall go to Rheims, of course, but also to my cousin, who has a property in Auvergne. Would you not like to come with me for a few days, Stephanie? It might be interesting for you.

"My nephew the Marquis de Quincy is refurbishing his estate in Auvergne. He is trying to marry . . . but it is difficult," Isabelle sighed. "Difficult to get a bride both noble and wealthy. He will have to look elsewhere. . . ." And both women thought, but did not say it: possibly a rich American.

"I'd love to go to France with you, Mom, but I'm planning on getting back to China real soon."

Isabelle left and Stephanie went shopping in New York. For Jen Yong, for Shaggin and Loumei, for Sa Fei and her husband Liu Ming, for Professor and Mrs. Chang, for David and Jessica Eanes, for Bamboo Shoot, and even for Party Secretary Pu, and for Comrade Lo, who had beamed at her so affectionately at her marriage ceremony. She bought sweaters and socks, sneakers and shirts, underwear, and baby clothes for Loumei's child.

Dr. Baxter had listened to her describe the shortages in Yenan and he had written a thick wad of prescriptions for sulfonamides and penicillin, the new wonder drugs, for her to take to China. She would not return empty-handed or only laden with frivolous things.

Michael Anstruther telephoned. "Stephanie, I've been trying to reach you. May I come round?"

"Of course, Michael. Love to see you."

Michael walked in and kissed Stephanie lightly on the nose. "How beautiful you are, m'dear. Quite recovered, I take it? May I have a Bloody Mary?"

"Of course."

He sprawled easily on the rug, tailor fashion. "My dear, don't get upset. Jack Service has been arrested by the FBI."

"Why?"

"You knew he was back from Yenan?" She nodded, he

202

continued. "Well, he kept on putting forward his point of view—the view of all us China experts, I suppose—that Chiang Kaishek is done for. That the future lies with those chaps of Yenan. He's now accused of passing diplomatic secrets and copies of confidential documents to a magazine called *Amerasia*. It's a radical publication. The editor and staff went to Yenan in 1937. . . ."

"Michael, I don't believe Jack would do something prejudicial to America . . . he just wouldn't."

Michael produced his inevitable Burma cheroot. "My dear, Roosevelt conceded so much to Stalin at Yalta, there's bound to be a reaction. The Pentagon, the air force, and a good many ordinary people are deeply worried about Russia now. And Russia of course means communism. So a blanket terror of communism is falling upon the land. And nobody is stopping to think, to say: 'But there are *different* Communists . . . the Chinese of Yenan are not the same breed as Stalin. . . .' Nobody makes any distinction now.

"You've probably seen some indications. The House Committee on Un-American Activities has started hunting down people 'soft on communism.' Republican and Democratic congressmen are flooding Washington with calls for an immediate showdown with Russia. 'We've had enough of Yankee liberals' is the slogan of the South—including your beloved Texas. . . .

"Stephanie, your country will now back Chiang Kaishek to the hilt. And the word is that Stalin has promised not to help Mao Tsetung. Of course. Stalin hates Mao. Stalin much prefers the weaker Chiang Kaishek. . . ."

All this spells war, Stephanie thought. Civil war in China. It's almost inevitable now.

"I'd better get back as quick as I can," she said.

ten

IN that summer of 1945, the Dakotas and Constellations flying the Atlantic were crammed with diplomats, officials of all kinds and of many nations, military staff in starched uniforms with top priorities, all of whom squeezed out the less important travelers.

Stephanie's plane landed at Tenerife in the Canaries with one of its engines burnt out. Spare parts would be flown in from either Cairo or Miami, but this would take ten days. Meanwhile, the passengers were free to enjoy the island, which basked in Atlantic wind and dazzling sun, shaded by wind-bent pines. The goats and shepherds on its arid dunes, its villages white and austere, enchantingly reminiscent of Greece.

Such long waits were not uncommon, one white-haired diplomat to the newly formed United Nations told Stephanie. He went for long rambles with her across the barren cliffs. The diplomat was head of a mission to process displaced persons in Europe.

"Fifteen millions, fifteen millions in Europe alone, m'dear, who in one way or another have lost their homes, lost their families . . ."

A trial of war criminals was to take place at Nuremberg. "I hope they hang the lot," he said. "They're monsters, not human beings, those Nazis."

Five days in Lisbon, at the Quasimodo Hotel, which opened its ochre facade and green shutters on a beautiful square heavy with eucalyptus of palpable shade. Here officers and officials from the nations of Europe congregated, and the most vociferous of the lot, demanding top priority, were the Poles.

Disheveled and vocal, temperamental and stimulating, the Poles were always raging. A difficult ally, a fierce enemy. They were raucous against the Yalta Agreement, which had unreservedly and without consulting the Poles given their country away to the USSR. The hotel resounded with their imprecations against America.

Another four days, then on to Cairo, where again there were long-drawn battles for plane seats. This time it was the British officials going to India, where a reshuffle of the Indian Civil Service was taking place.

Finally Stephanie landed in Calcutta. The heat struck at her, reminding her that this was the worst time of the year to go to Chungking.

Calcutta was awash with soldiers, many of them Australians. Stephanie was greatly pressed by some of these hardy and amorous warriors. The Anglo-Indian girls who went out with them were only occasionally accessible, and it was quite impossible for them to sleep with Indian women, except the prostitutes. A large epidemic of venereal disease had broken out among American GI's in the Philippines, and many were being evacuated for treatment in the hospitals of Calcutta.

On the streets of Calcutta hunger stalked the population. In the narrow side alleys great-eyed children with ballooned stomachs died mutely. When the bleary morning misted the herds of the poor on the pavements, large signs were seen scribbled on the walls: BRITISH QUIT INDIA.

In Calcutta Stephanie seemed stuck forever, for the weekly plane to China was always crowded: with trunks and wooden cases containing banknotes, and Chinese passengers, mostly official Kuomintang delegations back from missions abroad, loaded with luxury goods—jewelry, watches, cameras, furniture, and leather shoes—purchased with U.S. dollars that had been earmarked by the Lend-Lease Act for war equipment.

In that summer eighty-six thousand tons of goods went by plane over the Hump of the Himalayas between Calcutta and Chungking.

Calcutta sweltered. Violence and surliness was its temper, and one day Stephanie saw a procession of white-clad, chanting Indians, close-packed, winding down Chowringhee Avenue with banners: BRITISH QUIT INDIA.

"Stuff and nonsense . . . hotheads . . . why if *we* leave they'd be at each other's throats in no time." The talk of British businessmen within the clean hotel was that of a bygone era.

But not so the Americans. "There's no sense in fighting this war and not giving these countries their independence," said the American officers whom Stephanie met (and they were most meetable) in the lounge and the dining room of the Great Eastern Hotel.

Large V for victory signs were painted along the walls on the major roadways, but in the small back lanes, where Muslims grilled cow udder on braziers, chalked roughly in auburn and red on the walls, were other signs: LONG LIVE SUBHAS CHANDRA BOSE.

"Bose? That's the Bengal wallah who joined the Japanese. Wanted India to fight on *their* side against *us*." The mustachioed British colonel who one day sat at lunch with her at Firpo's was emphatic. Firpo's was the most prosperous and busiest restaurant on Chowringhee Avenue. All the officers, British, American, Australian, congregated there, for the drinks were excellent. Before the war Firpo's had amassed a great store of the best Scotch whiskey, and now dispensed it with enormous talent at hair-raising prices.

The colonel told her what he called a very "hawhaw" story. "I was in Germany this spring, and there's this American in charge of an occupation battalion who rings me up. Tells me that about twenty very dark chaps, claiming to be Indians escaped from a German prison camp and nearly starving, have come to him and what should he do with them? Told him I was busy but I'd get over in a few days and have a look at them. So for a week the blokes are fed and housed. This American turns some German family out of a villa to house them. I check with headquarters: no news of any Indian contingent in the battalion they claim to belong to. So I go over in a jeep with a couple of subalterns, and since I know the score, I could tell immediately they were Bengalis. And you can never trust a chap from Bengal. *We* know. *We've* been here long enough. More than two hundred years. Now give me a Rajput or a Punjabi—damn good fighters—also the Madrasees, wily but clever. But

Bengalis . . . all liars, all of them . . . That put the wind up me. Didn't say anything but pretended I believed their story. Then told the American to surround the villa with his troops, not let one of them out, we'd come back and pick them up."

"And then?" said Stephanie, when the colonel bent down to his plate of tandoori chicken.

"Oh, we shot them all, they were traitors," said the colonel. "A Bhose battalion, fighting with the Germans against us." He swallowed another mouthful of chicken.

On Chowringhee Avenue, a gentle babu, speaking in the rapid singsong English of Calcutta's clerks, told Stephanie of the Great Famine of 1941.

"It was the British, madam, who provoked it, to break our spirit. They took away the *paddi* rice, had it transported to their own cantonment. . . . Many people were extinguished in this vile manner. Almost a million people died of hunger in Bengal."

Calcutta. Would HERE magazine accept her article profiling the quagmire city? "I smell murder a-coming here." And slaughter, appalling slaughter would be the city's way of life two years later, when independence came at last.

At night Stephanie double-locked her room door and pushed the heaviest piece of furniture, a Victorian cupboard, against it. Randy Aussies, assaulting any female in sight, hurled empty beer bottles at her closed door throughout the night. Bleary, like spavined horses in the morning heat, they would apologize.

By spending a great many hours at the American Consulate, Stephanie managed at last to get a seat on a Dakota over the Hump to Kunming. The planes were not pressurized, and just as when she had léft five months previously, Stephanie became violently sick. Through tiny portholes the passengers watched great dazzling peaks claw the sky; between majestic summits blue-black troughs occurred into which the Dakota sank, only to stagger up again. Even the hardiest traveler arrived in Kunming shaken and pale green.

And there at Kunming airport was Michael Anstruther, so English in his impeccable safari shirt of Indian homespun, and with him, in a faded blue gown, wearing cloth shoes and white socks like a schoolgirl, was Yee Meiling. They waved at her as she stepped out, and Meiling hugged her, crying: "Oh, Stephanie, how well you look! I got here just before you, Stephanie, and Michael told me you were coming on this plane."

Meiling was in Kunming on Red Cross business. Since the reopening of the Burma Road, the American and other Red Cross organizations and the Quakers had been trying to send medical supplies to the hospitals of China.

"But we can't get them to Yenan, although the Red Cross is supposed to help both sides, distributing medical supplies equitably," said Meiling. "I've come here to see that not everything is confiscated by the Kuomintang, to be sold on the black market." Meiling was thinner, but radiant-faced.

"How can I get to Yenan?" asked Stephanie.

"I think correspondents do get through," Meiling replied. "But things are certainly a bit worse than a few months ago. Even my father is finding problems. And you know how he can deal with problems . . ."

With Meiling's voice speaking so lightly, and so much tragedy taken in a nonchalant way as everyday occurrence, Stephanie knew she was back in China. China, the most confusing, fascinating, and nourishing paradox of all. China. Unforgettable because of its people. The people. Admirable and infuriating, mendacious and loyal. Tender and totally ruthless. Fragile aesthetes, but capable of surviving hardships which would kill or drive mad anyone else.

Yong.

Meiling's voice led her back, back to that other self of hers, the self who had fallen in love with Yong. Though she was unaware of it, her body movements changed, change which was but another affirmation of her person. That other Stephanie reentered her, bringing her not emptiness but affluence, as if her life was a substance diffused in the air, absorbed by osmosis. Life more abundant and splendid in its magnanimity and its terror. Or was it that? A different tempo. Different perceptions. As the heart expands to admit the beloved once a stranger, so now Stephanie became again Spring Snow, the name that Yong had bestowed on her. Yong was once again vividly alive. She yearned for him now, yearned with the words of those ancient poems crafted in this land.

In spring snow, all women are beautiful . . .
My heart is empty, the sea tide enters it . . .

A three-storied brick building was the hotel for Americans in Kunming, the capital of Yunnan province. Here, on a plateau nearly six thousand feet above sea-level, clement weather was perpetual. Kunming never knew frost, nor the furnace heat of Chungking. And there was near-luxury, for over the Hump came all that was needed for the large American air base sited near Kunming, some of which filtered down to the Chinese. . . .

The sun shone on the temples above the city's lake and upon the great wall around the city with its drum-shaped towers like carved agate, which took on the roseate tints of sunset, the pearly tints of noon. And everywhere the brightly colored gowns of the tribal peoples. For Yunnan province was a great reservoir of people of astonishing diversity, language, custom. "We've got nineteen different ethnic groups here in this one province," said Meiling.

The Pais, the Miaos and the Yis and so many others: women turbaned and athletic and with collared necklaces of silver and turquoise and coral; men handsome and negligent, doing nothing but looking handsome, leaving the worry of the world to the women.

The men of the Pai race, once a mighty kingdom, were absurdly good-looking. Long limbed and slender, they lolled at ease on small ponies with bright eyes and beautiful heads that went up and down the slopes with alacrity, showing themselves off and parading their riders, clad in scarlet and blue and with great belts of turquoise. The Pais once had a kingdom here. Renowned as great artists and singers, they wore gaudy embroidered jackets. Their women had large brown faces, yelled their delight at each other, and carried everything, especially their husbands (of whom they were so proud), on their backs.

Stephanie gawked as, going up the cliff staircase to the famous temples carved in the rock face, she saw a Pai woman, her turban a marvel of tassels and silver filigree, great anklets of silver around her legs, carrying a man up the steps. "That's the Pai custom," said Michael. "Women do all the work and therefore own the land, the fields—and their husbands. A husband is a precious and beautiful and cherished sex *object* to them."

Yunnan province, with its medley of people, had provided all of Southeast Asia with their varied populations. From Yunnan had come the Malays of Malaya, and the Shans of Burma, and the Thais of Thailand, and many other races dubbed "native" by Western historians.

The Yis stalked the roads in long black pleated capes, fluted horns upon their headgear—or dawdled in an ecstasy of opium. Their area was the most opium-productive in China.

In the spring, the hills of Yunnan were covered with opium poppies, and at the time of harvest, like a great swarm of locusts, the army commanders of Chiang Kaishek swooped upon the province; their battalions were mustered to stand over the opium crop, gun in hand, to see that none of the brown gold was stolen by civilian bureaucrats. For the profits of the opium trade were fabulous.

With Michael and Meiling, Stephanie went to see the professors of the West China Union University.

An amalgam of six refugee universities from the coastal provinces, its staff and students had walked to Yunnan when the Japanese had invaded China.

Kunming, remote and barbaric (so said the fastidious intelligentsia of China's east coast), had thus become a great center of learning. And therefore, of agitation against Chiang Kaishek.

Michael Anstruther went about the campus, listening, smiling that engaging smile of his which invited confidence. And he took Stephanie around, introducing her to the professors of the universities as the wife of Dr. Jen Yong.

The professors were delighted to meet Stephanie. "I know the family of your husband. . . . Your husband . . . although young, he has already achieved much." Then, briskly, they began asking her about America's aims, about Russia . . . and she answered as best she could.

They treated her as their equal, a colleague, a friend, and delighted and charmed her. Through them Stephanie felt so near to Yong, so near. One day Yong would be like this old professor with his beautiful sculptured face, his gentle voice quoting Tu Fu, the Szechuan poet of the seventh century A.D.,

> *Yesterday night the Spring wind wafted*
> *The rank smell of blood to my nostrils.*

It was in Kunming that Stephanie came to understand the difference between the Chinese scholar-bureaucrat and the Western intellectual. The Western notion of an intellectual elite, whose business was ideas and ideals *detached* from the context of the functioning power, did not apply to the Chinese intelligentsia who had been for almost two millennia officials of the state. They were the curators of China's culture, possession of which was in itself a mandate from Heaven to ensure China's permanency. Any government which hoped to survive must cherish them.

From Kunming Stephanie sent telegrams to Yong and to Lionel Shaggin in Yenan, to David and Jessica Eanes in Chungking. She was restless and her nights were heavy with erotic dreams. This was a result of Kunming's six-thousand-foot-high elevation, its abundance of ultraviolet rays, its treacherous spring languor. She would turn in bed, hearing the clapper of the night watchman through the hours, an occasional violin, the burst of a sudden quarrel . . . and at dawn the birds, mad with joy at the streaming light.

On August 6, Stephanie boarded a Dakota for Chungking. Three hours later she saw below her the white and bone-bleached city, stepped into the steamy, clinging heat. There was the odor of manure, and white egrets squawked in the green rice fields.

Henry Wong had sent Secretary Hung to the airport to welcome her, and there also were Rosamond Chen and Jessica Eanes. They hugged her joyfully and exclaimed on her healthy appearance. "We missed you so much," said Rosamond.

Somehow Stephanie had hoped that Yong would also be there at the airport. But of course it could not be. He was still in Yenan.

Secretary Hung had a ministry car to take her to the city. He handed her an invitation from Henry and Meena to a cocktail party in their residence. As they sped towards

Chungking, Secretary Hung, turning to the three women, said conversationally: "I have to inform you that today the Americans have bombed Hiroshima. With an atom bomb. The whole city is destroyed."

"An atom bomb?" said Rosamond.

"It is like one million ordinary large bombs. Nothing is left of Hiroshima."

Jessica said, "Oh my God."

Rosamond asked, "Then the war is over?"

"The Japanese were already putting out peace feelers three weeks ago," said Secretary Hung.

Stephanie thought: Women, children, babies . . . a million times the massacre at River Fork. She felt queasy.

Jessica squeezed her hand. "I'm frightened . . . what have we begun?" she whispered.

Rosamond, however, was ecstatic. "The war is over." Her eyes shone. Stephanie knew she was thinking of Terry. Noticed too that her smoothness had gone. The jadelike unruffled face showed a lacy web of lines at the outer corners of her eyes. And knowing what she knew—of Terry's wife, of his assignment to Dublin—Stephanie grieved for Rosamond. And thought, Yong, I've come back to be with you . . . now the war's over, we can be together.

The surrender of Japan took place on August 15. Official celebrations were held in Chungking.

There were so many people at the Wongs' cocktail party that it was almost impossible to squeeze into the room. Everyone was present, all the diplomats from the various embassies, including the overwhelmingly numerous Russians. "It's wonderful, it's great" everyone said to everyone else.

The radio was on full blast, blaring out more news, the announcers excited or solemn. Every minister of the Chungking government put in an appearance, beaming, lifting their glasses and shouting: "*Kampei.*" Henry Wong said to Stephanie: "We'll be back in Nanking next month. Meena's started packing."

All the wives of government officials were packing to return to Nanking, Chiang Kaishek's capital. A rush for seats on American planes began.

There were dozens, scores of Liberators, Flying Fortresses, Constellations, Dakotas; an air armada, flying to all points of China, flying Kuomintang troops to the cities to take over from the surrendering Japanese garrisons.

Stephanie tried to be happy; she knew she should feel proud. But she could not. Could not rejoice. The staggering implications of Hiroshima gave her a queer sense of loss, of defeat. *I feel as if something has gone forever. . . .*

Alistair Choate greeted Stephanie with rapture. "Darling, how wonderful you look!" No longer lascivious but loquacious, bubbling over with anecdotes of war. Stephanie decided to forget his former rudeness. They danced, and Alistair told Stephanie he might be getting married. "She's tiny, you know, with small hands, a painter. Got a great sense of humor." He added, ruefully: "D'you know, I was quite crazy about you, Stephanie, at one time . . ."

"That was only too obvious," she replied. They both laughed, a friendly, forgiving laughter.

A few days later, came the news that Mao Tsetung, the Chairman of the Chinese Communist Party, was coming to Chungking from Yenan. A most important Party Congress had taken place in Yenan that April, and Mao had emerged the undisputed leader, while Stalin's appointees were relegated to minor roles in the Central Committee.

A sultry August afternoon, the end of the dog days of summer. The newsmen were marshaled in neat rows along the fenced enclosure of the airport. Gun-laden guards walked around, and the welcome party consisted of Kuomintang officials, and the Communist liaison office men.

A little farther off, a small crowd held up large banners:

UPHOLD THE UNITED FRONT!
FOR A DEMOCRATIC COALITION GOVERNMENT!

Mao's visit to Chungking was a momentous event. Should it be successful, should a coalition government be formed, there was hope of peace. Pat Hurley, the American ambassador, had flown to Yenan to persuade Mao and to bring him back to Chungking for these talks with Chiang Kaishek.

"There they are!" A speck in the sky, a Dakota sailing in, turning, becoming bigger. Landing. The plane door opened and out came Hurley, mustaches to the fore, a hunter bringing back his prey.

213

Mao Tsetung was right behind him, coming down the steps. Incongruously wearing a colonial sunhat—a topee. Where was it from? Who had given it to him? Why did he wear it? He was clad in a quilted jacket and must have been sweltering in it. He was pale-skinned, smooth-faced. He had the impassivity of a granite mountain. In his giant calm, he was all China's peasantry, and all along the airport road, all the way to the city, people were bunched, kept in order by armed soldiers, waiting to see him.

Mao was given a pleasant residence with a small garden, and during the next four weeks, large numbers of people would walk there to meet him, to talk to him.

On the third day after Mao's arrival, Stephanie walked out of the Press Hostel with Alistair, going to a press conference.

And Yong was there, ten yards from the gate, at the curve of the pathway. He sat on his knapsack. Waiting. He may have been waiting for hours, or only for minutes.

"Yong." Though her heart leapt, she stood still.

"Stephanie." He stood up. His eyes went beyond her, to Alistair.

She said: "Alistair, this is my husband, Dr. Jen Yong. Yong, this is Alistair Choate."

"How d'you do?" said Alistair carelessly.

Jen Yong shook hands and said: "Glad to meet you."

"I'll toddle off now, Stephanie." Alistair was suddenly very English, extricating himself gracefully. "I'll tell them you're busy, shall I?"

"Yes, do," said Stephanie, distracted and staring at Yong's face, which once again had begun to shut in.

She said: "I've missed you. So much."

The shadow went away from his face. "Spring Snow," he said. And the magic between them was roused, in their eyes and mouths, and their hands which now clasped each other.

And the parched feeling went from her. He had come back, they now moved together; the waters of love came welling up and they were one skin. "Come," she said. "Let's go in."

Stephanie walked back past the sentinels, but one of them stepped up smartly and put his rifle across Jen Yong's chest horizontally. "You must have special permission."

"I am a doctor from the hospital. Invited by this American lady," replied Jen Yong.

"Tell them we're married," said Stephanie, impatiently.

"Please ask the hotel manager to come. I am sorry to trouble you," Yong continued in his reasonable soft voice.

"I'll get the manager," said Stephanie.

"No, Stephanie, let the soldier do it, or he will lose face," Yong said to her in English.

They stayed side by side, waiting at the gate, while the soldier, with a grim face but inwardly softened by Yong's placating voice, walked into the hostel.

The manager came out, accompanied by Old Sung the waiter, who was all smiles when he saw Stephanie and Yong together.

"Dr. Jen," said the manager, bowing, "excuse the incivility of these ruffians . . ."

"The guards are merely doing their duty; they are most responsible," said Yong.

But the manager, whom Stephanie had never seen before, insisted on showing his authority. "This way, this way," he beamed, waving a hand towards the hostel.

"Dr. Jen, often have I heard of your great name. Now that your light deigns to appear to us we are honored. Old Sung, bring tea," he shouted, although Sung was just behind him. "Please to rest for a moment in the dining room, Dr. Jen."

He bustled away. Old Sung reappeared, carrying a teapot and two cups. Chinese green tea, which he never served to the foreign guests of the hostel. He put the cups down, ceremoniously, in front of Yong and Stephanie. His demeanor had changed; while retaining the guise of a classic family retainer, he was also an equal, a friend. When Jen spoke to him softly in the sibilant dialect of Shanghai, Old Sung answered. After he had left, Yong said: "Old Sung's eldest son is a newspaperman with a guerilla unit . . . I met him when I went to his guerilla base."

"You're the first Chinese to come into the hostel, Yong— except for the censors and the Information Ministry officials," Stephanie said.

He smiled slightly. "Because Chairman Mao Tsetung has arrived, the manager thinks I might be important."

"How would he know?"

Yong laughed. Showed her his knapsack: *Red Cross Committee—Yenan*. "His eyes travel swiftly, Stephanie."

Yong was here. He was here and the world was renewed, all staleness gone. She heard the afternoon rooks, cawing as they searched out a place to settle. Most curious of all, time slowed, moved contentedly, unhurried. No longer that restless clawing of life's fabric. There was time for everything. The clocks had stopped being significant. Time was the beat of her blood.

They sipped and talked, in short spurts: Stephanie of America, and spring in New York. Of landing at Tenerife, of Calcutta. Drifting talk. Words were not important. Like bird call, words merely implied consent to the bright unsullied moment which bound them in its newness. Words gave them time to listen to themselves.

Yong told of those months of walking, walking from village to village, walking in single file, carrying what he could. And reaching one village and then another. Everywhere he had met his trainees, and he knew his work had been valuable.

But here was his life . . . Stephanie. Spring Snow.

"I wrote you many letters—every day—but there was no way to send them. I brought them with me."

"So did I."

The first ripple of an unknown sea, speaking softly to their sea-body, and all the months of separation but an awkward drowsiness, a small sad sleep. In them rose the tide, singing, until their ears could hear it, and their mouths knew its savor, and they were melting, melting into the being of their love.

He listened to her rainbow voice, listened to the beat of his being gaining sway, authority. And no, he was not worried, he had known she would become well again in America. And yes, there had been a few battles, and he had operated, under shortages, no anesthetics—and oh, let us relinquish this parrot squawking of words and follow the wind gust, the tide whose sound is the sound of creation. . . . The perfect moment came and they rose and walked together to her room in silence and came together, no longer soiled with weariness, anxiety, waiting. No longer needing anything but each other.

"Spring Snow, we are going to my Family, in Shanghai."

They had slept after love, the sheet was damp with their

216

sweat. The fan above them whirred with the buzz of a wasp hive.

"When?"

"In a few days. As soon as possible."

Stephanie would never know how difficult it had been for him to extricate himself from obligations, duties. For her. For her.

"We are married, but no marriage is really acknowledged if the Family does not agree. I want us to get married all over again, in my father's house; otherwise some relative or other is bound to be dissatisfied. I want the whole of China to know you are my honored wife."

"And we'll also have to get married the American way, Yong. Because otherwise, we won't be married for *my* family. And you'll have to buy me a ring. Without a ring people in America don't believe there's been a wedding."

"How wonderful," said Yong, holding her. "I shall be marrying you again and again. Let's think of other ceremonies we can go through . . . a Buddhist ceremony to please my third great-uncle . . ."

"A Baptist ceremony for my father, a Catholic one for my mother . . ."

Yong stretched out, laughing at the absurdity of institutions built around love-making.

"We'll get married again every year. Will you be able to leave with me in, say, a few days? Less than a fortnight?"

"I'll manage," said Stephanie. "I'm working on an article about the chances of peace now that Mao Tsetung and Chiang Kaishek have met. I wish John Moore were here," she added. "I'd pick his brain. Alistair is no help. He says all that's happening is just window dressing."

"He may be right," said Yong, wincing slightly at the name of John Moore. But he was foolish. Stephanie must never know. . . . And Stephanie rose, slim and white, and started to pour water on herself, washing herself, a curtain between them.

"Yong, your face changes when you see me with another man, or when I speak of one of my colleagues. I feel a rumbling in you, like a sky preparing a storm."

He stared at the curtain which concealed her. "Yes, it is true, I am a jealous man. It's my upbringing . . . but please, never give in to me on this. . . ."

217

He came to her, took the towel from her hand to wipe her back, doing it with precision and care.

"If you give in to me, you throw me back into my own tradition, which is vilely possessive about women. We deny the woman any right to her own body; we men have all the rights, to theirs and to ours. But the revolution will change all that. It must change. I want this new equality between us. . . . I love you, Stephanie, and I *want* to love you, as an equal. And loving you I must accept that you make your own choices."

"Yong." He was giving her freedom . . . because he loved her he was making her a gift of his feudal pride, his medieval honor.

"I am the happiest of men," said Yong. "I have the privilege of loving you."

"I'll remember, Yong." Her hands cupped his face, and they kissed, feeling once again the invasion of desire. She had been afraid of the frailty of remembrance, which changes with the seasons and the place. But in the sweltering room, in Yong's arms, she felt invulnerable, immortal. Nothing could take away this moment. Nothing.

She completed the article for HERE the next day, abiding by the informal, chatty tone of the magazine. She wrote of the quiet power of Mao Tsetung's presence: "He seems sincere in his desire to seek a peaceful solution for China's tragic problems."

Alistair did not agree. "Had you interviewed Chiang Kaishek you would be just as impressed by his desire for peace, by a certain nobility in his deportment."

"But all the non-Communist intellectuals are going over to Mao, Alistair."

"They'll live to regret it, poor sods."

Yong nodded when she told him of Alistair and Michael's conviction that civil war was imminent. "I too hear the sounds of knives being sharpened," he said sadly.

That was why he had returned from Yenan, to be with Stephanie.

He had seen the preparations. The new recruits, the first guerilla convoys, on foot and with mule-pack trains, complete with propaganda teams of writers and musicians, leaving for Manchuria in June, two months before the Japanese surrender. The focus of the civil war to come would have to be Manchuria, with its arsenals and coal mines and hydroelectric power plants.

"Who will pluck the peaches of victory? We, who have fought the Japanese, or Chiang Kaishek?"

Mao Tsetung had said it. A number of Japanese garrisons were stranded in China, and the Communists and the Kuomintang had begun a race to take these over on the very day of Japan's surrender. But from August 16 onwards, hundreds of American planes flew Kuomintang elite corps to take over the surrendered cities, before the Communist forces, slogging on foot, could reach them.

"The peaches of victory are being handed to Chiang Kaishek by the Americans." The Communists were bitter, for all along they had hoped America would learn that the future of China had been born in Yenan. Instead, the Russians came.

In that same August, one hundred thousand Soviet troops entered Manchuria, as had been agreed at Yalta, and swooped into the north portion of Korea as far as the 38th parallel. As agreed between Russia and America, the 38th parallel became the demarcation line between them in Korea.

Everything was being prepared for civil war to come.

After so many months in Yenan, Yong had felt soldered, seamed to his own people. He had shared their lives, and he had felt tempted to go with them.

But there was Stephanie. He had known Stephanie would be coming back. And he had wanted to be with Stephanie. With his love. He wanted to have some months, some years with her, knowing now that every day of their being together would be threatened. . . .

So he did not volunteer to stay on.

Loumei had given birth to a son on the day of Hiroshima. "We shall call our son China Warrior," said Lionel Shaggin.

Lionel Shaggin did stay on in Yenan. He had shaken hands with Yong. "Give Stephanie our love, and best luck to you both." Landing in Chungking by truck, Yong had walked to the Press Hostel, to wait on the pathway for Stephanie.

And now, although "negotiations" still went on between Mao Tsetung and Chiang Kaishek in Chungking and hopes of peace seemed high, Yong knew that there would be war.

Yong and Stephanie were too drunk with the heady wine of love-making to worry overmuch; all that happened beyond the universe of their own bodies seemed slightly unreal. And so they said their goodbyes happily, and through Meiling Yee obtained two seats on a plane loaded with Red Cross personnel and medical stores going to Shanghai.

The presence of Stephanie, an American, prevented the plane from being commandeered by the cousin of the finance minister, with his grand piano, two large sofas, wife, children, and concubines.

The House was at the end of Eight Jewel Lane, paved with stones dating back to the previous century. It was surrounded by a stone wall ornamented in the fashion of middle China, where chimneys were adorned with carved bricks and roof tiles dovetailed to fashion flowers and birds.

The main gate was heavy wood, lacquered in black, with brass clappers. Three steps of stone led up to it. Standing below the steps was the gatekeeper, a young apprentice by his side holding a copper and glass coach lantern.

Stephanie and Yong alighted from their rickshaws. A third rickshaw carried their luggage. The gatekeeper peered, recognized Yong. "Eldest young master, welcome, welcome . . ." He turned to the young boy: "Quick, run inside, tell old master and mistress eldest young master has arrived."

"Old Fu, I am glad to see you strong and healthy," Yong greeted the gatekeeper.

"Eldest young master, all of us are joyful that you have brought back the light of your presence to us."

"This is where we live, Stephanie. Our House is called Willow Pool Garden."

Through a courtyard with sycamores flanked with neat rooms where the servants lived, on to a second courtyard, then through a round gate into the garden proper. A gallery covered against inclement weather zigzagged towards the main pavilion, the reception hall, with its curved roof, eaves lifting heavenwards a burden of small beasts and birds. Its inner size was concealed by the fact that the outer walls were angled and that its color was somber, brownish lacquer. It was—as were all the buildings in the garden—raised on a stone ledge of three steps. In front of the pavilion stood two girls and two men, also holding English coach lanterns, and on the steps was the Family. Yong's parents, then uncles and aunts, sisters and cousins, a score of other relatives.

Yong hurried forward, bowing to his father and mother and saying: "Father, Mother, we have come."

And Father advanced one step and said: "My son."

And Mother advanced two steps and hugged Yong and said: "Son, you are here."

And having thus established recognition, everyone unbent, everyone began calling the appropriate kinship name, while Yong turned to Stephanie. "Mother, I present to you my loved one, Lai Spring Snow."

There was a moment of stunned silence. *Loved one.* A shiver ran through cousins, uncles, aunts to the third and fourth degrees of kinship. A small giggle came from an untutored niece. *Loved one.* The term invented by the Communists to indicate a wife or a husband. Before Yenan, the very word *love* was an inner closet word, never to be used in public. . . .

But Mother smoothly placed her hands upon Stephanie's shoulders, drawing the girl to her, saying: "Welcome, you are most welcome, Spring Snow."

Father was just behind her. He shook her hand and said in the same exact, prim English which Yong used: "We are honored to have you come to our house, Miss Ryder."

Lai Spring Snow. Lai for Ry–der. No *r*'s in Chinese. No wonder, thought Stephanie, Yuyu had always addressed her as Miss Lighter. . . .

And Stephanie, feeling their genuine affection, gave them her heart. At that moment she entered the Jen Family. "Thy people shall be my people . . ." People, Family . . . Stephanie had rehearsed her manners. She bowed, replied in perfect Chinese: "My unworthy self is honored to be received in your house."

They went into the reception pavilion to drink the ceremonial tea of welcome. Electric lights hung in silk lanterns from the center of the high ceiling and also from the corners. Stephanie was enchanted: it was a beautiful room, uncluttered, with south China style carved furniture and on tall stands peony and fuchsia in porcelain flower pots. The windows, uncurtained, displayed lattice work of lacquered wood. Their centerpiece glass panes were etched to represent landscapes. Light could pour in, but it was impossible to see through from the outside.

There were also two European style sofas covered in pale brocade. Mother took Stephanie to the place of honor on one sofa, but Stephanie, who had learnt the ritual of seating (even in Communist Yenan there were "high" and "low" seats), said: "I dare not, I dare not," with proper bashfulness.

Mother beamed at her son and said: "Ah son, you have indeed brought a wise phoenix to us."

Father laughed and said to his twin daughters, Ling and Hu, Calthrop and Coral: "You must learn good manners from this accomplished lady." The servants came in procession and the tea cups were filled, but Father called to his daughters again: "Quick, bring the tea to our most honored visitor."

Yong had risen and with dutiful love had taken the cups to his father and mother. Like a ballet, but with smoothness and apparent casualness, the tea cups were distributed, and Stephanie remembered to receive hers with both hands.

Mother sat next to Stephanie, and Stephanie, as she sipped, tried hard not to stare at her. Mother was indeed beautiful, like white jade, without blemish. She had Yong's eyes, his nose, and the same tight-woven skin, as if she had no pores. Mother said: "My son is young and awkward. You must be indulgent, our teaching has been so inadequate."

Stephanie's mind boggled; she had tried to train herself in the ways of self-deprecation so necessary in polite Chinese society, but this left her speechless. And because she looked a little stunned, Calthrop and Coral immediately rose to refill her tea cup, saying: "Please taste our unworthy tea," and Father added anxiously, "Our tea is not very good, would you like some other tea?"

"No, oh no, this is wonderful, wonderful tea," Stephanie said and gulped, not knowing that Father had bought that very day some strong Indian tea and had also bought milk from the European dairy store (although the very smell of milk was repugnant to him, as a proper Chinese), thinking that perhaps Stephanie would be unable to drink Chinese tea.

And so the moment of awkwardness passed. "Now let us have the photographer," said Father, clapping his hands, looking young and happy. Not a white hair on his head, agile in all of his bones, as Yong was, and with the same eyebrows sweeping neatly outwards towards his temples. In him, Stephanie could envision Yong twenty, thirty happy years from now.

In came three men in black assisted by two servants who set up the tripod camera wrapped in its black sheet. With much cheer, Father fussed and everyone fussed, turning the occasion into a smooth comedy, all of it the product of an etiquette which makes an art of seeming inadvertency, of feeling the moment and the person by hint, indirection, a quiver in air, a gossamer lightness, so that long-planned events appear haphazard and important occasions seem unrehearsed fun.

Mother took Stephanie's hand in hers and said: "I feel I have another daughter, one of beauty and kindness." Father placed Stephanie by Mother, on her right. Yong stood at his father's left, and the rest of the family arranged themselves, falling into rank but without appearing to do so.

The photographer said importantly: "Smile, yes?" in English and started squeezing the bulb.

Photographs. Evidence that Stephanie was being accepted into the Jen Family.

Many, many photographs. The photographer was conscious of the importance of this occasion. He bobbed up and down, a little nervous, adjusting things, moving the peony and cassia and jasmine in their porcelain pots. After all, after fifteen hundred years of existence, the Jen Family was preparing to welcome a foreigner into its bloodline. Could anything be more worthy of immortal likeness-taking? Other families would come to the photographer to hear the story. The photographer would gain great face, especially when, retouching the product of his work, he would make sure that all the faces would be without blemish.

The photography session over, a sudden eclipse of persons occurred. Within a few minutes, the large room was almost empty. Mother now rose, a flowing movement as if she had no joints. She wore a dark blue silk dress, and on her wrists were a pair of apple green jade bangles. She said conversationally: "Did you know that my son's name is En Yong, Abundant Grace? But he uses only Yong; it is now the fashion among the young to shorten their names." And almost without stopping she continued: "But you must be very tired. Let me take you to your rooms." And led Stephanie out, through the garden, and around a small rockery which was like a screen separating the garden into several smaller ones, to a neat pavilion set between a grove of bamboo and a willow tree, with a pool at its feet. Two servants, Petunia and Peony, and the cook, Master Lee, were waiting.

The pavilion had windows of the same etched glass panes with latticed surrounds, as the main building. There were four rooms and a bathroom. The kitchen was separate, at the back with the servants' quarters. One room contained an enormous bed with a carved canopy, draped in a cobwebby mosquito net of silk. The bathroom had a marble floor, a bathtub, a modern toilet, and a faucet for cold water. The hot water would be brought from the kitchen, Mother explained. The living room had Ming furniture, the chairs lacquered in red. The sofa was covered in cream silk. On the walls were painted scrolls, one of them a thousand years old, Stephanie later discovered. There was a dining room and a study lined with books.

"Rest well, you have filled our house with joy," said Mother.

Dazed at the tranquil perfection around her, Stephanie allowed Petunia to lead her to the warm, scented bath which she'd prepared; and when Stephanie stepped out, an embroidered silk gown waited for her.

Finally Yong appeared, smiling, cheerful. "Stephanie, is everything satisfactory?"

"Oh Yong, Yong, such a beautiful house! . . . Such beautiful people! You never told me. I never guessed!"

Before retiring, Yong showed her the stone. It stood in the pool where goldfish played, a unique stone, three cen-

224

turies old, collected by an ancestor after much arduous travel in a hunt for stones of great beauty. "We love stones. They are ribs of earth, and the story of the centuries is told by them. We cultivate stones that bear moss, for moss clings to stone with the tenacity of love."

As I cling to you, Yong, Stephanie thought. And Yong said it, with his mouth and his arms.

The auspicious day for the marriage ceremony came.

At the propitious hour (confirmed by Father after consultation with the almanac of auspicious and nefarious times of day, and two astrologers), Stephanie was clad in vermilion jacket and skirt embroidered with pale pink cherry blossoms. Mother had personally supervised the embroidery. The red veil over her head was dispensed with. "These are new times . . . there must be *new* customs," said Father. After all, Yong had broken all custom by using the term "loved one."

She was then taken to the ancestors' pavilion—secluded and protected, its only access through the length of the garden, murmurous with willows and sycamore, Chinese oak and cassia, with trellises of wisteria and seven-mile jasmine. It stood raised on a stone platform. It had pillars of brown lacquer; its floor was black tiled. The altar was very simple. No god, no deity. Ancestors. Not their bodies, but their soul-tablets, denoting the imperishable spirit. Simple slivers of wood arranged by rank, each one inscribed with the name of the particular ancestor, each bearing a dot at the top, red for male, black for female.

Stephanie stood in front of the ancestors, her hair done up in a simple chignon, held by the thrust of jade and kingfisher-feather hairpins. And next to her, Yong in a blue robe. They bowed to Heaven and Earth and to the ancestors; bowed to Father and Mother, and to the Family. Bowed to each other, and drank wine from the same cup. And Spring Snow became First Daughter-in-law of the Jen House.

Stephanie lighted an incense stick, then poured tea from a prepared teapot and brought the tea cups to Father and to Mother, saying: "Father, Mother, please drink."

And they took it and Father said: "Eldest daughter-in-law," but Mother said: "My very dear daughter."

And now all was laughter, joyfulness, as three hundred people sat at thirty round tables in the courtyard in front of the ancestors' pavilion, so that the latter could rejoice to hear their descendants and bless the generation to come.

The ancestors' own share of the feast was set in dishes on the long table in front of the altar, and Mother called out their names, urging them to eat, before any of the living moved their chopsticks.

"Who does not know his ancestors does not know his posterity." This was written upon a lacquered wood tablet on one side of the ancestors' pavilion. On the other side was written: "He who does not respect the forces of Nature cannot travel long in time."

The day after her marriage Stephanie rose to bring early tea to Mother and to Father. And Mother embraced her and said: "Daughter, this is too old-fashioned; nowadays the bride is no longer required to perform such service."

Stephanie smiled. "Mother, I won't be able to do it every day, but whenever I'm up early."

And then both women laughed and hugged each other. "I am truly delighted, my son has chosen well," said Mother.

Mother was the ruler of the House. A ruler whose rule was hidden by apparent casualness. But nothing really happened in the House without Mother's knowledge, suggestion, approval. And Stephanie noticed the great love Father bore her, for he always looked at Mother, looked at her, as if his eyes never had enough of her.

Three days after the wedding, Mother gave a pendant to Stephanie. Jade carved with phoenixes sporting under peony trees, carving which had taken many months. All along the 24-karat gold chain were small jade emblems of good luck and prosperity. "This I give to you, dear daughter, as it was given to me—it has been in the Jen Family many years. . . ."

"Yong, your parents spoil me, you spoil me. I've never been so pampered. Three servants, just for the two of us . . . I can't even pick up my shoes . . . or wash a handkerchief. . . ."

"Let us enjoy it for a little while, a little longer," said Yong. "We do not know, my love, how long it will last . . . but each moment of happiness creates its own immortality."

Enchantment, paradise and no serpent.

Mother gave receptions for Stephanie. "A first daughter-in-law is a very important person," she said. Stephanie was amazed by the number of parties Mother managed to cram into a week. And so many varieties of parties! Western style, where couples sat side by side, and Chinese traditional, with the women at one table, the men at another.

This is worse than Dallas, she thought, changing her outfit for still another gala.

Mother had a superb tailor who created long, slim, high-collared Chinese dresses for Stephanie. He and his eleven apprentices turned them all out in a day, and each was exquisitely stitched.

"You have small bones," said Mother. "And no hairiness on your arms or legs."

"It's my Hungarian ancestor," laughed Stephanie. She knew how repulsive hairy skin was to the Chinese—how thankful she was that, like Isabelle, she'd never had to shave her legs.

Each day Stephanie discovered a new, often surprising, aspect of the Family—so traditional, yet so modern. Father, for instance, loved Western style music and dances and had a collection of the latest recordings from America; he also loved Brahms and Mozart, and played the Chinese flute.

Father also took on Stephanie at tennis: on the court he looked young and slim, and twinkled at Stephanie as he skillfully placed a ball just beyond her reach.

As for Yong, he suddenly revealed a talent for games: tennis and volleyball, mahjong and bridge. Like his father, he also loved chrysanthemums.

Stephanie would see him bent over the chrysanthemum beds, snipping away. (The old gardener, who had grown up with Grandfather and was still alive, was duly consulted, of course.)

Yong was also crazy about goldfish. "All Chinese boys are," he said simply. He had come back one afternoon from hospital duty carefully holding a round glass bowl in which flitted minute bits of aquatic life. Now, in silver and gold and carmine, with tails longer than their bodies, the goldfish waved lazily around the ancient stone in the rock pool.

And then one day Father gave Stephanie a landscape in a dish. A minute pear tree lay in its small pot in Stephanie's hand. It was five inches high and one hundred fifty years old. It had taken six generations of gardeners in the Jen Family to grow.

eleven

ON the roadway the students filed. A thin, but determined file between the rickshaws and honking cars. They would walk a long time, past the university, past the villas of Shanghai's ex-French concession, villas built by a Spanish architect. They carried banners in English and in Chinese: AMERICAN GI'S GO HOME.

It was summer, 1947. Stephanie stood with Calthrop and Coral, Yong's twin sisters, watching the students file past.

The twins were very excited. They had become intensely political and furiously anti-Chiang, as were all the young.

"America must not help Chiang Kaishek."

"Chiang is massacring students, professors."

There had indeed been killings. The Secret Police had kidnapped some students and buried them alive. In Kunming a famous professor and his son had been shot down on the steps of his university.

The twins were proud of Stephanie. They told their schoolmates that their American sister-in-law also deplored her government's policy. "I think we Americans have involved ourselves in a big mess and that we'll regret it," said Stephanie.

One earnest young man with a fresh rosy face and bright eyes detached himself from the procession and came towards the three women.

"Is she American?" he asked in Chinese, pointing to Stephanie.

"I am American," replied Stephanie in Chinese.

"We are not against the American people," said the student earnestly. "Please read this." He handed her a pamphlet and returned to his group, who raised their fists and chanted rhythmically: "American soldiers quit China."

Stephanie shivered though the day was warm. To hear people—Yong's people—shouting slogans against her country still hurt her . . . despite the ways America had been hurting China over the past two years. . . .

Since August 1945, American aid to Chiang's armies had shot up to nine hundred million U.S. dollars. He had also received $658 million from the United Nations Rehabilitation and Relief Administration (UNRRA). Plus three hundred thousand tons of goods, from food to medicines.

In Yenan, the Communists had received from UNRRA some medical aid and equipment totaling a million dollars altogether.

During 1946 and part of 1947, American policy had become increasingly ambiguous. It proclaimed the need for peace, but provided Chiang with the weaponry to wage war. And fifty-three thousand Marines were stationed in China, to hold strategic cities and harbors for Chiang Kai-shek.

When President Truman had appointed General George Marshall as his personal representative to China, Stephanie and her press colleagues had become once more sanguine with hope.

"America seems genuine in making one last effort to bring peace to China by sending a man like Marshall," wrote Stephanie for HERE. "But if military aid to Chiang continues, it will encourage civil war." Marshall tried to stem this aid but did not succeed.

For a year he labored: the U.S. wanted to bring about China's unification in a coalition government. A conference was called, and the Communists agreed to having only ten divisions, while there would be fifty Kuomintang divisions, in a reorganized and integrated Chinese Army. But American aid continued to Chiang.

"Marshall's mission appears doomed," Stephanie wrote, as local clashes continued. A letter from her editor at HERE stated: "You seem too involved with local politics . . . your public expects touching stories, humor and warmth. Human interest."

"Look at this, Yong. Too involved. Of course I'm involved

and *concerned* . . . it concerns my country, America . . . my people, and yours."

Yong continued to peel the juicy pears which a grateful patient had given him, pears which could not be found for sale anywhere in Shanghai. They came from Loyang, in the north, and were known locally as Buddha's temptation. He sliced one pear neatly and handed the plate to Stephanie, watching her eat, deriving pleasure from her pleasure.

"Mmm, they're good . . . they just melt in the mouth, don't they? . . ." She finished the pear and Yong started another. She tossed her head in that coltlike movement which Yong found utterly stirring. Every time, he wanted to make love to her. . . .

"Yong, what do you think? What should I answer?"

"Nothing," said Yong. "Perhaps you should *not* write too much about the military situation. People often are angry if one tells them the truth. . . ."

"But I've got to . . . you said it yourself."

"I said: Chiang will win all the cities and in the end he will lose the country. His armies are locking themselves into cities like rats into a trap." Yong did not tell her that at the Shanghai hospital where he worked there was a Communist underground. That the underground was everywhere. Secret Police searches in Shanghai had begun and it was better not to speak. "What counts is the peasantry, Stephanie. It's always been so. Chiang's soldiers are filling the cities; but they have to send armed battalions to wrest the harvest from the peasants in order to feed themselves."

"I guess it's useless for me to write that—they don't want to know," said Stephanie, a little aggrieved, but smiling and holding out her hand for another pear.

"Stephanie, the time may come when some people in your country will become very angry . . . for having failed. . . ."

"America is a free country, Yong. There isn't only one truth . . . there are always lots of different opinions."

It annoyed her that Yong couldn't seem to differentiate between the American tradition of free speech and the caution that was so necessary in China. "No harm ever comes from just *saying* what one thinks in America."

"Truth is not always palatable, Spring Snow," he replied with infuriating calm. "Americans also have pride and obstinacy. And to make a mistake rankles."

The afternoon drew closer around them, the fine-grained light of evening softening into lavender. "Oh Yong, don't let's quarrel." She shivered. "Here we are, in this small Eden, where your father plays the flute and raises orioles and chrysanthemums, and Mother, your mother is as indispensable to him as the air he breathes . . . and you talk so lightly of losing all this. . . ."

"I think we may lose it," said Yong. "But I have no doubt that we shall build again. Meanwhile, it is right to enjoy a time of beauty. . . ." They looked at each other; the light around them was the heart of an opal now, and Yong stood up, and together they entered their house.

They had now begun what happens to people who are married and in love. They grew in the ways of each other, learning and discovering more about each other every day, acquiring a treasure trove of memories. Memories of love, of passionate nights and mornings and afternoons, but also of a thousand small delights which made them a couple. Responding to each other, until Stephanie could tell by the sound of his footstep whether the day had gone well or badly for Yong. Badly meaning that he had lost a patient in an operation.

Yong's work at the General Hospital, where he headed the surgical department, was arduous. There was an enormous number of patients, and though organizations such as the Red Cross, the Friends (Quakers) Ambulance Unit, the China Welfare Fund, the UNRRA tried to help, only too often the medicines found their way to the black market and not to the hospital patients, just as in Chungking.

Stephanie was writing another book. Her first one, *Travel to Yenan*, had had very favorable reviews and sold well. In the second she was attempting to describe the dissolution of Chiang's rule.

Her work took her to the headquarters of the China Welfare Fund, whose president was none other than Soong Chingling, Madame Sun Yatsen, elder sister of Madame Chiang Kaishek. Soong Chingling, a tireless worker for the United Front in Shanghai, was extremely critical of her brother-in-law Chiang Kaishek and entirely committed to the spirit of Yenan. To her intense dedication she also brought an American passion for fairness and justice, and since she, like her sisters, had been educated at Wellesley and spoke flawless English, her eloquence was spellbinding.

Stephanie was fascinated with Soong Chingling. "This woman ought to be heard," she wrote. But it was her sister, Madame Chiang Kaishek—who would be going to America to ask for weapons and yet more weapons—who was being heard. . . .

Nevertheless, because of Soong Chingling, Stephanie found herself in Nanking, one bleak February day, watching a convoy of DC-2s being loaded to depart for Yenan.

On this momentous February day, the Marshall mission had finally admitted failure. Open civil war had begun, and the Communist truce teams were being withdrawn and returned to Yenan by American planes.

Stephanie watched medical supplies provided by the Quakers for Yenan being loaded. This would be their last medical convoy. A young American girl, fresh-faced and auburn-haired, climbed in with the cargo of medicines, and Stephanie spoke with her.

Margaret Stanley was from Minnesota. "I just volunteered to work *anywhere*, I don't even know *what* Yenan is." In Minnesota she had never heard a word about Yenan.

Shocked, and wondering if she and the other correspondents had simply been wasting their words on an America that didn't *want* to know, Stephanie tried to describe her own experiences in Yenan.

"Will you take some letters to my friends there?" she asked Margaret Stanley, and scribbled hasty notes to the Shaggins, to Bamboo Shoot, to Sa Fei. "It's been so long since I've had any news from them."

With a tightening in her chest, feeling bereft, she watched the planes take off.

Margaret Stanley, young and enthusiastic, was going to war without knowing it. Five days later Yenan would begin to evacuate its caves, and three weeks later, on March 21, it would fall to the armies of Hu Tsungnan, Chiang Kaishek's most trusted young general, the man who had blockaded Yenan with two hundred thousand troops for almost ten years.

In the large conference room of the Information Ministry in Nanking, Henry Wong, debonair and loyal, spoke of the great Kuomintang victory. "The Communist rebels will now sue for peace," he declared. There were banner headlines in the newspapers:

THE FALL OF YENAN
THE END OF COMMUNISM IN CHINA

All over Nanking, firecrackers exploded; joyful demonstrations organized by the Young Kuomintang League swore loyalty and devotion to Chiang Kaishek, *The Leader*. They goose-stepped a little, incongruously. "Modeled on Hitler's storm troopers," said Michael Anstruther, watching the procession from the hotel for correspondents in Nanking.

Michael had reopened the British press bureau and often called on Stephanie in Shanghai, bringing with him his urbane and seasoned wit, his knowledge and flair—and, always, an interesting young Chinese man.

"Well, it won't be long now," he said, as a particularly colorful float showing Communists prostrate before heroic Kuomintang soldiers went by.

"You mean . . . it's all over for Yenan?"

"I mean it's all over for Chiang Kaishek. The Communists planned, quite a while ago, to *let* General Hu Tsungnan take Yenan. . . . Now they're dragging him and his troops by the nose through the villages in hot pursuit. Hu wants to capture Mao Tsetung and Chou Enlai, but he doesn't realize he's been hooked. 'We have traded seventeen empty cities for six hundred thousand of Chiang's best troops'— that's what the Communists say."

"But Chiang has five times more troops, and so many weapons . . ."

"But he hasn't got the people," said Michael.

At home, Stephanie turned to Yong for an answer. But his hands lay loose in his lap. He looked remote, and there was

234

a sadness about him. And suddenly Stephanie knew that but for her he would now be walking away, singing, walking in another step, with the others of Yenan.

He had returned to Shanghai, where everything was for sale, everything including people's souls, because of her. He had wanted to take her to his family, to Mother. He had wanted to live with her and to love her. And now he felt heavy at heart, guilty.

They looked at each other, each knowing the other knew. They had each other, each other, and love like a great fire between them, dazzling them still. . . . Would it always be enough? And the tendrils of fear crept and grew in Stephanie, in her body and limbs. Perhaps one day . . . she sought Yong's hand.

By the summer of 1947, Chiang's government was nearing financial collapse. Inflation had raised prices to one hundred fifty thousand times what they had been in 1945. By mid-1948, they would be fifty million times what they were in 1947. Even the printing presses could no longer catch up with inflation.

In Shanghai, people trundled huge suitcases full of money, wheelbarrows packed with money, packets of money made up in bundles. Each packet was a million dollars. One never carried less than three million dollars, which was enough to buy a carton of cigarettes. Or a meal for one person . . .

"How do the people live? They walk about with these bundles of paper currency . . . they pay in packets, it takes too long to count single bills . . . all they want is to get rid of the money quickly, before it drops in value again. And so they buy and sell. All the time. Anything. Everything . . . automatically." This would be Stephanie's last article for HERE. It was May 1948. Her three-year contract was up and she did not want to renew it.

"Automatically, the crowds move . . . everyone has something for sale. Very often it is a child, a little girl. But it may be a bolt of cloth, a fountain pen, a blanket, a shirt. . . . Others buy, and hours later, they will sell what they have bought for more bundles of paper money. . . . This ghoulish, incomprehensible, frantic sell-buy exchange goes

235

on all the time. Sometimes there is direct barter . . . people squat on the pavement, their few possessions in front of them. Others crouch to look, handle, exchange a straw hat for a pair of slippers, a plate for a piece of cloth. The food lines are miles long. They start at 2 a.m. and family members relay to keep their place. . . . If they are lucky, they will buy something by nine in the morning. Others, those who are strong, or fortunate enough to have a bicycle, go to the villages to find food."

The Jen Family was lucky. It still had gold bars. Only gold bars and U.S. dollars were valid, were real. A family could live very well with fifty U.S. dollars a month. Stephanie had U.S. dollars from her royalties. She paid the salaries of her servants and their food, as well as the food for Yong and herself. But when she wanted to contribute something to the Family, Mother, smiling, stopped her. "Dearest daughter, it is not necessary . . . we still have some gold. . . ."

In 1948, a new, peremptory edict was issued, and a hunt to confiscate gold bars began. Anyone found with gold bars, or trafficking in gold, might be subject to the death penalty. . . .

"This is ridiculous," said Father, "ridiculous." Nevertheless, he would consult with his brother, Second Uncle. "Second Uncle will know, he has more brains than I," said Father. And, smiling, he knocked his forehead with a bent knuckle.

The government was offering to buy up the gold. A new Chinese dollar was to be created, linked to the U.S. dollar in a parity of two to one. Many small people, fearful of being investigated and hauled off to be shot, turned in their few small savings in gold.

But the wealthy did not. There would always be a black market way to sell gold.

Some families sent their servants to dig holes in gardens to hide their gold—or hid it in their ceiling rafters. Mother kept the gold bars in her room, in two very large, ornate, carved blackwood cupboards: both contained gold bars in their false backs and tops.

When Mother was absent from the house for any amount of time, Widow kept watch.

Widow was Sixth Aunt, Father's youngest sister. (The redoubtable Jen Ping, whom Stephanie first encountered in

Yenan, was Fourth Aunt and his elder sister.) Jen Jen was Widow's name: Patience.

Widow had indeed been widowed, but *before* being married to her intended bridegroom, so that she was also a virgin. Because precisely at that time Jen Ping had run away to join the Communists, and Grandfather had been infuriated. So the beautiful young girl had had to remain a chaste "widow," dressed in pale gray, almost white, the color of mourning; she wore no make-up and walked with a sidle, half in submission, half in revolt against her diminished life. Mother had urged that she marry, but Widow had now grown into her role and would not.

She kept watch over the gold bars when Mother was away. She sat on Mother's stool in front of the triplicate oval mirrors, trying to look like Mother. She tried to become Mother, touching her lips with delicate fingers, like Mother when Mother rouged her lips. She hovered among Mother's little boxes of pure almond cream for the skin, and among her eyebrow pencils, and the powder and rouge which were modern and from the West. Her fingers touched, pretending. Her face assumed an air of languor; she felt more beautiful then, turning her head with that infinite grace which Mother had . . . and then sometimes she would bury her face in her hands, or throw herself on the bed, and laugh, and weep.

By mid-1948, everyone knew that Chiang Kaishek had lost the civil war.

The Communists had recaptured Yenan in April. They had also captured or were besieging other cities on the railway lines running from north to south China.

In Manchuria, the cities occupied by the Kuomintang were starving, and the United States Air Force, the Flying Tigers of General Chennault, airlifted food to them.

The greatest black market of all was in barbed wire. Surrounded by the guerilla-infested countryside, the armies of Chiang erected barbed wire fences all around the cities they occupied . . . millions of meters of barbed wire.

Nevertheless, every day, over the radio: "We are brothers. Brother does not fight brother . . . join us . . ." And Kuomintang troops changed over, bringing with them

American guns and ammunition, American uniforms . . . whole battalions began to surrender.

Every Friday night, the top bureaucrats of Nanking (those who had not yet run away) still arrived in Shanghai by the special trains for their weekend of fun, of nightclubs and dance halls and gaiety.

In sleek cars, the wives of wealthy officials, twittering like birds, went to parties. So much luxury, so much wealth. So much extravagance. So many parties. Frantically gay parties that outdazzled each other. Parties that never stayed in one place. That was dull. They moved in throngs of people and laughter and small shrieks from one glittering entertainment to another. From ballrooms to dance halls, where girls sat primly on chairs: Chinese girls, three dances for only a million, the price of a cup of tea . . . they floated like clouds, weightless. Nightclubs and bars. Whatever one wanted in a woman, one could have: Chinese or Eurasian, White Russian or Korean. For the very select there were small private clubs where white women, Australian, French, even American—the bored wives of businessmen or army officers—prostituted themselves for the fun of it, but only to wealthy Chinese.

The beggars. They were now thick in the main streets. Every day the police would descend upon them with sticks, push them back into the small lanes. They seeped out again. More every day.

Corpses.

The scheme of the government for creating a new strong dollar failed. People who had lost their small gold hoard were angry. Nanking's big bureaucrats were now squeezing capitalists and bankers like Father.

Second Uncle, the financial brain of the Family, strove mightily to keep the Family financially afloat. He was taciturn, wore long robes with collars much too big for his thin neck, and had two long streaks of folded skin from nose to chin. His digestion was poor and he smelt of the herbal medicines he took. But he did manage to bypass the bureaucrats, or to bribe them efficiently.

As for Third Uncle, Father's young brother, he was a mathematician and went about in a dream. He had numerous children by a nice faded wife who played mahjong all day and half the night, only interrupting herself to breed another baby. And one day he did not return home.

It was discovered that he had been passing anti-government pamphlets and, being dreamy and vague, had done so standing on the bridge across the river, in broad daylight. The security police had seized him and thrown him into the river, bound and gagged and with a stone tied to his chest.

From habit, for an article which might never be printed, Stephanie took notes on what was happening to their world. . . .

Chiang Kaishek's top ministers now sent their wives and children away in U.S. planes loaded with furniture, antiques, jewelry, vases—and gold bars. The planes took them to Hongkong,, to America, to Brazil, where they bought land and houses and put their children in schools.

The Communists advanced, streaming towards middle China from the north. The cities of Manchuria fell to the People's Liberation Armies, and the businessmen and capitalists of the north started to move into Shanghai.

A stubborn myth persisted. Shanghai would never fall to the reds: it was the city of capitalist enterprise, of lucre and greed, crime and corruption, drugs and gangs and prostitution.

It was a brilliant city, with the largest concentration of intellectuals in China.

It was the most westernized city of China.

"Shanghai will be safe. The Communists will not dare to take Shanghai. The West will never allow it . . . it will come under United Nations protection."

Land values went up in Shanghai; the price of houses soared, the sky was the limit.

By May 1948, Yong was paid in rice, with an additional monthly stipend of money which allowed him to purchase two packs of cigarettes for Stephanie, who smoked occasionally. And she laughed uproariously, then he laughed—then they both rocked with laughter when he brought her his chief surgeon's wages for the month.

Father brought home Mr. Keng, benign, round-faced, chuckling. Keng Dawei was the Business King of Shanghai. Of all the capitalists in China (fifty thousand among nearly five hundred million people), Keng was one of the wealthiest.

Uncle Keng went directly to the heart of the matter. "I asked my dear friend," indicating Father, "to allow me to call," he said to Stephanie. "I happen to have met Mr. Ryder when I was recently in Dallas. A most successful man." He beamed.

Stephanie nodded uncomfortably at mention of her father.

"I'm sending one of my good-for-nothing sons to Texas to study oil prospecting. China will need technologists for the oil industry. Your father was most kind, promised to take my son to one of his oil fields. We must think big, think far, think to the day when today's small troubles are past. . . ."

Small troubles? thought Stephanie. . . . A universe in shambles . . . the now virulent anti-American processions almost daily . . .

"Temporary troubles," Keng said suavely. "I am not too worried. Already, I know, your country is withdrawing its Marines. . . . True, there will be rough passages," he beamed again. "But we've had many rough passages in China's five thousand years."

"Uncle Keng is the head of our chamber of commerce," said Father. Meaning that Stephanie should listen very carefully.

"History in China is a continuum through many contradictory situations," said Uncle Keng. "The contenders fight, but in the end, the result is neither to the victor nor to the vanquished. Victory belongs to those who have endured, who have known when to bend, when to straighten up. We shall have to bend for a while, but only to straighten up later. The important thing is to serve our country and our people.

"Chiang Kaishek has finished himself off. The next ruler will be Mao Tsetung. Look at me. I am a big capitalist. But I shall cooperate with Mao Tsetung."

He beamed again at Stephanie. "It is difficult for a Westerner to understand this," he said gently. "But you are very intelligent, you *will* understand."

"Uncle Keng has one son in the United States, one son with the Communists, and he will probably place a nephew to follow Chiang Kaishek to Taiwan," said Yong. He said it without rancor or accusation or even indignation. It just was the way it was.

They lay in the classical canopied bed where every night, for hours, they would talk, make love, talk again. Stephanie suddenly felt very American. Mention of Heston Ryder had triggered it. She seemed to withdraw into herself, there to discover another Stephanie lying in wait for her . . . a Stephanie full of righteous principles, who found it bewildering that Uncle Keng should use his progeny as pawns and safeguards, whatever the future might bring . . .

"I'd like to know why Uncle Keng went to see Dad."

"I think my father mentioned your name; Uncle Keng was going to the United States, he had business there."

"You should have told me. . . ."

"It wasn't certain that Uncle Keng would go to Dallas," said Yong reasonably.

"I wonder if Uncle Keng realizes how Dad hates the reds," said Stephanie. "Why, the very idea that Uncle Keng, a capitalist, is ready to work with them is unthinkable. . . . I bet he didn't tell this to Dad."

"Of course not," said Yong, seeing nothing wrong in Uncle Keng's many-sided conduct. It was the Chinese way. Survive all storms. Only China mattered, and for her sake, General Yee maneuvered. For her sake, Soong Chingling, the aristocratic and beautiful sister-in-law of Chiang Kaishek sided with the communists. And the Jen family. . . .

Yong slept. Stephanie reasoned with herself, tried to come to grips with another way of feeling, of thinking. But something in her rebelled, an unmelting core of defiance.

Daily the city's foulness increased. Cheerfully, Father went on pretending he was doing business; for to appear uncheerful would have upset Mother, and Mother was his universe, his heart, the marrow of his bones. He would not bring a frown upon her face. But of course Mother knew.

Father and his brother, Second Uncle, sought out all means of survival for their bank. Second Uncle was involved in obscure deals with a certain foreign religious mission, which benefited from ample foreign exchange and also owned pawnbroking shops. A trickle of needed foreign cash thus reached the enterprise, but it was not enough.

Stephanie returned one day from the Nantao district of the city, where she had witnessed a food riot with crowds assaulting the closed and barred gates of a hoarder's shop. Michael Anstruther had been with her, and his behavior taught Stephanie how to survive in a hostile and alien crowd. So long as she did not try to take photographs and remained at the edge of the gathering, it was all right; when the crowd grew restive, she and Michael had quietly walked away.

As Stephanie entered Willow Pool Garden, two men in long robes with black fans tucked into their collars, and behind them two coolies carrying a large vase, were walking out of the house. The vase with the pomegranate design was one of a pair in the living room. Outside was a wheelbarrow with straw and cardboard, in which the vase, well wrapped, would be laid.

Stephanie walked to Mother's pavilion. She stood outside the transparent matting covering the door. . . .

"Mother . . ."

"Oh, dear daughter, come in."

"Mother, why are you selling the vases?"

Mother looked at her, a little startled by Stephanie's abruptness. "Sit down, my dear daughter, you must be tired. . . . Bring tea for the young mistress," she told her maid.

The tea came. Mother, lifting her cup, politely signaled Stephanie to drink.

"Dear daughter, you know the government has passed an edict against gold bars. I still have a few, but very few . . . terrible are the bribes, the extortion . . . Father has to be careful, especially since he is not in the government."

Again she sipped, inhaling the scent of the tea. Outside the willows whispered with a small wind, rising and falling from nowhere.

"So we thought . . . we would sell the vases; one has gone, they will come back for the other. . . ."

"No," said Stephanie forcefully. "No. They are lovely . . . you cannot part with them."

She turned to look at the room. "How can you part with anything here?"

"They are only objects."

"Why won't you let me give you, say, a hundred dollars a month? We spend almost nothing, my royalties have come in and I've got several thousand dollars. . . . Mother, please . . ."

Mother shook her head. "You and Yong may need it."

"But we've lived here almost three years at your expense. . . . Why won't you let me do this, please, Mother?"

Mother's face was both joyful and sorrowful. "Oh, daughter Spring Snow, I wish they had not driven me into that embroidered palanquin when I was sixteen. . . . Then I might have worked as you do, and I could hold my head up. . . ."

"You're working all the time. You are the very heart, the bloodstream of this House; you keep the whole Family going. Everything you do . . ." Stephanie shook her head. "All the parties you gave for me . . . to make me feel accepted . . ."

"We cannot afford many parties now," said Mother, a little rueful.

"Please," said Stephanie, "*please* let me help."

Mother then made a very young gesture. She placed her hand gently upon Stephanie's arm. "My son has chosen well," she said. "He has chosen . . . my successor."

Stephanie looked at those hands, so pale. So strong. Mother had taken life strongly in those pale hands. She wove skillfully a web of living. Even Stephanie was now enmeshed in it. She had become so much part of the Family it would hurt her to be torn from them. . . . Strange, she thought, that I feel nearer to this Chinese woman than to my own mother, Isabelle. And yet Isabelle too, in her own way, had a claim upon her. With the help of distance, with the maturity of the last three years, Stephanie understood Isabelle much better, knew why her spirit had shrunk upon itself. Because Heston Ryder had given her too much wealth, and too little tenderness.

"Stephanie, do you not sometimes want to go back to America to see your family?"

"Of course," said Stephanie. She straightened her shoulders. "But I don't want to leave Yong. . . . He's so busy, it wouldn't be fair . . ."

"Then Yong must arrange it."

And Stephanie remembered that Yong had mentioned casually, about a week ago, that there had been a proposal from UNRRA that he should spend three months in the United States, on a medical tour. . . . "Oh, that'd be great," Stephanie had said, excited and happy.

"Three years is a long time to be away from your parents," Mother continued. "And with the little one coming . . ."

"Oh cripes," said Stephanie. "How did you know?"

"It's your hair, your eyes, your skin . . ." said Mother.

"Is there anything that isn't known to you in this house," said Stephanie, laughing. But she had wanted to tell Yong first. She had wanted to tell him that Dr. Wu had examined her.

"Petunia noticed . . ." murmured Mother.

"Of course." Alert Petunia had noticed. Stephanie had missed a period.

She *had* become a little homesick. And Mother had known. And that is why Yong had mentioned so casually UNRRA's invitation . . . Mother had already talked to Yong. . . . Would they always, always be a step ahead, always arrange and plan, arrange her life for her?

244

twelve

COLONEL Tsing, he of the bristling antenna sense, now in charge of countering Communist infiltration, had a brilliant idea: the creation of spurious Communist cells in Shanghai, where the red underground was loose and scattered.

Because the scheme needed a fair amount of money, Tsing had approached the Americans.

The old Office of Strategic Services (OSS) had given birth to the Central Intelligence Agency. In Shanghai, two lean, greyhound-handsome young men were running its embryo branch from a nondescript office on Bubbling Well Road. By the end of 1947, Washington had decided that the CIA should work closely with the Kuomintang secret service.

Funds were forthcoming. But Tsing had superiors, and a lot of the money stuck to their palms on its way to him.

Another brilliant idea came to Tsing. He discussed it with Lieutenant Colonel Hsu Towering Cloud, now a trusted subordinate.

"Realism is the essence of a wise man's conduct," he began, and Towering Cloud nodded in eager compliance.

The military commanders were restive. Especially those left in outlying areas with the riffraff forces, while the elite divisions sent to man the coastal cities benefited from American weaponry, uniforms, and finance.

However, the commanders could and did establish their own territories, extracting food and money from the cities and villages under the control of their divisions, now turned into personal armies.

It was possible for these men to prosper—and make

possible Tsing's own plans for the creation of an under-ground.

Drugs. Heroin.

The military commanders in the interior would provide the raw opium needed. On the hill slopes of Szechuan and Yunnan, miles and miles of poppy fields swayed in the breeze.

The soldiers would make sure the opium would be harvested. The officials of the Transport Bureau would ensure it being brought down-river, to Shanghai.

And everyone would cash in on the bounteous crop.

The Triads would collaborate. Both the Green and the Red Triads. They had a network all over China. All over Southeast Asia. Wherever there were Chinese, there were the Triads. In every Chinatown in America as well.

On his return to Shanghai, Lieutenant Colonel Hsu had been welcomed back by his brethren of the Green Triad, one of the most powerful of the secret societies. His father had belonged to it, and so had Chiang Kaishek.

The Triads had not only survived the Japanese invasion but expanded their operations into the heroin trade in all the occupied cities.

With the return of the Kuomintang, the drug traffic was muted for a few weeks; but swiftly the Triads restored their old alliance with the Kuomintang officials.

To begin training anti-Communist Communists, the Triads would be invaluable.

The Triad heads were realists. They were already preparing for the possibility of having to travel abroad, very shortly.

But not everyone could leave. The links must be kept alive. Couriers must be trained who would know how to evade all capture. Those who remained would have to endure, perhaps for decades, until the Triads could rise again in China. Hence they agreed that some of the "brothers" must become Communists.

Hsu began in a cramped, dusty office with two desks, two chairs, and one telephone. The small company was called the Crystal Import-Export Company; it ran loans and discount bills for several small trade unions in the Chapei district of Shanghai.

"No intellectuals," Tsing warned. "No students. And no dealing with big capitalists."

There was a loose web of people of wavering allegiance, neither Communist nor Kuomintang. They could be approached by well-trained simulators, agents with long experience of Communists. They would be trained and then "adopted" into the "underground," told they had become Party members. . . . "They must genuinely believe they *are* Party members," said Tsing. "We must borrow the red bandit wind to sail our own ship."

Crystal helped relations between workers and employers. It gave loans, did not collect contributions. Its members talked of "the patriotic united front" and the "liberation forces." Within a year it had succeeded in sending out couriers to several bona fide pro-Communist unions in the city underground with needed foreign exchange and gold. Thus good relationships were created. The Party needed gold and foreign money, especially U.S. dollars, and didn't enquire too deeply as to where it came from.

Hsu Towering Cloud became two people. Himself, and Party comrade Hsu Build-the-City. His fervor was great. He studied, devoured Communist literature. At times he almost felt he was a *real* Communist.

By the summer of 1948 the Liberation Army had overrun Shansi province and successfully persuaded its silver merchants—whose traditional trade had swung along the great Silk Road to India, to Persia, to Egypt—to cooperate with them.

The Kuomintang, on its return in 1945, had started confiscating silver, but the Communist armies who now marched in had refused to take even a token ingot.

So the silver merchants sent representatives with the Communist teams to talk with the capitalists of Shanghai.

"See," said the quiet and sober Party men, "you have nothing to fear from us. We *need* you capitalists. China needs you to progress. In Manchuria, the People's government is paying the debts of capitalists who went bankrupt! If you cooperate with us, we shall prevent your workers from striking, from occupying your factories and your houses. Ours is a new democracy. Capitalists are an indispensable part of our new democracy. . . ."

In Shanghai the capitalists, who were also patriots, were swayed. The cotton yarn king, the flour king threw in their lot with the Communists.

"We love our country first. . . . Our country needs us. Without us *they* cannot rebuild China. . . . We love our country. . . ."

Hsu Towering Cloud continued to love visiting airports.

To go to the airport, to watch the huge silver birds take wing . . . At least once a month he would indulge in this pleasure, gazing at planes soaring into the splendor of the sky, and dreaming.

Would he ever work himself into a position where he could collect enough money and authority for a plane ticket, a passport, a duly authorized one with the necessary visas?

Hsu feasted his eyes on the planes and dreamt of going to America. There to work for the CIA.

He also dreamt of foreign women. One saw them at the airport occasionally. One day, he must have a foreign woman . . . taste what it was like to penetrate, to smell a foreign woman, hear a foreign woman scream under his thrust, his mauling . . .

One day, Hsu entered the hall at Hungjao airport. Standing at the ticket counter was a foreign woman in a white dress. Her back was to him but there was something about her hair which stirred him . . . suddenly his heart was beating hard, and saliva came into his mouth.

The woman turned, looking around the hall. Her eyes fell on him. She looked away, then back at him. Not quite recognition, but puzzlement, a search for a face in her mind. He did not move. He could not drag his eyes away from her. The woman turned back to her companion. A Chinese, a slim man, filling in forms at the counter. She talked to him. Hsu turned, walked away swiftly. Out of the airport, into the sun, towards the guarded gate and out.

She had recognized him.

"I could have sworn I've seen that man somewhere," said Stephanie to Yong.

"All Chinese look alike," said Yong jokingly. He had turned at Stephanie's bidding, glimpsed only Hsu's back.

Stephanie persisted. "But I'm sure I've seen him, and he also knew me, he walked away."

Several hours later, in the Dakota, waking from a doze, Stephanie remembered.

"Yong . . . that man, that was the officer who hit me, in Chungking. . . . He's shaved his mustache, that's why I couldn't tell at first. . . ."

"Do you remember his name?" Yong groped in his memory. Had Colonel Tsing ever mentioned his name during his interrogation?

Stephanie shook her head and felt a cold shiver down her back. *Someone is walking on my grave.* Yong guessed her disquiet and squeezed her hand. "He cannot hurt us now, Stephanie. Never."

"He cannot hurt us," she repeated, comforted.

The lean, greyhound-elegant American in the small building on Bubbling Well Road pored over papers and documents.

"Married in Yenan . . . then registered again as married in Shanghai . . . registered also with the U.S. Consulate as married, September 1945 . . . I'm afraid they're well and truly married," he muttered.

"Check. See who they'll be contacting back home," said the other, who was just as lean, if more casually dressed.

"Apparently he's a whiz in surgery . . . invited by a Dr. Sam R. Dean, top surgeon at Mt. Sinai. Through UNRRA."

"You know what these eggheads are like. . . . Let's check Dean."

"Wonder how Heston Ryder will take it. He won't have anything to do with a red. . . ."

"He may get his Chinese son-in-law a good job in Dallas—most young pinks settle down once they begin to make some dough."

They were unprejudiced, meticulous. Their job to keep an eye on the politics of Americans in China. Stephanie Ryder, Mrs. Jen, was on their list of people to watch.

Heston Ryder welcomed his Chinese son-in-law with a nod and unsmiling blue eyes. Then he embraced Stephanie, and with an arm around her, took them to his car, a splendid silver Lincoln.

"Well, now, I didn't want to worry you, baby, so I didn't tell you . . . your mother's had a small operation, nothing to worry about . . . she's resting at home."

On the smooth highway which led to the city, Heston did his usual monologue. He had dressed to match in fawn pants and boots, a beautiful ten-gallon hat. He was acting the cowboy come to town. His eyes were flinty, his speech pleasant.

"Dallas has grown a lot more in the three years since you've been away, Steph." In front of them were the new factories; once again elegant cranes crowded the waiting sky. Heston pointed out this or that building, citing figures crisply.

"This is the biggest mill . . . and oh, here we've got the refineries . . . of course, we ain't big yet, only four hundred thousand of us in Dallas, but we're going to beat everybody you all wait and see. . . . They won't be calling us rednecks much longer, honey."

He's leaving Yong entirely out of the conversation, Stephanie thought resentfully, and turned to smile at her husband.

Heston was watchful, his whole skin aware of the other man, the man who possessed, owned his daughter now, to whom his daughter smiled (and oh, the sweetness of that smile rent him), who had made his daughter pregnant. . . .

She had written: "At last I've got what Victorians used to call Happy Tidings. I was just beginning to wonder whether there was anything wrong, knowing how keenly everyone expects babies, *loves* babies here. I guess my in-laws practiced heroic restraint."

A wave of furnace heat surged in him when he thought of it . . . in Stephanie's belly, a yellow brat . . .

Heston saw his daughter Stephanie give Yong a look, a smile. "Relax" said the smile, the look. "Don't worry . . . it's only Dad." He felt a shock of pure hate course in his body.

"Well now, we're getting into Dallas. . . ."

They passed the Ryder skyscraper. Heston made no sign; he waited for Stephanie to point it out to Yong.

"That's Dad's building," said Stephanie to Yong.

Courteously Yong thrust his head through the window and said in English, "It is magnificent. The greatness of technology."

The car went down Armstrong Parkway, purred forwards past the splendid houses which were just beginning, came to the gates of Ryder House, and went up the long avenue through wooded grounds to the mansion, built as a mixture of Schönbrunn castle and the Trianon at Versailles.

They walked through the hall and the main reception room to an elevator which took them up to Isabelle's apartments on the second floor.

Paintings of old and contemporary masters on the walls. Carpets underfoot. Lustrous magnificence. A house built in such meticulous detail, with such perfect material, that not a stone would move, no piece of wood would splinter or creak for many, many years.

Isabelle's bedroom. The alcove, the canopied bed raised high on a platform, swathed in brocade, fluted pilasters copied from a royal couch. The painted ceiling. And Stephanie could not help thinking, Dad's just gone overboard . . . . it's too much. . . . . The loot of centuries. The spoils of museums and palaces. A surfeit of treasures . . . .

In the middle of the huge bed, under a silver and gold brocade coverlet, Isabelle, shriveled, shrunk, her hair carefully done, her face made up.

"Oh Mom," Stephanie came forward. "Mom, you didn't tell us you'd been ill. . . ."

"Nothing much, my dear. I'll be up very soon. So this is your husband." She smiled at Yong. Her smile made her young, soft, a little eager.

Yong bowed and said: "Mother, my parents have asked me to convey to you their warmest regards."

He and Stephanie had brought presents for Isabelle and Heston. An old chest, inlaid and carved, a screen fashioned of silk *kesu*. Woven into the silk was a tale of love and sorrow, of a poor scholar and a love betrayed. For Heston there were two flamboyant phoenixes of pure white jade. Reverently Yong unpacked them himself, with highest courtesy presented them.

Isabelle lay back, smiling at Yong. "I am so glad you came, Yong. We must have a long talk . . . as soon as I am well. . . ."

Then they were in their own suite of rooms, walking on soft and beautiful carpets, the walls covered with silk damask.

"Yong," said Stephanie, "I'd have liked you to see our old house . . . there were magnolias in the garden, and white oaks. All of this is . . . just too much." Here the view from the windows was on a Versailles style park, with statuary and fountains.

"Your father is the emperor of a new, vigorous dynasty," said Yong. "All such founders have ransacked the world for treasure. It is a law of nature."

And then, "Your father loves you very much. I must make him accept me. For your sake, and for the sake of our child."

The child, Stephanie thought, awake but still.

The outside night spawned a million whispers, the murmur of a thousand insects. Through the open, screened windows came the night air, dispelling the odorlessness of massive entombment. Yong, who slept lightly, turned on his stomach; and then without waking, turned on his back again.

Her wonderful, considerate, young husband! Whose child she carried with such happiness. Who in the deed of love had so amply satisfied her. "Who taught you how to make love, Yong?" she would tease.

"You . . . and an old man called Lao Dze," he had replied, "who lived twenty-five hundred years ago." And went on to describe Taoism, the perennial philosophy, the one Confucius had fumed against so savagely. For Tao placed the female as the matrix of creation. Tao taught that man must learn of woman, letting the unconscious self take over. Tao had taught the inner eye of love. "You created me, Stephanie," Yong said. "*You* gave me all the magic of the universe. Without you I would wither."

And Stephanie had felt secure, as if love was a guarantee against a world of hate.

She knew it when around her she saw other women.

Women who were inculcated, molded into accepting a sense of inferiority, which stuck to them like hair shirts. Isabelle in this enormous house which was a monument to Dad's power, decaying quietly, her hands heavy with diamond rings, her eyes ringed with blue. It was awful to see her smiling so resignedly.

Just before bedtime Stephanie had gone to say goodnight to Isabelle. They talked about the child to come.

"Are you glad, Stephanie?"

"Yes, Mother, oh yes . . ."

"And your husband?"

"Yong . . . oh, he was nearly crying with . . . with emotion. Chinese men don't think it unmasculine to weep," she hurried to explain. It was the house, the presence of Dad, a weight upon her, compelling her to explain Yong all the time.

Because Yong, in this house, was not . . . was a trifle lost.

"I'm glad God has given you this child, Stephanie. I think He means the child and you to do His work in China."

"Oh Mom, you know I'm not religious-minded. . . ."

Isabelle lifted a hand. "My child, God's will is to lay a Calvary upon us . . . and your way also will be a Calvary . . . with a mixed-blood child."

She had said it.

Mixed blood.

Stephanie had heard it before. In Nanking. At a party. Some American woman, to her husband: "But we can't have him at our party, dear, he's a *Eurasian.*"

A Eurasian . . .

The British in Shanghai called them half-castes.

The Chinese called them mixed blood, as did the French.

She had seen them in Shanghai. There were a good many of them in Shanghai.

The girls. In the dance halls, in the bars. Very beautiful, striking. But . . .

She remembered that evening in Shanghai, in the Family House that was so exquisitely a blend of garden and room, that was its own soliloquy with the Universe. Yong had come walking through the first and second courtyard, along the small gallery which curved as it followed an invisible meridian, to where Mother and she sat, waiting for him.

Thus sitting, they resembled those figurines embedded

253

in lacquer on the chests and the screens. Women sauntering amid the leaf and blossom of early summer. Stephanie
knew better now than to rush at Yong or expect him to kiss
her. Not in front of Mother. Or anyone. He bowed and said
formally "Mother" and then he was smiling at her, giving
her all of himself.

"Stephanie."

She heard the shadowless flowers of love in her name and
smiled, saying formally: "You are back." And the servant
had come with another cup of Dragon Well tea.

And Mother had said, leaving them: "I have to look at
Sixth Aunt's new dress. . . ."

New dress. Always the same bleached noncolor; Widow
had two hundred fifty gray dresses.

Yong had sat by her and said: "Shall I tell you how
beautiful you are?"

She put her hand in his. "Yong, I am going to have our
baby."

For at least ten seconds he had gazed at her without
speaking. And she had seen in him . . . she had seen it in
him . . . elation, happiness, exultation, but also . . . also
something else. Fear.

And then he had folded her in his arms, whispering: "Oh,
my love, my love . . ." And she had felt his tears on her
cheek.

Now, in the Texas night, she remembered that something
else . . . that winglike shadow, the beating of a wind-
grieved ghost. A muted specter. And within her she was
numbed by his concealment. He wasn't hiding something
from her. But he strove to *rearrange* himself so that she
would be reassured, unworried: and that was a kind of
lie. . . .

At the Shanghai hospital there was Dr. Wu, whose wife
was American . . . and Dr. Hsieh, whose wife was Belgian
. . . their children Eurasians . . . Beautiful and intelligent
children, happy couples. Their children went to school in
Shanghai. Were bilingual. They had friends. Chinese
friends. They also had American and French and other
friends.

It was ridiculous to worry.

And even if there were a few silly people saying things
about mixed bloods, about Eurasians, what did it matter?

* * *

They planned to go down to the ranch for the weekend. "I won't be riding because of the baby, but I'll show you our horses," Stephanie said to her husband. After three days in the house, Stephanie was feeling the tension. Like singing wires strung taut between two poles, something was never still within her. Like the beat of a serpent's heart within her—tension. She found it difficult to fall asleep. She woke up suddenly, too early.

Making conversation, trying to talk things out, only made it worse.

"Dad, in Yenan, they gave Yong a Mongol pony to ride because he had miles to go to the hospital and back . . . a whole valley to cross each time."

"In that case, he can do some riding at the ranch," said Heston.

Stephanie knew Yong would not be able to ride a big horse. There was a world of difference between that Mongol pony and Dad's thoroughbreds. But Yong was saying: "I'd like to try."

"We'll make it a stag party, then," Heston had said. Decisive. And in Stephanie rose tension, fear. Yong—and Dad's friends. All like Dad, tall, with strong bones, muscular. Their talk a code, telegraphing to each other. The handmade boots and the deceptively simple shirts . . . Yong would look so . . . alien surrounded by these tall, burly, vital men with their thighs knit by knowledge of horseflesh, their bright eyes and slow drawls. . . .

Yong was trying his best to talk to Heston. To have a normal conversation. He asked questions about America, about Texas. Heston replied, and somehow each reply ripped off a bit of Yong's skin.

"Now if you're interested in business, you should talk to your friend, Eddy Keng. He's working in our oil outfit . . . smart guy. He's going to stay here. Yeah, maybe you ought to have a talk with him."

"Certainly," said Yong humbly. And did not tell Heston that Edward Keng was being an obedient son, staying in America at his father's behest, his father, Keng Dawei, who would cooperate with the Communists.

It was heavy going. Yong lapsed into stiff stilted Chinese-

English when he talked to Heston. He uttered deplorable generalities. It made Stephanie quiver with irritation—at Yong, and at her father for causing her husband to diminish himself.

"Business is very important in America," Yong would say simplistically, and Stephanie felt her skin crawl.

"You said it." Heston, lean and handsome and virile, looking at Yong with almost undisguised contempt. "Know anything about business, Yong? Need it, you know. Where d'you think all the money we're giving your country comes from?"

"We are grateful."

"You've got yourself into the right family to get your learning," Heston would say, and his tone would imply that Yong had known Stephanie was the daughter of a wealthy man.

"Yong's father is a banker," Stephanie would interject furiously.

"So you told me. What's he plan to do now with his bank? Give it to the reds, or move to Hongkong?"

"My father does not intend to move," said Yong.

"Just knuckle under and get more of our boys killed, eh?"

"Dad!" said Stephanie and then stopped. *I must trust Yong to handle this himself.* "I'm going upstairs to see Mom and let you men chew the political cud," she said, thinking, How heavy-handed I'm getting. And she walked out, feeling sick.

When she returned Yong was walking alone in the garden, looking with placid interest at the roses. He looked so much like his father, with that face which concealed hair-trigger emotion, that Stephanie felt her insides wrench. The Chinese speak of emotion as feeling their entrails cut, and it's true, it's the belly, not the heart, which is the churning vortex. That is where murder and love and all things godlike and beastly spring from. She put a hand on his shoulder, he turned to her with a cheerful face. "I enjoyed talking to your father," he said, and so won a victory which was perhaps a lie, but a victory all the same.

That evening Dr. Webster and a Dr. Padrewski turned up for dinner, with their wives. John Webster had been Stephanie's doctor for many years, and Stephanie felt at ease with him. Padrewski was a surgeon in the new hospital. Ryder Corporation had created a medical trust fund, and a new

256

wing, the Ryder wing, was being built with a hundred beds for surgical cases. Padrewski was the head of that unit and anxious to make a good impression upon Heston.

Seldom had Stephanie seen her father so virulent, though his tone remained polite. He chose to speak of what America had done for the world, of the blood spilt in the wars for freedom, of America's magnanimity towards Japan. It was a great paean, and a true and moving one. But he then went on with a denunciation of Bolshevism, fellow-travelers, and reds in America; Stephanie could hear the streak of cold paranoia in his talk.

"They're undermining the very foundations of our society. Communism is eating its way into our homes, crawling into every institution—even sacred ones. It's even gotten into the churches. Some of those missionaries . . . "

Webster was conciliatory. "Well, Heston, we're the giant of the economic world. . . . I don't think we should worry too much. . . ."

"I think we should, John. . . . In the hospital here no one should be employed who isn't loyal . . . there should be a loyalty oath, like in Washington for federal employees. Everyone checked before getting a job . . . that'll stop some of the rot. . . ."

Stephanie felt the now familiar bitter taste rising in her throat. Nausea. Though addressed to the table at large, her father's every word was a rapier thrust at Yong—a thrust, and a challenge. A challenge she silently screamed at Yong to rise to.

But Yong quietly continued to eat. He was having great difficulty with steak. It was too much, too large a piece, he almost gagged at the enormous mass of red meat on his plate. He was horrified by the rawness. He chewed a little of it slowly, cutting it into small pieces methodically. During a pause, he turned to Dr. Padrewski. "Dr. Padrewski, I've become interested in surgery of the blood vessels and nerves—the reattachment of severed limbs."

Eagerly Padrewski seized the opportunity. And now with technical talk and descriptions of the kind of surgery performed at the front in China under primitive conditions, with little or no anesthesia, the doctors' interest was aroused, and for a while they and Yong ran away with the conversation.

After dinner, everyone went up to talk to Isabelle, who had elected to stay in bed and not join the dinner party.

Jimmy came down to the ranch, on leave from the San Antonio Military Academy. Jimmy was lean and long as his father was, but there was something still unshaped, tentative about his face. His hair was thick and hung in a golden cowlick above his gray eyes, eyes that were too easily troubled, Stephanie thought.

"Hello Yong," he said hesitantly. A pool of quietness seemed to surround them on the large verandah with its Mexican tiles, its white cane furniture, and its black servants laying the table for lunch.

When Heston came striding out of the Packard, he saw them: Jimmy, Yong, and Stephanie, sauntering under the trees by the paddock. There was a sound of young syllables among the leaves. He felt something tighten in him. Then Stephanie saw him, and he watched her lips move, saying, "Dad's here," before she cried gaily, "Dad," and walked towards him, her walk still graceful, swift, all of her flushed and juicy with the new life growing in her.

She hugged him and he said, "Hi there, baby," automatically.

And Jimmy, smiling that nervous smile of his which irritated Heston, said: "Hi, Dad."

Yong said good morning. Heston ignored him.

"Well now, Jimmy—how long you going to be with us?"

" 'Bout a week, Dad. I got leave . . ."

"Well that's fine, that's great. How you doing?"

"Oh fine, Dad." Heston frowned. Jimmy's report cards in mathematics weren't all that good. And he hadn't made either the football or the baseball team. . . .

"Seen your mother?" Isabelle had remained in the house in Dallas.

"Thought I'd go tomorrow," said Jimmy. So he'd arranged to come on to the ranch first, Heston noted. To see Yong and Stephanie.

Again that queer slap and recoil of rage in him. He felt it in his brain, too. As if he were being pushed out, by the three of them.

He looked up at the sky. Breathed slowly. "Going to see

some horses tomorrow at the Gants . . . ride down there in the morning. Y'all want to come? It'll be stag."

Stephanie said: "I'll follow in the car." And foreboding hit her in a wave of nausea.

"That's Yong's Family House in Shanghai."

They sat in the living room after dinner. Stephanie had brought back with her a great many photographs, including a few taken in Yenan. Yong on his small Mongol pony, looking like an inoffensive highwayman, with the desert plain and the gullies behind him and his fur hat askew on his head. "Wow," said Jimmy, grinning. "They're smaller than our Navahos."

"Look, Dad," said Stephanie, "that's our rockery, with the goldfish." She rose, placing the album on his knees so he could see it better.

Heston glanced and then yawned. "Guess I'll turn in . . . had a tough day."

Jimmy was laughing, a joyous sound. "Oh Yong, what's that you're carrying? A hen?"

"Goodnight, Dad," said Stephanie lightly. Too lightly. That tense, coiled feeling again, arching her spine, adding its false gloss to her too-wide smile . . .

Heston heard again Jimmy's laughter and Yong's voice and Stephanie's rich chuckle. A long time afterwards he heard them come upstairs to bed.

Stephanie had a violent attack of morning sickness the next day. Heston phoned Dr. Webster.

"It's perfectly natural," said Webster.

"I want ya to come, ya hear?" said Heston. And to his daughter: "I'll call the hospital. Fly down a specialist."

"No, Dad, please. I'll stay in bed. I'll be fine." She smiled. How could she tell Dad that it was tension, that it was her being stretched, racked between him and Yong, which made her throw up?

Heston took Yong and Jimmy. "Like you said, you can ride, so we'll give you a horse," he said to Yong. Jimmy had to loan Yong a pair of boots he'd worn when he was fourteen.

"Now just hold on tight, that filly's a mean beast," he whispered to Yong. The three went off together.

As soon as they had gone Stephanie felt better. She called up Webster. "Dr. Webster, it's Stephanie. I'm all right now. I oughtn't to bother you. . . ."

"Well, Stephanie, morning sickness is natural, but I guess if you feel a mite under stress it aggravates."

So Webster had noticed. "I'm sure I'll be all right. Yong and I will be leaving the ranch in a couple of days . . . we'll be going to New York." She chatted on. Webster said he'd drop in, late in the afternoon. Stephanie realized that he, too, was under stress because of Heston Ryder.

"I didn't know he couldn't really ride," said Heston. And added: "Not much of a man, is he? Can't even finish a good piece of meat."

Yong had fallen off the horse and broken his collarbone. The next two days Stephanie vomited a great deal. Not only in the morning. Webster and the specialist gave her pills and more pills.

"Yong, let's leave."

Yong looked at Stephanie, lying on the bed; the cicadas' shriek rose and fell outside.

"Stephanie . . . it is my fault. . . ."

So he knew.

That unbroken blandness of his . . . If only he would shout, or break something. If only he'd turned on Heston, saying: "The saddle wasn't strapped on properly, and you knew it. . . ."

Jimmy had mentioned it to her: "Hate to tell you this, Sis, but I think on the way back the cinch was loose—someone was trying to play a trick on Yong. . . ." It wasn't Dad. It must have been one of the other men. Dad didn't do mean things . . . but he probably knew. . . .

On the third day she swallowed twice the amount of pills which had been prescribed and announced that they would have to leave for New York day after tomorrow.

"Yong's expected at Mt. Sinai," she said. Hoping Yong would not contradict. He did not contradict. He did not react at all.

"What's the rush, honey? Don't you like it here anymore?" Heston, drawling, so dangerously courteous. And to Yong, "Guess Mt. Sinai isn't all that keen, anyway . . .

least from what I hear . . . They can spare y'all for a couple more days. . . ."

"But perhaps I can learn something in New York which I cannot learn here," said Yong.

"What the hell is he talking about?" Heston asked his daughter.

"Yong knows more about surgery than most of the people down here," said Stephanie, savage, fighting him, and angry at Yong for *not* fighting him.

"Now I'm hearing sump'n," said her father, emphasizing the cowboy look, the cowboy drawl, the cowboy oh-me-I-don't-read look.

They went back to the big house in Dallas. Isabelle was up and about. She looked better. She picks up when Dad's not around, Stephanie thought, as Isabelle sat with them in the endless living room, built to hold at least two hundred people, and asked polite questions about China.

Heston walked out. Which created both relief and unease. Jimmy became almost garrulous when his father was absent. And when Isabelle went upstairs, Jimmy and Yong stayed together, talking, talking. And Yong would explain things to Jimmy that Stephanie longed for him to explain to her father.

It was Jimmy who drove them to the airport, and hugged Stephanie, and shook Yong's hand repeatedly. "Gee, I sure do hope to come to see y'all. Now take care of yourselves . . . and write to me."

They waved and waved at Jimmy, and he waved back until the plane began its takeoff run and his golden head was no longer discernible.

When they arrived in New York, for the first time in ten days Stephanie felt free of that corset feeling around her ribs. Her nausea and vomiting improved immediately.

But a rift between herself and Yong had been created. It was there. No larger than the hairline crack in a porcelain vase, but there.

She had wanted Yong to lash out at her father, to stand up to him . . . but Yong had done none of these things.

Invariably he had smiled, evaded, and parried. He had been dignified, and courteous, had given in. Heston had insulted him. Yong had looked vague. He had told Steph-

261

anie: "Entirely my fault," as his collarbone was being strapped.

He hadn't stood up to her father, and she knew that Heston despised him for it. Heston had almost said as much: "Well, baby, have a good time in New York—hear it's full of fags nowadays."

"What d'you mean, Dad?"

"A lot of foreigners around, too, baby . . . just be careful, will you?"

They stayed in Isabelle's apartment. Stephanie told Yong how she had been there three years ago and how John Moore lived not too far away. But John was now in Southeast Asia, doing a major report on the rising Communist wave in French Indochina and Malaya. "What a pity. He's good fun, you'd enjoy him," she said.

And Yong caught himself before his face could change, and closed his mind, as he had closed it since arriving in America, refusing jealousy, anger, refusing to be flawed in his love for Stephanie.

Yong's broken collarbone did not prevent him from attending the surgery course at Mt. Sinai hospital as Dr. Dean had arranged. He watched operations, attended seminars and lectures. He brought back books and read and took notes till very late at night.

It was in New York that Stephanie began to sense the mood of America. Or rather to smell it. For it was nothing open, nothing unambiguous enough to hang on to. There was still the reassuring, comforting feeling that every opinion was counterbalanced by a contrary view, that all was okay.

But what she smelt was a kind of sourness, an intangible, inexplicable discomfort, like the faraway stench of vomit in a bathroom. . . .

America, America . . . what's happening here? She was aware now of something which she would not, could not acknowledge.

An oppressiveness . . . an inexplicable apprehension . . . something disquieting in the air. She tried to shrug it off. But it wouldn't be shrugged off.

She telephoned HERE magazine. The secretary at first seemed enchanted. "Oh, I've read your book," she gushed. "*And* your articles. I'll get Mr. Mandel right away." Three

minutes later she was back. "He's in conference just now
. . . he'll call you as soon as he's free."

Halway Mandel called back, cheerful, too cheerful. It
oozed out of his voice. "Stephanie, great to have you
back. . . ."

They lunched. A small Italian restaurant off Second Avenue.

"What's happening here?"

"Stephanie . . . look, it's a kind of fear." He said the
word. "At the moment there's fear—not only in Washington,
not only among all those who've got to take the loyalty oath.
. . . There's fear in Hollywood; actors, and script writers,
and directors are being investigated. . . . And I'm telling
you, *we're* also fighting . . . for a free press."

Fear. That was the name of the thing. Inescapable.

Like the smell of excreta in Chungking. Everywhere.

In the book publishing houses. Among writers. Scientists. School teachers . . .

Newsmen, some of them now out of jobs because of what
they'd written about China.

Nineteen forty-eight was a presidential election year.
"The Democrats are soft on communism" was the Republican slogan. And much of the American press had
begun to veer as a ship in ocean veers, with deliberate
speed, so that its course does not appear to have altered.

On August 3, Stephanie, walking along Second Avenue,
bought *Look* magazine and the *New York Times* at the store
on the corner of Fifty-second Street. A headline screamed
at her: "Could the Reds seize Detroit?"

Fear.

The House Committee on Un-American Activities began
a much-publicized investigation of "spies in the government." Beginning that August, being subpoenaed by
HUAC led to the loss of one's job.

"What's happening—oh, what's happening to America?"

Dick Steiner, now a partner in Steiner, Finkelbaum and
Mann, a law firm on Lexington Avenue, tried to explain:

"Things have changed a lot, Stephanie . . . when I try to
say that I was saved by *Communists* . . . well I'm not saying
it now. God, even Charlie Chaplin's in trouble." He gave

263

Stephanie his business card. "Keep in touch." He grinned. "If you ever need me, I'll be there." She knew he meant it.

Vance Marston, her editor, was out of town. Stephanie saw an associate editor, a plump brunette, who made her think of ripe plums. Who was sympathetic, engaging. Who took Stephanie's manuscript with an exclamation of delight. Who listened to Stephanie with glowing eyes.

Stephanie felt understood, comforted. "I think you're great. . . . As soon as Vance is back from his trip we'll get on with your manuscript. . . ."

A week later the manuscript was mailed back to Stephanie with a very friendly letter from Vance. He'd been *so* busy . . . really the pace of work was so intense . . . and he also had two children going to school (what that had to do with Stephanie's manuscript she never did fathom). "We've greatly enjoyed reading your new manuscript; it truly conveys a good deal about China . . . but after much consideration, it's been regretfully decided that your book does not really clarify the perspectives in China. It is also—forgive me for being brutally frank—too political in its approach." However, if Stephanie wished to rework the book, of course Marston House would be more than happy to have another look at it. . . . "P.S. Do call me . . . I'd love to take you and your husband to dinner. . . ." This in Vance's own hand.

Stephanie did not call. She felt emptied, weary.

At Radcliffe, prim Professor Woodward was being investigated by the House Un-American Activities Committee. He had been to the USSR, had written a small book: *Introduction to Modern Russian Poetry.*

Stephanie rang up her friend Camilla Waring. Courageous, brilliant, blond Camilla, of the impeccable Pennsylvania background, was organizing protest meetings in Woodward's favor. "Count me in," Stephanie told her. She would go to Radcliffe for the meeting. Thank God, she thought, there is *still* freedom to dissent in America. . . .

After the meeting Camilla took Stephanie home to meet her husband, Gene, a quiet, humorous man who worked as an engineer in a federal project concerned with hydroelectric power production. After supper Camilla tucked the two children into bed, put on some classical records, and they sat and talked. About China. About America. About the hysteria being created in America. About a Communist fifth column.

Stephanie had brought her photograph albums. She talked of Yong's family, of capitalists willing to accept the new regime for love of country. . . .

Gene shook his head, dubiously. "It's a mentality quite different from ours."

Nevertheless, Stephanie went back to New York relieved, happier than she had been for many days. Thank God, some Americans were fighting back. . . .

In New York people did not stare at her and at Yong when they walked out together, as they had done in Dallas on the sole occasion when she had taken him to Neiman-Marcus. There was, about New York, the comfortable oblivion of the big metropolis which does not care. Yong was making friends at Mt. Sinai; young doctors and their wives came for a drink and stayed for dinner. They pooh-poohed the panic, the conspiracy theory . . . "It'll all blow over," they said.

Yong's collarbone healed. The rift between him and Stephanie did not. Increasingly, Stephanie, steeped in American forthrightness, fought back against the rumors of spy rings and conspiracy. She was now into her sixth month of pregnancy, it gave her a tough invulnerability; she felt ready to fight anything on earth. And she wanted Yong to fight. To speak up for Yenan, for Communist victory in China, speak up and defend . . .

But Yong did not. He would avoid the issue every time. "I believe some of your own newsmen have told you the truth," he would say. But when asked how it would all end, he would smile apologetically. "I am not a politician."

It angered Stephanie; it was shirking. She remembered Dad's sneer of contempt. Why was Yong . . . so afraid?

For he was afraid. She knew it.

He lay next to her, scarcely breathing. *He's trying not to irritate me*. For she was always irritable now, snapping at him, and then sorry for having snapped.

And one night she could not bear the silence building a wall between them. She put a hand out and he was there; he had waited for her hand, her arm across the bed. And now he was holding her tightly.

"Stephanie, you think I'm . . . a coward."

"It isn't that . . ."

"It is. You expect me to be . . . a little more American. Less . . . careful."

"All our friends say exactly what they think."

"I am not American and I'm not sure our friends won't change. . . . Yes, I *am* afraid of what's happening. . . ."

"But if we shut up, it'll get worse."

"True," he said meditatively. "That is true."

"Yong, with Dad . . . you let him ride roughshod all over you. . . ."

"I understand your father well . . . *why* he cannot bear me." He sat up. "I understand, but I do not think *you* do . . . but it doesn't matter." Now he was detached. "Stephanie, in a short while things will change greatly. Sometimes I worry . . . that you should be involved."

"But I want to be involved," said Stephanie. "I love you, Yong. I'm going to have your baby. . . ."

He sighed then.

And was silent for a long while, looking into the future. Trying to see all that *might* happen, all the possible anguish in store. And he wanted to tell her: Perhaps we should consider . . . perhaps the baby should be born here. . . . But he knew that something stubborn and proud in Stephanie would consider this also a lack of courage.

"Oh Yong," she said, "hold me." And he was there saying her name, caressing her, and whispering that he loved her, loved her.

And because she was angry with her father, bone angry, and defiant and reckless, she said: "Our child will be Chinese, and American. And proud of being both. I don't want our child to feel ashamed ever, of anything. I think he'd better be born in our home, with your ancestors watching over him. Then he'll always be proud of himself."

Another book publisher, Alfred Zimmerman, to whom Stephanie had sent her manuscript, took them to dinner. At the Algonquin. Stephanie explained to Yong the place of the Algonquin in American literature, and while they ate some people came up to greet Zimmerman, who introduced Yong and Stephanie. "I want you to write for me, too, Dr. Jen," he quipped. "Surgery in the wilds of China."

266

He too dismissed the red conspiracy theory. "There are some paranoiacs about, but believe me, we're not all that crazy."

Stephanie signed a contract then and there, and Zimmerman paid her an advance of five thousand dollars.

They would be leaving soon for China.

A Chinese couple came from San Francisco, another from Chicago, to call on them in New York, for the Chinese grapevine worked even in America.

Yong would say: "Ah yes, he is the relative of a classmate of mine." Or, "Oh, this is a relative of a friend of my father." And once there were a charming silver-haired lady and her daughter. The lady was the aunt of the husband of Yong's mother's sister. . . . This was the Chinese diaspora, with its links of family and friendship. They came, came visiting, cheerful and neat and *never* talking politics. Polite and beaming at Stephanie, delighted with her obvious pregnancy. They brought gifts and gave letters to take home.

Arthur Chee and his wife Millie also came. Both were overseas Chinese, doctors with prestigious positions in a Los Angeles hospital. And both had decided to return to China. They asked Yong to help them return.

"We want to serve our country . . . we have to go back . . . we know it won't be easy . . . the life will be hard. . . ." they said. And they looked at Stephanie with respect. With admiration. "You have joined our people in this great adventure, to rebuild our country. We shall see you in China." They would be returning by the end of the year. They were starry-eyed. Their ears heard the wind of Destiny blowing, their hearts heard the thunder of Creation. In China.

In late September Isabelle came to New York to spend a few days with them before their departure.

"I wish I could go with you. I've always wanted to see China. Such a mysterious country . . ." Suddenly she was very French, reflecting the French mirage of China, the stereotype of a land both fascinating and fearful. Isabelle asked: "How many Chinese are there? . . ." And with a little laugh, "When I was a child, we were all made afraid of the yellow peril. . . ." and "Do you still bind the feet of women?"

And Yong smiled gently, reassuringly at her. He accompanied her to St. Patrick's Cathedral, standing by her during the service, kneeling when she knelt, though the awkwardness of the constant movements startled him. And Isabelle expanded in the fine-grained air of his attentiveness. Her spirit gathered itself, as a convalescent draws strength from simple food, an orange, a cream cake. And without that usual fatigue which swathed her words, she told her daughter: "You did well not to come with me to France, Stephanie, three years ago. It was atrocious."

The Count de Quincy, her uncle, who had given receptions in his chateau for the German military commander, now lived in exile in Spain. And his two sons had been shot.

"It was ugly, dirty, but it's better now, the Communists have been bridled," she said. "The Resistance was full of Communists, you know. But," she said quickly, "the Chinese Communists . . . they are different. . . ." She gave Stephanie a scapular of the Immaculate Conception and a Holy Image to Yong. "I feel you will both come to God," she said. "I feel it. Jimmy has, but he hasn't told his father. . . ."

Jimmy. They sat at ease, talking of Jimmy, their love centered on his fair head. Jimmy had written, had telephoned. It was raining in San Antonio and the academy was all mud. There was chapel every day. "My son will become a Catholic," said Isabelle.

"I'll be coming to see you both in China," Jimmy wrote. And, "Yong, I've been reading up on goldfish. . . ."

The day they left America the newspapers were announcing the fall of all of Manchuria to the Communists. "The collapse of Chiang's army seems total."

Seven armies of Chiang Kaishek, four hundred thousand men, with all their American weapons and arsenals, lost . . .

Once again, Chiang Kaishek was sending his wife to plead for help. But the American government would no longer give. The GIs were being evacuated, the U.S. compounds in Nanking emptied. Only the autumn wind made incursions upon the lawns, planted with imported trees.

The Family was at the airport to welcome them home. Father and Mother, Second Uncle and Widow, and the usual bevy of youngsters. Uncle Keng was also there, patting Stephanie's hand and saying: "Tell me, did you see my son Eddy in Dallas?" And there, oh surprise, was Meiling Yee, excitingly elegant in a long narrow gown of dark brown velvet.

"Stephanie, it's been such a long time. . . ." Meiling was with a tall bespectacled young man. "My husband Sung Weichang," she said. "He is a journalist."

Mother was subdued and beautiful, her eyes going over Stephanie quickly, shrewdly. *True, I am carrying* perhaps *the eldest son of her son.* . . . Stephanie felt Mother's appraisal and was not offended.

She and Mother and Meiling squeezed into the car borrowed from Uncle Keng and were driven back to the House. And there were her servants, Peony, Petunia, uttering little cries of joy: "First young mistress is back!" Their quick eyes also caressed the beautiful round curve of her stomach.

Tradition, courtesy, cocoon of silk swathed her. But still there was the small heart bite. Dad. He had been so abrupt on the telephone. "You're going . . . Well, good luck, baby. Say goodbye to your husband from me." And he'd hung up.

"I'll win him back," she thought, carrying her heavy body proudly. She smiled at Yong.

thirteen

CARS splashing, the *kwadze*, shaped like a melon seed, moored onto the shallow overhang at Ichang. The boatmaster paid the trackers, who dispersed swiftly to smoke their evening opium. Shouting, jostling beggars fought to carry the luggage of disembarking passengers.

Little Pond stepped ashore.

For months, for three Spring Festivals and three Autumn Moons, Little Pond had followed his mother's murderer. Learnt his name: Hsu Towering Cloud. Learnt he was from Shanghai. Had seen him leave Chungking, with others like him, when the downriver people had gone back downriver, after the Americans had thrown Heavenly Fire upon Japan.

Feeding on garbage, fighting rats for offal, Little Pond had grown strong with the ferocious will to live.

Now in this year of 1948, year of the rat, his strong destiny had taken hold.

The *kwadze* had been there, sail furled. Ready to go downriver from Chungking; its passengers waiting in the mid-cabin. On deck the sixteen trackers, the two line-clearers, and the three deck hands, with the pilot and the boatmaster. But one of the deck hands, a small boy, was busily dying. The boatmaster was shouting: "I'm not taking corpses"; and the trackers flung the body on shore. Little Pond stepped up.

"*Laopan*, Old Master, take me, I'm strong. Never sick."

"You'll eat too much," shouted the boatmaster after one look.

"*Laopan*, one bowl of rice a day is enough for me." Little Pond struck his chest, rounded his eyes.

He had boarded. He learnt quickly, zealous and deft as his mother had been. Chopping vegetables, washing dishes, cleaning the deck, washing the passengers' clothes. When the *kwadze* stalled, he waded with the trackers, rope across his shoulders, pulling, pulling the boat until he felt his guts would burst, until his shoulder was rubbed skinless by the wetted hemp.

Every foot of the Great River was legend: the grim rocks where dwelt the mother of Yu Wang, King of the Waters; the walled towns on the cliff summits, where bloody battles had taken place seventeen centuries ago; the Heavenly Ford where passports to Heaven were sold to travelers; the Iron Threshold, where every passenger girded himself with an empty barrel, ready to jump in the stream, to float till help came, as the pilot guided the *kwadze* between the boat-killing rocks.

Wanhsien City, the city of myriads, where the river loops between fantastic peaks. It was there that a man came to talk to Little Pond.

And Little Pond thought, Perhaps he wants what the boatmaster wanted.

For the boatmaster had spent himself on Little Pond's body one night, hurriedly, while the trackers smoked their opium and the passengers were asleep. And Little Pond had clenched his teeth and endured.

This man was bulky, portly, round-faced. He stood and watched Little Pond, who was washing a great mound of spinach. Little Pond was watchful. *What does this rich man want with me?*

The man asked: "Eh, *hsiao kwei*, little devil, how old are you? What is your name? Where are your Pa and Ma?"

"I am an orphan. My name is Liang. . . . My father was pressganged . . . my mother died . . . I am eighteen years old. . . ."

"When you get downriver, what will you do? Have you any relatives? Why did you want so much to go downriver, little devil?"

"I wanted to see new places."

The man nodded, walked away.

Past the Dragon Rapids, which legend said required three victims a day; through Windbox Gorge, the Great

River cannoning against its rocky confines until the boat rang with the sound; through the Witches' Gorge, shrouded in the color of night even at midday and echoing with the screams of its golden-furred monkeys. Through the Ox Liver and Horse Lung Gorges, dread black rock shielding the narrows through which the *kwadze* must slide, through Lampshine Gorge to Yellow Cat Gorge, to Ichang.

Ichang. Where the Great River broadened, broadened, became a tranquil and mighty stream, until it reached the city built on the sea: Shanghai.

At Ichang the man came to Little Pond again. "Are you going further downriver, little devil? This *kwadze* goes no further."

By now Little Pond had watched the man for fourteen days. Watched carefully. Noted his quietness. Noted he did not drink, nor gamble, was always agreeable to everyone.

"I do not know, Great Firstborn. For us poor people the morning does not pledge the evening."

"Little devil, I think you have something else in you." His hand drew a little circle over his chest, over the heart place. And Little Pond broke the dam of his tongue. He said:

"I want . . . revenge."

The man looked at him. "That is good. This is fine. All of us want revenge."

He took a few steps forward, looked back to Little Pond. "Come then," he said. And added: "I will not do to you what the boatmaster did."

And Little Pond followed Prosperity Tang into Ichang city.

The American educator Leighton Stuart, now a diplomat, turned to General Yee: "I must thank you for all that you have done. . . . Your help was most valuable."

"It is we who thank you. Your task was beyond that of any man," said General Yee, who sipped tea and thought, It won't be long now. Nothing can save Chiang Kaishek. He said to Stuart, "Your name will not be forgotten by the Chinese people, by your numerous students through the land."

Stuart smiled wryly. "General, they curse me now." It hurt him very much.

General Yee said, "Each of us has to fulfill a role, a destiny. What is important is to do what has to be done."

Something very frail, yet very determined, then arose in the educator. The words recalled to him his work, the work of half a century.

Fifty years in China. Now he would leave, but China was his bones, and all else would be exile. Here in Peking, the lovely city he loved so much, he had founded China's most prestigious university. Yenching University.

It was in 1918 that he had left the Presbyterian seminary in south China where his parents worked, to undertake the building of this Christian university in Peking.

He had had to battle the fundamentalists of his own missionary group, intent only on training theological workers, but he had won. Yenching University would train doctors, scientists, writers, a new and necessary elite for China.

Tirelessly, he and another American missionary, Henry Luce, had canvassed friends all over America for money. He had donkeyed, bicycled, walked all around Peking's walls, looking for a site to build on, finding only cemeteries, private graveyards, which could not be moved.

Then a certain Warlord Yee, the father of General Yee who was to become his friend, had helped him. An enlightened man, alert and vigorous and believing that China must change, Warlord Yee had convinced the governor of Hopei province to part with one of his properties. And Yee had persuaded China's most prestigious families to send their sons and daughters to Yenching University.

Seventeen of Warlord Yee's descendants had been students there. Meiling Yee had been one of the most brilliant students in her class.

Yenching. The beauty of its campus, the excellence of its teaching famous all over China. An integral part of American missionary enterprise, it had refrained from ramming Christianity down its students' throats. It was this respect for the non-Christian which had brought so many great Chinese families and their descendants to it.

But—"Your teaching has bred anti-Christ!"—thus had

one American on the missionary board welcomed Stuart on his last visit to his own country.

"God works in mysterious ways . . ." he had replied meekly.

But now, he felt his work had indeed bred . . . a monster.

In the summer of 1947, General George Marshall, exasperated and exhausted, had called Stuart. "Can *you* understand the Chinese? I can't."

He had then labored, trying his best to bring about peace, going on his knees to beg God for enlightenment. He had failed, as Marshall had failed. And now the people he loved reviled him as a double-crossing, hypocritical imperialist.

"They will need you one day," General Yee repeated. Yee had a vision of China which went beyond wars and enmities, beyond dogmas and regimes.

But even with fifty years of China behind him, this was impossible for Stuart.

How could the Communists one day need a Christian like him? "Ah. You will also need them," General Yee said, suave, eclectic, and thinking of the centuries to come.

Like the Great River, China's history was tortuous, full of meanders. General Yee would stay with his people as so many of China's intelligentsia were doing. For almost three thousand years these scholars had served their country, taken in hand every foreign invader, tutored with supple inflexibility every barbarian ruler—just as generations of gardeners trained a five-hundred-year-old pine to grow no more than six inches, to adjust to a miniature landscape.

That was China's immortality. Chinese culture had cannibalized fourteen foreign rulers. Would it also digest the doctrine of communism? Of course it would.

Back in the gloom of his living room, Leighton Stuart took his worn Bible down from the shelf above his desk and read: "Behold, the sower went forth to sow . . ."

The years fell off him; he was again the young ardent missionary, working in the field of grace, bicycling among the dilapidated graveyards around the fabulous northern city, searching for a piece of land to build a university.

The next step in the war would be the red conquest of the southern cities. General Yee flew between the two sides, knowing that there could be no truce.

The Communist guerilla group outside Shanghai, and the underground within the city, were organizing. When the Liberation Armies would pour down from the north, there might be a hiatus, vacuum, a time of chaos. The Kuomintang in their retreat might loot and pillage, sacking their own cities. Citizens' groups were organized to maintain order. The spread of cholera and other infectious diseases must be averted. Meiling, with the Red Cross and the hospital doctors, was working on a program to make the city's health safe. To ensure an orderly takeover.

"We want to avoid epidemics in the cities if there is fighting," said practical Meiling to Stephanie as the devastatingly cold winter of 1948 set in.

Perhaps it was Meiling's marriage to Sung Weichang, the bespectacled newsman, which had changed her, made her so energetic. Or perhaps it was the imminent victory of the cause she believed in.

Yong was as buoyed with joy as Meiling. He was busy readjusting the surgical section of the hospital, in case there were battles over Shanghai.

As for Stephanie, she was entranced by the marvel of her own belly. It was now the Universe, the Milky Way and all its stars. In the security of her body, bolstered by the daily adulation of the Family, she contemplated the war with a detachment which would later puzzle her.

Chiang Kaishek's government, now back in Chungking, continued to broadcast messages of victory. "The Communists will not take south China. The great river Yangtze cannot be crossed by them. South China will remain with Chiang Kaishek."

No one questioned the broadcasts, since no one believed them. Everybody was busily preparing to welcome the conquerors.

The schools were busy. A victory parade was planned for the Liberation Armies when they came to Shanghai. Triumphal arches of bamboo and paper flowers were being made, thousands of schoolgirl hands busily making the paper flowers. Thousands of boys rehearsed for the victory march, learning the Communist songs and dancing the *yangko* dance, the planting seed dance.

Stephanie's and Yong's son was born on Christmas Eve, December 24, 1948, the day the Communist armies reached Yenching University near Peking.

The birth was easy. The obstetrician, Dr. Wu, made it so with his unfussed calm. Mother made it so with calm acceptance. Everyone made Stephanie feel that it was a joyous enterprise that she was undertaking with great success. Every physical detail was greeted with approval. Every gush of pain was a salvo of triumph for Stephanie.

Mary Lee, the head nurse who looked after her, was Eurasian. White Russian mother, a Chinese father. She spoke five languages, had been engaged to an American captain, and then, just a week before their scheduled wedding, JUSMAG, the Joint U.S. Mission, had issued an order against fraternization.

"Quite a few of us girls were caught that way," said Mary. "Jack had already bought the ring . . . he was shipped away and I had the baby." The baby turned out blond, with blue eyes, and Mary called him Wenceslas. "I don't know why," she laughed. Mary Lee was disaster's child, and disaster had stalked her life. But she lived with formidable gaiety. "I laugh so I don't have to cry," she told Stephanie.

Stephanie's waters broke. She heaved and pushed and Mary heaved with her. It was the hospital rule not to allow relatives during labor but Mary, who had no rules in her beautiful, unbreakable body, squeezed Mother in for a short while, and Mother was so soothing that Stephanie smiled and felt nothing could go wrong. She thought of Isabelle, her own mother, and suddenly knew a great, overwhelming pity for her. Had Isabelle been surrounded with such care and love? Or had she been alone, terribly, terribly alone in that hour of bliss and pain? Or had she been terrifyingly surrounded with only technical, clinical precision, treated as an object to be scientifically observed? No Mother, no Mary Lee, no Yong whose face writhed with worry and love and anguish, until she laughed because he was so comically helpless in his desire to mingle his voice with hers, to strain with her, to push the new life into being with her . . .

I know now why Isabelle always felt I was a stranger . . . I see it now . . . she'd given birth to something not hers.

Dr. Wu said: "Now just one more nice good push, Mrs. Jen," and quickly gave her a whiff of ether. And then they held up the child, slippery and screaming, his wet scalp covered in smooth black hair.

"A son, it's a son," cried Mary Lee.

And Yong was there, his hair like a worn toothbrush, and she said jauntily, for now she wanted to laugh, to laugh, oh, the world was so beautiful: "Your son's hair grows just like yours, Yong."

"Oh beloved, my love, our child," Yong babbled incoherently.

"Seven pounds and four ounces. A big healthy boy. Now you must be sleepy, Mrs. Jen. And now I must go to midnight Mass. Isn't it wonderful, a Christmas baby . . ."

Mary Lee was enchanted. *Another one of us, another Eurasian.* Washing the child, putting him in his cradle, she crooned, "They cannot stop *us* . . . *they* won't stop you, will they?" And went back for a last look at Stephanie, sleeping the untroubled sleep of her triumph, before going to midnight Mass with a heart full of gladness.

On Christmas day, everyone in Shanghai knew that Christian Yenching University's professors and students had sent a delegation to welcome the People's Liberation Army. A triumphal arch had been erected.

The Communist armies bivouacked in the village near the campus and astonished everyone by their good behavior. They requisitioned no food, animals, or men. They even helped the peasantry carry loads, drive their carts. "We have never seen such an army before."

The People's Liberation Army did not enter Peking, but waited outside the city. Waited for the Nationalist commander, General Fu Tsoyi, to "see the light," to surrender gracefully, thus avoiding slaughter.

General Fu Tsoyi had to be given time. He had to pretend to defend the indefensible, while at the same time withdrawing his troops in good order. Must be given food and money for his soldiers. Must be allowed all face and dignity.

Yong explained this to Stephanie. "Graceful yielding to reality" he called it. Stephanie wrote a short article and sent it to *Time*. "The Chinese concept of victory and defeat, of loyalty to a cause, is different from ours." *Time* did not print her piece.

In January 1949, through an intermediary who was a professor at Yenching University, General Fu Tsoyi and the Communist commander of the Liberation Armies arrived at a satisfactory understanding.

Thus on January 23, the Liberation Armies entered Peking. Michael Anstruther was there. "It all looked so easy. The soldiers walked in. The last plane flew off as arranged, carrying away the remaining Kuomintang officials. All exits and entries beautifully timed, like a Chinese opera."

Father came decorously to see Stephanie every evening, bringing the newspapers with him. The official *Singtao*, the *Takungpao*, and the English newspaper, the *North China Daily News*. Over a cup of tea he entertained her with cheerful remarks and compared the articles, wildly divergent, in the three newspapers. The *North China Daily News*, sponsored by the British banks and Jardine Matheson, he found fairly reliable.

Mother came in a little after Father, always bringing with her a special dish to strengthen Stephanie, or a present, a knitted jacket, shoes, a cap for the baby.

They filled the eyes of their heart with sight of their first grandchild. It was Stephanie who, with an *amah* carrying her son, should have called on them, to show them the baby, to teach the baby reverence of elders, to pay her respects. But they reversed the tradition.

Mother seemed young, yearning, as she looked at the baby. "He is a spring wind blowing alive the frozen tree of my life," she said. Both she and Father would look at the child with ravishment, and Stephanie, moved by that love, would place the child in the arms of Father and say in Chinese:

"Little Thing, bow to Grandfather." And lightly press the dark head forward. "Bow to Grandmother."

They held that squirming parcel of new life, who gurgled and bubbled and caught their fingers in its tiny grip and looked at them with the squinting attention of babies everywhere. The whole room would become charged with emotion as Father, holding his first grandson, would say tremulously: "I think he has our chin, my daughter. . . ."

"Do you think so? He has your eyes, Father. . . ."

Ritual, ritual, compliments and courtesy, but oh, how fulfilling, how satisfying, renewing the bonds and making them bonds of love and care between the generations.

Mother held the child with concealed expertise. Renewing her own youth by contact with the baby. And then, fearful of appearing too possessive, she would hand the child back to Stephanie.

They called him Winter Treasure. It would be his baby name.

There had been a minor crisis on Stephanie's return from the hospital. She had insisted not only on breast feeding her son, but looking after him entirely, changing him and bathing him, walking him up and down when he cried. "But dearest daughter," said Mother, "it will tire you so much. We have procured an *amah*. *Amah* Mu is excellent with babies. She is waiting in the outer courtyard for you to see her. . . ." *Amah* Mu was clean, sober. She reminded Stephanie somewhat of Teacher Soo in Chungking. (Oh, where was Teacher Soo now? She had never replied to a letter Stephanie had written. . . .) *Amah* Mu had worked in American families. "The other American ladies *gave* me their babies to look after, *entirely*. They went out, they went shopping, they went to parties every night . . . I stayed at home with the babies and nothing ever happened to them. . . ." said *Amah* Mu, obviously feeling insulted. "I came to the Jen Family because the Family has an excellent reputation . . . how did I know that without trying me the young mistress would deem me unsatisfactory?" She had lost face. Mother soothed and pacified her. Told her that the young mistress was *very* young, and this was her first child.

"Of course, my daughter, it is most praiseworthy of you to do everything for First Grandson. But in a month or so you will want to go out sometimes, to see friends. You will want to be with your husband. You have a book to finish, as you told me. At least *Amah* Mu can wash the baby's clothes, watch over him when you go out."

For three weeks Stephanie refused to hand Winter Treasure over. She only allowed *Amah* Mu to wash the baby's clothes, to clean the baby's small room, partitioned off from hers by a screen. And then she caught a cold. And so did Winter Treasure. And Winter Treasure became a great howler, howled just for the fun of it, not because he was hungry, and Yong rose and walked him up and down half the night. . . .

Stephanie lay in bed, nursing her cold, and *Amah* Mu padded on noiseless cloth shoes and changed the baby and brought him to be fed at the breast, but only after she had, gently but firmly, tied a white surgical mask over Stephanie's nose and mouth. And Stephanie gave in. Her possessiveness diminished.

The hormones of motherhood had awakened in her a hostility to anything strange, anything different. For a while she had been totally repelled by the idea of *Amah* Mu's hands on her baby. But *Amah* Mu, who spoke an extraordinary pidgin American, interspersing Chinese words with "oh yeh" and "okay" and "goddam," was truly expert, and Winter Treasure liked her, and gurgled and laughed and thrived mightily.

On the twenty-fourth of January, the child's first month was celebrated as tradition decreed. Eggs were painted red, dozens of them. Were distributed to all relatives and friends; and a rejoicing feast was held, twenty tables, two hundred relatives and allied families . . .

Winter Treasure was formally brought forth to bow to his ancestors. Jen Yong carried him to the pavilion where lived the tablets of the Honorable Ones. Spring Snow walked by her husband's side, wearing a dress and jacket of pale embroidered satin, fur-lined. Father and Mother walked in front of them, and Father struck a bell, to call the attention of the ancestors, lest they might be distrait or busy at something else. He cleared his throat, called the Honorable Ones respectfully, and introduced Winter Treasure by his proper genealogical name.

The book of genealogy had already determined, for twenty-four generations to come, the stem and root of the ideograms to be used for names.

"O Venerable Ancestors, the name of your unworthy great-grandson is Forest," said Father. Forest was to be Winter Treasure's official name. Jen Lin.

Forest was a lucky child. The eight circumstances of his birth had been most propitious, and the chief astrologer, who sat at one of the tables, said that the child would only have two difficult passages to cross in his life. One would be at eight years old, and one at twenty-five . . . But the configurations of the planets were such that he would cross them, and each would bring him advancement.

When the meal was eaten and the guests had departed, Stephanie and Yong returned to their own pavilion, Yong carrying his son, and Stephanie said: "And now, darling, we've got to have his American side attended to."

Yong nodded. "Of course, we'll give him an American name too."

"I don't mean that," said Stephanie, "he must also be baptized, made a Christian."

Yong handed the baby carefully to *Amah* Mu, whose face had now been totally restored and who had received many small envelopes containing gifts (even ingots of silver and silver dollars). Yong spoke slowly, deliberately: "Some of my friends say a Christian is taught to despise his ancestors, Stephanie."

"Oh Yong, how can you believe this? I'm a Christian, and I don't despise my ancestors or yours. . . . Where on earth did you suddenly get that idea? Why, you've been working with Christian missionaries all your life."

Yong looked away. He had a way, like Mother, of abstracting himself, of not being, which was quite maddening.

Stephanie sat in her fur-lined robe, the beautiful robe which Mother had given her, her hand stroking the silk, while she waited for Yong to return to her.

She would wait no longer—not this time. "We decided our child would be both of us. Remember?" she said, trying to sound calm, to still the sudden tumult of her heart.

"I remember." Yong came back, partly. Then Stephanie knew that he was again trying to fit her, and her needs and desires, into a universe where she did not exist. She felt the distance between them growing.

Yong also felt it. . . . Since the child's birth he had been away much of the time. Besides his work at the hospital, there was the training of emergency teams in case the war should be carried into Shanghai. He was now also a member of the Democratic League. He attended political debates and came home very late every night, rising early to go to the hospital. And, since returning home from the hospital, Stephanie's conduct had changed. She had become so immersed in the baby. The attention, the homage, the cosseting, the adulation she received from the Family had spoilt her, made her imperious.

Yong was an adoring husband, a devoted lover; had always thought of Stephanie first, afraid to hurt her. But now he reacted to her suggestion, thinking of all the implications, striving to fashion the words in which something so alien might be acclimated.

New York. That night they had clung to each other, fearful that they might lose each other. Yong knew that Heston Ryder dominated a part of Stephanie's soul forever. He had accepted the fact, because it could not be changed. He had almost asked that Stephanie remain to have his child in America. Because then the child would have been safe from any evil which might come . . . But he did not tell Stephanie of his fears, because Stephanie would have considered it cowardice—or opportunism. Of course it was . . . opportunism. But for China, for China. Because China was a universality. But in New York, he had been unable to explain this to Stephanie. And since her pregnancy, she had seemed almost to shut off the outside world, to shut him off. . . .

Finally, he turned towards her. Her face was lovely, and the satin gown chosen by Mother suited her so well. There were blossoms embroidered all over the jacket, very pale pink and gold, and the sleeves were cuffed with embroidered white satin. . . .

Stephanie, the valorous, who had not hesitated to fling herself into his arms. She had chosen to return with him, against her father, trusting him, trusting love, angry with her own father because of him. . . .

He came to her and took her hands and brought them to his chest. "Forgive me, my dearest. I am very tired and somewhat troubled. Of course he shall be christened as you wish. I shall tell Father and Mother. It will make no difference to them. Only some silly relatives will grumble, but we shall ignore them."

"I just don't see what's wrong with it," began Stephanie.

And then burst out weeping, and Yong spent the next hour soothing her, soothing her . . . No, he had never meant his son *not* to be christened, but he had felt that to do so before the child understood what he was being committed to was not fair to the child. How could one be automatically forced into a religion?

"If he has to become a Christian, he ought to be christened twice," said Yong, hoping to lighten her mood, "once for your father and once for your mother, and since they are of different Christian churches, he must be able to go to both." In fact, this is precisely what the eclectic Chinese had always done. For, almost thirteen hundred years ago, they had lumped all the creeds together. No one felt treacherous or inconsistent if he was one day a Buddhist, the next day a Taoist, and on the third something else.

Stephanie laughed. "In the West people have died for such details as whether Christ was in a piece of unleavened bread or not." For a Chinese this fanaticism was incomprehensible.

And so they came together, and she was satisfied, and melted into tolerance. "I guess I've just been nervous." All fears and doubts seemed resolved as their bodies, once more solaced by each other, came together.

But later, Stephanie lay wakeful, thinking of Yong's reluctant agreement to let their son be part of *her* heritage as well as his own . . . would it always be like this? A struggle not to lose her own identity—not to be completely absorbed by the seductive world she had married into?

Stephanie asked Meiling to be Winter Treasure's godmother. "You've been to a Christian university, Meiling, so it won't be strange to you."

"I'm delighted and honored," said Meiling, and suggested that Leighton Stuart should be the one to christen the new baby. "It will give him great pleasure. He's not popular at the moment, of course, but he's a good man. I used to sing in the choir, *The Messiah,* every Christmas, when I was at Yenching University, and he always came around to say hello. . . ."

Leighton Stuart came to the Jen House one quiet sunlit afternoon. Only Yong and Stephanie, Meiling and Michael

Anstruther were there. Michael was godfather. Winter Treasure was baptized Thomas Heston James, and behaved very well throughout the brief ceremony.

Isabelle wrote: "Your father hopes you'll be coming back to America with your baby, as we hear that events are worsening in China." Jimmy was now in his second year at the San Antonio Military Academy. "I don't think he really wants to be an officer. I am convinced that he has a vocation." Isabelle clung to the idea that Jimmy wanted to become a Catholic priest.

Jimmy's letters were always cheerful, although curiously empty of any information about himself. He wrote: "I'm looking forward to meeting my nephew, Thomas. I'll get him a real cowboy hat and boots." He would joke about the academy. "They keep on making us run and run with our packs on . . . bet they don't do that in China." Always he would include a note to Yong, short, shy notes. "I'd like a letter in Chinese, Yong, and of course the translation, and could you send me a Chinese reader? I've decided to start learning the language so when I get to Shanghai I won't be a stranger. . . ."

Stephanie wrote back to Jimmy, wrote at length, wrote about everything. She sent photographs of the Family, of Yong and herself with Winter Treasure, of the parents and of the House; and Yong also wrote: "Dear Jimmy, I *do* earnestly hope you will come to see us . . ."

On the night of April 20 the Communists crossed the Yangtze to Nanking. A dark night with patches of mist. All along the front the artillery broke open the darkness with fire and sound, and the Communist boats pushed off. Ten divisions crossed to capture Chiang's capital city, as lines of lorries loaded with Kuomintang officers and their baggage, furniture, and families pulled out, headed for Shanghai.

In the afternoon the People's Liberation Army made an official entry into Nanking and was welcomed by a delegation of university professors and dignitaries.

284

Shanghai would be defended to the bitter end, said the Kuomintang government spokesman when Nanking fell. Henry Wong, nobly mendacious, assembled the pressmen to tell them that Shanghai would be another Stalingrad.

Yet the docks of Shanghai were piled high with goods. The wharves were full of people leaving or trying to leave with all their possessions, embarking for Hongkong and Taiwan, for the Philippines and for America . . . taking everything they could take with them.

Brigadier General Tsing came to Shanghai to take charge of the city.

It was a job he did not relish. The orders from on high were inappropriate, messy, changeful, and only antagonized the people even more. But Number One Big Wind wanted to "punish," to "strike fear and weaken the bones" of the surly discontented people.

Chiang had ordered a "scorched earth policy" for Shanghai; the sinking of all the small vessels and river craft; a barbed wire fence around the city.

It became quite commonplace to see workers and intellectuals shot down in the streets. A child who was wandering along the railway line, because he was feebleminded, was shot as a spy. He was eleven years old.

This is madness, thought Tsing. But he had to obey. Loyalty. The greatest virtue of all. He would remain loyal to Chiang Kaishek. Distractedly, he fingered the top priority air ticket to Hongkong in his pocket.

The Family looked after itself.

More relatives now sought asylum in Willow Pool Garden, knowing themselves threatened. Threatened because of Yong. No one said it openly, but everyone knew. Along with many members of the Democratic League, Jen Yong was marked down for assassination. But Jen Yong was also their passport to the next dynasty, the Communist one.

Father assembled the inhabitants of the House and told them they must be careful. Especially after the "accident" to Third Uncle. They must never go out alone. After dusk and the curfew they must all be at home.

"Stephanie, you must not go out alone, it is too dangerous," said Mother.

"They will try to hurt you, just to provoke an incident, and say it was the Communists who did it," said Father.

The main gate of the House was kept tightly closed all day. So were the two back gates.

Father recruited bodyguards from among the younger members of the Family.

Cousins, two by two, patrolled the garden at night. People came in furtively, before curfew, and all business was transacted at home. The bank sent the mail by messengers. Uncle Keng Dawei came in his limousine with three armed bodyguards to confer with Father.

And everyone waited for *them*, to come and take over.

Hsu Towering Cloud/Build-the-City and the Crystal Trading Company were a success, Brigadier General Tsing noted. "Security teams" ingeniously fragmented into tiny cells, linked to each other only by one member, and that one usually a Triad brother, had now permeated the Communist underground cells which reached everywhere, even into police offices and government departments. Their people ran the post office and the railway yards, the factories. The Communists were very strong in the factories, and Hsu had penetrated a few of them.

Tsing was satisfied. He would make quite sure, tighten the links he had created with the Triads. So very little time was left.

In front of him, emanating from on high, were lists. Lists of people to punish for treason . . .

Dr. Jen Yong went to the hospital accompanied by a bodyguard. His father insisted on it.

The bodyguard, Hsiao, was the younger brother of the sister-in-law of a cousin twice removed of the Jen Family. But he was a playboy, his nickname was Wastrel. He had a concubine who cost him a great deal of money. His legitimate wife had five children below the age of eight. Tsing had sent one of his best agents to get in touch with Wastrel.

286

An accident to Jen Yong—that would be a good lesson for the members of the Democratic League, for the Jen Family, and that wild American woman they had taken into their bloodline.

At a busy crossroads at dusk, while people hurried in all directions, two men waited, waited by the barbed wire road block barring the main street.

Yong came walking from the hospital, Wastrel by his side. Wastrel saw the two men and made the agreed-upon sign, raising a hand to ease his collar, thus identifying himself. Then he drew his gun. And Yong would have died, but at that precise moment, as the killers came towards him, he turned to ask Wastrel a question, saw him, gun in hand and his face shaking like jelly, and knew. Yong threw himself flat on the ground, and as he did so the two men fired. They hit Wastrel. Wastrel's body fell on Yong. The men fired again and then ran away.

The frightened people in the street had cleared a wide space around the bodies, but some medical students rushed to the scene. Yong lay still. He was covered by Wastrel's body, Wastrel's blood. He was unharmed, but he let himself be carried, pretending to be wounded, back to hospital.

Very late that night, as the Family waited for Yong, the messengers Father had sent in various directions returned and told him what had happened. "He is safe. At the hospital. A watch is kept on his room." Stephanie wanted to go.

"No, you must not, Stephanie," said Father. "It is much too dangerous."

"But Father . . . I must!" She was weeping, weeping, unrestrained, fighting the hands that restrained her gently, but so firmly.

"Your going will not make him better if he's hurt . . . trust me . . . stay with Mother."

Father went, with two bodyguards, and came back. He decided that only Stephanie and Mother should know that Yong was untouched.

"But pretend that he is grievously hurt, daughter, otherwise they may try again."

Wastrel was dead. Father told Mother about his betrayal. No one else in the Family was to know. Father sent money to his widow. The concubine disappeared.

After that Father hired three White Russian bodyguards with wolf dogs to patrol the garden by night.

Coral and Calthrop stayed at their school and did not return to the House. "They are safe with other young people," said Mother, as if to convince herself. But she worried for her daughters, especially for Calthrop who was brash and talkative. "They are very patriotic and they are probably doing a lot of dangerous things."

Some girl students from a progressive school had been caught putting up posters welcoming the Communists and had been tortured. Hair, fingernails and, of course, vagina.

Another week. Another. Yong stayed in the hospital. Father refused to let Stephanie or Mother go to see him. "Too dangerous."

Stephanie withdrew to her own house, quiet, too quiet, and concentrated on her son. Winter Treasure was growing; he crowed and laughed. He was nearly five months old and a robust active child. Every day Widow came to exclaim:

"He looks entirely Chinese, how lucky!"

And Stephanie contained the resentment which rose in her.

Then one night there was the faint boom of guns, like a distant roll of mild thunder.

At dawn, smoke wreathed upwards from across the river—the Kuomintang were burning the villages. Later there was thicker smoke as the fleeing troops blew up some oil installations. The distant guns boomed occasionally, fitfully, and then stopped, were silent.

"They are coming," said Father.

They came into Shanghai. They wore sneakers and walked in single file, not marching, merely walking. Their officers also walked and were impossible to distinguish from the men. With them came cultural workers with megaphones, to talk to the people.

This army did not rape or kill or plunder, but it was said they would shoot all the wealthy, all who owned land, or who had worked for the Kuomintang.

"They are passing through this street," Calthrop told Stephanie. She and Coral went out. They had bands on their sleeves, indicating they were members of a team for maintaining order in the streets.

There were few people about. The houses were shut and the shops shuttered. The soldiers walked so quietly that they had nearly passed the House before Stephanie, standing inside the gate, saw them. Each of them carried, slung across his chest, a sausagelike cloth bag which contained his rice ration. Their guns were at ready. Fifty or a hundred men would pass. Then there would be a five- or ten-minute interval, and another group would walk in single file, passing the House. This went on all day.

They were well fed and round-faced, brown with the sun, heavier in build than the people of Shanghai. Their uniforms were rumpled but clean.

After some hours, as they continued filing by, people began to come out of their houses. Doors opened. Children came out. The soldiers smiled at the children. Then the women came out.

Someone began to clap hands and the soldiers clapped back. And then the soldiers began to sing. No one knew the song or the words, but it sounded fine.

Thus the city was taken.

"On the twenty-fifth of May," wrote Michael Anstruther, "the Communist troops of Commander Chen Yi entered Shanghai in perfect order, astounding the inhabitants with their discipline and decorum."

fourteen

IT was over a year since Stephanie had watched the first soldiers of the People's Liberation Army come shuffling in their sneakers into Shanghai; had seen their cavalry riding in, slow paced, on big-headed Mongolian ponies, as if they had come straight from the yellow cliffs of Yenan.

It had been an exalting, phenomenal year. Galvanized into action—inspired by colorful posters exhorting them to "GET ORGANIZED!"—the people of Shanghai had responded, volunteering to clean the streets and the alleys of offal and garbage that had collected during the last months of Kuomintang terror, repairing the crumbling houses, removing the barbed wire fences. Rice and oil and vegetables and meat came in from the countryside on peasant carts pulled by mules. And no one tried to jump the queues, no one pillaged.

The streets changed their appearance. No longer were there insolent cars honking their way through hordes of ragged and sullen bodies. The stores began to change their displays, for there were very few luxury goods.

At first the nightclubs and dancing halls remained open, but no one went into them anymore except foreigners and "imitation foreigners," meaning totally Westernized Chinese. One by one their bright lights went out.

Much of the glitter—and vice—that had made Shanghai such a seductive city was now being transformed.

Many Westerners, however, wanted to stay. They had lived in Shanghai almost all their lives; here were their friends, their servants, their houses, their clubs. In the past they had been exempt from taxes, had lived in sumptuous surroundings, walled off from the real China and its woes. The warlords, the Kuomintang, the Japanese, had not touched them. Life anywhere else in the world, especially life without servants, was unthinkable for them. But their indignation at being checked on, suspected, at having to pay their servants proper wages and give them a day off a week, was great. Some left, but a number of foreigners went on living in Shanghai, hoping that eventually a placid normality would prevail. And the *North China Daily News*, representing the interests of the British Empire, continued printing.

The nights were now peaceful family occasions and people went to bed early. Polite but implacably meticulous young men and women visited each lane, each house, each shop, registering the inhabitants, checking on the sick, the jobless, the visitors from out of city. The schools reopened and the children went to them in great singing groups. Volunteer student-teachers opened classes in temples and abandoned houses for the adult illiterate. Beggars were rounded up, fed and clothed and returned to the villages they came from.

From the start the Party moved strongly against the drug evil controlled by the Triads. Sector by sector, lane by lane, army trucks and lorries rolled in and arrested hoarders, traffickers, suppliers. They were summarily shot.

Within ten days drugs had disappeared from the city. Clinics were open to treat the addicts. An association of "opium smokers willing to rehabilitate themselves" was formed. Opium smokers and drug addicts were persuaded to report themselves, not to be shot, but to begin group rehabilitation to kick their habits.

A sense of overwhelming virtue now pervaded the city of sin and squalor and wealth.

UNITY IS STRENGTH. Posters showed young and old, men and women, a vast multitude, all with entranced faces lifted towards a radiance of red flags unfurled in the wind.

LABOR IS NOBLE, LABOR IS GOOD. The posters showed how great obstacles could be overcome by collective effort. Everyone wanted to roll up sleeves and *do something* now!

Father was organized into the Association of National Capitalists. "I have an aim in life," he said. "To rebuild my country." Each night he returned late, tired but exalted, from meetings for the reconstruction of China's finances. Uncle Keng Dawei presided over the meetings; a major plan was being drawn up for the economic revitalization of Shanghai, the leech city which had sucked off China's blood for foreign interests, now to be transformed into China's major asset.

A new currency was inaugurated, which would end the inflation. "We'll put *everything* right," said Father.

The mayor of Shanghai was Marshal Chen Yi, the commander whose troops had entered the city with such decorum. His goal was to rally every brain, every hand, to set the city upon its new course. He listened to all. He went to the universities to coax the professors. He called on scientists and engineers. He dined with capitalists. Everyone was amazed. If this was communism, then communism was a good thing, tolerant, enlightened. . . .

Father recounted how Mayor Chen Yi had told him and his fellow capitalists: "We'll have to learn from you. We don't know anything about cities, about foreign trade: *you* have all the experience."

The hospitals held meetings to discuss a plan to train doctors for the villages. It took eight years to become an M.D., and less than a thousand a year could be turned out. At that rate, and provided the population did not increase from its five hundred million, it would take a thousand years to have enough doctors for the villages, where eighty-five percent of the people lived. Yet some eminent physicians were angry at plans for turning out medical personnel more swiftly, for shortening courses, arguing that it would dangerously lower medical standards.

"They want to keep their bourgeois privileges," said Joan Wu, the American wife of Dr. Wu. She was round-faced, prim, and worked in the hospital pharmacy. She was enthusiastic about the new regime.

Medical teams went to the countryside to study the health requirements of the villages. They were conveyed in army trucks; they lived in tents. For the first time, some of the doctors, and many of the students, saw the true and appalling conditions of their own people. "We never guessed . . ." they said uneasily. Dr. Wu and some others volunteered to stay in the rural areas for six months to a year, to establish a proper midwife service. Baby care, mother care, was primitive. Too often the village midwife

292

was a dirty old woman using rusty iron hooks to tear out the child if there were difficulties. In some mountain regions, manure was still plastered on the navels of the newborn. In some provinces, the woman in labor was given no rest, was propped up straight, over two bricks, for many hours. . . .

A pervasive sense of guilt now infected not only the doctors, but many of the intelligentsia. True, they had fought for democracy, against Chiang. But had they really *done* very much about their fellow men?

Yong had been to Yenan, had worked at the front lines and in the villages; eating and sleeping and working with the peasants. Now he drew up plans for clinics at village level, where paramedical personnel could be trained in simple operations on work-related accident cases. The most important thing was cleanliness: sterilization of instruments, antitetanus injections, accurate diagnosis. "Eighty percent of common diseases and sixty percent of accidents *can* be handled at the local level," he stated. Provided there was efficient personnel, trained for two to three years, in recognizing what was serious, what was not. Thus medical costs would be radically pruned, and time gained to produce more doctors.

His twin sisters, Calthrop and Coral, now sixteen, were filled with a great ardor. "We want to lay down our lives to build a New China," they said extravagantly. "We gladly relinquish all private ambition." They both volunteered to work in the villages, teaching and helping in medical work.

Mother was also organized. All the women along the street gathered to discuss their responsibility to the community. A street committee was formed to supervise registration of everyone living in the street, hygiene, care of children, solution of family problems, reporting on antisocial behavior, such as clandestine prostitution.

Widow suddenly became what was called "an activist," indefatigable, exhorting all the other women of the street to cooperate.

She proved especially talented at spotting family problems. At No. 4 lived Mrs. Nieh, who mistreated her daughter-in-law, ordering her son to beat his wife. Out of filial duty, he slapped and kicked her energetically, and was indignant when the street committee expostulated with him. "But I am a filial son!" After all, tradition stated: "Only sweep your own doorstep. Don't worry about frost on the neighbor's roof." But Widow reported the case to the National Federation of Women. "He burnt her neck with a cigarette the other day."

How had Widow accumulated so much information about everyone in the street? Every woman wondered about this in the silence of her own mind. Nevertheless, Widow was soon surrounded by friends—she whom it had been bad luck even to meet—for no one wanted to become the object of her patriotic scrutiny.

Stephanie, being the only foreigner on the street, received special attention.

Two Party members came to investigate her. She received her registration card and was acknowledged as one of the Family. But she was not allowed to participate.

"I'd love to do something, to help," she said. But the street committee could not or would not give her any tasks to perform because she was a foreigner.

She started another book. About the changes in the city. She kept a diary. She walked about a great deal. She felt left out, ignored, abandoned.

And then one day there was a voice, an American voice, at the door. "Hi there, Texas." Lionel Shaggin, sunburnt and grinning, opened his arms wide, and Stephanie flung herself at him, hugging away her hunger for something American.

"It's been years," they said together, and laughed. Years. Since early 1945 when she had left Yenan, and now it was 1949.

Lionel Shaggin, Loumei, and their son, China Warrior, were evacuated from Yenan when the cave city fell to the Kuomintang in 1947. Now Lionel was posted to Shanghai, assigned to clean up Shanghai's venereal diseases. The basic principle was not to punish the women, but to catch and to punish the men who dealt in sexual slavery. Women's rights, equality between the sexes, were an integral part of the Chinese revolution. Prostitutes were victims, not criminals. They would be healed, educated, taught to work.

"You know, Lionel, I'd never thought about the matter in that way. . . ." An idea was forming in Stephanie's mind:

the American magazines wanted "human interest" stories—
well here was one. . . .

"Not only you, sister. Even I—when I started my medical
career—I wasn't clear about the whole nature of female
sexual slavery."

There was no trouble with the mail. It came regularly,
albeit a little more slowly, due to censorship on both sides.
Letters from Stephanie's editor, Zimmerman reached her,
and a cable from HERE asked her for a major article on the
"downfall" of Shanghai.

"It's not downfall, it's liberation," she wrote, and sent off
an article about Lionel's work with prostitutes. It was never
published.

One day, a group of four professors came to the House to
ask Stephanie to teach English and American literature at
the university. She was delighted.

"Yes, yes, I'll do anything I can."

At last, she too was useful.

Stephanie was also asked, with Mother and about five
hundred other women, to a tea party given by the new
National Federation of Women. The mayor was present and
shook her hand warmly: "You are a friend, you are welcome." The women were asked to study the draft of the new
marriage law, which was the Charter of Woman's Rights.
For the first time, there would be freedom in choosing a
marriage partner, and female infanticide would be severely
punished.

Stephanie also went to meetings to discuss reforms in
teaching literature and creative writing. There must be new
books, new stories, new fiction. What would the writers
write and for what audience? Stephanie wondered. Eighty
percent of the people couldn't read. She and the other
teachers were provided with political guidelines: a speech
by Mao Tsetung, made in 1941 in Yenan, on the relationship between the writer and his audience; on the obligation
of writing for peasants and workers, not only for an intellectual elite. Of creating heroic characters from among the
people, and "educating the masses" through literature.

Social-realist literature, thought Stephanie. But the
masses *still* couldn't read. She was dubious, but politely
refrained from commenting, and agreed eagerly when
asked to help the new Translation Bureau at the university,
translating textbooks in science, sociology, history, and eco-

nomics: it was an important first step towards the goal, "Mass education, mass literacy."

Stephanie felt herself on the threshold of an awesome experience. *Everything* had to be rethought. So much had to be started from scratch. "There is a great unfolding of initiative," she wrote in her diary. And then stared at the words she'd written, knowing that before experiencing China she couldn't have written them, could not have even framed the thought. And felt herself helpless, *limited* by her own education, in describing what was being attempted.

In July 1949 a great victory parade took place.

Along the streets of Shanghai—Bubbling Well Road and Nanking Road and Avenue Joffre—great dragons of silk and paper went twisting and writhing, each one supported by forty-eight men. There was the clash of cymbals, the deep voice of drums. Young girls and boys in colorful jackets and trousers danced the *yangko*. Floats were paraded: paper airplanes and paper ships, paper locomotives and motor-cars, paper skyscrapers . . . dreams and visions of the future, when China would become an industrial giant.

Units of the People's Liberation Army marched, weapon-less, each man holding a paper peony in his hand. The crowds laughed and clapped and jostled to tease the soldiers.

But by autumn, the strain of such immense change began to tell. And during the winter, some unpleasant incidents involving foreign and Chinese businessmen and their workers occurred. The workers demanded better labor conditions and higher wages. The revolution's heady slogan, "Power to the working class," seemed contradicted by the Government policy, which was to restore the shattered economy as swiftly as possible, and therefore to maintain the capitalist factories, run by their owners, and still demanding 362 days work a year from their workers—ten hours a day. A shortage of raw material developed and some factories closed down.

Inflation, curbed for a while, began again. Hoarders took

heart. "We'll have this new regime by the throat within the year."

One of the major problems of the new rule was the great scarcity of experienced administrators. In the municipal departments, in the banks, in most of the offices, the old employees of Kuomintang days had been kept on. They were needed. Nevertheless the Party faithful had to be rewarded, though many of them knew only how to fight and found dealing with forms and paperwork beyond them.

The majority of the Party men now in charge were peasant guerillas from the north. They did not even understand the Shanghai dialect, that sibilant birdlike chatter. Many had never seen a big city before. They did not know how to flush toilets, to turn water taps. Telephones, radios, refrigerators, and elevators made them feel transported to an alien and malevolent planet.

The municipal government combed the universities for more competent men and women. The Communists of the Shanghai underground were trained in conspiracy, but unable to run a bank or a commercial enterprise. Where would the *educated* administrators come from?

And thus, in such a city, so spread out and so complicated, with its five million people in 1949, the plan of Brigadier General Tsing of the Kuomintang Secret Police saw a measure of success. For now the demand for anyone who could read and write was so great that many people were hastily promoted as cadres, or even to Party membership, without too much scrutiny.

Within six months, Hsu Build-the-City had become the right-hand man of a weather-worn, broad-visaged, and broad-beamed guerilla woman from Yenan, Comrade Lo. She had been in charge of marriage registry and social welfare in Yenan. She was now assigned to Shanghai, in charge of registration of citizens in textile and spinning factories employing mostly women.

And because she was a peasant woman—good with a gun, but flurried by elevators and afflicted with vertigo when she stood higher than four floors—she listened to Comrade Hsu, recently appointed to help her because he knew Shanghai and was educated. He was such a willing young man, a little like a son to replace the boy killed in the war of liberation. He always walked her to the common dormitory where she lived. "There are still bad people around," he said gallantly. "Aunt Lo, you are too valuable to lose."

Hsu became her deputy, her right hand. He began to recruit his own subalterns, among them two of General Tsing's earliest recruits . . . Chaste Wisdom, now known as Comrade Bo, who, with her husband, Tsui Sea Dragon, had infiltrated Yenan five years before.

Comrade Lo was happy that Comrade Bo should be one of her assistants in charge of the education sector of the textile workers' unions . . . for Bo Chaste Wisdom brought back memories of Yenan. And Comrade Tsui Sea Dragon was in Peking, in charge of the middle schools in a sector of the capital. Thus—"If you need anything to be reported quickly in Peking, my loved one can help," said Chaste Wisdom.

Comrade Lo's own husband, Meng, was still in the army in Manchuria. Alone in Shanghai, Lo found comfort in the efficient help of Comrades Hsu and Bo Chaste Wisdom.

Six times a week, at 7 a.m., Stephanie would ride to the university on Yong's old bicycle, which he had used to go to college. Yong went to the hospital by bus until Lionel Shaggin procured for him an almost new bicycle from a departing American friend.

The first few times, the police stopped Stephanie to examine her papers. "I teach at the university, Comrade Policeman," said Stephanie politely, and showed photographs of herself with Yong and Winter Treasure. Photographs were most persuasive. The policemen now waved at her as she bicycled past.

Her university class was double the size admitted before liberation. Sixty students. "But at that time, Mrs. Jen, we had silly notions: 'Few, but the best' was our motto. We were completely divorced from the masses," the dean told her.

On her first day, the dean, thin and scholarly, had introduced her to her class: "Comrade Lai Spring Snow is helping us in the reconstruction of our country." The students clapped, two girls rushed forward with small bouquets.

After lessons the students surged around her, eager, full

of questions about America. Why had the Americans helped Chiang Kaishek? When would America recognize the People's Republic?

"Americans are not always well informed," Stephanie would start to explain—"Americans are terrified of communism, the very word stops them from thinking clearly. . . ." She would try to explain why, but found herself puzzled by her own country's growing hysteria.

The dean suggested that she teach Chaucer, Walt Whitman, Shakespeare, Dickens, and Mark Twain, considered "progressive."

"I thought Jane Austen would be a good introduction to literature. . . ." said Stephanie.

"We think *Huckleberry Finn* is a good example of progressive writing," countered the benign dean.

She returned home each afternoon, tired but satisfied, to be greeted by her son. Winter Treasure was now a sturdy toddler, cheerful, headstrong, and quick-minded. *Amah* Mu was punctilious in making him revere his mother. "Bow to your mother." "Ask your mother if she is tired." "Say: 'Mother, your unworthy son is glad to see you back.'"

Stephanie was happy—aside from occasional bouts of homesickness. She was needed here. She could contribute something useful. She also felt like a woman fulfilled, at ease in her skin. "I have everything . . . a husband, a son, a loving Family, and fascinating work. . . ." she wrote in her journal, and ignored the vague sense of . . . impermanence . . . that played in the back of her mind.

Shanghai was now a slow-paced, unstressful place. The running and scurrying, the breakneck hurry, had vanished. In old Shanghai people worked until their guts came out of them—pushing and shoving, carrying and pulling, a desperate agitation as if pursued by calamity to be outraced. Shanghai had been a jungle, as restless and clamorous at four in the morning as in mid-afternoon. All this had gone.

Individual swiftness was no longer a premium, speed no longer a desirable attribute. People waited on decisions from the collective, and the collective was themselves. There was a shedding of responsibility by the individual.

The stress of survival was lessened, tooth and claw urgency disappeared.

A certain apprehension of doing too much instead of too little now crept in. Stephanie noticed that to stand out with too much boldness, mordancy, was not well received by "the collective."

"It is as if a tranquilizing drug has been sprayed into the air, permeating everything," wrote Stephanie. "But despite this slowdown, remarkable things are being done."

"It is simply the pace of the countryside—of the peasants," said Yong cheerfully. "The peasants are taking over."

Stephanie's body also slowed down. It took her longer now to react to anything. Despite the fact that she was very busy with her teaching schedule, she sometimes had a feeling of being suspended between the yellow earth and the blue sky, in an expanded moment of living. A vegetable ease. She walked for pure pleasure, pushing her bicycle home after teaching. She imbibed the city, the city which was learning a new way of being. And in her class this mind-leisure reflected itself in her teaching. She came to understand Walt Whitman better in Shanghai than she had at Radcliffe.

Each of us inevitable
Each of us allowed the eternal purports of earth . . .

She tried to explain the meaning of the lines to her students. Abstract notions of being, states of anxiety and sentience, were most difficult to translate. But with patient metaphor she succeeded, her reward the moment when they looked at each other, and nodded, and smiled.

Despite the new security, their happiness, Yong and Stephanie had moments in which they felt precarious, vaguely threatened. There were constraints in the air, as yet nebulous.

It occurred mostly over trivia, such as wall posters, or a particularly virulent speech on the radio. Or the fact that slowly, but relentlessly, the city was emptying itself of foreigners.

In ones and twos and a dozen, ship by ship, by train when the trains started running again, the foreigners were leaving.

Yong would bring home friends, especially those friends who had foreign wives. The Shaggins, the Wus, the Hsiehs. He would ask professors from the university who had been in Chungking, in Yenan. Soon the Jen House was noted for its hospitality. From among these friends there sprang a loyalty, a need of each other, as if below the tolerant, enchanted ground they now trod, something threatening lurked, waited.

Trade had resumed with many Western countries, despite press fulminations against China. European businessmen maintained companies in Shanghai. Some Americans in Shanghai stayed on, including Henry Barber, a free-lance journalist and writer who printed a weekly *Newssheet*. They gathered fairly often, either at the Shaggins' or at one or another house, to discuss the possibility of a change in the American government's policy. They had been encouraged by President Truman's announcement that Korea was outside the perimeter of American defense in Asia. Perhaps, in time, there would be reconciliation. The Chinese Army was demobilizing. Mao Tsetung had openly declared: "At present, another world war is quite unthinkable."

Herbert Luger came to Shanghai on a visit, to reorganize the English-language programs of the Shanghai broadcasting station. He came to see Stephanie and launched into a denunciation of the United States because of persecution, witch hunts.

Colonel David Barrett, because he had been head of the Dixie Mission, had been deprived of advancement. John Service had undergone a series of loyalty hearings. He had been cleared in 1946, 1947, 1949, and had just been cleared again, but "they keep on harassing him . . . the imperialists won't be happy until they've got another war going."

Luger peered at Stephanie, tried to put his arm around her, which she avoided by moving away. "We need you, Stephanie. I know you're doing a fine job teaching, translating, but you could be more effective in our broadcasting service."

"I know nothing about broadcasting."

"We need an American voice. A woman's voice. To speak to Americans. If you could give a talk, say twice a week, at night, to catch the peak hour in Washington, that would be a great help."

His forcefulness, the jargon he used, were distasteful to Stephanie. And those pawing hands . . .

"I don't think I can do it."

"You don't have to do a thing. Not a thing. *We'll* do the writing. You just read it out. We've got several Americans, Australians, Britishers working for us. *Think*, Stephanie! It's a great honor, to refute the lies of imperialism point by point. We're engaged in a tit for tat struggle against the warmongers."

He was off on his monologue, his voice sonorous, pulpit-preachy. "The days of imperialism are numbered, but the imperialists will continue to try to make trouble. . . ."

"I'll have to think about it."

"Stephanie, where's your enthusiasm? This is a magnificent opportunity for you to show where you stand. . . ."

"Herbert, don't stampede me. Please." She rose. "I'll let you know tomorrow. It isn't all that rushed, is it?"

That night Yong came back late with dark pouches of fatigue under his eyes. Stephanie was wrapped in the house gown he specially liked, loose-sleeved silk, sculpturing her slim body. She wore her hair very simply, in a chignon; her face, chiseled and grave, was more beautiful in its maturity than it had been six years previously. And so he found her, in the cool lovely room, and his body became at ease, untired. "Oh my love, my love," he said, "the room is aglow with walking fire because you are in it. . . ."

"You're spoiling me with poetry." She smiled, then told him of Herbert's proposal.

"No," said Yong. "No, Stephanie, you are not to do it. . . ."

"It might help . . ."

"I don't think you should read broadcasts." He was angry and therefore spoke in a cold stilted manner. "Not unless it's your own words."

"All right. That's what I'll tell Herbert."

They sat, smoothing the unease over with agreement.

"Uncle Keng has invited us to go to Wusih for the summer," said Yong. "I used to go when I was a child, at the turn of spring into the hot season." Yong would not be able to stay longer than a few days, but Stephanie would go with Mother and Winter Treasure.

So when Stephanie's courses ended in mid-May—when the university students were "going down" to assist in land reform in the villages—she and Mother left with Winter Treasure and *Amah* Mu.

Wusih was a resort famous for its beauty, a painter's paradise. The willows and the camphor trees, the silver oak and the eucalyptus made a riot of varied greenness by the lake's edge. The jade of the rice fields spread to melt into faint azure hills girdling the horizon. The lake lay like all the silk of the world, rippling its sapphire blueness.

The front courtyard and side rooms of Keng Dawei's house were occupied by a school of painters. The new Academy of Art had borrowed part of Uncle Keng's house, and he had gladly agreed.

Artists were now on a monthly salary. They had security, and the new Government encouraged them to paint. "Before liberation we starved . . . now the Government gives us all we need . . ." was the chorus which Stephanie heard every day from writers, painters, and musicians. Now all they had to do was to produce. Produce in praise of the revolution.

The famous painter Tseng Shunte, a master of the southern school whose landscapes of Wusih were highly prized, was here with twenty of his students. The school intended to create collectively several large paintings celebrating the first anniversary of the People's Republic of China on October 1, 1950.

"Korea," said Mother. "Something seems to have happened in Korea." Stephanie, who had been out for an early morning walk, had missed the radio broadcast.

Tseng Shunte walked into their courtyard.

"Master Tseng, welcome, have some breakfast with us . . ." said Mother.

"No, no, I have eaten . . . have you heard the radio?"

"Yes, just now . . . Something has happened in Korea."

"The reactionary government of South Korea has attacked North Korea," said Tseng. He lingered. He looked at Stephanie. "The American government says they will help South Korea."

"Well, let's hope it will be settled soon," said Mother.

303

"President Truman said Korea wasn't in America's defense perimeter . . . that's what he said. . . ." Master Tseng sighed. "Things are unclear, unclear." He bowed and left.

That morning the students went out as usual to stroll around the lake, to choose shady corners for their easels.

Stephanie sat by the radio, and after a while the news came on again.

There had been "aggression." South Korea had launched an attack on North Korea. She twiddled the knobs to try to obtain Hongkong, the BBC, but there was nothing but spluttering sounds like frying fat.

That evening, from Hongkong, she heard that General MacArthur, the Supremo in Tokyo, had been instructed by the American government to support South Korea with warships and warplanes.

Mother came as Stephanie sat listening to the radio.

"What does it mean?" asked Mother.

"I don't know," said Stephanie. "I just don't know."

From Hongkong, a commentator's voice drifted in, ominous.

"This is where the democratic nations of the world must take their stand . . . otherwise the red tide will engulf us . . . Armageddon . . . a third world war. . . ."

Demonstrations against South Korean aggression began on a minor scale in the cities of China. Students, workers, housewives, mobilized through the network of organizations, held meetings, signed petitions against "aggression."

Stephanie walked in an uneasy, almost disembodied state; her only shield against anxiety was Mother's tranquility. Mother appeared unruffled. Only a slightly more demonstrative gesture towards Winter Treasure, a little more playfulness with the child, betrayed her.

But the art students no longer came to chat with Stephanie. Master Tseng and his pupils held meetings; they began to paint posters for the Korean War. They stretched large frames against the courtyard walls. Majestically, Master Tseng would begin a design, swiftly sketching people in throngs, surging heads like the bobbing waves of an ocean. . . . Red flags spreading above them, and haloed in light, a North Korean soldier, rifle in hand.

Master Tseng was now slightly distant, though still affable towards Mother and Stephanie. He never crossed the threshold of their courtyard, but stood outside it, chatting with Mother, appearing not to see Stephanie. He stroked the slight wisp of beard he cultivated and spoke of the diamond brightness of light upon the lake.

By July 7, the North Korean Armies had mauled their way deep into the south and threatened Seoul. At the United Nations, thirteen countries agreed to send armed forces into Korea, provided the United States did so first. MacArthur was appointed commander in chief of the United Nations forces in Korea.

Dry-mouthed, Stephanie said to Mother: "Perhaps we should go back to Shanghai."

"It is too hot in Shanghai," said Mother.

"I don't want Yong to worry," said Stephanie.

"It is so *very* hot in Shanghai . . ." Mother repeated.

Stephanie understood. In time of war foreigners automatically become suspect. In any country. And she was American. Better not be in Shanghai at this time . . .

Mother went to confer with Master Tseng, who agreed that Stephanie had shown herself indignant at the aggression by the imperialists. "Master Tseng, your word will count. Our gratitude will last a thousand years."

"A hundred will do," said Tseng, charmed by Mother. "I, Tseng Shunte, am also greatly distressed."

Amah Mu came back with Winter Treasure from his walk, chatting, as do all nurses, of her charge. "Oh, *we* have heard the drums and seen the dancers, they asked *us* to support North Korea against the aggressors," she said.

And Winter Treasure piped up: "Down with American imperialism! Down with the lackeys of imperialism!" He was a bright child, with a great deal of fluency and a quick ear. Too quick an ear, thought Stephanie dismally. His eyes were large and brown like Stephanie's, but he looked Chinese, his hair like his father's. He parroted the slogans, but also had sudden watchful silences. He had a way of tossing his head when he became stubborn which was pure Stephanie. But Stephanie caught him now and then staring at her in his grave, puzzled way. Perhaps he was finding out that she was different, physically different from *Amah* Mu, and Grandmother, and all the other uncles and aunts he met. . . .

305

She walked into her bedroom and closed the door. Leaned against it. Oh God, she thought, he's my child, my child. . . . But Mother came in, almost brusque, carrying Winter Treasure, placing the child next to Stephanie and saying: "Now, Treasure, hug your mother . . ."

And Stephanie held her son to her, fiercely, so hard that he squirmed a little. *Oh God . . . . don't let him be sorry that his mother is American.*

Winter Treasure came back the next day with his latest trophy of slogans: "Kill all the imperialists and their running dogs."

Amah Mu took on her fondly scolding tone: "Now, Treasure, you must not shout these things *at home*, they are only for people who parade in the streets."

"I want to parade. I want to parade." Winter Treasure strode up and down swinging his fists. "Down with American imperialism."

"You are too small to parade," said his grandmother.

"I want to be a soldier," said Winter Treasure. "I want to kill dogs. . . . I saw a dog, Mama. I saw it. It was being killed. Hahaha." Painfully, Stephanie swallowed the bile rising in her throat.

There was a massive hygiene campaign going on, to kill mongrel dogs and all strays suspected of rabies. But as usual, people went overboard and all dogs were being killed.

Mother looked at *Amah* Mu, who said: "We were walking by, we saw them kill the dog. . . ."

"You will be a doctor, like your father," said Mother to Winter Treasure.

"I want to be a soldier, a Liberation Army soldier!" clamored Winter Treasure, walking up and down and tossing his head like Stephanie.

"Whoever heard of anyone wanting to be a soldier? Good iron does not make nails, good sons do not become soldiers . . ." said *Amah* Mu.

"I want to fight," shrieked Winter Treasure, and *Amah* Mu quickly took him away, saying: "Silly little one, let us go and wash your face and hands."

On the train back to Shanghai, Stephanie was checked four times by the transport security police. At every station, the diligent train conductor would lead a pair of policemen to question her. Again and again, with grave courtesy, Mother explained; *Amah* Mu nodded, held up Winter Treasure, exhibiting him as living proof that Stephanie was not a spy, was married to a Chinese, was traveling with her Family.

But what was she doing in China? asked the persistent and puzzled young policemen. Stephanie's excellent Chinese made her suspect. They stared at her, then at each other. They addressed themselves to Mother. Where had she learnt her Chinese? How had she come to China from America? Stephanie told them that she had been to Yenan and showed them the photographs she always carried. Snapshots of her marriage in Yenan, and then a group picture. And in that group, in the front row, were several of China's leaders, their faces clearly recognizable, and behind them, the Americans of the Dixie Mission. . . . The train policemen then shook hands with Stephanie. "What an honor to have on our train a respected guest who has been photographed with our leaders!"

The train conductor sat with them for the last lap of the journey, basking in reflected glory. "This American comrade has seen Chairman Mao, Commander Chu Deh, Premier Chou Enlai," he told the whole carriage, and the passengers then crowded around to admire Winter Treasure. "He looks all Chinese," they said and smiled at Stephanie approvingly. They pressed sweets upon her and the child.

But when she came down from the train, a young man spat on the ground in front of her.

Shanghai was bombed from Taiwan. Chiang Kaishek used his American planes to do it. Among those who died was Stephanie's maid, Petunia.

Petunia went every Saturday to see her mother, who lived in Needle and Thread Lane in Chapei. There the houses were of wood, flimsy, uproarious with children. The lane was always crowded with women sitting outdoors, stitching, sewing, embroidering. They worked in pairs, or threesomes, and in relays. Their nimble fingers never stopped except when they slept. The birdsound of the Shanghai dialect in their high sweet voices mingled with the shouts and laughter of children playing in the *neelung*, as the lanes were called.

Petunia was a filial daughter. As soon as she arrived she would pick up the silk spool and a needle, and sit on a stool by her mother and sew. Her mother's fingers had never stopped, even when she said, "You are here, daughter."

And Petunia would say, "I am here, Mother," and start stitching. All the street praised Petunia, lauded her mother for having such a dutiful daughter.

The bomb fell upon the lane a little before noon. They heard its high whistle and some of the women raised their heads. Someone shouted in terror, "Aiyah," but the reaction of the seamstresses was slow. The clothes. The clothes in front of them. They rose, mechanically folding up their work, and the bomb came down.

"Unless everyone in the West starts to *think a bit*, we're headed straight into war," said Lionel Shaggin worriedly, "and war is the last thing China needs."

Lionel Shaggin's radio was a very efficient shortwave set which captured the many voices of the world: the BBC, the Voice of America, Tokyo, Hongkong . . . It was almost a ritual for Henry Barber, for Stephanie and Joan Wu, and occasionally other foreigners in Shanghai to congregate in the Shaggins' living room to listen to the broadcasts from the world outside China. Individually they listened to the Chinese radio every morning. Together they tried to piece together the contradictory things they heard.

"Truman is trying to control MacArthur," argued Henry Barber. "He's been told to keep south of the parallel, not to begin a new crusade."

But the Seventh Fleet was mobilized, under MacArthur's command, to patrol the seas and to protect Taiwan. "Protect Chiang Kaishek? Why?" said Lionel Shaggin.

South Korea was now declared vital to the West's defense. "It's contradictory with what President Truman said a few months ago," observed Joan Wu.

"Chiang has just offered America six divisions to invade China."

"Truman's in hot water . . . the Republicans are out to skin him alive if he doesn't show himself rabidly anti-Communist."

"At the moment there's an all-out assault, and the Democratic Party is scared. It's got to prove itself even more anti-red than the Republicans. . . ."

"Hysteria," said Lionel. "It's hysteria. Alger Hiss, and now the Rosenbergs . . ." Three weeks after the start of the Korean War, they'd been arrested on a charge of conspiracy to commit espionage.

"America is in shock, paranoiac. First 'the loss of China.' Then the announcement that the Soviet Union had the atom bomb. Now Korea . . . " said Henry Barber.

Michael Anstruther, who until now had circulated in China with almost miraculous ease, was expelled forty-eight hours after the war started in Korea, because his newspaper in London had sided with American policy. Michael took it philosophically. "It's the usual diplomatic way of indicating displeasure," he wrote to Stephanie cheerfully.

For Britain, too, had been shaken by the confession of Klaus Fuchs, a high-level atomic scientist, that he was a spy for the USSR.

"There is a red cancer in the American body politic . . . the government is now forced to obliterate it in self-defense . . ." ran an editorial in the Hearst press.

A certain Senator McCarthy was becoming increasingly vocal. On February 12, Lincoln's birthday, he had been assigned by the Senate Republican Committee to speak on "communism in the State Department." He attacked fifty-seven anonymous "card-carrying reds" and, by name, a scholar, Owen Lattimore.

"There is fear and intimidation. All over America people are afraid," a friend wrote to Henry Barber.

"China does not want a war with America . . . it's the very last thing she wants or needs," Henry Barber wrote—his weekly *Newssheet* continued to be published in Shanghai.

The Peking radio broadcasts were increasingly condemnatory. Listening to both sides, Stephanie became more and more heartsick. "Everybody seems to have gone crazy," she said.

309

Lionel attempted a weak grin. "The sound of fury is a form of communication in our modern age, sister. China doesn't want war, and most Americans don't want war either. So perhaps invective will be a warning."

Stephanie smiled bleakly. "In other words, when people swear at each other, it's love and kisses."

"That's one of our ancient Chinese proverbs," said Loumei, who refused to be disheartened.

All through July and August the news from Korea was of headlong retreat. Day after day, week after week.

"It's a debacle for the imperialist aggressors," shouted Herbert Luger. The North Koreans had Russian-made 35-ton tanks; the American forces—most of them untrained in combat, plucked from comfortable billets in Japan—were badly equipped. There was confusion and worse: pell-mell retreat, savagery. Along the wreck-littered roads, among the sawtooth ridges of Korea, the GIs fought and retreated, fought and—outgunned, outflanked—drew back.

Lionel said, "Our boys dying out there in Korea . . . it just hits me right in the guts."

Nor did the Voice of America try to minimize the stark defeat: "All around us bugles started blowing. They were right on top of us, in the hills, firing down at us. . . ."

"Tanks fired at us from our own motor pool."

"We ran . . . God, how we ran . . . We were cut off."

Herbert was radiant. "Hear them? Hear them? This demonstrates the superiority of our side. . . ."

"Herbert," said Lionel quietly, "shut up."

"But . . ."

"Shut up," said Stephanie. "We're all dying a little bit too. . . ."

In her class the students asked her—and if they asked, it meant they had reached a collective decision to ask—"Teacher Lai, what do you think of the great victories of the heroic Korean people against the imperialist aggressors?" The whole class looked at her. Mute. Expectant.

And Stephanie said, her voice shaking: "I hate to think of all the suffering for the people, on both sides—and I hope it's all over very quickly."

She knew it was the wrong answer. It was not revolutionary optimism. It was not . . . whatever the correct attitude was supposed to be. It was a bit like talking of the Japanese after Pearl Harbor as human beings, equally involved in deadly conflict. . . . Her hands knotted behind her back as she faced the young faces frowning disapproval at her attitude.

Stephanie wrote an article which she called "Letter from Shanghai," which Henry Barber published in his weekly *Newssheet*. It was a reasoned piece, trying to explain the Chinese attitude towards the conflict. "China wants peace, needs peace to build up China . . . the Government hopes that the war will not expand to involve China. . . ."

Herbert raged. "Are you hinting that the Chinese People's Republic is *scared*? What a typically bourgeois defeatist attitude. . . . Our Chinese comrades are *never* scared . . . this is the end of imperialism. . . . The forces of socialism are digging their grave in Korea. . . ."

Stephanie became allergic to Herbert's manner. Gooseflesh started on her forearms when he approached, his eyes bulging behind their thick glasses.

"Stephanie, you're always on the fence, a typical middle-of-the-road liberal. But you'll have to take a stand. It was, after all, the USSR and not the U.S. which won the last war."

"Balls!"

But though they argued, even violently, perforce they met, again and again, around Lionel's shortwave radio. Herbert could have listened to the news at the Broadcasting Center, where his Chinese colleagues received, on new equipment bought in Hongkong, every important radio station in the world. He said loftily: "This is such a waste of time. What the USSR and China say is good enough for me." Yet he continued to drop in and to listen. . . .

Stephanie's *Newssheet* article was mentioned in a column by John Moore, and by Michael Anstruther in a London newspaper. "Miss Ryder's article is a plea for sanity. It points to the danger of our excessive rhetoric," wrote John Moore.

And Michael: "Stephanie Ryder has given us the point of

view of a country which, although Communist, is palpably anxious not to become militarily involved."

Both were trying to give her encouragement. But in the Hearst press, Stephanie was savagely attacked: "A fellow-traveler—a new recruit to the reds . . ."

Stephanie wrote to her father, making several attempts at a coherent letter. "Dad, you've written to me of an immense red conspiracy. But I am convinced that it is not so." The letter, once written, seemed to her hollow, rhetorical. There was none of that particular bond, beyond intellect, which soldered her to her father. Not only distance, but a different meaning to the same words, now prevented any real communication.

She wrote to Isabelle, her mother.

"All is well here. A lot of people are upset about Korea, but I am sure everything must come out all right. . . . I'm fine, and so is Yong and so is our son."

And she wrote to Jimmy, though there had been no letter from him for a long while. But then Jimmy was at the San Antonio Military Academy. With the war on, perhaps it was difficult for him to write.

Meanwhile, at the university, the demeanor of her Chinese colleagues and her students became more and more distant towards her. A silent censure was obvious also in the Translation Bureau, in the way her foreign colleagues, a couple of Frenchmen, a couple of Spaniards, a Britisher, now walked past her without a greeting. As if she personally were responsible for the Korean War . . .

It hurt Stephanie, hurt her a great deal. Even the Chinese, she thought, did not behave in such a bitchy manner as did these foreigners, so goddam sure they were of being splendid revolutionaries. . . .

She cycled back and forth to the university. She taught, stolidly, doggedly. She braked her heart and mind to a thick numbness. She felt watched; she felt heartsick; but she went on.

fifteen

ON August 6, the retreat of the UN forces in Korea ended.
Large numbers of reinforcements combined with the mur-
derous pounding of American bombers—a continuous bat-
tering which destroyed nearly every village and town in
North Korea—halted the ten weeks of terrifying flight.

It was MacArthur's brilliant amphibious operation—landing the Marines at Inchon, near the western end of the 38th
parallel, and their drive eastwards, cutting in two the North
Korean forces—which made the new phase possible. The
tide of war had turned. Within the next fortnight the South
Korean territory was evacuated by the North Korean armies. On September 27, MacArthur entered Seoul in triumph.

Crouched over Lionel Shaggin's powerful radio, the small
band of Americans in Shanghai heard the news.

A hasty UN resolution was passed, which allowed Mac-
Arthur to cross the 38th parallel into North Korea. "Now
the fat's in the fire," said Shaggin. "Oh damn, oh
damn . . ."

Stephanie heard, loud and clear, Alistair Choate's
cultured voice reporting from MacArthur's headquarters in
Tokyo. "It's almost a joy ride. The morale of our troops is
very high. The Marines fighting in Korea are the veterans of
Guadalcanal and Okinawa, thoroughly trained in amphibious warfare . . . the North Korean armies are being annihilated. . . . Victory is in sight."

All resistance was crushed. American forces and their
allies advanced into North Korea at an astounding pace.
And now there was talk of reuniting North and South

313

Korea, under United Nations auspices. There were also apprehensive comments at the warlike rhetoric which poured from the Tokyo headquarters of MacArthur.

"The man sounds all set for a major crusade," commented Lionel, face creased with worry.

The Chinese Government was now reacting to the obvious threat to China; for MacArthur, on his own initiative, had visited Chiang Kaishek in Taiwan, and they had talked of future military cooperation and "final victory."

"Reconquest of the mainland is our aim," Chiang had proclaimed.

Each morning Yong and Stephanie listened to the local radio. "The Chinese people will not supinely tolerate seeing their neighbors invaded," said the radio.

The Indian prime minister, Nehru, sent warning messages to the American government. Should MacArthur's forces go beyond a certain distance into North Korea, China would have to intervene. . . .

But MacArthur almost openly avowed his intent to "destroy North Korean sanctuaries" wherever they should be. Worried by the unprovoked attack by MacArthur's planes on a Soviet airbase near Vladivostok in Siberia, President Truman flew to Wake Island on October 11 to meet with MacArthur.

The Yalu River was the border between China and North Korea. It supplied hydroelectric power to Chinese industries in Manchuria. If the American forces came too close, the Chinese would feel very threatened. The State Department and Truman denied any "extension of the hostilities," but Sygman Rhee, the president of South Korea reinstated by MacArthur, was saying: "The war cannot stop at the Yalu River." And MacArthur was going towards the Yalu, lifting all restrictions to his advance. . . .

Stephanie, Lionel Shaggin, Henry Barber wrote letters, sent telegrams to the American government, to friends they knew in America. Barber's *Newssheet* explained the Chinese point of view. Stephanie wrote to her father, wrote to her former editors, to her publisher, wrote to her friends, wrote . . .

There was no answer to any of those letters. Later she would learn they had all been confiscated. She penned them in anguish. "The Chinese do not want war with America," she wrote. "Despite the rhetoric, the Chinese have stated their willingness to sit down and talk with Washington . . . the last thing they need or want is a war. . . ."

She wrote also about Chinese attitudes to the Americans remaining in China. "Of course it is not 'friendly.' But it is not *racist*. They leave the Americans scrupulously alone; but this might change if the war continues."

The headlong thrust of the American forces continued.

"It is air power which has won," said Alistair's confident voice, "the blasting of all defenses from our aircraft carriers, blasting the cities and the roads and the railways of Korea . . . there is not a stone left of Pyongyang." Stephanie was sickened as she listened to him praise the screaming terror of those weaponed archangels of death.

The worst casualties were not soldiers, but civilians, since every village was suspected of being an enemy concentration. A million people would be killed in the bombings and the subsequent famine. The roads were thick with streams of refugees plodding everywhere and nowhere, and dying on the way.

"Some of the troops are black . . . seasoned battalions from New Guinea . . . when there is a lull in the fighting they make music . . . the most beautiful blues . . ," said Alistair. Strains of jazz came through, bringing tears to Stephanie's eyes.

From Tokyo emanated statements by MacArthur that the North Koreans must not be allowed "privileged sanctuary" across the Yalu River, which meant in China itself.

On the radio came Alistair's precise drawl: "It is clear that if the North Korean forces are allowed to crawl back into a sanctuary, there to lick their wounds and re-form their battered forces, another invasion might follow. . . ."

"Oh damn, damn, damn," muttered Lionel Shaggin.

President Truman declared: "We have never at any time entertained any intention to carry hostilities into China. . . ." Unfortunately the statement came ten days after the warlike noises from Tokyo, and by then it was too late.

"A mixture of honeymoon words and threats," spat Peking Radio, "to soften up public opinion for an advance right up to the Chinese frontier *and across it*."

Chinese volunteers crossed the Yalu River between October 12 and 20. The Yalu was already freezing, a highway of ice. Crossing by night, volunteers melted into the fields.

They had white capes and hoods, which would make them invisible once the snows began in November. Filing in small, thin threads of men, and then disappearing among the mountain ridges of North Korea, their number soon reached twenty divisions, two hundred thousand men.

The Chinese would say in November: "To help Korea in its resistance . . . is to defend our own country." The precedent of allied volunteers, they claimed, was initiated by Lafayette, during the American Revolution.

The Chinese hospitals prepared for a possible full-scale war.

"We can't just wait to be hit," said Yong, whose routine was grueling; not only with his medical duties, but because he had been co-opted to represent his hospital for the non-Communist parties in the Democratic League. Each night he came back exhausted, to fall asleep as one falls in a stupor, to rise from insufficient sleep and rush back to work. Stephanie wanted, *needed* to talk to him.

"Look, your country and mine . . . we're on the brink of fighting each other. . . ."

But Yong would reply tersely: "We must prevent it . . . " and take her in his arms, hug her fiercely, and rush away.

And so the war expanded, involving more and more men. A steady stream of GIs went to Korea. The UN called it a "police action," and this euphemism was to be preserved for the next three years.

Stephanie enrolled in a nursing course, together with Joan Wu, the quiet mousy American wife of Dr. Wu.

They joined a committee for the evacuation of children and pregnant women, in case of indiscriminate bombing of Shanghai. (A rumor had begun to circulate that certain senators in Washington suggested dropping atom bombs on Peking and Shanghai.) Since Shanghai was sited on a shallow mud bank, it was not possible to dig air-raid shelters, as had been done in the rocky cliffs of Chungking. There must be evacuation of the population, and this meant faultless discipline. Teaching each citizen what to do and where to go.

Mother wore a band around her arm saying "Health,"

and taught first aid to everyone in her district. She and Widow formed stretcher bearer units.

Almost every day there were demonstrations to "resist America and aid Korea." Patrols were set up to keep order and prevent looting, in case of mass bombing.

There was growing talk of the need for vigilance. Vigilance against Kuomintang agents, saboteurs, and spies. Spies . . . any foreigner was becoming suspected of spying.

"It can happen in any country," said Henry Barber, valiantly. He kept up an attitude of strong calm. But he was losing weight. As was Lionel Shaggin. As was Stephanie. Only Joan remained unimpressively the same, except that she often wiped her spectacles upon her skirt, as if the glasses blurred easily.

The foreigners had begun to leave, as a feeling grew among the people that *all* Westerners were against China. Were not UN forces from thirteen countries involved in Korea?

The small group of Americans remaining in Shanghai felt more than ever that they must do something, *must* do something to prevent a disaster.

In every city of China millions of people cheered volunteers departing for Korea. To the sound of drums beating, cymbals clashing, gongs booming, in a sea of red flags, young men adorned with ribbon rosettes climbed on army trucks and set off for training camps, for Korea. . . .

In Shanghai, industrialists marched at the head of their business staffs to offer gifts of money and clothes for Korea. Comfort teams of women made padded coats, trousers, knitted gloves and caps for the volunteers.

From every house, even from the poorest slums, people came out bearing their donations: silver or jade hairpins, a pair of bangles, a porcelain plate, or money . . .

Father donated lacquer scrolls and porcelain, paintings and calligraphy, and his last gold ingot. All these would be sold abroad, to bring in money for the war.

Mother gave practically all her jewelry, save her bangles. But she did not let Stephanie give away her necklace. "No, daughter, this you must keep. One day, when you too acquire a daughter, a wife for Winter Treasure, you will give it to her. . . ."

In Korea, Thanksgiving Day, November 23, 1950, was celebrated by the victorious United Nations forces with turkey, coffee, and mince pies. "The troops are looking forward to hanging their washing on the Yalu line," said a happy voice on Radio Tokyo. "The victory is total . . . they'll certainly be home by Christmas."

On the twenty-fourth of November the rout began.

The Chinese volunteers drove a massive wedge between the armies of MacArthur. Suddenly all the hills bristled with men. Thirty divisions hit the Western forces. On and on they came, and no amount of bombing seemed to stop them.

Once more a retreat began. Once again the radio voices documented it meticulously. This amazed Dr. Wu, who now came with his wife Joan to listen. "But we Chinese would never admit to such shambles, such a shameful retreat," he explained.

There was something odd about this second retreat. Henry Barber was perplexed. "They seem to run even before there's any enemy offensive." The havoc originally created by the previous advance of the UN armies was now compounded by their withdrawal. Everywhere ruin and desolation, millions of civilians homeless, fleeing, blocking the roads, bottling up all communications. The withdrawing troops competed against the fleeing civilian population for road space. Bridges, railways, and crossings had been demolished by the U.S. Air Force so thoroughly that nothing remained. And winter with its Siberian rigor now fell upon Korea.

Now exultation filled the Chinese air, while the voice of Alistair Choate in Tokyo was pitched to stern gloom as he somberly described "savage hordes rampaging down from the mountains upon our helpless remnants."

Once again the 38th parallel was crossed. Once again Seoul fell to the North Koreans and the Chinese volunteers.

But the new year of 1951 brought another upturn for the American forces. They fought back, fought their way across the 38th parallel. Seoul was retaken. And now both armies paused, breathless and spent.

Stalemate.

318

They were back where the war had begun, six months ago. Glaring at each other across a defense perimeter, at (almost) the 38th parallel.

Winter Treasure was two that Christmas of 1950. He had a toy train, a toy airplane, a toy rabbit. But war was his joy, for he heard of it on his outings and came back shouting with glee, his mop of dark hair dancing. "Down with American imperialism. Resist America, help Korea," he sang, waving the toy gun that *Amah* Mu had bought for him. Stephanie took it away from him and ignored his angry howling, but she could not ignore the words of hatred for her country that he mouthed so energetically, so innocently.

The child would play at bombing. He would run around the garden with his toy plane in hand, saying *boom-boom-boom* and *paah*, while his older cousins set off firecrackers, playing at war. In school the children were taught about bombing, to crawl under tables or desks when they heard the planes. For Chiang Kaishek's planes repeatedly strafed and bombed the coast, though Shanghai now had anti-aircraft guns, and his planes avoided the city.

"Pah, pah. Boom!" said Winter Treasure.

Stephanie remembered how Jimmy too had played at war, dressed in a cowboy hat, and at shooting red Indians with a toy gun. "You big bad Injun . . . bang!"

When Yong was able to leave the hospital early, before his son's bedtime, he would try to make the child play at something else than war. At games of skill with balls. At marbles. At trains arriving and leaving from railway stations. Anything to divert him from war.

"Kill," shouted Winter Treasure. "Run over him with my train . . ."

"No, son, the train is for carrying people to see each other. Let us take a train to go to see Grandmother." Stephanie would fall into the act, buy a ticket from Winter Treasure, board the train, and she would sing "Chattanooga Choochoo," which always made Winter Treasure laugh and laugh.

Thus they tried to round out a circle of happiness, of normalcy and quiet, away from the ever-present war, for themselves and their son. And Stephanie would watch the two heads bent over the toy train, so similar in their shape, both with the wilful abundant black hair, and her heart leapt like a gazelle.

Late at night, quiet love would come on noiseless feet, a blossom of light and calm. In this little pool of love, all else was abolished. Stephanie and Yong would cling to each other fiercely, silently, afraid to love so much, to love each other too much, frightened of the day when this love might become the weapon to wound each other. . . .

Sometimes Stephanie would cry very quietly at night, afraid to waken Yong, who slept the sleep of exhaustion. Awake, Yong would feign sleep, and soreness invaded his body. "It is my fault she is unhappy . . . what can I do to spare her?"

They made love gravely, leading each other from grief and anxiety to peace. At those moments sorrow slipped away, a garment discarded. Slipped away only to return the next morning, to adhere to them all day, to clothe them from head to foot with unease.

"Oh Heaven," prayed Yong, "let there be peace, quickly . . ."

"This war is destroying us," said Father, worried. "There were plans to disband the armies, they're a great burden, over thirty percent of the budget, and now it can't be done. . . ."

"We can't afford this war," said Dr. Wu.

Timidly, on the air, voices were raised. Speaking of a truce . . .

Mother had faint shadows under her eyes. Mother, always so elegant, now went out dressed in a blue cotton gown like a student, and wore flat shoes. And still looked elegant, matchless in line and gesture. She and Widow went from house to house to promote the sale of Government victory bonds. "To resist America and to help Korea."

Widow no longer sidled. She walked straight. She was competent. The street cited her as a model worker. She came to Stephanie.

"You must march with us," she said, "to demand peace in Korea. All our street housewives are marching today. . . ."

And Stephanie reluctantly said: "I'll walk for peace, but do not ask me to shout against my country, that I cannot do."

Widow looked at her coldly and said: "You have a responsibility—your son is Chinese—do you want him to grow up a traitor?"

Every day Widow expanded with new ecstasy, feeling wanted, useful. Her past sorrow changed into mystic grace. Her previous grief had been a testing, a preparation for today's glory, which was hers, all hers. No one else's. She owed nothing to anyone.

Mother had everything. A husband, a son. A beautiful house. But Widow was blessed by the revolution, fulfilled by it. She, not Mother, had become a leader and she would lead. Her long-suppressed hostility to Mother grew.

"She has fed on my sorrow, and now I shall make her bow her proud head to me. . . ."

At first Widow was not even aware that she felt this; it merely grew in her, a little more every day. She explained to her friends (and now every woman in the street wanted to be her friend) that Mother was not a wicked capitalist, only frivolous; that she liked parties and make-up; that all she needed was thought-remolding. Widow now walked as an equal with Mother. But at the meetings, when the applause came to her, wafted up to her in homage after a rousing speech (and how she loved making speeches, which followed exactly the latest editorial in the newspaper), she was irked by the faint smile on Mother's face.

"You did that very well, Sixth Sister-in-law," said Mother.

The pressures upon Stephanie grew. Unspoken, but felt. A miasmatic hostility. A wooden look when she appeared.

She made excuses to herself. "I can't blame them. It's natural. I'm an American and we're killing Chinese and Koreans. . . ."

It was Herbert Luger who brought it all to the surface in his usual manner. He appeared at the university after her class one afternoon. "I want a word with you, Stephanie. For your own sake. I think you should listen."

"I'm on my way home, Herbert. We could walk together . . . or meet at my house."

Herbert shook his head vigorously. "No, Stephanie, I won't step into your capitalist in-laws' house again." He folded his arms. "It's my duty to tell you that your behavior is a poor example for all of us. We're guests of China. All of us are marching for peace, are marching against the monstrous crimes against humanity committed by the imperialists." As if his pompous words were not enough, Herbert had brought with him a heavy folder filled with clippings, to show her that all over the world, eminent people, scientists, lawyers, writers, were protesting against the American conduct of the war. He put the folder on the table, read out some of the clippings.

Stephanie interrupted: "Herbert, I *have* protested. I have written letters. I've *said* we were wrong to go into North Korea . . . but I can't parade, mouthing slogans. . . ."

"*We*," Herbert picked up on the pronoun with relish. "*We* . . . Stephanie . . . are you identifying with the aggressors who are butchering the Korean people?"

Stephanie exploded. "Oh, sonuvabitch, I *am* American, and so are you! All this makes me heartsick, bonesick, so please leave me alone will you?"

Herbert wagged a finger and went on slogan-spouting. Even the Chinese must find him grotesque, thought Stephanie, and remembered that in Yenan his Chinese nickname had been the Centipede. Herbert Luger would always have to *prove* himself more revolutionary than anyone else.

"Stephanie, you're bugged with what you call balance, objectivity. Why, even your husband is at this moment submitting to criticism because of you." And seeing Stephanie gawk, incredulous and frightened, he continued gleefully: "He didn't tell you, did he?"

Stephanie no longer heard him. He was merely blur and noise. She ran out of the room and slammed the door on Herbert and yes, they were there, people, in twos or threes, small groups standing in the corridor. Listening. Or perhaps not listening. They did not move towards her. They did not look at her. She walked to her bike, upright in the cycle stand.

On the saddle was a piece of paper, stuck with glue, on which were scribbled words in Chinese:

"Imperialist spy, get out of our university."

322

When Yong returned home she was sitting, still muffled in her pale coat, in the half darkness of the bedroom lit by the embers from the open brazier. She did not turn her head.

He came to her, calling her name. Without looking at him she held out the paper in her hand, a small pitiful gesture. He read the scribble, put it down carefully on the table. To *destroy* it would be dangerous contempt for an expression from the collective will.

He put it in the drawer. He sat down and held her in his arms. And they felt grayed, invaded by grayness, moving in grayness. Their bright love turning to ash, turning gray.

"Forgive me," said Stephanie. "Forgive me, Yong."

"There is nothing to forgive, my heart. It is I who have done you great wrong."

"Yong . . . do you think . . . we'll be able . . . they'll let us be together?"

"Yes," he said, "yes . . . this will pass . . . you'll see . . . this will pass . . ."

That night they made love with a fierceness, a ceaseless passion which exhausted them, yet left them unslaked. Almost cruelly, they sought reassurance and peace from each other's bodies, only to fall back upon themselves. The dawn that came brought back grayness, in which love appeared to founder with a new taste of ashes.

Yong would go back to the hospital, and today a meeting was scheduled to criticize him publicly.

"Not only me, Stephanie. All of us doctors," he lied. "Because some of us felt unhappy about the volunteers in Korea."

Stephanie was astonished. "Who were they?"

"Some of us. But now we know we had to intervene. Yet it is costing the country so much—" He smiled, gently, sadly. "We have to endure it. It will temper us." He smiled at her. "Do not worry about this meeting. It does not bother me. You know, Stephanie, China is a very old country. We are very patient. . . ."

Yong did not tell Stephanie that his three best friends, Dr. Wu, Dr. Hsieh, and Dr. Fan (the latter back from Chungking and now with seven children), had been the ones to criticize him. Their wives, Joan Wu the American, Michelle Berbiest the Belgian, and Chinese Mrs. Fan carrying her ever-fertile belly, had marched in the procession of families of hospital employees shouting slogans against the Korean War. They had been congratulated. Their children, in Chinese schools, were cited for the meritorious action of their parents. Stephanie had not marched.

Dr. Wu had said to Yong: "You must not take it amiss, old Jen, that we should criticize you gently . . . it is better that *we* should do it rather than someone else, who might have called you a spy or counter-revolutionary." Dr. Wu and Dr. Fan had tried to keep criticism of Yong's conduct within the limits of "subjectivity, bourgeois ignorance."

They were concerned that someone else, at lower level, might interject wild accusations against Yong. "The hospital water-closet cleaner is given as much attention in what he says as I am," said Dr. Hsieh. "Remember that, Yong."

"Well, that's democracy," sighed Dr. Wu. "The rule of the people."

"I thank all my colleagues for their help," Yong said in his formal self-criticism. "I fully realize that it was my duty to help my wife understand the situation better. I did not do so. It is my fault, not hers." He cited Stephanie's letters, her concern. To shield Stephanie, who would not be able to endure a criticism session. "I must point out that my wife is a writer. Writing, not marching, is her way of showing her stand."

Every hospital, school, office, department, factory, bank, bureau, was now a unit, under a Party committee, responsible to itself and to the State for the conduct of each and every one of its members. Everyone in each unit was his or her brother or sister's keeper. The matter of Yong and Stephanie was everyone's business in the hospital's unit.

The unit declared itself satisfied by Yong's explanation.

And when Stephanie approached the dean of the university about the note on her bicycle, he said: "Of course you must continue to teach. You must not heed irresponsible accusations!"

Stephanie continued to teach. Though she now felt constantly watched. Malevolent, or simply curious eyes, stabbing at her like small but penetrating daggers.

Due to the Korean War, a resurgence of Kuomintang and Triad activity took place, along with rumors that Chiang Kaishek was going to reconquer the mainland with America's help.

The Party worried about unrest in the cities. The greatest fear of the Party was the fear of "losing the seals of office," if the village majority was to become dominated by the city intelligentsia.

It began to take measures to consolidate its position; beginning with life records: in every unit every person now had to write his autobiography, which would be cross-checked with that of other members of his family in other units, with the biographies of his peers and his colleagues in his own and other units, with his friends and acquaintances, with anyone he or she knew or had met in a lifetime.

In a land where there had never been any official registration of births or deaths, where everything depended on family history or on oral memory, on what one's contemporaries, neighbors, schoolmates, colleagues, friends, enemies, acquaintances would write or say about one, this process of checking everyone was an enormous undertaking, but also a very efficient way of putting everyone on file.

Nothing was therefore any longer private, personal, apart, separate, unconnected, irrelevant. No single act or thought in one's whole life was anything but a stitch in a pattern, interwoven, connected with the actions, thinking, motives of many others. In the end it was motive which was paramount, and which explained the pattern. What was the "thinking" which produced such or such a behavior? And if anyone's behavior was different from the behavior of the rest, then the unit pounced upon the difference—it was disharmony, a flaw, a discrepancy.

Faced with this scrutiny, self-examination, relentless because it took its time but never let go, a good many felt totally disoriented, unsafe, as if they trod water, unsafe because their familiar world and its known lineaments had abandoned them.

In every Chinese family there had always been a sense of

325

collective *responsibility*. No personal act was independent, since it would impinge upon the lives, the fates of others in the Family. There was always guilt by association. And now this was being extended, stretched outwards, beyond the Family, spread through every event in one's life, reaching every single person one had ever met.

"It's monstrous," said Stephanie, almost shouting, to Lionel, when she realized that everyone, including Yong, was busily writing out their lives down to the last detail. "Why, it's a total breach of privacy."

Lionel laughed. "Well now, Texas, it's happening everywhere. Privacy . . . that's a myth. Why in World War II, any American who'd been in the Lincoln Brigade for the Spanish government against Franco was barred from becoming an officer. And that was when we were fighting Hitler, fighting the Nazis, who'd helped Franco. And look at what's happening now . . . people being dragged in front of the House Un-American Activities Committee, just because they might've been to a party, twenty years ago, where there were some Communists. . . ."

"But how can this knowing everything about everyone help?" asked Stephanie.

"The modern state, whether in America or China, will have us all registered, docketed, filed," said Lionel. "You just wait and see."

"But, Meiling," Stephanie was once again the young woman hurtling herself at what she considered vicious, "we may have religious bodies in America who do just that, public confessions, being born again, but not on this scale, and not compulsorily . . ."

"We've always been private, too private," said Meiling cozily when Stephanie talked to her about this snooping into private lives. "Until now, to protect one's family was the highest duty. . . ."

And Stephanie thought: That is why Yong deals with situations the way he does. Not standing up to face issues, not . . . fighting for ideas, always thinking in terms of *people;* of what might happen to Mother, to Father . . . to *me* . . . if he said something . . . Oh, Yong . . .

Meiling was now pregnant, but still active. At least once a fortnight she came to see Stephanie. They would sit together and talk the evening away.

"You *must* go on teaching, Stephanie. You must ignore this scribble," she said, dismissing the note left on Stephanie's bicycle. "It is a hard time for you, but it will pass," Meiling said. "And besides," she smiled, "all of us gave you very good reports. . . ."

"All of us?"

"I mean all those who knew you in Chungking, in Yenan." She rose, patted Stephanie's hand. "Don't take things too hard . . . they will pass."

One April day came the news that MacArthur had been relieved of his command by President Truman.

"At last," Lionel said, "at last." He grinned hugely and started dancing, swinging Loumei around.

"You Americans," Loumei chided, "you are so full of emotion."

Lionel grinned. "Nothing seems to worry my wife. She comes back from a meeting where someone criticizes her for having married an American, and she listens and nods and lets them have their say. Then she explains that according to Chairman Mao, the American people are good, only a small handful of imperialists are bad. She sleeps blissfully, while I get insomnia from worry. . . ."

"We are puerile, like young volcanoes," said Henry Barber.

And one of Stephanie's students smiled quickly at her when she came to her class the next morning.

There was a big meeting in the university calling for peace in Korea. Stephanie joined it. She linked arms with Joan Wu and they were applauded by everyone.

In America the Korean War had produced an enormous economic boom, and an almost equal boom took place in Shanghai, with factories out to beat norms, to overfulfill quotas. Almost every day workers, clashing cymbals and beating drums, went out on the street with red flags to proclaim records in their achievements.

Father had never seemed so confident, for the measures taken by the Government to switch the factories to the war effort had been carried out in concert with the Shanghai capitalists, and most of them had responded well.

But the purchasing prices paid by the Government to the private industrial sector were going up and up. New factories sprang up, old ones worked overtime. The capitalists had not been so prosperous for many years. Because of the need for machinery and raw materials, smuggling on a large scale took place, smuggling through Hongkong.

"Smuggling for the revolution is meritorious," Uncle Keng Dawei said, his face wreathed in smiles. The Chinese Government pretended not to see any smuggling. "The Party keeps one eye shut, and one eye open," said Keng.

Nevertheless, the Party noted the fact that Shanghai, boom city, was once again becoming a predatory hydra through its wealth-making activity, a contradiction to any reform of the social structure.

Then—"The United Nations has placed an economic embargo on China. . . ."

The respite had ended. Hopes of peace were dashed. The war continued, and the mood once again turned ugly.

Until May 1951, despite the Korean War, trade with the West, and with the United States, had been eighty percent or more of China's total trade. Ten countries of the West had signed agreements with the People's Republic of China. But all this was now destroyed by the United Nations embargo in that month.

"America is rather immature," sighed Uncle Keng, talking to Stephanie. "Pushing us to depend entirely on the Russians, which is *not* what we want."

Whether capitalist or Communist, all Chinese disliked the idea of sole dependence on one country, even a "fraternal" country. Besides, the USSR was charging vast sums for its delivery of war material to China in the Korean War.

Now the smuggling from Hongkong became difficult because of the embargo. The United States established a large and hawk-eyed staff of watchers, investigators, inspectors in Hongkong to prevent machinery, medicine, or any material that could possibly be used in Chinese industry from reaching the country. It became impossible for China to sell her silks, antiques, jades, her ducks or duck eggs, Chinese medicines, and pig bristles—all traditional trades—through Hongkong. For anyone dealing with "Red China" was blacklisted by America.

Illicit smuggling took over, and the Triads, versed in all that was illegal, re-established some of their networks, making huge profits.

And gradually all the abuses, frauds, deceits, knaveries, trickery, wiles, indecencies of the past started once again. For many capitalists it was very easy to fall back into old habits. Shoddy goods for the war. Orders executed in a rush, at inflated prices.

"The State has to pay; the State has contracted with us to buy everything we produce, even if it is unusable."

"Party members can be bought, corrupted. They're mud bags . . . give them a feast or two, a padded jacket, a pair of shoes, and that's enough . . . you'll get the licenses you need, the permits you want. . . ."

The old way of life came back, habits of a lifetime of crookedness, as enthusiasm eroded with the stalemate in Korea and prices soared.

"It's saddening," said Professor Chang Shou to Stephanie, to Yong. He observed this resurgence of the past with some anxiety. "Some of the Party members have changed. They *expect* special privileges now. Expect their children to be specially cared for in the schools. Expect people never to argue with them, just approve and obey. No one can contradict them." He sighed. "They haven't enough education to resist corruption."

Professor Chang's two elder sons were scientists, the third was mentally retarded. They had been ashamed of him, but now he was a manual worker, and earned his living pushing handcarts. "He attends meetings at his factory," said his father proudly. "He pushes more loaded carts per day than anyone else. He no longer feels inferior to his brothers."

The Shanghai newspapers printed articles against corruption, bribery, nepotism. But now the factories were bogged down in a tangle of self-made red tape, with each Party bureaucrat inventing his own set of rules to give himself more power; and at every level there were forms to fill, seals to be brandished and applied to these forms. The only way to bypass it all was bribery. To keep their factories supplied, to obtain quickly the needed certificates and permits, the industrialists gave "presents" to Party men. Inspectors received gifts, to close their eyes at the right time, to make the necessary telephone calls.

Yong was worried. There was a shortage of medicines, of equipment. The Party committee of the hospital was under a man who was scarcely literate, and who looked with deep suspicion at the surgical instruments. "Why do you need so many?" he would say, looking at the rows of forceps. And now the best rooms were reserved for the higher-ranking Party cadres and, because of shortages, the best treatment went to the privileged higher Party officials. . . .

So swiftly has corruption infested the Party, thought Yong, and we haven't even begun to put things in order.

And, just as in America, where Senator Joseph McCarthy was riding high, strident and powerful on a witch hunt for reds everywhere . . . so in China, similar pressures mounted; talk of sabotage, of counter-revolutionary activity increased as the economic situation began to deteriorate.

Calthrop and Coral returned from helping the land reform movement in the countryside. They had stars in their eyes and sunburn on their faces. They refused to have sheets on their beds; they cut their own hair; they complained that there were too many dishes at each meal.

"We stayed with poor peasants," said Calthrop proudly. They had watched the trial of landlords, the execution of one of them. "Only one big 'tiger' landlord was shot," said Calthrop regretfully. "The others were given a chance to redeem themselves. But they wear black masks upon their faces when they work so that everyone should know they were a bad lot."

"The young are always for radical solutions—humanity seems to advance not through tolerance but through fanaticism," Mother mused to Stephanie. "If one were to add up each country's debt of blood . . ."

"My country would be no better, Mother," said Stephanie. "Look what we did to the Red Indians . . . what we're still doing to the Negroes."

"Mankind always creates beautiful theories and faiths to

330

tell itself how right its latest bloodletting is," Mother sighed.

Mother discussed her daughters detachedly, with humor and kindness. "Calthrop leads, Coral follows. Coral does not seek the limelight but Calthrop does."

Calthrop had taken to wearing large peasant straw hats, but Coral always took hers off.

At dinner one night Calthrop announced a plan to reform the Family thinking.

"Now that we have remolded our thinking by practice through land reform," she said a little fiercely, "another responsibility is upon us. We shall have to make sure which stand you take, Father, Mother. For or against the revolution. Everyone must come clean."

Coral nodded timidly. Coral loved her mother very much and clung to her, in a mute, childish demand for love; Calthrop seemed so much more brilliant, having been born half an hour earlier.

It was Calthrop who decided that, three times a week, the whole Family should assemble to study Marxism-Leninism together. Much to her mortification, everyone eagerly agreed. Yong with a very straight face said: "I suggest we begin to study at four in the morning—it is the only time everyone is at home together." He rose at five, to be at the hospital by 6:30 a.m.

At school meetings, Calthrop had "come clean" on her family and their class origin. "Our parents are capitalists. We are determined to remold ourselves, and also to change our Family . . . or otherwise to break with them!"

Having shouted this and been applauded for her performance, Calthrop came home pleased with herself.

"Mother, why do you still insist on wearing those dresses? You should go to work in a factory, to help Korea."

Mother replied serenely: "Calthrop, your hair is dirty. Don't you think it's time to wash it?"

"Oh, Mother, you only think of trivial things. What does washing hair matter? Do you think the volunteers in Korea wash their hair?"

"They certainly do," replied Mother with infuriating logic. "I am told our heroic People's Liberation Army has very high standards of hygiene. Not washing one's hair will breed lice, and lice bring disease. . . ."

The twins had applied to become members of the Youth

League. "I'm afraid we'll never be admitted because of our bad class origin," Calthrop said glumly to Coral. Ah, why had they not been born in an honest worker or poor peasant family?

Calthrop said to *Amah* Mu: "You should work in a factory. Let young mistress take care of her own child."

"Go fart," replied *Amah* Mu, bundling up Winter Treasure to go to kindergarten.

"*Amah* Mu is backward, she should be re-educated," said Calthrop to Mother.

"We must all be re-educated," agreed Mother, embroidering a bib for her grandson and a pair of slippers for Stephanie, because Stephanie was now pregnant again. Mother's heart followed the stitches of her needle, and stitch by stitch her spirit followed the needle, stitching a new pattern to her new life.

"I am ashamed to be your daughter," said Calthrop boldly.

Mother looked at her. "It cannot be helped, little one. We are what we are."

Calthrop said: "I want to spend my life teaching the peasants."

"That," said Mother, "is an excellent idea."

And because they could never get Mother flustered, the twins secretly admired her, but told each other how dreadful it was to be burdened by such reactionary parents.

Mother stitched and stitched, knowing life to be very long and man's theories and heroics very short. Some bad things might happen, and it was not the time for indulgence in one's own emotions. As one folds imperishable pure silk, Mother folded herself upon herself and waited.

Meiling gave birth to a daughter, a pretty child with a great wave of black hair and big round eyes. Meiling called her Round Round, Yuan-yuan. It was pointed out to her that this was the name of a famous imperial concubine whose beauty had caused disaster to China.

"I shall think of another name for her when she grows up," Meiling replied placidly.

Her husband was in Hongkong. "I'm not supposed to tell," she said to Stephanie. "The Americans forced that

332

resolution in the UN to ban all sale of war material. Now they are trying to force Hongkong not to buy anything from China. And anyone who trades with China is put on the blacklist. But the British are levelheaded. Anyway Hongkong would starve witout Chinese pork, Chinese vegetables, Chinese rice, and would die without Chinese water . . . even the Americans have to drink our water." Her husband had gone to Hongkong to talk quietly with the British about further trade.

Maternity had rounded Meiling's angles, softened her pixie looks. She and Stephanie reveled in this unspoken and shared plenitude of the body, the immense superiority of birth-giving.

Winter Treasure loved playing with Round Round, and Round Round crowed with delight when Winter Treasure carried her about, and he cried when she went home with her mother. "Your mama will give you a sister all your own one day," Meiling said to Winter Treasure.

"When they grow up, let us marry them to each other," said Meiling, already the matriarch. "I never told you, did I, Stephanie? But my husband's father is Old Sung, the waiter at the Press Hostel. He has been a Party member for many years."

A letter came from Rosamond Chen, in Peking. "Dear Stephanie, my mother is very ill. She lives in Shanghai and I have obtained my permit to come there to visit her. The Government is very good to be so concerned about my mother's health. I would like to see you if you are not too busy."

Stephanie cabled back: "Welcome." But when she told Meiling that evening, Meiling said:

"Rosamond is such a careless person."

"What do you mean by careless?"

Meiling's face was unmoved, bland. "She puts her own gratification above everything else."

"But, Meiling, she is your friend. . . ."

"She is," said Meiling. "But she has adopted a Western pattern of self first. And, you know, Stephanie, we do not think that way."

Rosamond arrived muffled in a quilt coat, a dark kerchief around her head. She had aged, around the mouth especially. Her loveliness was a little frayed, like silk that a cat has clawed at.

"Oh Rosamond," said Stephanie, "I *am* glad to see you. I've been counting the days."

Rosamond smiled, but her eyes did not smile; there was something opaque, fearful in them, and she spoke in a brittle, fast manner.

"So good to see you, so good to see you," she said in English as Stephanie led her across the garden to her own pavilion.

"What a lovely house you have. I think you're so lucky to have kept it, you must be very important people. The Government of course has *such* a good policy towards those who are *useful*." Words dribbled out of Rosamond, all in that nervous mechanical voice, as if she were not thinking or feeling her words.

Stephanie made tea. Since Petunia's death, she tried to do a little housework, although Peony and Cook Lee would not allow her to do much. "Young mistress has happiness in her," they said, meaning that she was carrying a baby and must be careful. Peony brought some biscuits and fruit, put the plates down, glared at Rosamond, and left.

Why is she so rude? thought Stephanie. And she noticed that Rosamond's features had shrunk a little more, as if Peony's insolence had been a blow.

Rosamond said: "I'm always cold now . . . it's not cold in your house, but at my mother's it's always cold." She held her hands out to the small brazier. Around her eyes was a cobweb of lines.

"You're looking young and beautiful, Stephanie. Meiling told me you had a wonderful baby boy . . . let's see, how old is he? We haven't met for seven years . . . yes, in Chungking, in August 1945, just when the bomb fell on Hiroshima, and now we meet again . . . oh, things have changed so much, so much. . . ."

"Indeed they have," said Stephanie a little loudly. As if someone was listening. Rosamond had brought with her that feeling of being watched. Something that hit one between the shoulder blades, even if there was no one in the room.

"Oh yes, yes indeed," said Rosamond, "d'you remember in Chungking, how we longed for liberation?"

She began to cough, took out her handkerchief. When she raised her head again her eyes were full of tears. "Oh Stephanie," she whispered, "I'm . . . I'm so unhappy. . . ."

Stephanie hugged Rosamond's thin shoulders. "Tell me, and blast anyone who eavesdrops," she said.

Rosamond's eyes swept the room with the unfocused stare of the blind. "I'm silly . . . I always feel watched . . . all the time . . . because of Carlos."

"Carlos?"

Taking deep breaths between her words, Rosamond told her story.

"You remember, Stephanie, we went to the American Consulate and you sponsored my application to go to the States? But nothing happened. The visas had to go through the Secret Police, and they refused me a passport. I wrote to Terry, and he sent me money. He said he would try to come and fetch me . . . and then . . . there were no more letters. . . ."

(Terry, in Ireland perhaps, with his wife, Blanche, and the children.)

Rosamond had gone to Peking and obtained a job there with an American firm. "That was in 1946. Terry stopped writing sometime that summer. And I—I fell in love with Carlos." Carlos was a Spaniard who also worked for the American company. And when the American staff left, Carlos was appointed delegate for the company, for he knew Chinese very well, and had lived thirty years in Peking.

"They arrested Carlos. About three months ago. At the same time as a German family in the same street. I don't know why," said Rosamond helplessly.

"The public security men asked me many questions and I told them the truth. They have now closed Carlos's house and put a guard on it. I wanted to send him parcels, food, but only *immediate* relatives—wife, son or daughter, father, mother—are allowed to send food parcels or letters. 'You are not his wife,' they said to me.

"So I asked to come to Shanghai, to stay with my mother. She's now very old. . . .

"Something must be done to get Carlos out of jail," said Rosamond, twisting her body in agony, knowing that really nothing could be done. How does one explain a Spaniard

335

living in China many years, perhaps as a spy? Spain had no diplomatic representative with the new Government, and was a fascist country.

"The new Government is very proud. Any interference by foreigners is resented. The more shouting the more they are *sure* that there has been what they call 'illicit connection,' spying . . . and that only brings worse trouble."

Nevertheless, Rosamond wanted to return to Peking. To be near Carlos. She could find work as a translator with the accredited embassies. "I must persuade my mother to come with me to Peking. But she's so attached to her coffin. She purchased it some years ago. I'll have to take the coffin along with her on the train."

Poor Rosamond, Stephanie thought after she'd left. For so many years, she's depended on a man—Terry, now this Carlos . . . What will happen to her? There is no place here . . . now . . . for a woman so alone, so needing. . . .

Dense autumn darkness, and cold, unstirring. Yong came back. And Stephanie knew something had happened.

"What is it, darling?" Her heart beat fast, fast . . .

"We are going to Korea, Stephanie. Dr. Wu, Dr. Fan, and myself. In a few days."

"How long will you be away?" Her voice shook. She would be alone . . . needing. . . .

"I don't know . . . I hope not too long," he said and took her in his arms.

That night they clung to each other, clung, every inch of flesh and bone precious beyond words, the only universe their own bodies, blind with passion, with hunger, with ecstasy.

Stephanie went with Yong to the airport to see him off. The doctors were flying to Manchuria. There, by army truck, they would travel to an undisclosed destination in Korea.

Joan Wu and Mrs. Fan had not come to the airport. Joan was too busy at the hospital pharmacy; Mrs. Fan had too many children to look after.

As Stephanie sat with Yong, waiting for the departure of the plane, the security police came to question her.

She showed her pass and Yong explained she was his wife.

"Foreigners are not allowed in the airport," said the security policeman.

"But she has a permit," said Yong. "She lives in Shanghai."

"We have to investigate the permit," said the policeman. He was even-voiced, scrupulous, a little severe.

Over the loudspeaker came the voice: "Passengers for the plane to Peking and Shenyang please embark immediately."

"Don't worry, Stephanie," Yong said. "It is just routine. . . . Make them call Father, call the dean at the university." He was very pale. He did not want to leave her. He stood, looking at her, at the policeman.

"I'm not worried. Take care of yourself, darling." Stephanie smiled gaily.

She had not come to the airport to spy . . . she had come to see Yong off. And now Yong was going, walking away. She watched him, watched his back going down the stairs, watched him turn, again and again, walk across the cemented area to the plane. She waved. Patiently, the police officer stood, letting her wave, until Yong was only a smudge climbing the ladder of the Ilyushin.

"Come with me please," said the police officer.

In the small office of the airport there were two other security men. They stared at her pass, stared at her.

"We'll have to check," they said.

"Where shall I wait?" asked Stephanie.

They looked at each other. All three of them were young. They did not know how to handle this situation. A foreigner at the airport, a foreigner who was *not* leaving, who was married to a doctor going to Korea.

An American.

Two of them had never seen a foreigner. They stared at Stephanie.

"She speaks Chinese," said one of them, wonderingly, to the other. "I even understand what she says. . . ."

"I would like to have a chair to sit on, comrades," said Stephanie. And added, knowing that this always made a great impression: "I am pregnant."

One of the young men immediately went to get a chair.

And Stephanie sat while they looked at her pass, over and over again, turning it up, down, looking at her.

"Do you know the telephone number of your unit?" one asked. Stephanie knew. She told them. Told them where she lived. And, as usual, exhibited the photograph of Winter Treasure. "My son," she said. And felt the glass cage melt. That glass cage which had sprung up around her when Yong had left, and from which all the oxygen was being slowly pumped out.

She waited fifteen hours. She asked for water to drink, and hot water was provided. She asked to be allowed to pace up and down outside the office, in the corridor, and was refused. There was no food to be had. She sat, a little lightheaded. The security men went off to lunch. She asked for the toilet. The security men discussed it while she waited. Finally an old woman appeared. The toilet cleaner. She went with Stephanie and gave her some paper. She stood inside the toilet while Stephanie urinated.

"Hai, you're made just like us," said the old woman.

It was almost midnight when the security officer, one of a new batch, just as young and uncertain as the others, said that she could go home.

"But how can I go home? It is night. I must telephone my family."

"No telephoning is allowed," said the security man.

"Then I shall have to stay here until morning light," said Stephanie.

"No," said the security officer. "This is quite impossible." He did not tell her, but she guessed that the office was also his bedroom. He would lie down, unroll a quilt on the floor. She had to leave.

"I will tell you," said the security officer kindly, "there are pedicabs, a pedicab garage, just about a third of a mile down the road from here."

Stephanie thanked him. She walked into the very dark hallway and out of the airport. She reached the flight of stairs going down to the road. The usual night rain and fog mixture had come upon Shanghai and everything was wet, almost oily with damp. She slipped, slid down five or six steps, landing on her buttocks. For a while she sat upon the last step. She picked herself up, rubbed her buttocks, walked on to the pedicab garage.

It was a rickety wood hut, disjointed planks filtering the brown gold of an oil lamp through its slits. The door was partly closed. Inside were some men sleeping, others play-

338

ing cards. Their pedicabs were garaged neatly under an awning. While she stood there two other men garaged their carriages and walked towards the door.

Now the men no longer pulled between shafts like animals. They had bicycle vehicles. They formed cooperatives. Their fares were fixed. Some of them were Party members.

And whereas they had been so poor, so despised that they could not marry, now the daughters of rural landlords, running away from land reform, tried through matchmakers to marry even pedicab drivers, to get themselves a new identity.

The two men fell silent, perceiving Stephanie, a foreigner, at this hour of the night, alone.

"Comrades," said Stephanie. "I was detained at the airport by the security police. But they have checked me and have released me to go home. It is very far. Will one of you take me?"

"Where is your home?" asked one of the men.

"Which is your unit?" asked the other.

Stephanie told them.

They looked at each other. It was indeed very far.

"If I do not go home," said Stephanie, "I shall have to wait until morning. And there is no place where I can rest."

They looked at her again, hesitant.

"Where is your husband?"

"My husband is a doctor. He went to Korea this morning, that is why I was at the airport."

The two men went inside the hut to discuss the matter with their colleagues. Stephanie waited. One of the men came out. "I will pull you home. A woman should not be alone in the street at night. Even though it is safe now."

"It is indeed safe now," agreed Stephanie.

After an hour and a half pedaling, Stephanie recognized the paved street leading home.

She had chatted with the pedicab man on the way. He had been born in Shanghai, his father was a peddler and had died of tuberculosis. The Government was now building flats for people like him. He was thirty-five. "I never had a roof over my head before, only the rain from the sky, only the sun."

Stephanie felt a rush of affection for him. He was not trying to force her to say anything, he pedaled, making small courteous remarks. And Stephanie thought: I feel at ease, I feel safe with him and people like him, safe and even happy. She told him about Yong and Winter Treasure. . . . *This man had waited all his youth for a roof. Why complain because I've been checked for fifteen hours? There's a war on.*

"Yes, comrade, I have a father and mother in America, also a younger brother."

"In the past," said the pedicab man, "the Americans used to get about twenty of us lined up and make us run races. They sat in our carriages. How we ran!"

"That was very bad," said Stephanie, feeling ashamed.

"It was for money, we were always so hungry," said the pedicab man, reasonable. "The Americans always paid. Some of the other foreigners did not." He was no longer hungry now. "But I do not think I can have a loved one . . . you see, I still have an old mother, very old and blind . . . young women today do not wish for such a burden."

He harbored no hate, no bitterness, no resentment against his life. From him came a great sweetness.

The gate of the House was open, Mother was standing there, frail and upright, a formidable wisp, watching, watching the street. Stephanie alighted. She felt a queer heaviness in her belly, a smoldering, wringing ache.

Mother said to the pedicab man: "Comrade, thank you for bringing my daughter back." She paid him the exact fare and he went off grinning, stepping delicately away, pushing his pedicab and then hopping onto the saddle.

Stephanie walked with Mother to her bedroom. Something odd was happening to her. A sensation of gushing warmth. And suddenly a cramp which twisted her in pain. The light was on. She looked down. Mother said: "What is it?"

Where Stephanie stood, on the tiled floor, some drops of blood, dripping slowly from between her legs.

sixteen

FROM Tokyo the Flying Fortresses winged their steady convoys across the storm-prone Sea of Japan to Kimpo. Dakotas took off several times a day, with men and guns, reinforcements to the interminable war in Korea.

Second Lieutenant James Ryder felt his lean buttocks numbed by the metal edge of the seating bench. He hitched his yellow Mae West and turned to peer through the porthole. The sea and the sky danced up and down, the Dakota lurched and bobbed as it began its descent towards Seoul.

They landed at Kimpo in the late afternoon and the freezing air whooshed into the opened hatch. Jimmy took a big gulp of it and said "Aaah." It was so clean, so clean after the pollution, the brownish miasma of Tokyo, with its odors of burning gasoline and rancid everything else. His lungs expanded, hungrily absorbing the oxygen purity. "I smell snow," said Jimmy.

A top sergeant, bulky and red-cheeked and straight out of the comics, waited to take the reinforcements to the trucks. Jimmy stared at the amethyst horizon in which a gold sun was dissolving beyond the mountains. "That's where the Chincoms dig themselves in, sir," said the sergeant amiably. "Now if you please, sir . . ."

The trucks roared along the road, docilely following the frozen Han River. The light changed, deepened into a shadeless lilac, and the icy stream sparkled between its white sand banks. "God, it's so beautiful," said Jimmy.

"What's beautiful?" asked Arch Cappuzzio, who had been sick in the plane.

"Everything," Jimmy said. "All of it." His hand swept up and down. "I never knew it could be so lovely . . . " He inhaled deeply again.

Arch laughed. "You ain't seen anything, buddy. It can be hell. Wait till the Chincoms start on you." In Tokyo Arch had heard many stories. About the Chincoms and the gooks, who materialized out of nothing, straight under your feet, shot at you, and then disappeared again. "They're right behind you when you think they're in front. They've got miles and miles of tunnels in the mountains. No bomb can touch them."

The American Army quarters stretched their barracks north of Seoul, and the trucks drove through the ruined city whose silence and empty streets absorbed the whine of the engines. Walls stood haphazardly about, delineating streets, as in an archaeological site. Windows blind with emptiness sometimes checkered a side alley. There was rubble in neat heaps, leaving the main avenues clear for military traffic. Seoul had changed hands four times in a year.

The officers' quarters were a few rows of Quonset style buildings. "Company G," said the sergeant. "Here you are." Jimmy and Arch tumbled out of the truck onto the familiar landscape of a U.S. military camp. Even the smells were the same.

But Jimmy did not want to walk into the warmth of the officers' quarters. He wanted to walk out, out of that prison of barbed wire, out into that gorgeous color which thickened the air, magenta night now that the sun had gone.

Captain Farady, face hacked into exact and trenchant grimness, gave the new companies their pep talk the next day. He lived in a small cubicle, at a desk strewn with papers. The walls of the cubicle were covered with maps. He seemed to know Korea only through these maps. Did he ever walk outside, walk until he would hit those blue mountains whose snow perfume reached Jimmy?

"I can smell snow," said Jimmy to Arch once again.

"I can smell chow," said Arch, who sometimes said things like that when he felt Jimmy was getting too far out for him.

Farady read out their names: Spellman, Cappuzzio, Hinckle, Ryder . . . pausing just to hear the smart: "Yes sir." Another bunch of our boys, he thought wearily. There had been talks of truce, ceasefire, since July 1951, three months after the President had fired General MacArthur. But still the war went on, and still GIs died, and new, fresh-faced young men came out to replace them. And Captain Farady didn't like it. He was a good soldier, careful of lives. Every GI who died wrenched a bit more of Captain Farady's guts out of him.

Crisply, Farady assigned duties, outlined the situation in sector H, the combat sector in which the reinforcement companies would operate. "We've got reason to believe the enemy might try a sortie along that edge of the front. They're holing up behind the mountains. So we're reinforcing the entire sector." The company would be assigned to hold a small valley which wound around northwards. No enemy presence had been detected there for some months. "We're strengthening this area because we feel they might try their steam-roller tactics again." All the villages in the valley had been destroyed, to deprive the enemy of cover or food or aid of any kind, and the hill slopes had been bombed and would go on being bombed.

He's trying to make it all sound too damn much like a walkover, thought Arch Cappuzzio.

Jimmy strained to look at the map. Found the "frontline" zigzagging athwart the spined and ridged valleys.

"Any questions?" Captain Farady looked around. Jimmy held up his hand. "Yes. Lieutenant Ryder?"

"Sir, I'd like to ask . . . what about the truce talks?"

Farady remained speechless.

"Sir, the territory indicated on this map seems to be a bit beyond the ceasefire neutral zone I saw on another map. . . ."

"Lieutenant Ryder." Farady, flushed and angry, bit out the words. "The enemy is acting in flagrant violation of any civilized conduct. Can't trust them. We've got to keep on hitting him. Got to hold on to territory . . . is that clear?"

"Yes sir, thank you, sir."

"Shit, you had a nerve," said Arch. "That map thing, buddy . . . how did you know the sector was beyond the neutral zone?"

"I read up on it all in Tokyo . . . it was in the Japanese papers in English, with names and all . . . I recognized the names."

"Aw c'mon, can't go by what *they* say," replied Arch. "Let's hope they don't send us climbing those mountain

343

slopes—that's murder, every time. Ever heard of Heartbreak Ridge? and how many of our guys . . ."

Jimmy and Arch walked in the streets of battered Seoul. A dead city, or so it appeared if one just stuck to the main roads. From time to time, Jimmy could see people, in and out, furtive like shadows, in rags: men, women, children. But they kept away. They lived among the debris.

Little boys, urchins with swift hands, flocked like eager starlings around them. "Hey, hey, GI, GI, shine shoes, shine shoes . . . GI, GI, want me shine you?"

In the midst of the ruins, strangely untouched, rose the incongruous granite dome of the capitol building, copied from some American state capitol; and behind it, the old Golden Palace of the emperors of Korea, its bright glazed roof tiles and the treasures of its rooms littering the ground around it. Jimmy walked its once-upon-a-time garden and picked up a tiny plate, Korean celadon, pale green glaze, with an under-glaze design. He put it in his pocket and touched it from time to time. It comforted him. It was a sign, a beckoning, like the mountains, like the air. . . .

Some buildings were being repaired. The gray brick of the United Nations headquarters, which had once been a ministry, was a-crawl with workers. Women in trousers, scarfs on their heads, were hauling planks, carrying baskets. . . .

"It's the women who do all the heavy work here, like in Russia," said Arch. Women sweeping the streets, carrying the garbage, hauling loads. The men wore white clothes, clean every morning, and waited, squatting, for the women to cook their food; the women spent their nights washing those clothes, beating them in the clear streams, beating and beating them with wood paddles to a resplendent white.

Women with flat, calm faces. Stolid and solid and strong. Enduring. Some worked with babies tied to their backs in blankets.

"I'm walking this land and I don't know anything about it, Arch."

"You'll learn soon enough, Jimmy."

Down the avenue to what had been the railway station.

Shacks of wood, with tarpaulin over their leaky roofs. Shacks lighted with hurricane lamps, blaring out music, grinding music from old Victrolas. And in front of the shack the women. Squat. Short legs. No waistline. Frizzy hair. Faces round and thickly covered with pasty white make-up. Blood-red mouths.

"Hey, GI, hey, American? Hey look here, give you a good time, a good time, only a dollar, only a dollar. Come, come . . ."

"They're Japs . . . brought out of Tokyo . . . can't trust the gooks," said Arch, exhibiting his Tokyo-acquired knowledge.

Gooks. That was the name for the Koreans.

Gooks not allowed in our trucks . . . kick them out . . . gooks not to come into the camps . . . gooks not to be trusted.

The music was nostalgic, almost greasy with nostalgia, catching at one's throat, one's belly, because it reminded one of home.

They stopped and like magpies the girls congregated, screeching, almost yodeling, pulling at their sleeves, their arms, even boldly patting their thighs, insinuating hands upon the crotch. In the light their masklike faces were all identical.

Jimmy tore himself away. Arch, surrounded, half liking it, half disgusted, pushed away the two girls who hung over him, yelling: "Hey, Jimmy, wait for me."

"Big boy, oh you big big boy, have good time with me."

Arch shook them off and followed Jimmy and the girls shrieked, then laughed, laughed at them, calling out obscenities they did not understand.

"It isn't as if we were going to fight," said Arch. "Hell, we're really just going on a holding operation. Then we'll go home."

"Sure," said Jimmy. "We won't have to kill anyone."

"Or be killed," said practical Arch.

The armored convoy and the trucks carrying Company G left Seoul and headed northwards, towards those snow-scented hills. Jimmy couldn't stop gazing at them.

Soon the road yielded to a faceless quagmire of frozen

mud, ploughed up by the wheels of so many vehicles. This had once been fields.

They went on. The land became contorted, sinuous, with sudden ridges erupting and twisting away.

In the months since July 1951, while the truce talks went on, it was reported that ten thousand GIs had been killed, wounded, or missing. Many of these casualties had been suffered in the first few months when ridges were taken which would later prove of total insignificance.

Now there was no more scaling of hills. Only holding positions. The truce talks were on, then off, and then on again, each side accusing the other.

The battle front had been stagnant for several months. No advance, and no withdrawal.

"Oh dear Jesus," prayed Jimmy every night. "I don't want to kill anyone."

Funny, but he couldn't hate. He ought to, but he couldn't. He didn't feel he was defending anything either. And that was all wrong. This non-feeling about the war. Only that the country was so beautiful, the devastated land, and his heart was wrung with pity.

Stephanie. And Yong. He was here because of his sister Stephanie . . . and Yong.

Back at school, coming into the locker room after the ball game, body feeling good, feeling the glow of muscle and blood now eased, the ecstasy of tiredness, the sweat agreeable on cooling skin.

He had heard.

"I tell you . . . his sister's fucking a Chincom . . ." And someone said: "Hold it . . ." He'd stood there and they were looking at him. And Arch had come up quickly, come and pushed him out.

"Now Jimmy, I've got to talk to you . . ." And over Arch's shoulder the guy pushing himself back into his trousers, whistling.

Arch had dragged him, linking arms, up and down along the quadrangle of the military academy, beneath the arches and then in the fields. Making him walk up and down, as if his life depended on it. "Aw, Jimmy, c'mon now, you know he's just a moron . . . don't pay any attention, c'mon, look, let's go get a cup of coffee. . . ."

"I'll kill him, Arch, I'll kill him . . . my sister . . ."

"Ah, Jimmy, he didn't really mean it. . . ."

346

"How long have they been talking, Arch? How long?"

"Never heard it before, Jimmy, it's the first time. . . ." Arch was lying.

"My sister's married to a Chinese doctor, Arch. He's not a red."

"Of course not, Jimmy, lots of Chinks around, not red . . . it doesn't mean a thing. . . ."

"I'll kick the guy's teeth in." And that evening he'd felt it. That thickness in the air. That elaborateness of gestures, the seeming naturalness. Talking of Stephanie. He could not stand it. So he'd gone to Captain Herzog two days later, and even now, now that he was cool and here in Korea, he could not quite remember how it was, because he had been in such a white, blind fog of pain. He only remembered telling himself: Hold it. Hold it.

"Yes, Lieutenant Ryder?"

Herzog's eyes. That film over them. He also knew.

"Sir. I'd like to volunteer for Korea. . . ."

They'd been waiting for this. A white blue, raging white heat shaking him.

"Feeling all right, Ryder?"

"Yes, perfectly well, sir."

Training camp. Six weeks of it. Live ammunition. He'd wanted to die, wondered what it would be like, he'd wanted to be hit. . . .

Then Arch Cappuzzio had turned up. "Kind of lonely without you around, Jimmy. Besides, I've always wanted to travel."

In training camp he'd heard the grapevine news. About casualties. About the coffins returning. Too many coffins. Too many generals eager *not* to stop the fighting. "Hell, war keeps the wheels of industry spinning . . . there's a boom on, they've got to keep the war going, so there won't be another depression . . ." said Arch. Accepting it all.

He telephoned Mom a few days before leaving for Tokyo. Must tell her that he would be going to Korea, but taking it easy, not making a big deal about it . . . .

Mom wasn't well. But it was something she didn't want to talk about.

"Jimmy, oh Jimmy," Mom wailed. "Oh, Jimmy why, but why? I thought you weren't going. . . ."

"I'll be back real soon, Mom . . . why, they're already talking about peace in Korea, so it's absolutely safe."

347

His jaws hurt with the part lie.

"Jimmy," sobbing. "It's Calvary, Jimmy, each one of us, each one of us has his own private Calvary . . . each one of us . . . may the Lord spread his grace upon you."

"Mom, please, don't cry . . . why, I'll be back real soon, everyone says it'll be over soon . . . and there's practically no fighting going on."

"Jimmy, Jimmy, perhaps it's God's will, but it's hard, Jimmy. . . . You won't forget to pray, will you?"

"No, Mom." He fingered the little cross Mom had put around his neck. "You bet I won't."

And later it was Dad on the telephone.

"Jimmy."

Quiet. Not imperative.

"Yes, Dad." He braced himself.

"I hear you volunteered, son."

"Yes, Dad. We're off to Tokyo. We'll be there for a bit, to acclimatize . . ."

"I see." Heston was thinking, thinking furiously. Jimmy heard the tick tick tick of his father's thinking. And now he was no longer uneasy about Dad. About the silence between them. There was no threat in the silence. He'd done it. On his own. Done something and it was a kind of victory over Dad.

And of course Dad was at the airport when they were enplaning for Tokyo. Trust him to call up the right people, to get the timing and everything perfect.

Dad looked Dad. Still so tall and handsome and bestriding the earth that was good to him; but as he came nearer Jimmy felt that some substance had gone out of his father, as if he were lighter, more fragile. He no longer awed his son or made him nervous, and his son now calmly watched him come towards him. Heston's eyes were steady and blue and he wore his ten-gallon hat, and Jimmy knew that he loved his father.

Heston said: "Time for a cup of coffee," and they sat on stools at the bar in the waiting room. The morning was brilliant, everything was sprayed with bouncing brightness like bright varnish. Jimmy dunked a doughnut in his coffee.

They did not talk very much. Of Mom, mostly. Jimmy guessed that Dad was worried about Mom's health. The doctors kept on saying there was nothing to worry about, but she was never really well. Now she was in bed again. "Give her a call whenever you can . . . will you?"

"Sure, Dad." And he had. Almost every other day, from Tokyo. And Mom always prayed with him:

"Almighty and merciful God, show me what to do . . . give me peace of mind. Thy will be done . . ."

"I think you did right, son. Stand up against evil." But Dad wasn't forceful on the word *evil* now. Not like before. As if he was tired of the word. "I'm told there isn't a city left standing in Korea. . . ."

"Dad," said Jimmy, "I . . . " Then he stopped. How could he tell his father he'd volunteered because of Stephanie, not to kill anybody? . . .

And as if guessing his thoughts, Dad said: "Seems to me we've had enough bloodletting . . . in that damn country . . ."

"Dad, you heard from Stephanie?"

The last letter had been a couple of months ago. Anodyne. Saying almost nothing except that all was well and not to worry. And Mom had replied, as usual.

Heston nodded, then gripped his son's shoulder with awkward affection. "Jimmy, take care of yourself . . ."

He wanted to say: I love you, but he could not say it. His eyes said it. And Jimmy said: "Dad, it's great you could come."

And then he was walking away, walking to the plane, lighthearted, walking off to the war just like going off to school.

In front of the outpost where Company G was quartered, the valley climbed to a rainbow curve of mountains leading into North Korea. There was no sign of life in the valley, which narrowed as it advanced among the rising foothills.

All the villages had been destroyed and the people had gone, or if they had not gone, they were now inoffensively dead, part of the earth and its rocks.

When Jimmy saw his first dead body he had not known what it was. Had thought it an animal, or a strange pulpy plant of some kind. At one end of a great blossom of purple-blue intestines was a triangular white blob. A face. That of a

349

girl. With long black hair. Frozen, with wide-open eyes and mouth.

There had been others. The kids were the worst.

Somehow their limbs were always so queerly set, at such odd angles. And always those open eyes, open mouths, frozen in a final gulp of that wonderful oxygen-full air . . .

"Heck, if we've got to stick around we'll have to organize a couple of cemeteries," said Arch.

But death is odorless in the preserving cold. And soon the men got used to the litter of bodies strewn among the debris . . .

Regular as clockwork, at certain times of the day, the Air Force exercised. Bombed the hills and mountains, blasting and pounding the folded and forested land. "Got to waste so much ammunition per day per man . . ." said Arch gravely, "to keep the war going." And Jimmy grinned at this parody of attack on the land, on the earth which took it all, and went on being.

The vehicles advanced, ploughing across what had been a patchwork of rice fields and was now crater-pocked frozen ground. Sometimes a bend would reveal a small copse of firs. Sometimes they went through charred anonymous copses. The ground was soft with dark ash, and bodies in imploring positions, arms raised to the sky, lingered among the cadavers of tree trunks.

"Napalm," said Arch.

"Arch!"

"Yes, Jimmy."

"They're not soldiers. . . ."

"Well, Jimmy, they're gooks . . . enemies . . ."

The camp was well protected with reinforced barbed wire. Protected by a small jut of promontory, upon which an observation post had been built, commanding the valley. Northwards the ground undulated gently into hills, into a fuzz of green pine, and above them was a range of snow-capped mountains, stark and brilliant and fascinating. Behind them lay the plain through which they had come.

No dogs, no people, nothing.

Below them, its back against a faint ridge which led nowhere, the usual ruined village. Yet not all that usual, for in its middle, among the heaped ruins, stood one small tiled roof, token of what had once been. The tiles of that magenta color which the gooks seemed to love.

How could this one roof, wistful eaves curling upwards, have escaped the bombing? Behind it rose a small rock, sheer, wind-buffeted to silver-gray granite.

Jimmy and Arch went to see it. There was no one around. Not even a corpse.

"First really clean place," said Arch. "It's nice."

The company settled in well. There was nothing much to do except reinforce the foxholes, and drill, and take turns watching, and do all the important trivia of a training camp.

"Guess we'll just sit here till the end of the war," said Arch.

In the afternoon the mountains sparkled and then in the lilac-turning sky they became infinitely clear. The temptation to get at them, to climb them, became irresistible. Jimmy and Gunnar Christiansen watched them from the promontory lookout and yearned to get at them. "God, how I'd like to be up there," said Gunnar, who had been a mountain climber and a ski instructor in Aspen, Colorado.

"They're called the Diamond Mountains," said Gunnar, his voice thick with desire.

And both thought: When the war's over, we'll be back, be back. . . .

At night, Jimmy and Arch and the men lay in foxholes, with pup tents above them. But no enemy plane ever strafed them. The men trained, as if for war. But here it all became a game.

And after a while, because of the silence, and nonactivity, a kind of contented torpor settled upon the camp. And the sun splashed its profligate splendor upon them and they basked in it. And the days lengthened, they could feel the angry stir and sap of burgeons yet unseen.

"Spring is coming," said Arch.

And the restlessness of spring with its mischievous tug at all one's nerves, one's body, the rise of humors and the brain's muted parleys with itself made their casual words significant.

Jimmy went almost every afternoon to the clean battered village in their rear and visited its miraculously intact curlicue roof of magenta tiles, which seemed to reflect a rainbow all its own in the sparkling light.

"D'you know that according to my reckoning we're almost a mile and a half beyond the agreed neutral zone?" said Gunnar. Gunnar loved maps, as he loved mountains.

He had procured a Korean grammar, a book of Korean fairy tales, and had begun to study the ideograms. He pored over the maps and he had worked out that the camp was just beyond the limit tacitly agreed upon at the last truce talks. But then the two sides always accused each other of going beyond the agreed line. It was part of the games of war.

Jimmy squatted with Arch and Gunnar, staring at the map. "Maybe that's why the Aussies who were here before us left," said Christiansen in his careful, methodical Swedish way.

One morning Jimmy fancied he heard singing. "I hear singing," he said to Arch.

"Oh come on." Arch listened. "I don't hear nothing." Arch himself produced music, blowing on his mouth organ the hit tunes of the year. Jimmy looked at the roof. It glowed. Suddenly he saw, propping up the roof, columns of painted gold. . . . But of course it was a hallucination, for now almost every day he walked to the ruined village and sat among the stones, thinking of nothing, and there were no golden pillars there.

But he had achieved an intimacy with that bit of unspoiled roof which he could not relinquish. It was significant, as the celadon plate in his pocket was significant.

He went to it across the stubbled havocked fields. Climbed a small wavery pathway which leapt at him from between the ice-filled bomb craters staring glassily upwards as did the dead. The pathway of irregular, packed clay steps bordered with short lengths of sapling reached a stone ledge in front of the intact roof, and Jimmy tried to imagine the village, the street, before it had been rubbed out, clustering around that magical stretch of magenta tiles which must have been the temple. It must have covered a fair sized room whose side walls were still vertical, though the front and most of the back walls had crumbled. Inside the room there was only rubble and a large bronze incense burner, bent and twisted, leaning on its side. In one corner of a side wall he could discern incomprehensible scrawls in black ink on the rough white plaster. Writing, or perhaps just those nebulous cloud patterns surrounding a Buddhist saint.

One afternoon Jimmy heard a bell tinkle.

"Arch . . . listen . . . hear that?"

But it had stopped.

"I don't hear nothing," said Arch.

But Jimmy knew. Hanging from one of the eaves there was a small bronze bell. It was meant to send out music when the wind blew. And now it had sent music.

But there was no wind. Perhaps a bird . . . but there were so few birds.

Again he fingered the plate. Maybe not a bird. Beautiful, the music of that small bell . . .

Late that day, just before the cold and evening set in, he walked, his limbs tingling with happiness, to the village. Sat down on what had been a wall, uncemented fitted stones lying upon each other.

The Diamond Mountains were so clear, eating up the sky, and the sun was going away. He raised himself, stood on tiptoe to touch that miracle of nondestruction, the small bell. It must have been a bird, its wing brushing it.

Pfc. Dryberg, on sentry duty, watched Lieutenant Ryder go for his accustomed afternoon walk, just before chow, and then no longer watched him.

Jimmy sat on the threshold of what he now called the temple. He felt the sun do its usual stunt: gold to green to crimson and then drowning in the gore it lavished upon the sky.

Here he could believe in God, in a way he could not when he was in San Antonio. Here God was evident, in His galaxies, His sun and its rainbow games, and the glistening mountains were there too, for God's pleasure, and man's. *Thank you, God.*

The cat came on dainty feet, to watch Jimmy. And Jimmy watched it walk, picking its way. Where had it sprung from? There was no life here, all life had been abolished, demolished . . . didn't the cat know it?

"Puss, puss," said Jimmy, wondering if it was a dream. The cat was small and dark as midnight with two white front paws. It seemed unafraid. It stopped and looked at Jimmy and mewed.

That was another miracle, like the bell, like the roof. Oh, this was the most wonderful miracle of all, the first living thing in so many days, the first noncadaver, and to confirm it the cat, rounding its back, walked around Jimmy and rubbed itself against his boots. Not mangy. Thin, but not skeletal . . . And not wild. Perhaps there were a few people still alive, huddled in some mountain crevice, who had

353

escaped the bombing; but cats always come home, and this village had been its home. . . . But I mustn't tell anyone, thought Jimmy. Because then we'll send out a search party, and search will be destroy; can't take chances . . . they may be spies.

The cat sat in its accustomed place on what had been the village street and was now a shambles of broken stone, and washed its face.

Jimmy squatted by it, making cooing sounds. His fingers tickled the cat just below the ear, and the cat purred. "Oh you funny little thing, how did you manage to *live*, huh?" asked Jimmy. And planned to bring food, but he mustn't tell anyone, mustn't tell . . . not even Arch. No one must find the cat.

The lilac shades of swift approaching evening deepened and the whole world changed color, and the sun began to paint its crimson city in the sky.

Jimmy picked up the cat, felt the vibrant fur, alive against his shirt. He stood there, filled with happiness as the shadows lengthened. Soon it would be shadowless dark.

There was a slight noise. Very slight. Something like the slither of a soft shoe crisp against dry grass.

Jimmy looked up. Framed by the yawning crumble of the back wall, in pale gray, with a fur cap upon his head.

Yong.

"Yong!" cried Jimmy, full of gladness. "Yong!"

The last sunlight dazzled his eyes and he walked forward, still holding the cat. Then behind the first fur cap he saw another, and another. And there was a noise in his ears, and suddenly night had fallen, and he was glad, glad, he had never killed anyone.

All hell broke loose as they came out of the tunnel they had dug, debouching behind the camp as another body of their men came down from the safe mountains. The camp was caught in the crossfire of machine guns.

The company fought bravely, the men firing as they ran for shelter, firing as they died. Arch Cappuzzio did what he could. He too died, wondering where Jimmy was. As suddenly as they had come, the attackers withdrew and night fell.

The bombers came and pounded the hills and their folds. They threw tons of bombs. But the tunnels were well-constructed and safe.

Comrade-in-charge Kang lay on his pallet that night, deep underground. He thought about the single American soldier and the cat. They had not expected the American there, but they could not delay. It had not interfered with the plan. Kang also loved cats, and had owned a kitten when he was a boy. It was a pity the cat could not be spared.

Why had the American walked straight toward him, holding the cat and smiling?

seventeen

SHE knew well the green-walled, gray-tiled corridor on the maternity floor. Winter Treasure had been born in this hospital, a little over three years ago. Now she was back, and she wondered whether Mary Lee the Eurasian was still working here.

Mother and Peony had made Stephanie lie flat in bed, anchored a pad firmly between her legs. But the bleeding went on, and the cramps; so with the first silver smudge of dawn Mother had taken her to the hospital, in Uncle Keng's borrowed car.

The nurse in emergency was abrupt. "She is a foreigner . . . this is not a hospital for foreigners."

"My daughter-in-law is the wife of Dr. Jen Yong who is a surgeon here. She had her baby in this hospital three years ago."

The nurse frowned. "What is her unit?"

"The university, department of foreign languages and literature," said Stephanie, showing her work card.

"Then you should have applied through your unit. Your unit should have referred you to us."

"That was not possible," said Mother. "The bleeding began very late last night. . . ."

"We must also report her presence to Public Security. She is a foreigner," said the nurse as if she had not heard. "All displacements of foreigners must be reported. . . ." She frowned heavily at Stephanie's university work card. "American. She must wait until we have received authority."

Mother put two wooden chairs together and made Stephanie lie down upon them. The pain was a dull one, not much worse than her period. From time to time it sharpened, like a hand groping then squeezing.

"I think I've stopped bleeding," she said to Mother. And dozed.

It was late morning when the young doctor turned up with another nurse. He also frowned heavily when he saw Stephanie. "This is quite irregular," he began.

Mother explained. Stephanie was the wife of Dr. Jen Yong. She had had a baby in this hospital. Dr. Wu could testify to it. "Dr. Wu is in Korea," said the young intern. "To normalize procedure we need authority from her unit."

"Doctor," said Mother, "please telephone the Party committee at the university. Here is the telephone number." The young doctor took the number and the new nurse looked at Stephanie and said:

"Would you like to drink some water?"

"Oh yes," said Stephanie.

Nurse held her up and said to her, "You speak good Chinese."

Now the pain was grinding, constant, precisely in the middle of her belly, and Stephanie wanted to curl up around it and sleep. Another hour went by. The telephone connection to her unit was hard to get.

Finally Mother came back with the young doctor who said: "Move the patient into ward three." He sat down to write a form. "You will have to be responsible for Public Security. You must report her being moved to the hospital," he said to Mother.

There was no stretcher available. The nurse and Mother helped Stephanie to walk to the ward. The ward held eight beds; one waited emptily for her, very clean and white. She lay on it, and screens were put around her. She was thankful for the screens. The other seven patients watched. They whispered: "A foreigner, a foreigner . . ." Nurse and Mother helped Stephanie to undress. The pads were soaked through with bright red blood. Nurse changed Stephanie, gave her an injection, wiped her face and hands with a warm towel.

The women sat up in their beds, heads turned towards Stephanie's screens.

"Why is she here?"

"This hospital is for Chinese, not for foreigners."

"Is she carrying germs? The Americans are killing our people with germs."

"We shall all get sick and die."

Mother held Stephanie's hand and said: "Try to sleep." The nurse took Stephanie's temperature.

"We shall all die of her germs. . . ."

The nurse came out from behind the screens. She said: "Big Sisters all. This is an American friend, she has no germs. Look at me, was I frightened to be with her?"

Mother sat on a chair by the bed. Faces peered between the screens. Many faces. One after the other. Stephanie closed her eyes. I mustn't mind, she told herself. I mustn't mind. Of course there's a war on and lots of people feel angry. In America, too, this kind of thing happens. Get a grip on yourself, Stephanie.

And then an older doctor was there, speaking in that light cultivated tenor, which distinguished the intellectual.

"Mrs. Jen, I am Dr. Peng, a colleague of your husband." Stephanie tried to sit up. Dr. Peng said: "Don't move. We are taking you to the examination room."

A stretcher took her to a small cubicle. Dr. Peng examined her gently. Then she was taken back to the ward.

Peony was there with two thermos flasks, one with tea, the other with boiling water, and a set of dishes, rice and soup and meat with cabbage, in those round boxes which fitted on top of each other. And some clean clothes. Peony said: "Old mistress was called away. She told me to come with the food now and again this evening. She will return to see you as soon as she can. . . ."

In the afternoon Stephanie was seized by stabbing pain, unbearable cramps. She was now passing blood in large clots. The nurse came, and Dr. Peng. He ordered some injections. And then suddenly it stopped, after a heaving tearing cramp, and Stephanie knew that she had lost her baby.

It was there, a little blobby red mass, just outside of her. It was over. And she was relieved. *I did not want this child. I didn't want to bring a new life in a world bereft of love.* She buried her face in her pillow and wept very quietly and only for a short time. It was over.

The next morning Calthrop stood by her bed, defiant and uneasy. She had brought Stephanie's lunch and also her dinner. The thermos flasks had been refilled. "All of us are

358

very busy with the new counter-revolutionary campaign," she said. "Mother has to care for Father. She cannot come."

"Tell Mother I am very well looked after," said Stephanie.

Calthrop chose to take this as an insult. "Why do you think we are barbarians, like *your* soldiers?" she said. "*We* have socialist morality . . ."

"I did not mean . . ."

But Calthrop had worked herself into a minor rage. "I hope in future you will show more clearly how you condemn aggression."

Stephanie closed her eyes. The young fury made her feel old, very old. Oh Yong, Yong, am I really harming you? Mother, am I really harming you?

"The Americans are now using bacteriological warfare," said Calthrop. "Spreading clouds of insects and bacteria. The whole world is indignant about it, condemning this atrocity."

"I did not know." Stephanie would feel the deep, deep pain later. At the moment she was limp. *It's good no child of hate will be born.*

Calthrop left and the nurse came in and washed her again, as she had done the night before. She was kind and brisk. She gave her an injection, and then she left. She had not uttered a word.

Dr. Peng did a competent curettage the following day. When she had recovered from the anesthetic he came to see her. She noticed then he had a tic. The left side of his face pulled out and up towards his eyes. The outer orbital muscles of the left eye also twitched.

Had he had this tic the first time she had seen him? Or was it only now that she had noticed it?

"Mrs. Jen, you can go home in two days' time. Rest at home as much as possible. There is nothing to worry about."

"I thank you very much, Dr. Peng."

He left. He had not smiled.

Peony was waiting to take her home. A nurse went down the corridor with them to the registration office where a middle-aged man sat smoking and reading a newspaper.

359

"What is this, what is this?" said the man importantly, riffling through the papers the nurse handed him.

"Patient returning home," said the nurse.

"Has the Public Security been told?"

"No," said the nurse.

"She cannot leave until the Public Security allows it." He was fussing, giving himself airs.

Stephanie said: "I shall report myself to the Public Security of my district on the way home."

"Ah, but you cannot leave the hospital," said the man importantly.

"Then someone must take the papers to the security, and I'll wait here," said Stephanie.

The man stared at her angrily. Such insolence! She was not humble, placatory, this foreigner. He would report her insolence. "I must have higher authority," he said.

Stephanie waited. Two, three hours. The man left, and another man came. And then suddenly Dr. Peng was there. He bent over the desk and whispered something to the man, who opened his drawer, took out the rubber stamps, and stamped Stephanie's papers. "You can go home," he said.

"At a meeting of the students and the university staff it was decided to suspend the course in American literature, to concentrate on the present movement against counter-revolutionaries," wrote the dean to Stephanie.

The letter was on the living room table, awaiting her. No other letters. None from Yong. The House and garden were empty of people except Cook Lee and the gateman. "Everyone is at the meetings," said Peony.

"The American aggressors are spreading germs to poison the people," said the radio, which Cook Lee had turned on to listen to the news.

Peony went to a demonstration against germs: how to recognize and eliminate them. Cook Lee had prepared all the dishes for the evening meal, and *Amah* Mu would help to serve them when she returned with Winter Treasure from the nursery school. Cook Lee went to the seminar for cooks, to learn how to prevent germs contaminating food.

I don't believe it, I can't believe my country would do

this, thought Stephanie. Total, black despair overwhelmed her. She wanted to stay in bed forever.

Had Yong known about this? Was that why he had gone to Korea? If he knew, why had he not told her? The women in the ward were muttering about the germs she carried . . . so he must have known, at least the previous day. Why had he not told her?

I can't believe it.

Lionel Shaggin turned up the next day, looking very grim and tired. He had big black punched hollows under his eyes. "Germ warfare. I find it hard to admit that my country would do such a horrible thing . . . but after the bomb, I suppose anything is possible. What could be worse than the atom bomb?"

"Somehow spraying bugs sounds more horrible. . . ."

"Stephanie, I've got to reserve judgment until medical evidence is irrefutable. But I'm fairly convinced. . . . Bubonic plague has broken out and there are thousands of victims."

"But are you sure, absolutely sure?" asked Stephanie.

Lionel looked at her, and then looked away. "Stephanie, what can I do but believe the reports of my colleagues who are out there?"

Late at night Mother came back. Her face was waxen pale. "We'll talk another day," she said. "Don't overfret yourself with excessive grief."

Mother went every day to the bank. Father was being held there, to answer to the investigations which were proceeding. *Amah* Mu, who felt part of the Family, stood holding Winter Treasure to salute his grandmother. "I always tell young mistress: eat well and improve your body, let go of your mind, then another little master will come."

Henry Barber came to see her. He also looked tired and was unusually abrupt. "The whole of China is suffering. So many projects, so many things the new Government planned on doing cannot be done because of this war. Somehow or other the Chinese Communists had expected America to help them. And now there's this germ business."

Don't yield, Stephanie. Oh, bridle your heart. Don't go

*in for self-pity. And be careful, for you are no longer alone.
There's Yong, there's Winter Treasure. Whatever you say or
do, they'll be involved.*

But it was difficult, and she fought the great tide of
bitterness, a salt and evil sea, which welled up in her, which
swamped her, which made her rampage in her room, made
her dread to face the world outside, a world suddenly
unbearably alien and hostile.

Stephanie bicycled to the university. She was stopped
three times by security policemen. Each time she exhibited
her work card.

There were new posters on the streets: Plague in Korea
and in North China due to American germ warfare. Colorful brawny Chinese men and women shook fists at miasmatic clouds dropping insects, each insect a small Uncle Sam
with top hat, striped trousers, and a dollar sign on his chest.

She noticed the new wood boxes. Like mailboxes, slitted.
Boxes for the people's letters. Anyone who had a complaint,
a grievance, a suspicion, would write. Put it in these boxes.
This was because of the ongoing campaign against spies,
hoarders, counter-revolutionaries, and Party members
guilty of fraud, corruption, nepotism.

A large banner stretched across the avenue leading to the
university. It was in English and Chinese. "I am convinced
there have been large-scale field trials in bacteriological
warfare" said the poster. It came from an eminent and
respected man, a missionary doctor.

Young women with white masks on their faces went from
house to house, inspecting the latrines and the sewers. At
crossroads, booths for inoculation were set up. Smallpox
inoculation had begun the previous year. Now people were
being inoculated against cholera, typhoid.

Posters proclaimed the disinfection of all trains. A reinforced campaign against flies, rats, mosquitoes would begin. Stephanie remembered how she had participated in
the previous year's campaign, going around all summer
with a fly swatter in hand.

The university billboards were covered with posters and
reports. Entomologists reported that in North China the
corpses of various insects which were not local had been

found. There had been clouds of chicken feathers and of dried leaves, all found upon the snow in freezing Manchuria. Also small containers stuffed with bacterial cultures.

There were mass meetings of scientists in Paris, London, Moscow, Brussels, and they all protested against germ warfare. Christians in China appealed to Christians in America. "Stop germ warfare."

Passing along corridors lined with the posters, Stephanie reached the university's secretarial office. The clerk who had given her her university work card some months ago appeared not to know her. She asked to see the dean.

After a while the clerk came back. "It is better you should write to him what you have to say." He lowered his head and began to write, so that she would not try to shake hands, not call him by name.

And Stephanie knew that she had been childish to come to the university. After all, she reasoned, what could I have said to the dean? Look, I'm not responsible for all this; I care for the students. It won't do any good to the war to stop my course. Look . . .

She'd got it all wrong. She'd *reasoned* the wrong way. She was not supposed to show herself. It distressed everyone . . . she was *forcing* the issue. The dean wanted to avoid unpleasantness.

They're protecting me by withdrawing me from circulation, putting me on the shelf. So they won't be accused of harboring an American spy, and I won't be accused of spying at the university.

Stay at home, and wait. You're in China, remember? They do things differently here. Accept. Anyway, you can't do anything else *but* accept.

There's a typhoon on, and it must wear itself out. Why rush out and get broken, like those tall poplars they tried to plant in south China (the Russians advised them wrong) uprooted by the wind like telephone poles? Just become invisible for a while . . .

"Comrade," said Stephanie, "do I have to give back my pass?"

"I have no instructions on the matter," said the young man, busily looking at his own pen.

And then Spring Snow *knew* that the dean *was* protecting her. And that she had just imperiled the dean, herself, the young secretary, Yong, Winter Treasure, and all the Jen Family. By mentioning her pass.

Stephanie, you're still an American, trying to fashion the world in your own image, aren't you? You're an idiot, Stephanie.

This young man goes to meetings. He *knows* your course has been suspended and that you should turn in your card. But the dean has not asked for the card. And this comrade would have conveniently *forgotten* you, your card, the course, had you not thrust yourself forward. . . .

Suppose that, suddenly aware of the omission, he now accused the dean of having introduced an American into the university, of having protected her by not withdrawing her pass? . . .

Wouldn't the dean be in a fix?

Idiotic, Stephanie. Stupid, stupid, stupid . . . Raging against herself, Stephanie cycled home.

"Rest," said Peony. "Young mistress must rest."

"Rest," said Mother, a little gaunt as she shuttled between the House and the bank.

Rest. As Yuyu and Panpan used to say.

Rest is sacred. Like the noon siesta. Even the Long Marchers (and their opponents) did not fight during the noon siesta. *Rest*, Stephanie. Don't see, don't talk, don't hear, don't go out. Ill health excused so many things. Enjoy, harbor, nurture ill health.

Rest. In quietness and nonaction, the Universe moves, to make all things well.

Become invisible, Stephanie.

"We are lucky," said Mother. "Our servants have stayed with us, save the gardener's two sons." They had enrolled at the newly open People's University. And now Stephanie weeded, trimmed the bushes, looked after the goldfish, cleaned the pond.

Manual labor was a solace. Squatting over the beds of juniper, trimming the chrysanthemums, Stephanie's mind became calm. Patience came to her as she lifted soil, turned it with a small spade around the brimming roots. Old Gardener taught her that every tree and bush had its own mood. Because Father was so busy being investigated, he and the bank, Stephanie also took to walking the thrushes and orioles in their cages, swinging the cages slightly to give their plumage the necessary shock of a nonexistent breeze, changing the water and filling the tiny porcelain bird bowls with seed, and covering the cages at night.

"Pah . . . pah . . . wooooooooo," shouted Winter Treasure. A new primary school had opened in Eight Jewel Lane. Winter Treasure ran into the street, hung around the fence of the new school. He could hear the children chanting, singing, and outside the fence he chanted and sang with them. Second Uncle and deceased Third Uncle's children played in the courtyard, played at war in the longer spring evenings, training their toy weapons at the target. And the targets were American devils, grotesque cardboard images of Americans.

The children saw films on the Korean War. Third Sister-in-law's children turned their part of the garden into a small battleground. They dug a trench and erected a small lookout of piled gray brick and stone. They bought strings of firecrackers and fired them.

One afternoon Stephanie heard Winter Treasure's voice, howling and screaming. The children had tied him up and were hitting him hard with sticks and with their fists.

"Hit him, hit him, he's American!" shouted K'uei, Third Brother's second son, a sturdy twelve-year-old. Since his father had died, killed by the Kuomintang, he was much spoilt by his mother.

"He's a spy . . . kill him," shouted K'uei. When they saw Stephanie the children stopped, and then ran away. Winter Treasure saw his mother and bawled afresh. And then Stephanie heard K'uei. *"Yang Kueidze,"* foreign devil, he chanted, his treble voice very shrill and high.

His mother came waddling, saying: "Oh, you wicked child, don't shout . . . what have you said? . . ." She gathered her brood, shooed them inside her pavilion. Then turned to Stephanie with a beaming face. "Pay no attention . . . he's only a child. . . ."

Stephanie unwound the string that bound her son's arms against his chest (that, too, was copied from the films). She took him to the bathroom and poured some warm water and wiped his face and hands with a warm towel. "Treasure," she said, "Treasure, don't cry."

"I want my *Tietie*," wailed Winter Treasure, crying for his father, looking away from Stephanie, and opening his mouth very wide. "*Tietie, Tietie!!*"

"*Tietie* is away curing the sick soldiers. . . ." She put her arms around him. But he would not look at her. "Come," she said, "we'll read the story book *Tietie* gave you."

"I don't want." Winter Treasure wrenched himself free of her arms. He ran to the servants, to Peony, to Cook Lee, crying: "I want *Tietie*, I want *Tietie*. . . ."

Stephanie cleaned the bathroom. She wanted to die. She wanted to pick up Winter Treasure and leave, to go away with him right now. To leave this House and this country that was tearing her heart out, taking her son away from her.

She cleaned and cleaned. Cleaned and scrubbed the floor tiles. Mechanical toil kept her mind from exploding. She clenched her jaws so tight that they hurt.

After a long time, or so it seemed, she came out. Peony was playing with Winter Treasure in the living room, cutting paper with her small scissors, with her deft hands folding paper frogs and paper birds, and sending them through the air. Winter Treasure was laughing. He appeared to have forgotten his sorrow. The next day Third Aunt was there, all smiles, with some small cakes and dried comfit peaches. And nothing was said.

But a week later Winter Treasure was back from the nursery, his big round eyes upon his mother. *Amah* Mu, who took him and brought him back, had a pendulous lip and was a little paler than usual.

She informed Stephanie that she needed *rest*. "I have headaches all the time. Besides, my sister is not well and has many children. I must help her. At the moment, with the political campaign, my sister has no time for the children. . . ."

Amah Mu had told Stephanie some two years before that she had no sister, no brothers. She was an only child. Stephanie had commiserated. But, of course, a sister was needed now, and it was ridiculous to make an issue of a small and very necessary lie. *Amah* Mu's sudden sisterliness saved face for everyone.

Stephanie understood perfectly why *Amah* Mu needed *rest*. That pause, that suspended moment, to give everyone time, including God, who arranges the future, and political drives, and wars, and consumes vast quantities of time to settle these things.

"You must rest," said Stephanie, rising nobly to the dialogue. "You have indeed been very fatigued lately."

Amah Mu breathed more easily. "It is very difficult for my sister."

"It is most difficult," agreed Stephanie, making her voice calm and agreeable. *Amah* Mu would go out saying: "She may be an American but she understood. . . ."

Amah Mu looked away. "The nursery is full of rude children. I did not want to disturb young mistress, but another school would be more satisfactory for the little master."

Understood.

Winter Treasure was no longer welcome at the nursery school. Because of the germ warfare in Korea.

The nursery school had been full of lovable teachers, all exclaiming with joy and smiling when she had first brought her son there, a little over a year ago.

Winter Treasure now spent many hours by the fence of the primary school, looking. He came back to play with his toy train. Twice in a week, he wet his bed. He had not wet his bed since he was eighteen months old.

He also stopped asking questions. He had always been inquisitive, and wanted to look through Yong's microscope. Yong had obtained and set up a small toy telescope for his son. Had taught him to watch the stars. His grandmother called him "a myriad whys" because he always asked so many questions. But now he no longer asked any questions at all.

Second Uncle punished K'uei. No play with the smaller children. He asked Stephanie to organize games for the children before they turned the garden into a replica of a battlefield. Stephanie made them play blindman's buff and treasure hunt, put up a volleyball net, and told them stories. "The Cat with Seven-League Boots" was a great favorite, and so was "Cinderella." The children acted out charades, but in the end went back to war games.

Unable to control them, Stephanie watched with tired

despair, thinking—people kill each other in war, people who might have been friends, even lovers. In war they hate and don't even know why. It was all so irrational. . . .

Insomnia. The large bed too large, hostile with Yong's absence. She read through the hours, after listening to the radio. Father and Yong both had extensive libraries. She read in Chinese, several hours a day—for although she spoke the language fluently, she had not mastered the written word. She found it required such concentration that all else faded from her mind. She mastered new ideograms, looking them up in the dictionary. Each time it was a pleasant small victory wrested upon that invisible, pernicious enemy which counseled despair, which filled her limbs with heaviness and tore her mind to shreds. The enemy which kept a gravelly terror in store for her at all hours, like those small puffs of wind which rise from nowhere, suddenly scooping up stiff sand to throw into one's face. The ideogram, which had survived the millennia, taught her patience.

Professor Chang Shou offered to teach Stephanie. Several years ago, on the eve of liberation, she had done him a favor. Chang's wife, a diminutive and shy woman, had cancer of the rectum, and he could not afford to pay the hospital fee. Shamefaced, he had asked for a small loan; Stephanie gave him a hundred dollars. Yong performed the operation without charge. The distinguished professor emeritus of Chinese literature and his wife were more than grateful.

Though nothing was mentioned, Stephanie knew that his offer to help teach her Chinese literature was his way of repaying the debt. And Professor Chang, on his part, was glad to have such an eager student. "You have made a good start," he told her. "Now I will help you progress."

And so, each week, Professor Chang would appear in the Jen garden at twilight, when he had finished at the university. His match-thin figure, no longer in a patched robe but in a neat jacket and trousers, exuded serenity. Sitting opposite Stephanie at a large desk, covering his mouth with his hand, a courteous gesture lest his breath fall upon her delicacy, he expounded on the philosophers, the classics, for two hours.

Stephanie sent small gifts to Mrs. Chang: talcum powder, some handkerchiefs, a cake she baked.

Mrs. Chang managed her colostomy well. She seldom went out to parties or even to see friends, feeling shy about her state. But now Stephanie learnt that the quiet, effaced woman was a poetess, publishing under the name of Autumn Breeze, small and perfect poems that were highly regarded.

Occasionally Professor Chang's daughter came by to bring him home. She was tall and quite pretty, with wavy hair and a soft mouth. She was twenty-seven, still unmarried. "At the moment, with all these political movements, it is best to leave such matters aside," said Professor Chang discreetly.

Learn from these people, Stephanie. They are going through great stress . . . but they do not inflict it upon you. Try to be like them. Keep your trivial complaints to yourself.

The counter-revolutionary purge which had begun in autumn 1951 had become a more refined and particular and specific campaign—or rather two: one against the five capitalist "evils" or poisons, and one against the three "evils" in the Communist Party itself.

The five evil-poisons in business enterprises were bribery of Party officials, producing shoddy goods, cheating on government contracts, establishing cartels and raising prices, and passing "economic secrets" abroad. The three evil-poisons in the Party were related to this corruption. But Party members would be punished much more severely than non-Party people.

Father and Second Uncle had been involved for many weeks in meetings and criticism sessions. They spent hours sifting the records of the bank and a small electric lightbulb and switch factory it owned, checking to see if contracts had been kept or if the State had been defrauded in any way.

The probes were meticulous, relentless. And of course there were victims. Both among the guilty and the innocent. And fear, groveling terror, grew and grew among the involved families and many other families related to them.

But not so Father. Strangely, he waxed strong in stature, in confidence. As if he had awaited these ordeals to show a mastery of distress, of anguish. "We welcome the campaign. We welcome all investigations. We have nothing to hide."

He confronted the investigation with unfaltering good temper, with a sense of humor so exquisite that anyone meeting him and hearing his gentle laugh wondered how this man could stay so unbothered.

Mother was always by his side. Since she too was a vice chairman of the bank, she insisted on being with him. She sat with the accountants, checking all the details, competent and accurate. And Second Uncle would sit with them, his fingers flying up and down an imaginary abacus, as he checked and rechecked the accounts of the factory and the bank.

But when they came home, they laid aside their cares, even Second Uncle, whose digestion was worse than ever. The House was sanctuary, inviolate. No sorrow or worry must be brought into it.

Stephanie, exchanging with her in-laws the daily affectionate courtesies, would remember not to ask questions. Not even to interrogate their faces with too demanding a glance.

"I'm living in the middle of a typhoon which is ripping up everyone's lives," she wrote in her diary. "But I'm living it secondhand."

At night she would muffle her small portable radio in a blanket, turn it down very low—always she remembered those boxes, on every street, denunciation boxes—to catch the voices from outside.

The voice of the BBC from Hongkong said:

> "A great many of Shanghai's capitalists are being jailed, dragged to struggle meetings, condemned to labor camps. . . . It is reported that several businessmen accused of fraud, corruption, bribery of Party members, producing shoddy goods for the State, and passing economic secrets have committed suicide. . . ."

The Voice of America commented on the "total terror" in

which Shanghai was plunged. An American "China expert" affirmed that around sixty million people had been killed within the past two years.

"According to sources from Red China, the famous multimillionaire Mr. Keng Dawei committed suicide by jumping from a high building on the bund. . . ."

"How is Uncle Keng, Father?"
"Dawei? Oh, he's very well. He's been completely exonerated." Father laughed joyously. "Lucky fellow. But then, he is so *needed*. . . ."
Mr. Tam, the Overseas millionaire who had retuned from Indonesia the previous year, was also not to be molested. "He's not even set up his factory," explained Father. "He and his family attend political courses in Marxism-Leninism three times a week." His children were setting a good example. Johnny Tam had led his class in demonstrations against germ warfare.

Yet sometimes the broadcasts contained truths which made Stephanie cringe:

"Among the many foreigners arrested in Peking since the Korean War began, the case of Mr. Carlos Annioli, a long-time Peking resident, seems to be one of the most serious. He has been held incommunicado for almost a year and a half. . . ."

Rosamond. Unlucky Rosamond. Was Meiling helping her? Her presence was dangerous to her friends. Knowing her was dangerous for Stephanie. And therefore for Yong, and Father and Mother.

"It is reported that the American wife of a Chinese obstetrician has been arrested in Shanghai," said the BBC.
"Joan Hesse, wife of Dr. Wu, the daughter of American missionaries, a graduate cum laude of Radcliffe, majoring in biochemistry. She met and married Dr. Wu in America. . . ."

Dedicated, selfless Joan. Joan of the myopic eyes and

scrubbed look. Who had entirely given up her American identity to merge with her husband's people. Why had she been arrested?

"There's no sense in these arrests, Loumei."

Loumei had come to visit with her son, China Warrior, three years older than Winter Treasure. He collected insects, and taught Winter Treasure how to catch fighting crickets.

"She will be released if she is innocent." Loumei, regular as a Swiss watch. "There are mistakes. People are arrested who should not be. The Party cadres are sometimes very ignorant."

At the university, a scientist in telecommunications had been arrested. The experimental panel he was working on kept producing winking lights which the Party man did not comprehend. He had been condemned to death as a spy . . . Two years reprieve, of course. That was the rule. To give everyone time to cool down, to reassess.

Loumei said: "The terrible thing is that the other scientists in his department did nothing at all to help. Lionel and I tried to reach someone to plead for him, but we were not in that unit so we were not heard. There will have to be an overhaul of all the condemnations. Of course so much injustice was done in the past, to so many, but sometimes the righting of past injustice produces new injustice."

Professor Chang Shou arrived, not at the usual twilight hour but in the middle of the morning, as Stephanie was busy in the kitchen.

"I'm sorry, Mrs. Jen, I won't be able to come for a few days."

It's me. He's been told not to see me anymore.

"No, no, it is not what you think," said Professor Chang, noting her stricken look. "It's my daughter. She has been arrested."

Relief, and shame at the relief.

Professor Chang accepted a chair. He drank a cup of tea, sighed.

"Forgive me," he said, "I have much disturbed you. I apologize . . ."

"Please, Professor . . ."

"Of course, all will be well . . . " His spectacles glimmered as he moved his head. "It is a rather silly story. Four years ago my daughter was sought in marriage by a young man. He seemed well connected, well educated. His family was equal to ours and keen on the match. My daughter and he met once, formally, and there seemed no great obstacle. My daughter was not in love, of course, but she is a good daughter. Her mother wanted her to get married.

"Then we found out that he was a member of Chiang Kaishek's blueshirts. His Nazi-trained supporters. So we broke off the match. But my daughter has now been apprehended because of this old story. Someone dug it up and wrote a denunciation."

Stephanie shuddered. "How awful!"

Professor Chang shook his head. "It is a time of testing. Beyond your experience, and beyond mine. But we must adjust to it. We must live with it."

One day, Father and Mother casually told Stephanie, "Daughter, tomorrow we have to attend quite an important meeting. We came to tell you not to worry. All will be well."

"There have been many meetings," said Stephanie. "Why is tomorrow different?"

"It is a class struggle meeting," said Mother. "Our whole Family will be present. The young people often do not wish to remain identified with our class. Because, you see, we have been the exploiters. . . ."

"But you're needed, you've been *told* you're part of the people, that you have voting rights, that you're indispensable," exclaimed Stephanie indignantly.

"We have to look at it from both sides," said Father brightly. "We are of the exploiting class, and we must remold ourselves, change our thinking. Our children must choose, for their own sake, to break off with us."

"Our children will not be capitalists," said Mother.

"No, they will be good workers for the State," said Father.

Stephanie pleaded: "Let me come with you, I'm also part of the Family. . . ."

Mother smiled. "Dear daughter, you are a foreigner, you are not required to endure this meeting."

"Spring Snow, don't fret your heart," said Father. "The

373

trials we are going through are to educate us, as well as to educate the people. It is for the good of our country."

"For the good of our country," echoed Mother.

Stephanie looked at them bleakly. Helplessly. Mother put a hand to touch her cheek. "All will be well, daughter," she said. "Remember. We live not for ourselves alone, but for the generations to come." Her voice was glossy with strength. But Stephanie noted that the jade bangles on her wrists were gone; somehow this distressed her very much.

Peony was also going to the struggle meeting. "I shall put in my word for the old masters," she said to Stephanie, striking her chest. "Too many people just want to create a commotion and slander. I will tell them the good of the Jen House. My voice is small, but piercing."

And, of course, her word would count. It outweighed the word of a capitalist, since Peony's father and mother were both workers, which made her class origin excellent and herself reliable.

"One must get used to equality of a new kind," wrote Stephanie in her journal. "At the moment, equality means the peasants and the workers are now the masters: but they have to be *taught* how to be masters . . . and I doubt if the right way is to stir them up against the capitalists, especially right now. . . ." But was not democracy sometimes perilously close to mob rule, unless its liberty was hedged by rules and constraints? "China is trying to evolve a whole new social system . . . there are no laws, no defined civil or criminal codes working . . . the link between freedom and the legal *uses* of freedom has not been worked out. . . ."

She started Winter Treasure's lessons. He did a little writing in the morning. Then he learnt more ideograms out of his reader, and copied them. Stephanie also began to teach him the English alphabet. He learnt very quickly, but whenever Stephanie spoke English with Lionel Shaggin or Henry Barber or Professor Chang, Winter Treasure would stand very still, and on his face would be that winged shadow which also swept, at times, across his father's face.

Shanghai now had its first children's newspaper and there were also many children's story books, well done, but cheap enough for all to afford. Stephanie and her son read the children's newspaper, which announced that there would be an exhibition in the park on health and how to avoid germs.

"I know all this already," said Winter Treasure. And his face shut.

"Then we'll play here together," said Stephanie. "And we'll cook our lunch. Cook Lee has gone to a meeting."

"I know," said Winter Treasure, still with his tight shut face.

Later, Winter Treasure sighed in his sleep, turned, and slept again. It was his afternoon nap, and Stephanie had laid him on her bed. He was losing his baby chubbiness. He would be lean, like his father, but his legs were long, long like those of Heston Ryder. Already an elegance of gesture inhabited him. Except for his eyes, and a glint of burnished bronze in his hair, he was all Yong. He had those flying eyebrows, and that silk-tight skin.

"He looks all Chinese . . . he looks like us," said Widow, and Second and Third Aunt, every time they saw Stephanie.

She sat by her son on the bed. He had not used the chamber pot. Perhaps she should wake him—she was worried about his bed-wetting. Oh my darling, my darling, she thought, my precious one, my beloved, don't hate me, don't hate me please, don't hate me . . . what can I do to keep you, to make you happy, to stop that brooding which comes to you when you look at me, and then at the others? . . .

Fiercely, gently, she put her arms around him, not waking him. And remained thus and prayed. Please God, dear God, spare him, and his father, and the Family; don't let me bring misfortune and pain to them.

"Daughter-in-law, we are back."

Stephanie rose from sleep. Deep night, Mother standing by her bed.

"Mother . . ." She rose, reached for her dressing gown.

Mother went to the study and sat in the chair where Professor Chang had sat. Her face was small and pale.

"Would you like some tea, Mother?" Fresh leaves, and boiling water from the ever-present thermos flask.

"This is good tea," said Mother. Her voice was very white, all color wrung out of it.

Stephanie said: "Was it bad?"

"No. Not too bad. Except for Jen Jen, your Sixth Aunt-in-law, Widow . . ." said Mother.

"Widow? Why? What did she do?"

Mother said in a tired voice, "She denounced us, and your Second Uncle has been arrested."

This campaign against the five poisons and the
three poisons has been for us like crossing
mountain ranges, passes, and gorges. Many false
accusations, on and on, without rest. And slanders
have been like jagged stones, cutting our feet, as
we walked on to reach safety.

With joyful faces we welcomed the new order,
knowing that we would be of use. And we love our
country. We too suffered the shame inflicted on us
by foreign conquests.

My son's father and I approached this testing time
without fear. We had attended thought-remolding
classes. We informed ourselves, and watched how
others performed. My son's father did well. He
wrote an essay: "I welcome being investigated."
Like his ancestors, he laughed at perils. He
rediscovered courage, and boldness.

My son's father is the only man I ever knew. I did
not love him for many years because I did not
choose him, and I was proud and rebellious. I knew
of countries where lovers choose each other. But
this was not my fate. I decided I would hostage my
body, but my mind would fashion him and I would
rule.

But with this ordeal, I discover a new man. As I
discover in myself unknown selves. He had
become, I thought, fixed in a happy, but dependent
youthfulness. He loved me and it was precisely this
love which diminished him, kept in embryonic state

376

those virtues which he now displays: a mastery of events. Shrewdness and skill.

And now, after thirty years together, I have fallen in love with my husband. Me an old woman, he an old man. In that war of resentment which I waged so long, I have now lost myself to love. And this is wonderful and terrible. For now I shall be so much more vulnerable. . . .

I kept Spring Snow from knowing too much of what was happening, because she is not accustomed to handling injustice and suffering without feeling indignation, without *showing* concern and anger. Which is dangerous for us.

Yet Spring Snow is quick to learn. She listens. I hope that my son will always be able to reach her heart, for her heart is exceeding fine and moves with her mind. But she must learn not to be so outspoken. She must learn to plan. In the end, she will save us.

Her miscarriage made it easier to keep her safe. The university suspended her course. It protected her from her own impetuosity.

Meanwhile we went through the testing and tempering of the five poisons. Were we guilty of one, or all, of the vices of our class? Luckily, we had many people saying good words for us.

My son's father went personally, with his accountants, through the accounts of the bank for many years. Day after day. We were confronted by our staff. Our bank clerks, the employees, the servants, all were assembled to give testimony as to our conduct.

This is democracy. The will and the opinion of the masses.

My son's father stayed in the bank for about two weeks, pointing out his own errors. I brought him

food and fresh clothes every day. I attended every
meeting, doing the adding and subtracting, using
the abacus as I had taught myself. We accepted the
criticism with bowed heads and expressed gratitude;
thankfulness to those who corrected our grievous
errors.

We were then confronted with our friends. Others
such as ourselves, such as our friend Keng Dawei.
He was being accused by people whom he had
thought his intimates. Envious of his success, to
save themselves, they heaped upon him their own
misdeeds. Use of unsalable yarn in the uniforms for
the volunteers for Korea.

Siphoning gold and foreign currency to Hongkong
to purchase smuggled goods. Manipulating the rice
trade. Creating food shortages. Keng Dawei came
out of it well. He laughed cheerfully when called an
unrepentant criminal. We stood by him. Those who
falsely accused him were undone. The Party
members bribed to give false evidence were taken
to prison. Some were shot.

The new rulers know our great weakness. The
weakness of the intellectual, the scholars, the
possessing classes, whether it be wealth or
knowledge we own. We seek to save ourselves, and
betray and denounce each other too easily. But
there are among us courageous ones who will not
yield, who will not betray friends. Of such is the
man I married.

We too found ourselves accused, slandered by
people we had thought our friends. Who had eaten
with us and played with us, in the old days.

My son's father laughed at them. His eyes shone with
strange delight, as if he had discovered something
which he had wished for all the days of his life.

Having successfully overcome several ordeals only
one more remained: Family confrontation.

The whole Family must attend. Each member's testimony must be checked against the others.

"My son is in Korea," I told them.

My son. He would have suffered greatly had he been with us. And someone would have brought up his American wife against him.

"Must my daughter-in-law attend?" I asked. "She is a foreigner."

"Being a foreigner, she cannot attend."

We decided to tell Spring Snow ourselves that she was not to attend. To reassure her, that in the end, all would be well.

The next morning we went to the old movie house now used for these struggle meetings. The walls were plastered with posters.

WE SHALL CRUSH THE VICIOUS CAPITALISTS WHO CHEAT THE GOVERNMENT!

DOWN WITH THE COUNTER-REVOLUTIONARY ORGANIZATION OF CAPITALISTS KNOWN AS THE TUESDAY CLUB!

DOWN WITH THOSE WHO HAVE SUCKED OUR BLOOD FOR GENERATION AFTER GENERATION!

NEVER FORGET CLASS STRUGGLE.

And the usual vivid drawings. I wonder whether our friend, Master Painter Tseng, whom we saw in Wusih two years ago, has trained the Art Academy students whose posters now decorate the walls?

We passed a friend and his family, waiting in the corridor for their turn. His head was lowered and he looked upset. But he put on a good face when he saw us. I think he has little chance of being proclaimed clean, because he is a member of the Tuesday Club.

The newspapers have written much about the club, condemning it as an association of businessmen to cheat the State, a cartel to fix prices, to make huge profits. The word *club* itself now is a bad word, connoting plots and conspiracies.

We stood on the platform, the curtains neatly pulled back. In front of us the audience, a few "cleaned" capitalist families, workers representing various industries, all the employees from our bank.

On a tribune, the Party secretary in charge of the proceedings, and other Party men. The Party comrade in charge asked whether anyone of us had anything more to confess. "If you come clean, you shall be treated leniently . . . if not, punishment will be severe. . . ."

That is the formula.

Recently, in these confrontations, certain young people have accused their parents. The young are overzealous. They believe that youth is a guarantee of revolutionary spirit. They have been told that by denouncing evildoing, even in their own family, they are serving the higher interests of their country, and are also helping to remold their backward parents. They are told our generation is perverse and lacking in ideals.

My daughters have disparaged us at their school meetings, but this I think all adolescents do, especially in a revolution. It is fashionable now to look upon filial veneration as abhorrent. "We shall never be able to become Party members with such a bad class origin," they have lamented. As if it was our fault that they were born to us.

380

I was prepared for the worst, and a certain thickness grew upon my soul like moss upon stone, clinging to me and cushioning me.

I consoled their father. "They do not understand the world, or even the revolution they profess to love."

"They are unfilial," he said angrily.

"Only a little excited. It will pass."

When he saw me so calm, he became unperplexed. "A new world to be born," said he, "and all births are painful." He had told Keng Dawei that it was a spiritual marathon race. "He who can walk to the end will win."

As we stood in front of the masses, I wondered whether my dear little daughters would say how sorry they felt for themselves, being born in such a capitalist family.

"Take it as the wind that passes, as flies that buzz," I whispered to their father. "It is not an arrow to fester in your heart."

"I shall not be like Ouyang," he replied.

Our friend Ouyang. Ouyang's son stood up in this theater and denounced his father. His middle school used to be the most snobbish, the most high-class and aristocratic school in Shanghai. It had the highest standards and was only for the wealthy. The school has now "turned over," is being born again; teachers and students are redeeming themselves by being most fanatical.

Ouyang did not take well to his son's harangue against him. He went home, swallowed poison, and died. And now his son does not know where to put his head. For even those of his classmates who

encouraged him to denounce his father want
nothing more to do with him.

And there is a girl who also accused her parents.
The Party committee of her unit praised her. But
no one will speak to her now, and she is having a
nervous breakdown.

The Party man in charge called upon Second
Brother's children to speak. But not one of them
would say anything except: "Yes, we are a Family of
capitalist origin. But we have welcomed the
revolution, and we love our country. I have never
found my parents to utter anything counter-
revolutionary." To a question about his mother's
habit of playing mahjong, the eldest son replied:
"But she never plays for money. And since the war
of resistance to help Korea she has not played, but
spent days and nights stitching clothes for our
heroic volunteers." This was only partly true, for
Second Sister-in-law cannot sew. I have done some
stitching for her and so has our tailor, who is loyal
to us.

I could see the Party secretary was happy. He did
not want to have any searching denunciations.
Suicides do not go down well with the masses. The
workers hate it. "It's not right for children to accuse
their parents. . . . What are these small imps who
spit on their ancestors?"

When it was our turn, Coral looked at Calthrop,
and Calthrop looked at Coral, and they both looked
at us, and Calthrop said: "Our Family has
welcomed the revolution, and we have never heard
our parents utter one word of counter-revolution.
Since we don't want to be capitalists, our parents
encouraged us to go to the rural areas, to go into
land reform. . . ."

And then Coral said "Mama" like a baby and flew
to my arms, weeping. And Calthrop stood, a little
jealous, because she thinks I prefer Coral, so I

extended my hand to her, and we stood with our arms around each other, and the people clapped as they do at a well-performed act, and I thought: It is over.

I had forgotten Widow. She now came forward and shouted: "But I have to say something. I have to declare the bitterness in my heart."

All restraint gone, all modesty forgotten, she told her story. Being a widow and a virgin. Being forced not to marry. She made it sound as if her brothers and I had forced her to celibacy. "I was like the living dead until the revolution liberated me," she cried. "And she, she . . ." she pointed to me, "all these years has fed on my sorrow. See, she has grown beautiful on it! She has had everything, a loved one, a son, and you should see her dresses, all the colors of the rainbow. . . ."

"Comrade Jen Jen, Comrade Jen Jen," the Party man interrupted her. "The masses here feel great sympathy for you. . . . But you yourself said in your life story that you had not wanted to marry again."

"I had to protect *them*," said Widow. "They used me. I had to look after the house, and the gold. *She* went out, leaving me to guard her gold, which was in her cupboards, in her bedroom."

"There is no gold with us now, comrade," I said. "This was before liberation, when we could not live without gold. When liberation came, we turned over all our gold to the State. We bought victory bonds. We have receipts for all the gold. You may search. There is no gold."

But Widow went on, to speak of trafficking with the foreign missionaries for gold and foreign exchange. I had not realized that she knew. She turned on Second Brother-in-law, accusing him of having taken part in this trafficking. And his wife is not a clever woman. Instead of smiling and shrugging, and saying: "This was before liberation," she began to scream at Widow: "Traitor, what face have you, you miserable slave? Have we not fed you all these years?" And of course this made a poor impression.

My son's father stood up. He said soothingly: "Comrades, before liberation, yes indeed we held gold, to save our lives. Both my brother and myself have fully explained these matters when we wrote out our life stories. This session is to investigate the five evils *after* May 1949, when Shanghai was liberated. We have not trafficked, nor bribed, nor defrauded the State nor any one of the State companies, nor any individual. As for my sister," he turned to Widow, "we entreated her many times to marry again. My loved one tried to arrange matches. . . ."

But now there was a commotion and some people cried: "Investigate, investigate the traffic with the foreign missionaries." And so we and Second Brother-in-law were to be reinvestigated.

And then, theatrically, one of the people in the audience got up and pointed to Second Uncle and said: "He went to the Tuesday Club. I saw him there." It was the doorkeeper of the club.

Second Brother-in-law was not allowed to return home with us. He was deathly pale, rasping through his nostrils as if he choked, when he was taken in custody.

Stephanie's throat was sore with indignation.
"What kind of system is this, which turns people against each other? Which encourages them to betray one another?"
"Widow did not feel she was *betraying*. She persuaded herself into the *right* kind of indignation. She could not resist being a heroine, because she had been a shadow for so long . . ." said Mother, sipping tea.
In the balmy, wisteria-scented night the two women sat by the willow pool. The darkness cradled their words.

"Patience was a kind girl, rescuing birds, cats. She wanted to become a Buddhist nun and for a while ate no meat. She kept a menagerie. Dogs, cats, parakeets. But with people, she was unlucky every time. Her fiancé died. She clung to Yong when he was a baby, but Yong grew into a wilful little boy, just like Winter Treasure," said Mother, smiling.

No, thought Stephanie, Winter Treasure is not like Yong. Yong's childhood was all of a piece. Winter Treasure has a crazy patchwork of things to assemble, to make a security for himself . . . and some of the nastiness will stick forever. . . .

"Widow then loved my twins, and was often with them. But the twins grew up, and they thought Widow old-fashioned, and gave her little time. Strange," mused Mother, "she said I fed on her loneliness. I did try to care for her, as for everyone in the Family. But perhaps I had assigned to her a place in the Family pattern. We should have done what she asked, build a small altar in the garden, to thank all living things who give us affection; but Grandfather refused, and after his death Widow did not ask again. The need for love was great in her, and no one ever did fill it."

Second Uncle's servants left when he was arrested, except the old cook and a cleaning woman.

They said they had jobs in factories. "Everyone wants to be a worker," said Mother.

The twins helped Second Aunt dust and clean her rooms and wash the children's clothes. Second Aunt had always been prone to quick grief. Now she could not stop crying, looking around her, waiting for things to be done for her. She was a slow woman, endowed with very white flesh, opaque and thick. Grief made her eat more.

Second Uncle became paler during the week of his interrogation, and the lines around his mouth deepened. Father worked tirelessly, calling on many officials he knew. "Your brother went to a meeting of the counter-revolutionary Tuesday Club. You never went," he was told. What had happened that day? Second Uncle would be confronted with other members of the Tuesday Club. Meanwhile, he was to write his life story all over again, as he had omitted this detail.

"The great counter-revolutionary movement is absorbing all the energies of the masses," said Father aloud at dinner. He looked fixedly at his sister, Widow, Patience.

On the eighth day of investigation, Second Uncle vomited a great deal of dark blood and was taken to the hospital.

"Why should we admit capitalists?" said the young male nurse in charge to Father and Mother, who had accompanied Second Uncle.

Father gave him a soft smile. "My brother has been sent here by the Party committee in charge of investigation," he said. "Here is the letter, comrade."

Second Uncle lay in bed in a semi-private ward. He was on an intravenous drip. In his thin face the two big folds running from nose down chin were more prominent. "I am not . . . too bad. No pain now . . ."

In the corridor a nurse sat under a poster advising relatives of patients in need of surgery to give blood. Calthrop and Coral gave blood. And Stephanie went to the hospital.

"I am also a relative," she said.

The nurse did not seem at all amazed that a foreigner should be there. "Yes, we do need blood, I'll register your name. We're trying to educate the masses to give blood, but many are still very scared."

Father afterwards chided her. "Daughter, we have given blood, it was not needful to give yours."

Second Uncle had a second, then a third massive hemorrhage. And now the Party committee was very worried. If he should die, they would be held responsible. A blood debt to pay. Hastily they cleared him. "He went to the Tuesday Club to see a friend . . . there was no illegal transaction." Second Uncle smiled faintly when he was told that he was cleared.

"It is a huge gastric ulcer . . . he must have had it for many years," said the doctors.

Second Uncle died suddenly, two weeks after having entered the hospital.

Arranging Second Uncle's funeral was not easy for Father. Cemeteries are never within a city. One has to go beyond the city walls, to the fields. The private cemeteries of the big families used to be there, at auspicious sites chosen by geomancers for their fortunate qualities.

In the old days, Second Uncle would have been transported to the burial place of the Jen Family, sixteen miles outside Shanghai. It was a new burial ground. A mere six generations lay there, the older graves being in the original village the Family came from, in Shantung province. They went back a mere fifteen hundred years, forty-nine generations.

But now there had been land reform, and all over China's countryside the burial grounds of the great families had been appropriated by the peasants, hungry for extra land. "Land for the living, not graves for the dead," clamored the peasants.

The families were notified. "Will you remove your tombstones and your ancestors' bones and find other sites? . . ." The Jen Family tombstones, with their inscriptions by the best calligraphers of the land, and the coffins were removed, reburied in a piece of waste land. But even this was precarious holding, and there was no ground left for another coffin.

"From now on we shall incinerate," said Father with that new firmness of his. Communist Party members were to be incinerated rather than buried, to set an example. But the rank and file of the Party, being peasants, were still hostile to the idea. They wanted earth burial.

Second Aunt wailed: "Burning burial is done in India, and by other barbarians. How shall I recognize my son's father when I too go down to the Nine Springs, if he is but a handful of ashes without a face?"

Mother said: "We shall keep the ashes of ancestors in urns. As the Japanese do, who have so little land to spare. The peasants will plough up the coffins of our ancestors if we do not remove them."

While the argument went on Second Uncle waited, in a coffin of best wood, the tall *lammu* which is cut in the mountains of Szechuan and floats in rafts over three thousand miles down to Shanghai. Second Aunt knocked her forehead on the ground in front of her husband's coffin. "Hear me, hear me," she wailed, "wait for me."

In the end Second Uncle was buried. No canopy, no mourners. Friends came and pronounced a funeral eulogy. There was no tombstone, because the stone cutters were too busy carving stones for museums and libraries and children's palaces and workers clubs.

"It is like the burial of a criminal," cried Second Aunt. But many people came to bow to the coffin, and she was mollified. All her children were there, wearing black armbands, as was the new fashion. Instead of being in rough white homespun.

Second Uncle's small tablet, adorned with a drop of blood from the index finger of the left hand of his eldest son, was placed among the ancestors. The Family gathered quietly and ate a meal, giving the ancestors their share. Renewing in this ritual of food-taking that cell and blood connection, which rides the tides of time and space and is continuity.

And Widow too was there. No one said a word to revile her. In fact no one spoke to her at all. Again she had become a shadow in the House.

Almost a week after Second Uncle's burial the postman brought two envelopes for Stephanie. One was a large brown envelope with censor marks all over it; inside was a telegram. It had been more than three months on the way.

The cable said: "Jimmy killed in an ambush in Korea March 18. Body recovered and shipped home. Dad."

The letter was from Isabelle:

My dear Stephanie,

Jimmy was killed in Korea. He had been there less than a month. He fell in an ambush on the front. Your father was upset, but he has his work, which absorbs him.

We, the creatures of the Lord, bow to His will, and praise Him, whether He administers to us joy or sorrow.

I know that God has a place in Heaven for the pure of heart. And Jimmy was pure. God will certainly take his intention to become a Catholic into account.

We spoke the last time you were here of Calvary. As our Blessed Lord gladly and wilfully took upon Himself the sins of the world, and made the supreme sacrifice of His life for us, so should all of us forever be mindful of the sins we have committed, and gladly accept, and rejoice, when we suffer. . . .

Her eyes blurred with tears, Stephanie crumpled the pages of her mother's pious words. "Jimmy! . . ." she whispered, and lay on her bed, wracked with sobs.

Much later, she smoothed out the letter and folded it and the telegram together and put them in the drawer where she kept Yong's sole letter to her of 1945, photographs of their wedding in Yenan, photographs of Winter Treasure. Since Yong's leaving for Korea she had had only brief, strained messages from him. Letters which said nothing at all. Censorship.

Jimmy. For days, months afterwards, she would feel the sharp stab of grief—suddenly feel transfixed with unbearable mourning. Never more to see Jimmy, the hesitant face, the gray wide eyes, and the golden cowlick.

Winter Treasure came running, shouting: "Mama, Mama, look, look!" On his lapel a medal, a small red flag. "Mama, Mama, Aunt Fan said I was a good child of Chairman Mao."

Stephanie knelt and hugged him tight, tight. "Who is Aunt Fan, my dearest?"

Winter Treasure squirmed a bit. "It's a new auntie. She has come to see you, Mama. . . ."

Stephanie smoothed her face, and went to welcome this unknown Aunt Fan who stood waiting at the gate.

She was a dark, quick-moving woman, very thin. Moving as do the women of the south, whose feet were never bound. She shook hands with Stephanie vigorously. "My name is Fan. I am now in charge of this district's nursery schools and kindergartens." Comrade Fan's darkness of face was immediately explained when she spoke. She was a Cantonese. She had the rude directness of the Cantonese, and all her syllables had hooks at their ends: k's and t's and p's . . .

"The three evils campaign in our Party has revealed a number of deficiencies in our work," she said. "We are now rectifying ourselves. I have heard of the incident about your son. It was incorrect. He should never have been sent home."

389

Stephanie said mechanically, copying Mother: "It is quite understandable. . . ."

"No," said Comrade Fan vigorously. "It is against Party policy. The children must learn internationalism. Now we must apologize. I have come to apologize to you. Your son is welcome back at the nursery. At seven he will go to the district primary school."

Stephanie called Winter Treasure. Teacher Fan said: "You are going back to school tomorrow, Winter Treasure. We are all waiting for you."

"I don't want to go," said the child.

Fan in her funny, quick way squatted by Winter Treasure. "You don't want to go because one child called you names . . . is that it?"

"I don't like school. I don't want to go." Winter Treasure's face was dark, shut. Just like Yong sometimes.

Teacher Fan said: "Look at me. When I was small like you, other children also called me names, and called my mother names; they said I was not Chinese. . . ."

It was as if the child had not heard. He kicked his foot on the ground.

"Tomorrow morning I will come here. You and your Mama and I, we will go together. Your Mama is welcome at our school. Then if you still don't want to go to school you may leave."

In the neat courtyard of the nursery school, eight hundred yards down the road, the children were lined up, clapping and chanting: "Welcome, welcome, Winter Treasure. Welcome, welcome, Auntie Lai." Behind them the teachers beamed and clapped. And there were two photographers who took pictures, as the teachers came up to shake hands with Stephanie.

Winter Treasure's classmates surrounded him. One little girl with an enormous pink bow took his hand and swung it. A boy tried to thrust four marbles, red and blue, into his other hand. Winter Treasure kept both fists closed. He looked at the other children, at the teachers, at his mother. . . .

"Winter Treasure," said Teacher Fan, again squatting down so that she would not tower above him. "Ming has kept these marbles specially for you. He cried when you left. . . ."

"Yes," said Ming. "I kept them for you."

"Ma," said Winter Treasure, "Mama." He saw his mother surrounded. He felt that she, like him, had been hurt. Hurt was a funny bad thing inside one. A beribboned girl was thrusting into Ma's hands a bouquet of dahlias. But it was the same girl who had shouted to him: "American, get out." And the teacher who was now smiling at Ma was the one who had said to *Amah* Mu: "We don't want American mixed-bloods in our school. . . ."

Comrade Fan made a small speech. "Chairman Mao teaches us that all the peoples of the world are good, only a very small number of exploiters are bad. Winter Treasure is the son of two very good people, Dr. Jen, who is with the heroic Korean people, and his mother, Lai Spring Snow, who has written good things about China and is our American friend. The American people are our friends."

Everyone clapped and clapped. The boy Ming again held out the marbles to Winter Treasure. "Take them, take them." Winter Treasure took the marbles.

In the main schoolroom trestle tables were laid, and there were sweets and peanuts and biscuits in small plates, and bottles of orange juice. On the walls the picture of Mao Tsetung looked down benignly upon the children.

"Today is a holiday, to welcome Jen Forest back," cried Comrade Fan. She came to sit by Stephanie. "Tell us, how are nurseries and kindergartens managed in your country?"

"I really don't know. We did not have one where I was born."

"We're going to build many, many, in China," said one teacher, shiny-eyed. "We want our children to grow up virtuous, healthy, loving their country and loving socialism."

Winter Treasure that night hugged his mother before she put him to bed. He had not hugged her for many days.

"Mama, I'll go to school tomorrow."

"Of course, darling. Teacher Fan will be so pleased. And all your friends."

"I have no friends," said Winter Treasure.

"Yes you have. One or two people just made a mistake. That's all. Everybody makes mistakes. . . ."

"Even you and *Tietie*?" asked Winter Treasure.

391

"Of course, darling . . . but if one's made a mistake one has to correct it . . . and all will be well."

He stood in the same way his father did, thinking.

"Mama." He put his head against her breast shyly, then pushing as if to enter her body again. "How far is America from our house?"

The poplars turned to rufous gold, and the sky's small clouds like errant yawls rode its blue wideness. The Autumn Festival came and Yong was back from Korea.

He came straight to Stephanie, bypassing his parents' pavilion. No one saw him except the old gateman, so knotted with arthritis now that he scarcely moved from his room next to the gate.

Stephanie was cleaning the living room. Now that Peony had so much to do for Second Aunt, Stephanie did as much of the cleaning as possible.

He stood helpless, helpless with love, so much in love, so painful now to be in love, watching her.

She lifted her head, and saw him.

He was so thin, so gaunt, so sad.

And so they remained, transfixed and frozen, tired with the agony of loving each other so much, and being afraid of this love.

Yong opened his small bag carefully. He took out of it a small plate of Korean celadon. It was very old, and under the glaze a phoenix shook its wings.

She took it. "It's lovely," she said.

"A man gave it to me. A Korean. He said: 'For your American wife.'"

She sighed. Her heart, her body, heavy with the torment of loving.

"Jimmy," she said. "Jimmy was also in Korea. He died there. His body's been shipped back home."

And Yong wept for Jimmy then, wept without restraint. Stephanie watched him weep, unable to go to him, comfort him. Her spirit was weary, and she could no longer lighten his sorrow.

They lay together but now they could no longer fervently reassure each other, neither by body gesture nor by the pulse of love. There was the savor of disaster, premonition of torment in their clasping.

"I love you," he said, "I love you."

And she said, "I love you."

And both turned their heads away to hide their eyes.

Winter Treasure asked his father: "*Tietie*, what does an American imperialist look like?"

"I did not see any, my son."

"Teacher says American people are good, like Mama. American imperialists are bad."

Talking to his son, because it was a way of talking to Stephanie, Yong said: "I did not see any imperialists. Only soldiers, and they only did their duty, fighting."

"Did you see them fight, *Tietie*?"

"Yes, son, sometimes."

"You did not kill anyone?"

"No, son. I even tried to cure the wounds of the American prisoners. . . ."

"Why, if they are bad people?"

"They are not bad, son."

"Then why do we kill them, and they kill us?"

"A lot of people get killed for nothing," said Yong.

Stephanie said, neutrally, to Yong in English: "Be careful, he may repeat this in school."

Then Yong knew that she had lost her impetuous innocence. That headlong audacity which made her rush into situations, not counting the cost. Which had made him love her, love her. Because it was so different.

Stephanie was now careful, careful. Her hands, resting in her lap, held tightness about them.

And he had lost the way to her. He knew it. A dissembling of rapture. Their words to each other now fell flat with the sound of coins on a pewter dish.

The purge of the five poisons and the three poisons, among the capitalists and in the Party, now ended. A verification of the verdicts would now occur.

Some people came out of jail; some were publicly apologized to for "wrong verdicts." Others were not so lucky.

393

Professor Chang Shou's daughter was released, and so was Joan Wu. Both of them had their salaries paid to them for the period they had been incarcerated, and their jobs were maintained.

"It wasn't that bad," said Joan Wu testily, emerging from jail. "We must try to understand the revolution. Such upheavals can't occur without a few mistakes."

"I don't think I'd have that kind of objectivity," said Stephanie, admiring Joan's fortitude.

"You're not a Marxist," said Joan with the glazed ecstasy of a missionary in a state of grace. The trouble had been her maiden name, Hesse, which was the same as that of a German spy arrested in Peking.

Rosamond's lover, Carlos, had been condemned to death, but had obtained the usual two-year reprieve. He was now expelled from China, while Rosamond was sent to a camp for thought-remolding through labor, for two years.

Meanwhile, the newspapers carried headline stories about the execution of Julius and Ethel Rosenberg, allegedly for having been spies for the USSR. Their execution had taken place in New York's Sing Sing Prison in June 1953, despite the pleas and protests of many eminent people, including Albert Einstein, who had called for a civil disobedience movement against the witch hunters.

And Stephanie once again was torn, torn with the realization that the same monstrous injustice could occur in her country as in China.

Then Senator Stuart Symington gave a major speech at Radcliffe, which Professor Moslyn sent to her. Although himself a member of the Investigations Subcommittee of the Senate Government Operations Committee over which McCarthy presided, he warned against "the new reign of terror" in America.

"My country is not immune from the virus of intolerance," wrote Stephanie in her journal. "But we at least have means to fight back. . . ."

Yong came back from the hospital with a joyful face. "Stephanie, I'm being transferred to Peking. To a new hospital for specialized neurosurgical operations."

The Shanghai hospitals were the best. Yong's hospital,

No. 6, specialized in brain surgery, in neurosurgery, and had begun microsurgery. Now it was required to spawn, establish branches in other cities, teach and train new doctors by the thousand.

It was the same in every sector. Scientists, engineers, skilled workers were in great demand, and the best were in Shanghai. Shanghai workers went to teach others in the new industrial complexes set up in faraway provinces.

Yong's transfer to the capital was recognition of his skill. He would go first; Stephanie and his son would follow, when he had found a house, a school for Winter Treasure.

Disappointed when Stephanie greeted his news with a polite, distant smile—and yearning for her to share his delight, Yong said, "There's a great need in the universities in Peking for foreign experts. I think it will be easy for you to be transferred, darling."

Apart from twelve thousand Soviet experts in China, building up China's heavy industry, there were four to five hundred other "foreigners"—everything from Czech experts on shoemaking to literature professors and translators—employed by the Chinese Government. They received very large salaries and were entitled to many privileges. All of them had at least one servant, if not two, at their disposal.

"Being a foreigner has its uses," said Stephanie bitingly.

He heard, received the insult, the bitterness of her.

She passed him as though he did not exist, going to the garden. She had planted tea rose bushes. Now they were heavy-petaled, the last crop of summer. Their perfume filled the air. She stooped to cut the stalks, to fill the beautiful antique vases in the living room with the last roses of summer.

Watching her, he knew again that he had lost her . . . just as she had lost part of herself, had coiled in upon herself, cautiously, fearfully.

How could he reconquer her? That which had painted each hour with enchantment had vanished. That which had been like the sway of the sea, a brimming gladness.

It will come back. I shall make it come back. I shall again feel my heart, a sonorous seashell, listening to the sea's return, her voice, her laughter, without which I die.

eighteen

IN Tientsin the school barracks were not far from the dock-yards of the port. The recruits they housed seemed unlikely material for education: children of peasant families starved out of villages, driven to beg. Orphans. Children unable to find their families. They came from all over, like Little Pond and his friend, Hsiao Wang, who hailed from far-off Szechuan province. The revolution took this human offal, transformed it into knowledgeable, dedicated cadres. Some of them would become outstanding scientists. Others bore in them the seed of statesmanship, of art, music, literature.

At dawn, after morning drill, when the bugles blew and the five-starred flag was raised, Little Pond felt his whole body shake with fierce love.

Every morning they repeated these words:

> "Oh, the Communist Party is dear to me; it has saved my life. It has nurtured me. I shall lay down my life to obey the Party. To build a strong, wealthy, socialist China."

Little Pond's whole life since Prosperity Tang had looked his way was living proof that the Party had given the subhumans—those ninety percent who had had no dignity, no worth, no value—dignity, worth, value, and hope.

Five years ago, in 1948 the Year of the Rat, Little Pond had followed Prosperity Tang, going eastwards, where the Great River widened into a universe of marshes. Tang left him with a rice merchant's household, in a small town. For three months he worked there, carrying rice bags, cleaning the shop, running errands, and keeping quiet. The rice merchant was a man who did not shout but said: "Come, little devil, I will teach you . . ." and then Little Pond knew that the rice merchant and Prosperity Tang were the same kind of people. People who were like those boxes within boxes within boxes. Or like onions. Peel a layer, there's another layer, on and on.

He was taught to count. To add and to subtract. To write numerals in a strange foreign script: 1, 2, 3, 4 . . . He knew one hundred, one thousand, ten thousand. He learnt to use the abacus. At night he trained himself, writing the numbers again with his saliva-moistened finger on the wood counter where he slept.

In the darkness, a barge would dock by the rice merchant's back door, which gave onto a stagnant stream. There would be the soft slap of disturbed water. Little Pond would rise, help to carry out rice bags, stow them on the flat barge which then was poled away. Not a word was spoken.

One evening the rice merchant said to Little Pond: "Little devil, you must now travel with the rice. Travel with the boat." And he had taken his place, squatting among the rice bags.

He helped to pole the barge. Two men sailed it, for two days and three nights, until they were traveling a large lake beset with tall reeds like a dwarf forest, thick and seemingly impenetrable. But between great stretches of reed were channels, a thousand meanders, uncounted small islands, thick hummocks of grass and damp soil. On some of them wore fields, trees and villages, thatched huts with boats moored near to them. In this semi-aqueous universe, the morning mist was like beancurd milk, thick and clinging. All was silence, save the cry of water fowl. The bankless water went on forever, and only those who knew the way could find the guerilla camp, nestling in the reed marshes. The villagers fished, grew rice, and nourished at least a hundred guerillas.

"Look out for the bones, little devil," the comrades said as Little Pond ate the first fish he had caught. He had never eaten fish before. He wore a gray uniform too large for him and straw woven sandals. He carried the big round iron pan in which the guerillas cooked their rice when they moved camp. Which they seemed to do fairly often.

397

He learnt to fish. To imitate the desolate threat of rook and the pompous squawk of duck. The querulous snap of water hens. He learnt to come up behind an enemy on soundless feet. He learnt to shoot. To kill.

Every morning there was drill, and then class. Reading and writing. The wonder of writing! He cut a reed and wrote on the sandy soil at the island's edge, entranced with writing.

"I want revenge." He told his story to the assembled guerillas at a "pour bitterness" meeting.

"We all want revenge," they said to him. But revenge could not be a single act, by a single person. It had to be "changing earth and heaven." It had to be total. So that never again would there be injustice on earth.

One morning as they stood at attention the comrade-in-charge said: "Today we march away. For that turtle's egg, Chiang Kaishek, is done for, and our armies are going to kick him out of his capital city of Nanking."

They cheered, laughed. Cheered and shouted: "Down with the turtle's egg! Long live the Party! Long live Chairman Mao!"

They walked. They got on to hard ground and walked, moving by night. They met other men in gray, all walking as they did, until it seemed the whole earth was walking, walking in the same direction.

And one night they saw spread on the horizon the red glare, that painted glow in the darkness which meant CITY.

And suddenly guns were booming all at once and the sky was peopled with soaring stars, and the first little wind of dawn crept over the land as a great scream rose and a hundred thousand men ran forward. Little Pond ran forward too, shouting: "Kill, kill." Shouting: "Hsu, son of a turtle, here I am, here . . ."

He almost imagined that he would meet Hsu, meet Hsu, and cut out his liver, cut it out. . . . And in no time at all it was morning, and they were there, they had won, and the comrade-in-charge was saying: "Now we walk into Nanking. Walk straight. Walk with our heads up. And remember: We are Communists, we never hurt the people. . . ." And so they had entered Nanking, the beautiful flat city with many maple trees, walking straight, not looking right or left.

But Little Pond did not stay very long in Nanking. He and others like him were reassembled and marched northwards, marching because no trains were running as yet, walking northwards for weeks until they reached the port of Tientsin. And all the way it was victory, all the way, and the villages welcomed them, and everyone spoke of liberation, and there were red flags everywhere.

And in one place Little Pond saw his first railway locomotive, a large monstrous thing like a huge worm's head, chomping impatient steam, pulling boxes with people stacked in them.

The school in Tientsin was army-run. Demobilized soldiers must help in production, but first they must be educated, to become low-level cadres or factory workers. They must learn—those who were still young enough to learn.

In the next three years Little Pond studied as a sponge absorbs water, doing the equivalent of four years' primary school.

The school grew its own food, had its own small repair shops for agricultural tools, its manure pits, its bricklayers and tailors and shoemakers, and carpenters who made all the benches and tables and beds. There were also cotton carders who made the padded winter jackets. The school teachers and students helped to tear down the slums which surrounded the port area. To build gray brick houses for the future workers of future factories.

Little Pond also studied culture and politics. Marxism-Leninism. Party pamphlets and booklets and directives. He studied music and singing. He was given a novel to read, but it puzzled him. It was from the great fraternal country of Russia, and the names were very long. In all things he strove, pushing his stout heart and his small body to master whatever tasks were his.

And one day he stood with ninety-seven others, selected to become Party members, having proved himself devoted and hard-working, disciplined and capable of self-criticism. As an orphan from the slums he was of good class origin, which also counted. He had eaten bitterness, a great deal of it. That too made him acceptable.

He raised his clenched fist when he took the oath, and his eyes were blurred with tears. This was the greatest honor of all, to become a Party member . . . if only his mother were alive, if only she could see him now! Truly, the powerful ones now groveled, and the downtrodden walked the earth as masters. . . . *Oh Ma, if you could see your son!*

399

His life had meaning, purpose. He fulfilled some cosmic plan of which he was but an infinitesimal part. But the wise, great, glorious Party would always know. For him the Party cared, and because the Party cared he was someone, not no one.

Because he was finger-deft he was put in charge of the repair workshop. The workshop was now growing. An engineer from Shanghai had come with plans. One day, it might even be a factory. Making bicycles, or even motors and generators.

He loved the tools he handled: he turned and twisted screws, oiled ballbearings, and he read about that wondrous magic, electricity. And a passion for knowledge stirred in him.

Little Pond dreamed of machines. He saw them on the posters:

LEARN FROM THE SOVIET UNION'S ADVANCED KNOWLEDGE!!!

CELEBRATE THE ANNIVERSARY OF THE HEROIC KOREAN PEOPLE!!!

EXPAND PRODUCTION, WORK ALL-OUT FOR A SOCIALIST CHINA!!!

Posters. Showing the new factories being erected in the city of Tientsin. Smoking chimneys. Locomotives and airplanes and trucks spewing from these factories. Textile looms, bright spindles weaving that wonderful future. Clothes for everyone!

A group of Soviet fraternal experts, conveyed in a large bus, roared along the avenue. Little Pond looked at them with respect, with awe.

The Soviet Union.

Great, fraternal, unselfish. Whose books were so learned that Little Pond could not understand them.

The Big Brothers always traveled in collective buses. Anywhere from six to twenty-five of them. Always together.

A team of Soviet experts had come to see the school. Nine of them.

For weeks beforehand preparation for their welcome had been made. Arches, banners in both Chinese and Russian;

the song team had rehearsed; the music team had torn the air with repeated shrill tuning of their instruments.

Little Pond had worked, worked sawing and planing and sandpapering wood to prepare the platform, the benches for the great, the wonderful guests.

They had come. A thick block of nine, sticking together.

They had listened to the speeches, clapped. Gone around the school, the Party committee hovering around them looking tiny compared to the huge Russians.

They ate prodigiously. Ate throughout that day. Ate. Little Pond would never forget their appetites. Their consumption of food had been the Russians' only outward sign of interest in the school.

Morning breakfast. Four eggs each. Then chocolate cream cake. Each one of them ate a pound of cream cake, made specially in what had once been the Kiesling German pastry shop of Tientsin and was now the Foreign Friends food shop.

Two bottles of liquor each. Milk. Red foreign tea. Three pounds of ham. Three of sausages. Five pounds of bread. Foreign jam, five pounds.

Never had Little Pond seen anyone eat so much. No wonder the comrades were large, so large. In his mind, eating well, being large, heavy, meant being upper class. And now upper class became confused with superiority in everything. Big Brother ate much because he was Superman.

Nevertheless, when they had gone, and the school put itself back together, and cleared the tables, and debated how to use the precious remnants of food, there was a silent, unspoken current of resentment among the students.

They ate so much. They had left crumbs on their plates, when crumbs were so precious. Not one grain of rice was to be wasted.

Perhaps one day the Chinese would eat as well, would eat four eggs just for breakfast together with ham and sausages and cakes and liquor and . . .

Afterwards for months the Party committee hoped that the Russians would write a letter of thanks. Would perhaps send a machine for their small tool-repair shop . . . would not forget them.

But nothing had come. Nothing. "Perhaps we have not

done enough," said the Party committee, resigned. And felt guilty. Perhaps they had failed in courtesy towards Big Brother.

One afternoon of late July, when the cicadas rub their wings and the heat soars, Little Pond and his friend Hsiao Wang went out on their usual once a month day-off stroll. And first they walked to the little noodle shop, under a mat shed, run by fat Aunt Lan, who always gave the young men heaping bowls of steaming, sleek noodles flavored with spinach and fragrant herb, which glided down one's gullet like velvet to fill the space between the ribs.

After they had eaten and carefully brought the empty bowls and chopsticks back to Aunt Lan, adjusting their caps and grinning at her sly jokes which made them blush (for she was bent on matrimonial matters), they sauntered away. Little Pond and Hsiao Wang had decided not to marry, although now even poor peasants could afford to marry, and workers were in high demand. So many girls of bad class origin wanting to marry a man of a good class origin! But until socialism was soundly established, Little Pond and Hsiao Wang would remain celibate, dedicating themselves to work for the country.

They walked towards the docks, for both of them loved the sound of water, loved to look at boats. They had nostalgia for the Great River, its russet junks and the turmoil of its water. Here in Tientsin the river was not beautiful as in Chungking. Here all was flat, and the water slow, turgid, silt-laden. The boats had to battle the muddy ooze to heave themselves away from land.

All along the road, posters flaming with color told them new things. Which furnished their minds as a house is filled with furniture.

WIPE OUT ILLITERACY.

Groups of little boys and girls radiant with laughter, their shining white teeth welcoming a big book haloed by the sun, their hands reaching for it, on an enormous poster by the new, mimosa-lined avenue.

"I had a sister," said Hsiao Wang, "she died of hunger in the famine. . . ."

I would have had a brother, thought Little Pond. What would little brother have looked like? Oh, he would now be one of those apple-cheeked, happy children, who did not have to work, who were not beaten, whose stomachs were filled, whose skin was clothed, summer and winter.

Ma would have clothes now, and beautiful pins for her hair. The neighbors would say: "Big Sister Liang, your son has brought honor to you. . . ."

Ma would smile, that gentle smile which curved her beautiful mouth. (His heart tightened with the memory. No other woman smiled with such loveliness.) He always looked for that smile when he looked at the young girls, now so free, so fearless, on the streets of Tientsin.

The dockyards were piled high with crates, and men unloading them. Machinery from Russia. Little Pond and Hsiao Wang showed their pass to the comrade policeman, handsome in his white summer uniform and cap with the red star on it.

They reached the end of the quay, listening to the gold-bronze water burping its undigested silt against the docks. And there a ship was moored, the gangplank lowered, at its foot a small crowd.

"Foreigners going away," said Hsiao Wang.

The foreigners, some fifty of them, waiting to board the ship, were surrounded by suitcases and bags and wooden boxes. A last checkup by the customs and by the security police. One by one, slowly, the foreigners went up the gangplank, and their belongings were hauled up behind them by the port staff. A fence of netted wire cut off the foreigners and their ship from the rest of the docks.

Hsiao Wang and Little Pond stared through the wire netting.

That ugly foreigner with glasses. He stooped a little. Bent over a suitcase, trying to close it after inspection. He wore a very rumpled white suit. By his side was a woman with graying hair, in a tired flowery cotton dress, much bleached with washing.

Taifu. Doctor. The foreign doctor who had taken him to see his mother that evening in Chungking. There he was. On the other side of the fence.

"Taifu! Taifu!"

Little Pond suddenly was again the Little Pond going to see his Ma, bowing low in the corridor to the ugly kind foreigner. *"Taifu!"*

David Eanes heard the words, heard the accent, the accent of Chungking, where he had spent half his life. He turned, saw a young man in a khaki jacket, high cheekbones, a broad nose. A Szechuan face. He took two steps towards the fence saying: "Are you calling me?"

But already the Public Security man had bounded forward. "Not allowed, not allowed," he bellowed. "Get back, get back." And angrily to Little Pond: "Who are you? What are you doing here?"

Little Pond took out his card. He continued staring at David Eanes. The Public Security man was frowning at his card. Was mollified by what he saw.

"It is not allowed to speak to foreigners. You must leave immediately. This is a breach of discipline which I must report." He took out his fountain pen and pad, and noted down Little Pond's name, unit.

"Let us go, let us go." Hsiao Wang pulled Little Pond away, pulled him. "Don't look back," he warned.

They walked away and the turgid water and the rumor of the ships faded and they were in a quiet street, in the muffled afternoon, with its hot pewter touch under the new trees.

Hsiao Wang sighed heavily. "Aiyah, Little Pond, I must criticize you. . . . Who was this foreign devil?"

"A doctor . . . he tried to save my mother . . . he gave blood for my mother. . . ."

"Aiyah. Who wants foreign blood?" said Hsiao Wang, appalled.

Chungking had been liberated, peacefully, in December 1949. David and Jessica Eanes welcomed the new power. Attended the processions winding through the streets, helped their colleagues erect a triumphal arch studded with paper flowers over the hospital gateway when the Liberation Army walked in.

And then, on June 25, 1950, the Korean War began.

The Eaneses, being Canadians, signed petitions against

American aggression. Their missionary board protested against the American bombing of civilians in Korea.

But in September 1951 the Eaneses were arrested. They remained under house arrest for a year.

During that year, they were interrogated many times. Had they not sent messages by radio, revealing what was happening in Chungking?

The months passed. The interrogations became relentless, taking several hours every day. The Eaneses' confidence ebbed. Fear and distress took the place of every other emotion. Fear, and distraught weariness.

"Some of the doctors and nurses have written reports saying that you have experimented on human beings," David Eanes was told.

David was stunned. "It is not true. I have never done any experiments on humans. . . . My religion looks upon human life as sacred." But this carried no weight.

This was a time when friend turned against friend, when colleague accused colleague. When there was treachery abounding. To save themselves, people invented things to say about others. It was happening all the time.

And David Eanes wept, wept bitterly when he was told that a colleague had accused him. "Dr. Wing says you trained him to do such experiments. . . ."

Jessica intervened: "Would Dr. Wing give exact details? On whom, where, and when did he and my husband do such evil things?"

The interrogators came back with questions: How many operations had Dr. Eanes performed in his twenty-five years? Why so many? How many had died after operation? Why had they died? He must make a list . . .

And then one day, in the autumn of 1952, all questioning stopped.

They learnt that a prominent Canadian, a member of the Peace Council, had secured their release. But they must leave.

They began to pack. Nine copies of the packing list of every item in their luggage. Declaration of all the monies they carried out. Notices in all the newspapers of their departure, a month ahead. Payment of all debts.

It took them four months.

The day before they left Chungking for Tientsin, now the only port through which foreigners were allowed to leave, they were visited by a bullet-headed man accompanied by two members of the Party committee in charge of the hospital.

The bullet-headed man had deepset eyes, wore a clean gray suit.

"*Taifu* . . . Do you recognize me?"

David looked. The face was familiar, but recently he had found his memory going faulty.

The man took an ashtray from the table in his left hand, hunched his shoulders, bent his knees slightly, and shambled forward.

"Old Wang," shouted David, "you're Old Wang."

Old Wang, the spittoon and bedpan cleaner. Now a cadre and, by his air of authority, in charge.

After the three poisons eradication campaign, about a million Party cadres had been demoted, sent to the countryside to labor, expelled, or criticized.

But Old Wang was among those promoted, replacing those who had succumbed in the cities to corruption and bribery.

"Things are very different now, *Taifu*. Our country has stood up, and nobody will ever insult us again."

"We are very happy about it," said Jessica.

"We shall always remember the kindness, the goodness of the Chinese people towards us," said David.

Old Wang nodded and left.

The Eaneses reached Tientsin without hindrance.

And now, with the ship on the high seas, they stood together under the stars, hearing the water's soliloquy. Feeling both relieved and sorrowful. For it was all their youth, their days of strength, which they were leaving behind, to become exiles in their own country.

"I've racked my brains trying to remember that young man . . . But I can't . . ." said David.

"But he remembered you, dearest, as did Old Wang," said Jessica. And this comforted them greatly.

"Fuck her mother," muttered Hsu Build-the-City, examining his hair, turning to watch the back of his head in the mirror. Even a young man would grow a few white hairs after all this.

406

Hsu still felt a terrorized emptiness within him, the gooseflesh starting in his cheeks, to his neck, down to the soles of his feet, when he thought of those weeks and months of the three poisons and five poisons campaign.

"It's the nightmares . . . " muttered Hsu, plucking at his hair, parting it to discover any errant white. Nightmares. They had begun when he had to write his biography, carefully prepared by Brigadier General Tsing. It had been checked. And rechecked. Some of the people he'd mentioned in it had not been found. But then so many Party members had changed names and identities . . .

But he still woke up covered with sweat, thinking of those boxes on every street, each with a slit through which people could shove letters, denunciations to be read, to be listened to. It was called "Listening to the opinion of the masses."

He sweated because he knew that when the accused, the suspect would confess, confess . . . sometimes they would say things that had not really happened at all, but which they now believed had happened. Thus the Crystal Import-Export Co. had been mentioned, and almost, almost, the people who confessed they had run errands for it blurted out that it had too much gold to give away, which of course was highly suspicious.

But somehow they had been unable to say how much. And the Party was just then extolling the sympathizers who had given gold, in times of distress, to Party organizations.

That night Hsu had found his first white hair. For many days he had walked, smiled, eaten with a thumping heart, though his impassive face showed nothing at all. That was what face was for. To conceal, to project *image*. Not to reveal.

Never was he found without a book in hand. Marx, Engels, Lenin, Stalin, or a pamphlet by Chairman Mao.

I am going through the eye of a needle, Hsu thought. Luckily, Comrade Lo had backed him. He was criticized only for a certain "commandism" by some of his subordinates. (Next campaign, he'd have their skins.)

Comrade Lo. That old mud lump, that rough-necked Ball of Grease, as Hsu called her to himself. But Comrade Lo was now preparing to go to Peking, and Hsu wanted to go with her.

"Little Hsu," she had said, her apple face still ruddy despite her city years, the cheeks blown red by the Yenan

wind on both sides of her minuscule nose, "my Old Partner
is in Peking, back from Korea. The Organization is now
shifting me there." Her Old Partner, which meant Meng,
her husband, was now an important member of the Party
and the Government. An army veteran. But Lo, of course,
always deprecated him, as she deprecated herself. "We're
just mud lumps," she would say, giggling like a young girl.
"I'm only a stupid mud lump . . ."

Everyone wanted to be in Peking. Peking was the center,
hub and heart of the Central Committee and the State
Council. Peking had become synonymous with "Party Center" and everything revolved around "the Leadership" and
"the Center" which had installed itself there.

Anyone who came from Peking or went up to Peking was
held to be privileged, a cut above mere provincial cadres.

Comrade Lo, enchanted with her husband's promotion,
played modest, even unhappy. She affected to be frightened. "Look at me, a stupid peasant woman, and my Old
Partner, a rough fighter. He and I ate sorghum roots during
our young days. We never had much schooling. What shall
we be doing in the capital city? I'm afraid I'll make a lot of
mistakes."

"Mother Lo," said Hsu, with his most charming smile,
"the Party really has good eyes. It knows how to choose the
good people, the fearless bone marrow of the revolution."

"Oh, what a flatterer," cried Comrade Lo, affecting to be
angry.

"Mother Lo, due to you, our outfit has done good work.
We have wiped out a great many counter-revolutionaries. In
fact, there is practically nothing left to do for your successor.
Had it not been for your guidance, all of us would have
committed a great many mistakes."

He must get Ball of Grease to ask for his transfer to
Peking. With her husband's elevated position it might not
be too difficult.

Hsu's first move was to insist that he must accompany
Comrade Lo to Peking to carry her luggage, to look after
her in the train.

"When we fought our way down to the south we only
caught the No. 11 bus" was Comrade Lo's favorite joke. No.

11 bus meant one's own two legs. "I've never been on a train in my whole life. As for an airplane, I think I would die of fright."

"Mother Lo, my heart will be at peace if I am at your side to see that you lack nothing on the train."

Comrade Lo was frugal and honest. She had never used Party funds for giving banquets, never abused any of the privileges which now came so easily, gravitated almost on their own to Party members. In queues at the doctor, Party members first. At schools, better care and extra tuition for their children. Easy tickets for trains, and to movie houses. And small gifts. Eggs, or a chicken, a head scarf. And many things done without payment: repairing a window, or the plumbing; bringing fresh vegetables, or scented mushrooms in winter from the south. But Comrade Lo staunchly refused all gifts.

And now it worried her that, to convey her old bones to Peking, two train tickets instead of one should have to be bought out of Party funds. And since she was a high Party cadre's wife, the Transport Administration had given her a soft-couch ticket, which she also felt uneasy about.

"I'll go hard," said Hsu, smiling. "We young people have to temper ourselves. And I shall repay the ticket out of my own salary."

One "hard" train ticket. It weighed on Lo's conscience like a small hill of stones. Of course, she was no longer young. She had quite a bit of luggage to carry, she had also bought a few things for Old Partner, and for her remaining son and daughter.

On the other hand, young Hsu was certainly entitled to a few days off work. Why, he had not even gone away for the New Year. He was an orphan, according to his biography. His father had died when he was seven years old. He only had distant relatives in Shanghai. At New Year's he remained in the office, checking on the files of the suspected counter-revolutionaries in the sector. Truly an exemplary young man. Also good-looking. Studious. Sometimes she thought: Would it not be a good thing if he married Little Pearl? She is near twenty-three now, still young, but in three or four years. . . .

Yet she hesitated over the train ticket.

Hsu knew that he must act. "Comrade Lo," he said

firmly, "you must be accompanied. You are no longer young, and a train journey is most tiring."

At the Peking railway station Comrade Meng, portly, gray-haired, in a cotton shirt and trousers, with a black fan in his hand, stood on the platform. He looked military all over from his very short grizzled crew cut to the way he planted his feet, in their cheap summer sandals, upon the ground. Hsu watched him carefully. The man was not naïve, not like Ball of Grease.

With him was a young girl, buxom, with pigtails, in army uniform.

The girl rushed up. "Mama, Mama," she cried, and threw her arms around Comrade Lo. The grizzled man smiled. The smile crinkled the corners of his eyes. He and Comrade Lo did not touch. "Old Partner," she cried to him. "How are you?" She beamed at him. He laughed, took the big bag she carried. In his outward reticence there was deep, unshakable love.

Hsu put down the last of Lo's numerous packages and suitcases on the platform. "Now that you have arrived safely, Comrade Lo, I shall go back by the next train."

"Why the hurry?" said Comrade Lo. "At least have something to eat. The next train will not go till midnight." She turned to her husband. "Comrade Hsu has taken so much care of me." Hsu felt the eyes of Meng rake him.

Protesting weakly, Hsu let himself be led. There was a big car waiting. For Comrade Lo's "old man" was indeed an important Party comrade, and fetching his old woman from the railway station came under the heading of a necessary public use of vehicle.

"A car," said Comrade Lo. "But we could walk." Her husband growled: "The Organization insisted."

Hsu thought: Using a ministry car to fetch his wife at the station, and filed this away for future use. In any subsequent campaign, this could be brought up against Meng.

The house allotted to the family was new. It had good wooden floors and a modern bathroom. There were two large bedrooms, a living room. Comrade Lo was pleased. Her daughter, Pearl, would have her own room. As for her son, he would sleep in the living room when he came home. She had learnt the use of a modern bathroom in Shanghai. Why, at first she hadn't known where to shit, where to wash her face!

While his wife and daughter were in the bedroom and the cook prepared a meal, Meng started to question Hsu.

He was a very tight, relentless inquisitor. Hsu kept a modest stance, but he felt the small, close-set eyes of the old veteran probe into him. Piercing his skin. Here was no flabbiness, either of body or of brain.

Which village had he been born in? When? What did his father do? His mother? Where had he gone to school? How many years? Name of his teachers? What had he done when the Japanese had taken Shanghai? When had he joined the Party?

On and on, minutely. He was dragged through his whole life, from the day of his birth up to how the unit had chosen him to accompany Lo to Peking. Really? It had been a unit collective decision? (Heaven, thought Hsu, I must get Chaste Wisdom to fix this when I return.)

Hsu began to sweat. He felt as if pieces of himself were now coming unglued, falling apart, and he could not put his life together—even though Brigadier General Tsing had prepared a "life" for him and he had learnt it by heart and even written it twice, and it had been accepted. It was the way Meng left a pause, his jaws chewing slowly, after Hsu's answer to each question. Letting the words sink in the water of silence, and then taking out the answer, repeating it, as if it was a stone he was observing.

Finally Comrade Lo emerged from the bedroom. "Now, Old Partner, have you given little Hsu some tea? And some peanuts? Oh, how forgetful you are . . . but now we shall have a meal . . ."

Throughout the meal Old Partner Meng kept silent. But his eyes never left Hsu's hands, nor his chopsticks. He just watched him. Watched the way he put the food into his mouth.

Hsu finally took his leave. Although the food was excellent, it weighed in his stomach, savorless.

"Old Partner," scolded Comrade Lo. "I speak to you and you don't listen."

411

They were both in bed, pillow next to pillow. An old couple, delighted with each other, totally accepting each other.

"I'm listening," said her husband affectionately, "but I was thinking about this Hsu fellow."

"What about him? He is a good young man. Hardworking. He has eaten bitterness in his youth. . . ."

Old Partner sighed. From the way Hsu wielded chopsticks, he *knew*, just knew he had not eaten bitterness. But he would not discuss it. When the water level drops, the stones appear, he thought. Let time do its usual work of showing what is true, what is not.

"I don't know what I would do without him," continued Comrade Lo. "I feel he should come up here to help me. Shanghai people are the cleverest and smartest, and they are all over China. They are much smarter than us northerners."

"Much smarter," agreed Meng smoothly. Comrade Lo was irked by something in her husband's tone. But she couldn't talk to him about her plans for Little Pearl. "Old silly, you are too suspicious," she said fondly.

When her week's leave to welcome her mother back to Peking had ended, Little Pearl left by train for Tientsin, to return to her engineering college.

The college had a part-time work, part-time study program; it trained technicians for the army. Pearl was proud to have been selected for the People's Liberation Army. She would drive and repair ambulances and trucks, possibly also tractors, if assigned to an army agricultural center.

On two Sundays a month, the students of Tientsin's colleges and institutes went to labor. The city had very few parks and the municipality had decided to convert a former slum, boggy with sewer dirt, into a park with flower beds, pathways, pavilions, artificial rockeries, and a small man-made lake. Many thousands of willing hands would work at it.

Pearl dug valiantly, sinking her spade into the fetid stagnant ditch which had to be emptied of its mud. There was not too much water but it had rained, and the spade was heavy. Pearl felt the ache in her arms, in her back; her muscles burnt. She slipped, fell into the ditch.

"Here, take my hand." A strong hand, a strong pair of arms, lifted her, pulled her up the slope. "I'll clean you. Don't move." The young man pulled handfuls of grass, wiped her trousers, her boots, her jacket. He bent to retrieve her spade from the filthy water, and cleaned that too. "You must level the ground where you stand when you dig," he told her. He showed her, stamping a small platform for her. He wielded the spade smoothly, filling her basket, then filling his. And then he slung them at both ends of a pole, heaved the pole on his shoulder, and started climbing the slope. "Take a few breaths before you begin to work again," he called out to her.

When work time was over they went back together up the slope. She said timidly: "You're very strong, comrade."

"Liang is my name. Liang Little Pond. I'm used to the sticky soil," he said, "it's like where I come from."

"I could tell by your accent that you came from Szechuan," said Pearl.

He grinned. "In our school we come from the four horizons," he said. He did not ask her name. Nodded briefly as they parted, going to their separate lorries. She looked at him as he walked off. He had a limp.

She thought: He has a square face, not a pointed face. She liked a square face much better than a pointed one.

nineteen

PEKING'S four-square houses crouch behind faceless gray walls, shutting out the world, entirely turned inward to their own courtyards. Each house repeats the three thousand-year-old plan of CITY: a hierarchy of walled squares boxed within each other, sited according to the cardinal points, north, south, east, west. CITY is symbol of the cosmos, equilibrium and harmony, and every house reproduces the city.

When liberation came in 1949 and many foreigners departed, their houses became vacant. Dr. Jen Yong, newly appointed chief surgeon at the new surgical unit of the New Hospital, chose a small, cinnabar-gated abode, No. 31 in Yellow Wall *hutung*, not far from what had once been a willow bordered moat lining the walls of Peking's Imperial City. These walls had been torn down in the 1920's, to make way for houses. Now only two sets of walls remained: the outer massive gray brick walls dating back to the 14th century, so wide that two carriages could drive abreast on their fortressed and crenelated tops, and the purple walls around the Ming dynasty palaces in the heart of Peking, known as the "Inner" or Forbidden City.

Yellow Wall *hutung* was seven feet wide. No car could turn in it. It was typical of the chicken entrail tangle of unpaved meandering lanes, impasses, paths connecting the dwellings with the paved or tarred avenues and streets crisscrossing the city. Every *hutung* was a spoor of dust, turning to mud in summer storms.

The gate of No. 31 was raised three stone steps above the

dust level. It was flanked by tail-flourishing stone lions standing on sixteen-inch-high stone pedestals.

Yong had chosen it as much for its courtyard garden as anything else—for Stephanie loved to garden. . . . The courtyard had two lilac trees, a Judas tree, some beds of juniper and phlox and dahlias, a forsythia, and a peach tree of great spread. Facing due south was the main reception-living room. On the west was the bedroom, on the east the dining room. Within these oblongs were ensconced a modern bathroom, a toilet, and smaller rooms, separated by carved wood screens. Beyond the kitchen (which boasted an iron stove imported from Europe in the early 1900's and an icebox), another small paved courtyard led to a back door for servants. And two rooms for domestics, one near the front gate, one next to the kitchen, were inserted into the structure without disturbing its harmonious squareness. A verandah paved with stone ran around the courtyard, showing off painted beams and purple pillars.

The owner had been a German scholar much in love with Chinese culture. He had died swiftly when back in his own land, now too alien for him. Before leaving, he had the house repainted, the roof tiles redone. And so had left behind him the perfume of affection.

Yong awaited Stephanie's reaction to the house with an emotion akin to panic. Would she like it, or would she be polite, with that pleasantness which ravaged him, for it was almost a lie? He wanted her to be once again the joyous, straightforward being he had fallen in love with. He could not afford—the weight of his tradition upon him—to be as utterly frank as she was. But that was precisely why he loved her, because she was so ruthless in her candor.

Let me plan and calculate, circumvent and compromise, making the way clear for you, he thought. But *you* stay as you are, my love.

"Oh, how gorgeous!" she said. "How did you manage to get this house?"

She stood, straight as a beam of sunlight, her pleasure unconcealed. And Yong delighted in her delight.

He heard a tremulous voice (his own) say: "The plumbing works, but not the electricity."

Stephanie walked to the peach tree and stood looking up at its boughs.

The peach tree had borne its load of fruit and was now

preparing autumn leaves. "Whoever designed this house was great," said Stephanie. "I feel good just looking at it."

"The cook . . ." said Yong, eager to disparage things in order to placate Fate, envious of too much human happiness.

"What about him?" Stephanie smiled at the cook.

The cook had served the German scholar for twenty-five years, and remained to look after the house. He stood behind Yong, giving Stephanie a crooked beatific grin.

"He can only cook German food. He makes potato pancakes very well . . ."

Stephanie laughed. Laughed until her belly ached. Releasing laughter, for the moment abolishing all doubt, sorrow, anxiety, strain. For the moment.

That night they made love on the large bed which was the only piece of furniture the German scholar had left behind him. And love was good and joyous and careless, unaffected and uncalculating, as it ought to be.

They slept and woke, and the house stirred with morning and put itself out to please Stephanie.

And Stephanie knew that, to recapture what had ebbed away—a certain magic between her and Yong—she must make this house her own, her very own, and his. Separate from the Family. Themselves alone, together.

In late and lovely autumn, misty with latter rain, Stephanie began to furnish the house.

She had not taken the furniture from Willow Pool Garden, although Mother had offered to send it. Besides, in Peking there were so many establishments selling genuine, or genuinely faked, Ming furniture, or the more ornate products of the Manchu dynasty which had come after the fastidious Ming. The managers of the furniture stores would tell her, with that new honesty that saw no point in lying since all prices were fixed: "This is a genuine fake, made eighty years ago, of a chair made five hundred years ago . . ." Buying furniture became a lesson in history, a roaming of the centuries, endless excitement.

"Utilize the past to serve the present" Mao Tsetung had urged. The Government was committed to preserving the past. Never had any regime, since the 18th century, done so

416

much to renovate, restore, maintain, and preserve the national treasures of all kinds. Rooting out the trees that had grown out of the Imperial Palace roofs, turning the neglected Ming palaces into museums, restoring the Buddhist frescoes, which dated from the 3rd to the 14th century A.D. in the caves along the Silk Road. Encouraging archaeological research. Not allowing old bronzes and jades and porcelain to be pillaged or taken out of China.

But other voices were strong. Those of people who had all their lives associated this search for beauty with their own exploitation. Those who said that, to work for the revolution, all "beauty" which was only a bourgeois reactionary value must be abolished. In many Party committees, there were fulminations against those who "only like old things, feudal and reactionary things . . ." Denunciations of aesthetes, their idolatry of "bourgeois living." To build "a splendid modern culture," there was only one model, the Soviet Union.

Ignoring this conflict of views about the political morality of aesthetics, Stephanie determinedly pursued her hunt for beauty; and Yong forbore to tell her that perhaps another political campaign might take place, when the possession of such relics would be unsound.

Stephanie bought snuff bottles, ivory statuettes, porcelain, old rugs, authentic Ming chairs and tables and chests. She conversed with the storekeepers, acquiring the history of each piece. Each object had been an object of love, going from owner to owner through the centuries; and the anecdotes about them were reverential. The act of buying became homage to a tradition preserved, despite the fact that the old world had cracked and lay strewn about like broken candy.

It seemed to Stephanie, in her new contentment, that a miracle might happen in China. The country might go from a universe of want to a universe of plenty, without too much destruction; with the preservation of what had been most worthy. In her buying frenzy, she did not stop to think that she might be trying to help shape this miracle—at least in her own life, and Yong's—by acquiring possessions . . . the familiar symbols of security as she had been taught it.

Yong too succumbed to the magic of Peking.

The bookshops were Aladdin's caves. Stored in dusty penumbral corners, stacked in disordered backrooms, lay hundreds of thousands of old books. Here congregated old scholars and young workers who had just begun to read. They pressed against the shelves, delved into corners, reading, buying. Five, six, ten centuries of books disgorged from private libraries. Yong would return from forays in the bookshops, his arms full of books, his pockets sagging with books—woodblock printed, 16th- or 17th-century treasures, which had come out of families fearful of being dubbed landlord, or capitalist, and who sold their libraries by weight of paper.

Meanwhile Yong was meeting new challenges for surgery. Problems which the Korean War had stimulated. New kinds of wounds. Napalm burns. Flesh torn by bullets inflicting horrible destruction. Care for wounded soldiers in the Kuomintang armies had been extremely limited; the People's Liberation Army devoted much attention to its wounded. And now there were the workers to be cared for. A total restructuring of hospitals, of surgery. Yong and his colleagues would specialize, for the techniques of surgery were becoming increasingly complex. Yong joined in the pioneering studies of microsurgical procedures, the reattachment of limbs, hands, fingers—an area of medicine that had particular importance in the new China. The loss of a precious worker because of a severed limb or finger was not to be tolerated; the country could not afford it. Great hopes were placed on the perfection of microsurgical techniques.

Many of Yong's colleagues would take up other specialties. Burns. Skin grafts . . . there was so much to do, and so few of them to do it. They would delve into China's old and little known medical lore, searching for old ways that might prove newly effective. Everything in the past of China was to be checked, to be sifted; the good preserved, the good which might lead to new breakthroughs of creativeness and discovery.

Stephanie was asked to help in the Translation Bureau of the Language Press, and thus became a "foreign expert."

This entitled her to an enormous salary—five times that of Yong—which she didn't need, and many privileges—which were less than useless to her because Yong couldn't share in them. Stephanie, for example, benefited from a month's holiday by the sea in summer, but Yong was not included in this holiday since he was Chinese.

"All because the Chinese are certain that no foreigner can or will endure Chinese living standards," she wrote in her journal. "So they strain to procure for us the luxuries they deny to themselves but which they imagine Westerners cannot do without."

As she wrote, she wondered if this was still another way of letting foreigners know that, however "useful" they might be, they would always be *foreign*.

They came to No. 31. Friends. Many friends.

Sa Fei followed by her unrelentingly adoring husband, Liu Ming. Sa Fei, now a vice chairman of the Writers' Union and of the Federation of Art and Literature, and yet critical of the heavily bureaucratic methods of the federation: "Every writer is also an official of the State. Just as in the imperial dynasties every poet became a mandarin. We have absolutely no tradition of a separate, individualistic intelligentsia," lamented Sa Fei.

Liu Ming did not bother about ideology. He wrote about what he knew best, the villages. He talked very little. Only smiled, and loved Sa Fei.

A few of Yong's colleagues also came to No. 31. Doctors, scientists, researchers, they also felt frustrated by the committees, layer upon layer of Party committees, all supposed to "guide" their work.

"They understand nothing of science, and any concept of scientific research is beyond their mental grasp," said one scientist angrily.

On occasion the air waxed thick with argument. Fundamental research. Chou Enlai was all for it, and his name was spoken with reverence by the scientists. "But a lot of Party people don't have his knowledge or perception," they said.

One or another of their guests, unable to describe some technical process in Chinese, because sometimes the words for it were not yet invented, would turn to Stephanie as "the language expert."

"Mrs. Jen, what would be the Chinese equivalent of a quark? Or a meson?" They teased her gently. They made puns and conundrums, and dared her to translate them.

Meiling Yee came to No. 31. As a vice director in the Health Ministry, she traveled on frequent missions to Eastern European countries. . . . One evening she invited Stephanie and Yong to dinner with her father, General Yee.

General Yee occupied a sumptuous "four-courtyard" mansion with pillars of carmine and raised marble balustrades around the verandah. This befitted his rank, which was that of a non-Communist minister, member of a dozen committees as well as a high-ranking member in one of the eight non-Communist parties which had formed the Democratic League, and now had seats in the National Assembly. The function of these parties was one of mild criticism of Communist errors, not opposition or challenge to Communist rule. Which made their status as "political parties" rather ambiguous.

General Yee spoke of the great achievements of the new Government. And gave his guests a splendid meal. "My father has one of the best cooks in Peking," said Meiling. The cook was not only good, he was also a member of the National Assembly, China's parliament, and he arrived in a motorcar, from the pool of vehicles reserved for officials, to cook for General Yee.

One of the guests that night, besides Meiling's husband Sung Weichang, who preserved a glum silence throughout the meal, was her husband's father, Old Sung, the ex-waiter at the Press Hostel.

"Old Sung!" Stephanie exclaimed with a spark of her old spontaneity. Just in time, she stopped herself from hugging him, and instead shook his hand warmly.

Sung raised his glass to Stephanie in both hands, and grinned affectionately at her and at Yong. He was now running "Friendship Hostel," an assembly of palatial-looking five-story buildings in which the Russian and East European experts and technical advisers, some two thousand in number, were housed. As were members of West European Communist parties.

He talked of the difficulties of providing enough milk, cheese, yoghurt, and sour cream for the Russians. "They eat things we cannot eat," he said. The very word *cheese*, Stephanie knew, made Yong turn pale. Many Chinese had the same reaction. Stephanie still yearned, occasionally, for a glass of cold, fresh milk. This secret vice she would indulge when no one was at home. Winter Treasure would not touch cow's milk. "It smells bad," he said, wrinkling his nose comically.

But though she and Yong occasionally went out, Stephanie preferred to hold "open house" at No. 31. She enjoyed the fact that their home was becoming a gathering place for Peking's intellectuals.

Hsiao Lu, the outspoken poet Stephanie had met at the Eanes's in Chungking, dropped in and entertained them hugely. He had remained an errant soul, eager to travel on the back of a small gray donkey throughout China. "Officialdom does not suit me." Like Sa Fei he found Peking oppressively bureaucratic, and agreed that the Party was becoming a new mandarinate. "I want to be unseizable, as the small dawn wind, removed from the vigilant eye of a comrade who frowns at my soul and its outpourings."

Hsiao Lu's father, the ex-warlord, was now much occupied in denouncing old habits, including his own opium-smoking. "He always tries to outdo me," sighed Hsiao Lu. "And he succeeds, even today."

Arthur and Millie Chee had returned from America in early 1955 in response to Chou Enlai's impassioned call to Chinese intellectuals abroad to return, to serve their country. One night they appeared at No. 31, bringing with them American noise, American exuberance, blended with their Chinese minds and bodies. They told Yong and Stephanie about the difficulties they had had in leaving the United States. Since 1952, only a dozen Chinese intellectuals had succeeded in eluding the stringent watch placed upon anyone suspected of wanting to go to "Red" China. Joseph McCarthy had then been at the height of his power.

The Chees had managed to leave, ostensibly for a holiday in Brazil. From Brazil they had set sail for Sweden, which had recognized the People's Republic of China; there the Chinese Embassy took them in charge and returned them via the trans-Siberian railway to the ancestors' country.

Arthur and Millie were radiant. Their eyes shone with stars and eagerness. They had been royally treated—only a few political-remolding lessons. "We'd like to get into the hinterland, start an epidemiology center . . ."

Other overseas Chinese called. A couple of delightful New Zealanders who had run away from their family to reach China. An engineer from Canada. They were remarkable both for their love for China, which stuck out of them like elephant tusks, and their wry realization that the China Chinese did not trust them; that being from "outside" their habits were different, and also their manner of thinking. "Every time there's a political campaign we're the targets for criticism," they said, puzzled but keeping their spirits high and clinging to their love, their love for the ancestors' country.

The house was thus cheerful with people, with laughter and talk. "Your doorstep is never cold," said Mother Huang approvingly. Mother Huang was the new cook. The German-trained male cook had been acquired by a Western embassy where they probably liked his potato cakes. Mother Huang, recommended by the street committee, now lorded over the kitchen, cooking good northern food, generous with garlic, and superlative noodles. She brought a niece to clean the house and to wash clothes. Nothing pleased Mother Huang better than "a warm threshold" and "hot and noisy air," which meant a party going on. She would stand, surveying the living room with a proprietary look, then decide how many more dishes she would make.

Stephanie's second book, which Zimmerman had published, had been hit by the McCarthy fury, and disappeared under vociferous abuse in the major newspapers. She had marveled then at the waywardness of the public in America. How easily swayed it was by critics who themselves walked in fear.

Yong bought a long narrow table on which he set out photographs of Stephanie, of their marriage in Yenan, of his parents, of Stephanie's parents, of Jimmy, of Winter Treasure. He enlarged the snapshots taken at the ranch by Jimmy—among them one of Stephanie, laughing, her hair blown about her in the wind, and behind her, sleek horses running in an emerald meadow. It was his favorite. He carried the original snapshot about with him, in the pocket of his jacket, everywhere.

Winter. Mornings opaque with white mist that filled the courtyard, blanketed the roof. The sound of sweeping. Each house owner was responsible for keeping clean that part of the *hutung* in front of his gate and walls.

Yong went off at 6 a.m. to the hospital, young-looking in his blue jacket and cap, looking like an ordinary worker running to catch the No. 14 bus which stopped in the avenue at the end of their *hutung*.

The postman. "Our green-clad friend has come," Mother Huang would announce. Her hands under her apron, she watched comrade postman leave his bicycle under the awning, cross the courtyard to deliver the letters to Stephanie. Stephanie would ask the postman to come in, to sit down. Mother Huang would bring him a cup of boiling water. He refused to drink tea, that would have been bribery. He would sit gingerly, on the edge of a chair, respectful and agog with curiosity.

Stephanie would look through the envelopes. Much mail for Yong. Some for her. With the end of the Korean War, the postal service between China and America had once again become efficient. She knew the postman would like to know about her letters, and she would hold one up and say: "Ah, this is from my mother."

"Your honored old lady . . ." the postman would say, sipping the water noisily, "how is her respected old body?"

Stephanie would open the envelope, glance at the copperplate handwriting. "She is healthy . . . she writes a long letter. . . ."

Stephanie would give him the stamps. The postman's son kept an album of foreign stamps. As Jimmy had done.

Isabelle wrote to her daughter once a fortnight. A new energy had come to her since Heston had been laid low with a mild heart attack at the end of autumn 1953. A heart attack, eighteen months after Jimmy's death. Isabelle's letters were a stream of comment on Heston's ill health. Because it was the foundation of her own new-found vitality.

"Your father was very affected by Jimmy's death," she wrote.

"He mourned quietly, trying never to show it. We are closing the large house. . . . Your father talks of giving it to the city in trust. . . .

"He will never work as hard as he used to; the doctors forbid it. I am taking him away for a holiday in Europe. . . ."

She was in charge now. In charge of Heston Ryder, creator and builder. Dad. Stephanie was swept by a great wave of love for her father, and resentment that his diminished state should now delight Isabelle so obviously. He'd appeared not to love Jimmy, but he'd cared very deeply. Dad had got himself tangled up in the fierceness of his love, the single-mindedness of his emotions. Dad loved and didn't let on. He'd loved her and then she'd gone away, and now Jimmy had died.

Isabelle. Her husband needing her had made her strong again . . . was it true, then, what Widow had said: Was one's strength founded on the loved one's weakness? "She has fed on my sorrow," Widow had said of Mother. . . .

Letters from Dad. His handwriting had changed. There was something assiduous, painstaking, less sprawling and confident about his short notes. She kept them with her sometimes a whole day before putting them away in the chest where she stored all her writing, and diaries, and letters from home.

Stephanie, you sound happy. Glad you seem to have no problems of any kind. I'm really perfectly fit, only a little tired . . .

Our national Big Mouth is getting too big . . . . I'm all for making America safe—the system, the freedom we've worked out are quite exceptional in the world, too valuable to endanger . . . but there are limits to be observed . . . he's getting plain cumbersome. . . .

A great admission on Dad's part. Dad no longer enthused about McCarthy. She showed the letter to Yong.

"I always thought your father was a sensible man," said Yong. "And one day he will be very useful to us. . . ."

"Useful? What do you mean?"

"I mean China will need the best there is in every kind of technology. And your father is a man of vision . . . he will understand, one day . . ."

Useful. Yong's father had once said: "Oh, nothing will happen to Uncle Keng. Keng Dawei is *useful* . . ."

Stephanie felt uneasy when Yong used such terms. As if people were gauged, measured by their usefulness, as if countries only thought in terms of self-interest. But America, too, catered to her national interests, real or imagined. Perhaps Yong was right, after all . . .

"But what about ideology? What about beliefs and faiths? Every day I hear praise of the USSR. Its unselfish fraternal aid, its high technology," she demanded.

"We have to lean to their side," said Yong. "After all, Stalin did help us . . . even if we did pay for the help. . . . Remember what Mao and Chou Enlai told John Service in 1945? 'Only America can really help to transform China.' "

"I know, you've always thought Dad would be here one day, shaking hands with Mao Tsetung," said Stephanie jokingly.

"I still think it. Stephanie, I *work* with Russian surgeons. They're good, but we are just as advanced if not more than they are. I've learnt better surgery from Western-trained surgeons, and I've seen it in America. I think America can help us with technology someday. And America will also need us." He spoke with such confidence that Stephanie was shaken.

How could America need China? Her Texas-bred patriotism rebelled at the idea of America *needing* anyone.

"In what way?" she asked, more sharply than she intended.

"Only America and China, together, can keep the peace," sighed Yong, aware of her defensiveness. "Otherwise the world will always be unstable."

In her letters, Stephanie tried to convey the mood of China to her father, describing the great stir of construction all over the country. Factories, new workers' blocks, new schools, new hospitals. Every day something was being done; and apathy, hopelessness, had disappeared.

"There's so much enthusiasm, because a lot is being done which was never before attempted," she wrote. If Yong was right, then Dad would pay attention, even if he did not like communism.

She attempted to amuse Heston Ryder with descriptions of Peking. "A city lovely to live in despite its mauling weather. Save for five weeks of autumn, the climate is most trying. From December to March the arctic wind howls. 'The walls talk with the wind,' that is the way the children describe that perpetual moaning and wheezing which is the dust rubbing itself against the stones. And then suddenly there is a truce, a few days of cerulean heaven, but this clemency always makes my cook predict disaster. 'The black frost will come, the soil will be cast iron, next year's harvest meager and we'll tighten our belts.' "

Stephanie also wrote to all her friends, to Professor Moslyn at Radcliffe. To Camilla Waring. Her letter to the latter was returned. "Her street committee should have her new address," said the postman, handing it back to Stephanie.

"There are no street committees in America, Comrade Postman."

She wrote again to Professor Moslyn, asking Camilla's whereabouts. "I have had no news of her for about a year," Moslyn replied. "She and her husband and children moved away some two years ago; I had a Christmas card from them, but nothing since."

Stephanie brooded over this letter, sensing a deliberate vagueness which disturbed her greatly, though she couldn't quite pinpoint *why*.

Three days before Christmas, Yong and Stephanie went back to Shanghai to celebrate their tenth wedding anniversary and Winter Treasure's sixth birthday.

At the railway station Winter Treasure was running along the platform as the train slowed down, running and peering through the windows. Her heart hungry with missing him, Stephanie could not wait. She sprang out of the still moving train and saw him stop, startled, and then rush to her arms.

"I've thought of you every day, Ma," he said with that seriousness of his which she both loved and feared. "And of *Tietie*." He looked bright-eyed up at Yong and there was no hesitancy then. He accepted both of them and Stephanie felt she had been foolish, as usual, to think he had paused, a fugitive reticence, seeing her. He took her hand and she felt blessed among all women.

Mother and Father, no older, not withdrawn into that internal cogitation of the elderly, welcomed them too.

Thus began contented days in warmer Shanghai, where no arctic dust wind blew, and the cold hovered bearably around freezing point, not twenty below as in Peking. Long grave discussions with Mother about Stephanie's skin. Mother's recipe for special almond cream to preserve her skin. Mother so very concerned that Stephanie should keep her beauty. "Oh daughter, the dust of Peking . . . I have friends who become hysterical, refuse to go to Peking even when their husbands are appointed to the capital. Peking makes their noses bleed and their skins rough, and they are perpetually hawking and spitting and coughing because of the dust."

And Father, discussing the nationalization of industry, of banks, which was on the way. Everything was to be nationalized. Banker Jen would remain, to manage what he had once owned. He would be paid a salary, and dividends upon the capital invested by the Jen Family, and compensation for whatever was taken over. "In this way I shall have no more responsibility," said Father brightly. "No longer be held accountable for mishaps . . ."

Contented days . . . except that Yong had to return to Peking, for unlike Stephanie—who had the privileges of a foreigner—he had no holidays, apart from a few days at Chinese New Year.

Lionel Shaggin and Loumei asked Stephanie to dinner and Lionel talked of the successful rehabilitation of the prostitutes.

He had put on some weight, looked younger, was enthusiastic about the results of the campaign. "Another five years and we'll have almost eradicated syphilis, and gonorrhea will follow. We've only got about ten new cases a month of syphilis in this city of five million people. . . ."

Joan Wu and Michelle Berbiest, Dr. Hsieh's Belgian wife, and Stephanie had a coffee session together at Michelle's apartment. Michelle baked two large cakes smothered in Belgian chocolate, homemade apricot jam, and cream. Michelle's housewifely talents had grown in proportion as her servants left her to go to the new factories.

With unswerving tenacity she reproduced in Shanghai the world of her Belgian home. Her children and her husband drank coffee, ate pancakes with plenty of homemade jam for breakfast. They ate with fork and knife, not chopsticks. She came back from the special food shop for Europeans in Shanghai loaded with meat, milk, and cheese. She deplored the fact that there were no strawberries.

And her children never told their mother of how their schoolmates said they stank of milk and shunned them. Stolid, large-boned, impervious, they thrived as foreigners, as did Michelle. She knew nothing of what was happening in China, never read a newspaper or listened to the radio. Totally self-insulated, she counted the rows in her knitting while her husband read, wrote, or worried; briskly folding her work and saying to her children "Bedtime," at nine o'clock.

Never did it seem to occur to Dr. Hsieh that his wife should change. And Stephanie wondered about herself. She had adapted, changed herself, become so involved. Had let Winter Treasure become totally Chinese. Perhaps she ought to have imposed her American way of life at home, perhaps. But she had not, she had not done so. On the contrary, it had been so exciting, so stimulating to learn Chinese, to dress, to eat, to almost *be* Chinese. Almost . . .

"*Amah* Mu came once or twice to see Winter Treasure," mother told Stephanie. "And Teacher Fan has been coming to discuss his studies." And thus gave Stephanie the aroma of public approval.

Comrade Fan came to see Stephanie, stayed a long time talking with her, talking of Winter Treasure and his precociousness. "He must become a scientist," she said gravely. "He will be valuable to our country."

Stephanie began to tutor Winter Treasure at home, and rediscovered her little boy even as she delighted in his intelligence. He could now read and write over three thousand ideograms. He had recovered his devouring curiosity about the sky, animals, insects, and machinery. But books for children were scarce. Many were printed, but ten thousand copies disappeared within the hour from the bookshops. So many readers.

Stephanie wrote to Heston and Isabelle for children's books, and Heston posted two dozen. Stephanie was called to the Central Post Office, and told by the supervisor that the books had to be returned.

"But, Comrade Supervisor, they are for my son. To train him as a scientist for China's reconstruction . . ." Her soft Texan accent added charm to her Chinese, and the supervisor sentimentally thought: Such a nice foreign woman, not arrogant.

Stephanie added even more softly, "Chairman Mao said: 'Things foreign must serve China.' My father, who is an engineer, thought these books might be useful to his external grandson."

The supervisor, thoroughly mollified, said: "I must consult higher authorities," which meant that he would plead for Stephanie.

After a week of very pleasant meetings with tea, peanuts, and sweets, between the Party committee secretary, the supervisor, the nine-person staff in charge of foreign mail at the post office, the censors, and Stephanie, an understanding was reached. Four of the books would have to be returned. They contained reactionary material. But Stephanie would be allowed to read them and transmit the useful scientific material in them to her son.

"We hope you will translate many useful books for our children," said the supervisor. Stephanie thanked him and promised. And made a decision.

A fortnight after Chinese New Year, when Stephanie returned to Peking, Winter Treasure came with her. He would now attend school in Peking.

With Winter Treasure at school most of each day, Stephanie continued to work at the Translation Bureau of the Language Press, which both excited and frustrated her. Old Chinese classics, as well as recent books by new authors, were being translated into English. But though many young writers were encouraged to write, what seemed to her best and most revelatory of China's fantastic changes was not being translated. One book in particular had captivated her: *Under the Old Mulberry Tree*, a story of land reform, with all its good deeds but also its mistakes and its terror. The complex struggle of a young man, guilty of nothing but loving a girl and cruelly tortured for it, was worked into it with great art.

"It's a good novel, with suspense and drama," Stephanie wrote, recommending it for translation. But it was frowned upon by the Party committee.

"Yet so many maudlin stories, pointless, flat, obsequious, *do* get translated," Stephanie complained to Sa Fei.

"I too am interested in the new, young writers," Sa Fei answered. "Some of our older writers scoff at the young, saying they are 'uneducated,' and their style is 'unpolished.' True, they haven't spent fifteen, twenty years reading three thousand years of the classics. But I'm sure that if a new Chinese literature is to emerge, the whole language must be rejuvenated. We must get away from this stubborn classicism."

Sa Fei brought to No. 31 a young writer of great promise, writing novellas both sarcastic and flawless. The bureaucracy of the Writers' Union had promoted him, made him assistant editor of some magazine. He was thus so busy with meetings about what and how to create, with reading other people's manuscripts, that he no longer had time to write.

"Every time a new talent is discovered, he is turned into an official, given a large salary, a house, paid for travels. This produces talentless hacks, not genuine writers," said Sa Fei.

"You're much too mordant," said Hsiao Lu. "Why, you yourself are a bureaucrat."

"It hasn't stopped me from producing . . ." said Sa Fei, defensive. But she had not written another major novel, only essays and reportage on land reform, since liberation. Liu Ming, who refused all official jobs, saying "I am not qualified, I'm only a primary school graduate," wrote a great deal, but his work was being scrutinized for political errors. He left for the villages, disappearing for weeks at a time, not even bothering to cash his salary.

"Liu Ming never was happy shitting in a modern w.c.," said Sa Fei. "He thinks of all that beautiful manure going to waste. It saddens him."

Nevertheless, old eminent writers were always asked to "correct" the style of young writers, and possibly because they resented the fact that the Writers' Union now grouped almost four thousand writers, where less than four hundred existed before 1949—many new writers never got into print.

"It is a mistake to 'improve' the style of any writer," wrote Stephanie in a memorandum to the Translation Bureau Party committee. "Who would try 'correcting' Hemingway to sound like Victor Hugo?"

But beyond the question of style loomed also the problem of politics, and this was indescribably elusive.

According to procedure at the Language Press, a Chinese translator first turned the original Chinese work into English. Then the "foreign expert," soon to be nicknamed a "polisher," went over it to make it readable.

Only after the polishing did the Party committee in charge of political purity of text review the translation for political reliability, to ensure that no adjective had been omitted, no word distorted. But since not one of the committee was fluent in the idioms of any foreign language, the foreign text had to be a word-for-word translation. Which, of course, made it read like nonsense. Stephanie, and the other foreign experts, tried to explain that languages differed in syntax, verb placement, phrase construction. But all to no avail. The Party committee was not convinced. The polisher would then begin polishing all over again. And so it went on, getting worse instead of better.

Most of the "foreign experts" fell into a state of chronic exasperation, followed either by resignation, a nervous breakdown, or total abandonment of any attempt to do good work. China was China, they said, and would go her own way. And it did not matter if no one in the world ever read a word of what they produced.

But Stephanie, tenacious as always, refused to give up. Her proficiency in Chinese made it possible for her to explain and to discuss the language discrepancies with the committee, after which she would redo the whole lot, translating it again. Until one day she realized that she was earning the hostility of the Chinese translators, making them lose face. And that was unforgivable.

Stephanie wanted to be transferred to other work, but this could not be. Her contract was for three years. However, because she had taught in Shanghai, she succeeded in getting co-opted to a language school run by a couple of amiable English teachers, Mary and Peter Wellington.

The Wellingtons were romantic Communists, in love with the distant paradise which revolution would create, a little abashed at the thousand petty or not so petty foulnesses on the way to fulfillment, but bravely carrying on nevertheless.

The language school had three thousand students. The teachers came from all over the British Commonwealth as well as the United States. Stephanie lectured four hours a day, three times a week, on American literature—and the confusion which the English language in its splendid variety could produce in Chinese minds became very real to her.

The Chinese students concentrated on word sound, tone, pitch, and pronunciation. Any variations, such as tom*ah*to instead of tom*ay*to, *ba*sin and *bye*sin, baffled them. Thus, the various accents—British, Canadian, Australian, American—sounded confusing, even chaotic, to their ears.

The Wellingtons coped. They proved that *basin* was *byesin*, that *skedule* was *schedule*, that *yeah* and *yep*, *yah* and *yes* were one word, and that Stephanie's Texan drawl and Oliver Todder's Cockney were one and the same language.

"English is a great tumult, an ocean with no rules," wrote one student. Stephanie had a wonderful time with the hardworking youths who soon grew to imitate her Southern intonations as well as the Australian, Scottish, London, and other varieties of English they were learning.

In August, Stephanie and Winter Treasure went for a month's holiday to the seaside, at Peitaiho.

The bungalow assigned to her was charming, and she taught her son to swim. His company was delightful; he was so grown up in certain ways, capable of much concentration, full of curiosity but also tenacious, pursuing a subject to its very end. What exactly was sand made of? Why did the sun change color in the evening? Why was the sea salty? She found a children's magazine called *Ten Thousand Whys*, printed by the million in China, which partly satisfied Winter Treasure's thirst for exact knowledge. She taught him English in earnest, but sought in vain on her radio for an adequate English program. Russian was *the* language being taught at the time, so she switched to Voice of America in Basic English. But when the Voice started to talk of Red China in unpleasant terms, she could not let Treasure listen. It made her squirm, as did the hostile references to America on Chinese broadcasts. A great emptiness would then seize her, and she would hold Winter Treasure tight, reassured by the physical beauty, the assurance of the little boy, who showed no trace of trauma.

432

With her son she walked the pine-topped hills rising above the white sand beaches. At three in the morning they watched the sun surging out of the sea. And the little boy clasped her, saying: "Oh Mama, Mama, it is so beautiful, it puts a fire in me." And she thought, hugging him to her, smelling his little boy smell, that she loved him, loved him and felt almost drowned in the great swoop of love.

Tsui Sea Dragon and Bo Chaste Wisdom, his wife, were reunited in Peking. Sea Dragon was now assistant supervisor in the middle school of a large city district in Peking.

And Bo Chaste Wisdom had been transferred from Shanghai to work under Comrade Lo in Peking at the same time as Comrade Hsu was transferred.

Simple, kind, devoted Comrade Lo, not an ounce of dishonesty in her, was unwittingly building her own "pyramid," or small mountain of power, in true bureaucratic fashion. All she thought of was to work more efficiently by recruiting able brains from Shanghai. But, all unaware, she was continuing a feudal practice, and a most corrupting one, that of compliant subalterns linked by relations of self-interest: a confederacy of sycophants, surrounding a "high cadre."

Throughout the bureaucracy, unshaken by political campaigns and by purges, this building of clusters and cliques around one or another high official went on. It was a pattern two thousand years old, hallowed by the Confucian tradition of *kuansi*, a relationship which so often had nothing to do with merit, or talent, or fitness, or hard work. The emperors had done it. The Kuomintang had done it. And now the Communists fell back into the old ways.

Thus Hsu Build-the-City was able to move into the very heart of things; Peking, the "center" of Communist Party power.

Winter Treasure took a sheet of paper from Mama's drawer. He climbed on her chair, pushing away her typewriter. Frowning a little, tossing his head, as Mama did, in utter concentration, he began to write.

"Darling, what're you doing?" said Mama, coming in.

Winter Treasure looked at Mama, coming back from work, her arms full of books. He wanted to run to her, bury his head in her belly, smell her. He would always love Mama, Mama so different, Mama so beautiful. He loved her, as *Tietie* did. *Tietie* and he agreed; they must both look after beautiful Mama.

"I am writing to External Grandpa," he said importantly, restraining himself from rushing headlong to her body. He was a *person*, not a little boy. Trying to be grave, serious, grown-up. Imitating *Tietie*, who sometimes looked at Mama from a distance, all the better to put all of Mama into his eye of love.

And Mama set her books down on a chair, laughing that crystal bell laughter which she gave to him and to *Tietie*, and took him in her arms and said "Oh, darling, darling. Yes, let's write to External Grandpa . . ."

He was all of six years old and he had begun to write in English, holding his pencil like a brush, and putting Chinese words when he did not know English ones.

"Respected loved Grandpa outside, i write my letrer to you mama sent you my facelike from the seaside, protect well you health external grandson Jen Forest Heston Thomas . . ."

And Stephanie said: "Oh, External Grandpa *will* be so happy with your letter. It's the first you wrote all by yourself in English."

Winter Treasure wanted to write External Grandpa's name and address on the envelope. All by himself. And then he began a letter to External Grandma.

"Respected loved External Grandma careful your body . . ."

Lighthearted, Stephanie took the letters to the post office and Winter Treasure settled down to wait for an answer, addressed to himself, to him, because he was now a *person*.

As many of the children of the intelligentsia, Winter Treasure had received so much private tutoring before going to school that he was three years ahead of the average child. Now, with the universities recruiting peasant and workers' children, there was added competition for places at the higher institutes of learning between the children of the intellectuals and the others.

"Education is important, nothing can replace it." Grandmother had said it back in Shanghai in her usual under-stated manner, unyielding as jade. In the end all systems thrived or failed by the number of the elite at their disposal.

"We have to supplement what the State, at the moment, cannot give us," *Tietie* had agreed, echoing his mother. He agreed totally with educating peasants and workers, but meantime he, as well as his parents, crammed Winter Treasure's mind. And Stephanie was also doing it, teaching her son English.

In the spring of 1955 another political hurricane swept the country.

For some months there had been veiled warnings in the newspapers about "mountaintopism," referring to in-dividuals creating their own semi-autonomous pyramids of power.

Now the explosion occurred. A rift in the Party. It was like a fissure in the sky, pieces of the sky falling to earth.

Two prominent Party leaders, Kao Kang and Jao Shushih, members of the Central Committee, were accused of con-spiring to split the Party. Their names were now anathema.

The rift did not affect non-Communists, only Party mem-bers. Yong merely received the documents, to read and discuss. "I told you that the hug of the bear was a dangerous one," he said to Stephanie. "Everyone knows the USSR back them, to take Manchuria away from us—but no one will say it. It's a state secret. . . ."

"You still think that Ryder Aircraft will be selling planes here one day?" Stephanie teased her husband.

"Uncle Keng believes it, I believe it . . . and I think some top leaders also think it will happen," said Yong, unruffled.

Then, in June 1955, the Hu Feng affair began.

Sa Fei came to talk about Hu Feng. A critic and essayist, he was a Party member who refused Party discipline and was unhappy with the political framework within which art and literature were confined. Hu Feng wrote "the political czars seem to be scared out of their wits by anything slightly unorthodox . . . they are so unsure of themselves that they

435

want to crush anyone who does not obey them with total submission." He expounded on, "the subjective spirit struggling for its own expression." He had written hundreds of letters, articles, and now his vitriolic correspondence was being made public in the press. Many other writers, recipients of his letters, were involved. But almost all of them were now recanting, recanting, expressing utter indignation at the content of the missives their friend Hu Feng had addressed to them.

There was a great debate in the Writers' Union on the case of Hu Feng, and Sa Fei was involved as well.

Yong said to Stephanie, in that quiet precise voice which foretold trouble, "I think it best we forget whatever Sa Fei has said in our house about Hu Feng. For her sake . . ."

"She hasn't said anything important."

"Nevertheless, we must forget every word." Yong went on, in his surgical voice, as if he were performing a meticulous operation. "The Party is shaken by the Kao Kang and Jao affair, and now there is this stir among writers, which is a threat to its power. I only hope the Party will not feel too insecure, and start another political campaign among the intelligentsia."

They were lying in the darkness, next to each other, but not touching.

What shall we do, Yong, if you are asked to bear witness against Sa Fei, or any other of our friends who have come and forgotten reticence and carefulness in our house because it is beautiful and mellow?

Stephanie's mind spoke the words, she almost thought she had said them aloud. But Yong slept on, or appeared to.

It *was* serious. Very serious.

Even the foreign experts were studying the Hu Feng affair. At the language school Peter Wellington called a general meeting to discuss it.

But there was no discussion—because Herbert Luger came to conduct the debate.

In September the campaign entitled "to ferret out hidden counter-revolutionaries both in the Party and among the intelligentsia" began. It would last eight weeks.

Yong attended political meetings every night.

Stephanie was now beset by a constant small anxiety, not yet apparent on her face, nor in her letters to her parents.

Anxiety. It moved within her like a caged animal, alien, unpredictable. It woke her with a start at night, as if the bed had jerked in one of those small earthquake shocks which occurred so often in Peking: when the lamps would swing, the tea in the teacups swirl. Anxiety was a sudden spasm, a twitch of the mind. She would find her hands knotting and unknotting, as she read or corrected a translation or looked over the composition of a student. She could not swallow through a suddenly constricted throat.

At those times Yong became unreal to her.

Did she imagine upon his face a certain transparent quality, too transparent, an assertive innocence, too assertive? He surrounded her more than ever with care, with tenderness. They went to the parks on Sunday, to see autumn fling its last gold upon the trees. He behaved as if he was thoroughly happy. Not a care in the world. It was too good to be true.

Anxiety grew. A blind, white, enormous worm. Growing. When cut in pieces each piece resurrected a total worm.

"I don't believe there *is* a Hu Feng conspiracy," she said to Yong. "I don't believe there are so many hidden counter-revolutionaries."

"I do not know," he replied, and sighed. He had taken to sighing. As if he too felt a *thing* sitting on his chest, weighting his breathing, and sought to dislodge it. By sighing.

The house was quiet. No one came, every unit, every department was seeking its own "hidden counter-revolutionaries," and every night there were meetings.

No one knew whether a colleague, a friend, or oneself might not be found counter-revolutionary in act, behavior, or thought. It was better to stay at home. For a visit to a friend could be interpreted as a plot.

At the language school, day by day discussions between the teachers and students had stopped. The students and the Chinese staff kept away from the foreigners.

At the Language Press translation work continued. Although the staff became hollow with tiredness. The translators and the foreign "polishers" continued to irritate each other with corrections and counter-corrections. Extra care was now lavished on choice of words, because a mistake might not be a mistake, but wilful sabotage.

And yet, courageously, the Minister of Culture, an eminent scholar and writer, approved a translation of classical poems. Although his own works were being subject to scrutiny for a whiff of counter-revolutionary thinking.

In Peking bookshops Sa Fei's works were still available, Stephanie noted, and drew comfort from it. From Shanghai, Lionel Shaggin wrote to her: "Cohn and Shine, McCarthy's aides, have been at all the U.S.I.S. libraries . . ." And Stephanie thought despairingly: But it's the same here, exactly the same, only more of the same, on a much larger scale . . .

There were ugly episodes. To clear himself, one poet betrayed his best friend; recalled some casual remark, evoked incidents to prove him a counter-revolutionary. His friend committed suicide.

There were a thousand names for such betrayals. Jealousy, cupidity, ambition, frustration, perfidy, sycophancy. But now it was all summed up in one word: counter-revolutionary. Everything had become *political*, all human weaknesses judged as political attitude, motivation.

Stephanie worried, worried. There were Yong's books, the house, the furniture. There were the friends who had talked; and there was herself. So much of it all could be interpreted as counter-revolutionary now. As deliberate attempts to restore the past, to instigate in visitors a yearning for bygone luxuries, to destroy socialism, to corrupt . . .

The worm of anxiety grew fat and sleek in her. She felt distraught, and all the more so because of Yong's extraordinary self-control. A self-control which was matched by many other intellectuals subject to grueling, exhausting meetings, to scrutiny of their writings, their words, their habits.

Paradoxically, that autumn of 1955 had seen a good number of literary celebrities from abroad visiting China.

For in April of that year at Bandung, Chou Enlai had launched a major foreign policy offensive to woo all the countries of the world. And throughout the left-wing intelligentsia of Europe, New China was being hailed as a shining hope.

Jean-Paul Sartre and Simone de Beauvoir came from France in that September. The campaign against hidden counter-revolutionaries was then at its height, but the eminent visitors would never know it. Not a word, not a grimace, not a bloodshot eye would mar the pleasant weeks they spent touring the country. Sartre's *The Respectable*

Prostitute was translated into Chinese, as a compliment to the illustrious visitor, and would appear in the November issue of *World Literature Translation* magazine, printed in Peking.

The commemoration of the 200th anniversary of Montesquieu's death took place in China. The 150th anniversary of Hans Christian Andersen was celebrated with an excellent translation of all his tales. For the first time there was an integral translation of Chaucer, and lectures on the lyrics of Byron took place. Emily Brontë's *Wuthering Heights* and Charlotte Brontë's *Jane Eyre* were published in translation, with first printings of fifty thousand copies of each. George Bernard Shaw's entire works were also translated. And so was Mark Twain, Fielding's *Tom Jones*, and Howard Fast's *Spartacus*.

Yong worked a full surgery day, six days a week and attending meetings each night. On Sunday he scanned political texts. When he came home Stephanie was quiet, apparently serene. He came home to forget anxiety, not to talk about it. He came home to joke, to forget, to love her for a few short hours.

She would hold Yong in her arms, for this is what he wanted. Gave him the boon and grace of loved body, reassurance. He strove to protect her, all the time, and she must be smooth-browed, light, gay. If she'd said: "What's happened, Yong? Can you tell me, because I can't breathe. I can't breathe properly," then he might have broken down, he might have drifted without a steadfast anchor onto the treacherous rocks of desperation. Perhaps he knew her serenity abnormal, but he was too tired to begin peeling off the mask of normalcy she wore, and which allowed him respite, allowed him to sag within himself, to sleep. Too grateful, also, for the mask.

They did not make love often during those eight weeks the campaign lasted. He needed tenderness, tenderness like a shield. A new womb in which he could gather his strength for the next day.

"Comfort me with silence, with quietness," said his body. And she did. And in this mutual deception their love both grew and withered: deployed with radiant wing, covering the dull earth and the sky, and crippled with the necessary permanent falsity.

As the weeks went by Yong grew inured to the perpetual

strain. Where others foundered or broke down, and there were many suicides, he became, as his father had become, more resilient, dulled with scabs in the right places.

Professor Chang Shou's eldest son, a scientist, was detained as "counter-revolutionary." He had been for a while, before liberation, an interpreter for an eminent English scientist who was also a staunch Marxist, a member of the Peace Council in Stockholm. While his interpreter was being detained, the Englishman came to China, as a most honored guest.

"Yong, how d'you explain that?"

"Ignorance, total ignorance at lower levels."

"Something must be done . . ."

But it took four months to get Professor Chang's eldest son released. The "lower levels" had not even bothered to read their own newspaper, featuring prominently the English scientist's name.

Millie Chee, the pediatrician wife of Arthur Chee, placed a pot of red geraniums on her desk. She was criticized by her colleagues because of the flower pot. Evidence of "bourgeois" tendencies. She had come to Yong, distraught. "I don't understand . . . what has this got to do with medicine? Or with the revolution?"

"Christ!" Arthur exploded, "what kind of people are they to take a geranium pot as proof of bourgeois thinking?"

Yong talked to them. Soothingly. Whispered advice to Arthur.

Millie stood up at the meeting. "We love China, these flowers remind me of China," she said.

The red geraniums stayed. No one could fault her on the sentiment. Now had they been *white* geraniums . . .

In November it was all over.

Yong came home early one night and said: "Spring Snow, it is finished." And went to the bedroom, lay on the bed, and slept twenty hours.

At the Language Press, it was over. Suddenly Chinese colleagues were friendly again and spoke to her.

"I think it is time we hear some music," the Party secretary had said when wearily, almost dragging themselves, the staff of the Press had assembled, each one slumping in

440

his chair, for yet another meeting. (No foreigners ever took part in these.) The Party secretary then put on a record and everyone had started talking to each other again (which they had avoided doing for eight weeks). Some of them had even begun to dance, led by the Party secretary. How could anyone explain this antipodean alternation between grimness and affability? Yet it had happened.

Around forty-five thousand "hidden counter-revolutionaries" had been "ferreted out" throughout the Party and the various units.

Now came the reappraisal of each case. A good many would be found innocent . . . but in the meantime some had died. Suicides. Especially among Party members.

"The purge has been too severe . . . professors in some universities simply refuse to teach any longer . . . scientists have been jailed merely for having equipment which the Party committee of their unit did not understand."

There was the story of a couple of photographers. The flashbulb of one of them had accidentally exploded during a meeting of some Party officials. They had both been arrested as counter-revolutionaries, intent on creating panic and killing top leaders.

There was the story of a man jailed because he had worked for a while with the Marshall truce teams . . .

Sa Fei was accused of many crimes by a posse of her fellow writers, but had somehow managed to survive, after having made a long self-criticism, recognizing her errors.

"They brought up anything against me, anything . . . said that I loved money, that already in Yenan I was trying to subvert socialism. Said I had written about not enough straw paper for the women's periods . . ." she told Stephanie.

"There was *not* enough paper," said Stephanie.

"Your fellow writers should know how much you've done—your books are immensely popular," said Yong.

"Ha, you don't know writers . . ." said Sa Fei. "They are jealous, jealous . . ."

"Well, it's over," said Yong lightly. Stephanie looked at Yong. His bland unwrinkled face, his smooth brow. And suddenly resented him. She had fallen in love with his people, his country, because of him. And this is what his people were doing. What his country was doing . . .

441

"Don't you find jealousy also among your colleagues?" Sa Fei asked Yong.

Yong at first did not reply and Stephanie knew that he had probably endured a good deal, which he would never tell her. Then he shrugged. "Human nature."

"Human nature. Ha! What is human nature?" asked Sa Fei.

Mother Huang came in to say: "We eat now." Now the threshold would again be warm with people, and she had made all of Sa Fei's favorite dishes.

"Too severe, the campaign has been too harsh. The leadership knows it . . ."

It was Jen Ping, Yong's Fourth Aunt, in faded blue cloth. A little shrunk, as if her bones had shortened, thinned, she had just been transferred to Peking after six years in Sinkiang.

She was now at the new Institute of Nationalities set up in Peking to train doctors and scientists and Party cadres from the fifty-odd national minorities of China. "Now we have a good policy," said Jen Ping. "Autonomy, cultural and religious freedom for the national minorities. But the trouble is implementation. We don't have the caliber of officials who understand how to work such a policy."

She talked briefly of Hu Feng. "In Sinkiang we have very few writers, and the Uighurs, the main national minority, had never heard of Hu Feng. They can't read Chinese. They read Arabic, and they are Muslims. Yet there were searches for Hu Feng sympathizers among them." For a moment, fleetingly, her face was weary, tragically tired. Then she was back to her usual composure. "You should go to Sinkiang, sister-in-law. To see it. We're making the desert there blossom with trees. And sinking wells for water, to stabilize the oases."

It was Winter Treasure's seventh birthday and Meiling came with her daughter Round Round.

Winter Treasure invited some children from his school. Stephanie baked a large birthday cake, decorated with seven pink candles. Mother Huang made steamed cakes and sweets and candied fruit. Winter Treasure brought out the microscope which his father had bought for him, and the children crowded around. They peered at his slides: foot of fly, wing of dragonfly, a hair.

Heston and Isabelle sent a telegram saying "Happy Birthday to you Dearest Tommy," and this made Winter Treasure very excited. His first telegram! He took out his maps. He had drawn maps of China and maps of America. In his American map Texas figured prominently. It covered almost half the territory. He explained Texas to the other children: "Texas is the biggest province in America. That is where my External Grandpa and my External Grandma live. It has many horses and cows and the village people wear big big hats."

"He's a real Texan," said Lionel, grinning.

Texas. The breathtaking spaces, the eye taking in all earth and the sky, no barrier, no fence, nothing to hinder the headlong thrust of man's energy or the measure of space. Stephanie, listening to her son, was overcome by a great yearning. For Texas. For America. She looked at Joan Wu, who had come from Shanghai to Peking for a seminar. She had dropped in to say "Happy birthday," to Treasure.

"Don't you feel homesick at times, Joan?"

"Homesick? Not at all," said Joan. "I wouldn't be able to *live* in America at the moment . . . such terrible things are going on . . ."

"Terrible things happen here too, Joan."

"Oh, it's not at all the same thing," said Joan. "In America ninety percent of the people are exploited; here we get rid of the ten percent of exploiters. . . ."

"How were things with you during the last campaign in Shanghai, Joan?"

Joan glowed with missionary effulgence. She described the campaign in terms approximating a Catholic novena. Stephanie's mind wandered. Total belief. Only One Truth. How odd to think Truth unique. Christianity had also laid fire and sword to many lands. In the name of a God of Truth and Love. Was it intolerance, and not liberal-mindedness, which propelled humanity forward? Religions thrived not through sweet reason, but through the fury of fanaticism. . . .

"I am personally convinced that this campaign will have proved useful," said Joan, sounding satisfied.

Treasure, his cheeks red with happiness, came back from seeing off his guests. Only Round Round remained, a stumpy little girl, madly in love with Winter Treasure. She crowed with delight, her face, arms, and legs moved with frantic pleasure when she saw him. In front of that dance of love Meiling and Stephanie felt almost shocked, then looked at each other and smiled reassuringly. Perhaps they would marry one day, Treasure and Round Round . . .

Winter Treasure basked in Round Round's adoration. It made him lustrous with vanity. He gave her his best marble, showed her his best slide—the butterfly wing. But Round Round looked at him and not at the slide.

"Meiling, what's happening to Rosamond, do you know?" asked Stephanie as Meiling was putting on her coat.

"Rosamond? Her two years of re-education are over," said Meiling, busily wrapping up Round Round.

"I'd like to see her again."

Meiling concentrated on fastening Round Round's belt. "It is best if you have nothing to do with her. . . ."

"But Meiling, she's a *friend*."

Meiling looked at Stephanie. "It won't do you—*or* her— any good for you to see her."

Winter Treasure hugged his mother when everyone had gone. "Do not fret your heart, Ma, *I* will look after you."

How did he know Stephanie fretted?

"Ma is sometimes stupid, little one. But Ma loves you, loves *Tietie*, Ma is just not clever . . ."

He nodded wisely. "But *we* still love you, Ma, even if you're not clever," he said, and padded away to bed.

In January of 1956, the centenary of Walt Whitman's *Leaves of Grass* was celebrated in Peking. Stephanie was chosen, among other Americans, to deliver a speech on Whitman. All the students of the language school were there.

Afterwards the students read aloud passages from *Leaves of Grass*.

The 350th anniversary of *Don Quixote* was also celebrated that month.

Stephanie was asked to help translate Hemingway's works. *The Old Man and the Sea* came off the Chinese presses. *The Sun Also Rises* and *For Whom the Bell Tolls* were to be translated.

Herbert Biberman's film, "Salt of the Earth," then blacklisted in America, was shown in the major cities of China.

Lionel Shaggin came from Shanghai with Henry Barber. They and other Americans would meet Albert Maltz, the writer. Albert Maltz, one of the "Hollywood Ten" who had refused to cooperate with the House Committee on Un-American Activities and had been given a jail sentence, was now living in Mexico. He had been invited to Peking.

The Americans got together and a reception was held, at which a great many of Peking's foreigners were present. The talk was of the Hollywood Inquisition and of how Joseph McCarthy had crumbled, destroyed by exposure on television.

"It was a judgment of the masses," said Herbert Luger solemnly.

"It was nothing of the kind. It's an American phenomenon," retorted Stephanie, who no longer tried to hide her dislike of Luger. "McCarthy destroyed himself through his own fanaticism."

Stephanie felt alternately very sad and very proud of her people. And a hunger took shape in her. She was homesick. For her own kind.

twenty

WHEN, in the years that followed, memory became obsession, Stephanie would pace the corridors of her mind, along which recollected events, departed acts, were aligned as for inspection.

If only I had . . . if only Yong had . . .

Strange how some years were clusters of strong days, shining like lit candelabra; and others drowsy, dim, morose, as somber as rooms at dusk.

It had begun in that January of 1956.

Oh, I am homesick after my own kind. Homesickness haphazard in intensity. It gnawed at the fabric of her being, but was not yet a drenching need.

The Family greeted the New Year with its usual gathering, display of festivity, mirth, enhanced by a new stir in the churning air of China's forever ongoing metamorphosis.

A new policy towards the intellectuals.

The leaders had made major speeches, delineating new relations between the Party and the difficult, indispensable, suspect, precious intelligentsia.

In the spring a document entitled: LET A HUNDRED FLOWERS BLOSSOM, A HUNDRED SCHOOLS OF THOUGHT CONTEND circulated in the universities and institutes. It reiterated the new policy.

The Party committees in charge of universities, institutes, hospitals now entreated the intellectuals under their care to criticize them.

"What does it all mean, Yong?"

"It means there must be more academic freedom, otherwise there will not be progress."

"Is that the only reason? Shouldn't freedom be necessary just for its own sake?" Stephanie's voice was sharper than usual.

"No freedom is absolute, there are always . . . constraints," said Yong.

"The revolution was meant to get rid of tyranny. Chiang's tyranny. Yong, that's what *you* worked for, that's what we believed."

She stopped herself. No, she must not hurt him. Not recall those shining days in Yenan, full of faith, of hope. She must continue to trust. To trust Yong.

But weariness now inhabited her, brittle weariness. The stepping stones to the future had become quicksand under her feet.

"The intelligentsia were promised certain constitutional guarantees, certain rights . . . that is why we rallied to the United Front . . ." said Dr. Fan, who was being co-opted to the new surgical unit in Peking.

Both Mao Tsetung and Chou Enlai made speeches on the "correct handling of intellectuals," which implied they had been incorrectly handled.

But the Party was not of one mind with regard to the intelligentsia. Chou and Mao might be for opening up, allowing discussion, divergence of opinion within the limits of the system. But the middle officials, the rank and file, were hostile. "*They* talk of freedom, of democracy . . . but only for themselves," said the cadres. "When one intellectual is jailed, there is a great furor. Ten thousand peasants die of hunger, and no one says a word."

"There are so many peasants in the Party, and we remind them too much of the mandarins who used to lord it over them," said Yong.

Hsiao Lu, the poet, and Sa Fei disputed this. "We are intellectuals of a new kind. We love our country and have made sacrifices for it; we've proved ourselves worthy of trust."

"But the Party does not trust us. It never will. Even if an intellectual is a Party member, he is *not* entirely trusted," Yong replied, matter-of-fact.

It was this matter-of-factness that disturbed Stephanie most: she no longer knew *what* Yong really thought, how he really felt. She had lost touch with her husband and, in so doing, had lost touch with the cause which had brought them together.

But Yong, unaware of her doubts, seemed possessed by a renewed spurt of hope. He spent long hours writing a report on the management of surgical hospitals, their needs, requirements. "We are now at a turning point, Stephanie. I want to do all I can to make things work better, at least in my sector. I believe the Party is sincere, and it's necessary for the Party to have a popular consensus among us. . . ."

Stephanie found herself unable to say to him: Yong, I'm no longer *able* to become involved—I'm bone drained. I want to go home. I feel . . . constricted, shrunk . . .

The house was lively with people's voices, with laughter. But in the afternoons its mistress paced the flowered courtyard, carrying her distress, gazing upon the gentle roof with unseeing eyes, seeking another sky, a seamless horizon.

"Let a hundred flowers blossom, a hundred schools of thought contend."

A beautiful, poetic sentence.

Professor Chang Shou came from Shanghai to Peking to attend meetings of the Democratic League. Exalted, he said: "I have been waiting for this moment to come . . ." Hundreds of intellectuals gathered to listen, to speak. There were, among China's six hundred million people, only five million of them, divided into upper and lower intellectuals; ranging from nuclear physicists through writers to engineers and biochemists, from archaeologists and geologists to doctors and middle-school teachers. Only around twenty percent of them were Party members.

> "In the past few years there has been a new growth
> of sectarianism and bureaucracy in the Party . . . ex-
> tensive rectification is absolutely necessary . . .
> everyone should listen with an open mind to the
> opinions of others . . . the right to reserve differ-
> ences must be permitted . . . non-Party people who
> wish to participate in this rectification should be wel-
> comed."

Thus ran a Communist Party document, encouraging non-Communists, members of the Democratic League and its eight non-Communist parties, to become involved.

"This is our country. Whether in or out of the Party, the affairs of the country concern every Chinese," said Jen Yong at the meeting.

But many were still reluctant to become involved.

Everything familiar had now become alien, hostile. The inescapable Peking dust drove Stephanie to a frenzy of irritation. She felt like screaming to Mother Huang, who had just cleaned the room: "Look, there's the dust again . . ."

But Yong sparkled, slept soundly, made love ardently. In the perceptibly relaxed atmosphere he thrived, and came home to tell Stephanie his plans for regular meetings of the hospital staff.

"If the habit of free dialogue is really established and accepted, if we can achieve a solidarity among ourselves on certain issues . . ." said Yong, dreaming of democratizing the Communist Party. "We are indispensable, Stephanie, they *have* to listen to us."

Such was his concentration on his work that he did not notice that Stephanie was not as enthusiastic as usual, only acquiescent. "How interesting," she would say, her mind elsewhere, her body yearning for elsewhere.

Even Winter Treasure became, at times, a stranger to her now. With a heart shocked into palpable staccato she would observe him, surprised. He had gestures she did not know. Attitudes, words that were strange to her. She loved him, loved him, but she was discovering how he changed, was changing. He was bright, courteous, adult in so many ways. And remote.

The texture of his mind escapes me now.

He was Jen. Not Ryder.

She would go to his room to smell his bedsheets, smell his little boy smell, and thus briefly heal herself, become whole once more. And then he would come in, and he was taller than she remembered.

At night, in the tenderness of love, her large store of remembered ecstasy served her well, enabling her to re-enact what had once been crystal delight, to give Yong pleasure, happiness. He slept, unsuspicious, and she stared at the darkness, swept by a narrow wind into an endless loss. *Tomorrow I shall tell him. Tomorrow.*

And then it was morning and Yong was up, like a small sunburst, eager with radiant hours of hope in front of him, and she could not tell him.

In February 1956 the news of Khrushchev's speech denouncing Stalin shook all China. A Chinese version of the speech circulated throughout the universities.

Yong showed a copy of it to Stephanie, and she felt all the more that she had to go home. *At the moment I don't make sense to myself and nothing makes sense to me.*

"Yong, don't you think that there's something wrong with the kind of system that allows such concentrated evil? *You* know that I always had a horror of Stalin."

"Oh Stephanie, dear heart, what shall I tell you? China is *not* going to have a Stalin . . . now there's more hope than ever."

He wrote till late at night. Surgical procedures. More efficient training. Management of operating units. Training of surgeons. Surgery in the villages. His dark, lean head bent over the pages; his brush traveled skillfully on the paper. He had brought back with him from America some books on hospital management. "I always thought that I might one day need to do something about hospital administration. China does not have enough trained personnel of any kind, and management is important to modernize quickly."

Afraid to disturb him, Stephanie gave herself reasons for not saying anything, while in her grew the thwarted need for another air, a space not China's, the sound of other voices, the smell of other cities.

All private enterprises were nationalized that year. Father, Uncle Keng Dawei, and Mr. Tam—a Chinese millionaire from Indonesia who, in an explosion of patriotic fervor had returned to China with all his assets to build factories—came to Peking to attend meetings for the second five-year economic plan. They wore big, easy smiles almost like uniforms.

Parades had taken place to celebrate this nationalization. The capitalists of Shanghai had marched, with flowers pinned to their jackets, to rejoice at the abolition of their own class. They held giant-sized envelopes in their hands containing their petitions to become "willingly amalgamated."

Father was almost alarmingly cheerful. He would become financial adviser to the national banking system, with a fixed salary.

Stephanie wondered how Dad would have felt if Ryder Aircraft had been taken over by the U.S. government. Dad would have fought it, fought to the last . . . gone off to the Rockies, taken potshots at the Feds who came for him . . . or would he?

In the autumn of 1956 trouble erupted in Poland, and then in Hungary.

Through Peking radio, through the foreign newspapers available at the Language Press, Stephanie read of the crushing of the Hungarian revolt by Russian troops.

The foreign experts in China, many of them belonging to Western Communist parties, were utterly confused, disoriented. They went about their work with a glazed look in their eyes. Like a tottering pier rotting under them, their moral convictions had given way.

"Loss of belief is a frightful experience," said Peter Wellington to Stephanie. "And some of us, including myself, we've been shaken. We've refused, for so many years, to believe that the Soviet Union could do wrong . . ."

But worse than anything was the fear of being thrown out of the Party—the Party which was family, security, friends, faith . . . That would be living death. "And so some of us stay, through habit. Hoping, still hoping, accepting through habit."

Stephanie thought of Isabelle. What would she do if the Catholic Church proved itself a hideous tyranny? Would she cling on, refusing evidence?

"I think I'm due for home leave," she said to Peter, changing the subject. "Can you tell me what to do?"

"The committee in charge of foreign experts handles it," said Peter. "Every few years, experts may return to their own countries. It depends on the length of your contract. It's three years at our school. Let's see—you've been with us since 1954, so by next year, 1957, you qualify for home leave. But you must clear it with Secretary Lung."

Secretary Lung was an amiable man who reminded Stephanie of Henry Wong, of those far-off days in Chung-king. "We want to assure your *safety*, Comrade Ryder. In the United States at the moment, progressive personalities are being greatly persecuted by the reactionary government."

"Comrade Ryder's parents are getting old, her father has been quite ill," said Peter Wellington. "She has been away almost eight years."

"Eight years is a long time," agreed Lung. "And doubt-less your parents do yearn for you." He twinkled, exactly as Henry Wong used to do. "I shall study the case and refer it to higher authority."

Yong watched Spring Snow as she tidied the cushions, emptied the ashtrays, then went into Winter Treasure's bedroom to make sure the blanket had not slipped off.

She came back, saw Yong looking at her. She smiled at him. He *was* handsome. More than handsome. He had some inner glow which made him the kind of man that would attract women anywhere.

It's his country . . . he loves his country.

The more one lived with a person, the more one had to remember to go on rediscovering that person every day, pausing to renew acquaintance. Otherwise a dullness of thinking crept in, the feeling that there was nothing new, that all had been deciphered. It was not so, but she had no more strength to try. . . .

"Yong, I've been to the Party secretary today to ask about home leave."

"Yes," he said, "yes." His eyes widened a little. That was all.

And then, with an effort, he said, "Of course, I should have thought about it before, I felt something bothered you . . . forgive me for being so stupid."

"There is nothing to forgive. You were so busy." She knew she was being abrupt; she didn't want to hear his eagerness to find fault with himself, his placation.

"I just want to go home for three months, maybe four, then I shall be back."

"Of course," he said, "of course. I understand. My heart's sinews would wither if I stayed too long away from China."

In the winter of 1956-57 the expanding bureaucracy moved into the industries and enterprises that had been nationalized. Their ex-owners saw with distress what was happening to their former possessions.

"Instead of one signature, now every document requires six to eleven seals of approval."

"We had expected more efficiency from the Party; instead, we now have lowered production, yet there is a vast inflation of personnel . . ."

"All heads of departments who are not Party members become ordinary employees, and Communists become heads of departments—even if they know nothing."

"Those who know nothing give orders and make decisions; those who know are not allowed to speak."

Father wrote: "I ran my bank with seven directors and vice directors, and one hundred twenty-five employees. Now there are twenty-five directors, fifty vice directors, and still only one hundred twenty-five employees."

Winter turned to spring. The trees blossomed and the rivers thawed.

Satiric stories denouncing the bureaucracy now appeared. Young writers, many of them Party members, wrote them. The bookshops were full of them. "We have Party men," wrote one satirist, "whose only talent is slogan spouting. When they've repeated a slogan a dozen times at meetings, they think they've done a great deal of work and quickly go home to sleep."

The criticism grew louder, more acerbic. The university students became restless, writing wall posters demanding more books, no more political studies, freedom to pick their own jobs after graduation.

Stephanie's students at the language school also produced the big character posters—wall posters that were affixed to walls, on the billboards, anywhere. Written by hand, these posters contained free opinions, suggestions, criticisms—of the system, of people. Anything they felt like writing. There were no libel laws. This was "the hundred flowers," total freedom of opinion.

They asked Stephanie questions. About Senator McCarthy, the Bill of Rights, law courts, the blacks, the red Indians . . . "Do you have wall posters as we do?"

Stephanie explained that even in McCarthy's time there had been dissent. She quoted I.F. Stone and others, and explained how the senator had been brought down. "Every country has this problem. The people have to fight to maintain their liberties, even when these have been guaranteed by a democratic government."

The newspapers printed editorials criticizing the Party and its "work style." Forums were held in the institutes and universities and were attended by journalists and also Party men. The Party men took notes. The journalists took notes.

People who are not experts should not "direct" people who are experts.

This was the main grievance of the intellectuals.

A large wall poster appeared in Peking's biggest hospital:

Party men who do not know medicine run the hospitals. They order X-ray technicians to work far too many hours. Refuse to acknowledge that it is dangerous. "X-rays? Why, it's like taking a photograph. How can it be dangerous?" they say in their ignorance.

"The Party has made a mess of everything and the leaders should submit to punishment," Stephanie read in one editorial.

"The Party is becoming corrupt. Another Kuomintang. It should share power with other parties," was an article which appeared in another national newspaper.

Yong shook his head dubiously. "I find this unrealistic. We're living under the Communist Party's rule. They've done good things and bad ones. We can't ask for total power."

But the tide had turned with a vengeance. The intellectuals were as eager as any in claiming "an eye for an eye."

Disquieting incidents took place. Strikes. Some Party cadres were murdered.

"University professors have no say at all in selection or promotion, in picking students to go abroad. Academic competence is not the sole criterion. Selection is determined by politics, and class origin," was the gist of one editorial.

In certain institutes of learning the children of workers and peasants were now being refused admittance. Wall posters blossomed in their precincts, alleging that education "suffered grievously from admitting the lower classes." Standards had been lowered to accommodate them. They were given jobs, even if their rating in examinations was lower than the sons and daughters of the previous elite. "Academic excellence no longer counts, only political class origin. Yet our country needs top-grade scientists of all kinds to modernize."

Winter Treasure was twice promoted at his school, skipping another two years.

"Mama, Teacher says I shall be a scientist. He would like to give me special tuition in mathematics."

Winter Treasure's calligraphy was elegant. He would enter into the all-China competition for calligraphy, for children of eight to fourteen.

He had a clear, wide gaze; a beautiful forehead and that extraordinary hair, black with a brown tinge and a wave to it. He read all the English books he could lay hands on, and was building himself a small radio. It was the latest craze; all youngsters were building their own radios.

"Are you still helping your friends with their lessons twice a week, Treasure?"

Because he was so bright, so advanced, he had been given a responsibility: to coach the slower ones in his class. He had done this with alacrity throughout one winter, and had made many friends.

"No, Mama." Winter Treasure grimaced a bit. "Teacher says: 'Let the peasants go back to planting, the workers to working.' He says they are stupid and will never be able to learn."

Stephanie found herself involved in real conscience searching. What was the choice? An elite with advanced skills, and the overwhelming majority of youths deprived of education . . . or making education available to all, but having to lower standards?

"China is a poor country; it cannot afford both an advanced elite and education for all," said Dr. Wu firmly. "It is better to have separate institutions, of lower standard, for workers and peasant offspring."

Yong countered: "We, the elite, are only one percent of

the population. Five million altogether. We cannot keep all education to ourselves and our children. And we're antagonizing the peasants and the workers."

The anti-Party clamor rose as April went into May:

"The Party is a new despot. It does not obey the Constitution."

May 1957 was effervescent, electric. Impassioned speeches, more wall posters. A rising infatuation with their own thoughts, heedless of consequences, was evident among some of the intelligentsia.

Yong remained sober, slightly apprehensive. "I think we are too prone to forget the past. We forget Chiang Kaishek. But the intelligentsia cannot run the country alone. They have no support among the ordinary people. We *must* establish a clearly defined relationship with the present power-holders. Laws, respect for the rights of the person. But to try to claim power for ourselves is utopian. Do you think any party would relinquish power, especially when it has fought for it so long, so hard?"

And Stephanie saw the reasonableness of Yong's views. Why even in America, one could not ask the East Coast liberals to *run* the country. There were always checks and balances. But China's intellectuals seemed carried away by their feeling of having lost face, by their resentment, their hereditary sense of superiority over the lower classes.

"Madame Lai, Madame Lai!!!"

Behind Stephanie, on the street, a woman, short, somewhat stout, young.

"You don't recognize me? I am Pomegranate."

Pomegranate, the diminutive child-servant of Rosamond Chen, in Chungking.

Pomegranate wore trousers and shirt of wash-faded blue; she could be a worker, or a primary school teacher, or just anyone in the new egalitarian clothing. She carried books in the crook of her arm.

"How you have changed, Pomegranate."

Pomegranate grinned. "The Party cared. Put me to

school. And now I shall be a teacher instead of a slave-servant." Proudly she showed Stephanie her books: a Chinese translation of George Bernard Shaw's plays, a book on hygiene in the factory. "I don't understand everything I read, but it's culture," she said.

"I am so glad," said Stephanie. "When we last met, there was Comrade Meiling Yee and Comrade Chen. Have you seen them?"

"I have seen the woman Chen," said Pomegranate stiffly. "I am helping her to remold herself. I go once a month to help her."

"Does she still live in the north district?"

"She returned two months ago."

Stephanie walked down the dusty *hutung* and was perceived by children playing in the lane, who ran to tell their parents. Women came out of their houses to stare at Stephanie. One of them called out: "Comrade Chen! A foreign friend has come to see you!"

In a neat gray shirt and trousers, looking like a student, a worker, anything but Rosamond, stood Rosamond. Her hair was short and there was no make-up on her face.

Rounder. All angles out. Her face calmer, though now visited by the discoloration of age.

"Stephanie, how nice of you to come. So far. So much trouble."

She said it in Chinese; and all around them the crowd, all those who could squeeze into the courtyard, watched the foreigner, and some asked each other: "Which country is she from?"

"I'm glad to see you, I was worried," said Stephanie.

"But you should not worry," said Rosamond with a lilt of surprise, leading Stephanie into her small room. "You should *not* worry. Everything is so well, so well with me."

A small neat room, a basin in the corner upon a trestle, a bed, a table, a chair, and a small mirror upon the table. And books. Three books. Under the bed a chest for clothes. The *People's Daily* spread upon the table. A thermos flask and four glasses.

Ascetic. No smell at all. A nun's room.

"Sit down please," said Rosamond, indicating the only chair. She put tea from a small canister into two of the

457

glasses, and poured boiling water from the thermos flask over them.

The tea leaves unfolded. Rosamond smiled serenely. There was nothing to say.

"How is your husband? And your son?"

"They are fine, very well."

Oh, there is nothing, nothing left of Rosamond. Perhaps she loved too much, perhaps not enough . . . who shall know?

"Where are you teaching now? I heard you were translating Hemingway . . ."

"I've finished polishing *The Old Man and the Sea*. I'm helping to compile a dictionary. I teach three times a week, at a language school."

Rosamond nodded. "I now understand myself much better. I was full of troubles, full of unhappiness. Now I have thrown all these away. I have turned over. I am a new person. Reborn." She suddenly became prolix, as if mechanical, clock-wound into a habit of satisfied self-description. "I had the wrong thinking, my thinking was bad, very bad, very reactionary. But now the Party is taking care of me. All my bones feel clean now."

"Where are you working?" asked Stephanie, blowing gently on the tea. It was difficult to hold the very hot glass, there was no handle.

"I am in No. 27 State Textile Factory. I did my two years of labor and thought-remolding there. The worker comrades were so kind, so patient—it was the first time that other women were truly kind, kind without wanting anything from me in return. They took me to their houses, as if I was as good as they were. They did not worry about my thought-sins."

"Your what?"

"Thought-sins," repeated Rosamond. "They treated me . . like their own family. There I knew the kindness of my own people. I felt safe. So I asked to stay on, as a worker. I want to be a worker."

There was nothing, nothing to say. The past had simply been annihilated. And Rosamond was happy.

"So kind, so very kind of you to come," Rosamond repeated, accompanying Stephanie across the courtyard, where children waited to catch a glimpse of the foreigner, and out the main gate.

"Goodbye, Rosamond. I'll come to see you again, if I may."

"It's too much bother, I'm not often at home . . . I'll write to you," replied Rosamond.

And then Stephanie knew that she too had been rubbed out of Rosamond's life. Rosamond did not really want to see her. Did not need her. Not now.

"Meiling, I saw Rosamond."

"Oh," said Meiling, her voice immediately patient, watchful.

"She seems well. A little fatter. She wants to remain a worker."

"What's wrong with that?"

Stephanie stared at Meiling. Meiling was still the corporal shape she knew, but also someone else.

"But Rosamond could teach, she could do other things."

Meiling pulled down the rolled-up sleeves of her shirt, buttoned the cuffs. "Comrade Chen has chosen, freely, to become a worker. Manual labor is ennobling. The working class is the basis of socialist society."

"But . . ."

"You do not know how vicious, how mean intellectuals can be towards each other," said Meiling. "Rosamond is happy. Let us leave her to be happy."

Meiling too had changed. Become peremptory, putting everything that was said, done, into a political framework. She was rapidly becoming distant, remote, and Stephanie felt incapable of reaching her. Stephanie, who refused to change, refused to become another Joan Wu.

In that May, Stephanie had missed a period. Her body nested another life. The grindstones of her cells, grinding out another human being.

Fierce, uncontrollable, the instinct to preserve arose in her. To protect. From everything. From everyone. For all around her now was alien, and threat. Even the Family. Even Yong.

Late May. The foliage of newly planted trees along the avenues provided welcome shade. Groups of factory workers went for a Sunday outing to the Western Hills. Peasants came from the villages, dressed in their best, came with their children in gay clothes. They were no longer hungry. They had security. The old ones, innocent and now well-fed, kowtowed, knelt in front of the Main Gate of the Forbidden City, topped by a portrait of Mao. "We have a new emperor," they said. "His name is Mao Tsetung." It was impossible to explain to them that this was not a new Imperial dynasty. They wanted the safety of being governed, ruled. By a benevolent emperor who would feed them.

But in the sophisticated cities, a maelstrom of "blossoming and contending" was still hitting the walls of the universities. Denunciations of the Communist Party.

"The Party has made a mess of everything."

"Sweep away the Communist Party."

"The Party will collapse very soon."

Scrupulously, the Communist press reported the vitriolic speeches made by certain eminent intellectuals in the Democratic League, speeches demanding to canvass workers and peasants for membership, and to vie in free elections for political power.

"What nonsense, what dangerous nonsense," said Yong.

It began on June 8 with an article titled "WHAT IS THIS FOR" in the *People's Daily*. It was couched as a complaint about an anonymous letter threatening a man who had defended the Communist Party. "We regard this letter of intimidation as challenging the political leadership of the Communist Party," said the article.

"I think," said Yong in the colorless pale voice that Stephanie recognized as disaster's gong, "that there will now be a counterattack . . . it will be bad, very bad . . ."

"What kind of counterattack?" asked Stephanie.

The morning was hot, a dustbowl heat which swung upon Peking and parched the skin. Only in the evening the public sprinkling machines, spraying water along the now tarred avenues, would bring a sensation of coolness. In the *hutungs*, every household threw water in basinsful to bring the dust down in front of the houses.

"The Communist Party cannot, will not tolerate a challenge to its power. It will overreact. The very fact that it allowed these articles to be printed shows that it has control of the situation."

"So," she said bitterly, "it's not turning out well after all. There's going to be another son-of-a-bitch campaign."

"Stephanie."

She turned on him, almost hissing. "*You* will weather it, Yong, you and your Family. Oh, you've weathered the centuries, or is it the millennia? Endure and survive. Smile and survive. You'll go on. And on. Every time you will adapt; you will compromise . . . but I . . ." Her voice broke, and she ran into the bedroom, threw herself on the bed in a fit of weeping.

Evening came and she was becalmed, as a ship in some quiet bay. I'm silly, she thought, I'm just silly.

Yong had left a message on the desk: "My very dear and beloved one, I have to go to work. I love you so much."

"I love you so much." Of course. But there comes a time when love is helpless, adrift in a country of rock and dead leaves.

Night. They made it up, sweeping heart's bane away. Made love. But Stephanie did not tell Yong: I am with child.

For now a sudden craftiness possessed her. She would be dispossessed if he knew. Dispossessed. By the Family. Their unquenchable solicitude would melt her.

Mother. All that care—it now appeared to her contrivance. It would weaken her. She would be taken in thrall, once again, if *they* knew.

She would keep her secret strength secret.

If Party Secretary Lung should know, he would be sure to fuss. To say: "Are you sure you can travel? In your condition?"

All, all of them were the same. They tied you in with a silken web of care, concern.

They thought *for* you. Planned *your* life, *your* likes and dislikes. They were always a step ahead.

And they would want to keep the child. A Jen. Belonging to the Family. Not to Stephanie Ryder. Suddenly she was beset by phantasmagoria. As if *they* were lying in wait, to take the child from her, their minds circling like far-seeing eagles, circling their territory, herself.

An undesirable and extremely evil sign marks the present rectification campaign . . . some are preaching liquidation of the Communist Party . . .

Criticisms are intended to strengthen socialism . . . not to destroy it . . .

On June 10, workers in Peking, Shanghai, Tientsin, Shenyang, Anshan, and twenty other cities held their own forums, and denounced "anti-Communist elements" among Democratic League members.

On June 11, the morning radio announced: "It is necessary to wage a struggle against rightist elements opposed to socialism." That was a new term. Rightist.

Stephanie and Yong were at breakfast. She said, pitching her voice to neutral: "Another purge."

"Yes."

"Luckily you didn't stick your neck out too much. They can't accuse you of being anti-socialist. . . ."

Yong did not reply. He was stunned by the malice in her words. Stephanie drank her coffee. Coffee was easily obtained at the food store for foreigners in Peking.

"This is a frantic attack on the working class, the Communist Party, and the whole nation. Without the Party, there would be no New China . . ." the radio went on.

Already many of the intellectuals who had made flamboyant speeches were retracting, retracting themselves, recanting, confessing.

"The vice chairman of the Democratic League thanked all those who criticized his erroneous views—he blamed himself for having misled a great many," reported the radio.

The vice chairman's voice, querulous, came on:

"I was misled . . . I now regret my errors. I listened to enemies of socialism. . . ."

Within the next five days, posters at the university denouncing the Party were replaced by posters praising the Party, condemning "rightists" and asking for "struggle" against them.

462

Yong returned one night looking haggard. He slumped in a seat and put his face in his hands. Never had Stephanie seen him give way to such discouragement.

"What happened, Yong? What is it?" She knew the surgeons had approved Yong's report on management of surgical hospitals and their requirements. But now she was suddenly violently afraid. *If something's happened, I won't be able to leave.* The thought streaked like lightning through her; and a moment later she felt the sear of hot shame.

She went to him and took his hands from his face. Solace she could still give him, her healing nearness.

"Dearest, what is it, tell me!"

He rubbed his arm across his face, as Winter Treasure did, wiping off desolation. "Spring Snow, I am ashamed. Almost everyone is now back-pedaling, retracting, and now we're looking among ourselves for scapegoats, for scapegoats . . . each one will find something to accuse someone else—saying they were misled, carried away, to propitiate the Party, to have its anger fall upon a scapegoat . . ."

He was no longer the calm, self-controlled man she knew.

He went to the side table, upon which rested a charming two hundred-year-old porcelain brushholder which he had bought some years ago. He took it in both hands and deliberately let it fall. It spilled fragments all over the floor.

"Communist Youth League members and all young people who love our country should improve their sense of smell," read Winter Treasure out of the *China Youth* journal, which he bought at the newspaper kiosk near his school.

"*Tietie*, does a rightist smell different from other people?"

"It's a figure of speech," said Yong shortly.

"In our class, there is a boy whose father is a rightist. I think he will leave the school. And we have a parade this afternoon. To struggle against rightist ideas."

Posters appeared in Stephanie's language school attacking those who had written criticisms of the Party, attacking "the abominable luxurious lives" and the "desperate, frenzied ambitions" of "bourgeois rightists who want to restore their ugly dictatorship. . . ."

On June 25 Stephanie arrived to give her usual morning course. She noticed a crowd denser than usual around the

463

poster board. Someone saw her and said: "She's come," and the students scattered very quickly as she approached.

Even from six yards away she could see it. In black brush characters, in Chinese, and below it in English, her name.

A poster against her.

Yong ended his operating schedule very late that day. He felt drained when at last he removed his gown. His shirt stuck to his back. It was not only physical exhaustion. The atmosphere was thick with furtive fear, slippery with evasiveness.

"We need a little rain," said Dr. Fan. This could be interpreted either as a remark on the weather, or as a political hint that things should cool down.

In the dim corridor Yong met Arthur Chee and said: "Hello, Arthur." These days few of his colleagues spoke to Arthur because they all expected him to be "hatted," labeled a rightist, any moment.

He was so *different*. An Overseas Chinese. With foreign habits, love of coffee. He had denounced political study classes as a waste of time. He had said the Chinese Government had no legal system.

"In the last campaign ferreting out counter-revolutionaries, it was arbitrarily set down that five percent in each unit would be counter-revolutionary. Everyone tried to reach that target of five percent," said Arthur. "In one small workshop I know, there were only nine people. How do you find five percent of nine people guilty of counter-revolution?"

People had applauded him then. But that was all of three weeks ago. Now everyone denied having ever agreed with Arthur Chee. Except Yong, and a few other brave souls . . .

There was no one in the common room where the surgeons changed. It too had its posters. Recent ones accused certain doctors of having "misled the masses." Others were confessions. "I was beguiled by the erroneous views of rightist elements . . ."

Then Yong saw the new poster, spread right across the room. With his name in big black brush characters. Dr. Jen Yong.

"I think it's disgusting," said Peter Wellington.

Herbert Luger shifted uneasily. "Now wait a minute, wait a minute. This is an expression of free opinion from the masses . . ."

"It's nothing of the kind. It's scurrilous and evil. Libel."

"In your country libel laws only work in favor of the exploiters," said Herbert Luger.

Peter Wellington stared at him. "My God," he said softly, "you'll forgive me for saying so, but you're a louse, Luger."

"Now wait a minute, wait a minute . . ."

But Peter Wellington had walked out.

He had seen the poster against Stephanie. Everyone had. He'd wanted expert opinion. Herbert Luger was supposed to be closest to what Chinese officials thought. Peter Wellington's fists rounded in his pockets. It was absolutely forbidden for foreigners to tear down posters, absolutely. Whatever they may contain. This was interference, obstructing the sovereignty of the masses. But Peter wanted to tear something apart.

Hsu Build-the-City savored his revenge.

A gentleman waits ten years for revenge. He had waited thirteen, less two months. He still remembered that blistering August day in Chungking. The slums. The furious lightning bolt of a woman. Hitting him. Him!

Because Comrade Lo had been the registrar of Stephanie's marriage in Yenan, her office had received a routine enquiry from Secretary Lung.

Lung had also sent an enquiry to the university in Shanghai where Stephanie was employed. He liked to keep his files in good order. Also, he liked to avoid decision making by sharing responsibility with many others. He wanted to help Stephanie. He had recommended she get one-third of her salary in foreign exchange and six months leave on full salary. He also wanted to arrange for another contract on her return to China. Her work was excellent. He fully expected good reports from every quarter.

All documents, inner Party directives, secret reports relating to intra-Party affairs that came to Comrade Lo now passed into the hands of Hsu Build-the-City. Since Lo was not overly inclined towards reading, Hsu read out the material to her.

When the enquiry on Stephanie came to Comrade Lo's office, Hsu gave it to Bo Chaste Wisdom. She pored over the letter. She remembered how her small campaign of gossip against Stephanie had failed in Yenan.

But now the old gossip could be resurrected, magnified, twisted, turned into a political matter.

Chaste Wisdom contacted Yellow Wall *hutung*'s street committee. The grandmothers in charge were only too eager to talk about No. 31 and what went on there. The people who came and went and made the *hutung* "hot and noisy." The important writers and doctors and scientists who came to the house.

"There is material here . . ." said Chaste Wisdom.

Her ability to convert seemingly innocuous events into suspect behavior had increased considerably. A gathering could always become a conspiracy. Against the Party.

Party Secretary Lung sent another letter asking for swift reply. "I have had favorable reports on Comrade Lai Spring Snow from other sources," he wrote.

Hsu ground his teeth. This was almost like saying: "We want a good report from you."

"Dangerous," reflected Chaste Wisdom. "We must get cover."

"Lai, the American girl," exclaimed Comrade Lo. Hsu could no longer delay the case.

"I do not know anything about this person," said Hsu meekly.

"I remember her well," exclaimed Lo, laughing. "A very good-looking girl. And Dr. Jen Yong. Really a handsome pair. I was glad when they married. I registered the marriage. The leadership was in favor."

Hsu listened to Comrade Lo extolling the marriage, while his heart sank. "Then I shall prepare an *entirely* favorable report," he said. "Of course, this is a great responsibility, Comrade Lo. To write that there was absolutely *no* criticism at all of this American nor of her loved one, though I understand their class origin is not very good . . ."

"There was some criticism. I believe we even held a meeting. Comrade Bo was there." And Lo proceeded to tell Hsu about the gossip in Yenan.

Hsu listened with rapt attention, noting down in his notebook what Comrade Lo said. To be used against her one day. To be used now in his revenge against Stephanie Ryder.

"Comrade Lo, I shall prepare the answer; and of course we must mention the idle gossip, for *your* protection," he said. "It will be up to the other unit to judge."

Little Pearl was going home to Peking for the summer holidays. She shouldered her pack, carried her bag. She would walk to the railway station to catch the train.

The People's Technical Institute where she studied was set up for the sons and daughters of workers and peasants who had been guerillas. The teachers were not eminent; the learning not accounted high-grade. But it was teaching; it was learning.

When "the hundred flowers" began, the institute committee had invited student leaders from a nearby prestigious university, an elite organization, to come, to tell them what their opinions were. Because they did not understand what the elite students were complaining about.

Little Pearl understood not a word of what these young people said. She *knew* the Party was good. The Party had rescued them. They would never have been able to eat, let alone read or write, without the Party. They would have starved, become white bones on some road. . . . What were these people complaining about?

Work was assigned to one when one graduated. Very early on, the students worked in the factories, applying what they had learnt. Of course. One went where the Party said one should go. Why feel that this was so terrible?

One day the Students Union of her Technical Institute had held a meeting with student delegates from other people's schools. And he had been there. Square-face. A delegate.

Liang Little Pond, Square-face, had said, in that slow but strong way of his, which Pearl liked, not at all the quick elusive way of the others: "What do they really want?"

Everyone had pondered.

"We do not know what they really want."

Liang Little Pond waited on the avenue leading to the railway station, under the mimosa trees which threw heady scent to the four horizons.

He had waited since early morning, fearful of missing her. There was a morning and an afternoon train from Tientsin to Peking. She was not on the morning train.

He waited.

They had met again, after the student meeting. They did not greet each other. Or talk. Someone might have noticed, might have passed comment. It would have spread and they would have been the butt of endless teasing. *They* knew. Sometimes looked at each other, but did not dare to smile.

After the meeting to discuss the hundred flowers, he had dragged his friend Hsiao Wang and talked with him, managing somehow to be within her earshot. And she had told a girl friend (needlessly) her intention to go to Peking for her holidays, and how on such and such a day she would take the train from Tientsin to Peking . . .

And he was listening.

Love was subterranean, an undersea marvel, yearning and darkness and mystery. Not *talk*. Especially not aggrieving, explanatory talk. Love was the color of sky and tree, the smell of earth. Words strained love with patches. Words were lanterns in the night, but the darkness was beautiful with becoming.

And so in silence and distance and the distinct knowledge of each other's existence they grew. As plants grow, wordless in the sun.

Little Pearl crossed the avenue, shifting her pack. The station was not too far now. Only a few hundred yards away. The scent of the mimosa came to her.

He was there, looking right and looking left.

He had brought his square face. Brought himself.

They did not have to reassure each other.

He walked towards her and took her pack off her shoulder and put it on his. His limped a little. They walked together to the railway station.

"It is getting very warm," he said.

"It will be warm in Peking too," she said. "It is quite cool in our house at No. 12 Coal Merchants *hutung*," she said, not appearing to give him her address but giving it. "There are two trees in front of the gate and a tree in the courtyard. They give coolness."

Now the mimosa trees came and went, one by one. Issuing from the ground and falling behind them. The trees kept on happening, all the way to the station.

Of course he could not enter the station, he had no ticket.

"I will walk to Peking," he said. "I shall start tomorrow. I have a teacher who knows a friend in Peking, and I want to see the capital. I will walk."

She said, "I am leaving."

He said, "You are leaving."

There was no need of anything else.

Party Secretary Lung was angry, uncomfortable, and also a little afraid. He stared at the poster against Lai Spring Snow. Outrageous.

"You say there is a similar poster at the Translation Bureau?"

"Yes. Another one has appeared in Shanghai University, almost the same. And one at the Surgical Hospital."

Party Secretary Lung reflected. This was serious. Was this evidence of "the opinion of the masses," or merely a cabal? And if the latter, what was its purpose?

A letter from Comrade Lo had come:

"Although in Yenan the Party leadership approved the marriage, there had been some unfavorable rumors about the private lives of both Dr. Jen Yong and the American woman. These were referred to the leadership by Party Secretary Pu. The marriage registration bureau did not deal with the matter."

Party Secretary Lung read again the poster against Lai Spring Snow:

LAI SPRING SNOW,
STEPHANIE RYDER,
AN AGENT OF AMERICAN CULTURAL
IMPERIALISM.

To protect the minds of our youth from bourgeois rottenness and filth is a major task for all of us who ardently love socialism. Yet for many years we have sheltered one of the worst examples of reactionary corruption and sexual license in our midst, entrusting this element with teaching and with translating, spreading poison frantically among our youth.

Lai Spring Snow, Stephanie Ryder, is an attractive American woman, who makes ample use of her charms. She is the daughter of a Big Landlord and Reactionary who sells airplanes to the bandit Chiang Kaishek to bomb our people. Brought up to indulge every wild fancy, Lai Spring Snow sneaked her way into China by becoming the paramour of several American newspaper correspondents. Living at the Press Hostel in Chungking she had affairs which were well known and encouraged by the Kuomintang lackeys of American imperialism. She caught the eye of Dr. Jen Yong, the uxorious son of a capitalist, and both indulged their lust with abandon.

Jen Yong was thus able to go to America, where he made a pact with American imperialism. Since then he has slavishly preached that American surgery is the best in the world, and begun to train lackeys to American imperialism in our hospitals.

Is it not time that this matter should be looked into?

Party Secretary Lung sighed. The poster also put him in a bad position—"Sheltering an agent of American cultural imperialism."

To Peter Wellington he said: "If Miss Ryder puts in an application for a holiday *because of ill health*, I think our committee would give her permission."

It was as if an earthquake was shaking her, shaking her. She lay in bed and the bed was rocking. She wanted to vomit, vomit her guts out. She went to the bathroom, and threw up. Clutched herself fiercely, clutched her belly, her life-giving belly, and her voice was loud, ringing in her own ears: "Get out, Yong. Get *out*. Leave me alone."

For he stood there, shrunken. He had returned from the hospital. "Stephanie . . ."

"Oh, so you know!" She had drawn the blinds and he stood, disaster dark, by the bed.

"Don't touch me," she said. *"Don't!"*

470

"Stephanie, please, darling, please do not feel so upset . . ."

She stared at him. "Upset? I'm not upset. I'm delighted."

"Oh please, my darling."

"Don't *darling* me!"

She was a continent of hatred. Disowning all that had
been. Trampling upon all that had been love, care. She
wanted to scream her hate, but he deprived her even of
that—he withdrew, hiding his hurt behind the mask of his
face.

He did not tell her of the poster denouncing him.

In the thick, deliberate dusk supplanting the striving
afternoon sun, rose not only the bile of her pregnancy but
also the bitterness of all memory. Oh, *he* had made her
blind, and deaf, and she, foolish, had raised no rampart for
herself. *I should have been like Michelle Berbiest, then it
would not have hurt so much. I hate you, Yong. Hate you.
You made me blind and deaf.*

Winter Treasure.

She must take him with her.

She could not take him with her. He was too much of a
Jen. He belonged to them.

She looked at her watch. Winter Treasure would be back
soon, very soon. He had gone to a Ping-Pong match.

He came, light-stepped, so much like his father in the
way he moved; his body had no stiff bones.

He *was* a Jen. He crossed the courtyard, looked around,
and walked into the bedroom, to her, saying, "Mama."

He knew nothing, nothing of what had happened. There
was this blessing: it was not broadcast about. Only in the
units where she worked. Not anywhere else.

"Mama, you are not well. Is your head painful, Mama?"

"Yes, darling. Mama was very tired today."

He smiled brightly. His face, Yong's face. A Jen. "Mama,
you work too hard—but it's summer, and we shall soon be
going to the seaside, won't we?"

"Yes, darling. But right now Mama just wants to rest."

Mother Huang came bringing tea, some cakes for Winter
Treasure.

"Mistress should take some strengthener, mistress is
worn out with work," said Mother Huang.

"I'm going to rest a few days," said Stephanie. (Had
Mother Huang guessed that she was pregnant?)

471

The bell rang. Mother Huang's niece went to open. It was Peter Wellington.

"I know how you feel, Stephanie . . . but please, please don't take it too hard. I mean, things like this do happen. There's always a streak of nonsense in these massive political campaigns. But they just wither away . . ."

"Thanks for telling me, Peter."

"Our friend Lung tells me that if you ask for sick leave, he'll be able to give it almost right away."

"Thanks, Peter."

"Stephanie." Peter was distressed. "We're all on your side. Please, come to the school, to say goodbye to the students. They'll appreciate it. They like you."

Everything was arranged very quickly.

Stephanie went to the language school one last time. A small reception was held, to wish her bon voyage. The students shook hands with her. Some gave her small presents: a fan, a pair of carved ivory chopsticks . . .

It was as if the poster had never happened.

Secretary Lung shook hands warmly. "Please write to us when you are feeling better," he said.

He made a little speech saying that Stephanie was not only an excellent teacher, but a wise wife and a good mother. He glared around him and repeated: "A wise wife and a good mother." Everyone clapped.

I suppose that means they don't believe the poster, thought Stephanie. This comforted her. She carried herself proudly, youngly, though her whole body felt bruised, as if she had been beaten.

She and Winter Treasure would go to Shanghai. Winter Treasure would stay with his grandparents; Stephanie would continue to Canton, to Hongkong. Yong had explained to his son that Mama was going back to see her parents. And the boy had listened, then looked at her steadily. "Mama, you will be back soon, Mama?"

"Yes, Treasure, as soon as I am all well again."

Jen Ping would go with her.

"Why?" asked Stephanie when Yong told her. "Why is she coming? Why not you?"

They did not talk to each other now, except in front of Winter Treasure. Yong went in and out of the house, to the hospital, returned. They lay stiff as tired ghosts by each other's side at night, not touching.

"Stephanie, I—"

Cold fury overwhelmed her. "You did not ask me whether I would like her company."

"Stephanie, please, please . . . " He came, took her hands in his, tried to get her attention. But she shook him off, glaring at him.

"Let go of me." She was icy. Glittering with fury, with contempt. He dropped his hands.

"I thought she might be useful."

That hated word. *Useful* . . .

"Let her come if she wishes, but I don't need her."

Again it was all arranged. All arranged. The Family. Jen Ping would be on the train with her. There was nothing she could do about it.

She did not know that Yong had been refused permission to go with her to Shanghai. By the Party committee of his unit. He did not tell her.

Smudgy heat clotted the evening and the smell of tar and smoke spread throughout the railway station. Railway stations were the same everywhere; they emptied one of feeling; one waited for the release of departure, a finality agreed to.

"Mama, Mama, I want you to take my present to External Grandpa and External Grandma." Winter Treasure waded through his bag, extracted the mysterious present, which had been a secret until now. A wooden box, decorated with his best seashells, those he had collected in his summer at Peitaiho. A heart, and below it, in English: "I lov you."

"I'll certainly take it, darling. Put it in Mama's big bag. It won't break."

Yong was looking at her. She turned to him again. The railway station master was blowing his whistle, soon he would raise and lower the green flag of departure.

"I'll write to you, Yong . . . I'll be back."

"Of course, Spring Snow. You will be back. I know." His voice sounded confident, but his eyes now slid beyond her, looking at another Stephanie just over her shoulder. "I shall always wait for you," he said.

"Yong, I *have* to go back."

His English was now once more the English he had used

in Chungking, precise and old-fashioned. "We are riveted together, you and I. Even your going away is part of our need of each other. We are in each other's hands, for all our days on earth."

It was time to board the train, time to leave. To wave hands, to wave a handkerchief. To wave to Yong who stood immobile on the platform, only raising his hand a little.

An hour later, when Winter Treasure was tucked in his bunk and Jen Ping and Stephanie were alone in the dining car, Jen Ping said: "Yong asked to go with you to Shanghai. Permission was refused."

"Why did he not tell me?"

"Because you did not guess it," replied Jen Ping.

Willow Pool Garden now seemed a little unreal; a fairyland gone shabby. Wrapped in a haze which was partly the heat, partly the fact that much of the House needed a coat of new paint.

Father shadowboxed every morning. Mother was entirely turned towards him, wrapped in a dazzle of love. Precious above all things is love in old age; the caring that comes with the years, precious beyond young passion. Stephanie saw them holding hands, walking the garden. They stopped by the wasted rose bushes she had planted. There had been a bad plague of aphids that year.

In the evening, Jen Ping sat with her brother in the study, talking. Reabsorbed in the Family. They talked about her. About Yong.

Winter Treasure would stay in Shanghai. "Until your return, dear daughter." Yong would not have time to care for him.

All was arranged. She felt superfluous. Widow hummed to herself, sidled in and out. Her sidling had reappeared. She was insubstantial, even in her various committees. Younger, sturdier women filled them with loud voices, with force and directness. Family planning. What to do about wife beating. Meals for children when the mothers worked. A women's magazine. Divorce procedures. Equal salaries. Whether women could become steelworkers.

Mother packed boxes of lacquer and small vases of cloisonné for Stephanie's parents. "We cannot give much of value nowadays, daughter. Please tell your respected parents we hope to see them when all misunderstanding has gone."

The understatement of the century, thought Stephanie.

The child in her. Three months. It did not show. She caught Mother looking, appraising. She hid from Mother her morning nausea.

Teacher Fan was delighted to see Winter Treasure again. "Please tell the American people we want to be friends," she told Stephanie earnestly. "The rightists want to destroy our great system. But without the revolution, I would be a beggar, rotting away somewhere."

But Secretary of State John Foster Dulles had just made statements in favor of the rightists.

Lionel and Loumei came with China Warrior who was now a tall boy, who played volleyball very well. "I'm glad you're having a break, Stephanie," said Lionel Shaggin. "Please tell them back home this country really wants to be friends. . . ."

"They won't believe me, Lionel."

"They'll have to one day. It's not hopeless. In Warsaw, the American ambassador is talking with the Chinese ambassador . . . has been doing so since 1955 . . ."

"Stephanie," said Henry Barber, "nothing is forever, especially in politics. There will have to be changes, in both countries. And you can help by explaining.

"You were in Yenan, way back in 1945. You know that Mao Tsetung and Chou Enlai wanted America as partner and friend. Not Russia. You know Jack Service and John Davies reported this correctly to the State Department and they've been hounded for it, their reputations torn to shreds, their living ruined."

"I feel pretty depressed myself at the moment with these political campaigns," said Stephanie.

"A revolution isn't easy, Stephanie. It goes through all sorts of trials and errors, terrible mistakes and fantastic discoveries. . . . But we've got to keep going. We wouldn't have had all this harshness in China if America hadn't changed course, way back in 1945," said Henry Barber.

"Oh, stop it, Henry!" she said savagely. "Stop apologizing for being American. Stop blaming America for all the problems in China—the Chinese aren't going to love you for it. You're still a foreigner to them."

Stephanie left for Canton, waving to Winter Treasure, who did not cry while she was blinking away her tears. Who said, imitating *Tietie*, "Take care of your precious body, Mama."

Shumchun, border station on the Chinese side between Canton and Hongkong. A narrow brook. A wooden bridge across it. On the Hongkong side, barbed wire looping above some low earth ridges. Everyone knew that China did not want to take Hongkong; but Hongkong still had to pretend that it kept the Chinese hordes at bay with a couple of English regiments. The greatest excitement for VIPs was a peek at the border between the Free World of Hongkong and Red China, across the barbed wire.

No trouble on the Chinese side. Her money was checked; she had two thousand U.S. dollars with her. Of jewelry, only the heirloom necklace Mother had given her. She walked the bridge. Her feet were leaden, her heart was lead. Yong. Yong. Winter Treasure. Already the uniformed policemen on the Hongkong side were saying: "Passport please."

Furrowed brows. Frowns. They stared at the passport, then at a black book in front of them. "Wait here," they said. She waited. The passport and customs lounge was small, very hot. Four armed policemen guarded the entrance and exit. There was no chair to sit on.

Half an hour later, a fair-haired Englishman came in, holding her passport in his hand. "Miss Ryder. I'm Wells, Special Branch. I'm afraid your passport's expired."

"But I thought . . ."

"We've been in touch with your consulate in Hongkong. They'll issue you a transit document, to put you on an American plane bound for America."

"That's where I want to go."

"I'm afraid you'll have to go to the airport right away. Under police escort. You can't stay in Hongkong without documents."

"When will there be a plane?"

"There should be one tomorrow afternoon."

"Couldn't I stay in a hotel?"

"Afraid you can't. You haven't any valid documents."

476

A Chinese plainclothes man bustled up to Wells, whispered something in his ear. They withdrew some distance, conferring. Wells returned. He looked surly.

"I understand you've been vouched for. A friend is waiting for you. He'll guarantee you."

Her luggage was on the platform, and also a young man dressed in a sumptuous Italian silk suit with a French silk tie. He shone from head to foot.

"Auntie," he said. "Welcome to Hongkong." And, seeing her puzzled, "I'm Eddy Keng, Keng Dawei's son. We met in Dallas, in 1948 . . ."

"Why of course." Dad said Eddy Keng was smart, a born businessman. Eddy Keng had been working for Dad, learning the oil business.

Porters materialized to carry her luggage. Wells frowned at Keng and said haughtily, "I say, you'll have to sign an affidavit, you know." But the Chinese policemen were now grinning and Eddy smiled beatifically.

"Mr. Wells, I know your boss. He tell me come here." He piloted Stephanie firmly to a gleaming midnight-blue Mercedes with a white uniformed chauffeur. "I borrow car from uncle," said Eddy loudly. "Everybody savvy my uncle. He Sir Henry Keng. He in London now, buy horses for Hongkong Racing Club. We stay by'mbye his house, Keng-stone."

Eddy Keng was talking pidgin English, making fun of Wells. Stephanie sat back in the air-conditioned Mercedes. It was cool, cool and restful. She was relieved, but also resigned. The Family, the connections. Uncle Keng. In China or out of China, that invisible, stretching gossamer web of relations, relations and connections . . . they looked after their own, right up until the end.

twenty-one

You were right to go away. You felt lost by so much
negation of constancy, the shadow of deception, growing doubt which made all things seem untrue. You left
in search of coherence because our love, the one
surety left to us, was dimmed by tragic uncertainty all
around us.

Uncle Keng arranged for his son to protect you in
Hongkong. So that you should not be hounded, insulted by newsmen agog for sensation.

My heart's darling, I am no philosopher, using apt
words; but poets have taught me that the tangible
world around us is never cast in an immutable pattern. It is forever dissolving and reassembling, a
ceaseless flow of time and change. Yet the human
spirit always hungers for stability, for a metaphysics of
immutable truth. How precarious some of these beliefs have proved!

And yet Belief is necessary to mankind. And men
have died when faith turned out to be a jest, a self-
delusion.

I shall have to undergo a certain ordeal, and I am
glad you are not here. I do not like to see your mouth
quiver, light fade from you as you try to guess what I
try to hide.

Knowing the probable outcome of the investigation
launched against me, hearing already that scurry of
rats which is betrayal, I shall think of you, back in

your country, safe, while on me fall the denunciations of my colleagues, of some of my friends.

I shall dream of you. Feel the wind of your American empty spaces stroking your hair. Hear your laughter fluffed like willow catskins in the blue and gold of your land. I see you move under the oak trees, silk-dappled with their shade. You are the bird of morning, and till morning comes I shall wait for you, happy because when I close my eyes you are there, just under my lids.

Yong wrote this letter, and never posted it.

Eddy Keng put up a bond of ten thousand dollars, enabling Stephanie to stay twenty-four hours in Hongkong, to rest. "You rest, Auntie. You sleep. I take care of everything."

"Oh Eddy . . ."

"Your father was good to me. He is a big man, Mr. Heston Ryder. He doesn't understand us Chinese, and he doesn't understand politics, but no matter. He thinks simple, black and white, red and not red. I tell him there's only one color, the rainbow. He laugh."

Kengstone was a vast pile of masonry, built in the semblance of a medieval English castle with crenelated towers. It was the abode of Sir Henry Keng, MBE, loyal pillar of Her Majesty the Queen in the Crown Colony of Hongkong, blood brother of Keng Dawei, multimillionaire, who was collaborating with the Communists in Peking.

Beyond the girdling stone wall, the padlocked iron gates, milled a mob of newsmen and camera and television crews, both Chinese and foreign, whose clamor might have reached Stephanie had she not been sound asleep, in an air-conditioned room.

Eddy Keng, smart in all the ways of Hongkong, had bribed hugely so that the policeman at Lowu Railway Station delayed for one hour, before releasing to the press the list of foreign passengers from Red China.

A day later, Stephanie was smuggled out of Kengstone at dawn. By the secret tunnel dug during the Japanese occupation of Hongkong. Many large Chinese mansions had such passageways leading into the hills.

At the airport Stephanie was hustled by two armed Hongkong policemen onto a Pan-American aircraft. Her passport, valid only for returning to America on an American plane, was not handed back to her, but to two lean, greyhoundlike young men who sat near her on the plane, one behind, one in front of her, both chewing gum.

"You are treating me like a criminal," she remarked. They did not reply. Their jaws worked methodically almost the entire trip.

In Hawaii, she was not allowed to deplane for transit. She remained on the plane, then was transferred to another. In San Francisco, two men in fedoras walked her through a side door into the airport building. There, another couple of men, more bulky, waited in a cubicle guarded by two armed policemen. Stephanie, bleary with fatigue, realized she'd forgotten how large-boned and heavy some Americans were.

Inside the cubicle, the questioning began. The voices were low, quiet, unhurried, relentless. On and on. Frequent long pauses between questions.

"Could I have a glass of water?"

"Look, I'm very tired, I've been traveling for forty-five hours . . ."

"I don't understand that question . . ."

"Yes, I was married in Yenan . . . yes, in 1945."

"But I've already told you all this . . ."

"I demand to see a lawyer . . ."

They were impassive, unresponding, unflappable. Her words, angry or reasonable, poured over them like slick water on granite. They went on. Page after page. Questions. Every twenty minutes or so, a tight-lipped, bespectacled, middle-aged woman came in, stared at Stephanie with contempt, and put down another sheaf of files on the desk.

She was being taped. One of the two men leaned back, fiddled with a tape recorder. When one man got tired, the other took over the questioning.

"Mrs. Jen, I'm warning you again . . . you're not being cooperative . . . now you're not leaving this building until we're satisfied."

"An American citizen suspected of treason is required to answer . . ."

"I'm not a traitor."

"That will be up to the Senate Internal Security Subcommittee to judge . . ."

"These interrogations admit only the person to be questioned . . ."

"This is not a trial . . . you can't ask for a lawyer."

Questions. Derailing the spirit. Her words came tumbling, jumbled, they knocked about; there was a steady drone in her ears.

After another hour, she felt that the men were receding; the cubicle blew its walls out, tipped over. She fainted.

White ceiling above her. Was she back in Yenan? No, it wasn't that kind of rounded, womb ceiling.

"Yong."

"Steph, it's Dad . . ."

"Dad." She opened her eyes, jerked herself up. Then she was in his arms. "Oh Dad, Dad, they kept me so long, so long . . ."

"Three hours, baby. I know. I waited. But it's over now, it's over."

Another pair of lean young men were there. She walked shakily down the corridor on Heston Ryder's arm, and the young men walked one in front, one behind her.

Her luggage was waiting by the door marked EXIT.

"Mrs. Jen, regulations won't allow the entry of any material from Red China . . . we've had to impound some of the things you brought. . . . "

They'd taken everything except her clothes. The notes, diaries, manuscripts, letters, gifts, the photographs of Winter Treasure, of Yong. Everything except her used clothing. Even Winter Treasure's little wooden box, with the seashells making a heart shape, and "I lov you."

"We'll give you a receipt for the material impounded. You can, of course, claim it as your personal property."

Heston's arm tightened around her.

"I'll get my lawyers on to this. Don't worry, baby . . . we'll get it all back. Yessir. All of it." His voice was confident.

"Mrs. Jen, U.S. regulations deny passport and travel facilities to those American citizens who visit Communist countries without due authority . . ."

No passport.

They were out of the building, into the sunlight. She looked up at Dad, her lips tremulous. He was answering the two young men who had come out with them, were noting the car number.

"My daughter will stay with me. My lawyers will notify you."

She looked at Dad.

Dad was old. He had an old man's ears, an old man's mouth. His body was still trim, he carried himself erect, but it felt different. She had been away too long, and he had grown old.

Spring Snow,

You told me once that witches had been burnt in your country, and not such a very long time ago. My country, trying to exorcise the past, is also doing a good deal of burning, though not of living people at the stake.

You have left a New Testament behind you. I read it. Christianity is based on a human sacrifice. A crucifixion, the torture and slow agony of a just, innocent man who wanted a world renewed, and was thus a danger to the Powers that be.

Perhaps what some of us are undergoing now is that same rite of purification as the one made sublime by the torture of the cross inflicted upon one man two millennia ago. I must believe that suffering has its own validity, even if it is anonymous pain. And that we, those of us here who forge a new world, *must* believe that we are also guilty, guilty by proxy. Upon us are heaped the sins and the crimes of our ancestors. Does not the Christian Bible also recognize hereditary guilt? Is not original sin, that curious concept, based on the notion of inherited culpability? I thus comfort myself with philosophy, and poetry, which are akin. What fear lurks in my inch of heart? None.

Hour after hour, day after day, Jen Yong stood with bowed head, listening. His attitude the required one, meek and humble. He would be allowed to reply by making a self-criticism. His life was not in danger. That was certain. But to be labeled a rightist was to become a non-person. And this danger loomed very large for Yong.

He looked around at the auditorium. Doctor after doctor, his colleagues, rising to accuse him. Like stoning. Some heaved big rocks at him, with intent to kill. Others threw bits of gravel, their hearts were not in it. Those were his friends.

But was it not odd that no one would say a word for him? Something *must* be found against him. And all those who had feared for themselves were relieved: he was the designated scapegoat in his unit.

Thus "evidence" could be collected, fabricated, accumulated, distorted, blown up, heaped against him, consuming time that might otherwise be spent looking for other men's errors.

Testimony. From Old Wang, now Second Secretary Wang in charge of the Party committee in Chungking Hospital.

"Dr. Jen Yong's ideas and behavior were always bourgeois. He would not listen to good advice. He recklessly pursued his romantic, lustful ideas, and thus put our Organization in danger. He avowed that 'love comes first . . .'"

From Nurse Sha, now head nurse in Tsinan No. 1 Maternity Hospital: "I worked for three years in the surgical wards of the Chungking Hospital. Dr. Jen Yong was a typical reactionary authority, haughty, arrogant, not concerned about us, the nurses. His private life was bad. Several times, an American woman came to look for him, even in the hospital wards. He would leave everything, to go with her to luxury restaurants . . ."

From someone who had shared a cave with Jen Yong in Yenan: "He left our Red Cross team when we reached Sian, and asked an army comrade driving a truck to take him to Yenan. Not because he was eager to work, but because he wanted to embrace lustfully his foreign paramour . . ."

Another: "The American guests in Yenan had single caves to themselves. He took advantage of it to indulge in debauchery almost every night . . ."

From a writer who had been brought by Sa Fei to Yong's house: "No. 31 Yellow Wall *hutung* was always full of people, many of whom are now being exposed as rightists. I was misled into going there once by that big rightist, Sa Fei. I was disgusted by what I heard . . ."

From another: "He purposely invited many writers to meet his wife, plied them with food and drink to fill their minds with hatred of socialism, with love for American imperialism . . ."

From a colleague: "He has slandered our great friend, the fraternal Soviet Union, and its unselfish aid . . . he said the Russians were not as advanced in surgery as the Americans."

Another: "He wishes to subvert the Party leadership . . ."

Only one good report, from a man called Prosperity Tang, now in charge of coal and steel production in a large district in Manchuria: "Dr. Jen Yong rendered service sincerely and unselfishly. . . . During his time in jail under the Kuomintang he was staunch, and struggled against the reactionaries in a correct manner. He is very hard-working."

Jen Yong read the posters against him. Spread in the hospital where he worked. Where he still worked; for surgery went on, and he still operated every day. Only now, no one spoke to him, even during the operations. He noticed that not one of the men who had been to jail with him in Chungking had written against him. And was glad.

And who was Prosperity Tang, sticking his neck out to defend him?

The hospital Party committee had not yet named him a rightist. But everyone behaved as if he would be labeled very soon.

Sa Fei had been named a rightist.

Articles against her and her "clique" appeared in *Clearness*, the newspaper of the intelligentsia.

Reading *Clearness*, its objurgations, its labored censoriousness, Yong reflected that writers were far more mean and petty and vicious to their own kind than other intellectuals. Engineers, physicists, mathematicians, archaeologists seldom talked about each other, but a good many writers seemed to thrive on mutual treason, stimulated by gossip and slander.

One writer was accused by a discarded wife: "He is a wicked man with a wicked heart, a corrupt mind. He told me: 'I shall always play safe by having a foot in both camps.' He has over one thousand pounds salted away in England."

Reading all this in *Clearness*, Yong thought wryly: The Party now knows our weakness. We have no solidarity.

Some eminent non-Party writers, who had kept sedulously quiet, were totally spared. They even had the honor of having tea with Chairman Mao. It was not recorded anywhere that they said a word in favor of their hapless colleagues.

Yet there were a few courageous writers. One of them wrote: "Many eminent authors and actors have kept safe by not doing a stroke of work for seven years. In the old society they would have starved; under the present system they are pampered, but Sa Fei has continued to write for the people . . ."

When anyone became a rightist, the family of the wife or husband strove to bring about a divorce. So that they would not be involved.

But Liu Ming would not divorce Sa Fei. "I shall remain with her all the days of my life."

They were sent to a distant village in Inner Mongolia. Sa Fei would do a little labor, but not too much. She would work as the village accountant. She would not be published again, not until she was rehabilitated. Which would take years . . .

"I never liked big cities," said Liu Ming, packing his and Sa Fei's clothes.

"Now I shall have time to think," said Sa Fei, packing her books.

The small autumn wind brushed the oak leaves, bowed the vigorous grass. The shining coats of the horses on their morning gallop glowed like starlight, and Stephanie could hear the clear syllables of the cowboys, the velvet sound of hooves. She might be subpoenaed to appear before some subcommittee or other at any time. Dad was doing his best. Writing to congressmen, to a bunch of senators, getting his lawyers to protest. But this threat hung above her. Someone had "evidence" against her, the FBI men told her. "You'll soon find out . . ."

Dick Steiner telephoned.

"Stephanie . . . there's been a couple of men here to ask me questions . . ."

"Dick, they come to our home regularly. Three times a week. To question me. But why pick on you? You never did anything . . ."

"I was there, remember? At River Fork." He laughed. "You need a lawyer, honey, but I'm doing conveyancing. Not the type of lawyer you need. And maybe I need one too. They're keen on having me say the killers at River Fork were Japanese, not Kuomintang."

"Why're they bringing that up now, Dick?"

"Want to prove that Chiang Kaishek was a great democrat all along, I guess. Or prove you were lying in your articles."

Dick was being subpoenaed as a witness before the House Un-American Activities Committee in a case involving a friend of his. Abe Collins was an ex-prizefighter, a writer, who had been in the Lincoln Brigade in Spain, then a GI who went to Officer's Candidate School. Two days before graduation, it was discovered he'd fought for the Loyalists in Spain, so he stayed a GI all through the war. And now he was being investigated in Hollywood.

Isabelle wanted Stephanie to go to France. "In France there is freedom, Stephanie. We condemn what is being done in America." She was poised, a great lady. Exhibiting much calm.

"I've got to see it through out here, Mom. After all, this is my country. I won't run away." *Not as I ran away from you, Yong.* "Besides, I haven't got a passport now."

As president of the Dallas Arts Committee, Isabelle had arranged a gala reception and concert. The maestro came from Paris, the French ambassador was flying down from Washington.

And then the news about Stephanie broke out in the press. Major articles, front page. Old photographs of Stephanie, from the dust jackets of her books. Quotations from her books.

Denunciations by a posse of "China scholars," many of whom were now writing for a CIA-sponsored publishing company.

Photographs.

A photograph of Jimmy in soldier's gear. "Miss Ryder's brother died in Korea, but this did not stop his sister from praising the aggressors who killed him."

Her marriage in Yenan; her acquaintance with the Dixie Mission—"Those men whose sycophantic reports on Red China are responsible for the catastrophe . . ."

Bonanza for the press.

The gala reception and concert had to be canceled. Refusals poured in. Along with insulting letters, some of them almost hysterical.

Snide, obscene telephone calls. Miss Birnbaum, Heston's secretary, coped with them firmly.

"Get off the line, you blubber," she said.

The FBI came. Two interrogators, three times a week. Refusal to answer their questions meant a subpoena to appear before the Internal Security Subcommittee.

The press called her "Red Stephanie."

That she was the daughter of Heston Ryder, Chairman of Ryder Aircraft, Dallas, made it all the more sensational.

"Stephanie Ryder maintains that what she wrote before and during the Korean War was 'just plain truth,'" one newspaper announced. Then went on to print truncated extracts from her books and River Fork articles, as if they had been written during the Korean War, and not five years before.

"Prominent Dallas society leader, Mrs. Stimpkin-Jones, president of the Daughters of Texas, said in an interview: 'We don't really want that kind of person here . . . the most charitable thing that can be said is that she was thoroughly brainwashed . . ."

Newsmen and cameramen hung about the house. Heston had the safety catches on the doors and windows reinforced. Enterprising newsmen perched in trees and trained telescopic lenses on the house.

Stephanie's pregnancy now made the press rise to greater heights of fantasy.

Stephanie's baby was that of a very high Communist Party leader.

It was to escape death that Stephanie had fled China.

Stephanie carried secret documents, directives to U.S. Communists to overthrow the U.S. government with agents suborned by the Chinese. The FBI had found these documents concealed in her luggage and were studying them.

One newspaperwoman claimed that she had smuggled herself into the house and found Stephanie, nude, being massaged by "a blind Oriental masseur."

Another claimed that Stephanie had given her an interview and said: "They drugged me . . . I didn't know what I was doing."

A national circulation women's magazine published an interview with Sybil Kersh. Sybil Kersh had left HERE in 1949 to become a scriptwriter in Hollywood, where she had teamed up with a Hearst pressman. She had turned evidence against Communist infiltration among her colleagues in 1951. She was appointed to a "rehabilitation" committee, publicizing the efforts of the film industry to purge itself of subversives and to clear repentant writers.

The interview, titled "The Agony of a Faithful Wife," was accompanied by Sybil's photograph, looking frail, wide-eyed—a loving mother with two grown children by her side—and took up three pages.

We were devoted to each other, Alan and I. But as a war correspondent he was often away . . . women found him attractive. He didn't want to hurt them. . . . Stephanie Ryder did her best to attract him . . . she wanted to go to China . . . she was already participating in pro-red meetings at Radcliffe.

Regular as clockwork, the FBI men.

"Mrs. Jen, you began doing propaganda for the reds way back in 1944 . . . those articles about River Fork village . . . You wrote two books, praising Red China, praising the Communist regime . . ."

"What were your relations with John Service?"

"Why did you collaborate with Henry Barber in his weekly *Newssheet* in Shanghai?"

"Mrs. Jen, during the Korean War you wrote letters to Americans, condemning the war and appealing for peace . . . You toed the line of the Communist-backed Peace Council in Stockholm . . ."

"You were a guest in Yenan for some months . . . yet you maintain you were not subsidized by the reds?"

"Some of your activities come pretty close to treason."

"Both of your editors have withdrawn your books from circulation . . ."

"If you'd only state that you've changed your mind . . ."

"You're being very, very negative . . ."

"You mean to say, you think the reds are right?"

"If you don't condemn them, you must be with them . . ."

"You maintain your husband's not a Communist. Then why doesn't he denounce the red regime?"

"We suggest a show was put on for you at River Fork village."

"Did you actually see those enemy soldiers? How d'you know they were Kuomintang?"

"You lectured at Radcliffe, praising the Communist guerillas when you came back in 1945 . . ."

"Can you recall the names of the Americans you met during your years in Red China?"

"Does the name Joan Hesse mean anything to you? Lionel Shaggin? Peter Wellington?"

"Here is a list of names. Now if you'll just tell us in detail specifically what these people are doing in Red China."

"You helped the reds to translate Hemingway and Walt Whitman . . ."

"Who else, besides you, went to see that movie 'Salt of the Earth'?"

"You are risking a jail sentence, we're warning you . . ."

Those letters she'd brought. It made her a courier for the U.S. Communist Party.

Her doctor, John Webster, found Stephanie becoming increasingly strained. He protested. "Mrs. Jen *must* have some rest . . . she is getting dangerously near to a breakdown . . . this may affect her baby . . ."

The two fedora-hatted men left. And Stephanie went down to the ranch to rest for a week. Horace would drive her, and Minnie would be with her. "We'll come tomorrow, after your father's had his checkup," said Isabelle, embracing her, looking beautiful in a new Paris frock. Heston was to have an electrocardiogram the next morning. He too was feeling the strain. He was still chairman of Ryder Aircraft. But the board was calling an emergency meeting to displace him.

"Look, Heston, what's happening is bad for the company. All this publicity! Shares are dropping."

Heston would be pushed out. It was in the fine print . . .

anyone whose conduct, or repute, was reprehensible or in any way conducive to undesirable effects upon the company. . . . Moral turpitude. That's what it was called. Damaging to the company's interests. He would have to resign.

Stephanie arrived at the ranch, and that very afternoon it began again.

The press mobbed the ranch. Horace and Minnie, and a couple of Mexican cowhands, kept them out. Stephanie stayed in her bedroom, behind locked doors. But an enterprising young journalist climbed on the roof, dropped onto her balcony, and began to photograph her through the glass door.

That evening she felt the first cramps, and her water broke.

Minnie telephoned Dr. Webster, and she and Horace bundled Stephanie into the car and drove her to the hospital.

A mob of pressmen pursued them closely. Took photos as she staggered into the hospital.

Isabelle and Heston arrived. Heston was so pale that he looked powdered over with thin frost. He paced outside the delivery room. He paced for the better part of the night. Isabelle stayed with him, brought him water in a paper cup. Isabelle took out her rosary and began to pray.

"Heston, God will hear us," she said to him. Heston sat down by her.

"Belle," he said. "Belle, I do care for you, you know that."

"I know, my dear."

He did care. Even more important, she was now strong—ever since his heart attack. He said: "Go in and talk to Steph, will you?"

That was better than sitting outside, going from bead to bead.

John Webster came out. "Stephanie's doing fine, doing fine . . . It's a bit early, though. She wasn't due till January."

This was mid-November.

Webster let Isabelle come into the delivery room to see her daughter. Stephanie's forehead was filmed with sweat; she was in pain, grunting; the baby was coming, coming quickly but very painfully. Isabelle stood by her, saying:

"Oh my dear, my dear." Stephanie could tell Isabelle really hated anything to do with blood, and flesh, and moans, with all the heaving and grunting which went with producing a baby.

"How's Dad, Mom?"

"He's well, Stephanie . . ." Isabelle left on tiptoe, as if regretfully, but actually relieved. Stephanie clenched her jaws and went on with having the baby. And so little Marylee, premature, was born and placed in an incubator.

Stephanie lay, spent yet unfulfilled. The nurses were efficient, and John Webster was kind and skillful; but no one had pushed *with* her. No one had been physically with her, made her feel the glory of childbirth, not as Eurasian Mary Lee had done in Shanghai. Not as Mother had done, *knowing* the ecstasy of childbearing pain.

And now like the advancing ocean tide she felt the memories surge up, roll up like waves pounding at her.

Yong, Winter Treasure . . . the sea came in, with that great hiss of water, and she was borne by it, and knew a tragic sense of unblessedness. I should not have left. I was a coward. But I just got so *tired*. . . . Still, I should have stuck it out. Yong, Yong. You should not have let me go so easily. *Why* did you let me go? . . .

He would have been there, and she would have said: "Yong, our daughter." And he would have looked both happy and distraught, his hair all mussed, and touched her with gentle fingers and cried with joy.

She wept then for her own fragmentation; and the tears burnt her to clearness. She would never be whole, in the sense of those who are whole because they have only that narrow space of living which never queries itself and carries no ambiguity. These happy many have not ventured on long explorations in other men's minds, gone into different worlds of thought and being, and come back, like Marco Polo, to bear tales that no one would believe. *Oh my heart to its folly comfortably yielded, and now like a captive fish loosed in the uncharted sea, to my marble basin I shall not ever return . . .*

And because of this yielding, she had brought to life children who would themselves be long-distance travelers, exploring the uncharted, and always strangers in a divided world. Winter Treasure, and now Marylee, on one side and the other of the sundering ocean.

Heston and Isabelle came in, and the tide ebbed silently away.

Isabelle had seen the baby in the incubator and she was moved to tears that did not fall from the corners of her eyes. "Oh Stephanie, she's so tiny, so precious."

"Her name will be Marylee, Mom. In memory of Mary Lee, the Eurasian nurse who helped my son to be born."

Isabelle felt it. The reproach. She winced but said: "It is a very pretty name."

Dad bent down, kissed Stephanie. He looked awfully tired.

"Want me to send a cable, baby? Guess I'll have to do it through Eddy Keng in Hongkong. He told us he'd take care of all the mail."

"Oh yes, Dad, please do."

Dad sat down and took out the silver ballpoint pen he carried. Stephanie dictated a cable for Yong.

Dearest

A little sister for Winter Treasure
Premature but healthy Please name our daughter

Spring Snow

"Yong will give her a Chinese name, Dad."

"Sure, you bet," said Heston.

Heston and Isabelle left. It was 9 a.m. and in the corridor a bustle of men stampeded: newsmen trying to take pictures, to interview the nurses, to reach the incubator, to get into Stephanie's room, to extract some filament of scandal for a jaded public.

They're like cockroaches, efficient scavengers, thought Heston, for the first time hating this swiftness, this efficiency.

There had been a hostile column about him in the local newspaper. About his resignation. Too bad they couldn't take his name off the corporation, or the hospital wing he'd endowed . . .

He sighed. He loved America, he'd really believed in a big red plot against America. But now doubts had come.

Steph. That lovely face of hers. The face of a woman, a beautiful woman who knew how to love.

Loving someone or something was an art, a learning, a vocation, a chimera to be made real.

While Isabelle lay down to rest, Heston walked into his study and dictated the telegram to his secretary, Miss Birnbaum. Then impulsively: "Take another telegram, will you, Miss Birnbaum?"

Dear Grandson Winter Treasure

You've got a pretty little sister

Love from your

External Grandpa Heston

He sat in his chair and sipped the coffee Miss Birnbaum kept ready for him. God, he was so tired. Shaky with tiredness. But happy too. Steph. Oh, Steph.

Now perhaps the FBI would let up on her. Those bastards. Harassing her. Couldn't they see she was innocent? She'd fallen in love with a man, and of course with his country. What was it the Bible said? "Thy people shall be my people." Steph was like that. She wouldn't stint her loving, she was a giver. Couldn't they see it? And she'd wanted to come home. And she hadn't approved of the Korean War, but even American generals weren't too sure now that the Korean War wasn't a mother-fucking blunder. One of them had even said it. The wrong war in the wrong place with the wrong people . . . But the FBI insisted on treating his daughter like a criminal, threatening her.

Heston had said to the FBI men the last time they'd come and tried to break Stephanie down: "I am ashamed of what you guys are doing . . . you're making me ashamed of being an American." He'd written to his congressman, telephoned a couple of senators. They'd promised to help. But the FBI had kept on coming.

Now there was this tiny bit of life, Marylee. Already had a mop of dark hair. Tiny, but cute, so cute. His heart kept on tap-tapping, an eager, violent heart, he could feel his whole chest wall vibrate.

He'd kept the letters from Winter Treasure, and now on his desk was that box of wood, with a heart, and "I lov you," made by his grandson, who was a Chinese boy. The lawyers had got that back, and also some photographs. There was one of Winter Treasure in a swimsuit, on a beach, looking in awe at a huge, stranded jellyfish. Such a good-looking boy. Maybe he'd come to America and go camping with him.

Oh, damn *all* politics. *I'm tired*. It was a lovely morning. In the garden, a concourse of wagtails and sparrows, and the linnets tuning up. Isabelle had been right to give up the big house. This one, near to a wooded copse, was happy with birds, was easier. The other would be turned into something useful. Annex to the hospital, or an art school. Or some institute for scientific forums. Because it didn't matter about these sons of bitches now. They were not America. Dallas would keep growing. Texas would be something on the map of the world. And Heston Ryder would keep on doing things to make it all happen. . . .

Having sent the telegrams Heston had dictated, and also opened and sorted the mail, Miss Birnbaum tapped gently and opened the study door.

Heston looked very peaceful and very young, looking at her with those blue eyes of his, sitting very still in his chair.

Tiny Marylee wanted very much to live. She bawled with a great voice and sucked with vigor, almost biting her mother's nipple. Isabelle attributed this to the fact that Marylee had been baptized a few hours after birth. Father Tremoine had come up to the hospital, and Isabelle had made Marylee a Catholic. Stephanie did not protest. "It really does not matter, Mom. But Marylee may object one day, since it was done without her consent."

Isabelle again felt humiliated by her daughter's offhandedness. But the death of Heston had dispelled all minor hurts, plunged both the women into grief. And once again there were assaults by the press.

Heston had died of sorrow.

The baby was abnormal . . .

However, the more sober newspapers mentioned that the child had been baptized a Catholic, and this seemed to turn the tide. Suddenly the filth stopped welling up. The ignoble forbore. The anonymous calls and letters dwindled. Except for one enterprising newspaper, which bribed a student nurse to take a photo of the baby being brought to Stephanie.

A birth and a death had purged evil. Heston's funeral was

attended by many people. The security guards hired for the occasion kept the press away.

Some friends came to call on Isabelle, bringing small gifts for the newborn child.

A month after Marylee's birth, Stephanie left Dallas with her baby and with Minnie. Horace drove them to Hot Springs and the next day to Memphis, where they boarded a plane to New York.

"I wanted to be away from Dallas," Stephanie wrote to Yong. "In New York I feel closer to you . . ." She waited, waited for a letter from Yong. But none came. She did not stay in her mother's apartment, which was known to the press. Dick Steiner rented her a new apartment, in the name of Mrs. Yates. The FBI paid her a visit, but the baby's presence made them desist. It was then the eighteenth of December.

Brigadier General Tsing, known affectionately by his friends in Washington as Reggie, pored over the reports on his nine-by-six-foot desk.

Tsing had a magnificent seventeenth-floor apartment on 51st Street, overlooking the East River. He worked closely with the FBI and the CIA, keeping close watch on the Chinese students and professors in American universities. The merchants, the traders of Chinatown, the restaurant owners were controlled by other Kuomintang organizations. They were not a problem.

Whereas intellectuals were always tiresome. Old Peanut had not known how to deal with them. Starve, suppress, kill. That was his way.

But the Communists were also in a quandary with the same intellectuals. They relied on long drawn-out thought re-education: they panicked at the slightest stir, then they steamrollered.

Tsing read the reports from inside China. He noted that Hsu had managed to get to Peking. Smart. He read about Jen Yong and about the posters.

Hsu had evidently intended to revenge himself on Stephanie Ryder. But such a poster was dangerous . . . the source of it might be investigated.

However, should Jen Yong be denounced as a rightist, the poster would help to denigrate his character. Tsing still resented the way Jen Yong had spoken to him the last time they had met . . . all of thirteen years ago.

Reggie Tsing had Stephanie's new address. Near Central Park. He felt a great urge to see her, to speak to her. The beautiful American wife of Dr. Jen Yong.

In the morning newspaper, Yong found his name. Labeled rightist for having denounced hospital management; for having sought to bring back "bourgeois" administrative methods; for having criticized the great and glorious, fraternal, unselfish Soviet Union.

But not a word about Stephanie. He felt relieved. Now he could write to her, tell her his condemnation had nothing to do with her.

He knew what lay ahead. He would go to the hospital. No one would talk to him. He would sit behind the others at meetings and seminars. He would eat alone. His medical writings, even if printed, would not bear his name, but would be attributed to a collective of surgeons. His salary would be cut.

At every political criticism meeting, he would have to be criticized all over again.

He would lose the house. He might be moved to some faraway hospital. In Mongolia.

He washed and dressed and knew that very soon he would begin to hurt like ten thousand furies. But at the moment he clung to ordinary gestures, trying to confuse the pain, the pain which was rising in him. He started cleaning his shoes. He must tell Mother Huang. Mother Huang had said: "Now the young mistress has gone, I will look after you."

He had better tell her. So that she could leave him without embarrassment.

The smell of steamed buns came from the kitchen. He must tell her . . .

The doorbell rang.

This was now so uncommon that Mother Huang came into the bedroom to ask: "Shall I open the gate?"

"Yes, Mother Huang."

It was Arthur Chee and his wife, Millie.

Arthur strode into the courtyard, making a lot of cheerful

noise. "Howdy, Yong! Millie and I thought we'd come and have some breakfast with you."

They knew.

Yong felt almost like weeping. "Arthur, you *are* a good friend."

Mother Huang walked in with dishes, which she set on the table. They sat down. Millie asked: "Any news of Stephanie?"

Yong smiled cheerfully. "Yes. I hear she's reached Dallas safely."

And then it began to hurt, to hurt abominably. He could not swallow, could only stare at Arthur and Millie Chee with an idiotic, desperate grin on his face.

General Yee pored over the lists of the rightists which his secretary prepared for him. The lists kept on lengthening, every day. He frowned. Too many. But a top leader had mentioned the figure ten percent, and the middle cadres would try to make it ten percent. Ten percent of five million. And the top leader had probably by now even forgotten his own words, as casual as flicking an ash from a cigarette.

Meiling came in, holding her daughter by the hand. Round Round was a noisy child, physically hyperactive, almost uncoordinated. "Grandpa, Grandpa," she shrieked at the top of her voice, throwing herself at him. Yee patted his granddaughter absentmindedly.

"Have you seen the list of rightists, Meiling?"

"Only the list of medical people, Father. Jen Yong is among them. Someone told me his report on hospital management was very reactionary . . ."

"It was a good report, I read it," said her father.

Meiling blushed. She had not read it. Too busy.

General Yee went to his committee meeting. A committee in charge of recruiting top scientists in every field. Under Premier Chou Enlai. The committee tried to make sure that nothing untoward should happen to these top brains. They must be protected, whatever their wrong political ideas. They were too useful.

Yee thought the list of "top" scientists far too small. More younger people should be co-opted. Dr. Jen should be among the protected ones. His work in surgery was quite remarkable.

There were others, even Party leaders, who felt like Yee. Who knew the value of intellectuals and came right out to protect them. "Why go nit-picking at them because they like Western music, or have had a love affair?"

The committee held its sessions in a large room, in a new, gray brick building. Only one man was there before Yee. Comrade Meng, in charge of the sector of research in design, aeronautics.

Vice-Commissar Meng had been a peasant, but he was astute. A natural learner. Very much aware of the need for expertise, he would come to Yee, asking him to explain this or that—unlike some Party members, who pretended to know everything, saying: "If you know Marxism, you don't need to learn anything else."

The two men greeted each other. "More names," said Yee. "I think that some of them should benefit from verification. When the time for verification comes. Dr. Jen Yong, for instance. His report was not anti-Party."

"I met him," said Meng. "He came to our frontline when I was there. Hard-working."

Yee said: "His wife is an American. A writer."

Meng said: "We must investigate every case. Unfortunately, it will take a long time."

Little Pearl went every day to the North Sea Park to sketch. She knew he would wait, wait outside the *hutung* she lived in. They would take the bus together.

She sat, sketching the white pagoda with its golden spire; the willow trees around the man-made lake; the lotus spreading its immense leaves; while Little Pond stood looking at the landscape. Sometimes they walked a little. And they talked. In short, easy sentences.

Little Pond had very little money but he was resourceful. There was a Szechuan restaurant in the East Market, and the cook had agreed that Little Pond might help in the evening, when the restaurant was full of people from Szechuan who had come to Peking and wanted the hot, chili-sharp pungent food of their own province. Food once a day; a place to sleep; no pay. Yet he could meet Little Pearl every morning at the bus stop. And walk with her to the North Sea Park, and look at her while she pretended to sketch.

Meng was busy reading Jen Yong and Stephanie's files when Little Pearl returned from the park at noon. He smiled fondly. His daughter looked so pretty now, with a new aliveness. "Your mother is bringing some guests, it's her afternoon off," he said.

"I'll help with the dishes," said Pearl.

Comrade Lo's loud voice arrowed across the courtyard: "Old Partner, are you there, the guests have arrived."

Meng rose, looked through the window. Frowned. That man again. And a couple.

He waited for them in the living room, holding the file, looking at them above his glasses, putting on his stupid look. Little Pearl came out of the kitchen, saw them, and immediately ran back. Meng felt a small spurt of contentment. His daughter did not like the fellow. "Good girl, a good nose."

The couple was unprepossessing. The man had a mole with a long hair on his chin; he was dressed in a gray jacket and trousers, very proper. The woman looked oiled, oily. She praised everything. "Oh, what a lovely house . . . we are most honored . . . Comrade Meng . . . your great repute has reached our lowly ears . . ."

Fart, thought Meng. The woman's eyes were keen, small buzzing screws, going zing zing zing . . .

Comrade Lo was scarlet with excitement.

"Little Pearl," she called. "Daughter! Come and bow to the guests."

Little Pearl came out, bowed mechanically, unsmiling. Bo Chaste Wisdom took her hand, started talking.

"Aiyah, such a nice girl, studying so hard . . . your father and mother have high renown, you must follow in their footsteps . . . without our young people to build socialism, who would be our successors? As Chairman Mao said, 'You are the morning of the world.'"

The dishes were served, but Little Pearl had not brought a chair for herself. "I am not hungry," she said, and withdrew into the kitchen.

Chaste Wisdom said: "Oh, what a good girl, so shy and modest, you have brought her up well, Comrade Lo."

Meng sat at table with his wife and her guests. The woman started to talk of Yenan and Meng suddenly paid attention.

"Ah, who could dream we would eat like this, when we were in Yenan," chanted Chaste Wisdom.

"We're old friends from Yenan," said Comrade Lo to her husband, meaning that Old Partner Meng must toast the good old days in the caves.

Meng toasted: "To the revolution. To the Party."

And now he waxed attentive—especially to Comrade Hsu, who had not been in Yenan.

Chaste Wisdom drank; her husband, Sea Dragon, drank. Their faces grew red and their tongues loosened.

"When we came from Chungking to Yenan, we felt we had entered heaven," said Sea Dragon.

"Ah," said Meng, looking in turn at all three. "All of you came from Chungking?"

"Not me," said Hsu hastily. "I was never in Chungking."

Chaste Wisdom then told how she and Sea Dragon had gone in peril of their lives for years. "To work in white areas under the Kuomintang was quite different from the freedom and security in a red base," she said.

"Yes," said Meng. "But I am only a rough soldier. I never was in any danger spot."

Chaste Wisdom airily mentioned Party leaders by name, as if she knew them well. And pretty soon, the talk veered to the rightists who, said Chaste Wisdom, "should be executed . . . they want to overthrow our beloved Party."

"Did you know Dr. Jen Yong from Chungking?" asked Meng. "He came to Yenan, and I saw him there. He's the son of a big capitalist, isn't he?"

"That rightist," exclaimed Chaste Wisdom, "how good that such people have now been exposed in their atrocious villainy!"

She was launched. Hsu, thoroughly frightened at her loquacity, tried to divert her. "Comrade Bo, let us talk of pleasant things."

But Chaste Wisdom went on about the foreign woman who had behaved so badly in Chungking—"everyone knew it"—and then married Jen Yong. "Two conspirators," she said, "plotting to bring American imperialism back."

"There was a meeting in Yenan about it," said Meng, looking at his wife.

"Comrade Bo Chaste Wisdom was there," replied Lo placidly. "She was the one who exposed the American woman."

"Not at all," said Sea Dragon, suddenly alarmed. "She only repeated what we heard."

Chaste Wisdom sobered down. "I only said what I had heard in Chungking."

"From whom?" Meng cupped his ear with his hand.

"A relative, who was a waiter at the Press Hostel," said Sea Dragon.

Meng refilled the glasses with a steady hand. How was it these people spoke evil of the American woman, when the Chungking underground had only good things about her in the files?

Comrade Lo was hurt. "I invite people and you are not polite to them."

Meng went on poring over the files.

"Are you deaf?" shouted Lo to her husband. "Answer me."

He smiled affectionately. "Old woman, old woman, I'm getting old, that's all."

But Lo was not mollified. "Little Pearl is really too stubborn," she said, changing the topic but attributing the stubbornness to Meng.

"Don't try to marry her off to Hsu, old woman. She doesn't like him."

"What do you know!" said Lo, thoroughly angry. "She'll do what I tell her to do."

"Not now. No coercion in marriage allowed. This is the new law," said her husband, pushing her gently into the bedroom for an afternoon siesta.

Little Pond was leaving Peking very soon. He had exactly fifty cents left out of the 3.50 *yuan* with which he had come to the city two weeks previously. He would walk back to Tientsin, the villages would feed him, he would help on the way, there was always something he could do.

Because it was their last morning together, Pearl and he lingered along the tree-canopied alleys of the park.

Little Pond told Pearl about his mother, Liang Ma; about the man who kicked Ma; about the American woman who hit him and took Ma to the hospital. "Hsu Towering Cloud," he said. "A Shanghai man. If he is still alive, I shall find him one day. Even if I have to overturn Heaven to do it."

They came to the gate of the park and turned to each other. She looked him full in the face and smiled. Her lips curved very gently. "Well, now you must leave," she said.

He looked at her smile. "I must leave."

In another fortnight she would be going back to school in Tientsin. He would see her then.

He walked away, turning back once, twice, to look at her.

Winter laid its unsurprising blight upon New York. In Central Park the leaf-shorn trees achieved a skeleton intricacy. Stephanie remembered how Yong and she, in 1948, had walked through Central Park, and Yong had thought it unkempt.

Christmas was five days away. Stephanie had cabled to Eddy Keng, again asking for news of Yong, cabled a message to Winter Treasure for his birthday. No letters from Yong.

Her son's birthday. He would be nine years old, and she would not be there. And no news from him.

"There is no direct postal communication with Red China," she had been told at the post office. But there was. Only the post office employees did not know it. Did not know the world's post office, oblivious of bamboo curtains, of political slammed doors, of the drums of war, *did* function. Through Hongkong. Through Switzerland, through London . . .

Stephanie began to doubt Eddy Keng's arrangements. She wrote directly to Yong in Peking, wrote to Lionel Shaggin, wrote to Mother, wrote to Peter Wellington . . .

Now she wandered in Central Park. The winter austerity of the almost deserted paths soothed her. A pair of lovers, undaunted by the cold, clasped each other on a commodious bench.

At the elbow bend of an alley, Reggie Tsing stood, watching the beautiful woman walk along in her unfussy beige cashmere coat with the sable collar. Oh, indeed she was lovely, with unconscious grace, and his heart was pinched with envy. Lucky, lucky Jen Yong. . . .

"Madame Jen." He bowed, courteous, presentable.

"Yes?" Lost in her thoughts, Stephanie had not noticed him. Now she saw he was Chinese, and for a moment thought: Perhaps a friend of Eddy's from Hongkong, come to give me news of Yong . . .

"Yes, what is it?"

"Madame Jen, my lowly name is Tsing. I knew your husband well, Dr. Jen Yong. Some years ago."

She saw the vicuna coat, the shoes, the pigskin driving gloves. But it was the way he talked. He talked . . . like the Kuomintang. Using those old ritual phrases.

She must not believe him, not believe him . . .

"I do not think you know Dr. Jen Yong," she said.

"But I do. We were intimate for several weeks. . . . I admired his courage, his loyalty. Alas, that he should now be condemned."

There was a dark door closing somewhere; the park was somber now, the quick light dimmed.

She said: "I am busy." She tried to walk on. But he walked with her, easily.

"You do not want to hear. Yet I tell you the truth. Your husband has been condemned. As a rightist. For having attacked the Party in a medical report. He praised American methods. You will never be able to go back to China now. The Communists will not allow it."

He saw that her shoulders had tightened. She walked away.

And he was discontented with himself. Somehow it had fallen flat. Perhaps she was weeping, but he derived no pleasure from it.

Stephanie walked between trees thrusting desperate fists towards the unhearing sky.

Yong. I saw you writing that report. You were so sure they would read it, that they would understand you wanted to help. But they didn't.

The nights he had spent writing.

Mechanically her legs moved, numb yet striding ever faster, faster homewards.

And halfway, she felt, she was certain, there was a message from Yong, or a telegram . . . something was waiting for her. At home.

The telephone was ringing in her flat, ringing as she unlocked her door. Minnie had taken Marylee out in the carriage. *Oh, don't let it stop.*

"Hello," she said, breathless, "hello?"

"Stephanie . . . it's John . . . John Moore . . ."

John. Relief, and also disappointment.

"John, it's so nice to hear your voice," she said.

"I'm in town, Stephanie, I live in New York now . . . any chance of seeing you?"

"Oh yes, John, please . . . " And suddenly she was almost crying, crying because it was not Yong, not Yong. Only John Moore. "I'd love to see you John. It's been such a long time. . . ."

twenty-two

THEY were again at the Algonquin, in the velvet glow of hooded lamps, the faint smell of old wood glossed with the fumes of good cooking and good talk. There is an emanation from such places, which colors the mind. No. 31, the house in Peking, had also been thus enriched, enriching.

John Moore looked at Stephanie. He would never love another woman. He had tried, hating this prison of the heart in which he was confined by the turn of her neck, the gold stars in her brown eyes. And now he was happily tormented, for she was here. They shared so much, their minds open to each other, if not their bodies.

Stephanie talked of Yong, talked of Yong, inflicting upon John Moore further harrowing while he toyed, impassive of face, with the stem of his wine glass. Her voice was grave and beautiful. "We were incapacitated by events beyond our control," she said. She spoke of Winter Treasure, and her voice shook, and tears pearled in her eyes. No word, no word had come directly from Yong or her son since she had landed in America, in late July. Only reassuring messages, from Eddy Keng in Hongkong, that "all was well," "not to worry." "As soon as there is anything definite will let you know." And, since reaching her own country, the various outrages inflicted upon her: "I believe my mail is being tampered with."

It was December 27. Stephanie had spent the three previous days immured in her apartment, waiting for a message, a telephone call. She had telephoned Eddy Keng in Hongkong, heard his voice, very faint. "Everything is fine, Auntie, yes. Yes, your son has had your message, he

505

thanks you, he says he has written to you . . . letters a bit delayed . . . your husband is not in Peking, but his health is good . . . do not worry . . ."

"Stephanie, postal communication is hazardous and there's a lot of censorship, three-way, four-way censorship," said John reassuringly. "All the letters from Red China to this country go via Hongkong. They're pounced upon, scrutinized. We've got three agencies and eight hundred agents working on it. And that makes for a lot of delays. And then there's the Chinese censorship as well. If I were you, I'd trust Eddy Keng. He knows. Probably your family is not writing to you because you've told them you've been harassed by the FBI, and they want to spare you further harassment. . . ." And to cheer her told her about a Chinese interpreter at the United Nations, a Mr. Bien, who had been hounded for the past six years. "He and his family are entitled to travel every two years to their homeland. That's UN regulations. So, in 1952, they went to China with their eight-year-old son. Since then the FBI hasn't left them alone. The son goes to school every morning accompanied by two FBI men. 'At least my son is safe,' says Mrs. Bien. 'Two bodyguards.' She and her husband find it funny to be awakened at 3 a.m. for questioning."

"You're joking."

"Truth. Mr. Bien told me so himself. He usually insists on giving the agents some tea."

Stephanie laughed, then she became serious again. "Now I feel rotten about leaving Yong. I should have stayed. That's what marriage is about . . . but Yong didn't hold me to it. He didn't *fight*, he agreed, immediately, too quickly. Now, I'm all confused . . ."

"So that you thought *you* were the cause of his troubles . . ."

John Moore put a hand upon her silk-sleeved arm. "Stephanie, don't tear yourself to bits. There's nothing one *can* do. It's like floods, or a war. Nothing the human will can change."

He went on. "You've always been impulsive, courageous. Remember Chungking, and the bastard you hit, and how it began your career? You've got guts, Stephanie. You don't let prejudice, timorousness, even common sense, stop you.

"You just couldn't take any more of those political campaigns. You were heartsick and homesick—and worn out.

506

And now you're being pressured to *denounce* Red China—which you can't do. Yong's there, and Winter Treasure. And so much good has *also* been done, along with the nauseating evil. Well, that's the dilemma of all history, isn't it? We're all caught in that ambiguity."

"John, what a good friend you are . . ."

"I'm not a friend, you idiot. I love you. Don't you understand?"

She made a small movement of her hands on the table.

He said: "You don't. I know. Now I've said it. I love you. Let's just file my feelings for the record. I'm happy being with you, and I hate to see you sad, and I'd hate to see you go back to China right now . . . but if that's what you want, then I'll try to help . . ."

Gratefully she smiled at him, and saw him then with other eyes: a little older, sinewed with experience, handsome with lines which featured his face better than his features had done.

They drank the end of the wine in silence. The place, the memories . . . and in the aftermath of strong grief, when the soul convalesces, a pleasant subsidence. And John, looking at her face with its luminous skin, that transparent quality which she owed to her mother, thought: Nothing will ever equal for her those years in China. Not only because of Yong, but because it had been such a trove of grief and joy, of passion and horror lived.

He too was marked by his China experience. A ferment, a stir within, as if despite the inclement reality a halcyon paradise could still be reached one day . . .

"All men whore after a vision, Stephanie," he said.

"A vision," she said, her eyes distant. "It seemed almost an accomplishment at one time, in Yenan. But at present things seem to fall apart, so much has gone awry . . ."

"When the vision becomes illusion, Stephanie, the price is hard to pay."

It was bitterly cold. They walked, she in furs, John Moore in the leather parka which he had been using for fifteen years. The wind waited at each street intersection to nip the legs of walkers, and white steam rose from the grids over the subways.

"I'll cable someone I know in Hongkong," said John.

507

"Hongkong's just crawling with agents . . . someone's bound to know something about Yong."

They parted at the door of her building, he kissing her cheek, and then walking away.

Damn, damn, damn.

He strode, restless. He'd ring up one of the two girls he dated. Madeline was much in love with him and hoped to marry him. Perhaps marriage was a cure.

Stephanie.

Stephanie's face, in love.

"Damn," he swore, and struck his fist hard against an insentient wall.

"Dr. Jen Yong, rightist, is to be transferred from Peking to Lingfu, near Shenyang, province of Liaoning." The Party committee's decision.

Lingfu was a new town, yet unmarked on any map, in Manchuria. An industrial town. Coal mines, factories, iron works, a new steel plant. Forty thousand workers. Population one hundred thousand with their families. Most of the workers were under thirty-five years old. The population would swiftly increase.

Yong had a week to pack. Jen Ping came to help him, obtaining three days' leave from her job at the Institute of National Minorities. She arrived punctually at seven in the morning, and set to work. The furniture. Stephanie's belongings. The books. Everything had to be crated, to be sent to Shanghai.

Dr. Wu and Dr. Fan also came to see Yong. Despite the fear of being labeled "sympathizers with counter-revolutionary elements." Dr. Fan had had a letter from Dr. Liu, once upon a time Yong's good friend in Chungking, who had now been reunited with his childhood wife. "Tell Jen Yong: do not despair." This made Yong happy.

But Joan Wu did not come to see him, neither did Herbert Luger.

Herbert, in fact, now went about saying: "I always suspected those two . . . I'm glad the masses exposed them. . . ."

Peter Wellington came to say goodbye. "If there's anything I can do . . ."

Jen Yong thought, If he writes to Stephanie about what happened, she will worry.

"I ask you not to write to my wife about me," he said.

Peter said, "I understand."

Professor Chang Shou and his sons were not rightists. His worker son took a week's leave from his factory in Shanghai to come to Peking, to help Yong with his packing. "My son is very good with his hands," wrote Chang Shou. The son was indeed excellent with nails, hammer, planks. He procured a handcart and he and Yong, pushing and pulling, transported the crates to the railway station. To be sent to Shanghai.

It was now mid-November. Yong would leave in another three days. The postman came with a large bundle of letters, walked into the courtyard, said: "*Taifu*, I hope you will return soon, washed white as snow."

"Comrade Postman," said Yong. "I am glad to have this opportunity to serve our workers."

They both paused, with a "but" in the air. But your foreign loved one won't be able to live with you where you go now, thought the postman, and Yong knew that he thought it, and whitened to the lips.

He opened the packet of letters, neatly tied together. His hands shook. Stephanie's letters, nine in all. A telegram relayed through Hongkong. Eddy Keng had removed the American envelopes of the letters.

He read the telegram. Read and reread it. Then carried it and the letters, in both hands, into the bedroom, and like a child lay on the bed with his treasure.

Darling . . . I was wrong to go away . . . I long for news of you, for the sight of your handwriting . . . it is hard to have nothing, nothing, since I left in late July, and now it is almost November . . .

I was pregnant . . . didn't tell you, forgive me . . .

I was afraid, I imagined all kinds of terrible things happening, because I'd already lost a baby once . . .

I am going crazy, no word from you, only Eddy Keng telling me all is well, all is well.

The FBI always comes in twos; they all have the

same look, the same clothes. They always ask the same questions. . . . Their questions sound unreal, surrealist. They want me to make a statement that I've changed my mind, that I've given up "communism." I tell them I never was a Communist, that you are not a Communist, they cannot understand—for them if you live in Red China you're red. . . .

Yong, Daddy's died . . . died when Marylee was born. I'm enclosing a snap of the baby, she's premature, so she's in an incubator. . . .

A little girl. Marylee . . . His daughter.
Oh Stephanie, Stephanie, you went back to your country, taking with you my daughter.
Now you ask me to name her. I shall name her.
I could not tell you what was happening to me, Stephanie. I was afraid of upsetting you. I have written to you: All is well, do not worry. But it was not true, and lying is a terrible crime in America. Americans wax indignant about it, few of them have outgrown Washington and the cherry tree.
Yet perjury is sometimes blessed by Heaven. Do you remember that American poet, Donald Hall, we read together, who wrote: "I lived to tell the truth, and truth was wrong . . ."
I sent you messages, short letters, through Eddy Keng. They do not seem to have reached you.
Mother Huang called him to eat. He rose, he ate, and went back to his treasure upon the bed.

"I love you," Stephanie wrote. "Yet I was beginning to hate you . . . because I could no longer accept what was going on around us. . . ."
Spring Snow. That is why I let you go. Had I pleaded, held you back, I would have destroyed our love.
Everything is now very clear.
Only in your own country can you deploy your talent, become what you can be. Not in mine. Here a good deal of your gifts, your intelligence cannot be used.
He must write to tell her this. Tell her that she must not return.
In her world, all the advantages were on her side. She

510

would make her mark. She could not *avoid* success. In America. Affluent America. A world where the heating was too hot; where the pace was swift, of mind and body; where there were so many mechanical creations to satisfy every wish, caprice, desire, fancy . . . except the inmost heart, of course, the inmost heart which the frenzy of consuming, devouring, employing, using, purchasing, owning, would sometimes dessicate.

But every possibility of talent-stretching and mind-stretching lay in America.

Why, you could run Ryder Aircraft if you put your mind to it, Stephanie. But then, of course, you will have become another *Stephanie, not quite the one I knew and loved so much, but not altogether a different being either.*

If you return to China now, you cannot be more than half the person you are. Teaching English literature, "polishing" translations. Writing mediocre articles. And you would not be published, neither in China, where your writing would not be "revolutionary" enough, nor in your own country, where you would be considered a red and expunged from all the libraries.

He had no right in the name of love to gird her with bitterness, hedge her with meanness, take away from her the things she *could* do, the person she could become.

Evening was there and the moon swelling her arc already. He lit the lamp on the table which, with the two chairs and the bed, was all that remained of the furniture. He lived and slept in the unheated bedroom. He wrote. Wrote out his heart. And then, because he could not send what he wrote to Stephanie, he put it with all the other letters he had not sent, with the photographs he would take with him, and began a letter that any censor might read.

Spring Snow,

So many things have happened, and I could not distress you with conjecture. Have no anxiety for my physical or mental safety and health. A conclusion has been reached in the campaign. I am being transferred to another city, a new city, not on any map. I cannot send you the address, but my parents will redirect letters.

You left in July. In October some of us were labeled

511

rightists. I am one of them. But my error is deemed light since I continue to work as surgeon. The reason was my reactionary report on management of surgical units. Nothing else was mentioned, so do not worry.

My heart rejoices to know that we now have a daughter. I understand why you did not tell me. A mother has impulses stronger than logic or convention. I am glad that we shall have an American-Chinese daughter as well as a Chinese-American son. Our daughter will be proud of her double heritage, as is our son. That is how we decided that it should be.

Our daughter's name is Swallow. This is the name set down for her in the book of genealogy.

Spring Snow, you must not return until all is well, until the baby is well grown . . . I am full of pain as I write these words. They are like a sentence of death upon me. But our time is out of joint, and only dismay can come from forcing something which has now gone awry.

You will remember that way back in 1945, America and the New China in Yenan almost came together. Together they could remake the history of the world. The leaders in Yenan said then: "Only America can help us. Help us now, and we can become democratic more quickly, and modernize more easily . . ."

But terror seized America; terror of a vast Communist conspiracy. And then there was the Korean War, and now it will take many years for our countries to find their way back to each other again.

Meanwhile, our countries will both undergo their Calvary, though in different fashions. America will not even perceive that she suffers, because she is so superbly affluent, so endowed. China will only too obviously, too dolorously go through her agonizingly painful march to the future. On both sides many people will die, and many will be broken in mind.

I do not want you to be broken. It would serve no purpose. I want your happiness, but even more, the fullness of your life. And to preserve the crystal clearness of our love, and our passion too, passion the narrow filigree root of love's unfading moment.

The year draws coldly to its end. Already the mole crickets chirp by Mother Huang's stove. As soon as this letter is posted, I shall regret having written it. My soul will cry: "Come back, oh come back, only once, only once more, oh my heart, my darling, hear me . . . " I am twisting the knife in my own entrails writing: "Do not return. Not yet."

I shall go on waiting. Perhaps my waiting will soften the heart of Heaven.

Night has arrived. But morning will follow, and till morning comes I shall wait for you, in this life, in the next, in all our lives to be.

General Yee and Vice-Commissar Meng discussed possible rehabilitation for some of the rightists in a committee meeting.

Altogether, 450,000 of the five million-odd members of the intelligentsia were labeled "rightists."

"Too many, too many condemned," repeated Yee.

"The time is too early, General Yee," answered the committee chairman. "A campaign of wall posters by workers and peasants is in full swing, denouncing the rightists. It is not possible to rehabilitate now . . . it would only confuse the masses. . . ."

The committee dispersed. Yee and Meng stayed on. Meng said: "About Dr. Jen Yong . . . " bringing up the subject himself, without circumlocution, which meant that he favored doing something.

General Yee said: "I think that I shall begin to investigate a little. On my own."

"Meiling, you are in the Ministry of Health. Why did you not write in favor of Dr. Jen Yong?" Yee asked his daughter casually, sipping tea.

"Father, we were told to write only critical things about other people, not favorable ones."

"But other Party cadres have stuck their necks out for him, so far as I know."

Meiling plucked at her nails. "I have been much criticized myself. I could not intervene."

"You are becoming a good official," said Yee, with unusual asperity.

Yee went to see Old Sung, father of his son-in-law. Old Sung sat in his managerial office at the Friendship Hostel and greeted Yee rapturously.

"General, do come in, please sit, sit here, in this corner there is no draft." He poured tea, his face wrinkled with smiles. He looked like a small, kind monkey. How was it that Old Sung, so ripe with tolerance, had produced such an arrogant son? thought Yee. Always talking of class origin, making Meiling nervous about *her* class origin.

Old Sung chatted, chatted; Yee appeared to have all day before him. Sung talked of his troubles at Friendship Hostel. "Such a huge assembly of buildings. One gets tired running from one to the other. . . . So many foreigners, all wanting different things, all wanting everything immediately . . . the atmosphere becomes quite strained at times."

The Party committee of the Friendship Hostel had wanted to institute discipline. Doors locked at 9 p.m. And no man-woman relationships in the rooms by inmates unmarried to each other. "It did not work at all, not at all." There had been most violent rows. "Some of the people from fraternal countries possess very choleric elements in their bodies," sighed Old Sung. There had been three divorces; at least forty unmarried couples were living together, and uncounted others had swapped partners so that no one could keep track of the permutations and combinations. And the Russians loved to break glasses. "Our breakage bill is enormous, General Yee."

"Talking of morals," said Yee, "someone asserts that Lai Spring Snow, whom you know well, the loved one of Dr. Jen Yong, behaved very badly in Chungking and that it was known to the waiters of the Press Hostel . . ."

"That is not true," exclaimed Old Sung. "Not true at all. Comrade Lai is a straightforward girl. Of course she laughed and talked and went to dances, but she was chaste," said Old Sung. "And I was happy that she chose a Chinese man, one of us. She never had any man in her room for immoral purposes. . . ."

Yee left with a list of the names of the waiters at the Press Hostel. Old Sung had a very excellent memory.

As Yee talked, Meng took notes. Yee told him also how he had warned Henry Wong, then Chief Information Officer to the Kuomintang, to make sure that Stephanie should not write the story of her encounter in the slums. "Of course, at the time I was with the Kuomintang," explained Yee.

"Of course, what else?" replied Meng, not at all perturbed.

Meng had kept in mind that a "spontaneous" meeting in Yenan to discredit Lai Spring Snow had occurred *after* Chaste Wisdom's arrival. Her husband Sea Dragon had said: ". . . a relative, a waiter at the Press Hostel . . ."

Now Meng had a list of the waiters.

It was no longer a case of Jen Yong and Stephanie Ryder. It had nothing to do with the morals of Stephanie. Meng was on the track of something else.

"What was the name of that young man Lai Spring Snow struck?"

"Hsu," said Yee, "Hsu. I have forgotten the personal name. A Shanghai man. His father belonged to the same Triad society in Shanghai as Tai Lee and Chiang Kaishek."

Meng looked above his glasses at Yee. "There is one more thing to do. We must go to Dr. Jen Yong. He may tell us more."

"*Taifu*," said Mother Huang, "I come to train with you. I stay until your train is out of my eyes."

"Mother Huang, you harm yourself, staying to look after a rightist."

"And what face would I have before my ancestors and before your loved one if I do not keep my promise? I told the mistress: 'I shall look after *Taifu* till you return . . .'"

And then Mother Huang threw her apron over her face, and wept behind the screen of her apron, wept with her eyes wide open.

"Aiyah, aiyah, such a nice family, now scattered to the four horizons . . ."

Yong wept with her, letting the tears streak down. "Mother Huang, I'll never forget your kindness, never . . ."

A little later when Mother Huang had gone to the market and Yong was packing two boxes with the medical books he would take with him, there was a ring at the gate. He went to open it. A driver, burly, stood with his finger poised on the bell button. A big car blocked the *hutung*, it had brown

515

veiling at all its windows. In it sat a corpulent woman, a body of thick, hard flesh clad in jacket and trousers of fine dark cloth. She had pulled one of the curtains aside and stared at Yong.

"We are looking for No. 31," said the driver.

"This is No. 31."

The driver turned to the woman. "Top leader's lady, this is No. 31."

"I can see," said the woman, continuing to scrutinize Yong. "Ask this man who he is."

"What is your honorable name?" said the chauffeur, who had good manners.

"I am Dr. Jen Yong." Yong added perversely, "A rightist. If you wish to see the house, come in." He turned away and went back to his packing.

The bureaucracy was growing, growing, and good houses were rare. There was a big demand for housing.

The corpulent woman walked about, trying to look like an army commander. Probably the wife of an army commander. She peered in the empty rooms, stamped on the echoing floor. Went to the toilet, to the kitchen. Peered into the rice pot. Then she came to the bedroom, looked around, as if Yong did not exist.

"Ha, this house is not well kept. The courtyard is too crowded with trees. The house is very old-fashioned. The peach tree is too old. I will have to come down."

And then still louder, as Yong went on packing his books: "The house of a rightist. Needs a lot of cleaning to make it fit again . . ."

His last day in Peking. The train left at midnight. He would hire a pedicab to take the two boxes to the railway station. He would walk behind the pedicab with his bedroll pack and his suitcase. Mother Huang had prepared a last meal. Dumplings, a chicken she had bought out of her own wages. She had also put more food in a dish carrier, so that he had enough for two days. "You have a long journey and who knows whether you will be able to eat in the train." That was true. Supposing the restaurant waiters refused to serve him? Not that they would know he was a rightist, but they might *smell* it. An intellectual. Traveling alone. People developed an uncanny sense of who's who in such situations.

Again the door bell. Yong went to open.

"General Yee, you should not have come." With General Yee was a grizzled, thickset man, and Yong thought: Another army commander to see the house.

"I am a rightist," he said aloud, mechanically. It was almost a habit now. Shun me. I am a political leper.

"Rightist or not, we want some talk with you," said Yee.

The grizzled man held out his hand. "You came to my guerilla unit, during the war with Japan, in 1945 . . ."

They stood in the courtyard and talked.

"Dr. Jen," said Meng. "You must tell us exactly what happened in Chungking, that day when your loved one, Lai Spring Snow, brought the woman from the slums. You must tell us everything. This is very important."

"Swallow, my darling," said Stephanie, feeding Marylee some baby food with a spoon. "Oh dear," said Stephanie to her voracious daughter. "You're going to be enormous!" She hugged the baby, laughing, kissing her. Swallow was now so sturdy, no one would have thought she had been premature. And how she bawled! Swallow. A beautiful name.

Yong's letters had come, at last, at last, a batch of them; also a batch from Winter Treasure, in a mixture of English and Chinese. "Mama-mama, you went away, to make me a little sister. Mama you must bring little sister when she is strong enough. Grandmother tells me that I have to be patient because little sister is very small, not strong. Mama, mama, I do so want to see your face, and to see the face of little sister, but I will be patient. Because *Tietie* has become a rightist the school did not want me to stay. But Teacher Fan has made them keep me. She said: 'Children should not suffer because of their parents.' Mama, I will be good. I will always be good now, and obedient. Then all will be well again and you will come back."

Winter Treasure's letter tore at her heart. "Oh John," she sobbed, "he's blaming himself for what's happened. I can't bear it. I can't. I *must* go back. I can't do this to him."

John said: "Stephanie, I can assure you that your son won't feel the trauma an American child might feel. Please trust the Jen Family. They will cope."

She was not to return. Yong had told her not to return

517

immediately. There must be a reason. *I won't cry. I won't cry.* Fiercely she hugged Swallow. And wept in utter desolation.

A door beating in her. A slammed door, tugged by the wind. There is no space but the space of sorrow now.

Time leafed its days through the spring.

Swallow grew strong, and began to bubble: "Mama, Mama."

And Stephanie grew out of desolation.

She had no passport. But with money one can do a great many things. She could smuggle herself out to Canada, or to Mexico. Money bought everything, everything, and she had money. Provided she avoided American consulates, and U.S. airlines, she could get herself to Europe, to France. To Sweden. From Sweden back to China.

She walked a great deal around New York. She was healing. Felt it in her, urgent strength, headstrong vitality. Sprouting in all directions. Wild.

The winter had gone, spring shed its petal hours and she listened to a great deal of music. The FBI no longer bothered her. They came only about every two weeks. But they kept her under watch. Her phone continued to be tapped. Her passport and impounded papers were still withheld, although the photographs had been returned.

Enjoy the season, lift your head,
Take your delight in momentariness . . .

Stephanie paced the streets. Returned to pace her living room. It was beautiful, with damask silk on the walls, and uncluttered furniture. She watched through the windows that particular splendor which comes to New York just before twilight.

Life went on.

There was Yong, and Winter Treasure. There was that endlessly changing country, China, with its unpredictable tumults. What would the next upheaval bring?

There was also another Stephanie. Growing, sprouting out of what she had been, what she had learnt, accumulated.

The mild warm air of May clasped the trees of the city, its buildings and enchanted spires.

And her body yearned, yearned in the way sap flows, buds burst, and the skeleton heart clothes itself in desire.

He has told me not to return. He has his reasons. His reasons are not mine. I must live with them, and with my own.

"Stephanie, would it make you unhappy to eat in a Chinese restaurant?"

"I don't think so, John. I often crave Chinese food; we had such excellent cooks. . . ." Quickly she shifted the landscape of her mind, not to fall back. She'd just heaved herself out of despondency.

The Scholar was elegant, with silk curtains, subdued wallpaper, paintings on the walls. It had a select clientele of diplomats from the adjacent United Nations. A press of elegant waiters assured a noiseless service. The only concession to American taste were the knives and forks, discreetly disposed—eating with chopsticks was still considered an exotic achievement. In the lobby was a large painted portrait of Chiang Kaishek, complete with mustache, baldness hidden in unctuous shading.

"Don't let that mug of his disturb you," said John. "In Chinatown all the restaurants hang his picture. Otherwise the local Kuomintang send rowdies to break up their kitchens. There's an apocryphal story going around that Mao's portrait is on the reverse . . . they'll just turn the picture over when the time comes."

"Aaaaah, my friend, my friend John, welcome!"

A mellow baritone, a portly man, arms extended. "And Stephanie Ryder. Welcome! Aaaaah!"

Henry Wong, beaming, a little overweight, shook their hands with genuine rapture.

"Stephanie Ryder, or should I say Mrs. Jen. Oh, this is the third happiest day of my life . . ." He seized John's arm, repeating, "My good, very good friend," led them to a table in a corner, under shaded lights. "So good to see you. I'll call Meena, she'll be so happy." He bounded towards the kitchen, while waiters produced beautifully laundered linen napkins, tea, and the usual iced water for Americans.

Meena came out in a white gown, like a doctor, and embraced Stephanie with squeaks of joy. "Oh such a long time, such a long time," she said, and her eyes brimmed.

She also had put on weight, her hair shone like lacquer, her face was round and young.

The dinner was succulent, a genuine Chinese meal, Henry ordering it and chopsticks being provided. Tea from Henry's own special store. "Comes from the mainland, the best, smuggled to Hongkong." He smiled mischievously, a small boy enchanted with a practical joke. "The only thing we do not provide is milk. Can you believe it, some Americans want to drink *milk* with their food!" For Henry Wong, gourmet, this was first-degree crime.

After the food he insisted on a nightcap in their own apartment, in the same building above the restaurant. "It's better for business to be always on the spot." Henry did not tell them that he now owned the building.

He had a large assortment of liqueurs and brandies. "Remember Chungking? My last bottle of brandy went on V-J Day," Henry reminisced. Chungking. The dirt, the heat . . .

"I'm a professor now. Political science. It's easy to be a professor in indefinites such as political science. Many Americans think if we're anti-Communist we *must* be endowed with special wisdom in politics." Henry had managed to stay neutral between the monstrous rocks of demagoguery. "Neutrality is genius. The Greeks were doing it all the time. They were civilized. I feel like Ulysses, too. I've had my Odyssey. Now I grow old. Taiwan's promised me a ministry if I go back; but I don't want to see Peanut again."

He helped in the restaurant on weekends and on holidays, otherwise he taught at Columbia, and occasionally at Yale.

"Stephanie, what about you?" asked Meena. And Stephanie told them, not avoiding the truth of that somewhat offhand disaster which was the wreck of her love. And speaking to these people whose lives were the salvage of a foundering, who had lost everything yet had created new selves, made the best of calamity without self-pity, she discovered a different proportion to her grief, another measure with which to measure its event. Tragedy lived with, de-dramatized, became the mainspring for something new.

The Wongs distilled around them that atmosphere of equanimity she had needed. Once outside, back in the

American street, Stephanie might become engulfed again in her own preoccupation, that anxiety she tried to hush.

"I'm afraid we Americans feel more easily shattered by what happens to one than you do," she said, almost apologetic.

"We can't *afford* the luxury of too much sorrow," said Meena. "We have to go on living."

Henry said, a little ponderously: "Your husband is a noble man, Stephanie. He loves his country, and he loves you. He has seen clearly for you. He does not wish you to be frustrated in China. He knows that he can't provide you with the opportunities you have here."

"What do you think I should do?"

"You should do the most intelligent thing. Which is to prepare the future. For your children."

"I won't give him up, Henry."

"Who talked of giving him up?" said Henry, surprised. "Of course not, Stephanie. But to go back *now* would be most frustrating. Foolish."

"We're not giving up," said Meena. "We'll go back *one day*."

"I don't think Chiang Kaishek will reconquer the mainland," said John. "Though he makes a lot of noise about it at the moment."

Said Henry: "Chiang will not reconquer anything. But things will change. By the way, the reds *are* talking with Old Peanut. Chiang Kaishek's third concubine is living in Shanghai. She's the go-between for them."

John slapped his forehead. "And here we are, talking of protecting Taiwan, Free China, and Chiang is screwing around!"

"You need a myth, you have it," said Henry comfortably, as if that settled the matter. He turned to Stephanie. "Put in a request to Peking, saying you do not give up your husband. That you are his wife and have a son in China. That you understand you cannot return *at the moment*. But that you don't give up."

"At the moment may last a long time, and what's the use of my writing: I don't give up?"

"So they'll know you're sticking to him," said Meena. "It's moral support. If you don't write, someone will say you've gone away because he was condemned as a rightist."

Yong my dearest,

After thirteen years, love had left me unarmored, a city without walls or weaponry. I now bend to a remaking of myself. Do I want to be with you? Yes. But once I am back with you, I shall regret what I left here.

Our summer of love would breed us no increase, and we might turn away from each other, in discord not of our choosing. You are right. I must not return at the moment.

I reknit my fragments into some coherence. I remember the porcelain shards upon the floor, the day you broke that bowl you loved so much. You have released me from the thrall of love, to become another me. But I am not released. I do not think I can be cured.

Around my neck your mother put a necklace of jade with gold links. A necklace handed down in your Family. And told me that I was her true successor.

I must begin to do what has to be done, in a world where dissimilar storms blow their particular destruction. Plan for our children's fulfillment. When what seems now most hostile will be welcome, what is now unreason will be reason.

Now let me write about America. America is changing. Americans do not take well to tyranny. The Internal Security Act still "legalizes" many things which are illegal according to the Constitution. The Subversive Activities Control Board set up by the act still holds Congress in fear of voting against it. But there is hope.

The Supreme Court has crippled the witch hunt. On June 17, 1957, a few days after the hundred flowers which seemed to promise so much began to wilt, the Court struck a great blow for a saner America. And despite the FBI, Hoover, and John Foster Dulles, Jack Service was again cleared. The Court voted unanimously in his favor against Secretary of State Dulles.

In my case, despite harassment by the FBI, despite the ignominious behavior of some members of the press, despite ugliness and fear, I will fight. Only by fighting can I help to make America healthy again.

China is a giant dragging itself up by its bootstraps out of poverty. We shut our eyes to the needs of this giant. But there is a strange logic coming out of these events. Our businessmen are grumbling: Why are we cutting ourselves off from the biggest market in the world?

I, like you, shall wait. Wait and work where I can work out a tolerable answer. I am not giving up.

In the flattering interviews which were heaped upon her in later years, she would say with a slight smile: "It all began in May 1958. When I decided that I would begin by learning something about my father, Heston Ryder, and his business."

In May 1958 Stephanie had flown back to Dallas from New York.

The firm of Casey, Hull and Ritchie, Heston Ryder's high-powered lawyers, awaited her with some trepidation.

The lawyers saw a slim, elegant woman walk into their offices, not the revolutionary maverick they expected. In clothes that made every other fashionable woman look over-dressed. No jewelry save a necklace, half hidden by the collar of her silk blouse. She smiled at them with instant friendliness, so that they felt both challenged and flattered. She listened quietly as they told her the provisions of the will.

Heston's will was unambiguous. A large amount of money in trust funds, in favor of Stephanie and her children. Sizable chunks of real estate, oil and other company stock to Stephanie. And a controlling interest as a major shareholder in Ryder Aircraft to Stephanie.

To Isabelle, Heston had left a considerable annuity, properties in Provence, on the Côte d'Azur, two apartments in Paris, one apartment in New York.

Isabelle had returned to France. There was no break between her and her daughter. But Heston's death had deprived them of both collusion and contention. The stress was eased, detached affection remained—satisfactory enough, requiring no effort.

The bulk of Heston's wealth was left to Stephanie. The large and the smaller house in Dallas; other properties in Houston and San Antonio; the oil land and its revenues. "I don't expect my daughter to do a man's job, I expect her to do better." Those were the last words in his will.

Mr. Casey, the senior partner in the legal firm, looked like Allen Dulles. He obviously disapproved of Stephanie. Hull and Ritchie were gazing at her with masculine interest, an evident desire to please. She decided to trust Casey.

"Mr. Casey, I do not know anything about business. I shall have to learn. I shall expect you to help me as you helped my father."

There was the matter of her father's employees. Heston had remembered them all, with annuities and cash gifts. Including the servants and the cowhands.

"Will you tell them," said Stephanie, "that if they wish to continue with me, I shall be most happy to employ them. Should they wish to leave, let them come and tell me, or telephone. I shall be in my home every morning from 8 to 11 a.m."

The auditors, the accountants, the banks . . .

Stephanie rose. "I intend to continue the work my father began. It will take me time. I shall make Dallas my main home."

Heston's library. Shelves of books; acres of them. Rows of scientific and business magazines. Doggedly, night after night, she went through them.

American business had also been crippled by the witch hunt.

All over America, businessmen were protesting that industrial and scientific progress was hampered by the security and loyalty checks, the snooping, the scares, the harassment. The terror generated among scientists. Many of the eminent scientists blacklisted were essential to American industry. Yet they were not allowed to work in aircraft, in nuclear projects, in other sensitive industries. A vast search for brains in Europe began, to replace the Americans hobbled by security checks.

"Industry is encountering considerable trouble and expense in handling its programs of personnel, physical and document security . . ." a report read. The witch hunt finally stopped at the factory door. Scientists, barred as security risks from government employment, were hired by private industry.

But government employees, from high to low, continued to be kept under constant surveillance. A loyalty case could never be *res judicata*, settled by the courts. The employee must be subject to new checks at any time "even though he may have emerged clean and clear from a score of investigations and as many hearings" wrote the Internal Security Subcommittee. Thus confirming its total illogic.

A lot of talent lying around, thought Stephanie. And talent, inventive capacity, was the rarest element of all.

She consulted her father's files. Heston had kept files, tabs, on all of America's scientists. On anyone who made a mark, who had an original idea. Even on so-called crackpots. She pored over them. She consulted Miss Birnbaum. Miss Birnbaum at first had wanted to resign on the ten-thousand-dollar gift and the life annuity Heston had given her. But Miss Birnbaum was also a romantic. When she came to tell Stephanie she would be leaving, there was Marylee being fed, her black hair already thick, gurgling with laughter all to herself. Miss Birnbaum heard herself saying: "I'll stay and help you, if you'd like me to."

Heston Ryder had wanted to create an organization whose main reason for existence would be devising new apparatus, new techniques, trying new ideas. A technology think-tank.

Miss Birnbaum assembled the papers, the letters, the list of names. "Mr. Ryder wrote to Dr. Clauwaitz; they were going to meet. Dr. Clauwaitz is a biologist."

"I'll see him."

She needed people around her she could trust. Not necessarily only experts. People who would hunt out brains and talent for her.

Dick Steiner. Eddy Keng. To begin with.

The telephone was still being tapped. She knew herself still under FBI surveillance. But she was no longer terrorized, miserable, afraid.

Not one of her friends in Dallas had called. Except John Webster and Dr. Padrewski. The latter to talk of the Ryder wing of the hospital.

"I intend to carry on as my father would have done. Let me know what is needed."

At noon the air was all cicada stridency and the sun a burst diamond in the sky. Under the full oak and camphor trees Stephanie walked the cool shade.

Power came to her. Dad had spoken of power coming to him "through the soles of my feet." In his youth he had paced the earth, and the boon of a fertile mind had been his. Stephanie paced the soil of Texas, and felt her mind moving.

At night the garden was fairylike under the milk-pale stars. Winter Treasure. He loved looking at the stars. His small toy telescope. He must one day look at the universe. With the best telescope in the world.

Light from the universe, falling on earth, falling in the net of men's eyes. Man's future was in space, in the stars, the last frontier of man.

Heston had listed the brains in astronomy, in space research; those employed, those blacklisted. For in that sector too there had been depredations.

"Miss Birnbaum, get me Dr. Hollingworth in Pasadena."

Electronic tubes. The first American computer, *Eniac*, was functioning, but there was more to come.

There had been the "numbers barrier" handicap. Complex electron tube circuits had a very short life, were difficult to assemble and maintain, and costly. But then in 1947 the transistor had been invented, and the way, via the semiconductor, to microprocessors was opened.

She would go into that field. Electronics, microelectronics, the new technological Revolution, changing society and changing man.

Camilla Waring, Brooklyn, New York. Through a private investigator, Stephanie finally obtained Camilla's address. She flew to New York one weekend. It seemed to her very important to restore Camilla.

Camilla lived in a small apartment in Brooklyn with her two children, ages twelve and fourteen. "Yes, do come, Stephanie, if you wish," she said when Stephanie telephoned.

A shabby building, a neglected environment. Houses

due for demolition. Camilla opened the door. "Stephanie . . . It's three floors up, there's no elevator." Her forearms were bare, the muscles showed under the skin. She was stringy all over.

The living room was small, with well-used furniture, posters, sneakers in a corner, a huddle of music records. Camilla went to the kitchen. "Cup of coffee? I baked a cake. D'you want a piece or are you dieting? Everyone is."

"I'm not. I'd love some cake and coffee."

Camilla, at the kitchen range, turned to look at Stephanie. The well-cut suit, unobtrusively expensive. Something like a frown came upon her face.

"How did you find me?"

Stephanie wanted to tell her, and then refrained. "Tell you some other time. How've you been?"

"As you can see. Not too good since Gene killed himself."

"Camilla! I didn't know."

"It was partly your fault, Stephanie."

"Mine? But that can't be true . . . Camilla, please . . ."

"Remember, you came to see us. You stayed with us one night. We were protesting about that professor . . . what's his name? . . ."

"Woodward. He'd written a book about Russian poetry. He was subpoenaed for un-American activities. . . ."

"I didn't tell you. Gene was on a hush-hush job. Government contract. They started on him right after you left . . . A security risk. He lost his job. And then he went through clearance tests. And then they began on me. The FBI went through all our things. Books, letters. Found your letters. We were Communist sympathizers, they said. And then one of our classmates, Rina Bowring, you remember her, we called her Rabbit, perjured herself. Said I belonged to the Communist Party. Mentioned *you* as contact. Mythomaniac. The student newspaper with which I was involved was stopped. Editor supposed to be a Communist Party member.

"We moved. Gene got another job. Then there was the Korean War. Lost his job again. And again. The FBI didn't stop hounding us . . ." Camilla talked in a dull metallic voice, enumerating facts.

"We moved again. Gene got another job. Lost it. We'd get to a new place and get set up and there they were. They kept on. All our money was gone. And then Gene again had to appear before some subcommittee. And one day he couldn't take it anymore. By that time the kids were out at school in California with my father, and I was working as a salesgirl at Macy's. I sold underwear. Gene was a night watchman, that's all they'd let him do.

"He tried to make it look like an accident. Drove himself down to Long Island. Hired a boat. He couldn't swim. But he messed it up somehow. Autopsy proved he'd taken some sleeping pills before drowning . . ."

"Camilla, oh, my dear, how dreadful, how utterly dreadful . . ."

Camilla stared at the wall. She looked forty. Her face was creased, and she had brown patches under her eyes.

"It's easier if one's got money, Stephanie. We didn't have any. Gene's family was poor. They threatened his father, who was Polish, with denaturalization. . . . He'd been over here thirty years. My mother got cancer and that took all of Dad's savings. Anyway, a professor of literature isn't very affluent. . . ."

"Camilla, I'm going to help you."

Camilla wiped her face with her hands. Her wide generous mouth twisted. "I'm sorry, Stephanie. I'm being silly. It wasn't your fault. It's just the system. Now the kids are growing up, but I'm worried. I'm worried if anything happened to me, who'd look after them."

"Camilla. I need you, need your help, need people I can trust around me. Will you come and work with me?"

She sketched her plan. To start her own business. Go around hunting for brains. Brain power. Talent. There was a lot of it in America. Technology. But also other things. Anything. And no race or color bar.

Camilla said: "But I'm on the lists of the House Committee on Un-American Activities."

"To hell with the committee," said Stephanie. "They won't touch private business."

They discussed the enormous powers of the committee. The committee's Congressional hearings, in the full glare of publicity, did not follow the guarantees of procedure which safeguarded individual rights.

"The committee sits as a kangaroo court and tries the victims for their loyalty, their political beliefs, or simply for their personal behavior," said Camilla.

"They won't touch you now," said Stephanie. She rose,

brisk, assured. "We'll fight this together, Camilla. Fight it *my* way. And you can help others, others who've suffered as you have. Just think it over."

She flew back to Dallas. And felt both triumphant and ashamed. She would fight. With money. Because she could do a great deal with the salve of money. Money really did change many things, in many ways. She would use money.

twenty-three

LINGFU New Town had a railway station, a lizardy main road full of crevices, smoke-choked factories which hummed with unstopping machinery, and clusters of four-story gray brick apartment houses for workers.

Just beyond those houses began the slag mountains from the coal mine of a steel plant. A pall of smog, sometimes russet, often black, from Lingfu's belching chimney stacks hung over the town.

It was almost midnight when Yong stepped onto the railway platform. A thin furious man rushed at him shouting: "I'm Dr. Szeto, in charge of Lingfu hospital. You're late, five hours late."

"The train . . ."

"Don't argue. You've no right to talk, you're a rightist." Szeto turned, walked off, leaving Yong to carry his two boxes, his bedroll, and suitcase.

Yong said: "I cannot carry all my gear."

Szeto glared venomously: "We are proletarians here. We walk."

"Is there a handcart?"

The stationmaster had a handcart and agreed to loan it. "The rightist will return it immediately," shouted Szeto. Fury was a perpetual state with him.

The main road was uneven with mud frozen into hard ruts. Needles of frost stung Yong's face. There were no street lights, but an indistinct gleam behind some windows showed the night shift workers were up.

Szeto entered a gray building. A smell of urine, all-pervasive, filled the hall, the staircase. He led the way to a small room, on the fourth floor, under the roof. There was no stove, no heating of any kind. A single bulb suspended by its wire from mid-ceiling. A narrow iron bed, table, and chair.

"This is your room."

Yong unrolled his bedroll, laid it on the sagging carcass of the bed, went to the small window, thick with dirt, which gave onto a high brick wall. The room would be dark, day and night. Yong was shaking with fatigue. Three days on the train. But he must return the handcart before he could sleep. The watchman downstairs waited to lock the main door after his return.

He came back, fell into a torpor, heard the clatter of doors, a running water tap, and woke. It was still very dark. He found the toilet, which was filthy. The plumbing did not work. A washroom nearby dripped its faucets of cold water.

He dressed, walked downstairs, finding the small dining room on the first floor next to the kitchen. A dozen round tables. Four men, in grubby white gowns, were eating breakfast at one of them. They were the doctors. At three others sat women and men, presumably the nurses. Lower hospital staff at other tables. Separation by rank. No place for Yong, the rightist. He waited, standing. One table became vacant and he sat. The young waiter who collected the dirty plates and bowls said: "You want to eat?"

"Yes, comrade."

The waiter went to the kitchen. The cook came out to look at the rightist. He had a huge protruding white eye. A cataract, now petrified stone.

The waiter came back with steamed bread, gruel, pickles. And then, reticently, a bowl of beancurd milk.

"Comrade, this is very good," said Jen Yong, surprised.

"The cook. He says he knows you."

Yong swallowed the beancurd milk, feeling its velvety warmth enter his stomach, and wondered about the cook. And then a furious voice at his back was screeching: "Still eating? I will not have this laziness . . . we start work right now." Szeto, white-gowned, a stethoscope around his neck.

"If I do not eat I shall not be able to work," said Yong, emboldened by the beancurd milk.

Szeto's mouth worked with rage. "You dare to argue," he shouted. "I will teach you to obey, cut off your arrogant capitalist tail . . ."

531

The first ten days were utterly vile.

Szeto gave Yong no respite. Insulted him in front of the patients, the doctors, the nurses. Put him on call at night. Made him clean the wards, the spittoons, and the bedpans. Sweep the corridors. Clean and wash the patients. And constantly harried him. "Rightist Jen Yong, come here . . . clean this mess . . ."

And Jen Yong remembered Old Wang, who through dedication had cleaned spittoons and bedpans for years, and lived in a filthy rat-infested basement. *I must have equal fortitude.*

He discovered the appalling state of the hospital.

Workers who needed operations, accident cases, lay untreated. Szeto's only remedy was a glucose saline drip. When they became too ill, they were sent home to die. Tuberculous cases were bedded in the same wards as other patients. A young worker with a broken back had been there for two weeks. No attempt had been made to put him in a cast. His legs were becoming paralyzed. Yet they could have been restored to function, had he been in plaster. . . . A cancer of the throat, slowly dying of suffocation, was sent home with some licorice. A young boy with an intussusception was given a laxative. . . .

The other four doctors were young, inexperienced. Recent graduates, sent here after six months' internship. Szeto terrorized them.

The maternity annex was overcrowded. The two midwives were competent enough, but an obstetrician was needed. "Doctor" Szeto said there was no need for one.

One hundred thousand souls in Lingfu. Many young people. Many babies being born.

From the hospital windows Yong stared at the mountains of slag. They kept growing. One day they might slip, bury the houses at their foot. Why had the workers' houses been built there?

One night a young doctor scratched at his door softly.

"Dr. Jen, my name is Teng. I have heard of you . . . I read your articles on surgery, before I came here. . . . You were famous. . . ."

"I am a rightist," said Yong.

Teng said: "My fiancée's father has also been 'hatted,' labeled a rightist. He was in education . . . a Party member. As I am. And now my fiancée will not marry me, because it would harm my career to marry the daughter of a rightist . . ." His eyes became red, but he sounded resigned.

Teng had graduated that June and been assigned to Lingfu. "I thought: To serve the workers of a new industrial town is a great task . . . I was enthusiastic. . . . But Szeto is not a doctor. He was a peasant 'wizard.' He used remedies handed down by his father who was a necromancer." Szeto had had six months' training in some provincial hospital and was then called "doctor." He came to Lingfu and as there was no one else here at the time, he became chief of the hospital.

"He is a dangerous madman," said Yong.

Four days later the three other medical men had come to Jen Yong's room.

"We cannot let things go on like this," said Yong. "We must write to the Health Department."

The others were frightened. "Don't mention us . . . we cannot associate with you. . . ."

"I shall not mention you."

Szeto heard of the doctors going to Jen's room. And decided to finish off the rightist.

One afternoon, as Yong was treating a young worker's bed sores, Szeto was there.

"You, rightist Jen. You're a surgeon, I have some cases for you to operate on. Immediately."

The operating theater was small, ill-lit, dirty. Yong stared at the autoclave. Was it functioning properly? What about sterile gowns, gloves? The nurses? The anesthetist?

On a bench outside the operating theater five people waited. They wore their own clothes, and on top of them hospital jackets and trousers.

"Two hernias, one case of hemorrhoids, one gallbladder. Dr. Teng will assist you. I shall watch to see that you do no sabotage, do not harm our beloved workers."

"I refuse to operate," said Yong.

"You refuse?"

"These patients are not prepared. I have not seen them. I don't know if they are fit for surgery."

Szeto was happy. Yong had fallen in the trap. "You are here to be reeducated, to submit to the masses, yet you refuse to work. . . ."

Patients had seeped into the corridor from the wards. Nurses appeared. Szeto turned to them: "You heard, all of you. The rightist insolently refuses to serve the masses. He must be struggled against . . . call a meeting to struggle against unrepentant rightist Jen Yong!"

The next afternoon the hospital assembled for the struggle meeting. Yong had been kept in his room. But the young waiter had come to give him a bowl of noodles. "Comrade cook says: 'Even rightists must eat.'"

There were around a hundred people jammed into the meeting room. Doctors, nurses, hospital staff, workers' representatives of the factories and the steel plant. Also the head of the Health Department for Lingfu New Town, Comrade Go.

Comrade Go was unhappy about this struggle meeting. His wife was one of the two midwives, and for over a year she had told him that Dr. Szeto was a danger, that the patients were not getting proper care. "The workers are not stupid. The young know that something is very wrong . . . several times we have had to explain to workers when the baby or the mother died. . . ." Comrade Go's wife had become very nervous and thin in Lingfu.

Szeto began a long denunciation of Yong. "Dr. Jen Yong has a big capitalist tail on him. He is arrogant and conceited. It is up to the masses to humble him, so that he confesses his crimes." Szeto always screamed. He could never just talk.

"Confess your crimes, stinking rightist," shouted one of the nurses, and the others took it up.

"Confess, confess! You dirty stinking rightist!"

Yong looked around him. Anger, long repressed, dammed to bursting point, now welled out of him. What more could he lose, except life itself? And what did he care now about living? Stephanie was safe, and Winter Treasure too, in Shanghai. But all his life Winter Treasure would have a shadow on him: the son of a rightist. He would be disqualified for university, for good jobs; even marriage would be a problem.

He stood straight as his father, and joyous as his father was under stress. Joy to be able to vomit his anger at last, spew it into the faces of those who persecuted him. Joy, happiness, not to worry about bringing woe to anyone else . . . nothing worse could happen now.

"I refused to obey Szeto, because I did not want to commit murder. It would be murder to operate under the conditions of Szeto. This hospital does not serve the people. All Szeto wants is that nobody should die in 'his' hospital. He does not treat anyone. He sends the patients home to die. No operations have been done in this hospital, and now, suddenly Szeto wants me to operate on patients he has chosen. If they die he will say I killed them . . ."

He pointed his finger at Szeto: "I have been here twenty days. I have seen these things done. Kill me if you wish . . . Send me to work in the coal mine. I prefer to dig coal. Digging coal is noble. I shall be proud to be a worker, digging coal. But to wear a white coat, and pretend to heal people, is to cheat them. Szeto is cheating you. He is not a doctor."

There was a stunned silence and then a murmur began. Low, and then swelling. Discordant. But the nurse who had first spoken began her prepared litany: "Beat the dog down!" And other nurses took it up, as a chorus.

"Beat the dog down!"

"He insults the Party."

"He insults the workers, the masses!"

"Let him never show his evil face in daylight anymore!"

Yong was taken back to his room. He heard the screamed slogans as he walked upstairs between two male nurses, who held his arms. Perhaps he would be sent to work in the coal mine. Probably without any salary. Perhaps for the rest of his life.

Health Department Chief Go woke up the next morning feeling queasy. He had been very upset about the struggle meeting. His digestion suffered. He felt feverish.

He swallowed some gruel, and then took some Chinese medicine to appease the heart.

The masses had condemned Jen Yong. And one was enjoined "never to pour cold water upon the red-hot fervor of the masses." That was the Party line.

Rightist Jen had indeed said very bad things about the

535

hospital. It also reflected upon him, Go. Upon his administration . . .

Now it was up to the Party committee to decide what
punishment to deal out to the rightist.

"But he is telling the truth," said Go's wife. She had
nagged him last night, nagged him since daylight. "You
cannot send Jen Yong to labor. You have to refer the case to
upper level. Otherwise there may be big problems one
day."

In his room, Yong wrote to Stephanie. Perhaps this would
be his last letter to her.

Spring Snow,

All is well with me, so please do not worry. I shall be
very busy in this new city, and not able to write
frequently. But I love you, and this is my happiness.
To love you. I am awake with tenderness, thinking of
you, and of our little daughter, and so happy that you
are safe, that you are well . . .

Department Chief Go vomited. He had much pain in the
belly, and he felt alternately hot and shivery.

He telephoned the hospital, asked for his wife. "Please
come home, I'm not well."

She came back and took his temperature. 101.4°.

"I'd better call the hospital," she said. "It could be appendicitis."

"Not Szeto," said Go, "not Szeto."

Now that his own life was concerned, he knew that Szeto
was a menace.

"But it's the regulations . . ."

Szeto came swiftly, with Dr. Teng. He put his hands on
Go's belly, then on his forehead. Listened to his heart with
his stethoscope. He asked, "Are you constipated?"

"The last two days."

"Then it is nothing. I'll give you a laxative, you'll soon be
all right."

"No, no." Go remembered the boy who had died after
Szeto's laxative. It had provoked much comment among the
workers.

536

"Dr. Szeto, I think it is an inflamed appendix," said Go's wife.

Szeto's fury rose but he checked himself. Suppose it really was an appendix? He might have to operate.

"I do not think it is an appendix . . . he has eaten something very bad, perhaps poison, which is causing this pain."

Dr. Teng in turn examined Go, and then said: "I think it could be acute appendicitis, Dr. Szeto."

Szeto said: "I am not a surgeon. You will operate then, Dr. Teng."

Then Go became suddenly very brave. "Call Dr. Jen. I want Dr. Jen to see me," he said.

Vice-Commissar Meng sat with furrowed brow, his eyes protected by a green eyeshade. Late night, but he could not sleep. He peered at his little notebook, and sighed.

Jen Yong had confirmed General Yee's story. Stephanie had indeed struck a man, a Major Hsu, of the Kuomintang Secret Police in Chungking.

Meng thought of Hsu Build-the-City. The only suspicious thing about him was the way he handled his chopsticks. Not at all in the way of a poor man who had eaten bitterness.

My Old Partner, thought Meng. She won't believe me.

When he was young, and the world simple, and revolution bright, he had fallen in love while training a girls' militia regiment in the village where he was quartered. Little Lo, Small Turnip, was the only girl who could never manage to hit the target, even by accident. Every time her shot went wild, she laughed uproariously, showing magnificent white teeth. Her lips were very red.

Everyone approved of their marrying, since both had good class origin. Poor peasants.

His blood still stirred, remembering those young nights when the untutored flesh knew what to do, bold in the darkness. Delight. Delight to make children out of that sturdy, responsive body. Yet they had never said one word, hinted at the pleasure they gave to each other at night.

War. Separation. Sorrow. They had shared so much. But

he could not share this matter with her. And if he pursued it, it might do her great harm.

For if Hsu, and Tsui Sea Dragon, and Bo Chaste Wisdom were Kuomintang agents, then Comrade Lo would be severely criticized for her lack of vigilance, for having trusted them.

And supposing the whole story was a fantasy, coincidence. Then he, Comrade Meng, would be in trouble. Slander against reliable comrades in the Party, based on the tale of a flighty American woman and her rightist husband!

What a muddle, what a mess.

Ha, how difficult it is to be an upright man!

Sighing heavily, Meng took up his brush and began to write a report to the Public Security officer. Very courageously, he signed the report, but did not indicate his rank, nor his address.

Again the restless land was astir.

It had begun in November 1957, when Chairman Mao Tsetung went to Moscow to talk to the Kremlin leaders.

Mao Tsetung and Chou Enlai had perceived in Khrushchev's speeches, in Khrushchev's wholesale condemnation of Stalin, not a "liberalization," but a trick. A bid to become "respectable." To soften the United States.

The Soviet Union was flexing its muscles. For total power. First woo the credulous Americans with words of "peace." Peaceful coexistence. If need be, use China as the whipping boy; talk of Chinese belligerence. The yellow peril. Then build up Soviet power, until it would equal, then surpass America's.

Khrushchev was angered when Mao asserted that there were "contradictions" between the people in a socialist state and the Communist Party in power. That there could even be contradictions between socialist states. "There cannot be," Khrushchev declared. Once "contradictions" were admitted between "socialist brothers," or within a socialist state, then how would the Soviet Union control its satellites in Eastern Europe? And what about the 1956 revolts in Poland and in Hungary?

The Soviet Union now pressured China for repayment of all the debts incurred for the Korean War, of all the aid given in the first five-year plan of 1952-1957. Repayment to be in food, in rare metals, at prices arbitrarily fixed by Moscow.

And there was no way out for China. The U.S. embargo was on. "Never, never shall we recognize the red regime," proclaimed John Foster Dulles.

And that is when the Great Leap Forward was conceived. An attempt to do without any help, from anywhere. *To accelerate* economic progress. Using China's only available wealth: manpower.

"We are going to speed up our modernization," Comrade Lo said to her office staff. Her eyes shone as she pinned to the wall of the office, and read aloud, the guidelines of the Leap:

To carry out the technological revolution together with the socialist revolution; to develop industry and agriculture simultaneously, central and local industries simultaneously, large, medium, and small enterprises simultaneously.

To narrow the gap between mental and physical labor, town and city, official and common man . . .

Speed up, accelerate. LEAP FORWARD!

Fully half of the officials in the ministries, departments, bureaus, committees would "go down," to do manual labor in the villages. To help in building canals, aqueducts, in digging wells and reservoirs, in afforestation, in road and railway construction, in setting up new industries in the rural countryside.

The village cooperatives would agglomerate into communes, large enough to mobilize thousands, to build dikes, and dams for electric power, even to detour rivers.

"If they send me to the countryside I'll die," thought Hsu Build-the-City.

Since that meal at Comrade Lo's house, when the wine had made Chaste Wisdom loquacious, Hsu worried. *Fuck her mother, why do women have such loose tongues?*

Now he often had a queer sensation between his shoulder blades.

Was he being watched?

He woke up one night with a start. He'd heard, dis-

539

tinctly, someone shout: "Hsu Towering Cloud!" Towering Cloud . . . he wanted to forget that name. . . .

If he did not volunteer to go down to labor, Ball of Grease would begin to wonder. She had volunteered. "It will make me young again to work in the fields. I don't like city life," she said.

Stinking mud dumpling, thought Hsu. Only happy when she treads shit.

"Comrade Lo, I am also volunteering," he had told her. She sparkled. "You young people are so enthusiastic."

Now he cogitated. How to avoid manual labor? Find a doctor to declare him tuberculous? Have a heart attack? Heart attacks were fashionable now.

He felt very lonely.

The plain was like a disturbed anthill, a-crawl with hurrying insectlike beings. Long files of men, poles on their shoulders, swinging baskets of earth, snaked up to the dike which rose like a wall, facing the unseen river, where sky and earth merged in the pewter blur of the horizon. Other men leveled the ground, tamping the earth, and chanting, "Hey—heng," as the smooth heavy stone was lifted by its ropes and flung down again. Yet others were planing the ground, removing the boulders which the floods had brought when the river burst out of its bed. Piling the stones in heaps. Still others, seated by the heaps, broke the boulders and filled baskets with the chips.

Almost half a million men were mobilized to build over three hundred miles of dikes to contain the silt-laden river. Another one hundred thousand on the dam, farther down the plain.

Little Pond was one of that half million and his heart was filled with a sensation of power. Who could deny the earth-shaking strength of the multitudes? Surely Heaven would now relent, would give such people, capable of such cosmic efforts, good days to come!

Half a million laborers sang:

> Oh there is no Emperor in Heaven, hai, hai,
> There is no dragon on earth, lo ho lo.
> Oh mountains make way before me, hai, hai,
> For here I come with my spade, hai lo lo.

Leaping with gigantic steps into the promised land. Building the paradise longed for, after centuries of pain and misery, hunger of body and soul . . .

Little Pond worked, carrying stones, dragging them to the heaps. The afternoon sun beat down, the ground shimmered with heat, and the smell and vapor of sweat rose from the barebacked, toiling multitudes. Each team had five hundred men, one red flag, one shed, four latrines. From team to team walked the water carriers, two at a time, large canisters of drinking water swinging on a pole between them. Each laborer had a mug, which hung from his belt.

Little Pond walked to a canister for a drink. He looked at the road, a brown gash across the plain. The army bulldozers had cut the road. Army lorries traveled it, filled with volunteers from the cities, cadres come to work at the dam three miles away. The dam which would give power, light to the villages and the cities of the region.

"Abolish the dark night of the mind!"

"Teach water to ascend to heaven!"

"Teach the sun and moon to change places!"

Those were the words of the Great Leap, painted upon rocks, bridges, walls, throughout the land.

Soon, so soon, there would be no more poverty, no more want, and he would say to Little Pearl: "Now we can marry."

Lorries with red flags stuck to their hoods growled up the road, packed with officials from the cities come to do manual labor.

Little Pond and other laborers cheered. The lorries slowed, going up the sloping road.

Little Pond saw him, saw him clearly. He was only thirty feet away. In the first lorry. The mole on his chin. He could even see the long hair growing from it.

His blood stopped in his body. The man. Who had been with Hsu, in Chungking, coming out of the restaurant that night.

Hsu, his mother's murderer.

The lorries picked up pace, wobbled away.

That night Little Pond left the mat shed where he slept with five hundred others. He said nothing to anyone, not even to his friend Hsiao Wang. He picked up his small bundle of clothes, his mug.

He began to walk along the road the lorries had taken to the dam.

The sky was fish-belly silver when he found the lorries, huddled as tame buffaloes, and as peaceful. Asleep. As were their drivers.

A hundred thousand men. Lying under mat sheds, asleep.

How would he find the man with the mole?

In the near distance, nebulous in dawn light, rose the dam, a skeleton of shafts and pillars.

The cooks came astir and banged their gongs, bang bang bang, calling the laborers out of their sleep. They rose, and all was commotion. Files for water, for breakfast, for the latrines.

Little Pond queued in one food line, hoping no one would question him. He was given the ration: two cakes of ground rye and millet, a bowl of cabbage soup.

The army supervisors blew whistles, and the men filed for work. Little Pond placed his bundle in a lorry shed, and walked, jacket buttoned up, like a minor cadre, as if he knew where he was going.

Where was the man with the mole?

He neared the dam, with men crawling all over it; and saw at its foot a cluster of officials. The man with the mole was holding a spade, being photographed shoveling earth. Click-click went the cameras. Two photographers.

Officials participating in manual labor . . . the working people looked at them.

Little Pond asked a young man at the edge of the cluster: "Where are they from?"

"Peking. Representatives of the Education Ministry."

The man with the mole talked, pointed, arm upraised, selecting another site for another photograph.

"Comrade, which province is that Education Ministry representative from?" Little Pond took out his notebook, his ballpoint pencil, as if he were a journalist.

"You mean Deputy Education Ministry Head Tsui Sea Dragon? I don't know," the young man answered, looking contrite, worried that he did not know.

"My newspaper wants to mention it."

He heard Tsui Sea Dragon laugh. The laugh reminded him of that night in Chungking, when he had scrabbled in the offal, and they had passed him, Tsui Sea Dragon, and a woman, and Hsu Towering Cloud, his mother's murderer.

He would follow Tsui Sea Dragon. To lead him to Hsu. He would find Hsu. . . .

Time dropped each day as a tree discards its falling leaves. Summer and winter and summer again. The Leap had failed. 1960, year of the rat. A bad year.

In the two previous years three hundred million peasants had left their villages at harvest time to do other things, such as making steel in primitive kilns, digging for reservoirs, making roads, opening new land. There had not been enough people in the villages to cope with the harvests. Much grain had rotted in the fields.

Now hunger stalked the land.

In Lingfu New Town a cinema, a park, a public hall, schools had been built. Houses for the workers, and more factories. The population was now one hundred fifty thousand.

The hospital had expanded. It had a staff of twenty-five doctors, two hundred nurses, and four hundred other personnel. There were two maternity clinics and an annex for children.

The Leap had brought a great many doctors out of the big cities, into the smaller ones, into the industrial new towns.

China's doctors were now confronted with the problems of industrial diseases and accidents, requiring new techniques.

It was in those years of the Leap that Chinese surgeons began to forge even further ahead. In the treatment of burns. In microsurgery. In the reattachment of limbs, of fingers. In fashioning thumbs out of toes. And Jen Yong would become one of the outstanding pioneers in that field.

Dr. Szeto was promoted out of Lingfu to become a major administrator in the department of Chinese herbal medicine at the provincial capital. There he could do no harm;

he could even wear a clean white gown, and even carry a stethoscope.

Comrade Go, elated by his small, neat appendectomy scar, had placed Dr. Teng in charge of Lingfu hospital. Because Jen Yong was a rightist, he could work, but could not be mentioned, nor share in any decision making, nor did he have any political rights. But Teng and Go consulted him all the time.

And the workers talked only of Dr. Jen and of his magic hands.

"Comrade Go was up in a week."

"He heals people by touch."

"Don't be scared of his knife. It cuts, but does not hurt."

The young worker who was becoming paralyzed was now comfortable in a plaster cast. He would walk again.

A Caesarean section gave the wife of a trade unionist a bouncing boy. Yong explained that the woman's bones were too small. She had had rickets in infancy.

Confidence towards Jen Yong grew. The workers of Lingfu did not care that he was a rightist. They shrugged when this was mentioned. "He is a good man."

Yong changed. His cheeks thinned, his cheekbones protruded. He looked older. He was a little harsher than he had been. But he worked as in a frenzy, and Lingfu hospital was improving.

He went to the provincial capital with Dr. Teng and Comrade Go, and hauled away some new equipment which was not being used—including an X-ray machine—from the main hospital there.

An obstetrician, two dentists, and three doctors with experience came to Lingfu, and all backed Jen Yong (whose name never appeared) in his demands.

The plumbing improved, though it was still capricious. Dr. Teng broadcast on the local radio, asking for vounteers to repair the hospital plumbing. A dozen plumbers turned up in an army lorry, clashing cymbals and waving red flags in a carnival atmosphere. The toilets and showers now functioned almost adequately.

Yong suggested that the slag mountains were dangerous. Comrade Go, thoroughly happy because Lingfu's successes were being cited on the national radio, went to look at the gray slag ridge towering above the houses.

New workers' houses were built on the other side of

town. The workers moved. And once again luck was with Lingfu. Three months after the removal of the last family, a tremor shook the region, a slag mountain vibrated, slid forward, and buried a quarter of the buildings which remained.

In winter of 1960 half of the factories of Lingfu came to a standstill as did the steel plant. In August the Russians had withdrawn all the Russian experts, and this stopped the large industrial plants.

The workers were getting paid, but there was not much work for them, just as there was very little food. Winter came and many people were sick, and babies and old people died. Stephanie sent boxes of vitamin pills and Eddy Keng got them into Shanghai, ostensibly for his father; and Yong gave them to the workers to combat beriberi.

Internists and surgeons from Peking and from Shanghai came to visit Lingfu; for Lingfu had people from all over China, and some had brought their parasites and particular diseases with them. Carcinomas of nasopharynx and esophagus, particular to other areas; cancer of the lung, now rising precipitately. . . .

One afternoon, as Yong was taking visiting surgeons from Shanghai around, Teng came to him, looking anxious.

"Dr. Jen, there's a worker downstairs. He's brought his hand with him."

Jen Yong ran down, asking Teng: "Right or left hand?"

"Right hand."

In the outpatient ward three workers surrounded a young man who sat holding his wrist. Someone had applied a tourniquet to it. The boy was pale, but tried to rise politely when he saw Yong. By his side was an enamel basin. In it was the young worker's hand, twisted off by a machine.

"Doctor," said the young worker. "You'll put my hand back for me, won't you?"

Jen Yong said: "I'll try."

The doctors from Shanghai organized themselves. Organized the work to be done.

The operation lasted eight hours.

Four months later, the young worker could use his hand. Hold objects, eat, even play Ping-Pong. Begin clumsily to write . . .

Between 1960 and 1962 some three hundred thousand
rightists were rehabilitated. Their positions and their salaries were restored. A certificate of rehabilitation was given
to them. In some cases the Party committee of their unit
offered them a "rehabilitation dinner." In others, a public
meeting announcing the rehabilitation was held.

Yong was rehabilitated in early 1961. He received the
notice fairly promptly. But nothing else was done for him.

He went to Peking, to ask for full rehabilitation.

In the Peking hospital where he had worked, someone
else had been appointed in his stead. It would be unfair to
the present holder of the post should Jen Yong be reinstated, argued the Party secretary in charge.

The "going down to the countryside, to the factories"
movement of the Great Leap Forward had now been reversed. Bureaucrats and intellectuals surged back to the big
cities. It was almost a stampede for jobs.

"Of course we shall reinstate you as soon as there is a
vacancy at your high level," said the Party bureaucrat. But
the Party committee did not hold an official rehabilitation
ceremony.

"They're so afraid of losing face, of acknowledging they've
made a mistake," said Dr. Fan to him. "That report which
you wrote still sticks like a fishbone in their throats."

Now his colleagues crowded around him, congratulating
him on being "washed snow white." He would have to
forget that some of them had helped to condemn him.

Yong went to Shanghai, to see his parents and his son. He
had not seen them since 1957.

On the train to Shanghai, he dreamt. If he was reinstated, if he found another house, then perhaps Stephanie
would come back, even if only for a visit, even if only for a
short while. . . .

*Oh Stephanie, my love, my love. Not a day has gone by
that I have not longed for you.*

He had written to her, written to her. Never telling her of
the humiliation, the discomfort. And so his letters had been
somewhat colorless. "All is well . . . we are working very
hard . . . the hospital is improving . . . all is well . . ."

And then he had written to her about the hand. Written with joy, with pride, with abandon . . .

Shanghai, Father and Mother, both a little older, but well; and by their side a tall boy, with those eyes, those eyes, Stephanie's eyes.

Looking at his son, Jen Yong was overwhelmed by a wave of bittersweet love and sorrow. *Oh, no day was really safe, no day was without recall of her. Oh Stephanie, come back, come back . . .*

"*Tietie,*" said Winter Treasure. He was in blue, he was thin. He was a little over twelve years old.

They came to his arms now, the old ones, Father and Mother, not caring about ceremony or who looked at them.

The House was in great need of fresh paint. The garden now grew vegetables, cabbages, spinach, some squash. In lieu of the peony, roses, chrysanthemums. The goldfish had gone; someone had eaten them. In one wood-fenced space there were hens, a rooster. In another rabbits in hutches, with wire netting around. "Everyone keeps rabbits," said Mother. Rabbits ate cabbage; there was a great deal of winter cabbage available, in great heaps.

"We have enough to eat," they said. The capitalists of Shanghai were allotted higher rations of protein, meat, sugar, and oil than the workers. The latter received more rice. Eddy Keng sent foreign money from Hongkong. "We can purchase extra food, we get extra food tickets with foreign exchange. As do the overseas Chinese."

From Hongkong, from all over Southeast Asia, from Canada, overseas Chinese sent money to their families in China. American overseas sent money through connections in Hongkong, in Singapore.

A letter awaited him, from Stephanie. "I knew you were coming here, son; I was afraid the letter might arrive in Lingfu when you were already here from Peking, so I did not forward it," said his mother.

"You did well, Mother."

Winter Treasure came in, holding the tea tray, serving his grandparents and father with tea, careful of the cups. Good tea in beautiful porcelain. Yong had not drunk tea for three years. In the north, people gathered the falling autumn leaves, brewed them for tea. They contained vitamin C.

"Special tea for overseas Chinese," smiled Mother. "The

money comes from Daughter. Please thank her again for us, when you write."

Stephanie sent money, sent parcels of clothes, sent books, sent soap, sent vitamin pills. For the Family, and for him. But he had said to his parents, "Do not post anything to me in Lingfu except vitamin pills." Parcels, food, coming for him, would have created a difference between him and the workers of Lingfu, the nurses, the other doctors. He gave the vitamin pills to his patients.

"The young are true believers," said Mother. "Winter Treasure sits with us, but does not eat all the dishes, only some cabbage, and a little white rice . . . he says he does not want any privileges . . . he scorns us for eating well . . ."

Winter Treasure had served the tea with perfect grace, but he had drunk none himself. "He only drinks boiled water," said Mother.

"I am proud of my son," said Jen Yong. "He is idealistic. As are all the young."

"But when the bubble bursts, then the young become bitter," said Mother.

Yong was tongue-tied in front of his son. His son who looked at him, looked with an exact measuring eye, unmisted by either love or dislike.

What went on inside of him?

He must have suffered a good deal when he knew his father had become a rightist. Would he ever talk about it to Yong? What did he think now, now that his father was rehabilitated? Who were his friends? The children of rightists often found themselves ostracized, friendless. . . .

"Read your letter, son," said Mother, rising, knowing Jen Yong was politely waiting for her to leave, to read it.

A small room had been made ready for him. "We have locked your pavilion, and all your furniture is safe," said Mother. He could not have endured being back in the pavilion where he and Stephanie had spent years of irretrievable happiness. It made him gag a little to see, across the garden, the winding path, the rockery, and beyond it the roof of their once-upon-a-time fairyland.

He opened Stephanie's letter.

He had waited to be in Shanghai to send her the good news: "Spring Snow, I have been rehabilitated . . . perhaps,

548

perhaps now you will be able to come, if only for a visit." That was what he planned to write to her.

Stephanie's letter. She wrote that she and John Moore were lovers. "I have to tell you, Yong, because we have never lied to each other. I do not love him. I love you. I shall always love you. But I could not remain alone. Can you understand?"

Always he had read and reread her letters, striving to guess, his heart reading between the lines. And now it seemed to him that he had always known. Known about John Moore. Known that this would happen. Known from the very day he held in his hand that crumpled letter in the jail of Chungking, while Colonel Tsing of the Secret Police explored his face for the agony he would read upon it.

After the evening meal Mother came to his room.

"All is well with Spring Snow?"

"All is well . . ." He fought down the explosion inside him, the flayed rawness. "She has found a good man. To care for her."

"The loneliness," said Mother.

She was very quiet, imbibing, sharing Yong's pain. Taking the pain into her.

"What about Winter Treasure? He yearns for her . . . will you tell him?"

"No . . . Not yet."

Spring Snow,

I have been completely rehabilitated. It is a good thing for our son. He is twelve, and he looks at me, measuring and gauging me, trying to fit this re-habilitation into his mind, as he had to fit my being a rightist. I look at him and I think: How can he join together all the fragments of the utterly incoherent events, pieces of the world in which he has to live?

I cannot write much about what you tell me. But it had to be. Of course. Should you wish for a divorce, so that you may marry again, please do not hesitate to ask me.

I thank you for the years and the days of love and happiness you gave me. Wonderful years which time cannot sully nor memory fade.

I think it best if, for the moment, you do not write to Winter Treasure about this matter. Some truths are best left unsaid. A twelve-year-old is very vulnerable.

The photographs you sent of Swallow are charming. She is such a pretty girl, and we all long to see her.

Because you send so much money, all our Family have more than enough. We are all very grateful to you. Things will go better next year. . . .

Yong spent the next two weeks in Shanghai and many friends dropped in to congratulate him. "You are washed white as snow," they said. "We are happy for you."

Winter Treasure listened. A young judge, making up his mind. About his father. About himself.

The twins Coral and Calthrop came and the House was once more like old times, with a froth of gaiety, and sorrows carefully concealed. Calthrop had become an actress much in demand in films at the Shanghai film studios. Coral had been admitted to the university. After graduation she would marry a biochemist who was doing research at the university research institute. "He does not care that I was the sister of a rightist."

Jen Yong went to see the fiancée of Dr. Teng. She told him that Teng's family had refused to receive her, because her father was a rightist. "It will hurt him to marry me," she said. "His family will cut him off."

"Marry him," advised Jen Yong. "Do not heed them. And do not repudiate your father."

Winter Treasure began to talk to his father. It had taken some days for him to make up his mind. A twelve-year-old thinks in absolutes and needs perfection. Perfection terrible like Death, like all absolutes.

Winter Treasure, angular elbows, knees protruding through his cotton trousers, mind haggling with unsolved problems.

"*Tietie,* you had a letter from Mama? She is never coming back, is she?"

"Son, let us wait another year, then we shall see. . . . It is not her fault . . ."

"She is not coming back. She could not endure it. Mama now has *her* child, and she does not want me anymore. . . ."

Jen Yong took his son in his arms.

"Son, Mama loves you, loves us. But Mama has many responsibilities. If she comes here, it may be difficult for her to return to her country. Her country may not let her go back. And our country may not let her come in. And your sister is a baby still, only three years old. It is I who asked your mother not to return too quickly."

"Over three years Ma has been away," said Winter Treasure. He was trying hard not to weep.

Then Yong opened the floodgates of his heart. He talked with his son. For many hours of that night, and again for the next day, and the next.

Yong told him about those days in Chungking and in Yenan, way back in 1944 and 1945, when the world was to be made anew, in hope, in candor. When it looked as if America would help the new aspirations for independence of the peoples of Asia. When Mao Tsetung and Chou Enlai were prepared to fly to Washington, and Yenan was full of Americans. He talked about Stephanie's courage, and her ordeal through the Korean War, and losing her baby then. About the dwindling idealism, and how hope still kept on, kept anchoring his soul; and how at one moment he had had to choose, choose between his country and Stephanie.

He spoke of the Jen Family, how it had weathered the centuries; of upright men exiled for rebuking a corrupt emperor. He spoke of the Jen tradition of loyalty and of patriotism.

"Love is to love in spite of, not because of," he said.

He told his son how the workers in Lingfu had not cared that he was a rightist. How they greeted him when he walked in the town, the women coming up with their babies, so that he should smile at them, as if he brought good luck. And how he felt warm, happy, because they truly cared for him.

"We serve our people, and our country," he said.

When he had done, the twelve-year-old boy had changed. His world had come together, had begun to make sense, even if it was a medley of contradictions and con-

551

flicts. "We must protect Mama," he said. "Also my sister Swallow. So I must quickly grow up, to be a man."

Yong was reinstated as chief surgeon in the Shanghai hospital, which was eager to have him back.

He left Lingfu with much regret. The Lingfu New Town committee gave him a farewell feast, and saw him in a body to the railway station. He had to tour the factories, to say goodbye to everyone there. The workers crowded around him, weeping, and his heart smote him. He wanted to stay with them! Oh, these were the people, his people, his own patient, obstinate, hardworking people, a great ocean of humankind turned towards the future. He would work for them until the day of his death.

"I promise you to return to Lingfu whenever I can," he said.

In Shanghai he lived in the hospital compound, the doctors' dormitory. So as to be easily accessible in case of any emergency. He lived with his books, Stephanie's letters, and a large photograph of Stephanie, at the ranch in Texas, the sun in her hair, the wind sculpting her and her laughter. And dappled bright horses in the meadows behind her. He kept the photograph in a drawer. He did not show it to anyone.

He wrote to Stephanie. Wrote to her every day, but kept the letters. He would never send her another letter. He kept all the letters in a chest under his bed. Until the day when he would have to destroy them.

twenty-four

LITTLE Pond did not return to his work site. He thus committed a crime, abandoning his work, his school, walking to Peking, two hundred fifty miles away. There he would have to hide from the security police, from the night patrols searching for vagrants not registered to live in the city.

He had no permission to live in Peking. No ration tickets. And in ordinary times it would not have been possible for him to be there. But during the Leap there had been such enormous movements of people, peasants and workers moving all over the country, in and out of the innumerable projects undertaken, that orderly registration was now disrupted.

"As long as I have two hands, two feet, I can work and I shall eat."

Nevertheless, he was almost starving when he arrived in Peking. For the harvests had been very bad, and the peasants kept all they had, and looked suspiciously at a young man who offered to work for a meal.

He had posted one short letter to Little Pearl. "I have found a friend of my mother's murderer. I shall not rest until I find Hsu Towering Cloud. Little Pearl, please wait for me . . ."

In Peking he went to the cook at the Szechuan restaurant where he had worked two years ago. "How can I feed you?" said the cook. "Food is so scarce this year. People come to eat, but there are no leavings, they scrape the bowls clean. . . ."

But Little Pond pleaded, implored, and Cook relented. After all, they were from the same province. And Cook needed a good pair of legs. If Little Pond went to the villages outside Peking to bring back some duck's eggs, a chicken, some precious beancurd, this would help Cook.

Every unit, every Government office during those three years of scarcity had organized a "food task force." The force reared pigs, chickens, or rabbits, made contracts with some villages to supply them with vegetables. All this was black market, free enterprise, but the Party wisely kept its eyes shut.

People must eat.

Winter was here. Winter making carcasses of the trees, and of those who died. A winter of want.

Little Pond served the clients, washed the dishes (licking the plates on the way to the kitchen), scrubbed the floors, ran errands, and in the backyard raised rabbits, sleeping with the small rabbits in a bag on his chest so that they would not die in the cruel cold which now tumbled down upon the city, twenty degrees below zero. And no heating, no coal. Cook kept warm by his stove when cooking was going on, but the stove was out at night.

The rabbits thrived. They ate cabbage. The only thing to eat that winter was winter cabbage. There were great heaps of them, white and green, in mounds at each street corner.

How could he find Tsui Sea Dragon?

"Old Man in Heaven, Old Man, be not deaf, be not blind. Listen to me. I am Liang Little Pond. Listen to the ghost of my unborn brother, of my mother, Liang Ma, for they cannot rest easy, they cannot rest until I have avenged them."

How could he find Hsu Towering Cloud?

The Education Ministry was a vast building. Soldiers guarded the gates, and he could not enter. He waited outside, waited to see whether Tsui Sea Dragon went in or out. Hundreds of people, thousands of people went in, went out. Not Sea Dragon.

There were branches, education departments, in every one of Peking's eighteen districts. Which one housed Sea Dragon?

Little Pond read the *People's Daily*. He went to queue for it in the freezing morning. He managed to scan it swiftly before giving it to Cook who gave it to the restaurant manager. For Little Pond was to remain invisible. He did not exist. The manager should not know he was there. In times of hardship, it is best to shut one's eyes.

When the manager had read the newspaper editorial aloud to his staff, he took the paper home. To stuff a jacket, a mattress, cloth shoes, to paper window cracks.

One day, Little Pond read an article written by Tsui Sea Dragon praising the indomitable spirit of the middle-school youths in his city sector, who had saved three hundred catties of rice by eating less every day for a month. This was due to the inspired leadership of the Party, wrote Comrade Tsui. And the enthusiasm of the masses for sacrifice.

Now Little Pond knew in which sector of Peking he would find Sea Dragon.

It took him fifteen days to find the street and the office building with its label: West Fourth Branch Committee of Ministry of Education. Another few days, watching and waiting, frozen-footed, and he saw Tsui Sea Dragon walk out of the building. Bulky in a coat, a fur cap with flaps on his ears.

Little Pond followed him home.

Sea Dragon lived in Cassia Fragrance *hutung*, in the dormitory for the Ministry of Education staff of West Fourth district.

One evening he saw Chaste Wisdom return, in a quilted coat with a hood. She looked well-fed.

He lay awake at night, nursing the rabbits, a pair of brood hens, and a piglet. He slept with them and they kept him warm. How would he force Chaste Wisdom or Sea Dragon to tell him where Hsu was?

It was another two weeks before he could follow Chaste Wisdom one morning to her office. She took the bus. Little Pond had ten cents on him. All the money he had. The bus cost him five cents. He climbed in after her. In the bus he almost touched her. She did not pay any attention to him, except to sniff a little. He didn't smell too good. The pig, the rabbits, the hens . . .

Chaste Wisdom alighted from the bus on Lamp Market Main Street, and waddled down it to a gate also guarded by soldiers. And then she stopped, raised her voice, peering into the smoke-fog which blotted the city in the morning. "Old Hsu, have you too been shopping?"

Little Pond heard Hsu's voice before he saw Hsu. The pointed face, the mustache emerging out of the fog. "Good

555

morning, Comrade Bo. Would you like some chicken legs? Mine are really choice."

Old Man in Heaven had listened to Liang Ma's son. At last.

Hsu Towering Cloud. In a pelisse, a worker's cap. He looked as he had looked when Little Pond had knelt, knocking his forehead in the dirt, begging that Ma would be spared, left in peace to have her baby under a roof, in her shack, not thrown out to have the baby in the open, in full view of everyone.

Hsu Towering Cloud. He and Bo entered the office, chatting and laughing, and the soldiers at the gate did not even look at them.

Little Pond would have to borrow Cook's hatchet to kill Hsu Towering Cloud.

The Spring Festival was coming. The year of the Tiger would begin, and the newspapers had said it would be a better year, all difficulties overcome, because Premier Chou Enlai had taken readjustment in hand. The crops would be better, the cycle of disaster would end.

Little Pond decided that he would kill Hsu on the eve of the Spring Festival, last day of the year of the Ox.

Cook's hatchet was a lovely thing. Short stubby handle to fit the grasp, a round hole like an eye, and what a glimmer to its razor-sharp blade! Cook did everything with it, skin and shred, cut and slice, hack and sculpt small pink radishes into flowers, eviscerate rabbits and chickens, debone meat, fillet fish. The hatchet was a living frolic in his hand.

Little Pond had five cents left and could not buy even a needle. Anyway, there were no needles and no knives for sale anywhere that year. Cook's hatchet was a precious thing, and Cook slept with the hatchet by his side.

Little Pond must take the hatchet in the morning, when Cook rose to go to the latrine. He must kill Hsu quickly, when Hsu left his dormitory to go to his office. Little Pond had followed Hsu to his dormitory, not far from the building where he worked. He must return the hatchet in time for Cook to prepare the midday meal for the clients.

And if he was a little late, he would explain to Cook why

he had had to borrow it. He would wash it clean before he returned it.

In the thick fog which froze one's lungs as it snaked its way inside one's body, Liang Ma's son waited, the hatchet concealed in his jacket.

But that morning, being New Year's Eve, Hsu had left his dormitory half an hour earlier, to go to the Muslim shop in East Peace Street to buy some cakes stuffed with ground dates. Only the Muslims made these cakes. Hsu would offer them to Comrade Lo, saying offhandedly: "Also for your thousand gold pieces." A thousand gold pieces being the courtesy way of saying "your daughter."

It was extremely difficult that year to get sweets, or sugar, or flour. Only the Muslims had some, and people queued at the shop, beginning at four in the morning. Each one could buy only four cakes. Hsu had paid in advance.

Little Pond waited. Waited, and then knew he had missed Hsu. And now it was too late to give back the hatchet. He must keep it with him all day. Kill Hsu tonight. He shuffled slowly to Hsu's office. Many people shuffled that winter. It was so cold, so cold.

He waited all day outside the office building. And in the evening dusk, in that indistinct light which digested color into monotonic grayness, Hsu came out, walking with an elderly woman. The woman held a parcel in her hands, warm inside knitted wool gloves.

When Hsu had given Comrade Lo the cakes, the latter had exclaimed: "Aiyah, you are too kind. My daughter is a silly, stubborn child. She is moping, moping. I do not know why. She has been moping since last summer. She has become thin, and she refuses to go out of the house, or to see a doctor."

"Perhaps she has been working too hard," suggested Hsu.

He knew Comrade Lo wanted him to marry her daughter, Little Pearl. He had now decided that he would do so.

The streets were uncrowded, everyone was hurrying home for New Year's Eve.

The street lights were on, very dim, to save electric power, but in front of them a gaunt figure stood, blocking their way.

Comrade Lo stopped. "Friend, are you looking for someone?"

557

Little Pond said: "I am Liang Little Pond. I am looking for Hsu Towering Cloud, who killed my mother."

Hsu immediately turned to run, run back the way he had come, but Little Pond was swift, his arm stretched out, he seized Hsu's pelisse collar, yanked hard, and Hsu slipped and fell on the ground.

"What are you doing? What are you doing?" cried Comrade Lo, and she tugged at Little Pond's jacket.

"Hsu, rotten egg, you killed my mother, now I'll kill you," screamed Little Pond. The hatchet gleamed in his hand, he swung it above Hsu's head and brought it down.

"Aiyah, aiyah," screamed Comrade Lo, pulling at Little Pond.

The hatchet missed, sliced off part of Hsu's cap and his ear, streaked down one cheek.

Blood spurted, Hsu screamed, Comrade Lo shouted: "Help, help, murder!" Little Pond raised the hatchet again.

"Die, die," he shouted.

But people were running towards them. They took hold of Little Pond. Hsu's hand went up, and the hatchet sliced at it, almost lopping off half the hand. Three men threw themselves on Little Pond, and brought him down. The hatchet fell to the ground.

"Old Partner, Old Partner, oh what a terrible thing, oh I nearly died!" Comrade Lo, back at home, supported by a young Public Security policeman.

"Ma, Ma," cried Little Pearl, and Old Meng rose. "What is it, what is it?"

Comrade Lo entered the room. There was blood on her coat. "A murderer, a murderer tried to kill Comrade Hsu."

"Ma, Ma, you're bleeding." Little Pearl rushed to her mother.

"Your Ma is all right, this is the blood of Comrade Hsu," said the policeman. "Now you are safely home, Comrade Lo, I'll leave." He saluted smartly, walked out.

Meng helped his wife take off her coat, poured some tea for her to drink as she fell in a chair. "There, there, calm yourself, Old Partner, calm yourself. Drink this . . . you're not hurt, are you?"

"No." She gulped. She told the story, gasping. "We were

walking out, Comrade Hsu and I, he'd given me some cakes—oh, I dropped them, dropped the box . . . and suddenly there was this young man standing in front of us, like a devil, and shouting: 'Hsu Towering Cloud, you killed my mother. I'll kill you.'"

"Ha, ha," Meng said. "Hsu Towering Cloud."

"He had a hatchet, he struck Comrade Hsu; Hsu was covered in blood," wailed Lo. "I don't know if he will live!"

"I must go to him, I must go to him," sobbed Little Pearl, walking towards the coat hangers near the door of their living room, and pulling her quilted jacket off its hook, tears streaming down her face, wailing like a little girl.

"Aiyah, I didn't know you had so much feeling for Comrade Hsu!" said her mother happily.

"Hsu, that turtle's egg?" Little Pearl suddenly was like a tigress. "It's Liang Little Pond, Liang Square-Face . . . I love him, Mama, I love him. And I must go to him now!"

"I'm going with you," said her father.

That very night of New Year's Eve, Meng and his daughter went to the Public Security precinct where Little Pond was held, bound hand and foot, a murderer.

Meng told the Public Security man on guard: "Comrade, this is not a simple murder case. Treat the prisoner well. I want to talk to your officer-in-charge."

The officer-in-charge was at home because it was New Year's Eve.

Little Pearl said: "I want to see Liang Little Pond."

"It is impossible," said the Public Security guard. "He is a murderer. Only close relatives may see him."

"I am his bride-to-be," said Little Pearl. The guard was startled. He looked towards Meng, the father. Meng kept silent.

Little Pearl said: "Papa, I want to see him."

The policeman questioned Meng with his eyes. Meng said: "I shall go with her."

And the policeman said: "Ten minutes then . . . and only because it is New Year's Eve."

Little Pond was in a very small cell, almost a hole, very dark. He was shackled, hands and feet tightly chained to the wall. A dangerous murderer.

The policeman opened the door, brought a lit candle. Meng saw a young man, very thin, with high cheekbones and large eyes, and his daughter held the man's chained hands in hers and sobbed: "Oh Square-Face, Square-Face . . . you should have told me more, told me more . . ."

"Little Pearl, how could I? I told you all I knew. But how did you find me?" He looked at Meng, surprised.

Meng thought: He's our kind, he's eaten bitterness. The story is true. And he was glad, and sad, because his loved one, Old Partner, might suffer.

Hsu Towering Cloud/Build-the-City made a full confession. His wounds were not mortal. His ear could not be stuck back, but his hand would heal.

Hsu threw himself on the mercy of the Communist Party. In these years in China, his heart had changed, he said. He was thinking of confessing everything. Now he besought the Party to be merciful to him.

He denounced Chaste Wisdom, Sea Dragon, and other people, in Shanghai, in Chungking, in Canton, the couriers, the remaining Triad members he knew.

Meng said to the police officer in charge of the case: "Comrade, I wrote to you over fourteen months ago about my suspicions. Yet nothing was done until this young man Liang Little Pond courageously attacked the Kuomintang spy Hsu."

But the bureaucracy is always right. The police had paid great attention, Meng was told. But they wanted to proceed cautiously, to catch the whole network, from low to high, "not only some small fry."

Tsui Sea Dragon and Bo Chaste Wisdom were arrested on the second day of the year of the Tiger.

Jen Yong was asked for his evidence, which he gave to the Public Security office in Shanghai.

Little Pond wrote to him:

Taifu,

Heaven has eyes, the Party has eyes. Good will win in the end. Heaven and Earth may break to pieces, but I Liang Little Pond shall always remember you, and your American loved one, Lai Spring Snow.

560

Chairman Mao has told us that it is the people who make history; we the once-poor should write the history of our own family. I Little Pond will do so, telling the good that you and your loved one have done to the Liang family, to live from generation to generation.

Hsu Towering Cloud, Tsui Sea Dragon, and Bo Chaste Wisdom were condemned to death. But because Hsu had revealed so willingly the network, he was given the usual two years' reprieve. If he behaved well and showed due repentance, he would have a life sentence at labor re-education. The other two were shot in the usual way, their faces covered with a mask, and a quick bullet put through the base of the skull.

Little Pond was angry. "Hsu must die . . . he should be cut in a thousand pieces, he should be boiled alive in oil!" he shouted in the court. But it was pointed out to him that his mother had committed suicide. Technically, Hsu was not her murderer.

When Little Pond saw that he could not move the assessors and the judge, he fell back into muteness. He set his heart and resolved that he would find out to which labor camp Hsu would be sent, and one day he would kill him. Cut his liver out and feed it to the carrion crows.

Little Pond had also committed serious offenses. Absconded from work, run away to Peking without a proper permit, lived in the city without being registered, stolen a hatchet.

He had to do a very thorough self-criticism for lack of discipline, disobedience, subjectivity, individualism, adventurism, not only in front of his own school but at a big meeting attended by other student representatives. However, he had become something of a hero, and the young cheered and clapped him. The Party secretary of the school tried to look severe.

"Comrade Liang should have reported to the proper authorities . . . the wisdom of the Party would have come into play . . . dismantling the Kuomintang spy organization."

He was condemned to a year of political study and manual labor.

In the next year, the year of the Hare. Little Pond and

Pearl were married, registering themselves, and then leaving for Tsinan where they had been assigned jobs in the same unit, a new telecommunications manufacturing plant. It was Prosperity Tang who had requested that Comrade Liang Little Pond work there, for Prosperity Tang was now an important leading cadre in the city.

As for Little Pearl's mother, Comrade Lo, she was let off with a long self-criticism, in which she did rather well. Her nickname became Mother Turnip, since the scoundrel Hsu had been like a turnip, outwardly red, and lily-livered white inside.

Nine years, thought Stephanie. And shut the door of her mind upon that place within her, crucible where passion and memory still blazed too easily, where disembodied grief stirred and would not die.

It's ridiculous. I still weep inside. . . . Mushy like a sixteen-year-old.

Evoke his name, and she altered, her limbs shorn of strength, in a chilly no man's land of her own choosing.

Twice a month the special courier of Keng Lai United Research Ltd. of Hongkong brought her the letters. Wherever she was in the world. Keng Lai. "Lai" the Chinese pronunciation of Ryder.

The letters were debonair, colorless, almost ominous in their reassurance. Underneath the smooth words was another world, the spell of a giant upheaval to which she no longer had access, in which she could not share. Deliberately, the letters kept her from entering it. They assured her: all is well.

At night came the dreams. An arched salt-white cave, and Yong. In his hands a rufous hen, and he turned to her, his face with its neat flying eyebrows, saying: "Eggs for your breakfast, my beloved." And somehow it was sinister, because the wind came rushing in with a great snarl, and carried him away, and she went pursuing the wind and calling: Yong, Yong, come back to me.

Or it was a railway station. The train was leaving, chugging a little, the wheels turned and all the people she loved were aboard waving at her and she was left on the platform, her luggage an enormous pile behind her, and there was no train, no station, only a long dark road banked by tall rye. And in the thick rye was terror.

Time, surely, had numbed her salient emotions. Something in her had forgotten. But something remembered, and was comfortless, and ate into her, every year a little deeper.

Yet on the surface time had dealt gently with her. She was forty-two in that May of 1966, but still looked in her early thirties. Money spared the body, kept the skin young, multiplied the mind's grasp, organized the days and the hours. Money had given her a multiple-level, efficient staff, extension of herself, to accomplish her decisions and desires. Travel, business, leisure, cutthroat board meetings; all meshed into her life. Culture and art and social contacts. Even love-making had its discreetly budgeted hours.

Even. The word a plastic Ping-Pong ball bouncing about in her mind. Love-making, to keep smooth the working of that efficient and fabulous structure, Stephanie Ryder, Inc.

The use of money did not require specific knowledge, but it required a special talent, made up of shrewdness, audacity, a gambler's instinct, a necessary illogic, a never-slumbering alertness. Heston had had it. Stephanie had it. The realization that brains were purchasable; swiftness in judging brainpower, original thought, and snapping it up. Taking risks coolly, letting down failures gently. This had created Space Time Research Inc., STRINC, founded on Heston's idea, carried out by his daughter Stephanie.

In those eight years since its inception, STRINC had spawned many successes. From telescopes to surgical lasers; from thermostats to space travel equipment. Stephanie could no longer follow the ramifications of her enterprise; this was taken care of by the staff, the board, and Dick Steiner, overall executive vice president. Stephanie had people in her pay hunting for new ideas, for the original innovative mind, the flight into fantasy that became achievable, became reality. They reported to her. She saw the potential, furnished the means. If something didn't work, she shelved it. But some discarded ideas had later proved useful, fitted in another context, became useful a year, three, five years later.

She was a warrior. Fierce, treacherous, vicious board battles left her unscarred. At Ryder Aircraft the board members had been determined to oust her. She'd fought, won, and got out. She never regretted it.

The Chinese experience had helped. Somehow, another way of thinking meant that every event, occurrence, could be explained in another way. It helped her, and also Dick Steiner, to see further ahead, beyond the momentary politics, the self-deceiving myths.

"When our perceptions fail to keep pace with events, when we refuse to believe something because it displeases us or frightens us, or is simply startlingly unfamiliar, then the gap between fact and perception becomes a chasm. And action becomes irrelevant and irrational."

Those words of Senator Fulbright Stephanie had had inlaid in gold on a marble slab in every office of STRINC.

"You have 21st-century thinking, Auntie," Eddy Keng said. He looked ahead, as his father Keng Dawei was doing, capitalist multimillionaire cooperating with the reds in Shanghai. As did his uncle, Sir Henry Keng, who never missed Ascot and Goodwood, and even ate Cheddar cheese, which made his nephew turn pear-green.

All went well then for Stephanie, save for that eye mote, smoldering cinder embedded in her heart. Cinder which so easily leapt into flame, threatening the workings of the perfect machine.

She rose from the peach satin-sheeted bed to look at herself in the mirror which paneled one bedroom wall. The one in which she slept alone. The other bedrooms held no such mirrors.

Slim. Trim. Luminous skin. Smooth. No tanning, that idiot sun compulsion, status symbol for the wealthy and not so wealthy, who worked with such desperate zeal at the trivia of strenuous idleness. "I don't dip into public pools," Stephanie had said, smiling, to a big fashion magazine. "She's filthy rich, she's filthy mean," they said of her. A female Howard Hughes. She was hated, because she was a woman, and she beat men at their games of greed and money.

Stephanie showered and dressed. Her hairdresser came once a week to shampoo and to trim her hair. Minnie looked after her wardrobe. Minnie Cole and Horace Washington traveled with her everywhere. Ever since that afternoon when they had bundled her into the car, taken her to the hospital where Swallow was born, she kept them near her. They knew her better than anyone else. They were people to her, not gadgets to be handled. They kept an eye on the servants, in the houses and apartments she owned. Twice a year she bought clothes, not many, from Gres or Balmain. She had her underwear, sheets, and house linen made in Hongkong.

Her passport had been restored to her in 1959, as well as her diaries, letters, and books. And the FBI had long ceased to worry her. Money. And the fact that she seemed reconciled to the business of making more money.

John Moore would be arriving this afternoon, back from an economic conference in Cairo. They would leave together for Hongkong in three days' time. Eddy Keng had assembled the Asian managers of Keng Lai Company, Ltd., which had branches in Singapore, in Manila, in Bangkok, in Tokyo, and Osaka. Keng Lai was also investing in Australian real estate and mines. "Long-term," said Eddy Keng, meaning that the profits would not be there for ten, fifteen, twenty years.

Stephanie had specified: "No business with Taiwan. I don't care how much money we lose. I won't have anything to do with Chiang Kaishek." And Eddy Keng had agreed. Although he also knew that Red China, one day, might use trade links to fetter Taiwan, its irredentist province, to be redeemed one day; and that what was heinous today would be acceptably *useful* tomorrow.

Things were changing, had changed. Despite the continuing irrationality in Washington, handicapped by policies based on old myths rather than current realities. Walter Lippmann was now opposed to the war in Vietnam, and so were other thoughtful Americans. But the mythmakers were still clamorous and strong, and the mythbreakers were hampered by their weak position as "red lovers."

"China is the enemy," McNamara screamed in 1965, to justify the bombing of North Vietnam.

"The Vietnam War will be over in three months," said the Pentagon, echoing MacArthur's "home by Christmas" bombast of the Korean War.

But things were changing, changing.

In 1961, the embargo on China had been breached by America's European allies. England, Belgium, France refused to be bound any longer *not* to trade with China. The blacklisting of firms dealing with China in Hongkong did not work. The businessmen of Japan were making their way to Peking. On the West Coast of America, a steady grouse was heard: "We're cutting ourselves off from the biggest market in the world . . . why?" Voices in Washington, in the *New York Times,* were being raised: "It is time for a reappraisal of our foreign policy. . . ."

The myth of a mighty and total red conspiracy was exploded. China had not only quarreled with the USSR; both countries spent more time insulting each other than vilifying America.

But there was the Vietnam War. The Vietnam War, that slide into an unsuspected quagmire, a hopeless bog of mental confusion, in which the best and the brightest of the East Coast intelligentsia, President Kennedy's stalwarts, would plunge. And as long as the Vietnam War went on, there was bound to be hostility towards China. Because China was bound to feel threatened. Vietnam was close to her borders, and if America crossed into North Vietnam, it would be a Korean situation all over again.

In China too there were changes.

In 1964 General de Gaulle had recognized the People's Republic of China. And now all of Europe's businessmen were flocking to China. Sir Henry Keng was assembling a delegation of British businessmen. Michael Anstruther from London was going to Peking to negotiate reopening a press agency.

By 1965, while the rest of the world went to China, the Vietnam War, and McNamara's warning that "China is the main enemy, not Russia," and the wrong-headed advice of the liberal establishment, which continued to exert its influence on President Johnson—all these factors combined to keep America and Americans isolated from the reality shaping itself across the Pacific.

But louder and more insistent were the voices in America asking for reappraisal. Only the war in Vietnam obscured all the issues. It was a war against the USSR, but it looked, to everyone, like a war against China, because the Vietnamese looked Asiatic, and Americans were not trained to think in terms of main issues. Only of appearances.

John Moore was also meshed into the structure of Stephanie Ryder, Inc.

By May 1959 she had been alone for almost two years. Her body knew it. Her temper grew short, she felt dumpy and scrawny at once, fussed irritably. Slept badly.

Then she had taken a three-month holiday. Gone to Europe, knowing consciously that she was looking for a lover, a male, someone to assuage the interfering flesh. She stayed with Isabelle in her beautiful chateau in Provence. Then went to Paris, Brussels, Copenhagen, to Stockholm and to Venice and to Monte Carlo.

She traveled with Minnie and Horace, taking her time, relishing the fact that she could see Europe with her own eyes, without being surrounded by the right people telling her how she should react.

The right people, from the right social slot. Brilliant, super-rich, or merely wealthy and fashionable. Her mother explained to her with that tactful daintiness of hers that those introduced by Isabelle de Quincy de Gersant were the "*vraie noblesse*," not the spurious ones, not those who bought their titles, not the *nouveau riche* like those Greek tycoons with their extraordinary destructiveness of other people's lives. "In the end, it is birth and breeding that count," said Isabelle. She now wore beautiful shades of difficult gray, and looked radiant.

Isabelle tactfully never mentioned Yong. Instead, she spoke of Winter Treasure, and of his letters. "He must be at ease, at peace. He sounds so mature. A large family around a child gives security."

Winter Treasure wrote to his mother, and to Isabelle, exquisite short letters in the kind of old-fashioned English, stilted and formal, which had been Yong's, and which Isabelle felt had *cachet*, an otherworldliness indicating breeding.

Europe neither amazed nor overawed Stephanie. She had known civility, refinement, sophistication, in Willow Pool Garden. In the House of Jen. Elegance, beauty, nobility. Not overtly based on money, not like the elegant predatoriness which characterized Europe's postwar elite, the jet set whose glittering eyes immediately calculated the price of her dress, her jewels, her shoes. She was aware of the vulgarity of their exclusiveness, the mediocrity of the organs of publicity, geared to make that vulgarity chic.

Men with just the right touch of silver at their temples had approached her, and she knew they were holding their stomachs in. Younger men in elegant whites on the tennis court gave her that filtered, sexy look between half-closed eyelids which was supposed to send her spinning, and she thought: Put myself in *those* hands? Never.

Yong, oh Yong. You have made it impossible for me to fall for the second-rate, the mediocre. . . .

Stephanie flew back to New York. "How was Europe?" asked John Moore, who had come in his Volvo to meet her at Kennedy Airport. "I've got an album full of newspaper clippings raving about the fabulously beautiful Texas sensation. You."

Stephanie smiled, looked at him, thought: It will have to be John, and replied, "I saw them with the eyes of another world. It was fun, but not really fascinating."

And when they reached her house in Sutton Place, she leaned back and said: "John, I came back to be with you."

There were so many things they enjoyed together. Paintings and painters, concerts, exhibitions. They could discuss so many topics, and John always had something to give from a well-furnished mind.

And through John Moore, as through Dick Steiner, both endowed with many friends, Stephanie acquired knowledge, expanded her interests, listened and was listened to in circles that otherwise would have ignored her.

Contentment came to her, an end to the tumult of the body's cells, which also creates havoc in the mind.

But contentment breeds its own litter of discontent. The fever of the bone remained, which no contact of flesh could allay.

She wondered if John would notice. He had been so happy, for many months. And then, gradually, a certain dissatisfaction arose in him. She had caught him looking out at the night through the windows which reflected her living room's objects and returned to him his face, blurred with sadness.

He deserved to be loved, deserved more than this facile compromise: the allotted time, the reserved evenings, the calculated holidays together . . .

And then one night in late 1960, a letter came from Yong. A letter very different from the previous ones. All about reattaching a severed hand, making it function. Words strong with joy, with precise knowledge: "Eight of us worked in relays . . . it took about nine hours . . . that was five weeks ago . . . today he has moved his fingers . . . we are so happy . . ."

She had rung up the chief surgeon at the hospital in Dallas. "Yes, Mrs. Jen, we know . . . we do get Chinese medical journals, we even send them ours . . ." He chuckled. "Excellent results, with such poor equipment, truly great surgery, and since 1958 new breakthroughs in treatment of burns . . . we'd like to send a medical delegation to Peking to learn how they do it."

That evening she had talked about the operation to John, exuberant because Yong had sounded so happy, so liberated.

John smoked quietly, watching her.

"Stephanie, I'd like to ask you a question."

"Of course, fire away." She poured herself a drink, uncautious with happiness.

"What am I to you, Stephanie? What do I represent in your mind?"

"John, I care for you, you know that, more than for anyone else I've met, except of course Yong. I've never lied to you . . ."

And then *click*, she had said Yong too often now and the ghost was back, and she was shaking, shaking and spilt her drink.

"I'm sorry," she said, "I'm sorry, I can't get rid of . . . it's like that every time . . ."

"Have you told your husband that you're sleeping with me?"

"No, I haven't."

"Stephanie, when I make love to you, do you imagine it's Yong?"

"No, John. I don't."

I couldn't. I couldn't. How could I? Just dreaming of him makes me cry out, makes me weak. I lock him out, lock him away. The heart's a jail too. Part of me is in that jail, with Yong.

"Stephanie, your husband's not a fool. He must wonder. He must spend hours thinking of you, thinking and imagining . . . as I do . . ."

"John, you're obsessed . . ."

"I *am* obsessed." He rose, went to pour himself another drink, lit another cigarette. "I love you. I want to marry you. I thought that in time you'd begin caring for me . . ."

"I do care."

"Yes . . ." He was going to say: As you care for your employees, your concerns, I'm in the scheme of all your enterprises; but he forbore. "It's not quite enough for me now."

She said in that grave and beautiful voice she had which belonged to the other Stephanie, the one he would never possess: "John, that's how things are."

He was suddenly angry. "How long will you go on lying to yourself? Pretending you can go back? Look at you, at all this around you . . . You can't give it up . . . you cannot live with him now in whatever godforsaken hole they've stuck him into. And you can't bring him out . . . because he'll never ask to leave China. Some do, some with families abroad. But no matter how badly China treats your husband he's going to stick to it. You know that. It's in his bones. Centuries of responsibility."

"I've got to lie to myself to go on living," said Stephanie. "Life's necessary perjury. That's what Yong called it."

She saw the thin gray strands curl up from his cigarette, like lazy question marks.

He sighed, and came to kiss her gently on the cheek. "You win, Stephanie. Faithful and faithless together, as we have to be. D. H. Lawrence. He knew it, and I guess we live it."

And then, in early 1961, she had written to Yong, telling him about John Moore and herself, at last.

He had replied. Offering her a divorce. Telling her he was rehabilitated. The letter had come to her when she was in Dallas. There was a children's party on, Swallow and her school friends playing in the garden. Their shrieks floated up in the mild warmth.

Rehabilitated. Then perhaps, perhaps his country would let her go to him. Perhaps her country would let him come

570

to her. She wrote: "I do miss you, miss you and Winter Treasure." But she knew that she was being equivocal, playing with dreams.

That had been five years ago and he had not written again. However, Winter Treasure continued writing, giving her news of the Family, of his father. "Papa is so busy with his new surgery. He travels much, going to many hospitals. The team of surgeons in Shanghai has become quite famous. Aunt Jen (Widow) says she remembers you. She thanks you for the coat you sent."

Meanwhile the war in Vietnam had expanded, extended. Meanwhile Kennedy had been assassinated in Dallas. Meanwhile more and more "military observers" had gone to Vietnam. There were, in 1966, 150,000 GIs in South Vietnam; and the generals were announcing, as was President Johnson, that there was light at the end of the tunnel, that the Vietcong would be definitely beaten by year's end.

John Moore and Stephanie flew to Hongkong in May 1966. From Hongkong, John would leave for Saigon, to have his own look at the Vietnam War.

twenty-five

HONGKONG was soggy with June heat. A cheesecloth sky spread its mildew over the harbor, and all the gold and turquoise of winter, its splendor of white-foamed islands rising from the rainbow sea, were drowned in a monotony of patchy gray. Indecisive clouds hung formlessly above the hills, and the crowded pavements were clammy with sweating people.

Hongkong was booming. A contract between its British-run government and China assured the Colony a constant supply of water from the mainland. The border with China at Lowu Railway Station still kept up its simulacrum of vigilance—barbed wire festoons and revolvered police. It continued to cater to tourists avid for a peek at "Red China." Daily, Chinese trains rumbled into Hongkong, loaded with live pigs, vegetables, fruit, poultry, ducks, to feed the Colony.

The business of certificates of origin flourished. Local factories produced them, as genuine looking as the ones required by U.S. Customs from American tourists making purchases in Hongkong.

The Vietnam War greatly increased Hongkong's prosperity. Since 1964 the British Colony had become a rest and recreation center for GIs from Vietnam. The GIs kept on increasing. There would be half a million of them in Vietnam by 1968. The bars, the brothels, and the drug trade flourished, and so did a new type of gonorrhea which was resistant to penicillin.

But it was not of boom-time Hongkong that Eddy Keng talked to Stephanie in his air-conditioned office on the seventeenth floor of the Keng Lai building, whose glass panes commanded a magnificent view of the busy harbor.

"Auntie, things not so good in China. Even my friends, the Communists in Hongkong, and the Chinese chamber of commerce businessmen, they don't understand too well what goes on . . ."

The Hongkong Communists were a sophisticated, seasoned group. Link and listening post for the People's Republic in a Hongkong stuffed with agents of all kinds and all countries, they operated with tact, delicacy, and discretion, under the exuberant, erudite advice of Mr. Wei, the manager of a prestigious left-wing newspaper. Mr. Wei's immense capacity for somersaulting over any political obstacle in true Chinese style commanded respect, admiration, and envy from every diplomat in the many consulates of Hongkong. But if even Mr. Wei was nonplused, then it was time to worry.

"Nobody can tell what is going to happen," said Eddy Keng.

It had all begun like a comic opera, in January 1966. With a major debate, full of long and twisted arguments, about the merits and demerits of a theater play. Suddenly it had turned into a major political struggle within the Party, massive denunciation of "revisionism" among some Party leaders. Revisionism was a word used in China to condemn the Soviet Union, its leaders and its policies.

Jungly with angry words and slogans, hallucinatory with vituperative argument, a stunning avalanche of newspaper articles condemning "people in authority IN THE PARTY who follow the capitalist road" and "freaks and monsters in commanding positions in culture, in education . . ." had followed.

"It's another political campaign," said Stephanie, already queasy with remembered anxiety.

"No, Auntie. My father, he writes: 'This not simple movement . . . this a real revolution.'" When thoroughly upset, Eddy Keng fell back into clipped Chinglish.

There were, he explained, two main factions in the Party. The story of the Chinese revolution was also the story of conflict between two major groups, whose protagonists varied, whose views and policies would also change, but who fought for leadership. And upon this leadership the very fate of the revolution had often depended.

573

Thus in 1935, after a long period of the most bitter infighting, it was Mao, his line, his policies, that had triumphed, during and after the Long March, against the Stalin-organized group of Party leaders known as the "Twenty-eight Bolsheviks," who rendered unconditional obedience to Moscow. Thus Mao had bitterly fought Stalin during those years for China's independence from the USSR. And now, it seemed, once again there was a big struggle within the Party as to the course to follow. But it was all so confused, so mixed up with domestic policies, with the shape of the economy, with the speed at which China could or should progress. . . . "No one really knows what's going on," Eddy concluded.

And this time, everyone would be involved, everyone was bound to be affected by this new earthquake in China.

As Stephanie listened she felt anxiety lurching alive inside her. That constriction which seized the throat, altered the voice, clutched all of her with a thick sluggishness. The insatiable worm of worry, awake and gnawing her substance away.

Yong. Yong was seasoned, had been rehabilitated. Yong knew how to maneuver. But Winter Treasure would only be eighteen years old in December. The vulnerable age, when youth is most foolhardy, intolerant, and careless, giving all of itself, and too easily disillusioned.

"What do we do, Eddy?"

"Nothing. Sit tight. Hold on. Wait and watch. Do too much, and trouble comes."

The Vietnam War was a complicating factor, obscuring the main issues. Would China link hands with Russia now because of the Vietnam War? Or would Mao's vision of America and China coming together in peace and friendship prevail at last? "Some high-ups in the Chinese Party want to have unity of action with Russia, to help Vietnam," said Eddy Keng. "But Mao, the old fellow, he get very angry. He say no. He say never trust the Russians, never. He say China help Vietnam, Russia help Vietnam, but not together."

And Stephanie understood. Her years in China had cleared her mind. Beyond the transient lies the permanent. Permanent was Moscow's desire to get America and China to fight each other. With "unity of action," Moscow might maneuver China to fight the Americans once again, as had happened in Korea, hobbling both China and the United States in Vietnam.

"It's another typhoon, this Cultural Revolution, Auntie. A very big typhoon," said Eddy Keng, laughing he-he-he, which he always did when he was upset. "My father say: 'Do not write. Letters from abroad dangerous. Do not write until typhoon blow away.'"

Keng Dawei felt correspondence was dangerous. Winter Treasure did not.

In the last four years, Winter Treasure had taken over the responsibility of writing to his mother on behalf of the whole Family, including his father. Twice a month, unfailingly, came his letters. Chatty, courteous, reassuring. But now he wrote twice a week, and in a hurry, as if he could not wait any longer.

"Chairman Mao has called on us, the young, to criticize the Party bureaucrats who abuse their power. Until now they could not be touched, could not be removed. Fierce as tigers whose tails cannot be tweaked! Mama, we feel proud and happy to have been entrusted with this great task: to renew the spirit of the revolution! . . .

"Some of these leaders are corrupt, their children have many privileges, they import foreign cars and television sets, whereas an ordinary person gets sentenced to re-education if he owns a jazz record.

"All over China we are now rising against those in the Party who are taking the revisionist, the capitalist road. . . ."

Stephanie was shaken. Her son, surely, must know that he came from a capitalist family. Had he then repudiated the Jens? His letter did not indicate this. Perhaps he made a difference between patriotic capitalists, like Uncle Keng and the Jens, and the new breed of "capitalists" whose capital was their Party membership, rank, power. . . .

Stephanie had learnt to read between the lines. She remained for two weeks in Hongkong, although it was unbearable to be so near to China, to see the trains chugging to Lowu, the boundary, a forty-minute journey, and to be unable to take it. She walked and walked the streets and listened to the radio, to the thousand and one surmises

575

about the "Cultural Revolution," the new upheaval in China. When the pressure upon her became too great, she explored the jade and jewelry shops and bought lavishly, spending money as catharsis. And found one day two bangles of the purest apple green jade, which she decided to buy for Mother because they looked exactly like the ones Mother once had. She also bought an opulent, queenlike, triple-rank necklace of pearls for Isabelle.

"We parade with flags and portraits of Chairman Mao . . . the Party has sent task forces, teams of investigators, into the universities to expose freaks and monsters . . . some professors, teachers, writers have been denounced, humiliated. . . . I do not think this is right . . . it looks as if someone in the Party is trying to protect the top Party cadres by turning us against inoffensive teachers . . ." wrote Winter Treasure.

In late July the task forces were denounced by Mao, who called their work "fifty days of enforced white terror" inspired by the "Khrushchev-like" person in the Chinese Communist Party.

It became clear that Mao was fighting for a pure, primitive type of populist communism similar to the early Christians who shared everything with each other, and that his own stratified establishment, the Chinese Communist Party hierarchy, he now considered had become a bureaucracy reproducing China's past mandarin tyranny.

In August, the Red Guards, millions of them, appeared. All dressed in neat regimental khaki, with red bands around their arms. And they could not have been created, organized so speedily, had it not been for the Minister of Defense, Lin Piao, who was now Mao Tsetung's chief supporter. Lin Piao had been a prestigious army commander during the Long March, and he was now considered Mao's heir.

Soon there were millions of Red Guards surging from every middle school, every university in China. They were seconded by Lin Piao's army units, conveyed in army lorries.

"Everyone of good class origin now becomes a Red Guard," wrote Winter Treasure. "Some of the Red Guards are not so young; they are over thirty years old. . . ." The age limit was supposed to be twenty-six.

And now there was a reversal. Those who had terrorized

576

the others were in turn terrorized. High-level Party officials were reviled, dragged to struggle meetings, had dunce caps put on their heads. The head of Public Security. Various ministers. Many high officials in the culture and education establishments as well as certain writers who enjoyed official favor were thus reviled, humiliated. And some of them committed suicide.

"The Four Freedoms of the Cultural Revolution have been proclaimed," wrote Stephanie's son. "Freedom to write our wall posters; to debate anything; to assemble; and to travel . . . We, the young, must abolish superstition, feudal behavior, all the old ways of thinking and acting which are detrimental . . . but no one quite knows what 'abolish' means. Some young people think it means that everything old is bad. Red Guards are assaulting old people, beating old writers, destroying old monuments. . . . Chairman Mao said the Cultural Revolution must be done without violence. But violence is becoming a bad habit. . . ."

Stephanie prayed: "Oh God, please don't let anything happen to Winter Treasure." Violence like drugs was habit forming. It got hold of a youngster and then there was no way out but more violence.

Lionel Shaggin wrote affable short notes to Stephanie. "This upheaval is to prevent China going the way of the Soviet Union. It gives the people the right to criticize officials, to dismiss corrupt cadres . . . but people are easily fooled, they fall into a pattern of obeying new tyrants who seem, for a while, to represent new freedoms. . . ." Lionel's wariness was obvious. It complemented Winter Treasure's guarded warnings at the increasing violence. "Some of the Red Guards are behaving so badly, the people do not like it . . . but our Family has not been unduly harassed. . . ."

"What does 'not unduly' mean, Eddy?"

"He means, little bit of trouble. Everyone still alive. Life important, Auntie."

True. The watershed came between life and death. The dead have no voice.

In October cases of violence and vandalism were reported from all the large cities. There were now hundreds of Red Guard groups and they were beginning to quarrel among themselves.

"The worst thing is that one group will already have searched a street, ransacked the houses for 'black material,' suspicious books, gold, guns; and then another group comes in and repeats the process," wrote Winter Treasure. "I do not think this is what Chairman Mao meant by the Cultural Revolution. . . ."

"My son China Warrior is a Red Guard; he keeps me in touch . . . we live very quietly . . . the situation is very complex and it is impossible at the moment to draw a clear picture . . ." wrote Lionel Shaggin.

Most of the Red Guards were youths from middle schools. They were sixteen, seventeen years old. Most of them had never seen a Venus de Milo, a Cupid, and considered these reproductions indications of high pornography and, therefore, of "revisionism" and "capitalism." Others simply became vandals and pilferers, cashing in on the Red Guard label but behaving like bandit gangs.

"Round Round, Aunt Meiling Yee's daughter, has become a Red Guard in Peking," wrote Winter Treasure. "And I too have become a Red Guard. My friends insist that not class origin, but good behavior, should be the basis for becoming a Red Guard. Our organization is dedicated to using no violence, to protecting the people, to scrupulous honesty . . . we go on searches, but we are glad to paint on the house doors: 'This house has been searched and must not be searched again.' This helps occasionally—many innocent people are being harassed."

Stephanie spent the Christmas and New Year holidays with her daughter Marylee in Dallas. Marylee was now nine years old. She was a pretty girl, with small bones, an inquisitive spirit, and a great toughness. She would never let go of any topic, but clung tenaciously to it until she was satisfied that no more could be said on the subject. And she had absolutely no fear of being hurt, either physically or mentally. At times, she seemed almost to resent her mother. "Why did you leave my father?" she would ask accusingly. And she would look at all the photographs, and ask and ask again about Winter Treasure. "I want to see my brother," she would say. "And my father."

"We shall, darling, certainly . . . but it is difficult at the moment."

"Because of the war, I know," said Swallow, meaning the Vietnam War. She had the problem—in the exclusive school

578

she attended in Dallas—of trying to make her two utterly different worlds fit, and she could only succeed by this surgical brutality she showed towards herself and others. "It doesn't hurt," she had said when once, leaping over a hedge, she had deeply gashed her leg on a rusty, jagged piece of iron, and hobbled home with a handkerchief tied around the wound. And in that refusal to be hurt, refusal to be lulled and petted, refusal to refuse the unpleasant, there was something so fierce and vital that Stephanie contemplated her daughter with wonder, wondering what she would become.

In school Marylee was respected because she was so tough and so forthright. She was told how wicked Red China was, how awful the Communists were, how they killed everyone, how there was no freedom in Red China. She would come home and interrogate her mother. "It cannot be so bad if my father is there," she said, frowning. Like many pre-teenagers, she adulated the absent parent, and had a large picture of Yong in her room. "Most people don't think in enough *detail*," she told her mother. "They like to smother everything in generalities." She would spend hours in the garden putting up a rockery and a pool. From Chinatown in New York, Stephanie obtained for her daughter goldfish of two kinds: the chrysanthemum-eyed variety and the gold and black translucent type with tails twice the size of their bodies.

In Marylee's school the Vietnam War was lauded; it was a great crusade against the forces of evil. Americans were sacrificing themselves for democracy, freedom, and Christianity. "In my class there is a girl whose father is in Vietnam, and he's sent her mummy the ear of a Cong," said Marylee. "Preserved in something. Her mother is so upset she's getting a divorce. Would my father do something like that, Mummy?"

"Your father is a doctor, Swallow. He does not kill, he heals. But the girl's father, maybe he's gone crazy with the war . . ."

Stephanie had dreaded the day when she would have to explain to Swallow that the world was fundamentally incoherent, savage, illogical, and this fundamental madness had to be lived with. But Marylee seemed born with the knowledge that the world was unfair. Perhaps because her rage for living was so great. And Stephanie found it easy to talk to her of paradox and inconsequence. "We do things for one purpose, and the result turns out just the opposite."

Swallow nodded sagely. "I know," she said.

And so Stephanie found herself comforted by her daughter, who seemed almost biologically capable of accepting a totally insecure state of world—the gods of hazard and necessity as its rulers—and did not require the ultimatum of a total conviction.

In January 1967 the Chinese Army was called out to restore order in the land. The confusion brought about by churning up popular resentment against the Party (Mao's doing) had spread to factories, and even to communes. "Chou Enlai is trying to keep things going, to keep China together," wrote Winter Treasure. "But the new power-grabbers are attacking him.

"The many Red Guard groups are battling each other. . . . They have been robbing the arsenals for weaponry, and also pillaging the trains with weapons for Vietnam."

Thus the letters came, relayed through Eddy Keng in Hongkong.

Spring went into summer. The Cultural Revolution in China as well as the Vietnam War escalated; both, in Stephanie's mind, began to assume a similarity, a resemblance in their paranoia which made them twin cataclysms, mirror images of each other.

In Vietnam, the slaughter, the body counts, the strikes, the defoliation, the burning with napalm, with phosphorus, the desolation inflicted, the cadavers aligned, the admitted torture of prisoners, became a daily chorus of madness, obscuring the fact that the war was *not* being won. South Vietnamese generals popped into prominence, were hailed as saviors of democracy, men of the hour, and lasted a few months. Fragging began. Frustrated GIs rolled live grenades into their officers' tents. A nightmare dimension invaded the reality of the war, and the pious cadences of those who argued for it began to sound like gibberish.

Meaningless victories were proclaimed in places no one knew, and which turned out to be rice fields; the endless rounds of self-persuasion on television, the moral immorality of scholarly experts, assuring the American public—by now restive—that light at the end of the tunnel was perceived, these could no longer cloak the reality. Young men rotting away in the endless putrefaction of the jungle, of their bodies, of their ideals . . .

In China too, the summer of 1967 saw the dominance of disorder. No one knew who was really fighting whom, which group was "revolutionary left" and which was not. All claimed to follow Mao, and battled each other. The army, told to support the "left," had to reverse itself quite often, and proved as confused as anyone else. Group after group came up to "seize power," to proclaim itself the one true reformer, only to go down in internecine battle with another group.

"This is almost a civil war," said Mao Tsetung.

In certain regions naïve youths filled with fine rage opened the jails and released the inmates, reasoning that these must be innocent, since they had been imprisoned by order of the "capitalist roaders" in the Party. And the criminals formed their own groups, and obtained weapons, and began their own random slaughter and pillage.

With the mounting disorder came increasing xenophobia. Anything foreign was suspect. The overseas Chinese were harassed, since they had "foreign connections" and had lived abroad. Arthur and Millie Chee were searched seventeen times. Every single book and letter they had was to be explained and to be translated to the inquisitors.

"Auntie," said Eddy Keng on the phone, his voice quavering, "I hope my dad don't keep any letters from any foreigners, not even from me, because I live in Hongkong."

I hope Yong and Winter Treasure have got rid of my letters, thought Stephanie.

John Moore was busy writing a book on Vietnam. He had been there three times within the year, and each time became more pessimistic about the outcome of the war. He wrote a series of articles that earned him the dislike of President Johnson and his entourage. Walter Lippmann had also drawn the President's anger. "Lippmann had thought that the Kennedy administration would perform the needed reappraisal of our role in the world," said John. "But the bright spirits around him proved more obtuse than many a Republican die-hard, and more dangerously so, for they kept on projecting a 'liberal' image, while launching America into this disastrous war. Johnson has to continue to live up to the Kennedy myth. It's not his fault."

In 1967 and 1968 the university campuses in America erupted into anti-war demonstrations. The question of Vietnam now affected, involved every single American household. No one was immune. Friends who had known each other for decades no longer greeted each other; couples who disagreed on Vietnam sought divorce as the only way out.

"Perhaps it is our tragedy, as it is China's present tragedy, not to have really come to terms with our own reality," wrote John Moore.

All over America seminars were being held about Vietnam. And perforce they would also involve a reappraisal of American foreign policy towards China. "The Chinese will accept neutrality in Southeast Asia," wrote John Moore. "Chou Enlai has made this very clear. The Chinese regard the USSR as the main danger; they see the Vietnam War as helping the USSR to establish itself in the region, and that is what they do not want. . . ."

"We have no credible policy for either winning the war or ending it," said Walter Lippmann, and John Moore repeated these words.

In August 1967 the British Embassy in Peking was burnt down by a mob of Red Guards.

By now it was clear that the Chinese Army was unhappy about the actions of these youths. Army commanders bore down hard on them, arresting them and carting them into camps. Within the army itself there were many commanders who wanted an end to the Cultural Revolution, and Mao would consult them in that August. Chou Enlai held China together, held it by the sheer force of reason and his own personality. He had tried to contain the movement within the schools and universities, as an expanded nonviolent debate. But the popular forces released by Mao were shaking the whole system, were weakening the Party.

Strikes occurred in Hongkong. Local "Red Guards" appeared. Three bombs were set off which blew up one car and killed five people. The wealthy panicked and some fled.

Much real estate was bought at a ridiculously low price by the banks and by shrewd entrepreneurs. Kengstone stood fast, and Sir Henry Keng said at a press conference in London: "Hongkong will not be taken over." He went about calmly buying what others gave up.

Joan Wu came out of China, to Hongkong, and proceeded to Canada. Her mother had breast cancer and was being operated on in Toronto, because Joan did not wish to set foot in her native U.S.A., where her passport might be taken from her.

Stephanie flew to Toronto to meet Joan, who looked as placid and unworried as she always had, and whose contempt for Stephanie, who had "run away," was obvious. "My, but you *do* look prosperous," said Joan, looking up and down Stephanie's expensive tailored suit.

"Joan, have you seen Yong? Your husband must have . . . can you tell me how he is keeping?"

Joan pursed her lips. "Dr. Jen Yong? I haven't seen him; we've all been so busy making revolution, we've had no time for social gatherings. I understand he was rehabilitated. He seems to have done good work in surgery. It did these bourgeois intellectuals a lot of good to be re-educated by the working class."

"There have been murders, and some people have committed suicide . . ."

"Sensationalism. You shouldn't believe all those exaggerations . . ."

Stephanie was patient. "I know there's always some exaggeration, Joan . . . and I don't feel good about Vietnam, I feel terrible. You must know that I've protested, refused to handle war contracts . . ."

Joan bridled angrily. "How can you compare the atrocities in Vietnam to the great proletarian Cultural Revolution?" she cried.

"I'm not comparing. I'm only saying it's strange, isn't it, that it's taking place together . . . starting almost at the same time. . . . I'm only trying to say that all killing is senseless."

"I do not agree," said Joan. She began to lecture. "In such a big revolution, there are some errors and mistakes; but there must also be firm handling of those who would like China to return to the past. . . . Now the people are really stirred up, and that's important. Why, for the first time we have a system of barefoot doctors, of paramedical personnel in every village . . . education is to be reformed, no longer only an elite in the universities. We want the children of workers and peasants also to have a chance, and not to be thrown out by the second year, as has happened so often, because the professors are in cahoots with the high officials. . . ."

Mollified by her own eloquence, she told Stephanie how she and Herbert Luger and other foreign experts in Peking had formed their own Red Guard group, assaulted and criticized other foreigners living in China who did not reach their own level of revolutionary fervor. "They were siding with the capitalist roaders, we settled their hash," said Joan with great satisfaction. Herbert Luger had personally gone through the bookshelves of a fellow expert and weeded out obnoxious material.

"Like Cohn and Schine," murmured Stephanie.

"How can you compare Herb's revolutionary behavior with McCarthyism?" shouted Joan furiously.

A sharp reply rose to Stephanie's lips. But she forbore. To antagonize Joan was not her intention. Mildly, she said: "Joan, please tell Yong that I've received all my son's letters; I understand I mustn't write, but I'm thinking of them all every day."

Joan nodded reluctantly, and then said: "When the revolution comes, your world will be swept away."

In mid-September Mao Tsetung returned from a tour of China and conferences with military commanders who were not happy with the incipient chaos. He now entrusted Chou Enlai with the winding up of the Red Guards. It was clear that Mao himself was disappointed with the behavior of the youth whom he had trusted.

Chou Enlai ordered the youth organizations to turn in all weapons, to return to their universities and middle schools, there to "make revolution within the institutions" not outside them.

"The Cultural Revolution is being wound up . . . order is being restored . . . " wrote the Hongkong newspapers. Eddy Keng, too, was heartened. "Maybe soon all over," he shouted over the telephone to Stephanie.

"So many of us are now disheartened, downcast. We had such high hopes. But now we feel that we have been manipulated in a power play between two factions . . ." wrote Winter Treasure.

This was the last letter Stephanie would receive from her son.

In early 1968 the army began restoring order by arresting a good many of the Red Guard leaders. Most of the young were heartily sick of chaos. They wanted to return to their studies. But a sizable proportion had acquired the taste for wandering, for wanton violence; the factional battles among the various groups and against the contingents sent to restore order would continue for another two years.

A formidable youth problem loomed. Every year more millions were born, and the economy could not absorb them. In the past, the infant mortality rate had been two hundred fifty per thousand. It was now around twenty-five per thousand, and work had to be found for all the young of China coming up on the labor market. For years the government had taken care of the problem by assigning jobs to young people, even if it meant four or five workers would do what could be done by a single person.

But now there were millions of middle-school adolescents who would never return to study. It would be another two years before universities and schools would reopen. And by that time, another crop of youths would enter them.

The only way to deal with thirty million redundant young was to employ them in the countryside, distributing them among the villages, in the communes. "They must be re-educated by the workers, peasants, and soldiers of China" was the slogan.

The trek of several million youngsters to state farms, to military-run agricultural estates, to communes, began in 1968.

Stephanie wondered whether Winter Treasure too had been sent out of Shanghai to some commune, to do manual labor. Meanwhile, she was opening yet another wing in a hospital for disabled veterans from Vietnam. And seeing these young men, crippled through a war they had not chosen, each one some mother's Winter Treasure, she felt again the tragedy of both countries—for if America had helped China way back in those early years when decision was fateful, there would have been no Korean War, no Vietnam War, and no Cultural Revolution.

Each one of these events had taken place because myth-making, rather than reality, had determined a certain course of action. Self-deception, which also meant deceiving others, had prevailed. And wrought its particular havoc.

Abruptly certain foreign experts living in China were arrested.

Among those jailed were Herbert Luger and his wife, Alicia.

Herbert Luger's radio broadcasts had been impeccable panegyrics about the Cultural Revolution. He was reputed to be a great friend of the rising power constellation. Then why had he been jailed?

"Possible spy mania," said Michael Anstruther when Stephanie telephoned him in London. "Our agency man in Peking is also under house arrest, as are a couple of West German engineers, invited by the Government to build a steel plant."

Stephanie began to pray. She now found herself daily praying for Yong, for Winter Treasure. Praying to God, not bothering whether he was Catholic, Methodist, or Presbyterian, merely praying, the prayer coming out of her spontaneously.

"Oh please, please, dear God, I should have stayed with Yong . . . I should have stayed . . . I have let him down, let them both down, please look after them."

Having no news, not a word from them, was almost unbearable.

"Mama," said Swallow. She said "Mama" with a slightly French accent. The result of holidays with Grand'mère in Provence.

"Yes, my darling?"

"Are you praying for my daddy and my brother? As Grand'mère prays for us every day?"

"Yes, my darling. I am doing what Grand'mère has been doing for many years."

"But is it *useful?*" asked Marylee. "I do not think God is a good person, Mama. Otherwise he would not let bad things

586

happen. I am not at all sure that God is smart to let them happen, and *then* make people beg him to stop."

"God always lets human beings use their free will, to do good or bad things . . ."

Marylee tossed her head as her mother used to do. "Today I hit a girl who said my daddy must be a bad man. I'll hit anyone who says it. . . ."

"Oh darling, darling," said Stephanie, "come, come here."

She could feel the small body pressed against hers, quivering, quivering with anger, and also hurt. "Oh God," prayed Stephanie, "please, please make it all come out right."

They stood in the lorry as it rolled slowly along the main avenue. Their bent heads met the stares of faces looking up at them. But there was no anger, no insult, nothing but silence, a transient interest, then its slackening, as the indifferent crowd paced away.

Each one of them had a board around the neck: "Bourgeois Authority." Yong had another word on his panel: "Unrepentant Rightist."

Shanghai was now under the "left" revolutionaries. There had been many such scenes, and the novelty had worn off.

Next to Yong was Dr. Hsieh. Dr. Fan stood farther towards the rear of the lorry. On Yong's other side was a colleague who had been particularly censorious about rightists, way back in 1957—over ten years ago. He was now taking his own exposure very badly. "A gentleman prefers death to insult," he mumbled. Yong noticed how bald he was becoming.

"Don't be ridiculous," said Hsieh to him. "To die does not arrange matters."

"When will it be over?" said Dr. Fan. This was the first time he was being paraded. Hsieh and Yong had been paraded three times already. They were used to the routine.

"Another hour or so," someone said. "They always stop at the river's edge, shout a few slogans, and then return us to the hospital."

"Bourgeois authorities, keep your heads down and don't talk," shouted the Red Guard with the megaphone.

The hospital had been "seized" by a new revolutionary committee. This was the third time in the year that a new and pure "revolutionary committee" was in charge of the hospital. The changes had come, however, without breakage of equipment or too much interference with medical work.

In the front lorry was the most recently dethroned revolutionary committee, its members with labels around their necks. As they had labeled their predecessors.

Yong yawned. There was work to do. Once again he had been labeled a "rightist." His previous rehabilitation had been done by "those Party people in authority taking the capitalist road" it was explained to him. Hence it was invalid. "But they were the same people who condemned me in the first place," Yong protested.

The parade ended and Yong hurried back to the surgical ward, to complete his unfinished work. Dr. Hsieh went home, and so did the bald-headed doctor, still muttering: "This is unbearable . . . a gentleman cannot lose face . . ." Some of the doctors went through a ritual washing of their faces and hands after the parade, as if the act of washing gave them back their face.

Dr. Fan whispered a funny story to Yong. Now that everyone was labeled something or other, all enduring the same harassment, no one cared whether Yong was a rightist and everyone spoke to him. "D'you know what happened when 'they' went to get . . ." he mentioned a famous comedian. "He was waiting for them with a big dunce cap he had made himself. 'I thought I would spare you the trouble,' he said, and put it on." Yong laughed. Dr. Liu, who had not been paraded this time, came in briskly, smiling and humming.

"I'd like to be jailed at the moment," said Liu conversationally. "I'm told one meets the very best people in jail. Everyone who is anyone in the Party is in jail. And when once again Heaven and Earth change places, it will be worthwhile having known all the best people." All the doctors guffawed.

When he had ended his check of the wards, Yong returned to his small apartment in the doctors' dormitory. The building had been a missionary compound in the 1920s.

Solid wooden floors, good windows. Apartments with one, two, or three bedrooms. His ground floor one-bedroom apartment had a small balcony on which he could sit in the evening. "Dr. Jen is thinking, looking at the stars," whispered his neighbors. And asked their children to be quiet and forbore to intrude, knowing that a man needs his own thoughts and dreams, especially when he faces the firmament.

What else could Jen Yong do? thought Dr. Hsieh, who lived across the garden. While his Belgian wife stolidly cooked the beef ragout in red wine which he hated but which she fed him, Hsieh would see the indistinct white shape, alone on the balcony. What else can a man do when he faces his own solitude?

Hsieh would watch until the thickening night took over. He would turn to his wife, his wife who had no idea what went on, whose only encounter with the turmoil had been the day a young boy on the street had thrown a large cabbage root at her. "I threw it right back at him," she had said. Someone else might have been arrested as counter-revolutionary, but the crowd had laughed, delighted with her. Hsieh's children had been systematically and completely uninvolved. "You are foreigners," they were told. They stayed home, read, and complained, and knew nothing of what went on. And Hsieh grinned, looking at the balcony, now empty. After he had been paraded on the lorry with the other doctors and had returned, he had told his wife. And her only remark had been, "You haven't caught cold, have you?" Catching a cold was, to her, the greatest calamity.

Night fell with that quick blackness of autumn which heaps its velvet into all the corners of its domain. Yong walked into his bedroom, did not turn on the light. He went to the wall which faced his bed and put his hand on it, lightly. "Stephanie," he whispered. "Stephanie."

Stephanie was there. Behind the gray wallpaper.

When the Red Guards had come the previous year, looking for "black" material, the walls of rooms had also been scrutinized. Some people had concealed old pictures and scrolls, family genealogy books, pasting them beneath the plaster.

The Red Guards had scraped every wall, tearing the wallpaper painstakingly. Yong had watched them. Stephanie had been pinned neatly between two leaves of wood, on the underside of a drawer. Winter Treasure and he had slit the wood and inserted the photograph.

After they had gone, Yong had repapered his two rooms, openly, not concealing himself. He had moved Stephanie's picture from the drawer to the wall. Furniture, chiefly desks, was now being requisitioned by the new revolutionary committee. Supposing his desk were taken, he would lose Stephanie . . .

"You will be safe," he had whispered to the photograph of Stephanie with her windblown hair, the laughter he could hear in the silence. "I do not see your face, my beloved, but I know that you are there, and now perhaps we shall have peace, you and I. . . ."

It comforted him greatly. Every night he touched the paper lightly, so lightly. With the tips of his fingers. "Stephanie, I shall now tell you what happened today, as I have told you every day since you went away. I shall write it all down. The letter will never reach you, but never mind. Every word of mine will have been alive, even if only for a short hour."

He sat down at the desk. He wrote. In the darkness. He had become adept at doing everything in the dark. By feel.

"Stephanie, shall I tell you again how much I love you, and how I go on living because I am waiting for you; and I have to give every hour that I can to the hope, the hope that perhaps, somehow, someday, I shall see you again in this life?"

When he had ended he carefully gathered the thin sheets of the letter and tore them up, tore them into small bits, very small. And put the shreds in the stove of the kitchen, among the ashes. In the morning he lit the stove to boil water for tea, to warm up a little rice gruel. He ate his other meals at the canteen. The letter would burn.

The nights were becoming cooler and now he used the light patchwork quilt that Stephanie and he had bought in New York, in a shop on Madison Avenue that sold American home handicrafts. He loved that quilt very much. It was, like Stephanie's picture in the wall, a thing he could keep. It made his solitude endurable. He had had to discard everything else.

Jen Lin, Winter Treasure, knew himself a man. He was almost twenty years old in that autumn of 1968, and he had grown well, having been initiated into manhood at twelve by his father, when his father had placed upon him the burden of his own life. Twelve is the right age for children to encounter adulthood, to discard childishness.

Children master sorrow and fear well. The shrinking away from grief, from pain, from horror, that sensitivity of the sinews and the brain, comes, as rheumatism does, with age. Children's fairy tales are terrifying and they teach a child to master his own fears. Winter Treasure had not needed fairy tales to know fear, to know how to live with it, circumvent it.

Winter Treasure understood that *Tietie* could not write to Mama. *Tietie* was afraid that writing to her would interfere with something nebulous to her son, which was called Mama's personal freedom. He accepted that Mama was good, that what she had done must not be commented upon, nor judged by her son. *Tietie* feared that Mama would be upset by his letters; and therefore Jen Lin, his son, must write for him. In the same way Grandfather and Grandmother sent good wishes, sent courteous messages through him. They did not write directly to their daughter-in-law, not wishing to impose the knowledge of their existence upon her. Jen Lin, man before his childtime was over, wrote to Mama for all the Family.

Only in the summer of 1967, because the post office was taken over by a revolutionary committee of the ultra-left, had he stopped writing.

"Illicit connections with the outside," screamed the newspapers. Letters to Hongkong were now opened, the stamps on the letters were unstuck in case messages were scribbled on their back.

Winter Treasure did not resume writing, despite the fact that in the autumn the disciplining of the Red Guards had begun.

Out of the thirty-million odd Red Guards now splintered into hundreds of groups, the vast majority, heartily sick of disorder, complied with the orders. Some of them, such as the group to which Winter Treasure belonged, had scrupulously adhered to the "no violence" directive.

Winter Treasure's group had disbanded. They had patrolled at night, intervening when they found other gangs dragging people out of their houses to beat them, to kill them. Some of them had been badly hurt in such encounters with gangs using spikes, spears, and knives. For about ten percent of the thirty-odd million Red Guards, violence had become a way of life.

Many of Winter Treasure's friends had been sent to State farms, to communes in the far north of Manchuria. Others, like himself, stayed in the city. The Government did not send away a "single child." Old people who needed care, who were disabled, were not to be deprived of the young who could care for them. Grandfather and Grandmother needed him; no other able-bodied adult was with them.

Twice a week, at night, Jen Lin scaled the wall of the hospital compound. He would scratch at his father's bedroom window. They would speak, very softly.

Once a month Jen Lin went to call on Uncle Keng. Since Uncle Keng was an old friend of the Family, this was not an illicit connection.

Uncle Keng was once again a "protected person," as was General Yee. That was Chou Enlai's doing. He tried to protect as many valuable people as possible. Scientists and nuclear experts and intellectuals of great achievement. Because of this, the new people in power hated Chou Enlai.

Uncle Keng had said to Winter Treasure: "Be careful about your mother. Do not tell foreigners about our troubles. Family grief is not to be aired outside. Remember that."

The Jen Family had survived the centuries; it would survive this typhoon.

Grandfather and Grandmother, *Tietie* and he had come together and decided to get rid of "black" material, feudal old things, illicit connections which might have excited the ignorant young.

The very good old porcelain and books and scrolls and calligraphy had been given to the museum which was a "protected place." The museum vaults contained many such heirlooms.

The Jens buried a few second-rate vases in the garden, at a fairly low level.

They buried the ancestor tablets and the Family records very deep.

They had Yong's pavilion sealed by Public Security.

And waited for the banging at the gate and the shouts: "Open, open, we are searching for 'black' material."

They were searched.

Some of the Red Guard groups were courteous, apologizing for their incursion, politely withdrawing after a cursory look.

But there were also posses of young from the provinces; to them all was abomination in Shanghai. Even running water faucets and the toilets were "foreign" and therefore to be destroyed. As were pianos, until Mao Tsetung's own wife intervened to save the pianos.

Such a band came down the street to Willow Pool Garden and roused Grandfather and Grandmother from sleep and kept them in their nightclothes on the verandah of their own pavilion for seventeen hours while they searched, and heaved, and threw furniture out, pulled drawers, tapped the walls, looking for hidden gold, hidden papers . . . anything.

They discovered the pavilion which had been Yong's and Stephanie's, which now housed their furniture and books and Stephanie's clothes. But there were great slips of paper pasted upon the door: "Protected by Public Security," and they did not dare to break the seals, which looked very imposing.

They dug up the garden very thoroughly.

Triumphantly, they dug up a vase; and Grandmother, confronted with it, exclaimed: "This must be very old. The archaeological department should be informed . . . we did not know that there was such a thing in our garden."

The Red Guards had to go to the archaeologists who said gravely that they would investigate the age of the vase.

Grandmother, watching them dig, had said pensively: "Poor children, so ignorant, it is a shame to cheat them . . . ."

The posse of young boys and girls, sixteen of them, stayed a week with the Jen Family. The house was pleasant, and there was a good bathroom. They used it abundantly. Baths make people friendly.

They investigated the ancestors' pavilion, found it empty. The girls moved in. They moved the two elderly people and

Winter Treasure to one of the servants' rooms, and invited five worker families to live in the pavilions.

For eighteen months, the three of them would live in that small room. "We have not been unduly harassed . . ." wrote Winter Treasure to his mother.

There was total unpredictability. The daughter of Mr. Tam, the millionaire from Indonesia, had married an American and they were never even visited by the Red Guards. But Mr. Tam's son, teaching in a school in an inland province, was arrested and beaten many times to make him confess that he was a spy for the CIA.

Winter Treasure made his grandparents comfortable. He slept on a pallet on the floor. He hauled water, coal, went to market, cooked on a small stove under an awning. At night he and his remaining friends met.

He went on studying. Textbooks, lecture notes circulated from hand to hand. A whole underground network of study was set up, functioned.

Round Round was in middle school when the Cultural Revolution began; she became a Red Guard, being eligible as the daughter of a fairly high Party cadre. She was a pretty, headstrong girl, dizzy with the idea of changing the world, rapturous, as many millions in China were rapturous then, with the promise of the Four Great Freedoms, an end to the stifling bureaucracy.

Round Round's love for Winter Treasure had not abated. She wrote to him, wrote to him often. She had loved him since she was four years old. Although her father said that Winter Treasure was a mixed blood and that mixed bloods were bad for the pure blood of the Chinese.

Her father also said that Round Round's mother was of bad class origin.

In the winter of 1966 Round Round's father had left for Shanghai. Her mother remained in Peking, and later was sent by the Ministry of Health on a friendship delegation to Albania, which supported the Cultural Revolution.

While Yee Meiling was away, her husband applied for a divorce, citing the fact that she was of bad class origin and he suspected her of conspiring with "the capitalist roaders in the Party."

"Comrade Sung's courageous exposure of Yee Meiling as a capitalist roader of bad class origin is to be commended. He has cut off all relations with Yee Meiling." He obtained the divorce in forty-eight hours.

Meanwhile Meiling's father, General Yee, left the big house where they all lived together and was staying with an army commander, a friend of his, in the south. Probably because he felt unsafe in Peking. But General Yee's palace was spared. Orders from Chou Enlai.

Round Round's group became increasingly violent. They began to beat people, selecting their victims haphazardly. Round Round followed and she too began to beat people.

The Ministry of Health was now seized by the "left." The previous administration Party cadres were paraded and their houses were searched.

Round Round lived as in a drugged dream, a drugged dream. She vomited and screamed at night. "You must temper yourself," the leader of the band told her. "This is revolution."

Meiling returned from Albania. She landed at the airport, not knowing that she had been divorced.

She was seized at the airport, where several of the seventy-nine Red Guard groups existing in Peking at the time were under the control of the Shanghai leaders.

She was taken to their headquarters. "But I live with my father, General Yee," she protested. General Yee was not available, they told her. "Let me send a message to my husband," she said.

"Your husband is in Shanghai, and he has divorced you," they told her. And showed her the clipping.

"My daughter Round Round is a Red Guard," she cried.

"Your daughter will be informed of your return. If she is a good Red Guard she will repudiate you."

"I don't believe it, I don't."

She was held in a cellar for three days and three nights, while the Red Guards relayed themselves in teams of four to question her, not letting her sleep, relaying themselves to make her confess that she had gone abroad to plot against the Cultural Revolution.

"But I was in Albania, Albania is a friendly country."

Ah, but she had been sent to Albania by the previous Health Ministry Party leadership, which now had been toppled and was being made to confess its crimes. Among

595

its crimes was that of sending a delegation abroad in order to plot against China.

"I want my daughter, Round Round . . ."

A meeting against her, and against the previous Party cadres in the Health Ministry, was held.

Meiling looked around. All faces she knew, all Party members, as she was, honest, scrupulous, some of them guerillas from way back, from the Long March, now lined up to be criticized.

In front of her were hundreds of people: the lower staff, the middle cadres of the Health Ministry. Many top jobs would now become available for these lower staff.

And there were the Red Guards. In one of the rows was Round Round.

"Round Round, daughter," called out Meiling, joyful. At last. But Round Round did not look at her. She kept her head down, her eyes fixed on the ground.

"Round Round, look, this is your mother . . ." she shouted, but then everyone was shouting, chanting slogans, and perhaps Round Round had not heard.

They were now being accused of this and that crime, but Meiling heard not a word. Her eyes stayed on Round Round who sat, sat, head bent.

And suddenly rose and, without looking at her mother, fled, rushed out, went down the runway between the seats, and was gone.

"Round Round."

Meiling felt better. At least Round Round had not risen to accuse her mother; she had fled, and Meiling was now worried that Round Round's peers would jeer, and scorn her, for being so sympathetic to a counter-revolutionary.

The previous ministry leadership would now clean the ministry rooms, do the menial work which they had inflicted upon others.

They were lodged in the basement of the ministry. Camp beds had been provided for them. Food and water. Army quilts.

One of her former colleagues said to her: "You were treated this way because your husband denounced you, otherwise it would not have happened to you. . . ."

"But my father . . ."

"Your father is in the south. It is reported that he is with a

596

group of the army that is against the 'left' and therefore he has no influence."

"I want to speak to my daughter," she told the Red Guards the next day.

"Your daughter will not speak to you. She has gone to Shanghai, to be with her father," was the reply.

Meiling cleaned, washed, scrubbed. Doing all things required very well, as she had always done her work well.

At noon on the third day, while all her fellow "criminals" were eating, and the new officials in power were also eating at the canteen, she walked up, up, up the stairs, to the top floor of the ministry building.

From the top floor there was a good view of the city, of the golden tiles of the imperial palaces. Of the massed green trees in the park.

She jumped.

She landed badly, on the marble verandah which girdled the lowest floor, in full view of everyone at the canteen.

Many of them screamed as the body came down.

It took some time to get a stretcher. To send for a doctor. Suicide was acknowledgment of criminal behavior. "Yee Meiling could not face the just verdict of the masses," someone said.

It took her an hour to die.

"Mrs. Jen," said the senator, "believe me, it's a great pleasure to meet with you."

In the quiet oak-paneled room with its beautiful antique furniture, its deep-set windows looking onto the mellow garden at the end of which a glimpse of the Potomac lay like a streak of light, were gathered well-known men, men of worth—and not always of one mind.

The time of reappraisal had come, a time painful and harrowing. Momentous decisions had to be made.

In April 1968 there had been a sudden announcement on television by President Johnson that he would not seek reelection.

"This may mean an end to the Vietnam War," John Moore said excitedly to Stephanie. "And certainly rethinking about China."

Washington was shaken with the implications of Johnson's

597

decision. The dream of a great society had yielded to what amounted to an admission of vulnerability.

In the months that followed, John Moore, Stephanie, and other Americans with a knowledge of China, but who until then had been looked upon as "biased," were asked to panels and to meetings with senators and congressmen, all anxious to learn.

Stephanie spoke with simplicity. "In my opinion, the Chinese have always been Chinese first. This does not mean they will give up easily what has been, for them, a tool for success. But they will Sinicize communism, adapt it to their own requirements. What they have sought is national independence and national prosperity."

"But what about those terrible political campaigns, what about the Cultural Revolution, what about these terrible extremist actions?" asked one senator.

And Stephanie replied: "My husband and myself suffered from these excesses, Mr. Senator. All I can say is that *if,* way back in 1945, my country had chosen to make an act of faith, to democratize China by working along with Mao Tsetung, then perhaps these things need not have happened. . . .

"China is a very old country, with a tradition of tyranny behind it. It has to *learn* democracy. We chose not to teach it at a very momentous time in history."

But the senators were still tangled within a web of stereotypes and assumptions. "Is your husband a Communist? If not, why did he stay in China when it became communistic? Would he come to America if we invited him?"

Stephanie saw Yong's face, his young face, glowing with that marvelous fire of love for his country. She steadied her voice, and replied:

"My husband comes from a very old family, Senator. Its members have traditionally served their country, through many different regimes, for the last twelve hundred years.

"There are millions like him in China. The non-Communist intelligentsia. Who elected to remain in Communist China. Because 'China is China is China.' Immortal, forever. Not because of communism.

"They do not believe that running away, to seek a secure and better life for themselves, is anything but treachery. They will not abandon their country and their people, depriving China of their knowledge, their brains, their contribution to her progress.

"They have seen the Communist Government at work. However abhorrent, authoritarian, crassly bureaucratic it is, it has also done an enormous amount of good for the ordinary people of China. For the ninety-five percent who were living in gross misery.

"The doctrine of communism is something which China has already begun to adapt, to transform to its own traditions. As she has adapted, digested so many things during her five thousand years of existence.

"China's break with the Soviet Union occurred precisely because Mao Tsetung vindicated China's right to go her own way, interpret communism in a fashion adapted to her own needs. A long time before Tito, way back in 1937, Mao Tsetung became a Tito, by refusing the dictates of the Comintern.

"My husband is Chinese. He loves his country and his people. He is a patriot, as are so many like him. Should we not understand, respect that patriotism?"

The senators were silent, and then one of them spoke up.

"Mrs. Jen, would you say that our perspective on China has suffered from a certain lack of realism?"

"Yes, Senator," said Stephanie firmly. "I would."

There is hope now, there is hope, sang Stephanie's heart. Up and down America, private business stirred.

At a board meeting of STRINC held in New York, Dick Steiner outlined what a possible "opening up" of China might mean for American business. "China will need a great deal in the way of computers and microprocessing apparatus. We've got a panel specially studying her needs in transport, in telecommunications. In fact, she can only solve some of her basic problems, such as, for instance, education and communication, book printing, etc., by utilizing the latest techniques." STRINC could now swing into a major project, applying its specialized brainpower to help solve these problems.

"Yong was right," Stephanie told John Moore. "He used to tease me, saying that one day my father would be going to Peking to shake Mao's hand, and to sell Ryder airplanes to the Red Army . . . and now it looks as if this is going to happen."

By now they had ceased to be lovers. They had become affectionate friends, in easy freedom and intimacy.

John had never been satisfied with his role as merely a surrogate, replacing an unreachable love. But because he loved Stephanie with an intensity which doomed other attachments, and because she had so greatly needed him, he had continued.

Swallow's growing up had also affected their relationship. Swallow had resented him. And shown it. Shown a jealous passion towards her absent father. And unconsciously Stephanie had reacted.

John Moore looked at Stephanie. She glowed, glowed with the hope that all would now be well, as in a fairy tale. She dimmed or became radiant from another source of light than his; the old and permanent claim of first love was still upon her. The years had not assuaged nor destroyed that once and forever fervor which transfigured her.

Now he had to be content with what had been. With the long autumn of his love. Perhaps he had had his share and enough. Better than nothing, better than most people in the world would ever know.

twenty-six

OF course.

It would be at night. The mouselike scratch at the bedroom window pane. The guessed whisper, neither wind, nor a dream. A shadow lighter than the darkness.

"Who is it?"

"Friends. Friends of your son Jen Lin."

Jen Yong did not switch on the light. He trod softly in his slippers to the kitchen back door. Opened it and walked along the brick wall, around the corner; saw the young man standing by his bedroom window.

This was the way Winter Treasure came at night. This was where he stood.

"Doctor, we have brought a sick man to you. . . ."

"Why to me? Why not to the hospital?"

"You will see who it is. . . ."

There was silence between the hedges of peas framing the pathway. Only the low stir of insects. By the gourd patch they stood, five of them in dark clothes, surrounding the prone figure on the ground. Yong had already caught the sound: stertorous breathing, a long-drawn sigh, then a pause, and then again that strained gulping which he knew so well, had heard so often.

". . . beaten, left for dead . . . we saved him and brought him to you . . ."

Yong was angry. A wild, blind, red rage. "Trouble for me, more trouble. Why come to me? To get me into trouble? Does my son know about this? Is the man a counterrevolutionary?"

"He was a high Party member, Doctor . . . you may know

his face . . . your son belongs to our group but was not with us."

The young man shone a pencil flashlight, cupping the finger-beam upon the man's face. The eyes flickered when the light touched them.

Yong knew him. His photographs had been in the papers. He was a good man. An important man. He had indeed incurred the wrath of the new power-holders by his forthrightness. And someone in power had hired a thug band to beat him to death. Such things still happened, such bands existed, although they were being hunted down.

"They left him for dead, we came, we fought them, they fled."

Yong was sarcastic. "Truly a heaven-sent gift," he said mordantly. But at the same time he knew these youths were brave and selfless. And he felt a surge of happiness too, that there was so much valiance and courage among the young, in his own son.

They placed the man upon Yong's bed. Four of them carried him, for he was thickset, a bulky northerner.

Yong examined him in the dark, with the aid of the pencil flashlight. No light must be seen, not a chink, and his curtains were worn, too thin, they let the light through.

Blood pressure was low, too low. Skin cold and clammy. Pulse unsteady, precipitate. In shock. Internal hemorrhage. He tapped the abdomen. Dullness. Blood in the cavity; the blows must have ruptured either a kidney, the liver, or the spleen. . . . It often happened.

And as his fingers touched the man, suddenly he felt he was back in Chungking, examining Liang Ma, and Stephanie was there, luminous, beautiful, her brown hair coiled upon her head . . .

The man's skull seemed intact. His pupils reacted evenly. He might be saved. A blood transfusion, a swift laparotomy to discover the source of the bleeding, remove the spleen, stitch up the liver.

But this meant operating on a "counter-revolutionary" now. A high army commander with cancer had not been operated on because he had opposed Mao Tsetung's heir, Lin Piao. The doctors had been too frightened. . . . If they had saved him, they would have been sent to the communes, to labor. . . .

It would be so easy for Yong to shake his head, softly to

murmur: "Nothing can be done, it is too late." The man was partly conscious. He would bleed some more, lapse into total unconsciousness. It would not be a painful death.

Refuse trouble; trouble which might also descend upon his son, his Family. . . .

He heard himself saying, and could not believe his own ears, "He is bleeding inside, but he can still be saved." That meant taking him to the hospital, lifting him on the dark cloth which they had used to carry him, and walking to the emergency room, five minutes away. "Two of you only. Say you discovered him on the street, that it was a street accident . . . a lorry."

But that did not take care of the main question. Why had they come to him? Why not straight to the emergency room?

"When you are in the emergency room do not say anything about me. I shall appear. I often stroll in at night, when I cannot sleep. It is a habit of mine." He did not tell them that he could not always trust the nurses now; some of them were almost untrained. And so he checked on the ward patients at night. Checked to see that all had been done. "I shall arrive in a few minutes. The emergency nurse is bound to ask my advice. . . ."

He told them to give the man a false name. And false names and false addresses for themselves. "Only one of us has a city resident card," said the young man who had scratched at the window.

"Then the others must go into hiding, and you too," replied Yong. And knew this advice superfluous.

Within the next three, four days they must find someone claiming to be a relative of the man, who would remove him before the gang who had tried to murder him returned to finish him off.

"You must remove him quickly," said Yong. He thought: They know many tricks I do not know. They will find something.

"We promise."

At three in the morning it was over.

The nurses seemed to believe the story. Yong had operated. A large boggy spleen from previous malaria had ruptured. The man's blood group had been simple to match. Since the Cultural Revolution, many people gave blood willingly; young Red Guards also gave blood, as did peasants in the villages.

Yong did not ask another doctor's help. Not to incriminate someone else, should the worst happen. The nurses could always plead ignorance. But the man's face was too well known for a doctor not to have seen it in the newspaper. . . .

Yong went back to sleep. At seven he would start another bout of surgery. He felt at peace with himself. Wrapped in the quilt, he let his mind roam. *Stephanie, I hope they will get someone to remove him quickly . . . the longer he stays in hospital, the more likelihood of someone snooping, talking . . .*

Within the next forty-eight hours the man showed signs of recovery. He was tough. He was also shrewd. He gazed calmly at Jen Yong. He did not talk, merely grunted, as if he were a rough peasant.

But someone must guess. Must. The man had bruises, black and blue welts on his back, on his body. "The lorry hit him quite badly," said Yong conversationally to the ward nurse. She did not reply. Perhaps she would not talk. . . .

Winter Treasure came on the second night and Yong told him: "You must not be involved. Have nothing to do with it. This is political . . . these young people must remove him."

"Do not worry, *Tietie*. I will manage it." Winter Treasure had such a tranquil assurance about him, as if he was at ease with the perpetual danger in which he lived. Winter Treasure told his father: "Round Round has come to Shanghai. She is staying with us because her father does not want her. He is getting married again."

Professor Chang Shou's wife had been criticized; one of her terse poems was:

> Sadness creeps in
> Although the peony
> Blossoms in splendor.

This was regarded as an insult to the Cultural Revolution. Because she had a colostomy some of the young had wanted to expose her, to show the phenomenon. "But we managed, she is in a hospital, no one can drag her out."

Winter Treasure left, walking with a light cool step, moving without disturbing the grass, the air around him, the darkness which cloaked him. And Yong thought: My son. Grown wise, and old, before his time. . . .

On the fifth morning, just as Yong was becoming almost haggard with worry, the man's bed was empty. The ward nurse told him: "His son and daughter came for him. They are in the army."

Yong felt light, light. He felt so well that he wrote down the episode for Stephanie. "I am glad there are so many good young people, among them our son . . . perhaps they will be able to master the furies now tearing our country."

Winter hobbled away and now the Jen Family pavilions were returned to them. The worker families were evacuated. Painters and carpenters began to repair what had been damaged.

But the universities were still the scene of battles between gangs of youths. Winter Treasure now went to a commune to work, because his cousins had returned and there were other relatives to care for the grandparents.

He left, taking his books with him.

Yong saw them before they saw him.

They were five, with masks over their faces made of khaki cloth with scissored openings for the eyes, and rods and spikes in their hands.

He saw them walking towards the dormitory; they passed under the lamp which swung between two poles above the pathway.

They were coming for him.

Oh Stephanie, Stephanie, I am afraid.

His mind went back to the Party official he had saved.

That had been almost six months ago; surely it could not be . . .

They stood behind his locked door. They talked in low tones to each other. Perhaps deciding what they would do next. If he did not open, they would have to break the door down. Then perhaps his colleagues would interfere. Dr. Hsieh, right across the garden . . . other doctors . . . but perhaps they would pretend to be asleep, or their wives would hold them back. "It's not your business . . . why go and get yourself in trouble? Think of the children."

What would they do to him?

They knocked. In an ordinary way.

"Who is it?"

"We represent the district revolutionary security. We have come to check your room." It was a high boyish treble; the voice of a fourteen- or fifteen-year-old.

That is a lie, he thought. The security bodies did not wear masks.

Stephanie, I'm afraid they're going to kill me. Stephanie, you always thought I was a coward, and it's true, I'm afraid.

He did not move. He stared at the wall and he could almost see Stephanie; she stood there, and he forgot them, almost, looking at her. He put his hand against the wall, and touched her, and began to dream. It was such a very long long time, so many years now; he dreamt more and more frequently now that she was back, she was back.

"Open, open."

They are not frightened, so they must have some powerful backer. That part of his mind which dealt with present reality told him. But the other part was adrift, drifting away, it carried his body to the bed, where he sat, fingering the patchwork quilt, and talking to Stephanie.

Stephanie, oh Stephanie, I remember Texas, the thrill of emptiness.

That was all he had of her, all that he had kept. The quilt. The photograph. Enough to keep him alive with resurrection of love. But now he knew that he might die. And he was so wearied, so tired.

Stephanie, I'm afraid we may not be able to see each other again. I'm sorry, my darling, somehow I've failed. I thought that there would be a miracle, and one day you

*would reappear, laughing and beautiful, and I would see
you with the eyes of my body. . . .*

But now it was not to be. He knew it. He must die.

They did not break down the door. They unlocked it. The
gatekeeper must have given them the key. Or perhaps they
had procured it without the gatekeeper knowing. Yong saw
the gatekeeper, small, old, with shaking hand unhooking
that big jangle of keys he kept above his bed, handing them
the one labeled: Dr. Jen Yong.

And there was no inner bolt to the door. All the bolts had
been removed when the Cultural Revolution had begun. To
let the investigating parties come in. But also in cases of
suicide, to make it possible to break in.

They came into the room and saw the thin man, so thin,
so gaunt, with graying hair, who now took off his glasses and
put them carefully on the bedside table.

They had a job to do and some of them did not like it, but
their leader had told them that this was revolution, and
they obeyed the leader.

They would first pretend that they were interrogating
him, pretend, by asking: "Counter-revolutionary dog, Jen
Yong, confess your crimes . . . where is the material you
sent to that American spy, your so-called loved one? Produce it or . . ."

Yong laughed. He began quietly, and then it was too
much. He was laughing, really laughing, heady with gaiety.
*Stephanie, did you hear them? Did you hear this silliness?
They are like gnats around the night lamp, moving to and
fro, to and fro, and not knowing why. . . .*

They wrapped him in the patchwork quilt. They stuffed
his mouth with the towel with which he washed his face.
And they began to beat him.

A routine. He thought: They must be one of the gangs
the army is hunting down. Our children, who went wrong.
My son might have been like them.

Now he knew why they had wrapped him in the quilt
Stephanie and he had bought in New York. So that no welts
would show. No broken skin. Then he would be pronounced
a suicide. Hastily.

And soon he was all pain, nothing but pain, a pain so
ample there was no space nor word for anything else,
nothing but this agony. He heard the dull blows upon him
and wondered that he could hear the noise, and the blanket

made it all last longer before he could lose consciousness. But he knew now that they were beating him across the abdomen, and across the kidneys, to kill him slowly, and it went on and on. It was a technique, too. And now they were breaking his ribs. It hurt . . . hurt . . . They struck him again and he did not react.

"Dead," said the high boyish treble.

"Not yet, but will die," said their leader. "Take off the quilt. And the towel."

They left him lying neatly on the floor. No disorder. No blood.

Their leader looked at the quilt. He folded it and took it with him. No one would miss it now.

They filed out and locked the door.

"Yong . . . Yong."

"Oh my beloved, I'm so glad you're back . . ."

It was her voice, but he could not see her.

He must go to her.

She could not be far away.

He could not walk, could not rise. They had broken the bones in his legs.

He crawled, dragged himself on one arm. The other hung useless. To the wall, where Stephanie waited for him.

See, my darling, I have kept your photograph. I pasted it into the wall. I knew you were there, I knew, and that was enough for me.

His breathing hurt. Hurt terribly. Liquid came up into his mouth. Blood, he thought detachedly. Blood and froth. Of course.

He reached the wall and clawed at it, clawed at it with his good arm to rip the paper, to reach the photograph.

But now a great darkness was coming, darker by far than the night. And wind whooshed in his ears, it was the wind of Yenan, bringing the huge darkness that was taking him away.

But Stephanie was there. Beyond the darkness. She had come, he could feel her smile, very soon he would see her, he would see her, and see the sun in her hair.

Hsu Towering Cloud, with money, a quilt, and some clothes, arrived in Canton to meet a "brother" of the Triad. A few more days, and he would be smuggled out, to Hongkong.

When he thought of his luck, his enormous good luck, his heartbeat quickened. He shivered with the wonder of his fate. Truly, such a fate meant he had a great future!

The Red Guards had come to the labor camp where he toiled, toiled at breaking stones for the new roads to be built.

They had released him and a thousand other men working there. They had shouted: "Long live Chairman Mao! Long live Vice Chairman Lin Piao!"

The young had believed their stories. Hsu knew how to talk. He was a good Party member; he had been unjustly accused by the "capitalist roaders" in the Party, he said, because he had exposed an American spy.

Hsu put a red band around his arm and joined the Red Guards. Soon he had become the leader of a small gang of youths; the youngest among them was fifteen years old.

There had been some good months. They wandered into small towns rather than the larger cities, shouting slogans, vowing to clean the area of all evil, of the filth of capitalism, of freaks and monsters. The searches were profitable. And after a time, they also raped.

But suddenly times became not so good. The Party was reforming itself. Chou Enlai issued the orders now; the army was systematically sweeping the cities clean of criminal gangs.

But it was still possible to hide. In the tangle of small lanes of Shanghai. Especially if one had a protector. And such a protector had surfaced.

A secret society man, of the same Triad as Hsu. Extremely clever, since he was now among the new power-holders. Comrade Ah Kao had gone through every net, had resisted every investigation, and was now quietly liquidating Party men who might prove troublesome to him. For this he needed a gang of small murderers; and who better than Hsu and his idealistic young followers, convinced that what they were doing was for the good of the revolution?

609

Hsu Towering Cloud had cleaned up several cases for Ah Kao. And Ah Kao had promised him help to reach Hongkong, where "brothers" were numerous and would also help him.

And then Hsu heard that one of his cases had not only survived but escaped. It took some months for the full story to reach him.

Jen Yong. That turtle's egg has once again crossed my path!

Comrade Ah Kao was now the vice-head of Shanghai's municipal revolutionary committee. He had provided Hsu with the necessary permits and money to reach the city of Canton, and thence to escape to Hongkong.

I shall revenge myself, thought Hsu. Before he left he would kill Jen Yong. To please himself. Then he would drop the youths who remained in his band; perhaps see to it that they would be caught for the killing, while he would be out of China, perhaps in beautiful America.

All his dreams would come true. He would get onto an airplane, and the great silver bird would carry him to America . . . there to find his former patron Tsing.

Hsu arrived in Canton and met with the Triad man in the city. Everything had been arranged. Only a few hours, and he would be in Hongkong.

The three men were waiting for him, with the light sampan. It was a very dark night, and along the coast with its thousands of bays and coves such a skiff would navigate safely. Cheerfully, Hsu threw his clothes pack and the quilt into the boat, swung himself into it. The men rowed, dipping silent oars wrapped in cloth into the water, gliding the sampan out into the dark waters.

When they were a convenient distance away, they moved upon Hsu. They stuffed his mouth with a towel, tied his hands behind his back, bound his feet, twisted a net with several large stones around his waist, and threw him into the water.

The Triads never forgive a traitor. And Hsu had betrayed several small brothers. . . .

The men returned with the clothes, the money, the quilt, and Hsu's shoes. Always they took away the shoes, so that the dead man's ghost would not be able to run after them.

twenty-seven

THEY had walked across the small wooden bridge spanning the rivulet which represented the border between Lowu Railway Station, on the Hongkong side, and the Shumchun, on the Chinese side.

The Chinese Army soldiers standing on the bridge had looked at their passports, and smiled, and said, "You are welcome," in English and in Chinese.

While they waited at Shumchun Railway Station for the train to Canton, lunch was served by pigtailed buxom waitresses, country girls who looked at Swallow and asked how old she was and exclaimed at her tallness. They gave her a present: a badge with the face of Chairman Mao upon it, to wear pinned to her shirt.

On the train, across the jade green fields which rolled so smoothly up to the tree-waving hills, they peered through the windows at the Hakka women, clad in black, with their wide circular hats, standing in the shallow rice field water, a breeze sculpting them, as if ready for tourist cameras—although there were, as yet, no tourists.

Stephanie leaned back in the comfortable upholstered train armchair, hugging to herself the bittersweet nostalgia which had inhabited her since she had crossed the bridge. Part of her hungered for and part of her dreaded this confrontation with herself, the coming together of two separate entities, both of them Stephanie: the one she had been and the one she was now.

Swallow was happy in a grave, serious way. She had said to her mother that morning: "It's something that's going to be with me all my life, Mama, isn't it?" At thirteen she claimed the right to make her own decisions; and perhaps it had to do with the adulation towards her absent, unknown father, which had been strong in her for the last three years. Grand'mère had helped. Isabelle, who had gone back to her roots in Provence, and took her granddaughter to Chinese restaurants, to the Musée Guimet.

"My child, you will never be totally yourself unless you also learn your Chinese side," Grand'mère had said.

Isabelle's aim was to thwart the American half of Marylee. Like so many of the French, Isabelle lived a resentment of dispossession. For France was now a small country, ruling cosmetics, wines, and fashion, not the world.

"Mama, will we really be in Shanghai tomorrow?" asked Swallow.

Sir Henry Keng, Eddy Keng, Stephanie, and her daughter were going to Shanghai together, to visit their families.

In a dramatic reversal, visas had been forthcoming. The ban upon talking to or having anything to do with Americans had ended as abruptly as it had begun. Everything that had been impossible, unthinkable, now became astonishingly normal. "Of course you wish to visit your family," the China Travel Agency manager had exclaimed, as if it were now the easiest thing in the world to do. Helpful hands, smiling faces surfaced everywhere.

It was 1971. Henry Kissinger, a portly cupid borne on wings of political statecraft, had spent some hours in Peking and talked with Mao Tsetung and Chou Enlai. President Nixon would be going to Peking within a few months. To shake hands and to talk with the leaders of Red China. The amazing, the unbelievable had come to pass, become accepted fact, and everyone forgot why it had never been possible to perform these simple gestures before.

Meanwhile, the Vietnam War still wound its weary way to perdition. It had even escalated into a frantic and useless extension of slaughter to Cambodia. The impossible military victory sought by the Pentagon became ever more nebulous.

In China, the Cultural Revolution was not ended; another earthquake had taken place, another dramatic reversal. The heir, Lin Piao, head of the "left" power clique, had attempted to flee to the Soviet Union and died in the crash of an airplane in the wastes of Mongolia.

The news would remain officially secret for many months, but already Eddy Keng was saying: "Auntie, all of us hope that Premier Chou Enlai lives a long, very long time, so that everything can be set right in China."

In deference to Chinese Cultural Revolution fashion, which had also pervaded Hongkong, Sir Henry Keng had bought several copies of the Little Red Book of Mao's quotations at the Chinese bookstore in the Colony, and gave one to each of his fellow travelers. He kept the Little Red Book in his hand and waved it at everyone he met. Only to discover, to his astonishment, that this was no longer being done.

In Canton, they went walking through the sultry evening, away from their comfortable but stifling hotel, which had been built on the Russian model for arctic weather. They strolled by the Pearl River, aglow with its famous translucence, watching the sampans go out to sea and the sun melt tenderly into the water.

Sir Henry met old friends. Sir Henry had friends everywhere; they sprang up wherever he was, as grass springs underfoot on an English lawn. And now these friends took them to a fish restaurant on a boat anchored off the small island of Shameen, and all was whipped cream lightness of talk, not a word about strife or trouble.

At the banquet, Sir Henry was approached by someone very important in the province and asked to start some discussions on expanded trade and commerce with Hongkong.

"Good thing for us, Auntie," said Eddy Keng to Stephanie. "Make very very light tennis shoes. Sneakers. Make millions of them. In China. Low labor cost. Introduce aerospace knowhow into light sport shoes. Take away weight; people jump higher, run quicker. Chinese can make millions of shoes for us, also for themselves. . . ." He already dreamt of an aero-sneaker company, a subsidiary of Keng Lai, in China.

On the plane to Shanghai the next morning, a young woman who sat next to Swallow began to talk with her. Soon she had whipped out a little notebook and begun a lesson in English with Swallow. "Airplane. Mother. Friend . . ."

The girl laughed a great deal, showing two dimples, and complimented Stephanie on her Chinese. "I did not have much time to study; I have been working in a commune for three years. . . ." But she was returning to visit her parents in Shanghai. She showed her hands, tiny, agile hands. "I have planted rice. I want to learn modern agriculture."

The plane landed and they filed out; and there was yet another check of their passports and visas by a policeman, who then said "Welcome" and motioned them towards a closed brown door.

Behind that door people waited for the airplane passengers. Behind that door was Stephanie's past, and also her future, and she felt herself falter, her knees weak. She gripped Swallow's hand hard, too hard. "Ouch, Mom," said Swallow, and then squeezed back, smiling.

Her blue-black hair streaming unrestrained from forehead to shoulders. The flying eyebrows and the small straight nose. Yong's daughter . . . and each step made it more obvious. *Oh Swallow, what will happen when you meet your father, your brother?*

And then they had passed the door and she saw him, saw him dressed in a white short-sleeved shirt, those he wore in the summer, with those arms she remembered, the hands, that tight-knit skin, no seam, no pores.

"Yong," she cried, "Yong . . ." She forgot everything, and rushed forward, letting go of Swallow, letting go of the years, each step taking away the years and the pain, and she was again twenty-one and in Yenan, seeing Yong standing by the quilted door of the dancing hall, and she had rushed to him as she did now, gone to his arms and had perhaps never thought that it would be forever, but it was forever.

She reached him and he said: "Mother, you are back."

Her son. Tall, taller than she by half a head. Long legs, slim body, taller than his father had been.

"Mama, so long we have waited for you, so long."

She clutched him then, clutched him to her, and smelt him, and remembered his little boy smell, and all the years without Yong were there, between them, and she already knew, but still hoped, still . . .

"Your father . . . he is . . . is he . . ."

"Mama, you must not grieve. *Tietie* is no more. We did not tell you because you were far away, and we did not want you to grieve alone."

And Stephanie was almost angry, almost saying: But why didn't you let me know? And then she realized that of course, of course, it was silly to say it. For what could she

614

have done? They had been kind, thinking that it was best to wait till she was back; when her grief would not be borne alone; when she would not be left solitary with the specter; when there would be the comfort, the reassurance of a whole family grieving with her, surrounding her with their own spacious sorrow, so many of them.

"Grandfather and Grandmother and many others are waiting for you at home, Mama," said Winter Treasure. "There was not enough transport for us all. . . ."

And then she felt the little tug at her skirt, and was remorseful, for she had forgotten Swallow, forgotten her. "Oh, this is your brother, Swallow, Marylee, this is Winter Treasure. . . ."

"Hi," said Swallow, very American.

"Little sister," said her brother, more formal, and smiling at her, and then she threw herself in his arms, tossing back her mane of black hair so much like his.

"Many people have come to see you, Mama."

This was not the time, not the place for sorrow; and Stephanie, still shaken, still quivering with tumultuous emotion, now saw them pressing forward, those who had been able to come to the airport to greet her. And manners, the ritual of courtesy took over.

Keng Dawei had come to greet his brother, Sir Henry, whom he had not seen since 1949. And Eddy Keng was bawling, almost like a child, *"Tietie tietie,"* and bowing to his father. For he too had been away for almost two decades. And throughout he had obeyed, obeyed his wise and fore-sighted father. Now he was sobbing like a child, because this was home, where the heart can be naked. And his father patted his respectful and prosperous son, patted Stephanie's hand and Swallow's hair, and rested in the serene glory of his age.

Lionel Shaggin and Loumei were there with their tall son China Warrior, who was a factory foreman. They too ap-peared unaltered, Loumei only a little heavier, Lionel affa-ble as ever, saying, "Welcome home, Texas."

And there was Joan Wu, bustling up, hugging Stephanie, and saying: "Now we expect great things from you, we expect you to do great work for friendship between China and America. . . ."

Beyond these stood a young man who limped a little, who had a high cheekboned face and said: "You will not recognize me . . ." He had a broad accent and Stephanie knew it.

"From Chungking . . ."

"Liang. Little Pond. You saved my mother, Liang Ma, it was twenty-seven years ago."

"Comrade Liang has come from his factory in Tsinan where he is chief engineer to thank you, and also to weep for my father," said Winter Treasure.

"We shall remember you, and *Taifu*, from generation to generation," said Little Pond.

And then two women, prim and precise, looking as Teacher Soo had looked, dressed almost in identical sober cotton suits, advanced upon her. "Madame Ryder, you will not remember, but we do. We were in the same motorbus on the way to River Fork village in September 1944. We read in the newspaper of your coming and we are glad to welcome you." At last they told Stephanie their names, and wrung her hand, and then effaced themselves, and disappeared.

And *Amah* Mu was there, wizened, come to greet Young Mistress, and she stroked Swallow's hand and said: "Aiyah, I missed looking after this one!"

Calthrop and Coral, surrounded by some of their children, now hurried forward, and there with them was a young girl with a round face and large eyes.

"Mama, this is Round Round, Yee Meiling's daughter," said Winter Treasure.

And Stephanie was just going to say, Meiling, how is she? But then something stopped her. Meiling was not here, and Round Round's face had something, something shocked and tragic and wavery; it *moved* too much, that face. . . . She would be told, later. By her son. This was not the place to ask.

Eight Jewel Lane was now tarred, and a good many of the houses were new tall brick buildings. There was no gatekeeper at the gate, which had been newly repainted, but Father and Mother stood on the raised stone threshold, and on both sides of them were arranged the various relatives, tall and short, fat and thin, old and young, according to rank and generation.

Stephanie came down from the car and walked up to them, and Mother held out both her arms and said, "Daughter, oh daughter, you have returned." Her voice was slightly breathless, age had faded its vibrancy. But she was still Mother, beautiful, her presence a fluid grace unbreakable as water.

And Father, much older he, with a cane, but happy, happy . . .

Everything arranged, orchestrated, streamlined by centuries of proper ritual, of organized behavior. Emotion exhibited in the proper way, at the correct time, in the appropriate place.

And so, after Swallow had bowed to the elders, and to the generation above her, and said Grandfather, Grandmother, and called out the respective uncles and aunts by their rank in the hierarchy of the Family, the little procession went through the garden, a garden now unkempt, neglected, although someone had swept its pathways and men were repairing the gallery which wound across it. Went to the pavilion where Jen Yong and Lai Spring Snow had lived, in that time that was no longer but was forever.

The stone with its clinging moss was still there, standing in the dry pool, although the moss had prospered. The pavilion doors were open, the paper seals having been removed. In the living room, with the furniture in its proper place, hung a portrait of Yong.

It did not look altogether like him, being the work of an enterprising photographer who had tried to soften and to round off the features, to mold them with soft flesh. An ancestor's picture must exhibit the dignity of wrinkleless debonair propriety.

And now the time to grieve came. Father stood in front of his son's picture, and his body shook a little as he said: "Son, oh son . . ."

The time to grieve had now come. A great burst of lament rose from all those present, a winged sorrow to wind its way into the universe to find the hovering ghost who had waited, waited, was waiting so long and so faithfully for this hour. . . .

And so each one called upon the dead, called with the appropriate name: Father and Mother called him son, and Winter Treasure called him *Tietie*, and wept; and others too

617

called him cousin, or uncle; and Liang Little Pond screamed loudest of all, calling *Taifu, Taifu.*

Mother took Swallow's hand and said to the portrait: "Son, your daughter Swallow has returned." Swallow and Winter Treasure stood together, lighted some incense sticks, and placed them in a small burner in front of the photograph and bowed together and said: *"Tietie, Tietie."*

Then it was over.

They walked back to the pavilion of the parents, Mother saying conversationally to Stephanie: "For a while, during the early months of the Cultural Revolution, the three of us lived in one small room, but now we have been given back the House, and the Government is repairing it at their own cost." Widow had volunteered to work in a commune; and now she had married. At last. "Married an old Party cadre also sent down to labor . . . she seems very happy," said Mother.

The furniture in the living room was much worn and the silk covers patched, but it was still a beautiful room, and the porcelain had been returned to the shelves, the scrolls and paintings hung in their accustomed places.

"Sit down, dear daughter," said Mother, "sit down." Meanwhile, Winter Treasure and Swallow had gone together to the kitchen, and they came back bearing the teapot and the teacups, to serve the elders with tea.

"Yeh yeh, Nai nai, please drink some tea," Swallow said, shyly, using the Chinese words for grandfather and grandmother.

And her grandmother looked at her with pleasure, saying: "Oh how young my heart becomes when it perceives such youth."

Stephanie rose to take the cups from her daughter's hands, placing them in front of the elders, and saying: "It makes me young again, Father, Mother, to do this for you. . . ."

They sipped and talked in carefree unfrowning civility, since all bonds were now duly acknowledged in front of the mighty dead who had created them and Lai Spring Snow was reintegrated within the Family.

They told Stephanie (and Winter Treasure translated for his sister Swallow) how Yong had died, how the gang that had murdered him had been caught.

"There are still wicked people around," said Father.

"There will be trouble still, but . . . " his brow cleared, "I am hopeful, daughter. China is China. Is China. She has gone through so much tumult, so many centuries of upheaval. She endures. We shall endure."

And Jen Lin, Winter Treasure, sat there, respectful and shy, and totally in control. It came out of him, this maestro surety, the fact that he was heir, provider, continuator, watchful for both old and young, fully assuming responsibility but saying little, saying nothing. Until his mother asked him and respectfully he replied that yes, he had been studying electronics and English, on his own, and also mathematics, and that now two research institutes in China were asking for his services.

"I have tried not to waste time, Mama," he said.

All those young minds, thought Stephanie. Those marvelous young minds. She could help them now, could provide the opportunities, the money. . . . "Winter Treasure, you must come to America to study," she said to her son.

"Certainly, Mama, but I shall return here; China needs so many things, she is still so backward . . ." he replied, and she knew it was a warning. A warning to her. He said it in the same way that Yong had said, all of twenty-seven years ago: "Our country is so backward; we need so many things. . . ."

He would not yield to the easy, to the obvious. Already he was taking Swallow in hand. . . .

And Stephanie felt both sad and proud, wondering what the future held for her son, her son, who looked at her with grave and watchful eyes, and was in charge. In charge of the Family.

Mother and Father's presence was still serenity. Gentle words came from them, telling her, telling her. Sa Fei and her husband were still under a cloud, but they had been moved to a small city. . . . Rosamond Chen had married, married a worker, a widower with three children. She seemed happy. "She writes that she has grown fat, and that she will come to see you as soon as she gets leave."

Winter Treasure bent to his grandfather's ear, whispered, and the latter nodded, sprightly, clapped his hands, and said: "And now we must take some photographs."

Duly then they all arranged themselves, in rows according to hierarchy in the generations, and the photographer who had been waiting came in, carrying his camera, no longer an unwieldy box sheathed in black cloth but the Chinese copy of a Rolleiflex.

They stood. They sat. They smiled. They paused. Click, click went the camera. Everyone murmured gently, happily. As if there were not a care in the world.

And in Stephanie rose then, fierce and sure, a great clearness. As if the morning sun had come, dispelling all darkness. Morning which reached out everywhere, making the whole world new.

A whole new world to make. And she could help. She would not wither, her heart mummified, her mind amassing wealth with pointless energy.

There was so much to be done, so much. And she was committed, involved, as never before. Not only by the memory of the dead, but even more so by the living.

Winter Treasure, Swallow. Her children. Yong's children. She would not fail them. Love had come home to her, at last.

HAN SUYIN was born under the name Chou Kuanghu in the Honan province of China in 1917, the daughter of a Belgian mother and a Chinese father. At the age of 15, after her mother refused to let her continue her studies, Han Suyin began work at the Peking Union Medical College where she worked for two years as a typist before entering the prestigious Yenching University in Peking. After two years at the University, she obtained a scholarship to Brussels University, Belgium, from which she graduated as a doctor with top honors in 1938. Despondent over the Japanese invasion of China that year, she abandoned her medical career to return to China where she met her husband, Tang Paohuang. As her husband rose in the hierarchy under Chiang Kaishek, Han Suyin served as a midwife in the Szechuan province (during which time she wrote a book called *Destination Chungking*), until 1942 when her husband was appointed military attaché to London.

During her years in London with her husband, who had been named a colonel, Han Suyin became disillusioned with the Chiang Kaishek regime, having observed corruption and cruelty within it. She also decided to resume her dream of becoming a doctor, refusing to return to China with her husband when he left England in 1945 so that she could study medicine at the Royal Free Hospital in London, where she graduated in medicine with highest honors in 1948.

While Han Suyin supported herself and her adopted daughter, Yungmei, with a scholarship and a part-time job as a typist, her husband was killed in Manchuria in 1947 when his soldiers deserted him. In 1949, unable to bear her separation from China, Dr. Han again abandoned her promising medical career to return to Hong Kong. However, she was not permitted to return to her homeland because China was in the throes of the Communist Revolution, and though she sympathized with the need for communist liberation of her country, she represented the old regime to them. During her estrangement from China, she worked as a doctor in Hong Kong, and wrote the modern classic love story, *A Many-Splendored Thing*, as a result of a love affair she had at this time. It was made into the ever popular film, "Love Is A Many Splendored Thing" starring William Holden and Jennifer Jones. The book is still in print in 25 countries.

In 1952, Han Suyin went to Southeast Asia where she practiced as a doctor in Malaya and Singapore, eventually marrying Leonard Comber, an Englishman who is now director of Heinemann's Publications in Hong Kong. Practicing medicine by day, she wrote by night during the next twelve years, producing such books as *And the Rain My Drink*, about the guerilla war in Malaya which is still used as a reference book in some American and European universities; *The Mountain Is Young*, a love story set in Nepal and India; *The Four Faces; Cast But One Shadow;* and *Winter Love*.

In 1956, she finally obtained a visa to return to China where she met Premier Chou Enlai and spent the next twenty years interviewing and talking with the Premier and many other Chinese leaders. During the McCarthy era, she was blacklisted for having returned to China for her father's death in 1958—a situation that was not corrected until almost twenty years later when Han Suyin finally convinced American officials to remove this ban.

Having made a practice of spending two to five months each year in China since her readmission, she began in 1964 to write a saga based on her family and its endurance through the century of China's revolution. That saga was published in several acclaimed volumes: *The Crippled Tree, A Mortal Flower, Birdless Summer,* and a final volume, *My House Has Two Doors* which covers the period from 1949 through 1979 and describes her meetings with Chou Enlai, Sukarno, Nehru and many other leaders of the Third World including Mao Tsetung's wife, Chiang Ching, who tried to destroy Han Suyin by branding her a spy for America.

Han Suyin worked on a major study of Mao Tsetung and his policies which were incorporated into two books, *The Morning Deluge* and *Wind in the Tower*, which are now valuable reference books on the spirit and policies of China from the start of the twentieth century until Mao's death in 1976.

Today, Han Suyin is a world recognized lecturer in the West, the Third World countries and China, where she speaks to many universities and institutes. She is now married to Colonel Vincent Ruthnaswamy and spends most of her time in Lausanne, Switzerland.

"IF YOU LOVED THE FAR PAVILIONS—*AND WHO DIDN'T*—*THIS WILL BE YOUR DISH TOO."* —Cosmopolitan

ZEMINDAR

The Award-Winning Novel by

Valerie Fitzgerald

A magnificent love story unfolds against a backdrop of exotic splendor and stirring deeds as young Englishwoman Laura Hewitt journeys to the East to the fabled fiefdom of the Zemindar, Guardian of the Earth. He is Oliver Erskine, hereditary ruler of his private kingdom, commander of his own native army—and brother of the man she loves. As a tidal wave of civil war engulfs even the enchanted reaches of Oliver's estate, Oliver invades Laura's soul—and claims her as his own, forcing her to confront her own divided loyalties, her own mutinous heart.

Buy ZEMINDAR, on sale July 15, 1983, wherever Bantam paperbacks are sold or use this handy coupon for ordering:

Bantam Books, Inc., Dept. ZE2, 414 East Golf Road, Des Plaines, Ill. 60016

Please send me _____ copies of ZEMINDAR (22845-5 • $3.95). I am enclosing $_____ (please add $1.25 to cover postage and handling. Send check or money order—no cash or C.O.D.'s please).

Mr/Ms _____

Address_____

City/State _____ Zip _____

ZE2—6/83

Please allow four to six weeks for delivery. This offer expires 12/83.

THE LATEST BOOKS IN THE BANTAM BESTSELLING TRADITION

☐	23291	JERICHO Anthony Costello	$3.95
☐	23105	NO COMEBACKS Frederick Forsyth	$3.50
☐	22749	THREE WOMEN AT THE WATER'S EDGE Nancy Thayer	$3.50
☐	23028	WINDBORN Victor Brooke	$3.50
☐	23026	CAPRICE Sara Hylton	$2.75
☐	22924	PUBLIC SMILES, PRIVATE TEARS Helen Van Slyke w/J. Edwards	$3.95
☐	23554	NO LOVE LOST Helen Van Slyke	$3.95
☐	23071	A RAGE TO LOVE Liz Martin	$2.95
☐	22846	THE DISINHERITED Clayton Matthews	$3.50
☐	22838	TRADITIONS Alan Ebert w/Janice Rotchstein	$3.95
☐	01415	FLAMES OF GLORY Patricia Matthews	$6.95
☐	22751	A PRESENCE IN A EMPTY ROOM Velda Johnston	$2.50
☐	22577	EMPIRE Patricia Matthews w/Clayton Matthews	$3.50
☐	22687	THE TRUE BRIDE Thomas Altman	$2.95
☐	22704	THE SISTERHOOD Michael Palmer	$3.50
☐	20901	TRADE WIND M. M. Kaye	$3.95
☐	20833	A WOMAN OF TWO CONTINENTS Pixie Burger	$3.50
☐	01368	EMBERS OF DAWN Patricia Matthews (A Large Format book)	$6.95
☐	20921	TANAMERA Noel Baker	$3.95
☐	20026	COME POUR THE WINE Cynthia Freeman	$3.95

Buy them at your local bookstore or use this handy coupon for ordering:

Bantam Books, Inc., Dept. FBS, 414 East Golf Road, Des Plaines, Ill. 60016

Please send me the books I have checked above. I am enclosing $_____
(please add $1.25 to cover postage and handling). Send check or money order
—no cash or C.O.D.'s please.

Mr/Mrs/Miss_____

Address_____

City_____ State/Zip_____

FBS—5/83

Please allow four to six weeks for delivery. This offer expires 11/83.

PATRICIA MATTHEWS' LATEST BLOCKBUSTER!

EMBERS OF DAWN

In the fiery afterglow of the Civil War, Charlotte King was penniless, her only possessions a ravaged farm and a cache of prized tobacco. Two men kindled her dreams, ignited her ambition, fired her passions—and torn between their love, Charlotte fought to see her beloved South reborn.

Don't miss any of these Patricia Matthews' bestsellers!
- [ ] *TIDES OF LOVE* (22809-9 • $3.50)
- [ ] *FLAMES OF GLORY* (01415-3 • $6.95 ($7.95 in Can.))—*A large format paperback*
- [ ] *EMBERS OF DAWN* (23107-3 • $3.50) *On sale April 15, 1983*

Buy these books at your local bookstore or use this handy coupon for ordering:

Bantam Books, Dept. EM2, 414 East Golf Road, Des Plaines, Ill. 60016

Please send me the books I have checked above. I am enclosing $_____ (please add $1.25 to cover postage and handling, send check or money order—no cash or C.O.D.'s please).

Mr/Ms _____

Address _____

City/State _____ Zip _____

EM2—3/83

Please allow four to six weeks for delivery. This offer expires 9/83.

SAVE $2.00 ON YOUR NEXT BOOK ORDER!

BANTAM BOOKS

Shop-at-Home
Catalog

Now you can have a complete, up-to-date catalog of Bantam's inventory of over 1,600 titles—including hard-to-find books. And, you can save $2.00 on your next order by taking advantage of the money-saving coupon you'll find in this illustrated catalog. Choose from fiction and non-fiction titles, including mysteries, historical novels, westerns, cookbooks, romances, biographies, family living, health, and more. You'll find a description of most titles. Arranged by categoreis, the catalog makes it easy to find your favorite books and authors and to discover new ones.

So don't delay—send for this shop-at-home catalog and save money on your next book order.

Just send us your name and address and 50¢ to defray postage and handling costs.

BANTAM BOOKS, INC.
Dept. FC, 414 East Golf Road, Des Plaines, Ill. 60016

Mr./Mrs./Miss/Ms. _____
(please print)

Address _____

City _____ State _____ Zip _____

Do you know someone who enjoys books? Just give us their names and addresses and we'll send them a catalog too at no extra cost!

Mr./Mrs./Miss/Ms. _____

Address _____

City _____ State _____ Zip _____

Mr./Mrs./Miss/Ms. _____

Address _____

City _____ State _____ Zip _____

FC—2/83A